DATE DUE

JUN 0 1 1995	
OCT 2 1 1995	
FEB 2 2 1996	
JUN 1 1 1996	
NOV 1 0 1995	
DEC 2 2 1997	

GAYLORD

PRINTED IN U.S.A.

The *Year's Best*
Fantasy and
Horror

The *Year's Best*
Fantasy and
Horror

SIXTH ANNUAL COLLECTION

Edited by Ellen Datlow
and Terri Windling

WITHDRAWN

ST. MARTIN'S PRESS NEW YORK

This year's volume is dedicated to Gordon Van Gelder for all his faith and support.

E.D. and T.W.

Contents

x   Contents

Acknowledgments

I am grateful to the publishers, editors, writers, artists, booksellers, librarians, and readers who sent material and recommended favorite titles for this volume; and to *Locus*, *SF Chronicle*, *Library Journal*, *PW*, and *Folk Roots* magazines, which are invaluable reference sources.

Special thanks to the Tucson and Chagford public library staffs; Tucson's Book Arts Gallery; to Lawrence Schimel, Jane Yolen, and Wendy Froud for story recommendations; to Robert Gould, Charles de Lint, and Ellen Kushner for music recommendations; to Beth Meacham, Tappan King, Ellen Steiber, Robin Hardy, and Munro Sickafoose in Tucson; to Rob Killheffer in New York; and, in particular, to our packager Jim Frenkel and his assistant Nevenah Smith; our St. Martin's editor Gordon Van Gelder; our cover artist Tom Canty; U. of A. intern and editorial assistant Brian McDonald; and my hard-working co-editor and friend Ellen Datlow.

—Terri Windling

I would like to thank Robert Killheffer, Gordon Van Gelder, Lisa Kahlden, Merrilee Heifetz, Keith Ferrell, Linda Marotta, Mike Baker, Matthew Rettenmund, Matthew Bialer, and Jim Frenkel for all their help and encouragement. Also, a special thank-you to Tom Canty and Terri Windling. Finally, I appreciate all the book publishers and magazine editors who sent material for 1992.

(Please note: It's difficult to cover all nongenre sources of short horror, so should readers see a story or poem from such a source, I'd appreciate their bringing it to my attention. Drop me a line c/o *Omni* Magazine, 1965 Broadway, New York, NY 10023.)

I'd like to acknowledge Charles N. Brown's *Locus* magazine (Locus Publications, P.O. Box 13305, Oakland, CA 94661; $50.00 for a one-year, first-class subscription [12 issues], $38.00 second class) as an invaluable reference source throughout the Summation; and Andrew I. Porter's *Science Fiction Chronicle* (S.F.C., P.O. Box 2730, Brooklyn, NY 11202-0056; $36.00 for a one-year, first-class subscription [12 issues], $30.00 second class), also an invaluable reference source throughout.

—Ellen Datlow

The packager would like to thank Nevenah Smith for her help in making this book possible.

Summation 1992
Fantasy

Fantasy, for those new to the field of fantastic literature, is a trickster of a term. To publishers, bookstore managers, and all the salespeople in between whose job it is to get books from an author's imagination into a reader's hands, the term *fantasy* means one thing: a convenient label with which to classify and market a narrow group of "genre" books. To the reader, however, it means another: fantasy fiction permeates the whole field of literature, for works of fantasy can be found in every genre—including the category labeled "mainstream fiction"—and in every area of the arts.

The Year's Best Fantasy and Horror annual anthology is intended for the readers, not the marketers, except wherein they be readers too. Thus, in these pages, our definition of fantasy is a reader's definition. For our purposes, *fantasy* is a broad and inclusive range of classic and contemporary fictions with magical, fabulous, or surrealistic elements, from novels set in imaginary worlds with their roots in the oral traditions of folktale and mythology, to contemporary stories of Magic Realism in which fantasy elements are used as metaphoric devices to illuminate the world we know. You need never have read the works of J. R. R. Tolkien or his imitators to have read fantasy fiction, for the field also includes magical works as diverse as Shakespeare's *The Tempest*, poetry by W. B. Yeats, tales by Oscar Wilde and James Thurber, modern novels by Joyce Carol Oates and Gabriel García Márquez.

Because there is so much fantastic fiction published each year, both within the fantasy genre and without, it is the purpose of this anthology to seek out stories and poems from as many different sources as possible: newsstand magazines, literary journals, anthologies and collections, mainstream books, small-press books, children's books, poetry journals, foreign works in translation, and any other publication in which a magical story might be found. The best of these are gathered together in this volume along with a brief overview of fantasy in the contemporary arts in 1992.

This anthology ranges, like the field of contemporary fantastic literature, from the dark magics of horror fiction to the luminous poetics of pure fairy tale. This range shows the many, many ways fabulous elements can be used in modern fiction to explore the shadows of the world we live in, or the shadows of the psyche, or of the human heart. We do not expect every story to be to every reader's taste, but they all share one important trait: the assertion that an appetite for wonder and mystery is not irrelevant in our modern lives.

In the last several years, the works of the late folklore scholar Joseph Campbell (popularized by the Bill Moyers' TV interview series *The Power of Myth*) have done more than even Jungian psychology or the efforts of fantasy fiction writers to bring our world heritage of myth and folklore back into modern consciousness. The mythopoetic men's movement spawned by Robert Bly's *Iron John* is another area in which myth and magical stories are used as metaphors to explore the complexities of modern society—and while one may agree or disagree with Bly's particular ideas on the subject of gender relations, he has certainly tapped, like Campbell, into the late-twentieth-century hunger for the pan-cultural traditional stories that connect us to the centuries of men and women who have walked the earth before us.

In 1992, Clarissa Pinkola Estés's mythopsychological study *Women Who Run with the Wolves* hit the best-seller lists. Touted by some as a woman's answer to *Iron John*, it is in fact a book written not only for women but for the men who live and work beside them, and for the feminine aspects within every man as well. In addition to her psychological credentials, Dr. Estés is an experienced oral storyteller, and the book is full of magical tales gathered from many cultures—including cultures native to our American continent. Written in the personal, poetic language of a traveling storyteller rather than a clinician, *Women Who Run with the Wolves* makes a compelling case for the importance of honoring Story, Myth, and Dream in daily life.

In *The Power of Myth*, Joseph Campbell states: "A dream is a personal experience of that deep, dark ground that is the support of our conscious lives, and myth is the society's dream. . . . Myth must be kept alive. The people who can keep it alive are artists of one kind or another. The function of the artist is the mythologization of the environment and the world."

Susan Cooper, in her essay "Fantasy in the Real World," elaborates upon this idea:

> [Campbell is] saying that artists have inherited the mythmaking function of the shaman and the seer, and of course he's right. Where the art of writing is concerned, his point applies most of all to the poets and to the writers of fantasy. Both deal with images, and with their links to and within the unconscious mind. And the fantasist—not one of my favorite words— deals with the substance of myth: the deep archetypal patterns of emotion and behavior which haunt us all whether we know it or not.

It is interesting to note that in late-twentieth-century American society, the collective myths and symbols that are most pervasive in our culture are the dark ones: vampires, ghosts, demon children, supernatural serial killers, and ghouls risen from the grave. The steady popularity of the books of J. R. R. Tolkien and his successors is greatly overshadowed by the vast multimedia popularity of darker fantasies in the form of horror fiction, comics, and films.

In mass-market publishing, horror fiction is usually published under a separate imprint from fantasy fiction—yet much of the best work written in the last couple of years in the fantasy genre is dark fantasy, falling somewhere in that twilight realm that lies between the two fields. It is interesting that works with a dark, horrific edge are automatically considered by some critics to be more adult, more serious, more sophisticated than even the most poetic and well-written magical fantasy tale. Is it a product of human nature, or merely the times we live in, that as a society we are quicker to believe in and take interest in the portrayal of violence and evil? Or that these things are hip and sexy, while tales of wonder and the miraculous are pushed to the children's shelves?

Fiction is a place where all things can be faced, all issues explored; dark fantasy and horror are important in this regard, and I mean no disrespect to the makers of those arts. But it is of interest to me how much more difficult it is to persuade the modern reader to "suspend disbelief" (to use Coleridge's phrase) for the miraculous in life as well as for the horrific. And how difficult it is to write mythic or magical fantasy that is as complex and as vivid as the world around us.

Ursula K. Le Guin commented ten years ago (in a 1982 symposium talk titled "Facing It," published in her 1989 collection of essays, *Dancing at the Edge of the World*):

> I see much current fantasy and science fiction in full retreat from real human needs. Where a Tolkien prophetically faced the central fact of our time, our capacity to destroy ourselves, the present spate of so-called heroic fantasy, in which Good defeats Evil by killing it with a sword or staff or something phallic, seems to have nothing in mind beyond instant gratification, the avoidance of discomfort, in a fake-medieval past where technology is replaced by magic and wishful thinking works.

The worst of the fantasy books published today are just such simplistic tales. Critics decry the endless series books published in the genre—yet dividing a story into several books is merely a form, a device, neither inherently good nor bad. It is what the author does with the form that counts. Unfortunately, what some writers choose to do is merely attempt to mimic Tolkien or some other favorite writer, rather than crafting stories out of their own experience, their own history and heart. As readers we should expect more—and support those attempts to offer us more. We sometimes forget that we are not the passive recipients of whatever the publishing industry chooses to send to us; we have vital input into the publishing process every time we put our money down for a well-written book rather than a shoddy one, or give a new and unfamiliar author a try.

It is a truism among genre editors that a bad fantasy story is one of the easiest things to write (as the stacks of unsolicited manuscripts in publishing offices can attest) and a good one is one of the hardest. Nonetheless there *are* many writers using the fantasy form to tell complex, thought-provoking, and thoroughly adult tales—although to find them you must sometimes stray beyond the genre shelves. The modern English-language Magic Realists (inspired by such foreign writers as Isabel Allende, Italo Calvino, Naquib Mahfouz, and Gabriel García Márquez, who have never felt themselves constrained by a need for strict realism) are proliferating in the literary mainstream. Fantasy is flourishing outside of the genre; now, what does this mean for the genre?

The tools of Magic Realism have appeared within the genre as well, as writers like John Crowley, Gene Wolfe, Megan Lindholm, and Charles de Lint—to name but a few—use fantastical elements within a tale as a way of illuminating both the dark and the bright of modern life. In an interview on fantasy in *Locus* magazine (April 1992), Ellen Kushner commented:

> Now my generation, we're all hitting late thirties to mid-forties. Our concerns are different. If we stick to fantasy, what are we going to do to fantasy? Traditionally, there's been the coming-of-age [novel] and the quest which is the finding of the self. We're past the early stages of that. I can't

wait to see what people do with the issues of middle age in fantasy. Does
fantasy demand that you stay in your adolescence forever? I don't think so.
Tolkien is not juvenile. It's a book about losing things you loved, which
is a very middle-aged concern. Frodo's quest is a middle-aged man's quest,
to lose something and to give something up, which is what you start to
realize in your thirties is going to happen to you. Part of the rest of your
life is learning to give things up.

Adult fantasy as a distinct publishing genre came into existence in the late sixties
and early seventies with the republication of Tolkien's Middle Earth opus, and the
novels published under the Ballantine Sign of the Unicorn imprint. Without ignoring the fact that there are always new young writers and new young readers coming
into the field, the genre as a whole is indeed coming into a more mature age in the
1990s. It is up to us—readers, writers, publishers, booksellers—to determine
whether age means growth or decay, and to define the field in the years to come.
My guess is that the best fantasy fiction will share the same qualities as the best of
literature as a whole—for we are one branch on that tree, not a different or lesser
tree altogether. As we move toward the changes the twenty-first century will bring,
and the need for myth and fiction to address them, I suggest we keep in mind Annie
Dillard's reflections on *The Writing Life*:

Why are we reading, if not in hope of beauty laid bare, life heightened
and its deepest mystery probed? . . . What do we ever know that is higher
than that power which, from time to time, seizes our lives, and reveals us
startlingly to ourselves as creatures set down here bewildered? Why does
death so catch us by surprise, and why love? We still and always want
waking.

Fantasy at its best is a dream from which we wake refreshed, enlightened, or
transformed. It takes us away from the world we know only to return us to it again
with a deeper understanding of its dark shadows, and a clearer vision for its wonders.

In 1992, despite cutbacks by the larger publishers, there was no scarcity of fantasy
fiction; a large number of dreadful-to-excellent fantasy novels appeared and disappeared on the bookstore shelves. A number of the most intriguing novels were
published outside of the fantasy genre—which is a change from past years when
the genre publishers were providing the most consistent publication opportunities
for innovative magical fiction. Yet the genre lists of 1992 should not be ignored,
for they have provided several potential award-winners as well.
    The following list is a baker's dozen of well-written, entertaining works showing
the diversity of the fantasy form. While I can't claim to have read *every* work of
fantasy published here or abroad, I hope that through my experiences working as
an editor with writers and artists across this country and England I can lead you to
some books you might have overlooked or some new authors whom you might
enjoy. These are books no fantasy lover's shelves should be without:

The Haunting of Lamb House by Joan Aiken (St. Martin's Press). A haunted house where Henry James once lived provides the setting for a literary ghost story by one of Britain's most distinguished writers.

Lord Kelvin's Machine by James P. Blaylock (Arkham House). This witty, eccentric Victorian story has elements of fantasy, horror, and science fiction and thus defies easy classification. Blaylock is a true original, and one of the finest writers in the fantasy field.

The Gypsy by Steven Brust and Megan Lindholm (Tor). Two of the field's best writers team up in a dark contemporary fantasy/mystery woven with elements of Hungarian folklore.

Cherokee Bat and the Goat Guys by Francesca Lia Block (HarperCollins). This was published as Young Adult fiction, but don't let that put you off. Set in the same punk-fairy-tale Los Angeles as Block's *Weetzie Bat* and *Witch Baby*, this novel shows that her books just keep getting better and better.

The Goblin Mirror by C. J. Cherryh (Del Rey). Cherryh—an award-winning writer in the science fiction field—creates a rich imaginary-world fantasy with a Slavic touch in her latest novel (which, I should note, is not a part of her recent "Russian fantasy" series).

The War of Don Emmanuel's Nether Parts by Louis de Bernieres (William Morrow). Although written by a British writer, de Bernieres' novel reads like Latin American Magic Realism à la Márquez, set in an imaginary Latin American country full of magic . . . and thousands upon thousands of cats.

Turtle Moon by Alice Hoffman (Putnam). Hoffman, author of mainstream novels such as *Seventh Heaven, Fortune's Daughter*, and *At Risk*, has written a wonderful contemporary novel with ghostly elements, set in a small Florida town.

The Course of the Heart by M. John Harrison (Gollancz, U.K.). British writer Harrison is a master of subtle, pervasive fantasy woven into the fabric of contemporary stories. This book is his best yet, the one we've all been waiting for.

A Song for Arbonne by Guy Gavriel Kay (Crown). Canadian writer Kay is one of the better craftsmen working in the traditional fantasy mode. In this new novel he evokes the flavor of a mythical twelfth-century France.

The Mountain Made of Light by Edward Myers (Roc). An intriguing, old-fashioned lost-race novel set in the Andes in the 1920s by a talented new writer in the field.

The Famished Road by Ben Okri (Cape, U.K.). Nigerian writer Okri won the 1992 Booker Prize for this marvelous, magical tale of modern Africa told from the point of view of a "spirit child."

Last Call by Tim Powers (William Morrow). Powers brings Arthurian myth (in the form of the Fisher King and his heir) to the gangsters of modern Las Vegas in this strange, funny, and brilliant novel. (It's also available from Charnel House in a beautiful limited edition.)

Divina Trace by Robert Anton Wilson (Overlook Press). The history of a small West Indian island is told through the tale of a child who "was born a man, but above the *cojones* he was a frog." Utterly delightful.

Briar Rose by Jane Yolen (Tor). This extraordinary book is a tour de force, weaving fantasy in the form of the fairy tale Briar Rose (the Sleeping Beauty legend) through a contemporary tale about a young American journalist, and a historical tale about the horrors of World War II.

Two additional books that aren't fantasy, but rather are about the makers of fantasy, are also highly recommended:

Was by Geoff Ryman (Knopf). A modern realist novel about the real Dorothy Gale in Kansas, brilliantly intercut with narrative exploring the growth of the Oz legend.

Love's Children by Judith Chernaik (Knopf). A clever and fascinating epistolary novel about Mary Shelley and her circle from the time the novel *Frankenstein* was begun in Geneva to the winter in which it was finished in Italy two years later.

Flying in Place by Susan Palwick (Tor) has my vote for the best first novel of the year—as well as for one of the very best novels of the year, *period*. It is a beautiful, brutal, but ultimately redemptive tale that no fantasy reader should miss.

The runner-up for best first novel is *Photographing Fairies* by Steve Szilagyi (Ballantine); a fantasy/mystery novel involving Arthur Conan Doyle's famous fairy photographs.

Other interesting first-novel debuts in 1992: *Unicorn Highway*, by David Lee Jones (AvoNova); a gentle midwestern fantasy set in 1947; and *Demon Drums*, by Carol Severance (Del Rey), fantasy set in the South Seas by an author who has distinguished herself previously with a handful of memorable short stories.

The "Best Peculiar Book" distinction goes to *The D. Case or the Truth About the Mystery of Edwin Drood*, by Charles Dickens, Carlo Fruttero, and Franco Lucentini (HBJ), a strange and wonderful novel about a conference of literary detectives—Holmes, Nero Wolfe, et al.—who compete to solve Dickens' unfinished mystery. The runner-up is *Augustus Rex*, by Clive Sinclair (Andre Deutsch, U.K.); an intelligent, peculiar, but surprisingly successful work in which Swedish playwright August Strindberg rises from the dead after making a deal with Beelzebub and becomes, of all things, a hero uniting Scandinavia.

Other titles published in 1992 that are particularly recommended:

Imaginary-World Fantasy:

Zimiamvia: A Trilogy by E. R. Eddison (Dell). An omnibus volume by this master of the language includes his classic works *Mistress of Mistresses, A Fish Dinner in Memison,* and *The Mezentian Gate,* with a new introduction and notes by Paul Edmund Thomas and a foreword by Douglas E. Winter. This edition contains never-before-published text from the unfinished third novel. If you haven't yet read Eddison . . . well, shame on you.

Chronicles of the King's Tramp #3: The Last Human by Tom de Haven (Bantam). This ends, more or less, a fantasy trilogy that is witty and surprising, a distinct cut above the rest.

Belden's Fire by Midori Snyder (Tor). As with the de Haven book above, this is the third and final volume of a distinctive and superior trilogy, rich with subtlety and fascinating characterization.

Songs of Earth and Power by Greg Bear (Legend, U.K.). An omnibus volume of Bear's two excellent contemporary magical fantasy novels *The Infinity Concerto* and *The Serpent Mage,* with some new text.

Domes of Fire by David Eddings (Del Rey) and *The Magicians of the Night* by Barbara Hambly (Del Rey). These two authors are among the best writing series fantasy, and are a good argument against quick dismissal of the series form.

The Avengers by Louise Cooper (Bantam). This adventure fantasy, the last of Cooper's "Chaos Gate" trilogy, has a very nice Moorcockian touch.

The Last of the Renshai by Mickey Zucker Reichert (DAW). A coming-of-age fantasy with a Norse flavor and memorable characters; and *Lightning's Daughter* by Mary Herbert (TSR), standard adventure fantasy set among nomadic clans, but told with a fresh voice. Neither of these authors sets out to write High Literature, they set out to tell entertaining tales—and have succeeded.

Urban Fantasy:

Spiritwalk by Charles de Lint (Tor). Canadian writer de Lint returns to the magical-house setting of *Moonheart* in the Urban Fantasy novel *Ghostwood,* published in this fat volume with three connected shorter pieces.

Elsewhere by Will Shetterly (Tor). A novel from the Borderlands "punk fantasy" series; Shetterly has used the magic-and-rock-and-roll setting to tell a poignant story about a young man's search for his brother, and himself.

Historical Fantasy and Alternate History:

The Sheriff of Nottingham by Richard Kluger (Viking). A recasting of the Robin Hood legend with a sympathetic sheriff based on a real historical figure: complex, detailed, and fascinating.

The Angel of Pain by Brian Stableford (Simon & Schuster, U.K.). Excellent dark fantasy set in nineteenth-century London.

My Sister the Moon by Sue Harrison (Doubleday). Set in Alaska in the eighth century B.C.

The Spirit Ring by Lois McMaster Bujold (Baen). Bujold draws upon Renaissance Italy and the biography of Cellini to create an entertaining tale of political intrigue.

Lion of Macedon and *Morningstar* by David Gemmel (Legend). Good historical adventure fantasy set in ancient Greece.

The Empress of the Seven Oceans by Fiona Cooper (Black Swan). A literary fantasy set in the seventeenth century.

Resurrections from the Dustbin of History by Simon Louvish (Bloomsbury, U.K.). A political "alternate history" fantasy set in 1968.

The Lost Prince by Bridget Wood (Headline, U.K.). Dark fantasy mixing Celtic myth with a grim future Ireland.

Byron's Child by Carola Dunn (Walker). A peculiar confection in which a modern historian goes back to Regency London and becomes involved with Lord Byron's daughter.

Fantasy from Other Traditions:

The Painted Alphabet by Diana Darling (Houghton Mifflin). A beautifully produced little book based on a Balinese epic fantasy poem.

The Gates of Noon by Michael Scott Rohan (Gollancz, U.K.). A mix of contemporary fantasy, Indonesian myth, and adventure on the high seas.

Last Refuge by Elizabeth Ann Scarborough (Bantam). Darkly humorous Asian fantasy.

Oriental Tales by Robert L. Mack (Oxford University Press, U.K.). Two fantasy novels published in one fat volume along with two shorter works.

The Chalchiuhite Dragon by Kenneth Morris (Tor). A lost fantasy classic, loosely based on the Quetzalcoatl legend, brought into print more than fifty years after the author's death.

Blades from the Willows by Huanzhuloushu, translated from the Chinese by Robert Card (Wellsweep, U.K.). The first volume in this Chinese fantasy/martial arts series from the forties.

Arthurian Fantasy:

The Grail of Hearts by Susan Shwartz (Tor). Shwartz mixes the Grail legend and the Fisher King with history of the Crusades and Jewish lore.

Herself by Fay Sampson (Headline, U.K.). A historical fantasy about Morgan Le Fay; Book V of "Daughters of Tintagel."

The Camelot Chronicles edited by Mike Ashley (Carroll & Graf). A fine collection of eighteen Arthurian stories including seven original to the volume.

Grails: Quests, Visitations and Other Occurrences, edited by Richard Gilliam, Martin H. Greenberg, and Edward E. Kramer (Unnameable Press). A collection of Arthurian and other stories produced in a lavish edition.

Humorous Fantasy:

A Sudden Wild Magic by Diana Wynne Jones (AvoNova). Witty, silly, magical adult comedy from a terrific author best known for her excellent YA fantasy novels.

Lords and Ladies by Terry Pratchett (Gollancz, U.K.). New from the master of the British humorous fantasy form.

It's Been Fun by Esther M. Friesner (Pulphouse). Issue #23 of the Author's Choice Monthly short story series.

Noah and Me by Antonia Holding Schwed (Evans). A charming, funny, and bittersweet fantasia about the patients of an animal psychotherapist.

Practical Demonkeeping by Christopher Moore (St. Martin's Press). A strange black comedy of a demon and his keeper in a small California town.

The Vicar of Nibbleswicke by Roald Dahl, illustrated by Quentin Blake (Overlook Press). The first U.S. edition of what is, or at least should be, a modern classic.

Ye Gods! by Tom Holt (Orbit, U.K.). A humorous contemporary fantasy about the offspring of the god Jupiter.

Flying Dutch by Tom Holt (St. Martin's Press). First U.S. edition of this quirky contemporary fantasy.

Fantasy Mysteries:

Humans by Donald E. Westlake (Warner/Mysterious Press). A literary fantasy about an angel sent by God to bring about Armageddon.

Lempriere's Dictionary by Lawrence Norfolk (Harmony). Murder, intrigue and intricate historical detail set against a background of classical mythology.

The Wrong Rite by Charlotte MacLeod (Morrow). A mystery novel with delightful fantasy overtones, the latest in the Madoc Rhys series (published under the pen name Alisa Craig) about a Canadian Mountie and his eccentric family.

The Testimony of Daniel Pagels by Vickery Turner (Scribners). Though not quite fantasy, this courtroom drama uses Native American mysticism and quantum physics to explore such large concepts as time, space, and the nature of reality. Fascinating.

The Hangman's Beautiful Daughter by Sharyn McCrumb (Scribners). A lovely Magical Realist mystery novel set in the Appalachians.

Absences by Steve Rasnic Tem (Haunted Library, U.K.). Five tales about a psychic sleuth.

Dark Fantasy:

Heart-Beast by Tanith Lee (Headline, U.K.). Dark fantasy about a shape-changer, from a master of the macabre.

Forest of the Night by S. P. Somtow (AvoNova). An excellent, hard-to-classify book that falls between several genres.

Imajica by Clive Barker (HarperCollins, 1991—not read until this year). Complex, sensual, richly imagistic dark fantasy.

Alembic by Timothy d'Arch Smith (Dalkey Archive Press). Literary fiction mingling dark fantasy and elements of SF and horror into an intriguing tale about the British government's secret alchemy bureau.

Conglomeros by Jesse Brown (Random House). Contemporary fiction with dark fantasy elements set in New York; poetic and disturbing.

Her Monster by Jeff Collignon (Soho Press). A contemporary dark fantasy novel loosely based on the Beauty and the Beast story.

Fantastic Tales by I. U. Tarchetti (Mercury House). The collected tales of an Italian dark fantasist.

Memories of the Body: Tales of Desire and Transformation by Lisa Tuttle (Severn House, U.K.). This collection of fifteen stories includes some dark fantasy.

Fantasy in the Mainstream:
The Journey of Ibn Fattoume by Naquib Mahfouz (Doubleday). A parable set in a mythic Middle East by a winner of the Nobel Prize for Literature.

At the Sign of the Naked Waiter by Amy Herrick (HarperCollins). A literary fantasy about a woman's search for love in a contemporary but magical world.

Leviathan by Paul Auster (Viking). Suspenseful literary fiction exploring a distinctively American mythological landscape.

Charlie Peace by Paul Pickering (Random House). A peculiar literary fantasy novel about two children who grow up listening to stories by a man who might be God.

The Good Fairies of New York by Martin Millar (Fourth Estate, U.K.). A peculiar literary novel about Celtic fairies exiled to New York City.

Voice by Tim Wynne-Jones (New English Library, U.K.). A literary novel set in a haunted castle.

Outside the Dog Museum by Jonathan Carroll (Doubleday). The first U.S. edition of the latest Magic Realist novel from this original and often brilliant writer.

The Cornish Trilogy by Robertson Davies (Viking). An omnibus volume of three novels: *The Rebel Angels, What's Bred in the Bone,* and *The Lyre of Orpheus.* These are entertaining and beautifully written novels with some fantasy elements.

The Man in the Window by Jon Cohen (Warner). A literary fantasy romance set in a magical town.

Young Adult Fantasy:
The Girl with the Green Ear: Stories About Magic in Nature by Margaret Mahy (Knopf). Short fiction by one of the very best writers in the field. Recommended.

A Bone from a Dry Sea by Peter Dickinson (Gollancz, U.K.). Excellent fantasy about an archaeological dig.

The Mark of the Cat by Andre Norton (Ace). A sweet coming-of-age story based on Karen Kuykendall's fantastical drawings of cats (found in *The Cat People* and *Tarot of the Cat People*).

Damnbanna by Nancy Springer (Pulphouse/Axolotl). A memorable and hard-hitting young adult novella.

Searching for Dragons by Patricia C. Wrede (HBJ). Sequel to her delightful *Dealing with Dragons.*

Tongues of Jade by Laurence Yep (HarperCollins). A collection of eleven stories based on Chinese folktales, illustrated by David Wiesner.

The Thief of Always by Clive Barker (HarperCollins). YA fantasy, with illustrations by the author, by a writer better known for his horror fiction.

Dark Moon by Meredith Ann Pierce (Little Brown). The sequel to *Birth of a Firebringer.*

The Land of Gold by Gillian Bradshaw (Greenwillow). Fantasy set in ancient Egypt.

A Plague of Sorcerers by Mary Frances Zambreno (HBJ). A standard but sweet fantasy tale.

Seven Strange and Ghostly Tales by Brian Jacques (Philomel). Darker than his "Redwall" novels. He also published a new "Redwall" book (that's the talking rodent series, remember?), *Mariel of Redwall.*

Child of the Ancient City by Tad Williams and Nina Kiriki Hoffman (Atheneum). An Arabian Nights–style vampire tale.

Hobkin by Peni R. Griffin (Macmillan). A magical contemporary story about two runaway girls on an old farmstead. Generally light and entertaining, the novel has more serious undertones as Griffin explores what it is the children ran away *from.*

Tristan and Iseult by Rosemary Sutcliff (Farrar, Straus, & Giroux). A reprint of an excellent Arthurian novel.

The Thirteen Clocks by James Thurber (Dell Yearling). A new edition of the classic fantasy tale.

1992 saw the publication of excellent work in the area of short fantasy fiction. Ellen Datlow and I read a wide variety of material over the course of 1992 to choose the stories for this volume. I found that the best anthology of the year was published in Britain: *Caught in a Story*, a collection of modern literary fairy tales and fables edited by Christine Park and Caroline Heaton. (I am indebted to Wendy Froud for pointing it out to me.)

The following story collections stood out among the rest and are particularly recommended for all lovers of good short fiction:

After the King: Stories in Honor of J. R. R. Tolkien, edited by Martin H. Greenberg (Tor). Nineteen original stories written in honor of the creator of *The Lord of the Rings.*

Conjunctions 18: Fables, Yarns, Fairy Tales edited by Bradford Morrow (Bard College/Random House).

Letters from Home (The Women's Press, U.K.). Short stories by Pat Cadigan, Karen Joy Fowler, and Pat Murphy.

The Daedalus Book of Femme Fatales edited by Brian Stableford (Daedalus, U.K.). Contains both reprint and new material.

Visions and Imaginings: Classic Fantasy Fiction edited by Robert H. Boyer and Kenneth Zahorski (Academy, Chicago). A "best of" anthology from their five previous collections.

The Magic of Christmas edited by John Silbersack and Christopher Schelling (Roc). A lovely holiday collection.

Alternate Kennedys edited by Mike Resnick (Tor). An "alternate history" anthology that asks the question, "What if . . . ?"

In addition, there were quite a number of excellent collections specializing in women's fiction in 1992. The best of these were:

Secret Weavers: Stories of the Fantastic by Women of Argentina and Chile edited by Marjorie Argosin (White Pine Press).

The Lifted Veil: The Book of Fantastic Literature by Women edited by Susan Williams (Xanadu, U.K.). An excellent collection from the past to the present.

Modern Ghost Stories by Eminent Women Writers edited by Richard Dalby (Carroll & Graf).

Herzone: Fantasy Short Stories by Women edited by Norma Brown, Jane Boughton, and Di Williams (Crocus, U.K.).

One Hundred Years After Tomorrow: Brazilian Women's Fiction in the 20th Century edited and translated by Darlene J. Sadlier (Indiana University Press).

The following is a baker's dozen of the Best Single Author collections to appear in the past year:

The Sons of Noah & Other Stories by Jack Cady (Broken Moon Press). A truly extraordinary collection, highly recommended.

Storyteller by Jane Yolen (NESFA Press). A limited-edition collection of poems, stories, and an essay, with an introduction by Patricia A. McKillip.

Iron Tears by R. A. Lafferty (Edgewood Press). A reprint collection of this highly original author's tales.

And the Angels Sing by Kate Wilhelm (St. Martin's Press). Stories by one of the field's finest stylists.

Bear's Fantasies by Greg Bear (Wildside Press). A lovely limited edition.

The Collected Short Stories of Roald Dahl (Michael Joseph Pub., U.K.). A complete volume of this late author's short works.

The Armies of Efland by Poul Anderson (Tor). A collection of eight stories from a Grand Master of fantasy.

The Bone Forest by Robert Holdstock (Avon). The first U.S. edition of this lovely collection, including the title story, which is a part of the "Mythago Wood" sequence.

Storeys from the Old Hotel by Gene Wolfe (Tor). Splendid surrealistic and stylish fantasy tales.

Untold Tales by William J. Brooke (HarperCollins). Witty and wonderful fractured fairy tales.

Let the Dead Bury Their Dead by Randall Kenan (HBJ). Stories with Magical Realist elements set in a small North Carolina town.

Killing Color by Charlotte Watson Sherman (CALYX Books). American Magic Realist tales by a distinctive and lyrical writer.

Mrs. Vargas and the Dead Naturalist by Kathleen Alcalá (CALYX Books). Mexican and American Magic Realist tales that roam across the border between the two lands.

A selection of works of nonfiction and folklore published in 1992:

Strategies of Fantasy by Brian Attebery (Indiana University Press). A study of fantasy in relation to postmodern literature.

More Real than Reality: The Fantastic in Irish Literature and the Arts, Donald E. Morse and Csilla Bertha, eds. (Greenwood Press, Connecticut). Sixteen essays.

The Novels of Charles Williams by Howard Thomas (Ignatius Press, California). First U.S. edition.

Forbidden Journeys: Fairy Tales and Fantasies by Victorian Women Writers edited by Nina Auerbach and U. C. Knoepflmacher (University of Chicago Press).

Explores the darker, subversive side of familiar tales refashioned by nineteenth-century women writers.

Victorian Fantasy Literature: Literary Battles with Church and Empire by Karen Michalson (Edward Mellon Press, N.Y.). An exploration of Victorian attitudes toward the fantastic.

Wisewomen and Boggy-boos: A Dictionary of Lesbian Fairy-lore by Jessica Amanda Salmonson and Jules Remedios Faye (Banned Books, Austin, Texas).

The Wise and Foolish Tongue: Celtic Stories and Poems collected and told by Robin Williamson (Chronicle Books).

Pacific Mythology: An Encyclopedia of Myth and Legend by Jan Knappert (Aquarian).

The Feminist Companion to Mythology edited by Carolyne Larrington (Pandora Press). A collection of essays on myths around the world.

Arthur the King: Themes Behind the Legend by Graeme Fife (Sterling). A nicely illustrated edition.

The Romance of Merlin edited by Peter Goodrich (Garland Press). An anthology of stories, poems, and criticism on the subject.

Fairy Tale Romance: The Grimms, Basile and Perrault by James M. McGlathery, ed. (University of Illinois Press). A critical study of romance and eroticism in fairy tales. The subject is fascinating and McGlathery has some intriguing ideas to raise, but the book is most unfortunately marred by the author's peculiar views on women. I'd recommend *The Erotic World of Faery* by Maureen Duffy or Jack Zipes' many critical fairy tale studies instead.

Fire in the Dragon and Other Psychoanalytic Essays on Folklore by Geza Roheim (Princeton University Press).

Mayan Folktales: Folklore from Guatemala translated and edited by James D. Sexton (Anchor Books/Doubleday).

The Brocaded Slipper and Other Vietnamese Tales by Lynette Dyer Vuong, illustrated by Vo-Dinh Mai (HarperTrophy).

Haunting the House of Fiction: Feminist Perspectives on Ghost Stories by American Women edited by Lynette Carpenter and Wendy Kolmar (University of Tennessee Press). A collection of essays.

A Sampler of Jewish-American Folklore by Josepha Sherman, illustrated by Jacqueline Chwast (August House).

Lilith's Cave: Jewish Tales of the Supernatural by Howard Schwartz (Oxford University Press).

Children's picture books are an excellent source for magical tales and for some of the loveliest fantastical artwork created today. Some fine editions were published in 1992 and are well worth seeking out by adult collectors. The best of the year's crop was *White Nineteens*, written and illustrated by David Christiana (Farrar, Straus & Giroux), a thoroughly whimsical, witty, and original tale, with lively, intricate paintings that are a pure delight. I hope the World Fantasy Award judges will keep this and other picture books in mind when they nominate artists for the best work done in the 1992 calendar year.

Also particularly recommended are:

The Wretched Stone by World Fantasy Award–winner Chris Van Allsburg (Houghton Mifflin). A picture book for all ages by this brilliant author/artist about a mysterious glowing stone from the sky.

Wings with poetic text by World Fantasy Award–winner Jane Yolen, beautifully illustrated by Dennis Nolan (HBJ). Retells the story of Daedalus and Icarus.

The Children of Lir, an Irish legend retold by Sheila MacGill with intricate and richly detailed art by the great Russian artist Gennady Spirin (Dial).

Hans Christian Andersen's Fairy Tales selected and delicately illustrated by the peerless Viennese watercolor artist Lizbeth Zwerger (Picture Book Studio).

The Fairy Tales of Oscar Wilde in a handsome edition illustrated by Michael Hague (Henry Holt).

Red Riding Hood in a new edition retold and charmingly illustrated by Christopher Coady (Dutton).

The Canary Prince, a sweet fantasy tale with text and art by Eric Jon Nones (Farrar, Straus & Giroux).

Moonhorse by Mary Pope Osborne with illustrations that mark an impressive artistic debut by S. M. Saelig (Farrar, Straus & Giroux—a 1991 book not seen until this year).

William Tell retold and illustrated by Margaret Early with paintings printed in rich colors and gold ink, beautifully reminiscent of a medieval Book of Hours.

Thirteen Moons on Turtle's Back: A Native American Book of Moons, lyrical, mystical text by Bruchac & London with lovely paintings by Thomas Locker (Philomel).

Mathew's Meadow by Carinne Demas Bliss, illustrated by Ted Lewin (HBJ). A magical story about a boy and a hawk.

Three titles to be found in the children's picture-book racks but really geared more to adult tastes are: *Beauty and the Beast*, the story retold by Nancy Willard with stark black-and-white illustrations by master book artist Barry Moser of Pennyroyal Press (HBJ); *The Necklace* by Guy de Maupassant, and *The Legend of Sleepy Hollow* by Washington Irving in well-designed editions with an art deco flavor, illustrated by Gary Kelly (Creative Editions).

Conversely, *Here Be Dragons* and *Way Up High* are two children's stories published in the adult list of Donald M. Grant, Publisher, with text by Roger Zelazny and distinctive illustrations by the late artist Vaughn Bode.

Other art publications of note:

Chronicle Press in San Francisco has published a sequel to last year's extraordinary epistolary art book *Griffin and Sabine* titled *Sabine's Notebook*. It has all the charm of the first volume, and the promise of more volumes to come.

Fantasy and science fiction artist James Gurney has released his utopian art book *Dinotopia* (Turner Publishing) to much acclaim and the delight of dinosaur lovers of all ages. Expect to see an animated feature version of Gurney's created world forthcoming.

Viking has published *A Foot in the Grave*, a collection of stories by Joan Aiken based on the fantastic paintings of Jan Pienkowski.

Gollancz has published *The Luck in the Head*, a graphic novel by M. John Harrison based on the story from *Viriconium Nights*, with art by Ian Miller.

Donald M. Grant has released *Double Memory*, a lavish collection of collaborative paintings and computer-manipulated images by Boston artists Phil Hale and Richard Berry (with behind-the-scenes input from designer/painter Sheila Berry).

Unwin Hyman, U.K., has published a calendar of Tolkien paintings from last year's gorgeous anniversary edition featuring the work of master watercolorist Alan Lee.

Pomegranate Press has published a new "Goddess" calendar of haunting images by the mystical American southwestern artist Susan Seddon Boulet.

And for the many Pre-Raphaelite fans among fantasy readers and artists, I recommend seeking out *Rossetti and His Circle*, a collection of Max Beerbohm's wicked watercolor caricatures of Guggums, Ned, Topsy, and the lot—available in a facsimile of the original 1922 edition from Yale University Press.

The adult comics field is another area in which to seek out fantasy tales and artwork—yet much of the work published in this form falls into the dark fantasy/horror category and is more aptly covered in my co-editor's summary. Among these titles, I'd suggest fantasy readers take a look at the wonderful *Books of Magic*, written by Neil Gaiman, and the *Ring of Roses* series set in an alternate history London, by Das Petrou and John Watkis (DC).

Despite commercial constraints that severely limit artists working in the area of book jacket design and illustration, there were still some exceptional works that stood out from the rest on the shelves in 1992, most particularly Dennis Nolan's striking design and painting for Susan Shwartz's *The Grail of Hearts* (Tor).

To note a few of the other memorable cover treatments in the past year: Gary Lipincott and Trina Schart Hyman's work for the Jane Yolen Books imprint (HBJ); Alan Lee's surprising painting on the cover of *Poems and Stories* by J. R. R. Tolkien (Unwin Hyman, U.K.); the surrealistic Remedios Varo painting used effectively as the cover of *Secret Weavers* (White Pine Press); J. K. Potter's photographic treatment of *Lord Kelvin's Machine* by James P. Blaylock (Arkham House); Thomas Canty's photographic treatment of Jane Yolen's *Briar Rose* (Tor); Lynette Hemmant's homage to the decadent artists of the fin de siècle on *The Daedalus Book of Femmes Fatales* (Daedalus, U.K.)—which makes an interesting comparison to Canty's current work on *Snow White, Blood Red* (AvoNova); David Bergen's luminous painting for Charles de Lint's *Spiritwalk* (Tor, and Pan, U.K.); and Kinuko Craft's beautiful work on Guy Gavriel Kay's *A Song for Arbonne* (Viking Canada). Tim Hildebrant, best known for his Tolkien illustrations painted in collaboration with his brother, published in the 1970s, was given the World Fantasy Award for Best Artist in 1992. We are indebted to these and many other illustrators for laboring within tight publishing restraints to bring artistic vision into the fantasy book publishing field.

Traditional folk music is of special interest to many fantasy readers because the old ballads, particularly in the Celtic folk traditions, are often based on the same folk and fairy tale roots as fantasy fiction. The current generation of worldbeat musicians, like contemporary fantasy writers, are taking ancient, traditional rhythms and themes and adapting them to a modern age.

Listeners new to this kind of music might begin with the new Green Linnet label release *Hearts of the Gaels*, a collection of music from Ireland, Scotland, Brittany, Canada, and the United States (a sequel to Green Linnet's *The Celts Rise Again*).

Featured on this new CD are Altan, Patrick Street, Skylark, Capercaille, Sileas, Milladoiro, Rare Air, and others—some of the best contemporary Celtic bands and solo performers working today.

One of the most intriguing bands to come out of the British "roots movement" is The Barely Works, who describe themselves as a "neo-primitive jug band." Using flute, fiddle, dulcimer, tuba, and anything else they can get their hands on, they play an eclectic and wonderful blend of folk, jazz, hiphop, and funk. Likewise, I recommend The House Band, three musicians who explore roots music in innovative ways on their CD *Stonetown*.

Cherish the Ladies is an all-woman Irish band named after an Irish jig; their new release of dance tunes and songs is titled *The Back Door*. Also from Ireland, Altan has followed up their first CD, *The Red Crow* with *Harvest Storm*, and this time they've added wonderful harmonies and Gaelic choral singing to their instrumental expertise. Fiddle wizard Kevin Burke (from the Bothy Band and Patrick Street) has released a new solo CD titled *Open House*; Pat Kilbride (the only Irish musician in Scotland's Battlefield Band) also has a new solo CD out called *Undocumented Dancing*. Ron Kavana, whom some call the best singer-songwriter to come out of Ireland in recent years (he's good, but my vote is still with sexy Luka Bloom), has released *Home Fire* (featuring Terry Wood of the Pogues on mandolin).

Scotland's Tannehill Weavers have released *Mermaid's Song*, full of songs and reels featuring superb highland piping. Scottish singer Dick Gaughin's classic album *A Handful of Earth* has been released on CD, as has British singer June Tabor's classic *Ashes and Diamonds*. Tabor has a new release as well, titled *Angel Tiger*, featuring her steady touring partner Huw Warren on piano. Texas native Ingrid Karlins, who mixes her ancestral Latvian music as well as American lullabyes into her compositions, has her first major release out now titled *A Darker Passion*. Singer Connie Dover teams up with Scartaglan on their new release, *Last Night's Fun: Irish Music in America*, recommended to those who love music of Capercaille's ilk.

Milladoiro is a band that plays the Celtic music of Spain; they've followed up last year's lively *Castellum Honesti* with a new release, *Calicia No Tempo*. Skin the Peeler is an excellent new Franco-Anglo worldbeat dance band that has been touring the folk festivals of Britain lately; keep an eye out for a commercial release from these folks.

Abana Ba Nasery (The Nursery Boys) bill themselves as the guitar and soda bottle kings of Kenya. Their first Western release, *Nursery Boys Go Ahead!*, was recorded in London with contributions from Ron Kavana, Three Mutaphas Three and the Oyster Band—and it's a real treat. Vocalist Mili Bermejo and classically trained acoustic bassist Dan Greenspan have teamed up with guitarist Mick Goodrick for *Ay Amor*, a collection of traditional and contemporary songs from Argentina, Cuba, Mexico and Venezuela.

On *Fanafody*, Tarika Sammy—four young musicians from the Indian Ocean island of Madagascar—plays the unique and magical music particular to the tribes of their country. On *Tribal Voice*, Yothu Yindi, a tribal band from Australia, mixes the rhythms of aboriginal music and the lowing strains of didgeridoo with the dance beat of modern rock and roll. They've just completed a successful U.S. tour to introduce American audiences to their unusual and infectious style of music. On *Warriors*, Robert Mirabal mixes didgeridoo and Australian rhythms with his own

Native American flute music to a haunting, eerie, and mythical effect. On R. Carlos Nakai's *Spirit Horses*, this extraordinary Navajo/Ute musician plays traditional Native American flute in a most untraditional way against a background of cello and full orchestra.

Andrew Cronshaw and the people who created last year's excellent charity compilation, *Circle Dance*, have now produced *All Through the Year*, a collection of performances by Maddy Prior, Fairport Convention, The Home Service, Richard Thompson, and others. Finally, if you were lucky enough to catch Canadian Celtic singer/harpist/songwriter Loreena McKennitt on her American tour this year, I expect you'll agree with me that it is well worth making a special effort to catch her on her next swing through the states. McKennitt has a truly exquisite voice, and a preference for songs (such as her rendition of the Yeats poem "The Stolen Child") imbued with romance and magic.

The 1992 World Fantasy Convention and Awards Ceremony was held in Pine Mountain, Georgia, over the weekend of October 30–November 1. The Guests of Honor were writers Anne McCaffrey, Michael Bishop, and John Farris, anthologist Martin H. Greenberg, and artist/film producer Robert Gould. Winners of the World Fantasy Award (for work produced in 1991) were as follows: *Boy's Life* by Robert R. McCammon for Best Novel; "The Ragthorn" by Robert Holdstock and Garry Kilworth for Best Novella; "The Somewhere Doors" by Fred Chappell for Best Short Story; *The Ends of the Earth* by Lucius Shepard for Best Collection; *The Year's Best Fantasy and Horror: Fourth Annual Collection* edited by Ellen Datlow and Terri Windling for Best Anthology; and Tim Hildebrandt for Best Artist. Special Award/Professional went to George Scithers and Darrell Schweitzer of *Weird Tales* magazine; Special Award/Nonprofessional went to W. Paul Ganley of *Weirdbook*. The Life Achievement Award was given to Edd Cartier. The judges for the awards were: Gene Wolfe, Robert Sampson, John Jarrold, Arthur Byron Cover and Jill Bauman. The 1993 World Fantasy Convention will be held in late October in Minneapolis, Minnesota.

The 1992 British Fantasy Awards were presented at British Fantasy Convention XVIII on October 4, 1992, in Birmingham, England. My co-editor reports on these and other awards in her summation.

The International Conference on the Fantastic in the Arts was held in Ft. Lauderdale, Florida, in March. The Writer Guest of Honor was Philip José Farmer, the Artist Guest of Honor was Kelly Freas, and the Scholar Guest of Honor was Jack Zipes. The Crawford Award for best first fantasy novel was awarded at the conference to Greer Ilene Gilman for her novel *Moonwise*, published by Roc.

The Fourth Street Fantasy Convention was held in Minneapolis, Minnesota, in June. The Writer Guest of Honor was Megan Lindholm and the Editor Guest of Honor was Betsy Mitchell. There will be no Fourth Street Fantasy Convention held in 1993 as the convention organizers shall be working toward the Minneapolis World Fantasy Convention in October.

That's a brief roundup of the year in fantasy; now on to the stories themselves.

As always, the combined word count of the best stories of the year ran longer than we have room to print, even in a volume as fat as this one. Each year when

I send the list of fantasy stories to our packager, Jim Frenkel, he calls me up to gently remind me, "We can't fit them *all*." So the following are stories I consider among the year's best and would strongly suggest you seek out if you haven't read them:

"A Beauty in the Beast" by William J. Brooke from Brooke's collection *Untold Tales*.

"Ghost Dancing" by Annie Hansen from *Kenyon Review* Vol. 16.

"The Monster" by Scott Bradfield from the *Los Angeles Times Magazine*, June 28, 1992.

"Things of this World, or, Angels Unawares" by Randall Kenan from Kenan's collection *Let the Dead Bury Their Dead*.

"Bringing Sissy Home" by Astrid Julian from the *Writers of the Future Volume VIII*.

There were also several other excellent stories in the anthology *After the King*, edited by Martin H. Greenberg, in addition to the two chosen for reprinting in this collection. I particularly recommend the Yolen, McKillip, Beagle, and Tarr contributions.

I hope you will enjoy the tales that follow as much as I did. Many thanks to all of the authors who allowed us to collect their work here.

—Terri Windling

Summation 1992
Horror

Nineteen ninety-two will be remembered in the horror field as the Year of the Vampire. The latest volume in Anne Rice's vampire chronicles, *The Tale of the Body Thief*, made the national best-seller lists, and Francis Ford Coppola's film version of Bram Stoker's *Dracula* dominated the media for months, pre- and post-release, even though the film itself failed to perform up to expectations (despite its operatic beauty). These two major works were just the most visible in yet another apparent resurgence of popularity for the vampire. Vampires and vampirism have continually retained a hold on the imaginations of readers and film-goers (particularly since Anne Rice's *The Vampire Lestat*), but 1992 seems to be a peak as anthologies, novels, short stories, movies, and related nonfiction books combined to reach a new high.

For me, though, the most exciting event of the year in horror was the Academy Awards' honoring Jonathan Demme's film of Thomas Harris's psychological horror novel *The Silence of the Lambs* with five Oscars: Screenplay, Actor and Actress, Direction and Best Picture. Another SF/horror film, *Terminator 2: Judgment Day* deservedly dominated the technical awards.

The first U.S. trade paperback edition of Salman Rushdie's *The Satanic Verses* was published by "The Consortium, Inc.," an anonymous collection of publishers, with the support of writers and rights groups. It appeared March 25, in a reported print run of 100,000, to initially lackluster sales. In the meantime, negotiations between British and Iranian officials about lifting the *fatwa* (death sentence) against Rushdie failed to make progress in May. Despite this, Rushdie made unannounced public appearances in Spain, and Boulder, Colorado.

And in the final year of the Bush administration, censorship got in its last licks, with the ban of certain "offensive" trading cards. In April, before Eclipse even issued their *True Crime* trading cards, *The New York Post* screamed "Pols Vow Crackdown on Cards of Killers" and ran a photograph of the mother of a murdered young woman under blow-ups of the Charles Manson, Richard Speck, and Jeffrey Dahmer trading cards. By June, Nassau County, New York, banned the sale of the cards to children under seventeen and legislatures around the United States were trying to do the same.

Former President Bush's opinion to the contrary, the recession was still in full swing, causing a major upheaval at Bantam where new president and publisher Irwyn Applebaum cut the mass market list from thirty to twenty titles, cut the hardcover list by a third, streamlined the company by combining hardcover, trade paperback, and mass market responsibilities, and laid off between forty and fifty full-time and contract employees. This transpired only months after *Isaac Asimov's Science Fiction Magazine* (now called *Asimov's Science Fiction*), *Analog Science Fiction/Science Fact*, *Ellery Queen's Mystery Magazine*, and *Alfred Hitchcock's Mystery Magazine*, their inventory, plus subsidiary rights in published stories, were sold by Davis Publications to Dell Magazines, part of the Bantam Doubleday Dell

Publishing Group. The new publisher is Christopher Haas-Heye, president and publisher of Dell Magazines.

Pulphouse Publishing virtually collapsed, at least temporarily, as a major player in the fields of science fiction, fantasy, and horror by the end of 1992 with the departure of crucial members of the editorial and production staff for different parts of the country. Production has slowed to near-zero until a new crew is trained. *Pulphouse* magazine, which skipped its December issue, will continue to be published under the editorship of Jonathan Bond. All book production has been put on hold, with about ten short story paperbacks plus three Axolotl Press novellas planned for 1993. Pulphouse has also dropped production work for other publishers. Only time will tell whether or not the corporation will return to its former prominence.

The Abyss horror line edited by Jeanne Cavelos for Dell Books published its first hardcover in October under the Delacorte/Abyss imprint. It was *Lost Souls*, a first novel by Poppy Z. Brite about vampires.

Weird Tales decided to drop its oversize-digest format for a more conventional 8½-by-11 size and return to saddle-stitched covers. The new format will be much cheaper to produce and is preferred by advertisers and distributors; *Space and Time*, the long-standing small-press fiction magazine edited by Gordon Linzner, has been sold to Jonathan Post's Emerald City Publishing. Linzner continues as editor, and the magazine, which publishes fantasy, science fiction, and horror, will maintain its twice-yearly schedule but switch to a 96-page perfect-bound format; John Pelan, founder and former publisher of Axolotl Press has announced the founding of a new company, Silver Salamander Press, issuing limited editions in variant states, following "the same editorial direction that made the first several Axolotl titles so successful." Pelan plans to release "no more than three or four titles per year."

Publishers Weekly ran a half-page ad from Zebra Books on June 15, announcing the withdrawal of two horror novels by a pseudonymous writing team, explaining that sections of each novel were found to be plagiarized from Dean R. Koontz's 1983 novel *Phantoms*. Koontz took legal action after a fan alerted him to the copying in a letter giving specific instances of plagiarism and similarities to his novel. The ad was part of a legal settlement.

British news:

The various publishing imprints once owned by Robert Maxwell's Macdonald Group have been absorbed into Warner/Little Brown with Macdonald and Scribner's to become Little, Brown; Sphere and Futura will become part of the new Warner imprint. A few imprints will remain unchanged, including Orbit, the SF/fantasy list. Victor Gollancz, Ltd., at one time the leading British SF publisher as well as a publisher of quality fiction, has been sold for the second time in three years, this time to British publisher Cassell. The acquisition means Gollancz will become an imprint, ending its distinguished sixty-three-year history as a separate company; the new British SF line, Millennium, part of Anthony Cheetham's Orion group, launched its first list in September 1992 with simultaneous hardcovers and trade paperbacks of three American science fiction and fantasy titles. Cheetham also bought Chapmans, a general hardcover trade publisher started three years ago by Ian Chapman, former head of Collins. Chapmans publishes about forty trade books per year, and some will feed the Orion mass market line launched in July 1993. *Fantasy Tales*, the twice-yearly paperback anthology, is negotiating with a new distributor. In light of possible changes in format, price, and frequency, the eighth issue has been delayed. Savoy Books has had partial success in its appeal against the 1989 seizure and destruction order against the novel *Lord Horror* by David Britton and the comic *Meng & Ecker*. In a Manchester court ruling July 30, 1992, the novel was declared not obscene, reversing the order for the book's burning; however, the ruling against the comic stood.

The British Fantasy Awards were announced in Birmingham, England, over the weekend of October 2–4, 1992, at FantasyCon XVII. Jonathan Carroll's novel *Outside the Dog Museum* won the August Derleth Award. The other awards were: Anthology/Collection: *Darklands*, Nicholas Royle, ed; Short Fiction: "The Dark Lands," Michael Marshall Smith; Artist: Jim Pitts; Small Press: *Peeping Tom*. The Icarus Award for best newcomer went to Melanie Tem, and a special award went to Andrew I. Porter. The awards are voted on by the British Fantasy Society.

The Second Annual World Horror Convention was held in Nashville, Tennessee, the weekend of March 5–8. Approximately five hundred fans, writers, artists, editors, and other professionals attended the event. Brian Lumley was Master of Ceremonies, Richard Matheson was Writer Guest of Honor, Richard Christian Matheson was Media Guest of Honor, and Harry O. Morris was Artist Guest of Honor. Stephen King (who did not attend) was named Grandmaster.

The Bram Stoker Awards, given by the Horror Writers of America at a banquet in New York, June 20, 1992, were received by Robert R. McCammon for his novel *Boy's Life* (Pocket Books); Kathe Koja and Melanie Tem for their first novels, *The Cipher* and *Prodigal* (both Dell/Abyss) respectively; David Morrell for his novelette "The Beautiful Uncut Hair of Graves" (*Final Shadows*); Nancy Holder for her short story "Lady Madonna" (*Obsessions*); Dan Simmons for his collection *Prayers to Broken Stones* (Dark Harvest); Stephen Jones for his nonfiction book *Shadows in Eden* (Underwood-Miller); and Gahan Wilson for life achievement.

Winners of the Readercon Small Press Awards for 1991 were: Novel: no award; Collection: *Wormwood* by Terry Dowling (Aphelion Press); Anthology: *Tales of the Wandering Jew* edited by Brian Stableford (Dedalus); Fiction Magazine: no award; Nonfiction Magazine: *Science Fiction Eye* edited by Stephen Brown; Nonfiction Book: *The Science Fantasy Publishers* by Jack L. Chalker and Mark Owings (Mirage Press); Cover Illustration: Alicia Austin, *The Edges of Things* (WSFA Press); Interior Illustration: no award; Value in Bookcraft: *The New Neighbor* by Ray Garton (Charnel House). Judges were Arnie Fenner, Donald Keller, Stephen Pasechnick, Stuart Schiff, Carter Scholz, and Michael Walsh.

In horror more than in any other literary field, specialty presses have taken an active role in publishing and have become important sources of good reading material. In order to avoid repetition in this summation, I have done the following: If a book published by a specialty press is mentioned under a specific category (such as anthology or collection) it will not be repeated in the section on "specialty presses."

Following is a biased and eclectic sampling of novels I have read and enjoyed during the year. I'm afraid I found many of the genre horror novels I read dull and unchallenging, so the majority of what follows, although containing horrific elements, would not necessarily be considered horror. However, I suspect readers will enjoy some of them as much as I did:

In the Blood by Nancy A. Collins (Roc) is the follow-up to the Bram Stoker Award–winning *Sunglasses After Dark*. Sonja Blue, the unique *living* vampire from Collins's first novel, vengefully tracks down Morgan, the Lord Vampire who raped and "created" her when she was a teenager. Collins skillfully integrates creatures from myth, legend, and fairy tale to populate this page-turner (for example, one character employs an ogre as bodyguard). Not only does this novel stand on its own, but I feel it's better than the first because Collins has gained more control over her craft.

Beauty by Brian D'Amato (Delacorte) is an amazing first novel about an artist who pioneers a way to remold faces with artificial skin. Unorthodox and untried medical procedures and an obsession with physical beauty move this novel into the realm of horror. The first-person voice of the narrator is reminiscent of that in Scott Spencer's excellent first novel *Endless Love*, in which everything the guy says sounds perfectly logical and rational—until you think about it. The downward slide of the protagonist is inevitable. Well-written, sharply satiric, funny and horrific, *Beauty* deserves bestsellerdom. Highly recommended.

The Shrine at Altamira by John L'Heureux (Viking) is another novel concerned with obsession and its consequences. Maria Corazon Alvarez wants desperately to escape the ghetto and to do so marries a sweet Anglo named Russell Whitaker. What ensues is believable (in fact, the focal point of the story is taken from horrific real-life events) and ultimately quite moving. The major problem is that Maria comes across as selfish, shallow, and crass—which may not be the author's intention.

Flying in Place by Susan Palwick (Tor) is an excellent first novel about how a young girl, Emma, learns to cope with and overcome an abusive childhood with the help of her sister's ghost. Palwick manages, with grace, the dual feat of creating art out of an inherently depressing fictional situation and of writing from the point of view of an adult looking back on childhood, with remarkably little feeling of intrusion. Highly recommended.

Bad Brains by Kathe Koja (Dell/Abyss) is the second novel by the co-winner of the Bram Stoker Award for first novel. The opening pages, about a young man who hits his head in a freak accident and ends up in the hospital, are terrifying. Like the male protagonist of *The Cipher*, Austin is more acted upon than actor in his own life. He is a blocked artist, depressed over his recent divorce and still in love with his ex-wife. An absence within him invites a terrible presence into his damaged brain. The novel is about art and creativity and taking responsibility for one's own life. Readers tend to love Koja's writing or hate it. I happen to think she's terrific.

Wallflower by William Bayer (Jove) is a meticulously written psycho-killer thriller by the author of *Blindside* and *Switch*. The unusual structure makes for a more interesting novel. Detective Janek, infamous for his success in solving the bizarre "Switch" case, knows the victim of what seems like a random murder in Central Park. This killing is initially linked to the "happy family" killings, in which the victims, all members of supposedly happy families, have had their throats slit and their bodies mutilated. Halfway through the novel, Janek seems to have solved the crime. Then, the real fun begins. The story is retold from another person's point of view, someone intimately involved in the murders. Finally, the two tellings converge. Janek behaves believably and responds realistically to the violence around him. As a thriller, love story, and search for self, this fine novel succeeds on all fronts.

After Silence by Jonathan Carroll (Macdonald, U.K.) is perhaps Carroll's most successful novel so far. Max Fischer, a popular cartoonist, is missing only one thing from his life—a great love. He finds it, along with a built-in family, when he meets Lily Aaron and her son, Lincoln. Carroll's writing is more controlled than in the past but just as quirky, imaginative, and riveting as in any of his other work. The novel is full of stories within stories but the main theme is how secrets, even with good intentions, can destroy. *After Silence* is a compulsively readable tragedy. Highly recommended. (I've only read the British edition, which differs slightly from the forthcoming U.S. edition.)

Whisper by Carolyn Doty (Scribner's) was something I initially put down after about twenty pages because I didn't like the opening situation or the characters. But because a friend recommended it, I was determined to give the book a second chance. I found myself sucked into Dorothea's (the object of desire) strange stories, as is Ben Hastings, and was compelled to read on. A successful young businessman becomes obsessively involved with a mysterious older woman who may or may not be his dying father's mistress. The strange subtle sinister texture, as well as references to *The Turn of the Screw*, give *Whisper* the feel of a Victorian ghost story, suggesting that evil and psychological corruption lurk on the edges.

The Hangman's Beautiful Daughter by Sharyn McCrumb (Scribner's) is even better than her first Appalachian mystery, *If Ever I Return Pretty Peggy-O*, and this one has supernatural aspects to it. Laura Bruce, pregnant wife of the town minister (who is serving in the Persian Gulf) is called by the sheriff to give comfort to the survivors of a scene of inexplicable carnage at the Underhill house. What happened there and why is only one strand in this rich novel that transcends its genre. The sheriff, dispatcher, and deputy return from the earlier novel. McCrumb has great respect and love for her characters, even the most marginal ones, and seems to know the region and understand its sensibilities. A beautiful, evocative, moving mystery. The supernatural elements (second sight and ghosts) are seamlessly integrated into the story and the lives of her characters. Highly recommended.

Her Monster by Jeff Collignon (Soho Press) is a marvelous retelling of Beauty and the Beast, in which Edward, the protagonist, is indeed a monster—at least physically. He is born horribly deformed, is hated by his father (who tries to kill him), and is then hidden away in the mountains by his mother, the only person who knows of his existence. Edward publishes Conan-like adventure novels quite successfully under a pseudonym and has never spoken to a woman other than his mother until Kat, a young orange-haired punkette, comes to stay with her uncle, who dates Edward's mother. It is the kind of novel wherein the reader wants everything to work out, knowing it can't possibly, given the nature of society and people. *Her Monster* may not end happily, but is very satisfying. Highly recommended.

Tribes by Alexander Stuart (Doubleday) is a short, searing novel about contemporary England—an England of skinheads, racism, and soccer riots. Nick Burns, a young film producer, is both attracted and repelled by the violence he witnesses around him. He and his partner are procuring film rights to a futuristic play about warring soccer gangs called *Tribes*. Nick's life is about to undergo a major upheaval as a result of two actions: his increasing involvement with his employee, Jemima, and her daughter; and his spur-of-the-moment decision to hire Neck, a young thug hanging around the set of his current production. The book is about violence, aggression, dominance, tenderness, and love. It's also about the ease with which a seemingly peaceful group of people can suddenly divide into warring groups. Stuart keeps fine control over his writing, veering at will from sexual to violent intensity. This novel is a powerful follow-up to *The War Zone*, Stuart's controversial first novel, which won the prestigious Whitbread Prize in England and was subsequently stripped of the prize when one of the judges objected to the book's treatment of incest. (*The War Zone*, published in the United States by Doubleday in 1989, is a terrifying novel about a family on the verge of disintegration.) Although neither novel is within the horror genre, both will appeal to readers who enjoyed Ian McEwan's and Iain Banks's early novels. Highly recommended.

The Secret History by Donna Tartt (Knopf), a first novel, is a heady, slightly twisted trip into existential Hell with six college students. The small, select group studies Greek with a dapper, brilliant, fatherly figure. Four of the impressionable students immerse themselves in Greek thought, culture, and religion—which leads them to a deadly experiment. The consequences of this naïve act on all members of the group are devastating. The story unfolds from the point of view of Richard, the outsider, who joins the close-knit group of four boys and one girl (twin to one of the boys) late. It is Richard who reveals, from the opening, one small bit of what has transpired. Richard (and author Tartt) manage to tantalize the reader through 500-plus pages of sly obliqueness, carefully crafted characterizations, and secret histories. A brilliant first novel. Highly recommended.

The Course of the Heart (Gollancz, U.K.) by M. John Harrison is a novel based on Harrison's story "The Great God Pan" (reprinted in *The Year's Best Fantasy and Horror: Second Annual Collection*). It too emanates from a secret ritual enacted by credulous college students and their mentor, but *The Course of the Heart* goes in an utterly different direction from *The Secret History*. The four main characters of Harrison's novel are so guilt-ridden that they can't remember what it is that they've done, but spend the next twenty years trying to escape its consequences. The narrator hides out in his successful life—happy with career, wife, and child. Yaxley, the mentor, slips into perversion, magic, and despair. And Pam Stuyvesant and Lucas Medlar, both of whom see visions, marry. During their marriage they attempt to comfort each other by reading the mysterious autobiography of the travel writer Michael Ashman, who writes of a country called the Coeur that only exists under the most special conditions, and is a place of visionary splendor where anything is possible. While Tartt's novel is concerned with earthly issues and tangible consequences, Harrison's is more intent on mining the unconscious, the intangible, the mystical. Less accessible than the Tartt but very much worth the effort, *The Course of the Heart* is a visionary and brilliant combination of horror and fantasy. Highly recommended.

Ghostwright by Michael Cadnum (Carroll & Graf) is a satisfying psychological suspense novel by the author of *Nightlight*, *Sleepwalker*, and *St. Peter's Wolf*. Taut and lean, yet with the poetic language of *St. Peter's Wolf*, *Ghostwright* displays

Cadnum's most fascinating characters. Hamilton Speke, a songwriter and playwright considered "brilliant and a genius" by his contemporaries, is successful, charming, and seems completely in control of his life, as he lives idyllically on his estate with Maria, his wife of a few months. One day his old friend Timothy Asquith reappears after ten years, accusing Speke of stealing his ideas, his talent, his very life—and Asquith demands it all back, in spades. Cadnum walks a tightrope with this chilling novel that moves with the unpredictability of charming, deadly insanity. Highly recommended.

Breaking the Fall by Michael Cadnum (Viking) is a short YA novel about Stanley, a teenager at a crossroads. His friend Jared entices him into "playing the game," a dangerous nighttime quest that terrifies him yet makes him feel alive while everything else in his life seems out of control and deadening. There are no traditional horror elements present, but the momentum and edginess built into the fast-moving story might interest readers of horror, and certainly will interest Cadnum fans.

Lost Souls by Poppy Z. Brite (Delacorte/Abyss) deservedly attracted a lot of attention as one of the best first novels of the year. Brite tells the story of an adolescent vampire named Nothing in rich, evocative prose that alone makes the book worth reading.

The Werewolf of Paris by Guy Endore (Citadel) was first published in 1933, and was later the first book ever published by Pocket Books. It still reads well today and this new edition, which features an introduction by Robert Bloch, is well worth finding.

Other notable novels published in 1992 were *Borderland* by S. K. Epperson (Donald I. Fine); *Less than Human* by Gary Raisor (Diamond); *Death's Door* by John Wolfe and Ron Wooley (Abyss); *The Serpent's Kiss* by Daniel Ransom (Dell); *Homecoming* by Matthew J. Costello (Berkley); *Liquid Diet* by William Tedford (Diamond); *Seven Kinds of Death* by Kate Wilhelm (St. Martin's); *Chiller* by Randall Boyll (Jove); *Reprisal* by F. Paul Wilson (Jove); *The Stake* by Richard Laymon (St. Martin's); *Master of Lies* by Graham Masterton (Tor); *Practical Demonkeeping* by Christopher Moore (St. Martin's); *The Holy Terror* by Wayne Allen Sallee (Ziesing); *Gerald's Game* by Stephen King (Viking); *Dark Chant in a Crimson Key* by George C. Chesbro (Warner/Mysterious Press); *Wolf Flow* by K. W. Jeter (St. Martin's); *Burying the Shadow* by Storm Constantine (Headline, U.K.); *Child of the Light* by Janet Gluckman and George Guthridge (St. Martin's); *Dark Channel* by Ray Garton (Bantam Falcon); *Belladonna* by Michael Stewart (HarperCollins); *Red Bride* by Christopher Fowler (Little Brown, U.K.); *Anno Dracula* by Kim Newman (S&S, U.K.); *Fantastique* by Marvin Kaye (St. Martin's); *Valentine* by S. P. Somtow (Tor); *Dr. Guillotine* by Herbert Lom (Sinclaire-Stevenson, U.K.); *Transition of Titus Crow* by Brian Lumley, with illustrations by Judith Holman (W. Paul Ganley); *Gone* by Kit Craig (Little, Brown); *Dolores Claiborne* by Stephen King (Viking); *Homme Fatale* by Paul Mayersberg (St. Martin's); *Incident at Potter's Bridge* by Joe Monninger (Donald I. Fine); *The Werewolves of London* by Brian Stableford (Carroll & Graf); *The Cry from Street to Street* by Hilary Bailey (Constable, U.K.); *Photographing Fairies* by Steve Szilagyi (Ballantine); *Wilding* by Melanie Tem (Abyss); *The Thief of Always* by Clive Barker (HarperCollins); *Lost Futures* by Lisa Tuttle (Abyss); *Dark Journey* by A. R. Morlan (Bantam); *Anthony Shriek* by Jessica Amanda Salmonson (Abyss); *Dark Dance* by Tanith Lee (Abyss); *Snake Eyes* by Rosamond

Smith (Dutton); *Mama's Boy* by Charles King (Pocket); *Silent Witness* by Charles Wilson (Carroll & Graf); *Grace Point* by Anne D. LeClaire (Viking); *In the Heart of the Valley of Love* by Cynthia Kadohata (Viking); *Kissing the Gunner's Daughter* by Ruth Rendell (Mysterious); *Body of Truth* by David Lindsay (Doubleday); *A Dangerous Energy* by John Whitbourn (Gollancz, U.K.); *Gone South* by Robert R. McCammon (Pocket); *Sin Eater* by Elizabeth Massie (Pan, U.K.); *Lost Boys* by Orson Scott Card (HarperCollins); *Unholy Fire* by Whitley Strieber (Dutton); *Leviathan* by Paul Auster (Viking); *The Blood of the Lamb* by Thomas F. Monteleone (Tor); *The Count of Eleven* by Ramsey Campbell (Tor); *The Ice-House* by Minette Walters (St. Martin's); and *Drowning in Fire* by Thom Metzger (Signet).

Anthologies:

The original anthology market continues to hold steady with more in print in 1992 than in the previous year. Anthologies from the United Kingdom, Canada, and Australia added to the number. (To purchase foreign anthologies, try mail-order catalogs or query publisher for U.S. prices plus shipping costs.) The best horror continues to be published in anthologies rather than in magazines, but I'll get into that a bit more later. In no particular order:

Dark at Heart edited by Karen Lansdale and Joe R. Lansdale (Dark Harvest) is exactly what it claims to be: "All new tales of dark suspense." Some are horrific, some are meant to be but don't quite work. This is a satisfying anthology with excellent stories by Norman Partridge, Steve Rasnic Tem, Thomas Sullivan, Stephen Gallagher, Ed Gorman, Chet Williamson, Ronald Kelly, David J. Schow, and David Morrell. Highly recommended. The hardcover, with a jacket by Peter Scanlon, is available in a trade edition at $21.95, and a 400-copy signed, limited edition at $45 plus $2 postage. (Dark Harvest, P.O. Box 941, Arlington Heights, IL 60006.)

Shock Rock edited by Jeff Gelb (Pocket). If one were judging rock 'n' roll short horror fiction solely by this anthology, one would have to conclude that there's nothing original to be said about the subject. Deals with the devil seem to dominate. There are a few good solid horror stories in here, by Stephen King, Richard Christian Matheson, and Thomas Tessier, but not enough of them, and none of them terribly original.

In Dreams edited by Paul J. McAuley and Kim Newman (Gollancz, U.K.) is a welcome antidote to the above. The editors have taken what might appear to be a peculiar idea, "the celebration of the seven-inch single in SF and horror," and put together an enjoyable crossover anthology with contributions from both sides of the Atlantic. My favorite horror or borderline-horror stories were those by Alastair Reynolds, Christopher Fowler, Mark Timlin, and Graham Joyce, although the entire 447-page book was quite enjoyable. Unfortunately, it has not been reprinted by an American publisher, although book dealers such as Mark Ziesing or Dream-Haven might have copies of it. Highly recommended.

The Dedalus Book of Femmes Fatales, edited by Brian Stableford (Dedalus) is, like last year's "wandering Jew" anthology, a combination of classic reprints and originals. Included are stories and poems by Keats, Baudelaire, Poe, Swinburne, and Vernon Lee as well as a contemporary reprint by Thomas Ligotti and excellent new stories by Storm Constantine, Brian Stableford, Ian McDonald, and Steve

Rasnic Tem. A nice mix. This one is not available in the United States either except perhaps from the book dealers mentioned above. Highly recommended.

The Weerde Book 1, devised by Neil Gaiman, Mary Gentle, and Roz Kaveney (Roc, U.K.), is a British anthology I was prepared to dislike because of my bias against "shared world" anthologies. I was pleasantly surprised. The premise is that an ancient race of shape-shifting predators lives among humans. The writers have been given enough leeway (and, I presume, encouragement) to pursue utterly different paths in writing about these creatures, with excellent results from Roz Kaveney, Paul Cornell, Christopher Amies, Josephine Saxton, Michael Fearn, Storm Constantine, and Liz Holliday. Highly recommended.

Souls in Pawn, edited by George Hatch (Noctulpa #6), is not quite up to last year's *Guignoir* but there are good stories in it by Adam Meyer, Norman Partridge, and Carrie Richerson, and good illustrations by Nicholas Scarcy. Recommended.

Dracula: Prince of Darkness, edited by Martin H. Greenberg (DAW), contains literate but lackluster stories with minimal resonance. Few of the stories get beyond cliché or delve into the ramifications of vampirism or the effect of the vampiric lifestyle on the vampire itself. The most ambitious story is by Brian Hodge, though the cop-out ending leaves its promise unfulfilled.

Abortion Stories: Fiction on Fire, edited by Rick Lawler (MinRef Press), boasts a provocative title that promises more than it delivers. What surprises most about this anthology is how unimaginative the stories are. The editor might as well have gone for the jugular, as the subject itself is inherently so controversial. The best stories are those that have the least to do directly with abortion, e.g., L. Crittenden's boringly titled "GP Venture," about extracting embryos for later adoption. Excellent stories about abortion *have* been published elsewhere in the past couple of years, such as Poppy Z. Brite's "The Ash of Memory, the Dust of Desire" and "The Murderer Chooses Sterility," by Bradley Denton.

MetaHorror, edited by Dennis Etchison (Dell Abyss), is a thick anthology of original horror fiction. While on the whole it doesn't seem quite as sharp as its predecessor, *Cutting Edge* (one of the major horror anthologies of the 1980s), it is still a remarkable achievement with a line-up of some of the best writers in and out of the field. Every story is first-rate; three are reprinted in this volume and all of them are well worth reading. Highly recommended. A hardcover deluxe, slipcased edition is available, designed, and illustrated by Thomas Canty. Limited to 1000 numbered copies signed by Etchison, Canty, and the contributing authors (all but Joyce Carol Oates). $100 plus $2 shipping. The art, atypical Canty, consists of photo collages in black and white, effective and horrific (Donald M. Grant, Publishers, Inc., P.O. Box 187, Hampton Falls, NH 03844).

Borderlands 3, edited by Thomas F. Monteleone (Borderlands Press), is the third installment of this ambitious anthology series. The stories in this volume are more consistently successful than those in *Borderlands*. Monteleone has set himself what is probably an impossible task, aiming to take readers to the "cutting edge" and over. Building an anthology series around such a vague premise seems doomed to disappoint, given the scarcity of writers who ever come close to the "cutting edge." Despite this caveat there is excellent fiction by Poppy Z. Brite, Thomas Tessier, John Maclay, Ed Gorman, Michael Cassutt, Kathe Koja, and Steve Rasnic Tem. Highly recommended. The hardcover anthology is available in a trade edition for

$20, and a slipcased, signed (by all but Avram Davidson) limited edition of 750 copies for $65, both with a dust jacket by Rick Lieder. Highly recommended (Borderlands Press, P.O. Box 32333, Baltimore, MD 21208).

Narrow Houses, edited by Peter Crowther (Little Brown, U.K.), is an excellent original anthology with "superstition" as its nicely broad theme. There's a good mix of British and American writers, and the stories are consistently interesting and varied. Most of them made my recommended list, and two are reprinted in this volume: those by Nicholas Royle and Stephen Gallagher. Highly recommended. *Touch Wood: Narrow Houses Volume Two* is scheduled for 1993.

Psychos: An Anthology of Psychological Horror in Verse, edited by Michael A. Arnzen (Mastication Publications), is consistently interesting with fine poetry by Steve Rasnic Tem, Don Webb, Robert Frazier, and Thomas Wiloch and good illustrations by Renate Muller. The only flaw is an unnecessary "final note" from the editor. $6 ppd: Michael A. Arnzen, c/o Mastication Publications, P.O. Box 3712, Moscow, ID 83843-1916.

Still Dead: Book of the Dead II, edited by John Skipp and Craig Spector (Bantam Falcon), is more consistent in quality than their first volume of flesh-eating zombie stories. I would have liked to see a few more "zombie as metaphor" stories but there's an excellent contribution by Poppy Z. Brite (reprinted here), and many others made my recommended list. Unfortunately, the introduction suffers from the self-congratulatory tone of the editors. Recommended. Mark Ziesing published a beautiful hardcover of the anthology, with full-color cover and interiors by Rick Berry, for $29.95 for a trade edition, $85 for a signed, slipcased edition. All books are plus $2 postage (Mark V. Ziesing Books, Box 76, Shingletown, CA 96088).

Freak Show, edited by F. Paul Wilson (Pocket), is the second Horror Writers of America shared-world anthology and must be judged two ways. As an episodic novel it works, and Wilson has done an admirable job integrating the pieces. Yet despite the overall quality of the writing, the book—as a showcase for members of the HWA—is an ill-conceived disaster, muting the writers' individuality. Why doesn't the HWA propose a non-theme anthology to show off the many diverse voices of its membership instead of continuing to produce these stifling wastes of talent? A limited hardcover edition of *Freak Show* was published by Borderlands Press with cover and interiors by Phil Parks, slipcased and signed by contributors and limited to 750 copies. $75. This is a beautifully produced book, much more attractive than the paperback.

Grails: Quests, Visitations, and Other Occurrences, edited by Richard Gilliam, Martin H. Greenberg, and Edward E. Kramer (Unnameable Press), was given out free to the membership at the World Fantasy Convention in Pine Mountain, Georgia. It's a very large anthology that stays a little too close to the Arthurian motifs of the "grail" theme for my taste. The most interesting stories are those that branch out into the "other occurrences" of the subtitle. There are some good dark pieces, but the book is weighted more toward fantasy. Unnumbered copies are available for general sale and a mass-market edition is forthcoming. Write to Unnameable Press for information: P.O. Box 11689, Atlanta, GA 30355-1689.

Midnight Graffiti, edited by Jessica Horsting and James Van Hise (Warner), is an anthology consisting half of reprints from the magazine and half of original stories. *Midnight Graffiti,* the anthology, is a spotlight for the magazine's flaws. Very few of the stories disturb in more than a superficial way, and the satires usually lack grace and subtlety. Despite this there's a terrific original by Neil Gaiman (reprinted here) and a very good original by John Shirley. There are multiple factual errors and misstatements on the book cover and in the blurbs, and there seem to be a lot of typos in the book itself. How about some truth in advertising from blurb writers?

Northern Frights, edited by Don Hutchison (Mosaic Press), is a solid dark fantasy anthology from Canada. It's the first volume in a projected series "inspired by the unique geography of the Canadian imaginative landscape." This nice-looking hardcover features reprints by Robert Bloch, Charles de Lint, and Terence Green, originals by Steve Rasnic Tem, Garfield Reeves-Stevens, Lucy Taylor, and others. There is good writing here with a few stand-outs, but the illustrations routinely give away too much of each story.

Intimate Armageddons, edited by Bill Congreve (FIP), is an Australian horror anthology with impressive stories by Robert Hood and Terry Dowling, the most recognizable of the contributors. The anthology is, on the whole, quite literate while not breaking new ground in style or content, and it unwisely includes an overly long reprint by the editor. Fire Island Press Associates, P.O. Box 1946, Wollingbong NSW 2500, Australia. Write for information.

SPWAO Showcase 8—All Aboard! edited by Mike Olson (Small Press Writers and Artists Organization) is disappointing, with even those writers who have broken into professional markets contributing less than their best work. ($8.95 including postage to Michael A. Arnzen, Director, SPWAO Publication Dispersal, 1700 Constitution #D-24, Pueblo, CO 81001.)

Bizarre Sex and Other Crimes of Passion, edited by Stanislas Tal (TAL Publications), is an anthology of erotic horror with good work by John Edward Ames, Lucy Taylor, and Wayne Allen Sallee, so-so works by others ($9.50 plus $1.50 shipping to TAL Publications, P.O. Box 1837, Leesburg, VA 22075).

Red Stains A Lexicon of Lesions: Bible of Blood, edited by Jack Hunter (Creation Press), is a strange, repellent anthology from England. The plots are minimal, the descriptions disgusting, but structurally there's some interesting experimentation within the stories. The only contributors with whom I'm familiar are Ramsey Campbell (whose reprint is by far the best piece in the book) and D. F. Lewis (£5.95 to Creation Press, 83 Clerkenwell Road, London EC1 U.K.)

Dark Voices 4 edited by David Sutton and Stephen Jones (Pan). Even though this series is never as interesting or scary as I'd like, there are always a few standout stories in each volume. This year they were by Christopher Fowler and Graham Masterton, both reprinted here.

Temps, devised by Alex Stewart and Neil Gaiman (Roc, U.K.) and *Eurotemps* (Roc, U.K.)—a pair of British shared-world anthologies several cuts above their American counterparts. The hook is that the Department of Paranormal Resources keeps their "talents" on tap as temporary workers as the need arises. Clever, sometimes horrific stories. Very enjoyable, particularly *Eurotemps,* with excellent stories by Jenny Jones, Storm Constantine, and Roz Kaveney.

Darklands 2, edited by Nicholas Royle (Egerton Press), is the second volume of the British dark fantasy/horror anthology series. It is a solid follow-up to last year's volume. Most of the writers are unfamiliar to me, but all the stories are good. (£4.99 to Egerton Press, 5 Windsor Court, Avenue Road, London N15 5JQ, U.K.)

Lovers and Other Monsters, selected by Marvin Kaye (GuildAmerica Books), features stories on the "darker and supernatural aspects of love." A handful of original works by Steve Rasnic Tem and various unknowns includes some good pieces. Among the reprints are stories by Gorky, Lovecraft, Sturgeon, Bradbury, de Balzac, Poe, Rosetti, and Hammett. A nice package created for and available only through the Literary Guild.

Cat Crimes II and *III* edited by Martin H. Greenberg and Ed Gorman (Donald I. Fine): Volume II has fine stories with horrific overtones by Richard Laymon and Sharyn McCrumb, a charming fantasy by Charlotte MacLeod and some real dogs (if you'll excuse the expression). Not as much for horror readers as for cat fanciers. Volume III is the best and the darkest of the series so far, with more variety than usual and several hard-hitting stories, including a nasty by Barbara and Max Allan Collins.

New Crimes 3 edited by Maxim Jakubowski (Carroll & Graf) came out in 1992 despite the 1991 copyright. Generally, this series isn't dark enough to call horror, but there are invariably a few horrific stories in each volume. Volume 3 had excellent contributions by Norman Partridge and Steve Rasnic Tem.

Constable New Crimes 1, edited by Maxim Jakubowski, seems to be the same series as the above but now is being published in the U.K. by Constable instead of Robinson—hence the numerical confusion. This volume of dark suspense opens with a powerful story by Mark Timlin, a writer with whom I'm familiar only through his stand-out story in *In Dreams*. Although there are a few weak contributions, on the whole the anthology is very readable, with excellent stories by Wayne Allen Sallee, H. R. F. Keating, and Ed Gorman.

Short Circuits: Thirteen Shocking Stories by Outstanding Writers for Young Adults edited by Donald R. Gallo (Delacorte). In his introduction Gallo strangely admits to hating being scared and that he avoids frightening stories and movies. So why a *horror* anthology? Gallo has previously edited three mainstream young adult anthologies, and I presume his publisher, perceiving the popularity of horror, requested the book. The criteria for Gallo's choices were that each contributor "write a story that focused on a teenage character and that was creepy, scary, weird, horrifying, or shocking in some way." There's some creepiness and a lot of weirdness but no shocks or horror. Even so, almost half, particularly those by Robert Westall, Vivien Alcock, and Joan Aiken are good, interesting fantasies.

Writers of the Future Volume VIII, edited by Dave Wolverton (Bridge), is generally considered a science fiction showcase for new writers, but VIII had more horror than usual. There were good stories with horrific overtones by Sam Wilson, Maria C. Plieger, Bronwyn Elko, Stephen Woodworth, and Astrid Julian.

Sisters in Crime 5, edited by Marilyn Wallace (Berkley), doesn't have any actual horror, but it does contain two very dark, effective stories by Joyce Carol Oates and Susan Taylor Chehak.

Aladdin: Master of the Lamp, edited by Mike Resnick and Martin H. Greenberg (DAW), has no actual horror but includes two excellent dark pieces by Pat Cadigan and Barry N. Malzberg.

The Magic of Christmas: Holiday Stories of Fantasy and Science Fiction, edited by John Silbersack and Christopher Schelling (Roc), is entertaining although there is only one horror story and one sweet ghost story.

The following original or mostly original anthologies cross genres and contain some horror: *Sword and Sorceresses IX*, edited by Marion Zimmer Bradley (DAW)—stories by Bruce Arthurs, Mary Frey, and David Smeds; *Dragon Fantastic*, edited by Martin H. Greenberg and Rosalind M. Greenberg (DAW); *After the King*, edited by Martin H. Greenberg (Tor), published stories in honor of J. R. R. Tolkien, with two, by Peter S. Beagle and Stephen Donaldson, veering toward the horrific; *Universe 2*, edited by Robert Silverberg and Karen Haber (Bantam)—Kathe Koja; *Villains!*, edited by Neil Gaiman and Mary Gable (Roc, U.K.)—Graham Higgins and Charles Stross; *New Worlds 2*, edited by David Garnett (Gollancz)—Simon Ings.

The following anthologies used mostly reprint material. Not all of them have been seen by me personally, particularly some of the British ones:
Kingpins: Tales from Inside the Mob, edited by Cynthia Manson and Charles Ardai (Carroll & Graf), reprints stories from *Ellery Queen* and *Alfred Hitchcock's Mystery Magazine* and includes stories by Stephen King, Andrew Vachss, Brian Garfield, Raymond Chandler, and Keith Peterson; *Women of Mystery: Stories from Ellery Queen's Mystery Magazine and Alfred Hitchcock's Mystery Magazine* edited by Cynthia Manson (Carroll & Graf); *Fifty Best Mysteries*, edited by Eleanor Sullivan (Carroll & Graf); *The Best of the Rest 1990*, edited by Stephen Pasechnick and Brian Youmans (Edgewood Press—a 1992 book despite the '91 copyright); *Modern Ghost Stories by Eminent Women Writers*, edited by Richard Dalby (Carroll & Graf), includes stories by A. S. Byatt, Penelope Lively, Jean Rhys, Ruth Rendell, Antonia Fraser, Edith Wharton, Joan Aiken, and other, lesser-known writers; *A Taste for Blood: Fifteen Great Vampire Tales*, edited by Martin H. Greenberg, Robert Weinberg, and Stefan R. Dziemianowicz (Dorset), includes stories by Clive Barker, Robert Bloch, Tanith Lee, Dan Simmons, and H. P. Lovecraft; *Weird Vampire Tales: 30 Blood-chilling Stories from the Weird Fiction Pulps*, edited by Robert Weinberg, Stefan R. Dziemianowicz, and Martin H. Greenberg (Gramercy), includes stories by Clark Ashton Smith, Robert E. Howard, C. L. Moore, Lester del Rey, A. E. van Vogt, Robert Bloch, William Tenn, and Charles Beaumont; *Foundations of Fear*, edited by David G. Hartwell (Tor), the monumental companion volume to the award-winning historical survey, *The Dark Descent*, reprints novellas by Daphne Du Maurier, John W. Campbell, Jr., Clive Barker, Richard Matheson and the first full-length publication of Scott Baker's "The Lurking Duck"; *Dark Crimes 2: Modern Masters of Noir*, edited by Ed Gorman (Carroll & Graf), includes stories ranging from 1950 to 1992 by David Morrell, Lawrence Block, Marcia Muller, Joe R. Lansdale, and John Shirley (and glaringly omits Ruth Rendell and Patricia Highsmith); *Future Crime: An Anthology on the Shape of Crime to Come*, edited by Cynthia Manson and Charles Ardai (Donald I. Fine), reprints stories from *Ellery Queen's* and *Alfred Hitchcock's Mystery Magazines*, as well as from *Asimov's Science Fiction Magazine* and *Analog Science Fiction/Science Fact Magazine*. It has original stories by C. J. Cherryh, Alan Dean Foster and

George Alec Effinger—but nothing dark enough to call horror; *The Mammoth Book of Vampires*, edited by Stephen Jones (Carroll & Graf), had a few originals, the exceptional novella "Red Reign," by Kim Newman, and two good ones by Steve Rasnic Tem and Graham Masterton. The reprints included stories by Clive Barker, Brian Lumley, Richard Christian Matheson, David J. Schow, Melanie Tem, Howard Waldrop, and Nancy Holder; *The Year's 25 Finest Crime and Mystery Stories: First Annual Edition*, edited by the staff of *Mystery Scene* (Carroll & Graf), reprints stories from 1989 and 1990, including those by Sue Grafton, Ruth Rendell, Andrew Vachss, Joe R. Lansdale, Faye Kellerman, and Charlotte MacLeod; *Best New Horror 3*, edited by Stephen Jones and Ramsey Campbell (Carroll & Graf); *The Year's Best Horror XX* edited by Karl Edward Wagner (DAW); *Great American Ghost Stories*, edited by Frank D. McSherry, Jr., Charles G. Waugh, and Martin H. Greenberg (Rutledge Hill Press); *Strange Tales of Mystery and the Paranormal*, edited by Cecilia Heathwood (Excaliber Press, U.K.), a collection of thirty-one occult stories and essays, originally published in the magazine *Ireland's Eye*; *Fairy Tales and Fables from Weimar Days*, edited by Jack Zipes (University Press of New England—according to *Locus* published in 1989)—twenty-seven fairy tales translated from the German by Zipes with a lengthy critical and historical introduction; *The Oxford Book of Gothic Tales* edited by Chris Baldick (Oxford University Press, U.K.), an anthology of thirty-seven Gothic short stories dating from the eighteenth century to the present including contributors as diverse as H. P. Lovecraft, Patrick McGrath, Eudora Welty, Jorge Luis Borges, Joyce Carol Oates, and Ray Russell; *The Second Dedalus Book of Decadence: The Black Feast* edited by Brian M. Stableford (Dedalus, U.K.); *The Little Book of Horrors: Tiny Tales of Terror*, edited by Sebastian Wolfe (Barricade), an anthology of seventy short-short horror stories, poems, and cartoons; *Best of the Midwest's Science Fiction, Fantasy & Horror*, edited by Brian Smart (ESA Books), an anthology of twenty-one stories that originally appeared in small press magazines—1991; *Forbidden Journeys: Fairy Tales and Fantasies by Victorian Women Writers* edited by Nina Auerbach and U. C. Knoepflmacher (University of Chicago Press), an anthology of eleven nineteenth-century fantasy stories by women writers with introduction and commentary by the editors; *Great Ghost Stories* edited by John Grafton (Dover), an anthology of ten classic ghost stories with an introduction by the editor; *Chilling Christmas Tales*, ed. Anonymous (Scholastic, U.K.), an original anthology of ten young-adult horror stories, including pieces by Joan Aiken and Garry Kilworth; *Great Irish Stories of the Supernatural*, edited by Peter Haining (Souvenir Press, U.K.), twenty-eight Irish supernatural stories; *Murder on the Menu: Cordon Bleu Stories of Crime and Mystery* edited by Peter Haining (Carroll & Graf), stories by P. D. James, Ruth Rendell, Michael Gilbert, Patricia Highsmith, and Roald Dahl; *Reel Terror* edited by Sebastian Wolfe (Carroll & Graf), an entertaining collection of stories that inspired some of the great horror films. The book includes Richard Matheson's "Duel," which, as a film, was Steven Spielberg's directorial debut; "Spurs," a story by the now-obscure Tod Robbins that strongly influenced Tod Browning's great film *Freaks* (it's interesting to compare the two versions—Browning's goes much further and is far more shocking than the original story). Also included are stories by Angela Carter ("The Company of Wolves"), John Cheever ("The Swimmer"),

Philip K. Dick ("We Can Remember It for You Wholesale," on which *Total Recall* was based), George Langelaan ("The Fly"), and Robert Bloch ("Psycho") among others; *Tales of the Lovecraft Mythos*, edited by Robert M. Price with an amusing cover by Gahan Wilson (Fedogan and Bremer); *The Puffin Book of Ghosts and Ghouls*, edited by Gene Kemp (Viking, U.K.); *Quick Chills II*, a hardcover anthology edited by Robert Morrish and Peter Enfantino (Deadline Press), the best horror stories from the small press published during 1990 and 1991. The book includes excellent fiction by Nancy A. Collins, Adam-Troy Castro, Norman Partridge, Susan M. Watkins, and Nancy Holder, among others. Limited to 575 signed, numbered copies. $45 (Deadline Press, 4884 Pepperwood Way, San Jose, CA 95124); and *The Definitive Best of The Horror Show*, edited by David B. Silva with a cover by Harry O. Morris (CD Publications). $25 for the trade edition.

As usual, few large publishing houses seem to be willing to take chances on single *living*-author collections, preferring those authors whose work is in the public domain, with specialty presses continuing to take up the slack.

The following single author collections contain horror or crossover material:

St. Martin's Press published *Geodesic Dreams* by Gardner Dozois, which despite being mostly science fiction is certainly dark enough to be enjoyed by horror aficionados. Ironic, moving, and literate, Dozois' work should be read and savored. He has been one of the major short story writers in fantastic fiction. Another important collection from St. Martin's is Kate Wilhelm's *And the Angels Sing*. Wilhelm's well-crafted stories are often moving and magical. She writes subtly about relationships and how technology affects us personally for better or worse.

The Overlook Press published Tanith Lee's *The Book of the Dead: The Secret Books of Paradys III*, a collection of eight very dark fantasies. Historical fantasy at its best, with a disquieting blend of sexuality and horror.

HarperCollins-U.K. brought out Lisa Tuttle's *Memories of the Body: Tales of Desire and Transformations*, which includes her recent sexual-political stories "The Wound," "Husbands," and "Memories of the Body." Tuttle does "alien sex," that is, the opposite sex as "other," well, if not better than almost anyone else around. Angry, sharp, stylish stories. Available in the United States from Severn House, 475 Fifth Avenue, New York, NY 10017.

Grove Weidenfeld published Dennis Cooper's *Wrong*, his darkly original collection of short stories about gay life in the fast lane. (See his novel *Frisk* from last year.) Although they are more vignettes than actual stories, and there is nothing supernatural or overtly horrific in them, nonetheless, Cooper's short works will startle, disturb, and perhaps horrify.

Nightmare Flower, Elizabeth Engstrom's first collection, includes several original stories, most in her trademark baroque style. It was published by Tor.

The Burning Baby and Other Ghosts by John Gordon was published by Walker-U.K. for young adults. Too old-fashioned for my taste; the stories seem a bit pallid. I much prefer Robert Westall's and Joan Aiken's young adult ghost stories.

Honeymoon with Death by Bridget Penney was published by Polygon in Scotland. A mainstream collection with dark, edgy material that might interest readers of Mary Gaitskill, although not as consistently violent and flaky.

Bantam published *The Complete Fairy Tales of the Brothers Grimm*, translated and with an introduction by Jack Zipes. This trade paperback includes eight stories not in the 1987 hardcover edition.

Carroll & Graf published *The Collected Ghost Stories of E. F. Benson*, edited by Richard Dalby, claiming that this is the first time the stories have been "reprinted in one volume, bringing together material that has not been available for over forty years."

Mercury House brought out a beautifully illustrated edition of I. U. Tarchetti's *Fantastic Tales*, translated from the Italian by Lawrence Venuti. Written in the nineteenth century, Tarchetti's eerie and macabre stories were the first Italian Gothic tales. This is their first publication in English.

Ecco Press published a new collection by Joyce Carol Oates, *Where Is Here?*, including stories from such diverse venues as *Omni*, *Self*, *Triquarterly*, *Yale Review*, *Seventeen*, and *Savvy*.

CALYX Books published Kathleen Alcalá's collection *Mrs. Vargas and the Dead Naturalist*. It has original fantasy stories with occasional horrific elements and reprints from *Isaac Asimov's Science Fiction Magazine*, *Black Ice*, *The Seattle Review*, and other magazines and anthologies.

Jack Cady's *The Sons of Noah & Other Stories* came out from Broken Moon Press. These are mostly reprints by an underrated crossover writer who started in the mainstream with quirky novels like *The Man Who Could Make Things Vanish*, *The Well*, and *McDowell's Ghost* but only began attracting attention in the horror field with his short fiction, specifically his powerful Vietnam novella "By Reason of Darkness," published in Douglas E. Winter's anthology *Prime Evil*. Since then his short fiction has been published in *Omni*, *Fantasy & Science Fiction*, *Final Shadows*, and *Glimmer Train*. $13.95 from Broken Moon Press, P.O. Box 24585, Seattle, WA 98124-0585.

Cemetery Dance's first foray into book publishing is Ed Gorman's cross-genre collection *Prisoners and Other Stories*. These stories, mostly reprints, give the reader a good overview of Gorman's style and range. $20.95 plus $1.05 shipping and handling. Trade hardcover. CD Publications, P.O. Box 18433, Edgewood, MD 21237.

In conjunction with Pat Cadigan's guest of honor appearance at Disclave in 1992, WSFA Press published a collection of four of her stories, *Home by the Sea*, illustrated by David R. Works, in a 500-copy edition signed and numbered in slipcase. $49.95 plus $3 shipping. WSFA Press, Box 19951, Baltimore, MD 21211-0951. A beautiful piece of bookcraft as well as good fiction.

In honor of Jane Yolen's guest of honor appearance at Boskone in 1992, the NESFA Press published *Storyteller*, a collection of nineteen stories, six poems, and one nonfiction piece, with interior illustrations by Merle Insinga in a 1000-copy numbered edition, the first 200 signed and slipcased. $32 to NESFA Press, P.O. Box G, MIT Branch Post Office, Cambridge, MA 02139.

Broken Mirrors Press collected eighteen vintage R. A. Lafferty stories in *Lafferty in Orbit*, which contains all of the stories by this odd fantasist that appeared in the *Orbit* anthology series. Very little of it qualifies as horror, but it's definitely of interest. $13.95 + $1 postage from Broken Mirrors Press, P.O. Box 473, Cambridge, MA 02238.

Donald M. Grant, Publisher, Inc., brought out a handsome 500-copy limited edition of William Hope Hodgson's uncollected short fiction entitled *The Haunted Pampero* with illustrations by Arthur E. Moore. $30 plus $2 shipping.

Norman Partridge's 30,000-word debut collection, *Mr. Fox and Other Feral Tales*, was published by Roadkill Press. It contains mostly original material from this up-and-coming writer and is illustrated by Alan M. Clark with an introduction by Edward Bryant. The signed paperback, limited to 500 copies, can be ordered for $8 plus $1 shipping.

Roadkill Press also brought out Edward Bryant's collection *Darker Passions*, with an introduction by Dan Simmons and illustrations by Melissa Sherman. It has two reprints and an original, "Human Remains" (reprinted here). The signed paperback, limited to 500 copies, costs $6 plus $1 shipping. (Little Bookshop of Horrors, 10380 Ralston Road, Arvada, CO 80004.)

Mindwarps is John Maclay's second collection and contains twenty-three stories, three of them originals. It comes as a signed hardcover and can be ordered for $9.95 plus $1 shipping through Maclay & Associates Publishers, P.O. Box 16253, Baltimore, MD 21210.

Horror's Head Press published *Chronicles of the Mutant Rain Forest* by Robert Frazier and Bruce Boston with Potter-influenced illustrations by Frazier and an introduction by Lucius Shepard. Many of the poems, about an imaginary rain forest in which dreams are manifest and strange things happen, have been published before. $8.95 to Horror's Head Press, 140 Dickie Avenue, Staten Island, NY 10314.

Iron Tears collects stories by R. A. Lafferty from 1973–1988. The paperback, with an introduction by Michael Swanwick, costs $10 plus $1.50 postage from Edgewood Press, P.O. Box 264, Cambridge, MA 02238.

Neal Barrett, Jr.'s *Slightly Off Center* is introduced by Joe R. Lansdale and is published by Swan Press. Barrett writes weird stuff, very American and only rarely horrific, but his characterizations alone make his work worth reading. A few original stories are included in this paperback. $9.50 to Swan Press, P.O. Box 90006, Austin, TX 78709.

Satanskin by James Havoc was published by England's Creation Press. While they are consistently disgusting, I'm not sure I'd describe these "stories" with their minimal plots as horror. They don't frighten or disturb—except in their appalling misuse of the English language. The writer attempts to go beyond the Marquis de Sade in his exotic depiction of violent eroticism. Energetic but barely readable for any but the most tolerant of "experimental" prose combined with gross descriptions of the corruption of flesh.

Anamnesis Press published a collection by Keith Allen Daniels called *What Rough Book: Dark Poems and Light*. Limited to 1000 trade paperback copies at $12.95 (Anamnesis Press, P.O. Box 1351, Clute, TX 77531).

Necronomicon Press published Steve Rasnic Tem's wonderful Lovecraftian triptych, *Decoded Mirrors*, illustrated by Eckhardt, for $4.95; Brian Stableford's story, "The Innsmouth Heritage," which extends the concepts of H. P. Lovecraft's supernatural horror fiction "into the brave new world of contemporary scientific rationalism," also illustrated by Jason Eckhardt for $4.50; and Scott Edelman's collection of two original horror stories, *Suicide Art*, illustrated by Robert H. Knox, for $4.50. The press also published *The Brain in the Jar and Others: Collected Stories and*

Poems by Richard F. Searight, reprinting five macabre stories and twelve poems for $5.95. All the above are paperback, and can be ordered from Necronomicon Press, 101 Lockwood St., West Warwick, RI 02893.

TAL Publications published *Edward Lee's Quest for Sex, Truth, and Reality* by Edward Lee. These three tales of erotic horror have cover art by Rick Lieder, interior art by Gene Gryniewicz, and an introduction by Jack Ketchum; and *Unnatural Acts*, three powerful raw stories of erotic horror by the impressive Lucy Taylor, with an introduction by Edward Lee and art by Kim Colson; $5.95 plus $1 shipping payable to TAL Publications. Address is under "Anthologies."

Jessica Amanda Salmonson's *Sorceries and Sorrows (Early Poems)* appeared as Drumm Booklet #42 and includes a bibliography of Salmonson's work. $3.75 to Chris Drumm, P.O. Box 445, Polk City, IA 50226. Another Salmonson book is the lovingly designed and produced hardcover containing short stories, vignettes, and parables, *The Goddess Under Siege*, illustrated by Jules Remedios Faye from Street of Crocodiles. (Price not available.)

Talisman published t. winter-damon's "visionary texts and collages," *L'Heure D'Hallucinations* in an attractive paperback edition well worth the $5.95 price. Subconscious surreal images; winter-damon's work is better in these small exquisite doses than in his full-blown texts. Talisman, Box 321, Beech Grove, IN 46107.

Jazz Police Books, the new imprint of Wordcraft of Oregon, plans to publish speculative poetry books and chapbooks. Its first publication is *House on Fire: The Poetry and Collage of David Memmott*. Memmott is consistently interesting as an artist and poet, and this book includes a Rhysling Award–winning poem. $9 paperback, $20 hardcover to Wordcraft of Oregon, P.O. Box 3235, La Grande, OR 97850.

The following collections I have not seen: Robert Hale–U.K. brought out *Creeping Fingers and Other Stories of the Occult*, a collection of fifteen original supernatural and ghost stories by Mary Williams, and *Charles Dickens' Christmas Ghost Stories* edited by Peter Haining; Macmillan-U.K. published Robert Westall's YA collection *Fearful Lovers and Other Stories*; Alfred A. Knopf published *The Girl with the Green Ear*, a collection by Margaret Mahy of nine young-adult fantasy stories previously published in various British Mahy collections. *The Horror of the Heights and Other Tales of Suspense* by Arthur Conan Doyle was published by Chronicle Books; *The Chilling Hour: Tales of the Real and Unreal*, a young adult collection of eight horror and dark fantasies by Collin McDonald, was published by Penguin/Cobblehill; and Penguin/Signet published Charlotte Perkins Gilman's *Herland and Selected Stories*, consisting of twenty stories, including macabre and ghostly tales; Vintage published *Edgar Allan Poe's Selected Tales*, seventeen stories plus the novel *The Narrative of Arthur Gordon Pym of Nantucket*, with an introduction by Diane Johnson; Viking-U.K. published Robert Westall's collection of two supernatural YA novellas, *The Stones of Muncaster Cathedral*; *The Uncollected Stories of Mary Wilkins Freeman*, edited by Mary R. Reichardt, was published by the University Press of Mississippi, collecting twenty of the author's uncollected stories; The Ghost Story Society–U.K. published *Out of the Past: The Indiana Ghost Stories of Anna Nicholas*, a collection of three ghost stories edited and introduced by Jessica Amanda

Salmonson (no price available); The Haunted Library–U.K. published Alan W. Lear's collection of four original ghost stories, *Spirits of Another Sort* for £2.50.

The magazine field continues to be in terrible shape. The problem is not a lack of magazines—I read issues of more than forty different magazines during 1992, several of them new—but the questionable quality of most of them. Only a handful consistently published readable fiction and provided adequate design (by which I mean readable type, not necessarily beautiful design elements). Since the advent of desk-top publishing, just about anyone can produce a magazine. Unfortunately, too many people with lots of ambition and good intentions—but no experience and little talent—are doing so. This is the reason why most of the horror stories chosen for *The Year's Best Fantasy and Horror* come from anthologies.

No matter what the pay rate, or how slick a magazine looks, it cannot be considered professional unless it keeps to a regular schedule. Under this criterion the only professional horror magazine is *Weird Tales*. *Midnight Graffiti*'s sole 1992 issue was a year late when it came out in December and *Iniquities* didn't publish in 1992 at all, although a new issue is scheduled for the first half of 1993. And only a few other magazines seem to be able to stay on any kind of a regular schedule. The following is a sampling of the best professional, semiprofessional, and small-press magazines that publish at least some horror fiction:

Weird Tales publishes fantasy and dark fantasy but rarely out-and-out horror stories. The best stories in 1992 were those by Ramsey Campbell, Tanith Lee, Robert J. Howe, and S. P. Somtow. The editor is Darrell Schweitzer. Schweitzer and George Scithers (who is now publisher) won last year's World Fantasy Award in the Special Award–Professional category for their work on the magazine.

Amazing Stories rarely publishes horror intentionally, but occasionally a story or two will verge on the horrific. Good work in 1992 by Tony Daniel, Ian McDowell, Barry N. Malzberg and Jack Dann, Susan Wade, and William F. Wu. The editor is Kim Mohan.

The Magazine of Fantasy & Science Fiction began publishing increasingly interesting horror fiction toward the end of Ed Ferman's editorship. The trend continues under Kristine Kathryn Rusch. Excellent horror by Nancy Farmer, Edward Bryant, Victor Koman, Rick Bowes, Algis Budrys, Carrie Richerson, Joyce Thompson, Marc Laidlaw, Joe Haldeman, Ian Watson, Rick Wilber, and Kit Reed.

Asimov's Science Fiction concentrates more on science fiction and fantasy but published good horrific fiction and poetry by W. M. Shockley, Paul Hellweg, R. Garcia y Robertson, Maureen F. McHugh, Ace G. Pilkington, Jamil Nasir, Diane Mapes, Esther M. Friesner, John Kessel, and Melanie Tem. The editor is Gardner Dozois.

Alfred Hitchcock's Mystery Magazine seems to be moving toward somewhat darker suspense stories that occasionally verge on the horrific. Good stories by David Braley, P. K. Schossau, Dan Crawford, Ashley Curtis, Frank Michaels, Esther J. Holt, Maggie Wagner-Hankins, and Don Marshall. The editor is Cathleen Jordan.

Ellery Queen's Mystery Magazine also seems edgier. It had good fiction by Martin Naparsteck, June Thomson, Jiro Agawa, Jo Bannister, Joyce Carol Oates, Betty Rowlands, David C. Hall, David Dean, Peter Lovesey, Deanne Jordan,

William Beechcroft, Bill Pronzini, and Donald Olson. The editor is Janet Hutchings.

Interzone, Great Britain's premier science fiction magazine, also published good horror fiction by Nicholas Royle, Stuart Palmer, Stephen Blanchard, Stephen Baxter, M. John Harrison, David Garnett, Diane Mapes, Ian R. MacLeod, Brian Aldiss, T. J. MacGregor, and Elizabeth Hand. *Interzone* is edited by David Pringle.

New Mystery, edited by Charles Raisch, put out two issues in 1992, one on the cusp of 1991–2 and covered by me last year. The third issue, published on the cusp of 1992–3, had a good story by Lisa Cantrell and useful reviews of several crossover titles. The full-color covers are attractive. It remains to be seen if this newest and slickest entry into the mystery/suspense field can keep on schedule.

Midnight Graffiti #7, edited by Jessica Horsting, was finally published late in 1992. It looks as good as ever and there's some good—and bad—fiction. The general look at what's going on in horror discovers it is rife with factual errors, misspellings, and confusions. Jeanne Cavelos, editor of the Abyss line, is interviewed, and throughout the interview her name is misspelled.

The following is a sampling of the best small-press magazines specializing in horror:

Cemetery Dance's editor, Richard Chizmar, deservedly won the 1992 World Fantasy Award for Special Award: Non-Professional. This quarterly is now the most regular and consistently readable of the small-press magazines, though I don't feel the cartoony covers or the interior art do the magazine justice. Thomas Monteleone's column is often provocative, sometimes annoying, but always entertaining, and the reviews are usually informative. The fall issue had an especially good column by Charles L. Grant. While not always outstanding, the fiction is generally literate. This is *the* small-press magazine to watch. The magazine published excellent fiction by Norman Partridge, Brian Hodge, Gary A. Braunbeck, C. S. Fuqua, Pamela J. Jessen, Stephen King, and Adam Corbin Fusco. $15 for a one-year subscription (4 issues) payable to CD Publications and mailed to *Cemetery Dance*, P.O. Box 18433, Baltimore, MD 21237.

The Urbanite: A Journal of City Fiction and Poetry is a new entry edited by Mark McLaughlin. It's attractive and had very good fiction in this second issue, subtitled *The Party Issue*—with slumber parties, book parties, cocktail parties, dinner parties. Good use of theme. It would be nice if author biographies were included in the future. $5 for a single issue, $13.50 for a three-issue subscription payable to Mark McLaughlin, P.O. Box 4737, Davenport, IA 52808 (IA residents add 6% tax). Irregular publication schedule.

Grue only published one issue in 1992, but #14 looks good, with professional-looking typesetting, an effective cover by Rick Lieder, and unusually high-quality interior art for the small press. Excellent stories by Melanie Tem and D. R. McBride. The editor is Peggy Nadramia. $4.50 for the current issue, or a three-issue subscription is $13 payable to Hell's Kitchen Productions, Inc., P.O. Box 370, Times Square Station, New York, NY 10108-0370.

Deathrealm has survived its close brush with the recession and been given a new lease on life by TAL Publications. Stanislaus Tal is now publisher, and Mark Rainey remains as editor. The large-format magazine had good covers and interior art by Jason van Hollander, Harry Fassl, Timothy Patrick Butler, Alan Clark, Jeffrey

Osier, and Phillip Reynolds, and very good fiction and poetry by Brad Cahoon, Kristopher Kane, Chad Hensley, Dan Crawford, Lisa Wimberger, and Jessica Amanda Salmonson. $4.95 per single copy, one year (4 issues) $15.95 payable to TAL Productions, P.O. Box 1837–Dept S, Leesburg, VA 22075.

Crypt of Cthulhu, edited by Robert M. Price, is a must for those with an interest in Lovecraft and his mythos. Scholarly essays and reviews of related material: #80 has Price doing Derrida, getting into the spirit of deconstruction, and in #82 Donald R. Burleson deconstructs the name "Lovecraft" (now *this* is four pages of silliness, but he seems to be serious). Good fiction by Mark Rainey. *Crypt of Cthulhu* no longer accepts subscriptions. Instead, request that Necronomicon Press place you on their mailing list. *Crypt* appears three times a year, each new issue to be announced in the thrice-yearly catalog. Necronomicon Press, 101 Lockwood Street, West Warwick, RI 02893.

After Hours, edited by William G. Raley, has stayed on its quarterly schedule for the last couple of years, and in addition to providing book reviews and interesting interviews with editors, writers, and artists of the pro and small press, has become a consistent forum for literate horror fiction. Good stories by S. R. Gannon, Rebecca Lyons, Benjamin Gleisser, Suzi K. West, Ty Drago, and Stephen M. Rainey. $4 per issue, $14 annual subscription payable to *After Hours*, P.O. Box 538, Sunset Beach, CA 90742-0538.

2AM, edited by Gretta M. Anderson, is now perfect-bound. It looks increasingly good, with clean and readable type. The fiction in 1992 struck me as too soft for a horror magazine but there were effective stories by Ronald Kelly and Linda Lee Mayfair. Single copies $4.95 plus $1 postage and handling. To subscribe, send $19 for four issues payable to Gretta M. Anderson, *2AM* Magazine, P.O. Box 6754, Rockford, IL 61125-1754.

The Tome, edited by David Niall Wilson, began to use full-color covers in 1992. The paper went from good heavy stock in spring to pulp in the summer, but the art and the fiction improved. There was good fiction and poetry by James S. Dorr, Brian Hopkins, Gary Braunbeck, and Elizabeth Massie. This semi-annual publication can be ordered for $3.95 per single issue, $12 for a year payable to Grub St. Publications, 454 Munden Avenue, Norfolk, VA 23505.

Eldritch Tales is edited by Crispin Burnham. The two issues published during 1992 had very good stories and poems by Kathryn Ptacek, Denise Dumars, Bentley Little, Judith R. Behunin, and John F. D. Taff. It's a nice-looking magazine and was effectively illustrated by Augie Weidermann, Ron Leming, and Harry O. Morris. $6 per copy plus $1 postage and handling or $20 for four issues plus $4 postage and handling payable to Crispin Burnham, Eldritch Tales, 1051 Wellington Road, Lawrence, KS 66049.

Sequitur: A Journal of Consequences, a quarterly edited by Rachel Drummond, made an auspicious August debut with an interview with artist Harry O. Morris and portfolio of his work, an article on true life weirdness by Ed Bryant, and a historical view of the devil by Anya Martin. This attractive, brown type on cream, perfect-bound digest-sized magazine is very promising, although the nonfiction was more interesting than the fiction, and the brown and cream colors don't do justice to Morris's art.

Sequitur has not yet kept to its proposed quarterly schedule, but Drummond hopes to get on track with the June 1993 issue. $3.50 for a single issue, $12 for a year payable to R&D Publishing, P.O. Box 480146, Denver, CO 80248-0146.

Fantasy Macabre, published by Richard H. Fawcett and edited by Jessica Amanda Salmonson, always provides an excellent combination of the classic and contemporary weird tale. Good stories by D. F. Lewis, Amy Nelson, Ruth Berman, and Miroslaw Lipinski. $4.50 single copy, $12 for a three-issue subscription payable to Richard H. Fawcett, 61 Teecomwas Drive, Uncasville, CT 06382. *Fantasy & Terror* is also edited by Salmonson and is attractively designed. Number 13 collects morbid poems by Harriet Beecher Stowe and others, famous in their time but virtually unknown today. $3.50 single copy, $12 (4 issues), same address as above.

Palace Corbie, edited by Wayne Edwards, is a nicely produced perfect-bound digest with a good mixture of poetry and prose, containing some good stories, most cross-genre rather than strictly horror. The best were by Sean Doolittle, James S. Dorr, and Michael A. Arnzen. The artwork throughout is by Eugene R. Gryniewicz and is often attractive. Keep an eye on this magazine. $6.95 single copy, $11 for two issues payable to *Palace Corbie*, Merrimack Books, P.O. Box 158, Lynn, IN 47355-0158.

Expressions of Dread, edited by Spencer Lamm, is a new slick fiction and nonfiction annual. The first issue is fifty pages and features a four-color cover illustration by Joe Coleman and color and black-and-white art inside. The nonfiction is more interesting than the fiction with several interviews, including one with the chief medical examiner of New York City, one with Wayne Allen Sallee, another with Philip Nutman, and more. There is also an essay on the tradition of graphic violence in horror fiction. This promising magazine has a third issue (100 pages) scheduled for spring 1993 but no price set. Write for information to *Expressions of Dread*, 300 Mercer Street, Suite 17-B, New York, NY 10003.

The Stake: Humor & Horror for a Dying Planet #2, edited by Bill Meyers, is a new quarterly satirical magazine that has some amusing items in it, including "The First Days of Christ the Umpire" (a parody of the weird novel *The Last Days of Christ the Vampire*) and "The Snopeses Go Camping." ($12 for the next four issues to III Publishing, P.O. Box 170363, San Francisco, CA 94117-0363.)

Other magazines that rarely publish horror but did contain good horror fiction during 1992 were *Playboy, Omni, Pulphouse, Aboriginal SF, Glimmer Train, Space & Time, Back Brain Recluse, Aurealis* (Australia), *Jabberwocky, Story, Eidolon, Raritan, Event, Gauntlet, Fiction International, Conjunctions, New Pathways* (now defunct), *Strange Plasma, CWM, On Spec, Celestial Shadows,* and *Tales of the Unanticipated.*

And good horror stories and poetry also appeared occasionally in *Midnight Zoo, Ghosts & Scholars, Weirdbook, The Silver Web, Terror Australis* (now defunct), *Forbidden Lines, Elegia, The Magazine of Speculative Poetry, Fantasy Tales 4, Mean Lizards, Prisoners of the Night, Aberations, Vlad the Impaler, Premonitions, Dreams & Nightmares, Weirdbook, Doppelganger, Bizarre Bazaar, Chills, Thin Ice, Haunts,* and *Dementia 13.*

Another source for short horror fiction is the single story chapbook published by various specialty presses. Usually published in a signed and limited paperback edition with cover and interior illustrations, these are often good buys, although the reprints might appeal more to collectors than to the general fiction reader. Some of the more interesting ones follow:

Elizabeth Massie's Bram Stoker Award–winning novelette "Stephen" has an introduction by Brian Hodge with cover/interior art by Keith Minnion. $5.95 plus $1 shipping from TAL Publications (see address under "Collections"); Wayne Allen Sallee's original story "For You, the Living" with cover/interior art by Alan M. Clark is $6 plus $1 shipping; Melanie and Steve Rasnic Tem's original story "Beautiful Strangers" illustrated by Melissa Sherman is $5 plus $1 shipping; Joe R. Lansdale's reprint "Steppin' Out, Summer, '68" with cover/interiors by Mark A. Nelson is $7 plus $1 shipping; Nancy Holder's original story "Cannibal Dwight's Special Purpose," with cover/interiors by Melissa Sherman is $5 plus $1 shipping; and Robert Zasuly's "Kill Shot" and Pamela J. Jessen's "Cuttings," two originals in one volume illustrated by Melissa Sherman, is $5 plus $1 shipping—all payable to Little Bookshop of Horrors (address under "Collections"); Joe R. Lansdale's "God of the Razor" features an introduction by Lansdale and artwork by eight artists, including S. Clay Wilson, Michael Zulli, Stephen Bissette, Mark Nelson and others. $15 postpaid, and Nancy A. Collins' original Sonja Blue novella, "Cold Turkey," which features an introduction by Joe R. Lansdale and art by Mark Masztal, is $13 postpaid—both payable to Thomas Crouss, Crossroads Press, P.O. Box 10433, Holyoke, MA 01041-2033. Wayne Edwards's "Mr. Oblivious," with artwork by Eugene Gryniewicz, is $3 from Merrimack Books. P.O. Box 158, Lynn, IN 47355-0158. The British Fantasy Society published Mark Morris's original short story "Birthday" as Booklet Number 19, in honor of the Fantasycon XVII. $3 to Peter Coleborn, 46 Oxford St., Acocks Green, Birmingham, B27 6DT, U.K.

Pulphouse's Short Story paperbacks, before being put on hold after number 60, published horror reprints such as Pat Cadigan's "My Brother's Keeper," Robert Bloch's "The Skull of the Marquis de Sade," Nancy Holder's "The Ghosts of Tivoli," Joe R. Lansdale's "Tight Little Stitches in a Dead Man's Back," and "The Bingo Man" by Joyce Carol Oates. $1.95 each. And also published, under the Axolotl imprint, Nina Kirki Hoffman's novella "Unmasking," $10 for trade paperback to Pulphouse Publishing, P.O. Box 1227, Eugene, OR 97440.

Other horrific works published by various specialty presses were:

Donald M. Grant, Publisher, Inc.: *Double Memory: Art and Collaborations*— paintings and sketches by Rick Berry and Phil Hale, friends and collaborators for twelve years, inspiring and influencing each other's art. They seem influenced, too, by Francis Bacon and Marshall Arisman. The book itself is a magnificent work of art, produced on high-quality paper and well designed. With cryptic quotations, dark, lush paintings done solo and collaboratively, this is a book to linger and dream over. Berry is best-known for his illustrations for the Donald M. Grant edition of Peter Straub's *Mrs. God*; Hale is best-known for his work on the Donald M. Grant edition of Stephen King's *Drawing of the Three*. Trade edition: $34.95. The deluxe, slipcased edition is signed and numbered with an extra signature containing four custom duotones and a signed and numbered lithograph from an edition of eight. $100 plus $2 shipping; *The Waste Lands Portfolio* illustrated by Ned Dameron has twelve full-color illustrations for Stephen King's *The Dark Tower III: The Waste*

Lands. Available in a trade edition for $20 plus $2 shipping or an artist-signed and numbered edition limited to 2000, which includes a print of the painting used as the endpaper for the book as well as the jacket design on cover stock ($30 plus $2 shipping). For address, see under "Anthologies."

Mark V. Ziesing: Wayne Allen Sallee's impressive first novel, *The Holy Terror*, with a dark *noir*-ish cover by Lainey Koepke in two editions: a trade edition for $29.95 and a slipcased 250-copy limited edition for $65; and Richard Laymon's short novel of psychic suspense, *Alarms*, with cover by Lainey Koepke in a $24 trade edition and $60 signed and slipcased edition. All of Ziesing's books are meticulously designed by Arnie Fenner. For address, see under "Anthologies."

Underwood-Miller: *Virgil Finlay's Strange Science* is a great-looking book with quality reproductions of Finlay's detailed black-and-white illustrations of aliens and monsters originally drawn for the pulps. The book has a foreword by Robert Bloch and an introduction by Harlan Ellison. Hardcover $24.95. Paperback $14.95 plus $2 shipping. PA residents add 6% sales tax. (Underwood-Miller, 708 Westover Drive, Lancaster, PA 17601).

Lord John Press: *Children of the Night* by Dan Simmons is available in a limited signed edition of 900 numbered copies, slipcased, for $125; 250 deluxe copies, ¼ leather, slipcased, for $250; and 26 lettered copies, full leather, $500. And also by Dan Simmons, *Summer Sketches*: Simmons's notes and sketches of his travels have brought such diverse places as Calcutta, Gettysburg, and Romania to vivid life. This book is a fascinating look at semiraw material transmuted and integrated by the author into his fiction, available in a trade edition of 2000 copies for $25; a limited signed edition of 750 numbered copies for $100; 200 deluxe copies, one-fourth leather-bound for $250; and 26 lettered copies, full leather-bound for $500 (Lord John Press, 19073 Los Alimos Street, Northridge, CA 91326).

Borderlands Press: A 500-copy limited edition (sold out) of *Captured by the Engines* by Joe R. Lansdale with cover by Alan M. Clark and interior illustrations by Mark Nelson, signed by the author and artists. $3 shipping and handling per title. See address under "Anthologies."

Pulphouse/Axolotl: Nancy Springer's horror novella "Damnbanna" in three editions: $10 for the 525-copy trade paperback, $35 for the 300-copy hardcover edition, and $60 for a 75-copy leather-bound edition. All states are signed by the author. (Pulphouse Publishing, Box 1227, Eugene, OR 97440.)

Necronomicon Press: *An Index to the Fiction and Poetry of H. P. Lovecraft* by S. T. Joshi is an index of proper names used by Lovecraft in his fiction and poetry. $5.95; *The Battle That Ended the Century/Collapsing the Cosmoses* (sic) by H. P. Lovecraft and Robert H. Barlow—two short-story collaborations. $2.50; *The Lady of Frozen Death and Other Weird Tales* by Leonard Cline—a collection of five stories that appeared originally under the pseudonym Alan Forsyth. $6.50; *H. P. Lovecraft Letters to Richard F. Searight*, edited by David E. Schultz, S. T. Joshi, and Franklyn Searight. $9.95; *On Lovecraft and Life* by Robert H. Barlow. $3.95; *Autobiographical Writings by H. P. Lovecraft*. $4.95; *Demons of the Sea* by William Hope Hodgson, edited by Sam Gafford, reprints ten stories and an essay. $8.95; *H. P. Lovecraft: Letters to Henry Kuttner*, edited by David E. Schulz and S. T. Joshi. $5.95. Address under "Collections."

Maclay & Associates: Ray Russell's (the author of *Sardonicus*) new horror novel

Absolute Power is in an attractive 500-copy signed, boxed limited edition. $49. Find address under "Collections."

Charnel House: *Last Call*, by Tim Powers, adds a poem and is a slightly different textual version than the trade edition from William Morrow, beautifully illustrated by Peter Richardson with slipcase art by J. K. Potter. Signed and numbered boxed edition of 350 copies for $150 (Charnel House, Box 633, Lynbrook, NY 11563).

Dark Harvest: In 1992, Dark Harvest moved away from horror toward dark suspense, publishing Thomas Tessier's *Secret Strangers* in a trade edition at $21.95; F. Paul Wilson's *Nightworld*, the third book of the follow-up trilogy to *The Keep*. $21.95; a first novel, *Frost of Heaven*, by Junius Podrug. $19.95; and Lawrence Block's first Matthew Scudder novel (in hardcover for the first time), *The Sins of the Fathers*, with an introduction by Stephen King. $19.95. See address under "Anthologies."

Wildside Press: Reprinted Alan Rodgers' novel *Night* in a 250-copy limited, signed, and numbered hardcover edition. $35 (Wildside Press, 37 Fillmore Street, Newark, NJ 07105).

Fedogan & Bremer: Published Basil Copper's novel *The Black Death* with cover and illustrations by Stefanie K. Hawks in a hardcover trade edition, $32 plus $1.50 postage. Payable to Fedogan & Bremer, 700 Washington Ave., SE, Suite 50, Minneapolis, MN 55417.

W. Paul Ganley: Publisher: Published *Iced on Aran & Other Dream Quests* by Brian Lumley, a collection of five stories with art by Stephen E. Fabian in a hardcover trade edition for $25 plus $1.50 to W. Paul Ganley: Publisher, P.O. Box 149, Buffalo NY 14226-0149.

Certain nonfiction magazines provide news and a much needed critical eye. I've included ordering information for those difficult to find at newsstands. For overseas prices, query first.

That old standby *Fangoria*, edited by Tony Timpone, now has, along with its usual blood and guts, a lively regular column by David J. Schow and perceptive reviews of some of the more interesting books of fiction and nonfiction related to horror. The September issue was devoted to vampires, covering Coppola's *Dracula* in detail in addition to critic Linda Marotta providing an analysis of her ten favorite vampire novels; the November issue had an interview with Candace Hilligas, star of the classic horror film (recently reissued) *Carnival of Souls*. *Fangoria* also published a special *Dracula: The Complete Vampire* issue including material on the making of the Coppola movie, the history of Dracula movies, books about Dracula, and upcoming vampire movie releases. The special also ran an interview with Christopher Lee, had an article about Dracula in comics and the by now standard article on the *real* Dracula. It's an impressive issue with contributions by Linda Marotta, David J. Skal, and Raymond McNally.

Cinefantastique, published and edited by Frederick S. Clarke, is bimonthly and more upscale than *Fangoria*. The February issue's cover story was *The Silence of the Lambs*, with detailed articles by Dan Persons on the acting, screenwriting, directing, and producing of the Academy Award–winner. The articles are good, particularly those on production design, for which Kristi Zea and her crew conceptualized variations of some of the most powerful scenes, including "the shot from hell" (as it was called by the crew) in which the police officer's corpse is flayed and lashed to Lecter's cage. Zea admits to being heavily influenced by Francis Bacon's paintings, and one can clearly see this in the sketches. There's also a piece on moth-wrangling. *Cinefantastique* is an excellent magazine for readers serious about their cinema. Highly recommended.

Psychotronic Video is an invaluable source of material on horror videos, nonfiction books, and personalities. Issues in 1992 interviewed actors Timothy Farrell and Brad Dourif, and Zalman King, producer of *9½ Weeks* and *Wild Orchid*. Highly recommended. A six-issue subscription to this quarterly costs $20, payable to publisher/editor Michael J. Weldon, 3309 Route 97, Narrowsburg, NY 12764.

Filmfax: The Magazine of Unusual Film & Television brings out lots of interesting articles on horror films in its bimonthly issues. Some of 1992's highlights included a piece on the Tod Browning movie *The Unknown*, an interview with Paul Naschy (star of *Curse of the Devil* and lots of other films), and an excerpt from David J. Skal's forthcoming cultural history of horror, *The Monster Show*. $25 (six issues) from *Filmfax*, P.O. Box 1900, Evanston, IL 60204.

Reflex (now *Nerve*) was primarily a music magazine, but also covered other types of "alternative" entertainment. Last year there were articles on Philip K. Dick's novels, Neil Gaiman and Dave McKean's graphic novel collaborations, interviews with Anne Rice (illustrations by J. K. Potter) and Brian Eno (illustrations by Dave McKean), a piece of fiction by David J. Schow, and book reviews of oddball titles. Legs McNeil has just taken over the editorship from Lou Stathis and, judging from the first issue (which doesn't acknowledge its predecessor), I'm afraid the intelligence and multimedia mix that made *Reflex* so interesting and entertaining is gone.

Afraid: The Newsletter for the Horror Professional is back, now edited by Mike Baker. The first five issues in its new incarnation were informative, with articles and columns by Gary Brandner, Brian Hodge, and a good article by J. F. Gonzales about semi-pro magazines. However, #6 was disappointing, as the newsletter's demeanor began to veer toward the less professional and became more petulant. A professional newsletter is no place for bashing writers by name. And what's the point of reviewing Stephen King's novels? How about giving lesser known writers the exposure? One year subscription (12 issues) $25. Checks payable to *Afraid*, 857 N. Oxford Avenue #4, Los Angeles, CA 90029.

Nexus is a good new newsmagazine out of the U.K. edited by Paul Brazier. It runs some fiction, lots of mini-reviews, and a roundup of news in the field of SF with crossover into fantasy and horror. The magazine is meant to appear quarterly, but so far it's been late and I've only seen the first two issues. Potential U.S. subscribers might want to hold off a while to make sure it stays afloat, although you can probably buy a back issue to check it out. Subscriptions are $25 payable to SF Nexus Subscriptions, P.O. Box 1123, Brighton, BN1 6EX, U.K.

Gila Queen's Guide to Markets edited by Kathryn Ptacek is a 24-page monthly devoted to giving up-to-date publishing and marketing information in various genres. ($20/year payable to the *Gila Queen's Guide to Markets* or Kathryn Ptacek, P.O. Box 97, Newton, NJ 07860.) Highly recommended.

Mystery Scene, published by Martin H. Greenberg and Ed Gorman and edited by Joe Gorman, which has gone back to pulp format with #35, seems to have made horror a low priority, and has shifted to four regular book columnists instead of using free-lancers (which might be good, as there was so much overlap in the past). The magazine will now appear every seven weeks. Subscriptions are $35 for seven issues from *Mystery Scene*, P.O. Box 669, Cedar Rapids, IA 52406-0669.

The New York Review of Science Fiction, published monthly by Dragon Press and edited by David G. Hartwell et al., publishes articles and reviews on horror, as well as science fiction and fantasy. It's intelligent, literate, and only occasionally opaque. Dragon Press, P.O. Box 78, Pleasantville, NY 10570. $2.50 per copy. Annual subscriptions: In U.S., $25; $29 Canada; $33 First Class. Highly recommended.

Scarlet Street: The Magazine of Mystery and Horror, edited by Richard Valley, is an attractive and entertaining magazine specializing in old movies. It also carries appropriate book reviews. Issue #8 covered vampire movies. Subscriptions are $18 (4 issues) from R.H. Enterprises, P.O. Box 604, Glen Rock, NJ 07452.

The Scream Factory, a quarterly edited by Peter Enfantino, published an especially fun issue #10 featuring "the worst horror in the world": the worst horror novels of all time, the worst horror on TV, the fifty worst monster movies—you get the idea. Comprehensive and incisive with an amusing cover illustration by Allen Koszowski. The magazine made good use of contributors such as Stefan Dziemianowicz, Bob Morrish, Peter Enfantino, and William Schoell among others. Schoell's informative "Hidden Horrors" column delved into old pulps, bad novels, and Lovecraft, but I don't see how the horror is "hidden." Morrish's welcome new column "What Ever Happened to?" discusses the work of writers who have seemingly disappeared from the field after an early important appearance or those who have not received the attention they deserve. Jere Cunningham is the focus of the first installment, Jack Cady of the second. To subscribe to this quarterly send a check for $19.50 ($21.11 CA residents) to Deadline Press, 4884 Pepperwood Way, San Jose, CA 95124.

Necrofile: The Review of Horror Fiction, published quarterly by Necronomicon Press, is edited by Stefan Dziemianowicz, S. T. Joshi, and Michael A. Morrison and continues to be the most important critical magazine in the horror field. During 1992 there were thoughtful reviews by Steve Rasnic Tem, Michael J. Collins, Douglas E. Winter, Brian Stableford, and S. T. Joshi (the latter asking "what the hell is dark suspense?"). Particularly good is a review by Tony Magistrale of Stephen King's *Needful Things*, questioning *The New York Times*'s consistent tendency to choose reviewers who have axes to grind against King. There's a good column by Tem about creating effective horror and how the marketing of "horror as a genre category" has damaged the field. The magazine regularly lists American and British horror titles. Highly recommended. (Necronomicon Press, 101 Lockwood St., West Warwick, RI 02893. $10/year—specify which issue you would like to begin with.)

Carnage Hall #3, edited by David Griffin, is much better than last year's generally disappointing issue. Griffin's editorial makes important points when it doesn't lapse into hyperbole. He compares the genrefication of science fiction in bookstores with that of horror. But he asserts mistakenly that suburban chains have nothing but brand-name authors with "one tiny notch reserved for 'literature,' usually some exorbitantly priced printing of *Our Mutual Friend* released in faux-leather binding. . . ." Most suburban bookstores I've been to have "literature" or "general fiction" sections stocked with everything from cheap paperback editions of Dickens to J. G. Ballard's newest novel in hardcover and Vintage reprints of his old ones. The issue also has a good interview with Thomas Ligotti. No subscriptions but individual issues can be bought for $3.50 plus $.50 postage to *Carnage Hall Magazine*, P.O. Box 7, Esopus, NY 12429, checks payable to David Griffin.

Gauntlet published its third and fourth issues, edited by Barry Hoffman. The idea of a journal on censorship has always been a promising one, but *Gauntlet*, in its third year, only succeeds intermittently. Issue #3, "The Politically (In)correct Issue," maintains an insufferable tone of "we're more righteous than thou." The worst example is Dave Marsh's "dissent" to Steve Lopez's article about NWA— Niggers with Attitude. Marsh's rant completely ignores the legitimate issues Lopez presents. And in his "The Year in Censorship," John Rosenman censures a waitress who "chastised a customer for reading *Playboy*." Why? Isn't *her* free expression protected? She didn't take the magazine away from the customer; she expressed an opinion. Her comments may have been rude, but they weren't censorship. And in the same article, "Note that at Stanford, student law associations for Asians, Blacks, Indians (Whoops!) . . . I mean 'native Americans,' Asian Americans, and Jews now advocate speech codes to combat racism and sexism." Sarcasm trivializes the problem rather than confronts it. Sloppy language and sloppy thinking throughout make it hard for me to take *Gauntlet* seriously. Issue #4 had some good fiction, but nothing that couldn't be published elsewhere. While there are usually a few good articles in each issue, *Gauntlet* gives too many hysterical contributors a forum for ranting. (*Gauntlet*, Dept. SUB92A, 309 Powell Road, Springfield, PA 19064. Issue #5 for $9.95 plus $2 postage and handling. One year [2 issues] $18 plus $2 postage and handling.)

Scavenger's Newsletter, edited by Janet Fox, is a reliable source of material most useful to the beginning writer, listing small-press, mostly non-paying or minimal-paying markets. There's also a good (albeit completely subjective) section with comments from readers on editorial policies and problems with various magazines. In general I think the reviewers are far too kind to mediocre material (a consistent problem in the small press). (Janet Fox, *Scavenger's Newsletter*, 519 Ellinwood, Osage City, KS 66523-1329. $12.50/year [12 issues] bulk mail, $16.50 first class).

Tekeli-li!: Journal of Terror, edited by Jon B. Cooke, is in its second year and is slightly late. Issue #3 had a cover date of fall '91 but appeared in early 1992. Issue #4 had an excellent interview with Thomas Ligotti and a very good column by Gary Braunbeck about horror in the mainstream. Excellent art by Jim Koney, Blair Reynolds, and H. O. Morris. Digest-sized with a nicely slick cover, it looks quite professional. Highly recommended. (*Tekeli-li! Journal of Terror*, c/o Jon B. Cooke, 106 Hanover Avenue, Pawtucket, RI 02861, $20 payable to Montilla Publications for the next four issues. RI residents include 7% tax.)

Science Fiction Eye, published and edited by Stephen P. Brown, although still not quite on schedule, is one of the major nonfiction genre-oriented magazines around. Issue #11 has 120 pages with cranky letters, Jack Womack recounting his recent trip to Russia, Paul Di Filippo interviewing Thomas M. Disch, Richard Kadrey covering the music front, great art, and provocative reviews. Highly recommended. $10/year (three issues) payable to *Science Fiction Eye*, P.O. Box 18539, Asheville, NC 28814.

Science Fiction Chronicle and *Locus*, the oldest and best news-magazines covering science fiction (primarily), fantasy, and horror, cover books published, give market reports for the U.S. and the U.K., relate domestic and foreign publishing news, and carry convention reports and listings. Ordering information for each are in the acknowledgments at the front of this book. Andrew I. Porter is editor and publisher of *Science Fiction Chronicle*, and Charles N. Brown is publisher and editor of *Locus*.

Graphic Novels:

The graphic novel continues to grow as a distinct art form, and there are so many interesting things available that it's impossible to cover them all. So here's a sampling of those I found particularly interesting or ambitious that incorporate horror aspects:

Bone Saw #1, edited by John Bergin and James O'Barr (Tundra), is an anthology of edgy material along the lines of *Taboo*. I like the art, but as in too many graphic novels, I found the prose inconsistent in quality. *Bone Saw* mixes illustrated stories with stories dominated by prose with a few illustrations. A mistake, I think—it's difficult for readers/viewers to switch gears between the two forms of expression. Although there is an overabundance of pieces by co-editor Bergin, his "Monkey Fear" is quite good as are pieces by Rene J. Cigler, Duvivier, and Michael Manning/ Misha. Definitely worth a look.

Some of the best illustrative work produced in the horror field can be seen in graphic novels. Tundra's sketchbook series has showcased several fine artists in the past two years. Two I missed previously were *Noodles: Sketchbook Stuff, Random Drawings and Telephone Squiggles* by Michael Zulli and a "Special Edition" *Kent Williams: Drawings and Monotypes*. Both artists have developed recognizable styles. While in his sketch book Zulli occasionally seems overly influenced by the romanticism of Jeff Jones, he is currently working with Neil Gaiman on a *Sweeney Todd* project that looks to be excellent. The sketches and doodlings in these two books show the artists honing their techniques and having fun; Paul Mavrides' *Sketchbook #10 Skull Farmer* could only have come out of the head of a founder of the Church of the Subgenius. One whole color page is used to show different types of ray guns. Excerpts from comic strips, caricatures, parodies. A manic and entertaining mix; Tom Kidd's *Sketchbook #11* shows his detailed drawing techniques and includes sketches for his Gnemo series in addition to providing informative commentary on his own work. Excellent.

Tales from the Outer Boroughs Volume #1, written and illustrated by Douglas Michael (Fantagraphic Books): "Mister Seebring" is the story of the eponymous hero and his talking dead dog, Lucky (run over by a train) and their arrival at the Khoelmacher household. Strange deadpan humor that cuts like a knife. "Lame Dog" is a convoluted tale of an abused child (or two), a clown disguise, a vicious murder, politicking, and, of course, a lame dog. Worth a look.

Taboo 6, edited by Stephen R. Bissette (Tundra), isn't as provocative as some of its past issues but has some excellent material including the next installment of Moore/Campbell's *From Hell*, an old unpublished piece by Charles Burns, and a collaboration by Neil Gaiman and Michael Zulli; *Taboo 7* gets back on track with episodes of *From Hell*, a prologue to the new Neil Gaiman/Michael Zulli *Sweeney Todd* collaboration; and another new collaboration that looks interesting—*Afterlife*, by David Thorpe and Aidan Potts. But there were a few losers in this one, too: "The Music-Loving Spider" made no sense to me, although I liked the art, and I'm afraid I find most of Joe Coleman's work overblown and obvious.

Omnibus: Modern Perversity (Blackbird Comics) is a good-looking, reasonably priced series that starts with five pieces of sexual horror. Lewis Shiner's "Scales," illustrated by Carlos Castro, is the most comprehensible and the best drawn, although "Zoo" by Mark London Williams, illustrated by John LeCour, is interesting.

Batman: Night Cries, by Archie Goodwin and Scott Hampton (DC), with Batman as the dark knight, focuses on Police Commissioner James Gordon. The text, about child abuse and its far-reaching consequences, perfectly matches the art by Scott Hampton, whose work gets better and better. He illustrated Robert E. Howard's "Pigeons from Hell" and *Tapping the Vein* for Eclipse, neither of which prepared me for his dark, moody work on *Night Cries*. Highly recommended.

Tell Me Dark, by Karl Edward Wagner, Kent Williams, and John New Rieber (DC), is a sumptuous, dark love story about an American rock star and his doomed lover in the decadent depths of London. It is Williams's best artwork to date—he was the artist of *Blood*, written by J. M. Matteis, and demonstrates exquisite technique. Karl Edward Wagner has disavowed this book because it was rescripted without his approval. Despite this, I have to recommend it for its beautiful look. Highly recommended.

The Residents Freak Show (Dark Horse). If you've never seen the Residents perform, you've missed a treat. They are best known for their giant eyeball costumes, but they've been reinterpreting musical artists from Frank Sinatra and Ennio Morricone to Elvis. *Freak Show* is their concept album, each song about a different freak—each artist in the anthology, a fan of the Residents, was given a copy of the album and asked to visualize one of the freaks. While the art is all pretty terrific, the texts vary in successfully capturing the artists' visions. It has a Charles Burns cover and art by Dave McKean, Brian Bolland, John Bolton, and others.

The Acid Bath Case by Stephen Walsh and Kellie Strom (Kitchen Sink). Nat Slammer is a cop in the fifties, and society is on the cusp of social change—symbolized by the appearance of fast-food restaurants; bad food changes into bad *fast* food. Several gruesome murders have been committed and Slammer is assigned to solve them. This is an interesting but unsatisfying story. Unless I missed it, there seems to be no motive and there is no resolution. But the cover art and interiors are wonderful.

Batman Gothic, by Grant Morrison and Klaus Janson with an introduction by F. Paul Wilson (DC), is a compilation, appearing for the first time in book form. Morrison again proves himself one of the finest writers of the graphic novel with this Faustian story of an ancient evil about to be unleashed on Gotham by a conscienceless immortal. And Batman as the dark knight is obsessed with fighting evil while trying to control his own dark instincts against which he must constantly struggle. The art bombards the reader with contemporary visions of urban decline and effectively uses monochromatic color to show dream sequences and flashbacks. My only complaint is that the characters bear too much physical resemblance to each other. Highly recommended.

Fast Forward 2: Family (Piranha Press), the second in the series, and the better, has six pieces. Kyle Baker's story is about a man bedeviled by the walking dead, making it exceptionally difficult to get a date. "Brothers and Sisters" is simple, bittersweet, and effective. "Hostage," by a cousin of Terry Anderson, is good, but the story doesn't seem to fit the theme.

Skin, by Peter Milligan, Brendan McCarthy, and Carol Swain (Tundra), is more interesting as a historical document/political statement condemning the greedy drug companies that sold thalidomide in the U.K. with insufficient testing than as an artistic statement. Martin Achitson, a thalidomide baby, is an early skinhead (the introduction explains that originally the gangs weren't racist; in their "golden age" these working-class thugs usually just beat up on each other). The authors write that *Skin* was commissioned and then rejected by Fleetway productions for its "adult comic" *Crisis*. They surmise it's the deformity that was the problem (shades of K. W. Jeter's *Dr. Adder*?), but the objection might just as well have been to the book's anti-establishment stance and colorful depiction of violence. Martin's bitterness and hatred is far more understandable than that of most of his peers in the book. I'd like to think the self-congratulatory afterword by McCarthy is a joke.

Mr. Arashi's Amazing Freak Show by Suehiro Maruo (Blast Books) is about a "normal" orphan taken in by a traveling freak show in Japan. This is not the warm, supportive, family-type atmosphere that pervades Tod Browning's movie *Freaks*. In Mr. Arashi's show, even within the freak show it's a cold and cynical world. A powerful, tragic story with excellent black-and-white art. Also from Blast Books (1989) comes *Panorama of Hell* by Hideshi Hino, a shocking story of post-nuclear Japan as told by a mad painter who uses his own blood as material. Bloody, grisly, perverted and sad, it puts to shame most American graphic novels that are meant to shock.

The Sandman: Season of Mists, written by Neil Gaiman and illustrated by various artists (DC Comics), is the compilation of issues 21–28 in which Dream travels to Hell to bring back an ex-girlfriend he condemned in anger to stay there. To his surprise, Dream finds Lucifer tired of it all, ready to empty Hell of its inhabitants, give up his kingdom, and give Dream the keys to do with as he will. Supplicants from all faiths then visit Dream to blackmail, bribe, tempt, or cajole in order to extract the keys for their own use. Good storytelling and intelligence permeate this charming mini-epic.

The Luck in the Head by M. John Harrison and Ian Miller (VG Graphics). First off, let me say I'm a fan of Harrison's writing and of Miller's art. But I think it's best to consider this more as an art book than a graphic novel. The art is wonderfully lurid and grotesque, with images of violence taken from Harrison's collection *Viriconium Nights*. Unfortuantely, the text, already obscure, is done in a script and design virtually impossible to read.

Other graphic novels of interest are:

The Minotaur's Tale by Al Davison (VG Graphics, Dark Horse); *Peter Kuper's Comics Trips* (Tundra Sketchbook special); *Fast Forward: Phobias* (Piranha Press); *The Dreams of Everyman* by Joe Lee (Rip Off Press); *Doghead* by Al Columbia (Tundra); *Snake Eyes* No. 2 (Fantographics Books); J. N. Williamson's *Masques 1 & 2* (Innovation); *The Cabinet of Dr. Caligari*, adapted from the film by Ian Carney and Mike Hoffman—three parts (Monster); *Freaks*, adapted from the movie by Jim Woodruff and F. Solano Lopez (Monster); and *Dracula: A Symphony in Moonlight & Nightmares* by Jon J. Muth (Nantier Beall Minoustchine).

Art Books:

Coppola and Eiko on Bram Stoker's Dracula (Collins-SF/Newmarket). If you enjoyed the newest film version of *Dracula* and appreciated its operatic and romantic qualities as much as I did, you might find this book a nice complement to and souvenir of the film. The Japanese designer Eiko Ishioka, costume designer for the film *Mishima* and the play *M. Butterfly,* was commissioned by Francis Ford Coppola to "make the costumes the set." In interviews and in their respective journals Coppola and Eiko discuss the cultural and historic influences on the costumes— for example, the Turkish influence on Dracula's clothes, various European and more exotic influences on the cosmopolitan Lucy Westerna. The photography and art in this coffee-table book is breathtaking, mixing the original sketches with the final designs on high-quality paper. Photography by David Seidman, edited by Susan Dworkin.

Bram Stoker's Dracula: The Film and the Legend, by Francis Ford Coppola and James V. Hart (Newmarket Press), is notable for its inclusion of the complete screenplay of the film. This is the book to buy unless you can't bear *not* to have those incredible costumes photographed in their full glory. This book is twice as long and $10 less and includes most (if not all) of the same text—excerpts from the journals of Eiko and Coppola on the thought behind the creation of the costumes.

No Man's Land: A Postwar Sketchbook by George Pratt (Tundra Special Sketchbook), with an introduction by Marshall Arisman. These sketches were for a graphic novel entitled *Enemy Ace: War Idyll,* an antiwar novel on World War I. Despite Pratt's being born in 1960, the viewer gets a realistic and stark vision of life in the trenches through his sketches and studies of individual and groups of soldiers. The book design is especially notable—clean, uncluttered sketches take center stage with quotations, poems, and observations of battle by writers such as Wilfred Owen, perfectly complementing the visuals. Beautiful.

Faces by Nancy Burson (Contemporary Arts Museum, Houston). Burson is a photographer who works with computers to create unusual effects in portraiture. She has used generated composites of faces to make political and cultural statements: a set of two photographs of women, beauties of the fifties and sixties, are compared. Each is made up of composites of five beauty queens of the decade.

Burson has since moved into age updating, which has helped in identifying missing children. And most recently, she has been photographing children with progeria (premature aging) and cranio-facial deformities. When before she made composite photos of deformed children to help create a distancing effect, she now says, "I want this group of images to be about what is normal and abnormal . . . If my photographs make it easier for anyone to look at any of these children, then I will feel that I've done my job . . . if my two-year-old grows up knowing that the real ugliness in the world comes from within people, then I will also have done my job." Hard to take, but this is a powerful little book.

Beauty and the Beast, by Nancy Willard and Barry Moser (Harcourt, Brace), is a glorious rendition of the fairy tale. Willard's prose updates the story, bringing it to New York City and the Hudson River Valley. Moser's woodcuts are lovely—In the past he has illustrated *Alice's Adventures Underground* and *The Wizard of Oz* (with Nancy Reagan as the Wicked Witch). Highly recommended.

Fitcher's Bird, photography by Cindy Sherman, based on a tale by the Brothers Grimm (Rizzoli), is a variation of Bluebeard. Fitcher kidnaps and murders young women. Sherman photographs what look like mannequins, but being aware that she often uses her heavily made-up self as a model, one can't help wondering if *she* is Fitcher. In any case, he's creepy and waxen-looking, and his massive beard almost becomes a character in itself. Oddly disturbing.

H. R. Giger's Necronomicon II (Morpheus International) is the oversized hard-cover book's first publication in English. In it are designs for *The Tourist*, an aborted film project, designs for the album cover of Blondie's *Koo Koo*, some of Giger's biomechanical paintings, photographs of his furniture and sculpture. Giger's dream-(or nightmare-) generated art jumps off the page at the viewer. Additional biographical material on Giger, a few profiles, and an interesting interview with him by Deborah Harry and Chris Stein make for a striking package.

Nonfiction:

Vampire: The Complete Guide to the World of the Undead, by Manuela Dunn Mascetti (Viking Studio), is a beautifully designed book using great art, but it maintains the unfortunate point of view that vampires are real. Mascetti gives "true" historical accounts of vampires and vampirism and mixes them haphazardly with fictional pieces such as "Carmilla" and the uncredited Fritz Leiber classic "The Girl with the Hungry Eyes." The result is beautiful but dumb.

In sharp contrast is the scholarly yet fascinating *Vampires, Werewolves and Demons: Twentieth Century Reports in the Psychiatric Literature*, by Richard Noll (Brunner/Mazel), a book of case histories that explores the "vampiric" behavior of the patient as generally a manifestation of one aspect of their psychopathology. For example, one who engages in "clinical vampirism—which consists of the periodic craving for blood, association with the dead, and no certain identity" drinks blood (sometimes her own) as a ritual that brings mental relief, not as a means of attaining immortality. And even though a patient may claim to be a werewolf and might behave as an animal, slobbering, crawling around on all fours, and howling at the moon, he looks no different to an objective observer. Dry, but an excellent antidote to the Mascetti book.

Vampyres: Lord Byron to Count Dracula, by Christopher Frayling (Faber & Faber), is a thorough history of the vampire in literature up to and including Bram Stoker's *Dracula*. Frayling briefly surveys the novel's literary forebears; charts a "Vampire Mosaic" in folklore, prose, and poetry, 1687–1913; and reprints Polidori's "The Vampyre," Lord Byron's "Fragments of a Story," and pieces by Dumas, E. T. A. Hoffman, Fitz-James O'Brien, Alexis Tolstoy, and others. Also, in a readable, gossipy way, Frayling corrects popular misconceptions (some passed on by the actual participants) about the infamous weekend at the villa Diodati on Lake Geneva during which Mary Shelley's *Frankenstein* and Polidori's "The Vampyr" were born. Finally, Frayling shows some of Stoker's research notes taken before and while writing *Dracula*. Highly recommended.

Cut! Horror Writers on Horror Film, edited by Christopher Golden (Berkley), is on the whole entertaining, illuminating, and diverse. The book includes dissections of specific films, analyses of directorial work, interviews with the famous, etc. *Cut!* begins with a refreshingly different interview of Clive Barker by his friend and colleague Peter Atkins on horror in movies that are not horror; Stephen R. Bissette writes intelligently on three 1990 films about the afterlife: *Ghost*, *Jacob's Ladder*, and *Flatliners*. Other good pieces include Ramsey Campbell on the quality of terror in film, Nancy Holder on why *The Haunting* is so effective, and Philip Nutman analyzing David Cronenberg's "families." Stanley Wiater's list of the thirteen most disturbing films ever made and Skipp & Spector's recommended list of all kinds of films are also entertaining. But the most ambitious and perhaps best piece in the book is Katharine Ramsland's article on *Angel Heart*—the journey to self as the ultimate horror. Good show. In addition to the paperback, Borderlands Press published a signed (by all but Anne Rice) slipcased limited edition of 500 numbered copies for $65.

Dark Visions: Conversations with the Masters of the Horror Film, by Stanley Wiater (Avon), is a decent introduction to some of the less-familiar names associated with horror film-making: producer Gale Ann Hurd, screenwriter Michael McDowell, make-up artist Dick Smith, screenwriter Joseph Stefano, and others more familiar such as Roger Corman, David Cronenberg, Tom Savini, and Robert Englund.

The Grim Reaper's Book of Days: A Cautionary Record of Famous, Infamous and Unconventional Exits, by Ed Morrow (Citadel Press), has at least one death for every day of the year. Although many of these exits are not exactly obscure, Morrow provides a wealth of fascinating details and does occasionally include the less famous ones, such as the death of Mary Bradham Tucker, the Pepsi Girl; and the actor, George Zucco, who basically scared himself to death. Fun for dipping into.

John McCarty's Official Splatter Movies Guide Vol. II by John McCarty (St. Martin's Press). If you enjoy reading movie synopses as much as I do and enjoy trash, splatter, and assorted weird movies, this sequel is for you. McCarty covers movies from *Fury of the Wolfman* to *Die Hard* to *Revenge of the Living Zombies* and *Don't Torture a Duckling*.

Nuclear Movies by Mick Broderick (McFarland & Company). The subtitle defines what's included: *A Critical Analysis and Filmography of International Feature Length Films Dealing with Experimentation, Aliens, Terrorism, Holocaust and Other Disaster Scenarios, 1914–1990*. Comprehensive, it makes for fascinating reading. Broderick's introductory essay claims that "unlike the 'serious,' 'well-intentioned' parables of the nuclear age, the bulk of the movies which have been condescendingly described as 'illogical visions (with) hooded, deformed villains, giant insects and other monsters' remain the most influential treatments of nuclear themes, largely bypassing audience predispositions using metaphor and allegory to depict 'the unthinkable.' " Maybe so, but when I was a pre-teen watching *On the Beach* on TV for the first time, it terrified me far more than any monster movie I've watched since. The filmography goes by year, and with the extensive cross-referencing the reader can discern patterns in movie-making. ($35 for this hardcover with library binding from McFarland & Company, Inc. Publishers, Box 611, Jefferson, NC 28640.)

Nightmare of Ecstasy: The Life and Art of Edward D. Wood, Jr. by Rudolph Grey (Feral House). For those unfamiliar with Ed Wood's career, this biography, told by interweaving interviews with family, friends and colleagues, might prove puzzling. But for those in the know, this book will prove a gold mine. Wood was notorious for two things—his unbelievably schlocky films like *Plan 9 from Outer Space*, *Orgy of the Dead*, and *The Sinister Urge*, and his penchant for cross-dressing (although he was heterosexual and married for many years), particularly in angora sweaters. The latter behavior showed up in his film *Glen or Glenda*, a sympathetic (if strange) portrayal of a man tormented by his secret yearnings to wear women's clothing. Wood was an alcoholic and a real character, whose chutzpah far outweighed his talent or money. He used the increasingly ailing Bela Lugosi as an actor until Lugosi's death. Wood—director, screenwriter, pornographer, and producer—died of a heart attack at fifty-four. ($14.95 plus $1.75 shipping from Feral House, P.O. Box 861893, Los Angeles, CA 90086-1893.)

Cronenberg on Cronenberg, edited by Chris Rodley (Faber and Faber, U.K.), wisely allows the director of such movies as *Scanners*, *Videodrome*, *Dead Ringers*, and *The Fly* to speak for himself. Cronenberg is articulate about his work, and the book makes a good companion volume to *The Shape of Rage*, a 1983 book of essays edited by Piers Handling that analyzed Cronenberg's films up to *The Dead Zone*.

Murder & Madness: The Secret Life of Jack the Ripper, by David Abrahamsen, M.D., F.A.C.Pn. (Donald I. Fine), uses the author's experience as a forensic psychiatrist to analyze all available evidence, including previously unreleased files from Scotland Yard, to prove that Jack the Ripper was actually two men working together, who they were, and their motivation. I have no idea how new this evidence actually is, but it's quite convincing. Abrahamsen's analysis of the killers themselves is interesting and illuminating, yet I'm troubled by his determinedly Freudian evaluation.

The Body of Frankenstein's Monster: Essays in Myth & Medicine, by Cecil Helman (Norton), is an entertaining book when the author sticks to his theme of medicine's relationship to myth and other fantastic fiction. Helman discusses the parallel of Frankenstein's monster to the contemporary use of donated organs; portrays Lycanthropy as madness or metaphor for our animal natures breaking out, and sees "germs" transformed into a powerful symbol of all kinds of unseen yet disruptive contagion, and as a metaphor for sudden social change encompassing everything from "an epidemic of crime" to the Asian flu. Occasionally he stretches the metaphor to breaking, such as when he describes a poor sick old man who has died in front of his television set as being turned to stone by the "medusa machine."

Guillotine: Its Legend and Lore, by Daniel Gerould (Blast Books), is not a historical view of Dr. Guillotine's merciful inventions, but rather concerns itself with the "guillotine as a cultural artifact and . . . its representation in the arts both high and low." It was last used in 1977, by which time it had long been an embarrassment to the French. Even in the nineteenth century, at the height of its power, the guillotine was never named in any government documents, instead being called "the instrument of death" or "the timbers of justice." Once the "reign of terror" was over, its orphans threw wild debauches dubbed "victims' balls," with women wearing slim red ribbons around their necks to simulate the blade mark. Interestingly, Samuel Taylor Coleridge complained that the representation of horror in literature came into vogue as a result of the "reign of terror" because public taste had been utterly debased by overexposure to the atrocities of the French Revolution. (Doesn't this ignore the fact that public execution by torture was a popular entertainment until the guillotine was invented?) All in all, an entertaining book.

Men, Women and Chain Saws: Gender in the Modern Horror Film, by Carol J. Clover (Princeton University Press), "explores the relationship of the 'majority viewer' (the younger male) to the female victim-heroes who have become such a conspicuous screen presence in certain sectors of horror," for example, *I Spit on Your Grave, Ms. 45, Halloween*, and *Texas Chainsaw Massacre II*. Until Clover began this project she'd rarely seen a slasher or revenge movie, so she comes to the movies with a fresh eye. Her analyses, which begin with De Palma's *Carrie*, the hit horror movie of 1976, seem right on the mark. She compares the widely banned exploitation movie *I Spit on Your Grave*, wherein the heroine takes the law into her own hands and kills her attackers, with the more mainstream movie on the same subject, *The Accused*, in which the actual hero of the movie is the female lawyer who uses the law to put the attackers behind bars (a less final punishment). This fascinating book is a must for those interested in the questions of who watches certain types of horror films, and why they watch them. Highly recommended.

Other interesting nonfiction titles (some not seen by me) are: *Orwell: A Biography* by Michael Sheldon (HarperCollins); *Out of the Night and Into the Dream: A Thematic Study of the Fiction of J. G. Ballard* by Gregory Stephenson (Greenwood); *Science Fiction & Fantasy Book Review Annual 1990* (not out until 1992), edited by Robert A. Collins and Robert Lathem (Greenwood)—a valuable reference work covering the field; *The James Gang* by Rosemary Pardoe (Haunted Library, U.K.)— a bibliography of writers in the tradition of M. R. James; *Presenting Young Adult Horror Fiction* by Cosette Kies (Macmillan Twayne); *Salem Is My Dwelling Place: A Life of Nathaniel Hawthorne* by Edwin Haviland Miller (University of Iowa Press); *Fairy Tale Romance: The Grimms, Basile, and Perrault*, edited by James M. McGlathery (University of Illinois Press, 1991)—a critical study of erotic passion in the literary folktale; *Horror Film Directors* by Dennis Fischer—covering 51 directors from around the world, illustrated, and nearly 900 pages long in hardcover ($75) and *Cinematic Vampires* by John L. Flynn—$39.95 (McFarland); *Scorsese On Scorsese*, edited by David Thompson (Faber and Faber); *Science Fiction, Fantasy, & Horror: 1991*, edited by Charles N. Brown and William Contento (Locus Press); *Reference Guide to Science Fiction, Fantasy, and Horror* by Michael Burgess (Libraries Unlimited); *Stephen King, The Second Decade: Dance Macabre to the Dark Half* by Tony Magistrale (Twayne); *The Dark Descent: Essays Defining Stephen King's Horrorscope*, edited by Tony Magistrale (Greenwood Press); *Black Forbidden Things: Cryptical Secrets from the "Crypt of Cthulhu,"* edited by Robert Price (Starmont House); *Discovering Classic Horror Fiction I*, edited by Darrell Schweitzer (Starmont House); *Lovecraft: A Look Behind the Cthulhu Mythos* by Lin Carter (Starmont House); *Fear to the World: Eleven Voices in a Chorus of Horror*, edited by Kevin E. Proulx (Starmont House); *Haunting the House of Fiction: Feminist Perspectives on Ghost Stories by American Women*, edited by Lynette Carpenter and Wendy K. Kolmar (University of Tennessee Press, 1991)—12 original essays on a woman's tradition in ghost stories; *Dead Secrets: Wilkie Collins and the Female Gothic* by Tamar Heller (Yale University Press); *A Web of Relationship: Women in the Short Fiction of Mary Wilkins Freeman* by Mary R. Reichardt (University Press of Mississippi); *The Changing Face of Horror in the Nineteenth-Century French Fantastic Short Story* by Gary R. Cummiskey (Peter Lang Publishing, 62 W. 45th St., New York, NY 10036)—academic; *Step Right Up! I'm Going* to *Scare the Pants Off America: Memoirs of a B-Movie Mogul* by William Castle (Pharos Books)—a reissue; *Serling: The Rise and Twilight of Television's Last Angry Man* by Gordon F. Sander (Dutton); *Edgar A. Poe: Mournful and Never-Ending Remembrance* by Kenneth Silverman (HarperCollins); and *Edgar Allan Poe: His Life and Legacy* by Jeffrey Meyers (Scribners)—the latter two much-needed biographies of the troubled father of the macabre.

Odds and Ends:

The Frog Prince Continued, story by Jon Scieszka, paintings by Steve Johnson (Viking). So what happens after the princess kisses the frog? Do they live happily ever after? Of course not. They both get bored and the prince wanders off on a journey to find the right kind of witch to turn him back into a frog. Charming, with great illustrations.

The Stinky Cheese Man and Other Fairly Stupid Tales (Viking) is by two of my favorite collaborators: Jon Scieszka and Lane Smith. Fractured fairy tales with editorial and other interruptions throughout. Another charmer. Highly recommended.

Little Pig, by Akumal Ramachander and illustrated by Stasys Eidrigevicius (Viking, U.K.), is a moral tale by an international collaboration, Indian and Lithuanian (the latter now lives in Warsaw). The illustrations are startling: each page has a color photograph of a person with a woman's face (Mary of Mary's Pig Farm) superimposed over the actual head, looking almost, but not quite, like a mask. Recommended to everyone, but especially pig lovers.

This Is Your Final Warning, by Thom Metzger (Autonomedia), is a strange little book of rants, fake biographies of Martin Bormann, Lon Chaney, Sr., and Jr., and others, vignettes, stories, and other weird or satirical stuff by the author of *Big Gurl.* A good-looking production. Autonomedia also published a rash of other titles in 1992 including *Cassette Mythos* edited by Robin James, a resource guide to the independent cassette underground, Semiotext(e) Architecture, and *Columbus and Other Cannibals* by Jack D. Forbes.

Crime Beat, edited by T. E. D. Klein, is the magazine for true crime addicts. All the details behind the headlines. It's informative and looks interesting graphically, but read too much of it and you'll get really depressed. It's like reading only the bad news in the newspaper.

Finders, Keepers; Eight Collectors, by Rosamund Wolff Purcell and Stephen Jay Gould (Norton), is a beautiful and appropriate follow-up to their collaboration *Illuminations: A Bestiary.* The guardians of natural treasures are called "curators" in the U.S. and "keepers" in England, hence the book's title. *Finders Keepers* is a coffee table book about eight collectors with lush photographs of their unusual collections. Louis Agassiz's single-mindedness at collecting fossilized fish drove away his first wife and family; Willem Cornelis van Heurn collected "boxes of perfectly pressed skins of rabbits, rats, dogs, cats, pigs, and moles," and Purcell describes him as "insatiable and out of control"; Walter Rothchild, with the assistance of two taxonomists, collected nearly every known species of Bird of Paradise, including seventeen he described for the first time; Frederick Ruysch collected fetuses and wrapped them in beads, to create beautiful, if morbid, works of art. A grotesque and gorgeous book. Highly recommended.

The Mütter Museum 1993 Calendar "presents the work of a distinguished group of photographers who have turned their attention to the unexpected art inherent in the study of medical photography." Included are photographs by Joel-Peter Witkin and Rosamund Wolff Purcell. In 1858 Dr. Thomas Dent Mütter formally presented his collection to the College of Physicians in Philadelphia. As a professor of surgery he gathered a teaching collection of anatomical and pathological specimens and models: the tumor removed from President Grover Cleveland's jaw, skulls and wax models of eye diseases, a plaster cast made from the bodies of the famous Siamese twins Eng and Chang, and a radiograph of a toy battleship stuck in the esophagus of an infant. Published by The College of Physicians of Philadelphia, 19 South Street, Philadelphia, PA 19103 for $14.95 (possibly more with postage).

1992 The Year in Darkness is the second edition of a monthly wall calendar showcasing original horror stories and illustrations by writers and artists from the small press. This year is "the all-editor issue" with stories by Jessica Amanda Salmonson, Crispin Burnham, Richard Chizmar, William Raley, Peggy Nadramia, and others. Art by John Borkowski, Allen Koszowski, Alfred R. Klosterman, and others. For the 1993 calendar, inquire, including an SASE to Montgomery Publishing, Agency and Studio, 692 Calero Avenue, San Jose, CA 95123.

H. R. Giger Calendar of the Fantastique (Morpheus International) takes note of the birthdates of fantasy/horror writers, the surrealist movement, the world premiere of *2001: A Space Odyssey*, Aleister Crowley's joining of the occult group The Hermetic Order of the Golden Dawn, and other pertinent dates. The art is stunning and gorgeously reproduced.

The Autonomedia Calendar of Jubilee Saints is a fourteen-month calendar beginning with October 12, 1992—Anti-Columbus Day. With its ever-sharp eye on the coming millennium, Autonomedia has declared every day a high holy day, a day of zero work and celebration. The publishers sent out a "Call for Nominations to Sainthood, and continued to collect names, birthdays, portraits of saints, unusual holidays, etc., until they had enough for a 1993 Jubilee Calendar." A fun calendar with snippets of information about the known and the obscure people whom the publishers feel worthy (with a decidedly left-leaning slant). $6 plus $2 postage to Autonomedia, P.O. Box 568, Brooklyn, NY 11215.

Evidence by Luc Sante (Farrar, Straus & Giroux). While researching his nonfiction book *Low Life*, Sante looked through archival material to get a feel for New York City in the early part of the twentieth century. He was directed to the Police Department Photo Collection, where he found a visual record of death in the tenements by murder, suicide, accident. Some of the stark photographs were captioned, some not. Fascinated, he chose fifty-five evidence photographs for this book. They are shocking, beautiful, revelatory. A dead dog lies in what looks like a subway station. It is pregnant and unmarked. Two detectives peer at the camera from a back room while the front room is bare, except for what might be bloodstains on the floor. Sante tried to ascertain the circumstances behind each photograph from newspaper articles of the period. Sometimes, when there's no information available he speculates from the details in the photograph. He also tells the history of evidentiary photography and ruminates on the possible reasons for the existence of such photos—occasionally there has been obvious manipulation of the crime scene. I hesitate to call this grim book beautiful, but it is. Highly recommended.

Extremes: Reflections on Human Behavior by A. J. Dunning (Harcourt, Brace) is "a series of tales about the extremes of human behavior, true events in which rational, normal people have yielded to passion, to a compulsion out of all proportion to the situation." The author compares the eating habits of St. Catherine of Siena to those of some teenage girls today; comments on the sacrifice made by the *castrati* (usually not of their own choice) for the sake of Italian opera, concluding that the practice ultimately died out because in the "long run the price of two testicles for four octaves proved to be too high"; compares Joan of Arc to Gilles de Rais, and immaculate conception in lizards to Jesus Christ's mother, Mary. Written in a clear, accessible, enjoyable style. Highly recommended.

Man-Eater: Tales of Lion and Tiger Encounters, edited by Edward Hodges-Hill. (Cockbird Press, U.K. Seven Hills Book Distributors, 49 Central Avenue, Cincinnati, OH 45202—$12.95 plus $2 postage and handling.) This book is about man-eating lions and tigers in East Africa and India with gripping first-person accounts by hunters, and occasionally victims (few people survive the septicemia of a tiger or lion bite). The accounts are written between 1909 and 1991. In his introduction, Hodges-Hill maintains that the "universal spread of firearms in the nineteenth century through the 1930s saw a higher proportion of the lion and tiger population becoming wounded and maimed and, unable to pursue their normal prey, turning to the native human population for food." One man-eater, taking a human a day (occasionally in broad daylight from the center of a village) could paralyze an entire area with fear. The reader is provided with the inadvertent bonus of a cultural commentary/history of Western colonialism that seeps into the stories of "great white hunters," implicitly revealing an uneasy relationship between Europeans and natives.

The New Murderers Who's Who by J. H. H. Gaute and Robin Odell (International Polygonics Ltd., 1991) is the first U.S. publication of this classic reference work on murderers. The oversized trade paperback features a foreword by Colin Wilson, black-and-white photographs, drawings, and newspaper cuttings, and most important, straightforward accounts of murders covering more than 160 years. The murderers are listed alphabetically. This is not a sensationalized tabloid-type book. Highly recommended.

World Encyclopedia of 20th Century Murder, by Jay Robert Nash (Paragon House), is an expensive but impressive-looking hardcover containing more than 1,000 entries and over 400 illustrations representing all types of homicides and slayers. The in-depth entries are similar to those in the book above, but some go into greater detail, and the book occasionally covers killers not included in the above-mentioned volume. Highly recommended.

Serial Slaughter: What's Behind America's Murder Epidemic? by Michael Newton (Loompanics Unlimited), is a serious, detailed, and frightening book about the epidemic of serial and mass murders abounding in America during the 1980s and '90s.

Although the existence of serial killers has been documented throughout American and world history, the last decade saw a massive increase in this kind of random murder. Newton delves into possible causes, provides statistics classifying different types of killers, and statistically delineates their early childhoods and upbringing. Especially powerful are the words of the killers themselves, taken from police interviews. A useful companion volume to Newton's earlier book (volume 1 is just out in paperback) *Hunting Humans: An Encyclopedia of Serial Killers*, the "who's who" of serial murder.

Whoever Fights Monsters by Robert K. Ressler and Tom Shachtman (St. Martin's Press) is a page-turner by the FBI man who coined the term "serial killer" and who for twenty years has developed and modified criminal profiling to accurately describe unknown serial killers. Much of Newton's material for *Serial Slaughter* (see above entry) comes directly from the statistics gathered by Ressler and his trained teams, who have interviewed some of the notorious murderers in the United States for their research. The best parts of *Whoever Fights Monsters*, the individual cases, read like a novel: we're right there when Ressler goes to actual crime scenes and deduces, from what he finds there, almost exactly what the murderers will be like—age, occupation, living conditions, how far they live from the crime, etc. Ressler's autobiographical material is less interesting but doesn't detract from the rest of this fascinating book. Highly recommended.

Violent Legacies: Three Cantos, by Richard Misrach with an introductory fiction piece by Susan Sontag (Aperture), is part of a project Misrach has been working on since 1979 "searching deserts of the American West for images that suggest the collision between civilization and nature." He creates art from juxtaposing decay, destruction, and the barren beauty of the desert. This set of photographs is about "militarism and cultural violence." The first section is called "Project W-47 (The Secret)"—formerly Wendover Air Base in Utah, a secret training and planning site for the atomic bombings of Hiroshima and Nagasaki. The beautifully composed photographs show a desert scarred by shrapnel, abandoned bunkers, bomb-loading pits, and buildings. "The Pit" focuses on county-designated dead animal pits and trash dumps where locals in the Nevada desert are encouraged to deposit dead livestock. This section is a series of disturbing images, taken between 1987 and 1989, of hundreds of dead animals. The dumps might be on old radioactive test sites and might still be contaminated, an allegation currently under investigation. Last is "The Playboys," a series of old *Playboy* magazines used for target practice by unknown persons on the fringes of a Nevada atomic bomb test site. Cover girls seem to have been the principal targets but other cultural icons were inadvertently shot as well. The Sontag piece is a minor and unnecessary parable. On the whole, a beautiful and disturbing coffee table book.

Version 90:3 is a strange hip journal published annually out of Allston, Massachusetts. I picked up the 1992 issue specifically for the interview with photographer Joel-Peter Witkin.

Graven Images, by Ronald V. Borst (Grove Press), is a wonderful visual romp through the history of horror, fantasy, and science fiction in movie-poster art. The personal reminiscences of each decade by Clive Barker, Robert Bloch, Ray Bradbury, Harlan Ellison, Peter Straub, and Forrest J Ackerman vary in effectiveness and are almost incidental. Stephen King's introduction lists his favorite horror films and his favorite horror posters. The sheer amount (500-plus) and variety of the poster collection and Borst's captions are what make this book outstanding.

Trading cards continue to be popular, especially the "true crime" cards that have generated so much controversy. *Incredible True Life Murderers!*, by Bad Otis Link and the Pizz (Rigamor Press), was the very first set of cards dedicated to the subject of murder. In 1992 the Philip Morris Corporation filed suit against Rigamor because the original trading card package was made to look like a pack of Marlboros. Subsequently, the cards in that edition were pulled off the market and a second edition has been released in new boxes. The cards are black and white, snappy in style, and light in attitude. Rigamor also put out *The World's Most Hated People*, illustrating "the twentieth century's most despised tyrants, politicians, criminals and entertainers," including people such as Morton Downey, Jr., Milli Vanilli, Satan, George Bush, Jimmy Hoffa, and many others. *Bloody Visions*, by Richard H. Price (Shel-Tone), takes the subjects of mass murder and serial killing more seriously and illustrates perpetrators in black and white and red. The best art is in the color work on the various true-crime series from Eclipse: *G-Men and Gangsters*, series 1, is by Max Allan Collins and George Hagenauer with art by Paul Lee. Series 2 is *Serial Killers and Mass Murderers* by Valerie Jones and Peggy Collier with art by Jon Bright. Series 3 is *Crime and Punishment* by Bruce Carroll with art by Bill Lignante. Other series that came out in 1991 or 1992 and are still available are *Crimes Against the Eye* by Robert Williams (Kitchen Sink Press)—36 full-color reproductions of the artist's work, and also from Kitchen Sink: *Hollywood Characters* and *More Hollywood Characters* by artists Charles Burns, Rick Geary, Drew Friedman, and others; *The Ed Wood, Jr. Players* drawn by Drew Friedman; *The Saucer People* drawn by Steve Bissette, Charles Burns, and others; and *Republicans Attack!: A Paranoid Fantasy in 36 Parts* by James Vance and Mark Landman.

—Ellen Datlow

Horror and Fantasy in the Media: 1992

Usually I'm griping because most of what happens in the field of SF/fantasy/horror film is exceedingly conservative and predictable. The movies may be highly crafted, but so infrequently do they hit the screen with any sense of real adventure. That's too often left to the vagaries of mainstream film and the marketing of same. Indeed, in 1992 Neil Jordan's *The Crying Game* came nearly unheralded to U.S. screens; but then succeeded wildly because of an astonishing word-of-mouth campaign combined with a collective, consensual oath of silence taken by the mushrooming audience. This mainstream movie was a mixture of political thriller, contemporary romance, and something more. It wasn't SF. Fantasy? Some in the audience thought so. Horror? Well, without violating the audience's conspiracy, let me just say that at *that* particular point in the plot, the audience reaction almost invariably was shockier than any of the screams you ever heard in *Psycho*. There was probably no film in 1992 that galvanized more viewer self-examination of assumptions and triggered more post-theater discussion. All this from the director of *A Company of Wolves*, *The Miracle*, and—as looks more and more likely—the long-awaited *Interview with a Vampire*.

Anyhow, as I said, that was a high-water mark in the mainstream. I could rhapsodize about *Unforgiven* and a variety of other nonfantasy films as well, but, in this venue, I won't. I just wanted to establish a high point or two for comparison.

So what was cool down here in the ghetto—especially allowing a few expansion seams in the walls of the genre? I want to start with *Rain Without Thunder*. This is a highly political, non-car-chase, no-special-effects, very talky science fiction drama. Talking heads, even? Yep, but I still found it more provocative, more involving, more entertaining, than, say, *My Dinner with André*. Director and writer Gary Bennett is also a lawyer, a background which makes itself readily apparent in his debut film. *Rain Without Thunder* (the title's from a Frederick Douglass quote) takes place fifty years from now in what seems at first to be a kinder, gentler America. Prisons, for example, have been euphemized into the appearance of country clubs. But don't be fooled. A mother and daughter (Betty Buckley and Ali Thomas), imprisoned for fetal murder, are serving as the test case for the Unborn Child Kidnapping Act. It seems the mom and mom-to-be went to Sweden for an abortion ("termination," in future parlance), in a time set twenty years after abortion has been made illegal in the U.S.A. The film is structured as a futuristic documentary, setting up its story by intercutting interviews with a variety of interested parties. Jeff Daniels plays the women's defense attorney; Linda Hunt is the head of the Atwood Society; Frederick Forrest plays the warden of a prison for convicted fetus-murderers; Graham Greene is a coldly bizarre cultural commentator; Sheila Pinkham effectively evokes an elderly twentieth-century feminist who, in her middle years, watched everything go down the tubes. What makes this film highly effective science fiction is the quality of its extrapolation. Gary Bennett's take on the future is not simplistic, however sympathetic it is to women's rights. *Rain Without Thunder* is a complex and balanced piece that offers empathy to all sides. The writer/director knows the cutting edge of change is a serrated blade. He fleshes out a future dangerously close right now to coming into existence. This is remarkable filmmaking that should be seen by everyone interested in issues, drama, or political vision. My screening pass said, "This film leans toward the pro-choice view which may be uncomfortable to some." Ah, I thought. A can't-miss-this-one. I was right. What about that lack of car chases? Go flip on Cinemax and watch *Freejack* ten or twenty times.

The funniest SF-horror flick I saw in the last year was Jean-Pierre Jeunet and Marc Caro's *Delicatessen*. This French post-apocalypse farce is as dark as the shadows a hundred yards from the deli/apartment house where the film is set, and as sharp as the shining cleaver the Butcher (Jean-Claude Dreyfus) uses to slice and dice a steady stream of new handymen hired by this bastion of civilization in a tired, depressed world. Then comes a new handyman (Dominique Pinon) who is brighter and more resourceful than his unlucky predecessors. He even falls in love with the Butcher's cellist daughter (Marie-Laure Dougnac) and joins her on duets playing the saw. Many of you will have previously seen Pinon playing a killer in *Diva*. Working from a script credited to the directors plus Gilles Adrien, the filmmakers craft a deliciously gross comedic extravaganza in which weird intelligence is always in ample evidence. If this movie were a storyboard, the pictures would have to be by the Far Side's Gary Larson. Or maybe John Callahan. There are endless wonderful touches, but for me the high point is the physical comedy of the gradually flooding bathroom scene. This is WC humor at its very best, and I'm not talking the Benny Hill variety.

Not quite as funny (or lucid, or, um, tasteful) but even more manic, is *Phallus in Wonderland*, a one-hour music video SF/heavy metal parody by GWAR. GWAR is a bunch of Richmond rockers and art students who decided to put on the whole metal industry with outrageous costumes, over-the-edge lyrics, and consummately tasteless—but hilarious—stage shows. GWAR uses all the best conventions of pulp fiction, SF, and Lovecraftian horror to, er, mount their productions. The video incorporates much of the music from GWAR's third album, *America Must Be Destroyed*. The plot deals with the final conflict between the alien GWARriors and the (presumably fundamentalist, tight-assed, ultraconservative) Morality Squad. There is a lengthy trial scene that's *not* a whole lot like, say, the one in *A Few Good Men*. GWAR singer Oderus Urungus has his penis chain-sawed free by Morality Squad goon, Corporal Punishment. The penis, also known, among other things, as the Cuttlefish of Cthulhu, has its own cheerful identity and is put on trial for obscenity. Wrapping this all together is a truly astonishing amount of over-the-top violence, cheesy effects, and sublimely grotesque puppet work. I watched this with jaw occasionally agape, and frequent laughter bubbling up like dead rats surfacing in ichor. A lot of this is akin to Clive Barker meets Abbott and Costello. Great stuff. *Phallus in Wonderland* made it onto the final ballot for the Grammies in the long-form video category, but was beaten out by Annie Lennox's *Diva*. Go figure.

While we're on strange, I want to mention Joe Christ's new short film, *Crippled*. This is rebel filmmaking. Not *Profoundly Handicapped*. Not *Really Differently Enabled*. But *Crippled*. It's about a paralyzed woman who, after being subjected to an inattentive home-care person, goes and hires a *really* abusive one. I mention this amiably savage little movie because among the cast, Nanzi X. Regalia, Margaret

Petrov, and Joe Christ, there is a pseudonymous horror writer who would be instantly recognizable to you all, who's making an interesting film debut.

Other strange ones. David Lynch's *Twin Peaks* prequel, *Fire Walk with Me*, was a tragically mixed bag. The film depicts the sad last week of Laura Palmer, the character whose violent death catalyzed all the convoluted happenings of the surreal TV series. The best thing about this feature is that Sheryl Lee gets to play her character alive. She's awfully good. But as for the rest of the movie, I think it would be acutely difficult to follow for anyone not familiar with the TV series. Something like watching A *Few Good Men* dubbed into Albanian.

Stranger and more rewarding was David Cronenberg's bizarre tackling of William Burroughs's *Naked Lunch*. Working with producer Jeremy Thomas, Cronenberg adapts Burroughs in a hallucinatory take that isn't so much a direct translation of the novel—were that even possible—as it is a separate-but-equal plumbing of the kinked-out depths of a writer's soul. Peter Weller plays the writer. Roy Scheider does a nice turn as a not-nice doctor. For those who relish the grotesque, the picture's full of bug-powder snorting, weird mugwump creatures, a dream Tangier and the even spacier Interzone, and typewriters that melt down into fleshy, insectile, talking goo. The key word to *Naked Lunch* is hallucinatory. But as weirded out as the film appears to be, ultimately it seems to make sense. Cronenberg did a good job.

There were two pictures that tried to capture the shadow-haunted social/political dreamscapes of deepest, darkest Europe. Steven Soderbergh followed up *sex, lies, and videotape* with *Kafka*. Essentially this is a fictional construction in which Kafka the Man and Kafka the Worldview are merged. In other words, this movie puts Franz Kafka into the literal world he reflected in his writings. Soderbergh gets some mileage out of the same sort of black-and-white to color and back to black-and-white sandwich that worked so well in *The Wizard of Oz*. Jeremy Irons as Kafka is, as one would expect, wonderful. But the film never quite makes it over the top, suffering, as it does, from a critical lack of obsessive conviction. I don't think Woody Allen has that problem in *Shadows and Fog*. This is another foggy, nighttime, Germanic fantasy. Shot in black and white by Carlo Di Palma, it claustrophobically evokes a crumbling European city full of maze-like streets. There's a killer loose in the fog and vigilantes are out to get him. And director/writer Woody Allen is in the middle. The music by Kurt Weill and Bertolt Brecht effectively evokes the mood Allen wants. Part of the fun in this one is trying to spot the cameos by Madonna, Jodie Foster, and a variety of others. At the same time, *Shadows and Fog*, whether or not you suspiciously want to see it as a metaphor for Woody Allen's own peculiar mind, is an effective evocation of strangeness. And no, it's not as funny as his early movies. . . .

Wim Wenders got in on the act with an odd science fiction film called *Until the End of the World*. It's a near-future road picture in which William Hurt's on the run in a landscape crumbling at the seams all the way from Europe to California to the Australian Outback. You *do* have to swallow the notion that an Indian nuclear-power satellite is about to go critical, and when it does, the EMP will do some pretty weird things. Everything works well until the ending. Blooie. Meltdown time. It's sort of like no one was quite sure what it really was all supposed to mean.

The much-touted biggies for the year were Francis Ford Coppola's *Dracula* and

Tim Burton's *Batman Returns*. Naturally neither one could match the incredible density of rumor and hype surrounding each. *Dracula* is one of 1992's most beautiful films; set design, art direction, and cinematography are all breathtaking. I had the opportunity to hear Francis Ford Coppola speaking in person about the making of the movie. He claimed that he had paid much attention both to researching the historical Dracula and to translating the Bram Stoker novel conscientiously. He should be given points on both counts. The only trouble is, the shoehorning of the historical Vlad theme sticks out of the whole movie like, well, a sore fang. It's not fatally intrusive, but it does jar and distract. The worst problem is casting. Keanu Reeves plays Jonathan Harker as a refugee from Bill-and-Ted Land. That's terrifying. Winona Ryder, whom I love dearly, can't seem, as Mina, to generate all that much chemistry with Gary Oldman's Dracula. And the wonderful Anthony Hopkins goes way over the top with Van Helsing. He eats so much scenery that Allan Rickman in *Robin Hood*, by comparison, seems the very soul of restraint. At the same time, to be fair, I have to grant a lot of credit to Tom Waits for his portrayal of Renfield. This year the ever-fertile field of vampire film was blessed with two first-rate Renfields (the other being Paul Reubens in *Buffy the Vampire Slayer*). But the distinguishing characteristic of Coppola's treatment of Stoker was its operatic quality. Overblown and passionate, *Dracula* shared this approach with 1990's *Godfather III*. With both films, audiences little accustomed to grand opera in the Italian manner got solid lessons in operatic structure. Not little tasty tidbits, mind you, but full seven-course, three-act feasts.

As sequels go, *Batman Returns* wasn't too bad. At the same time, director Tim Burton didn't exactly invest the big-budget production with a lot of soul, and Daniel Waters's script could have used a bit of wit. Villains Danny De Vito (the Penguin) and Christopher Walken (developer Max Schreck) together didn't generate as much heat as Jack Nicholson's Joker did in the first film. The brighter note in *Returns* was Michelle Pfeiffer as Selina Kyle and her alter ego, Catwoman. And I did appreciate yet another askew Paul Reubens cameo as the Penguin's father. All in all, the movie was interesting to watch for Burton's trademark quirkiness and striking design, but it never was terribly involving. More actual passion seemed to be raised by the animal rights movement's protest of *Batman Returns* for alleged cruelty to penguins. Much of the wind was taken out of those sails when Burton pointed out that the penguins wearing weaponry and rocket packs were aquatic seabird robots, and that the *live* bird-actors had not been kidnapped from Antarctica, but rather had been recruited from zoos just down the Pacific coast. . . .

Then there was a big sequel that had an intensely difficult time finding its own identity. It seemed like *Alien³* had taken forever to put together. Zillions of dollars in development money had been spent on director after director, script after script, before a millimeter of film was shot. Scripts came from both William Gibson and Eric Red, among others, and all were discarded. There was the famous premise of a handmade wooden planet inhabited by monks. . . . And then it evolved to the cheerless world of Fiorine, a prison planet inhabited by a colony of convicts-turned-fundamentalists. British rock video director David Fincher helmed, using a composite script from Larry Ferguson, Walter Hill, and David Giler. Initial critical and audience response was not terrific. People hated the initial disposing of all survivors of the previous films, save Sigourney Weaver as Ellen Ripley. People didn't like seeing good actors like Charles Dance getting lunched within ten or fifteen seconds of generating some audience interest and sympathy. Viewers especially seemed incensed by Ripley's *Terminator 2*-ish departure from the whole depressing *Alien* saga. At least in *T2*, the viewer was allowed to feel a lump in the throat. . . . But as I said above, I think the problem was identity. *Alien* was the consummate tekkie nightmare of Gothic sexual violence. *Aliens* was a best-of-breed, rock 'em, sock 'em adventure. Both directors, Ridley Scott and James Cameron, had a coherent and compelling vision of what they were trying for. I'm not so sure David Fincher did. *Alien³* was not, I really feel, the disaster so many claimed. But I can understand the disappointment of so many. Whatever territory Fincher and his screenwriters tried to carve out, it simply did not sufficiently engage the heart or the brain. It was indeed good to see Lance Henriksen get some on-screen time; but that didn't make up for the plot's clumsiness, Ripley's thankless role, or the whole sour feel of the production. And it was probably a really bad idea to allow the aliens so much on-camera time in full view, in good light. But although *Alien⁴* seems a doubtful project, there are ways. . . . What if Ripley's daughter didn't *really* die, and grows to adulthood wondering whatever truly happened to her mom, and then goes against the wishes of the PR guys at the Company and picks up a gun and a credit chip and goes looking? And it turns out that Jonesy the cat has begat about ten generations of kittens, and one goes along with the woman who looks so uncannily like her own mother? Never mind.

For less pretentious big-screen science fiction, Geoff Murphy's *Freejack* looked just the ticket. And indeed, it has its moments. Based *very* loosely on Robert Sheckley's *Immortality, Inc.*, this is lite adventure SF of the predictable variety. Emilio Estevez is a contemporary race driver who's yanked away from the very moment of his death in a spectacular crash and transported to the year 2009. Kidnapping healthy bodies from the past seems to be the SOP for important honchos in the future—since there's a means by which they can have their mentalities implanted in the new bodies. Estevez finds himself on the run from a very rich industrialist (Anthony Hopkins). The guy actually doing the pursuing is Mick Jagger, looking very much as if he's genuinely getting a kick out of the role. It's all fun, but it's still pretty silly stuff.

For more silly stuff, I trust you saw *Buffy the Vampire Slayer*, directed by Fran Kuzui from Joss Whedon's script. This was a reasonable B-movie approach to the burning question: What if the latest in an unbroken line of vampire slayers down through the ages should turn out to be a perky val-girl, a California blonde? Kristy Swanson certainly looked the part as Buffy. Rutger Hauer, however, didn't get nearly enough screen time as the chief bloodsucking antagonist. Paul Reubens continued his comeback with a wonderful turn as a Renfield, and performed one of the all-time great death scenes. Unfortunately "silly" never quite evolved into either chilling or consistently funny. Lots of wasted opportunities here.

And for something even sillier . . . How about Jean-Claude Van Damme and Dolph Lundgren in *Universal Soldier*? Roland Emerich's slam-bam action B-movie concerned American soldiers killed in Vietnam, then resurrected as a bionic, superhuman, counter-terrorist force. But then programming goes screwy and a badass cyborg zombie (Lundgren) has to pursue-with-intent-to-kill a good cyborg zombie

(Van Damme). It's comic-book violence. Fun, but requires you to shift your higher functions into neutral.

Ditto, but without the violence, can be said for *Encino Man*. Les Mayfield's comedy about a prehistoric dude (Brendan Fraser) unearthed in Southern California by a couple of high school guys (Sean Astin and Pauly Shore) has its moments when the jokes work, but still makes you nostalgic for *Wayne's World*.

Speaking of which . . . Penelope Spheeris struck a three-bagger with her comedy vehicle for the *Saturday Night Live* team of Wayne and Garth (Mike Myers and Dana Carvey). The saga of these hapless suburban metal fans and underground TV stars is funny and even occasionally affecting. And, as everyone now knows, the "Bohemian Rhapsody" sequence brought immense new life to Queen's album sales, though, sadly, not to Freddy Mercury.

While I'm talking about hits, *Aladdin* should definitely be mentioned. Disney released this one for Christmas. It's top-quality, classic, Disney animation. It's also one of the highest-grossing, fastest-breaking Disney animated features ever. Robin Williams gets a lot of the credit with a fantastic off-the-wall performance as the voice of the Genie. The Arab-American antidefamation organizations have protested the film for stereotyping Arabs, but they appear to be the only folks not buying tickets.

Robin Williams didn't do nearly as well, either in his performance itself, or by carrying the day, in Barry Levinson's *Toys*. This well-intentioned comedy about a former military officer taking over a toy factory, then determining to swing production from happy playthings to war toys, before being thwarted by Williams and his friends, just sagged to the ground and flopped around for a while. Maybe it was the lack of a backbone. *Toys* tried very hard, but it just couldn't match laughs with all its good intentions.

A third Christmas holiday movie was *The Muppets' Christmas Carol*. Directed by Jim Henson's son and heir, Brian, this was a sincere and pretty accurate translation of the Dickens classic. Playing off against the likes of Kermit and Miss Piggy, Michael Caine did a fine job as Scrooge. This was successful enough; it'll probably become a perennial Christmas classic on video.

So how would you like to see a combination of splatter and political consciousness? Talk about baking a cake and then eating it with a big knife . . . Polish director Richard Bugajski's *Clear Cut* tackles that challenge, but not particularly well. Written by Rob Forsyth from M. T. Kelly's novel *A Dream Like Mine*, the movie shows lots of great Canadian wilderness scenery. Ron Lea plays a liberal lawyer representing the interests of American Indians trying to keep a logging company from clear-cutting their pristine home. The good guys lose in court, and Lea finds himself trapped in the mysterious machinations of an enigmatic trickster-figure (Graham Greene). Greene's character kidnaps the timber boss and takes him out into the boonies in company with the lawyer. The attorney has expressed a desire to see the white logger pay; Greene carries out the wish. Thus we get to see a graphic depiction of the timberman's lower leg being flayed alive. The movie's earnest, the scenery's gorgeous, but the metaphysical depth is shallow and confused. Too bad.

You could see even more spiritual melodrama merged with an American Indian backdrop in Michael Apted's *Thunderheart*. The cast is pretty fine in this tale of a young FBI agent (Val Kilmer) dispatched to a Sioux reservation to investigate a murder. Kilmer doesn't even look like Kilmer for the first twenty minutes or so. He plays a repressed young quarter-Sioux man who is more than a little wary about getting in touch with the inner ancestor. The ubiquitous Graham Greene is present as a tribal cop, along with Sam Shepard as Kilmer's FBI partner. Sheila Tousey does very, very well as a young teacher who adds tension to Kilmer's life, but without the cliché of developing a relationship. The film's heart is in the right place, though the New Age/spiritual touches aren't always convincing. For frequent-flier travelers, the picture starts a touch confusingly when Kilmer is sent from Washington, D.C., to Denver, there presumably to catch a commuter plane to Rapid City. Thanks to the oblivious convenience of stock footage, he's routed through LAX. Or maybe that's just another Magic Realist touch.

Last year the so-called director's cut of *Blade Runner* was selectively released. This year the version without Harrison Ford's voice-over narration and the tacked-on happy ending got much wider distribution. Once again viewers could discover that Ridley Scott's loose translation of Philip K. Dick was sadly underappreciated a decade ago. If you hadn't seen it before, I hope you caught this re-release on the backswing. If you didn't, catch this version on videotape and wish you had access to a huge wraparound screen and multitrack Dolby.

For a very-far-back-in-the-pack *Blade Runner*–inspired wannabe, you could try *Split Second*, directed by Tony Maylam from a Gary Scott Thompson script. This is a British low-budget production that looks swell and tries very hard to work. In those regards, it is reminiscent of last year's *Hardware*: handsome and dumb. *Split Second* is set in the early twenty-first century in a grungy London being drowned slowly by global warming. There's a serial killer wired into astrological patterns. Turns out the killer also is capable of incorporating the DNA patterns of its victims. The critter's nemesis is a rebel cop played by a sadly chunky Rutger Hauer. Turns out as well that the killer and Hauer are somehow on a psychic wavelength. Kim Cattrall plays Hauer's girlfriend; Neil Duncan does an amusing turn as Hauer's latest partner (much as with Dirty Harry, being this sort of a cop's partner is not a great career move); and Michael J. Pollard spritzes up the flooded London sewers as a rat catcher. The creature is eventually unveiled as something of an Alien with cool shades (Gargoyles, no doubt). That's about it for revelations. This could have been a hell of a picture if only it eventually made sense.

There were two Clive Barker–associated films this past year. One, *Hellraiser III: Hell on Earth*, was so-so. The other, *Candyman*, was close to an unqualified triumph. The problem with *Hell on Earth* was that it veered completely off the track of the fascinating twisted curve established in its two predecessors. Gone is the gradual seduction and corruption of the Kirsty character (Ashley Laurence). *Hell on Earth* does fine with manic weirdness for its first half, but then degenerates into pretty standard monster schlock. In other words, it starts with a sweetly corrupt dish; then turns to hash smothered in tomato sauce. It does, I must mention, have one of the best, most accurate visions of a rock club ever committed to film; but perhaps that's only praising with faint damns. I'm afraid director Tony Hickox and screenwriter Peter Atkins got off on a kick of adding lots more Cenobites, but in the process, lost track of the primal Barker vision.

Bernard Rose's *Candyman* is *much* more interesting. One suspects Clive Barker had greater contact with this film, since he was the executive producer and Rose's script was based on Barker's own story, "The Forbidden." Music video–director Rose previously distinguished himself with the horrific childhood fantasy, *Paperhouse* (1988). The film moves Barker's decaying British urban blightscape to an even grungier Chicago and the Cabrini-Green wasteland. The landscape's scary already; it gets worse when an urban folklorist (Virginia Madsen) gets on the trail of an urban myth come to life. The Candyman (Tony Todd) does multiple duty, lurking in darkness and springing out through mirrors. He's the archetypal inner-city image of deep-voiced, smiling death, drugs in one hand, a razor in the other, oblivion always the final result. The tension is great in this movie; the nastiness, delicious. If it has a fault, it's in the increased degree of plottiness the script adaptation adds to the original story. The addition rings a bit false. And the Philip Glass score is magnificent.

The year saw a trio of Stephen King pictures, more or less. He had nothing formally to do with *Pet Sematary II*, Mary Lambert's follow-up to the mild hit scored by her first adaptation of King's "Monkey's Paw" homage. The filmmakers whack away at King's vital theme—the parental fear of losing children—and do a creditable, if not entirely on-target, recap of the original *Pet Sematary*. Anthony Edwards and Edward Furlong do a decent job as father and son relocating in Maine (though shot in Georgia). It's all watchable, has its moments, but doesn't quite hit one out of the park.

King had even less to do with *The Lawnmower Man*, going so far as to litigate successfully to have his name removed from advertising for the film. One short scene depicting a guy getting mowed to death is about all that remains from King's original short story. What the story mutated into has to do with what the producers think is virtual reality research. The released feature is damned close to incoherent. Rumor has it that the video release has another 20 minutes or so, and actually makes sense. I'd like to believe that.

Stephen King himself wrote the script for Mick Garris's *Sleepwalkers*. This was another good B-movie entertainment with little pretention. I wanted to like it much more than I actually did, because of a few plot and character relationship problems. The story's about an ancient family of murderous shape-shifters living among us since time immemorial. It seems that only cats are able to sense these creatures' hidden identity. The cast is pretty good. Alice Krige (remember her in *Ghost Story*?) plays the mama shape-shifting demon. Madchen Amick plays the high school girl who finds herself attracted to the hunky young shape-shifting son. The cast's real standout is Clovis, a big gray-striped tom, who gets the lion's share of cat-lines. The picture also boasts cameo appearances by such as King and Clive Barker, and some great morphing, not only by the shape-shifters, but by automobiles as well. Cool stuff. And it's nice to see the kitties on the side of all that's good and virtuous.

Let's look at a few loonies. Larry Drake gets to play one in the low-budgeted *Dr. Giggles*. A directing debut by Manny Coto, the movie shows some nice Portland area scenery. And star Drake gets to be a psychopathic doctor fixing family grudges against the community by icing a bunch of irritating teens in all the time-honored atrocious ways. Much of this is supposed to be funny; it sometimes reaches amusing. The movie won't put you to sleep, but neither will it galvanize much paranoia about your next doctor's appointment.

John Lithgow gets to go berserk—in more ways than one—in Brian De Palma's

Raising Cain. As with so much of De Palma's work, the plot can easily be decon-
structed to sheer silliness. But the pace of De Palma's own script and direction keeps
this one going. In its unreeling of revelation after plot revelation about multiple-
personality disorder, the filmmaker stuffs this one with endless visual nods to Alfred
Hitchcock. But then, that's nothing new with De Palma. I can't say this is a
magnificent film, but it *is* a hell of a lot of fun.

I think *Stay Tuned* was supposed to be extremely funny. I'm not so sure about
the percentage of successful guffaws, but the picture is still amusing in an incredibly
lightweight way. Peter Hyams directed from a script by Tom S. Parker and Jim
Jennewein. John Ritter and Pam Dawber play a couple of parents who run afoul of
a demonic plan to steal souls through a giant home theater setup lusted after by
unwary consumers. Essentially what happens is that prospective victims get sucked
through the set and into a sequence of Satanic virtual reality shows. Some of
the set-pieces bite the big one; others are hilarious. But Dawber and Ritter are
stereotypically suited for this sort of role.

Death Becomes Her was supposed to be *the* big-budget supernatural comedy, star-
loaded and helmed by Robert Zemeckis. It was pretty good, but didn't come across
with all it promised. Meryl Streep and Goldie Hawn play lifelong competitors
coming to grips with worldly success, aging, and physical decrepitude. A major
issue between them is the man Streep steals early on from Hawn (Bruce Willis).
Willis does wonderfully well—he plays his role as a weak-willed plastic-surgeon-
turned-Beverly-Hills-mortician in a way that never reminds you of, say, the hero
of *Die Hard*. The fantasy element enters in the form of Isabella Rosselini, a
mysterious woman offering the gift of both rejuvenation and physical immortality.
The film's satiric core is this dark grappling with the American desire for constant
youth and physical attractiveness. All that's fine so far as it goes. The script by
Martin Donovan and David Koepp and the lavishly gross special effects work on
the surface. But the movie just isn't funny enough. You keep watching situations
and listening to scenes that ought to make you laugh. But they don't. Or at least,
not enough. Somewhere along the way, the nervous tissue of this film has broken
down. The funny bone and the head bone are no longer connected, alas.

But then things can always be worse. *Honey, I Blew Up the Kid*, for example.
Rick Moranis and his wild and wacky family are back. This time a techno-booboo
causes their infant son to grow to *War of the Colossal Man*–size in Las Vegas. I
wanted to laugh. Really I wanted to.

For real laughter, let me sneak two associational pictures into the middle of this
pop culture catalog. Jon Avnet's *Fried Green Tomatoes* is pretty wonderful. Fannie
Flagg and Carol Sobieski's script gives Kathy Bates, Jessica Tandy, Mary Stuart
Masterson, and Mary-Louise Parker an opportunity to shine in this low-budget
comedic drama with some tense, some tear-jerking, some very funny moments.
There are touches of Southern Gothic, too. I mean, *Alive* isn't the *only* recent film
to deal with cannibalism. . . . The other funny—however bitter the laughter—
picture is Robert Altman's *The Player*. Credit goes both to Altman and his writer,
Michael Tolkin, adapting his own novel. This is a merciless insider's view of the
Hollywood process. The terrifying thing is that it's not satiric exaggeration. Every
shot taken, every point scored, is, if anything, an understatement of the madness

that is Hollywood and the movie biz. *The Player* should be required viewing for any of you who wish to become a star on The Coast.

Now, continuing with the theme of human monsters and acute horror (what a segue), I enjoyed more than one of the year's psychodramas. Things started off with a bang—and a slash, and a ka-clunk!—with Curtis Hanson's *The Hand That Rocks the Cradle*, a low-budget melodrama about a mad nanny. Rebecca De Mornay is effective as a woman who believes she's been hideously wronged and is determined to take out her ill feelings on a yuppie family. It's not a terrifically suspenseful plot, but I did admire the makers for letting the villain die at the end and not letting her lurch back through four or five false climaxes Jason-style.

Jonathan Kaplan's *Unlawful Entry* is half of a really neat movie. The paranoid plot conceit is great: What better psycho to menace you and your family than a crazy cop (Ray Liotta) with "Preserve and Protect" on his car and a large-caliber pistol in his belt? Kurt Russell and Madeleine Stowe are a nice young couple who find themselves enmeshed in a decreasing spiral of violence with Liotta after their house is broken into. The first half plays quite well as the whole setup is put in place; then the second half loses its equilibrium and topples over into simplistic melodrama.

But my favorite—and for my money, the most dangerous—crazed killer epic of the year was *Basic Instinct*. Remember all the publicity, both pro and con? The bondage and the ice pick? The rough sex? The question of what the film had to say about lesbians and bisexuals? The interrogation-room scene? Ah, sweet nostalgia. Now we've got *Bad Lieutenant* to deal with. But back to *Basic Instinct*. You can argue whether Joe Eszterhas got paid too much for the script ($3 million). You can debate whether Eszterhas and director Paul Verhoeven ran the plot too long, and needlessly (and hopelessly) convoluted it. But none of that stops the movie from being hot, dynamic, and seductive. Michael Douglas plays something of a sleaze as the homicide detective. There are only two sympathetic characters in the primary cast. One is George Dzunda as Douglas's aging urban cowboy partner. The other is Sharon Stone, the presumed killer. But wait, you say, how can she be sympathetic, being the twisted, maddened, stone-cold ice-pick killer she presumably is? Well, consider this: In a world portrayed as inhabited by guys who are dick-directed dufusses, Stone is an intelligent, self-possessed woman with a sense of humor and in control of her life. She understands, controls, and enjoys her own sexuality. She's a strong and independent character. So, yes, she does have that *one* eensey-weensy little foible about sharp objects, but hey, *no* one's perfect, right? In any case, I think the case can be made for Stone's character being the one good role model in the movie. So there.

There were a couple of really good and solid low-budget *noir* flicks. The first is Carl Franklin's *One False Move*. Billy Bob Thornton and Tom Epperson's script has a small-town Arkansas sheriff (Bill Paxton) joined by a couple of LAPD cops (Jim Metzler and Earl Billings) after a pair of stone killers (Thornton and Michael Beach) and Thornton's girlfriend (Cynda Williams) have slaughtered a passel of Los Angelenos in a drug rip and are headed back south-by-east. The film's wonderfully rich and tight. The violent episodes are leavened with tenderness and humor in other scenes. Best of all, the script writers rarely do anything we expect them to.

The movie is full of surprises as the layers of the characters' personalities start to peel back. Everyone has secrets, it seems. In its dealing with changing attitudes about race and other issues, *One False Move* is not only a crackling, taut suspense film, it's an adroitly and carefully textured portrait of the New South. It's memorable.

Equally memorable is Quentin Tarantino's *Reservoir Dogs*. You never actually find out in the film what the title means. But you get some ideas. This is another of those low-budget shockers that drove people out of screenings at film festivals. Just not what some people were expecting, I guess. Freshman director Tarantino keeps his focus tight and taut. After half a dozen men are recruited by a money guy to pull off a jewelry store heist, the robbery goes bad and the surviving crooks realize that one of their number is a traitor, a police informant. Much of the movie hinges on unstinting efforts to find out just who the mole is. There is a scene involving torture, mutilation, and a radio playing Stealers Wheel that will ensure you never hear "Stuck in the Middle with You" without thinking of this scene in *Reservoir Dogs*. It's a classic case of imprinting. A large part of why the movie was made at all was due to Harvey Keitel's clout. Keitel plays one of the gangsters, and is party to a surprising love story integral to the film's plot and its outcome. Maybe it's not as startling as *The Crying Game*, but it's still a beautifully unexpected (but believable) quirk. Spare and incredibly *noir*, *Reservoir Dogs* suggests much good to come in Quentin Tarantino's future.

Barbet Schroeder's *Single White Female* is something of a brisker, more crowd-pleasing version of what you might expect Roman Polanski to direct in this vein. Don Ross's screenplay is drawn from John Lutz's novel *SWF Seeks Same*. Bridget Fonda plays a young Manhattan career woman who splits from her boyfriend (Steven Weber) and needs a roommate. She interviews a whole series of young women and finally accepts Jennifer Jason Leigh. Leigh has been a remarkable young actor, whether in *The Hitcher, Miami Blues*, or any number of others. Here she plays a subtly disturbed, apparently vulnerable young woman who obsesses on her more glamorous, more accepted friend. Fonda finally notices that Leigh is looking more and more like her—hair style, clothing, attraction to the old boyfriend, *everything*. The film does do a remarkable job of turning Leigh into a ringer for Fonda, other than the latter's being about half a head taller than the former. This is a good, intelligent thriller, though the climax has some of the all too frequent usual problems in melodramas of this sort: Is the killer dead? I mean, is she *really*? Or is she only faking—urrrkkkgggh!

The Vast Wasteland Revisited: The SciFi Channel debuted at long last after nearly being stifled in its cradle. Being acquired by the USA Network gave the cable service the marketing clout it needed. Most of the programming is reruns of all your old favorites, or perhaps not-so-favorites. The service's original SF dramas have been a disaster. But then the Harlan Ellison commentaries on the Buzz show have been wonderful. So all the returns aren't in. The SciFi Channel just might make it.

"Quantum Leap" just keeps leaping along. "Beauty and the Beast" died and stayed dead. So did "Twin Peaks," mercifully. "The Simpsons" are still the Simpsons, and not nearly so dysfunctional as the Bundys. Creator John Kricfalusi apparently got kicked off his own show, "Ren and Stimpy." Not a good move on management's part. "Northern Exposure" continued on, just fine (did you see the Thanksgiving episode in which we got to view a beautifully elaborate and highly unusual American Indian commemoration of the white man's holiday?), and has been joined by another quirky series, "Picket Fences" (and the "Twin Peaks" episode in which their favorite Little Person, Michael Anderson, guest-starred with the liberated elephant?).

"Star Trek: The Next Generation" placidly motored along, and most of the country continued to be saturated with reruns of the original "Star Trek." Then came the end of the year, the beginning of the next, and suddenly the national TV screen was ablaze with all sorts of new SF shows. "Star Trek: Deep Space Nine" was to show us the grittier side of the Roddenberry universe. Less Star Fleet spit and polish. The cast is very solid, but the stories are pretty much the same. Nothing radical here. Since all three ST series are aired in most viewing areas, it's sort of like picking six-packs off the soft-drink grocery shelf: Star Trek Classic, Star Trek Lite, and Star Trek Crystal.

"Space Rangers" appeared. And disappeared. It couldn't decide whether it should be more serious, or more tongue-in-cheek. At least superficially like "Battlestar Galactica" in tone and characters, the series' Linda Hunt thanklessly got to play the Lorne Green role. As for "Time Trax," well, why *not* have a weekly series of a cop from two hundred years in the future back here in the present trying to track down the nastiest crooks from his own epoch? It's all lightweight, but occasionally has some nice touches: the cop taking in a prisoner and being jeered in the America of 2193. The mob screams, *"Blanco, blanco!"* It's an America in which white folks are the distinct minority. And then came the long-awaited "Babylon 5," J. Michael Straczynski's creation for Warner Bros.' new syndicated network. This is intended to be direct competition for "Star Trek." The pilot looks absolutely wonderful. The effects are state of the art, though produced with high economy. The acting, however, comes out of a redwood forest.

As ever, the music scene varied enormously—and pleasingly—in terms of fantastic content. I don't think any human being could keep up with the amount of death metal retropunk thrash grunge and still remain sufficiently lucid to get all the references to death, mutilation, blood-sucking, and chain-sawed passion down on paper. I won't even try, but will, instead, suggest the span of weirdness in this past year's tunes.

One way to gauge the spectrum is simply to mention the two best country songs about ghosts. Billy Ray Cyrus didn't sing either of them. The narrator of Alan Jackson's "Midnight in Montgomery" (*Don't Rock the Jukebox*, Arista) runs into a familiar gent in a big hat (no, it's not Garth Brooks) at, no kidding, midnight in Alabama's capital city. It'll be interesting to see if Hank Williams, Jr., covers it. The other, niftier, ghost tune is an upbeat spectral ballad by Concrete Blonde, "Ghost of a Texas Ladies' Man" (*Walking in London*, I.R.S.). It's a mutant rocker that has a country flavor, but isn't really.

In terms of associational stuff, there was a variety of soundtrack albums of interest. *Cool World* (Warner Bros.) included David Bowie, Ministry, Electronic, The Cult, and others. Sadly, Ralph Bakshi's movie was much better for listening than for watching. *Until the End of the World* (Warner Bros.) was a good deal sharper with the likes of Lou Reed, Patti Smith, Elvis Costello, and Nick Cave and the Bad

Seeds. But, of course, for real sensation (I mean, with a parental-advisory label for explicit lyrics) there was GWAR's *America Must Be Destroyed* (Metal Blade). This was the album that supplied the music for *Phallus in Wonderland*. One lyric in "The Morality Squad" says, "You're even grosser than 2 Live Crew." Indeed. There's something in these songs to offend just about everyone. But the album's also very sharp and funny. Lighten up, morality squad!

My favorite associational album of the year was *The Turtles—Featuring Flo & Eddie—Captured Live* (Rhino). This is a mixture of some of the instant-recognition tunes the Turtles play at their nostalgia gigs ("Happy Together," "She'd Rather Be with Me") along with less familiar material. The associational part applies because the band includes horror collector Howard Kaylan (he's one of the lead dudes—Eddie—along with Mark Volman—Flo) and drummer Joe Stefko, the publisher of specialty press Charnel House. This album is something eager fans can get autographed at horror conventions. Forget about massive King and Straub tomes—tapes and CDs are far more portable! And this one's first-line fun.

My rock journalist buddy Mark Barsotti offered a few suggestions. In his album *Burning Questions* (Capitol), vintage British rocker Graham Parker shows he's still got the touch. "Release Me" is about voodoo. There are sharper edges on "Short Memories" (war) and "Here It Comes Again" (the war on drugs). Jesus Jones's *Perverse* (E.M.I.) features "Zeroes and Ones," a nice tekkie rocker about cybernetics. Alice in Chains's entire album *Dirt* (Columbia) is more than adequately dim and gloomy, perfect background for reading serial killer novels. Consolidated's *Play More Music* (Network) is listenable, rappoid, high-density message music. "Infomodities," for instance, is a kind of 1984-ish virtual reality nightmare. Lotsa words, but good ones. As a bonus on this album, you get "You Suck" by the Yeastie Girls, an ode to cunnilingus and a very funny, sharp, subversive anthem. Listen to this and you'll wonder why you ever thought Dolly Parton's "Romeo" was rad. . . .

Writer Gary Jonas came up with some suggestions I largely agree with. Warrant's "April 2031" (*Dog Eat Dog*, Columbia) is one of those earnestly green cautionary songs. Saigon Kick's "Peppermint Tribe" (*The Lizard*, Atlantic) is chock-full of sweet, tangy violence. "When Darkness Calls," from Lynch Mob's eponymous album (Elektra), is about just what the title suggests. Testament's "Return to Serenity" (*The Ritual*, Atlantic) seems to be about redemption and death, but heavy on the death. *Green Jello Suxx* is a single. On it, Green Jello does the Three Little Pigs updated, along with "Obey the Cowgod." Very funny stuff.

Saigon Kick's "Chanel" is a romantic antiromance piece about a lover's disillusionment and fantasies of burying his former beloved. Faster Pussycat's "Body Thief" (*Whipped*, Elektra) takes an even more frenzied gander at psychokillers, suggesting that even Ed Gein can sell out.

On Ugly Kid Joe's *America's Least Wanted* (Stardog/Mercury), check out such cuts as "Goddamn Devil," "Come Tomorrow," and "Madman," a '92 remix of the group's old mass-murder ditty. Also note Jeff Healy's "Evil and Here to Stay" (*Feel This*, Arista) and "Christmas with the Devil" on Spinal Tap's *Break Like the Wind* (MCA). Then there's Kiss's "Unholy" on *Revenge* (Mercury). Note Pearl Jam's "Jeremy" (*Ten*, Epic). It's horror indeed, about an abused kid; the video's a killer.

Okay. My personal favorite rock 'n' roll death song was a pointed, if fairly traditional, rocker by Dave Alvin (late of the Blasters and then X, now in the Pleasure Barons) on his *Blue Blvd* (Hightone) album. "Haley's Comet" is about the despairing and depressing death of Bill Haley in Harlingen, Texas. It's an imagistic cautionary tale for anyone in the arts. I also have to admit a soft spot in my heart for Social Distortion's "99 to Life" (*Somewhere Between Heaven and Hell*, Epic), a sweet, high-octane foot-stomper about the fatal consequences of a lovers' quarrel gone wrong. Social Distortion's a sort of garage-band wall-of-metal group with a pronounced country tinge. A favorable mutation.

Stealin Horses was originally a great Kentucky band with a debut album out from Arista. Then the band moved to Oklahoma and cut a second album with a very small label called Waldoxy. Now the band's defunct and lead singer Kiya Heartwood's out on her own, getting ready to cut a solo album. I mention all this history not because Stealin Horses sings about ghosts and chain saws, but rather because Kiya Heartwood, if the cards fall her way, could become the Melissa Etheridge of country. She is fantastic. And Stealin Horses's music has the kind of raw, elemental power that's perfect for triggering the imagination and the writing process.

Aside from GWAR stage performances, perhaps the most extravagant live musical event impinging on the lives of fantasy fans came at the climax of the American Booksellers Association meeting on Monday night, May 25, 1992. This was the debut (but apparently not the last) appearance of the Rock Bottom Remainders, a literarily oriented supergroup formed for this occasion. The concert took place at the Cowboy Boogie, an Anaheim, California, C&W club. This was a charity gala with proceeds from the $10 tickets going to three worthy causes: pro-literacy, pro–homeless writers, and anticensorship efforts. The magnitude of the event was awesome, eventually requiring the volunteered services of scores of professionals, not just the musicians on stage, but also the men and women from the book trade who served as drum, guitar, and microphone techs, and as roadies in general. Project instigator Kathy Goldmark, founder of the primary Bay Area literary guide/escort service, allowed on the phone as how the benefit concert "became a Frankenstein's monster."

Fortunately the monster was benign, and possessed a definite rough charm. The center-stage musical group consisted of humorist Dave Barry on lead guitar, novelist Stephen King on rhythm guitar, thriller writer Ridley Pearson on bass, Magic Realist Barbara Kingsolver playing keyboards, spiritual guru Robert Fulghum on mandocello, and a pair of terrific "ringer" session musicians on drums and sax. The band was bracketed by two vocal groups. The Critics' Chorus included commentator Roy Blount, Jr., rock and culture writers Greil Marcus and Dave Marsh, cartoonist Matt Groening, and others. The Remainderettes, in gloves, lush tumbled curls, and sexy black dresses, consisted of Kathy Goldmark, AP correspondent and book author Tad Bartimus, and novelist Amy Tan. Très slinkster cool.

Ah, but the music itself? No one had reason to be ashamed either to listen or to participate. There were two sets, each about an hour. The Remainders played rock covers, "Sea of Love," "Last Date," all that sort of thing, occasionally with mutant lyrics. The instrumental work was all first-rate and tight. The vocals varied quite a lot, but less, I think, from a lack of native talent than from the expectable flopsweat. Nervous tension affected performers' pipes, particularly in the first set. It's only reasonable with a group of writers playing out a genuine rock 'n' roll fantasy. If a prize were awarded for the best combination of stage presence and musical ability it would probably have gone to Amy Tan.

Enormous credit should be given to the musical director, Al Kooper. Kooper, seminal sixties blues-rocker (The Blues Project, then Blood, Sweat, and Tears) and prominent producer, reportedly drove his charges hard for three days of concentrated rehearsal before the performance. Considering that brief a prep time, the results were something akin to miraculous.

It was not hard to discern at ABA that the concert's great drawing card was Stephen King. Certainly he was, in more ways than one, the most visible of the participants. It was to his credit that he did not hog the mike or the limelight. The event came through as a true ensemble performance, both as a social cause and as an entertaining event. And it gave the audience a chance, for one brief manic evening, to forget the vicissitudes of publishing.

Later in the year, BMG (the record club folks) brought out a $20 video documentary on the concert. There's a lot of interesting interview material presented through performer sound bites, but it's intercut with bits and pieces of the performance itself. You get no songs complete. Too bad, since the music wasn't *that* bad. So what you're finally left with is a long series of interesting tastes, but no full meal.

Now. Maybe in 1993 we can have a battle of the bands with the Rock Bottom Remainders, Social Distortion, GWAR, and the Pleasure Barons. And maybe all four could collaborate on the score for Neil Jordan's *Interview with a Vampire*.

Dream on.

—Edward Bryant

Obituaries

Each year marks the physical death of a number of those gifted people who create fantasy and horror in lierature and other media. In 1992 one of the most durable and important fantasists died. **Fritz Leiber**, 81, was a true giant of the field. It is difficult to gauge accurately the full scope of his influence upon other writers, but a list of his own writing, which would take up more space than we may devote to it, is impressive not only for its size, but also for the breadth of his range of styles and creative direction. He wrote fantasy and horror of many sorts, including his well-known Fafhrd and the Gray Mouser stories. These were typical of his work in that they can be read as exciting sword-and-sorcery, but Leiber's trenchant wit and sure sense of both the absurd and the tragic make these readable on deeper levels than most sword and sorcery.

He won many awards in fantasy, horror, and science fiction, including seven Hugos and four Nebulas, and was honored as a Grand Master in Science Fiction and for Life Achievement in fantasy. He wrote numerous seminal works in all three fields, including *Conjure Wife*, a brilliant novel of modern witchcraft, *Our Lady of Darkness*, urban dark fantasy or horror, depending on your critical stance, *The Big Time*, science fiction that reads more like existential fantasy, *The Wanderer*, SF that really was a great "disaster" novel, and a number of other works, long and short, of lasting beauty and modern sensibility.

His story, "The Girl with the Hungry Eyes," is a classic vampirism story, well ahead of its time; this is just a single example among many pieces that explored themes and were innovative in style and technique. Perhaps a reason for the lack of greater critical acclaim for Leiber's work lies in the ease and natural storytelling manner of his fiction. While Leiber was certainly a conscious artist, he didn't make the reader notice his craft, preferring to be unobtrusively artful, letting the story come through without drawing attention to the author.

Fritz Leiber was a cat person, and put cats into his fiction, perhaps most spectacularly in *The Green Millennium* (1952). That novel also contained more sexual excitement than did the works of virtually any other SF or fantasy writer of that time. Sex has caught up with the rest of the field long since, but Leiber was ahead of his time in this as well.

Leiber wasn't as commercially successful as the best of his peers, but none of them was more brilliantly gifted or creative. Born into a theatrical family, he was at one time an actor himself, and until his death remained a formidable stage presence whenever called upon to read publicly. He will be missed, but as is true with those who create art, his legacy is a gift to all future generations.

William M. Gaines, 70, was publisher of *Mad* magazine. In 1947 he inherited the EC comics line and transformed it from Educational to Entertaining, breaking new ground in the graphic format, publishing a wide range of titles, from *Tales from the Crypt* to *Weird Science Fiction*. When in 1954 Dr. Frederic Wertham published his anticomics tract, *Seduction of the Innocent*, which asserted that comics like Gaines's corrupted youth, turning kids into juvenile delinquents, Gaines, after a series of U.S. Senate hearings, was forced to drop virtually all of the comics. The one exception was the satire, *Mad*. He turned it into a magazine, and it quickly became nothing less than the most popular and culturally influential magazine for adolescents (and many adults as well), as it still is today. Nothing was or is safe from the wicked pens of *Mad's* "usual gang of idiots" (their staff artists and writers). It remains an American institution.

Angela Carter, 51, was a writer whose sharp, graceful prose and keenly insightful writing infused her plays, poetry, and fiction with an uncommon edge. She was known for her sense of the unusual in life, and her fantasy works included *The War of Dreams*, *The Passion of New Eve*, the screenplay of *The Company of Wolves*, and other works.

Not a writer of fantasy, but certainly influential to a generation of writers of the fantastic was **Isaac Asimov**, 72, who wrote hundreds of books and was widely known because of his incredible range of subject matter from fiction to nonfiction in dozens of fields. His first love, however, was science fiction, in which he was a Grand Master and won many awards. He also was involved with the magazine that bears his name, *Asimov's Science Fiction*. While there have been other magazines named for people, none is quite like this one. Until his death he continued to write the editorials, answer reader mail, and be actively involved. He was a writer completely obsessed with writing. He was famous for writing every single day, even on vacations. His *Foundation* trilogy was for many years the most popular SF series by far. When he wrote the fourth book, *Foundation's Edge*, years later, it became an instant best-seller, taking mere months to outsell the previous three volumes, which had taken decades to reach their audience. After that, Asimov was a consistent best-seller on national lists, though his work had passed its peak. He remained one of the best-selling SF authors until his death. An unassuming man who never claimed to be a great writer, Asimov was a firm believer in the essential goodness of mankind, and his works, imbued with that belief, inspired and encouraged several generations of readers.

Hal Roach, 100, was a filmmaker who began in the silent era and continued to make a variety of films, mostly comedies, for at least four decades. His studio was the starting point for many gifted comic talents, and his work encompassed fantasy as well as realistic works. Certainly the Little Rascals were fantasy! Another film-maker died, **Jack Arnold**, 75, a director who was known for a number of low-budget horror and science fiction films, including *It Came from Outer Space*, *The Creature from the Black Lagoon*, and many others. Actor **Robert Morley**, 84, was known for his droll, witty performances in numerous films and on stage. **Anthony Perkins**, 60, didn't deserve to be remembered only as the mad killer, Norman Bates, in Alfred Hitchcock's classic film, *Psycho*, but that success followed him for decades after he created the role. Before and after that film he was a character actor who played a variety of roles in dozens of films. Perhaps his other most memorable role was as major league baseball player Jim Piersall, in the biographical film, *Fear Strikes Out*.

Children's book author and artist **James Marshall**, 49, whose inspired work included such hilarious and affirming works as *The Stupids* books and the *Miss Viola Swamp* books, among many others. He worked a lot with Harry Allard. He was a bright light of silliness in the juvenile universe. **Mary Norton**, 88, was a well-known and well-loved children's book author. She wrote the "Borrowers" series, which became enormously popular as books and also as films. Another well-known work of hers was *The Magic Bed-Knob,* which was adapted for film as *Bedknobs and Broomsticks.* **Alvin Schwartz,** 64, was the author of many successful children's books, including *Ghosts,* and his *Scary Stories* series.

R.(eginald) Bretnor, 80, was a writer of fantasy, science fiction, humor, essays— but perhaps best known for his short pieces, many published in *The Magazine of Fantasy & Science Fiction,* featuring Ferdinand Feghoot. These appeared under the pseudonym Grendel Briarton, and was absolutely, irredeemably punnish. His other series, the Schimmelhorn stories, was also quite charming. He also wrote several novels, but never became as famous as his skills would have suggested.

Rosemary Sutcliff, 71, was a highly regarded British historical novelist, and author of the acclaimed Arthurian classic *Sword at Sunset.*

Michael Talbot, 38, was a talented fantasy and horror writer who in his short career wrote some very effective and creepy novels, including *The Delicate Dependency, The Bog,* and *Night Things.*

A number of people connected with publishing died in 1992, including **Samuel Walker,** 65, the founder and publisher of Walker Publishing, which has published a fair number of good science fiction and fantasy works, despite never having a terribly large budget; **Sidney Meredith,** 73, the brother of literary agent Scott Meredith and the vice president and treasurer of their famous agency; antiquarian bookseller **Eric Kramer,** 58, who had an enormous number of hard-to-find books in his Manhattan-based Fantasy Archives; **Jack Tannen,** 84, who was a bookseller and later the publisher of Canaveral Press. He published, with the editorial directorship of Richard A. Lupoff, a number of Edgar Rice Burroughs works. He also published Lupoff's biography of Burroughs; and **Roberta Bender Grossman,** 46, co-founder and publisher of Zebra Books.

Many other writers died in 1992. **Millea Kenin,** 49, was a writer published in many anthologies and magazines, in addition to being a designer, poet, and editor; **Barbara Comyns,** 83, was the distinguished author of a number of Magic Realist novels, including *The Vet's Daughter* and *The Juniper Tree*; **Richard Burns,** 33, was the author of the fantasy novel *Khalindaine* and its sequel *Troubador,* as well as other works in the mainstream; **M. F. K. Fisher,** 83, noted essayist and author of the fantasy novel *Not Now, But Now*; and **Edouard Roditi,** 81, essayist, poet, and translator associated with the surrealists.

Joe Schuster, 78, was the co-creator, along with Jerry Siegel, of *Superman.* **Martin Goodman,** 84, was the founder and longtime publisher of Marvel Comics. **Dwight V. Swain,** 76, was an early fantasy and science fiction writer who started out in the pulps. Many latter-day writers were influenced by his vigorous work.

Artist **Joseph Magnaini,** 79, was a great artist who did the classic covers of Ray Bradbury's work for many years, among many other fine pieces. He was also a filmmaker. **Francis Bacon,** 82, was a controversial artist whose distorted, macabre images of the human body were inspiring to generations of fantasy and horror artists. **Anton Furst,** 47, a special effects and production designer whose most famous work was on the design of the film *Batman*; **Robert Peak,** 64, was a celebrated illustrator who was a giant in the field of movie-poster art. Among his best known fantasy posters was the one he painted for John Boorman's *Excalibur.*

Many creative people connected with fantasy and horror in the media died in

1992. Actors who left the scene included **Klaus Kinski**, 65, who was known for his dark, effective portrayals in a number of fantastic films; he appeared with his daughter, actress Nastassia Kinski, in *Cat People*; **Denholm Elliott**, 70, was a versatile, distinguished stage and screen actor whose credits included television productions of *The Strange Case of Dr. Jekyll and Mr. Hyde* and *Dracula*, as well as many other diverse roles; **Paul Henreid**, 84, was a fine actor of many films, including his memorable turn in *Casablanca*; **Cesare Danova**, 66, was a character actor in a number of productions over many years; **Mae Clarke**, 81, co-starred in *Frankenstein* with Boris Karloff, and appeared in many other films; **Morris Carnovsky**, 94, was a stage actor and appeared in films, including *Siren of Atlantis*, before being blacklisted. He resumed his career in the 1970s; actor/director **Ray Danton**, 60, was a character actor in many films and television projects. He also directed a number of low-budget projects, including *Psychic Killer*; **Dick York**, 63, was best known as the co-star of the TV series *Bewitched*. He also acted in numerous other television shows; **Cleavon Little**, 53, was in a number of films and television shows, including the film *Once Bitten*. He's best remembered for his memorable role in *Blazing Saddles*; **Neville Brand**, 71, was known as a bad guy in the movies. A much-decorated World War II hero, he was in dozens of films, mostly the target for the good guys' fists; **Jack Kelly**, 65, was well known to television viewers. He also appeared in a number of films, including *Forbidden Planet* and *Cult of the Cobra*; **Arletty**, 94, was a French actress featured in, among other films, *Les Enfants du Paradise*; **Malcolm Aterbury**, 85, was in *I Was A Teenage Werewolf*, and many other films and television shows; British character actor **Tutte Lemkow**, 73, appeared in numerous films and television productions, including *Raiders of the Lost Ark* and *Theatre of Blood*; character actor **Ian Wolfe**, 95, appeared in numerous films, mostly in sinister roles, including ones in *The Raven* and *The Return of Dr. X*; **Paul Maxwell**, 70, was featured in many films, including *Blood of Dracula*. He also did much voice work; **Barbara Morrison**, 84, starred in *Bedknobs and Broomsticks*, and other films; **Marshall Thompson**, 66, starred in the classic chiller *Fiend Without a Face*, and appeared in many film and television productions for many years; **Brian Oulton**, 84, starred in the 1963 horror film *Kiss of the Vampire*, and appeared in many other productions; **Georgia Brown**, 56, a British singer and actress, was best known for her stage performance in *Oliver!* She appeared in the film *A Study in Terror*, and other films. **John Anderson**, 69, was a character actor for many years. He was in *Psycho*, and played parts in hundreds of television shows.

A number of screenwriters also died. **Edmund Beloin**, 82, wrote the screenplay for *Visit to a Small Planet*, based on the original play by Gore Vidal; **Robert Kaufman**, 60, was the screenwriter of, among other films, *Love at First Bite*; **Frederic Rinaldo**, 78, was a screenwriter who penned, among other films, *Hold that Ghost*.

Behind the camera, many others died this year. **Satyajit Ray**, 70, was best known for *Pather Panchali*. He was India's foremost filmmaker; **Hans Koenkamp**, 100, was a cameraman for Mack Sennett in the silent era, and became a special-effects man, working on *The Wizard of Oz*, among other films; producer **George Edwards**, 67, made *Frogs* and other low-budget fantasy-horror films; Puppeteer **Richard Hunt**, 40, was best known for his work on *The Muppet Show*; set designer **Ruby Levitt**, 84, created the *Addams Family* television series sets. She was an Academy Award nominee for some of her film work; film editor **Arthur Milford**, 89, won an Academy Award for editing Frank Capra's production of *Lost Horizon*; **Howard Christie**, 79, was a prolific producer for Universal Studios in the 1950s. He was responsible for a number of Abbott and Costello films; **Anna Johnstone**, 79, a costume designer for stage and film productions for over forty years, created the costumes for the Broadway production of *Bell, Book and Candle*, and many other productions, including the film *The Wiz*; Disney animator **Jack Kinney**, 82, contributed to many of Disney's classic cartoons; **Albert Taveres**, 39, was a stage and screen casting director, performing that duty for Disney's *Beauty and the Beast* and *Aladdin*. He also cast the original off-Broadway production of *Little Shop of Horrors*.

All these people contributed in their own ways to bring us the gift of entertainment and, in the case of many, edification. Their work lives on.

SILVER OR GOLD
Emma Bull

Emma Bull is a leading light of the modern Urban Fantasy field owing to her delightful first novel, *War for the Oaks*, set in the Minneapolis rock-and-roll scene, as well as her work in the Borderland "punk fantasy" anthology series. Bull is also the author of two excellent science fiction novels, *Falcon* and *Bone Dance*. Her latest is a Borderland novel titled *Finder*. Bull, who is also a rock musician and editor of the sporadic PJF journal *The Medusa*, lives with her husband, author Will Shetterly, in Minneapolis, Minnesota.

"Silver or Gold" is a more traditional work of fantasy than we're accustomed to seeing from this versatile writer—a lyrical, imaginary-world tale written for the anthology *After the King* (Martin H. Greenberg, editor)—a tribute volume to the late J. R. R. Tolkien.

—T.W.

Moon Very Thin sat on the raised hearth—the only place in the center room out of the way—with her chin on her knuckles. She would have liked to be doing something more, but the things she thought of were futile, and most were undignified. She watched Alder Owl crisscross the slate floor and pop in and out of the stillroom and the pantry and the laundry. Alder Owl's hands were full of things on every crossing: clean clothes, a cheese, dried yellow dock and feverfew, a tinderbox, a wool mantle. She was frowning faintly all over her round pink face, and Moon knew that she was reviewing lists in her head.

"You can't pack all that," said Moon.

"You couldn't," said Alder Owl. "But I've had fifty years more practice. Now remember to cure the squash before you bring them in, or there'll be nothing to eat all winter but onions. And if the squirrels nest in the thatch again, there's a charm—"

"You told me," Moon sighed. She shifted a little to let the fire roast a slightly different part of her back. "If I forget it, I can look it up. It's awfully silly for you to set out now. We could have snow next week."

"If we did, then I'd walk through it. But we won't. Not for another month." Alder Owl wrapped three little stoneware jars in flannel and tucked them in her wicker pack.

Moon opened her mouth, and the thing she'd been busy not saying for three days hopped out. "He's been missing since before Midsummer. Why do you have to go now? Why do you have to go at all?"

At that, Alder Owl straightened up and regarded her sternly. "I have responsibilities. You ought to know that."

"But why should they have anything to do with *him*?"

"He is the prince of the Kingdom of Hark End."

Moon stood up. She was taller than Alder Owl, but under that fierce gaze she felt rather stubby. She scowled to hide it. "And we live in Hark End. Hundreds—*thousands* of people do. A lot of them are even witches. They haven't all gone tramping off like a pack of questing youngest sons."

Alder Owl had a great many wrinkles, which deepened all over her face when she was about to smile. They deepened now. "First, youngest sons have never been known to quest in packs. Second, all the witches worth their salt and stone have tried to find him, in whatever way suits them best. All of them but me. I held back because I wanted to be sure you could manage without me."

Moon Very Thin stood still for a moment, taking that in. Then she sat back down with a thump and laced her fingers around her knees. "Oh," she said, halfway between a gasp and a laugh. "Unfair, unfair. To get at me through my pride!"

"Yes, my weed, and there's such a lot of it. I have to go, you know. Don't make it harder for me."

"I wish I could do something to help," said Moon after a moment.

"I expect you to do all your work around here, and all of mine besides. Isn't that enough?" Alder Owl smoothed the flap down over the pack and snugged the drawstring tight.

"You know it's not. Couldn't I go with you?"

Alder Owl pulled a stool from under the table with her foot and sat on it, her hands over her knees. "When I travel in my spirit," she said, "to ask a favor of Grandmother, you can't go with me."

"Of course not. Then who'd play the drum, to guide you back?"

Alder Owl beamed. "Clever weed. Open that cupboard over the mantel-shelf and bring me what you find there."

What Moon found was a drum. It was nothing like the broad, flat, cowhide journey-drum, whose speech echoed in her bones and was like a breathing heartbeat under her fingers, whose voice could be heard in the land where there was no voice. This drum was an upright cylinder no bigger than a quart jar. Its body was made of some white wood, and the skins of its two heads were fine-grained and tufted with soft white hair around the lashings. There was a loop of hide to hold it with, and a drumstick with a leather beater tucked through that.

Moon shook her head. "This wouldn't be loud enough to bring you home from the pump, let alone from—where *are* you going?"

"Wherever I have to. Bring it to me."

Moon brought her the drum, and Alder Owl held it up by the loop of hide and struck it, once. The sound it made was a sharp, ringing *tok*, like a woodpecker's blow.

Alder Owl said, "The wood is from an ash tree planted at the hour of my birth. The skins are from a ewe born on the same day. I raised the ewe and watered the tree, and on my sixteenth birthday, I asked them for their lives, and they gave them gladly. No matter how far I go, the drum will reach me. When I cannot hear it, it will cease to sound.

"Tomorrow at dawn, I'll leave," Alder Owl continued. "Tomorrow at sunset, as the last rind of the sun burns out behind the line of the Wantnot Hills, and at every sunset after, beat the drum once, as I just did."

Moon was a little shaken by the solemnity of it all. But she gathered her wits at last and repeated, "At sunset each day. Once. I'll remember."

"Hmph. Well." Alder Owl lifted her shoulders, as if solemnity was a shawl she could shrug away. "Tomorrow always comes early. Time to put the fire to bed."

"I'll get the garden things," Moon said. She tossed her cloak on and went out the stillroom door into the night.

Her namesake was up, and waxing. Alder Owl would have good light, if she needed to travel by night. But it would be cold traveling; frost dusted the leaves and vines and flagstone paths like talcum. Moon shivered and sighed. "What's the point of having an able-bodied young apprentice, if you're not going to put all that ableness to use?" she muttered to the shifting air. The cold carried all her S's off into the dark.

She pinched a bloom from the yellow chrysanthemum, and a stalk of merry-man's wort from its sheltered bed. When she came back into the house she found that Alder Owl had already fed the fire and settled the logs with the poker, and fetched a bowl of water. Moon dropped the flowers into it.

"Comforter, guard against the winter dark," Alder Owl said to the fire, as always, as if she were addressing an old friend. She stirred the water with her fingers as she spoke. "Helpmeet, nourisher of flesh and heart, bide and watch, and let no errant spark leap up until the sun should take thy part."

Firelight brushed across the seamed landscape of Alder Owl's face, flashed yellow in her sharp, dark eyes, turned the white in her hair to ivory. *Tomorrow night*, Moon thought, *she won't be here. Just me.* She could believe it only with the front of her mind, where all untested things were kept. The rest of her, mind and lungs and soles of feet, denied it.

Alder Owl flicked the water from her hand onto the hearth, and the line of drops steamed. Then she handed the bowl to Moon, and Moon fed the flowers to the fire.

After a respectful silence, Moon said, "It's water." It was the continuation of an old argument. "And the logs were trees that grew out of the earth and fed on water, and the fire itself feeds on those and air. That's all four elements. You can't separate them."

"It's the hour for fire, and it's fire that we honor. At the appropriate hours we honor the other three, and if you say things like that in public, no educated person in the village will speak to you." Alder Owl took the bowl out of Moon's hands and gathered her fingers in a strong, wet clasp. "My weed, my stalk of yarrow. You're not a child anymore. When I leave, you'll be a grown woman, in others' eyes if not your own. What people hear from a child's mouth as foolishness becomes something else on the lips of a woman grown: sacrilege, or spite, or madness. Work the work as you see fit, but keep your mouth closed around your notions, and keep fire out of water and earth out of air."

"But—"

"Empty the bowl now, and get on to bed."

Moon went into the garden again and flung the water out of the bowl—southward, because it was consecrated to fire. Then she stood a little while in the cold, with a terrible hard feeling in her chest that was beyond sadness, beyond tears. She drew in great breaths to freeze it, and exhaled hard to force the fragments out. But it was immune to cold or wind.

"I'd like to be a woman," she whispered. "But I'd rather be a child with you here, than a woman with you gone." The sound of the words, the knowledge that they were true, did what the cold couldn't. The terrible feeling cracked, melted, and poured out of her in painful tears. Slowly the comforting order around her, the beds and borders Alder Owl had made, stopped the flow of them, and the kind cold air wiped them off her face.

At dawn, when the light of sunrise lay tangled in the treetops, Alder Owl settled her pack on her back and went out by the front door. Moon went with her as far as the gate at the bottom of the yard. In the uncertain misty land of dawn, Alder Owl was a solid, certain figure, cloaked in shabby purple wool, her silver and black hair tucked under a drunken-brimmed green hat.

"I don't think you should wear the hat," Moon said, past the tightness in her throat. "You look like an eggplant."

"I *like* it. I'm an old woman. I can wear what I please."

She was going. What did one say, except "Goodbye," which wasn't at all what Moon wanted? "When will you come back?"

"When I've found him. Or when I know he can't be found."

"You always tell me not to try to prove negatives."

"There are ways," Alder Owl replied, with a sideways look, "to prove this one."

Moon Very Thin shivered in the weak sun. Alder Owl squinted up at her, pinched her chin lightly. Then she closed the gate behind her and walked down the hill. Moon watched her—green and purple, silly and strong—until the trees hid her from sight.

She cured the squash before she put them in the cellar. She honored the elements, each at its own hour. She made cheese and wine, and put up the last of the herbs, and beat the rugs, and waxed all the floors against the coming winter muck. She mended the thatch and the fence, pruned the apple trees and turned the garden beds, taking comfort from maintaining the order that Alder Owl had established.

Moon took over other established things, too. By the time the first snow fell, her neighbors had begun to bring their aches and pains to her, to fetch her when a child was feverish, to call her in to set a dog's broken leg or stitch up a horse's gashed flank. They asked about the best day to sign a contract, and whether there was a charm to keep nightshade out of the hay field. In return, they brought her mistletoe and willow bark, a sack of rye flour, a tub of butter.

She didn't mind the work. She'd been brought up for it; it seemed as natural as getting out of bed in the morning. But she found she minded the payment. When the nearest neighbor's boy, Fell, trotted up to the gate on his donkey with the flour sack riding pillion, and thanked her, and gave it to her, she almost thrust it back at him. Alder Owl had given her the skill, and had left her there to serve them. The payment should be Alder Owl's. But there was no saying which would appear first, Alder Owl or the bottom of the sack.

"You look funny," Fell said.

"You look worse," Moon replied, because she'd taught him to climb trees and to fish, and had thus earned the privilege. "Do you know those things made out of wood or bone, with a row of little spines set close together? They call them 'combs.' "

"Hah, hah." He pointed to the flour. "I hope you make it all into cakes and get fat." He grinned and loped back down the path to the donkey. They kicked up snow as they climbed the hill, and he waved at the crest.

She felt better. Alder Owl would never have had that conversation.

Every evening at sunset, Moon took the little drum out of the cupboard over the mantel. She looked at it, and touched it, and thought of her teacher. She tried to imagine her well and warm and safe, with a hot meal before her and pleasant company near. At last, when the rim of the sun blinked out behind the far line of hills, she swung the beater against the fine skin head, and the drum sounded its woodpecker knock.

Each time Moon wondered: Could Alder Owl really hear it? And if she could, what if Moon were to beat it again? If she beat it three times, would Alder Owl think something was wrong, and return home?

Nothing was wrong. Moon put the drum away until the next sunset.

The Long Night came, and she visited all her neighbors, as they visited her. She brought them fir boughs tied with bittersweet, and honey candy, and said the blessing-charm on their doorsteps. She watched the landscape thaw and freeze, thaw and freeze. Candle-day came, and she went to the village, which was sopping and giddy with a spell of warmer weather, to watch the lighting of the new year's lamps from the flame of the old. It could be, said the villagers, that no one would ever find the prince. It could be that the King of Stones had taken him beneath the earth, and that he would lie there without breath, in silence, forever. And had she had any word of Alder Owl, and hadn't it been a long time that she'd been gone?

Yes, said Moon, it had been a long time.

The garden began to stir, almost invisibly, like a cat thinking of breakfast in its sleep. The sound of water running was everywhere, though the snow seemed undisturbed and the ice as thick as ever. Suddenly, as if nature had thrown wide a gate, it was spring, and Moon was run off her legs with work. Lambing set her to wearing muddy paths in the hills between the cottage and the farmsteads all around. The mares began to foal, too. She thanked wisdom that women and men, at least, had no season.

She had been with Tansy Broadwater's bay thoroughbred since late morning. The foal had been turned in the womb and tied in his cord, and Moon was nearly paralyzed thinking of the worth of the two of them, and their lives in her hands. She was bloody to the elbows and hoarse with chanting, but at last she and Tansy regarded each other triumphantly across the withers of a nursing colt.

"Come up to the house for a pot of hot tea," Tansy said as Moon rinsed soap off her hands and arms. "You won't want to start out through the woods now until moonrise, anyway."

Moon lifted her eyes, shocked, to the open barn door. The sun wore the Wantnot Hills like a girdle.

"I have to go," she said. "I'm sorry. I'll be all right." She headed for the trail at a run.

Stones rolled under her boots, and half-thawed ice lay slick as butter in the shadows. It was nearly night already, under the trees. She plunged down the hill and up the next one, and down again, slithering, on all fours sometimes. She could feel her bones inside her brittle as fire-blasted wood, her ankles fragile and waiting for a wrench. She was afraid to look at the sun again.

The gate—the gate at the bottom of the path was under her hands. She sobbed in relief. So close . . . She raced up through the garden, the cold air like fire in her lungs. She struggled frantically with the front door, until she remembered it was barred inside, that she'd left through the stillroom. She banged through the stillroom door and made the contents of the shelves ring and rattle. To the hearth, and wrench the cupboard door open . . .

The drum was in her hands, and through the window the sun's rind showed, thin as thread, on the hills. She was in time. As the horizon closed like a snake's eyelid over the disk of the sun, Moon struck the drum.

There was no sound at all.

Moon stared at the drum, the beater, her two hands. She had missed, she must have. She brought the beater to the head again. She might as well have hit wool against wool. There was no woodpecker knock, no sharp clear call. She had felt skin and beater meet, she had seen them. What had she done wrong?

Slowly Alder Owl's words came back to her. *When I cannot hear it, it will cease to sound.* Moon had always thought the drum would be hard to hear. But never silent. *Tell me if you can't hear this,* she thought wildly. Something else they'd said as she left, about proving negatives—that there were ways to prove the prince couldn't be found.

If he were dead, for example. If he were only bones under the earth.

And Alder Owl, beyond the drum's reach, might have followed him even to that, under the dominion of the King of Stones.

She thought about pounding the drum; she could see herself doing it in her mind, hammering at it until it sounded or broke. She imagined weeping, too; she could cry and scream and break things, and collapse at last exhausted and miserable.

What she did was to sit where she was at the table, the drum on her knees, watching the dark seep in and fill the room around her. Sorrow and despair rose and fell inside her in a slow rhythm, like the shortening and lengthening of days. When her misery peaked, she would almost weep, almost shriek, almost throw the drum from her. Then it would begin to wane, and she would think, *No, I can bear it,* until it turned to waxing once again.

She would do nothing, she resolved, until she could think of something useful to do. She would wait until the spiders spun her white with cobwebs, if she had to. But she would do something better than crying, better than breaking things.

The hide lashing of Alder Owl's drum bit into her clenched fingers. In the weak light of the sinking fire, the wood and leather were only a pale mass in her lap. How could Alder Owl's magic have dwindled away to this—a drum with no voice? What voice could reach her now?

And Moon answered herself, wonderingly: *Grandmother.*

She couldn't. She had never gone to speak with Grandmother herself. And how could she travel there, with no one to beat the drum for her when she was gone? She might be lost forever, wandering through the tangled roots of Grandmother's trees.

Yet she stood and walked, stiff-jointed, to the stillroom. She gathered up charcoal and dried myrtle and cedar. She poured apple wine into a wooden cup, and dropped in a seed from a sky's-trumpet vine. It was a familiar set of motions. She had done them for Alder Owl. She took down the black-fleeced sheepskin from the wall by the front door, laid it out on the floor, and set the wine and incense by it, wine to the east, charcoal to the south. Another trip, to fetch salt and the little bone-handled knife—earth to the north, the little conical pile of salt, and the knife west, for air. (Salt came from the sea, too, said her rebellious mind, and the knife's metal was mined from earth and tempered with fire and water. But she was afraid of heresy now, afraid to doubt the knowledge she must trust with the weight of lives. She did as she'd been taught.)

At last she took the big drum, the journey-drum, out of its wicker case and set it on the sheepskin. The drum would help her partway on her travels. But when she crossed the border, she would have to leave body, fingers, drum all at the crossing, and the drum would fall silent. She needed so little: just a tap, tap, tap. Well, her heart would have to do.

Moon dropped cross-legged on the sheepskin. Right-handed she took up the knife and drew lightly on the floor around herself as if she were a compass. She passed the knife to her left hand behind her back, smoothly, and the knife point never left the slate. That had been hard once, learning to take the knife as Alder Owl passed it to her. She drew the circle again with a pinch of salt dropped from each hand, and with cedar and myrtle smoking and snapping on their charcoal bed. Finally she drew the circle with wine shaken from her fingers, and drank off the rest. Then she took up the drum.

She tried to hear the rhythm of her breathing, of her heart, the rhythm that was always inside her. Only when she felt sure of it did she begin to let her fingers move with it, to tap the drum. It shuddered under her fingers, lowing out notes. When her hands were certain on the drum head, she closed her eyes.

A tree. That was the beginning of the journey, Moon knew; she was to begin at the end of a branch of the great tree. But what kind of tree? Was it night, or day? Should she imagine herself as a bird or a bug, or as herself? And how could she think of all that and play the drum, too?

Her neck was stiff, and one of her feet was going to sleep. *You think too much,* she scolded herself. Alder Owl had never had such trouble. Alder Owl had also never suggested that there was such a thing as too much thinking. More of it, she'd said, would fix most of the world's problems.

Well, she'd feel free to think, then. She settled into the drumbeat, imagined it wrapped around her like a featherbed.

—A tree too big to ever see all at once, one of a forest of trees like it. A tree with a crown of leaves as wide as a clear night sky on a hilltop. Night time, then. It was an oak, she decided, but green out of season. She envisioned the silver-green leathery leaves around her, and the rough black bark, starry with dew in the moonlight. The light came from the end of the branch. Cradled in leaves there was a pared white-silver crescent, a new moon cut free from the shadow of the old. It gave her light to travel by.

The rough highroad of bark grew broader as she neared the trunk. She imagined birds stirring in their sleep and the quick, querulous *chirk* of a squirrel woken in its nest. The wind breathed in and out across the vault of leaves and made them twinkle. Moon heard her steps on the wood, even and measured: the voice of the drum.

Down the trunk, down toward the tangle of roots, the knotted mirror-image of the branches above. The trunks of other trees were all around her, and the twining branches shuttered the moonlight. It was harder going, shouldering against the life of the tree that always moved upward. Her heartbeat was a thin, regular bumping in her ears.

It was too dark to tell which way was down, too dark to tell anything. Moon didn't know if she'd reached the roots or not. She wanted to cry out, to call for Grandmother, but she'd left her body behind, and her tongue in it.

A little light appeared before her, and grew slowly. There were patterns in it, colors, shapes—she could make out the gate at the bottom of the garden, and the path that led into the woods. On the path—was it the familiar one? It was bordered now with sage—she saw a figure made of the flutter of old black cloth and untidy streamers of white hair, walking away from her. A stranger, Moon thought; she tried to catch up, but didn't seem to move at all. At the first fringes of the trees the figure turned, lifted one hand, and beckoned. Then it disappeared under the roof of the woods.

Moon's spirit, like a startled bird, burst into motion, upward. Her eyes opened on the center room of the cottage. She was standing unsteadily on the sheepskin, the journey-drum at her feet. Her heart clattered under her ribs like a stick dragged across the pickets of a fence, and she felt sore and prickly and feverish. She took a step backward, overbalanced, and sat down.

"Well," she said, and the sound of her voice made her jump. She licked her dry lips and added, "That's not at all how it's supposed to be done."

Trembling, she picked up the tools and put them away, washed out the wooden bowl. She'd gathered up the sheepskin and had turned to hang it on the wall when her voice surprised her again. "But it worked," she said. She stood very still, hugging the fleece against her. "It worked, didn't it?" She'd traveled and asked, and been answered, and if neither had been in form as she understood them, still they were question and answer, and all that she needed. Moon hurried to put the sheepskin away. There were suddenly a lot of things to do.

The next morning she filled her pack with food and clothing, tinderbox and medicines, and put the little ash drum, Alder Owl's drum, on top of it all. She put on her stoutest boots and her felted wool cloak. She smothered the fire on the hearth, fastened all the shutters, and left a note for Tansy Broadwater, asking her to look after the house.

At last she shouldered her pack and tramped down the path, through the gate, down the hill, and into the woods.

Moon had traveled before, with Alder Owl. She knew how to find her way, and how to build a good fire and cook over it; she'd slept in the open and stayed at inns and farmhouses. Those things were the same alone. She had no reason to feel strange, but she did. She felt like an impostor, and expected every chance-met traveler to ask if she was old enough to be on the road by herself.

She thought she'd been lonely at the cottage; she thought she'd learned the size and shape of loneliness. Now she knew she'd only explored a corner of it. Walking gave her room to think, and sights to see: fern shoots rolling up out of the mushy soil, yellow cups of wild crocuses caught by the sun, the courting of ravens. But it was no use pointing and crying, "Look!," because the only eyes there had already seen. Her isolation made everything seem not quite real. It was harder each night to light a fire, and she had steadily less interest in food. But each night at sunset, she beat Alder Owl's drum. Each night it was silent, and she sat in the aftermath of that silence, bereft all over again.

She walked for six days through villages and forest and farmland. The weather had stayed dry and clear and unspringlike for five of them, but on the sixth she tramped through a rising chill wind under a lowering sky. The road was wider now, and smooth, and she had more company on it: Carts and wagons, riders, other walkers went to and fro past her. At noon she stopped at an inn, larger and busier than any she'd yet seen.

The boy who set tea down in front of her had a mop of blond hair over a cheerful, harried face. "The cold pie's good," he said before she could ask. "It's rabbit and mushroom. Otherwise, there's squash soup. But don't ask for ham—I think it's off a boar that wasn't cut right. It's awful."

Moon didn't know whether to laugh or gape. "The pie, then, please. I don't mean to sound like a fool, but where am I?"

"Little Hark," he replied. "But don't let that raise your hopes. Great Hark is a week away to the west, on foot. You bound for it?"

"I don't know. I suppose I am. I'm looking for someone."

"In Great Hark? Huh. Well, you can find an ant in an anthill, too, if you're not particular which one."

"It's that big?" Moon asked.

He nodded sympathetically. "Unless you're looking for the king or the queen."

"No. A woman—oldish, with hair a little more white than black, and a round pink face. Shorter than I am. Plump." It was hard to describe Alder Owl; she was too familiar. "She would have had an eggplant-colored cloak. She's a witch."

The boy's face changed slowly. "Is she the bossy-for-your-own-good sort? With a wicker pack? Treats spots on your face with witch hazel and horseradish?"

"That sounds like her . . . What else do you use for spots?"

"I don't know, but the horseradish works pretty well. She stopped here, if that's her. It was months ago, though."

"Yes," said Moon. "It was."

"She was headed for Great Hark, so you're on the right road. Good luck on it."

When he came back with the rabbit pie, he said, "You'll come to Burnton High Plain next—that's a two-day walk. After that you'll be done with the grasslands pretty quick. Then you'll be lucky if you see the sun 'til you're within holler of Great Hark."

Moon swallowed a little too much pie at once. "I will? Why?"

"Well, you'll be in the Seawood, won't you?"

"Will I?"

"You don't know much geography," he said sadly.

"I know I've never heard that the Seawood was so thick the sun wouldn't shine in it. Have you ever been there?"

"No. But everyone who has says it's true. And being here, I get to hear what travelers tell."

Moon opened her mouth to say that she'd heard more nonsense told in the common rooms of inns than the wide world had space for, when a woman's voice trumpeted from the kitchen. "Starling! Do you work here, or are you taking a room tonight?"

The blond boy grinned. "Good luck, anyway," he said to Moon and loped back to the kitchen.

Moon ate her lunch and paid for it with a coin stamped with the prince's face. She scowled at it when she set it on the table. *It's all your fault*, she told it. Then she hoisted her pack and headed for the door.

"It's started to drip," the blond boy called after her. "It'll be pouring rain on you in an hour."

"I'll get wet, then," she said. "But thanks anyway."

The trail was cold, but at least she was on it. The news drove her forward.

The boy was right about the weather. The rain was carried on gusts from every direction, which found their way under her cloak and inside her hood and in every seam of her boots. By the time she'd doggedly climbed the ridge above Little Hark, she was wet and cold all through, and dreaming of tight roofs, large fires, and clean, dry nightgowns. The view from the top of the trail scattered her visions.

She'd expected another valley. This was not a bowl, but a plate, full of long, sand-colored undulating grass, and she stood at the rim of it. Moon squinted through the rain ahead and to either side, looking for a far edge, but the grass went on out of sight, unbroken by anything but the small rises and falls of the land. She suspected that clear weather wouldn't have shown her the end of it, either.

That evening she made camp in the midst of the ocean of grass, since there wasn't anyplace else. There was no firewood. She'd thought of that before she walked down into the plain, but all the wood she could have gathered to take with her was soaked. So she propped up a lean-to of oiled canvas against the worst of the rain, gathered a pile of the shining-wet grass, and set to work. She kept an eye on the sun, as well; at the right moment she took up Alder Owl's drum and played it, huddling under the canvas to keep it from the wet. It had nothing to say.

In half an hour she had a fat braided wreath of straw. She laid it in a circle of bare ground she'd cleared, and got from her pack her tinderbox and three apples, wrinkled and sweet with winter storage. They were the last food she had from home.

"All is taken from thee," Moon said, setting the apples inside the straw wreath and laying more wet grass over them in a little cone. "I have taken, food and footing, breath and warming, balm for thirsting. This I will exchange thee, with my love and every honor, if thou'lt give again thy succor." With that, she struck a spark in the cone of grass.

For a moment, she thought the exchange was not accepted. She'd asked all the elements, instead of only fire, and fire had taken offense. Then a little blue flame licked along a stalk, and a second. In a few minutes she was nursing a tiny, comforting blaze, contained by the wreath of straw and fueled all night with Alder Owl's apples.

She sat for a long time, hunched under the oiled canvas lean-to, wrapped in her cloak with the little fire between her feet. She was going to Great Hark, because she thought that Alder Owl would have done so. But she might not have. Alder Owl might have gone south from here, into Cystegond. Or north, into the cold upthrust fangs of the Bones of Earth. She could have gone anywhere, and Moon wouldn't know. She'd asked—but she hadn't insisted she be told or taken along, hadn't tried to follow. She'd only said goodbye. Now she would never find the way.

"What am I doing here?" Moon whispered. There was no answer except the constant rushing sound of the grass in the wind, saying *hush, hush, hush*. Eventually she was warm enough to sleep.

The next morning the sun came back, watery and tentative. By its light she got her first real look at the great ocean of golden-brown she was shouldering through. Behind her she saw the ridge beyond which Little Hark lay. Ahead of her there was nothing but grass.

It was a long day, with only that to look at. So she made herself look for more. She saw the new green shoots of grass at the feet of the old stalks, their leaves still rolled tight around one another like the embrace of lovers. A thistle spread its rosette of fierce leaves to claim the soil, but hadn't yet grown tall. And she saw the prints of horses' hooves, and dung, and once a wide, beaten-down swath across her path like the bed of a creek cut in grass, the earth muddy and chopped with hoofprints. As she walked, the sun climbed the sky and steamed the rain out of her cloak.

By evening she reached the town of Burnton High Plain. Yes, the landlord at the hostelry told her, another day's walk would bring her under the branches of the Seawood. Then she should go carefully, because it was full of robbers and ghosts and wild animals.

"Well," Moon said, "robbers wouldn't take the trouble to stop me, and I don't think I've any quarrel with the dead. So I'll concentrate on the wild animals. But thank you very much for the warning."

"Not a good place, the Seawood," the landlord added.

Moon thought that people who lived in the middle of an eternity of grass probably *would* be afraid of a forest. But she only said, "I'm searching for someone who might have passed this way months ago. Her name is Alder Owl, and she was going to look for the prince."

After Moon described her, the landlord pursed his lips. "That's familiar. I think she might have come through, heading west. But as you say, it was months, and I don't think I've seen her since."

I've never heard so much discouraging encouragement, Moon thought drearily, and turned to her dinner.

The next afternoon she reached the Seawood. Everything changed: the smells, the color of the light, the temperature of the air. In spite of the landlord's warning, Moon couldn't quite deny the lift of her heart, the feeling of glad relief. The secretive scent of pine loam rose around her as she walked, and the dark boughs were full of the commotion of birds. She heard water nearby; she followed the sound to a running beck and the spring that fed it. The water was cold and crisply acidic from the pines; she filled her bottle at it and washed her face.

She stood a moment longer by the water. Then she hunched the pack off her back and dug inside it until she found the little linen bag that held her valuables. She shook out a silver shawl pin in the shape of a leaping frog. She'd worn it on festival days, with her green scarf. It was a present from Alder Owl—but then, everything was. She dropped it into the spring.

Was that right? Yes, the frog was water's beast, never mind that it breathed air half the time. And silver was water's metal, even though it was mined from the earth and shaped with fire, and turned black as quickly in water as in air. How *could* magic be based on understanding the true nature of things if it ignored so much?

A bubble rose to the surface and broke loudly, and Moon laughed. "You're welcome, and same to you," she said, and set off again.

The Seawood gave her a century's worth of fallen needles, flat and dry, to bed down on, and plenty of dry wood for her fire. It was cold under its roof of boughs, but there were remedies for cold. She kept her fire well built up, for that, and against any meat-eaters too weak from winter to seek out the horses of Burnton High Plain.

Another day's travel, and another. If she were to climb one of the tallest pines to its top, would the Seawood look like the plain of grass: undulating, almost endless? On the third day, when the few blades of sun that reached the forest floor were slanting and long, a wind rose. Moon listened to the old trunks above her creaking, the boughs swishing like brooms in angry hands, and decided to make camp.

In the Seawood the last edge of sunset was never visible. By then, beneath the trees, it was dark. So Moon built her fire and set water to boil before she took Alder Owl's drum from her pack.

The trees roared above, but at their feet Moon felt only a furious breeze. She hunched her cloak around her and struck the drum.

It made no noise; but from above she heard a clap and thunder of sound, and felt a rush of air across her face. She leaped backward. The drum slid from her hands.

A pale shape sat on a low branch beyond her fire. The light fell irregularly on its huge yellow eyes, the high tufts that crowned its head, its pale breast. An owl.

"Oo," it said, louder than the hammering wind. "Oo-whoot."

Watching it all the while, Moon leaned forward, reaching for the drum.

The owl bated thunderously and stretched its beak wide. "Oo-wheed," it cried at her. "Yarrooh. Yarrooh."

Moon's blood fell cold from under her face. The owl swooped off its branch quick and straight as a dropped stone. Its talons closed on the lashings of the drum. The great wings beat once, twice, and the bird was gone into the rushing dark.

Moon fell to her knees, gasping for breath. The voice of the owl was still caught in her ears, echoing, echoing another voice. *Weed. Yarrow. Yarrow.*

Tears poured burning down her face. "Oh, my weed, my stalk of yarrow," she repeated, whispering. "Come back!" she screamed into the night. She got no answer but the wind. She pressed her empty hands to her face and cried herself to sleep.

With morning, the Seawood crowded around her as it had before, full of singing birds and softness, traitorous and unashamed. In one thing, at least, its spirit marched with hers. The light under the trees was gray, and she heard the patter of rain in the branches above. Moon stirred the cold ashes of her fire and waited for her heart to thaw. She would go on to Great Hark, and beyond if she had to. There might yet be some hope. And if there wasn't, there might at least be a reckoning.

All day the path led downward, and she walked until her thighs burned and her stomach gnawed itself from hunger. The rain came down harder, showering her ignominiously when the wind shook the branches. She meant to leave the Seawood before she slept again, if it meant walking all night. But the trees began to thin around her late in the day, and shortly after she saw a bare rise ahead of her. She mounted it and looked down.

The valley was full of low mist, eddying slowly in the rain. Rising out of it was the largest town Moon had ever seen. It was walled in stone and gated with oak and iron, and roofed in prosperous slate and tile. Pennons flew from every wall tower, their colors darkened with rain and stolen away by the gray light. At the heart of the town was a tall, white, red-roofed building, cornered with round towers like the wall.

The boy was right about this, too. She could never find news of one person in such a place, unless that person was the king or the queen. Moon drooped under a fresh lashing of rain.

But why not? Alder Owl had set off to find the prince. Why wouldn't she have gone to the palace and stated her business, and searched on from there? And why shouldn't Moon do the same?

She flapped a sheet of water off her cloak and plunged down the trail. She had another hour's walk before she would reach the gates, and she wanted to be inside by sundown.

The wall loomed over her at last, oppressively high, dark and shining with rain. She found the huge double gates open, and the press of wagons and horses and pedestrians in and out of them daunting. No one seemed to take any notice when she joined the stream and passed through, and though she looked and looked, she couldn't see anyone who appeared to be any more official than anyone else. Every-one, in fact, looked busy and important. *So this is city life*, Moon thought, and stepped out of the flow of traffic for a better look around.

Without her bird's-eye view, she knew she wouldn't find the palace except by chance. So she asked directions of a woman and a man unloading a cart full of baled hay.

They looked at her and blinked, as if they were too weary to think; they were at least as wet as Moon was, and seemed to have less hope of finding what they were looking for. Their expressions of surprise were so similar that Moon wondered if they were blood relations, and indeed, their eyes were much alike, green-gray as sage. The man wore a dusty brown jacket worn through at one elbow; the woman had a long, tattered black shawl pulled up over her white hair.

"Round the wall that way," said the man at last, "until you come to a broad street all laid with brick. Follow that uphill until you see it."

"Thank you." Moon eyed the hay cart, which was nearly full. Work was ointment for the heart. Alder Owl had said so. "Would you like some help? I could get in the cart and throw bales down."

"Oh, no," said the woman. "It's all right."

Moon shook her head. "You sound like my neighbors. With them, it would be fifteen minutes before we argued each other to a standstill. I'm going to start throwing hay instead." At that, she scrambled into the cart and hoisted a bale. When she turned to pass it to the man and woman, she found them looking at each other, before the man came to take the hay from her.

It was hot, wet, prickly work, but it didn't take long. When the cart was empty, they exchanged thanks and Moon set off again for the palace. On the way, she watched the sun's eye close behind the line of the hills.

The brick-paved street ran in long curves like an old riverbed. She couldn't see the palace until she'd tramped up the last turning and found the high white walls before her, and another gate. This one was carved and painted with a flock of rising birds, and closed.

Two men stood at the gate, one on each side. They were young and tall and broad-shouldered, and Moon recognized them as being of a type that made village girls stammer. They stood very straight, and wore green capes and coats with what Moon thought was an excessive quantity of gold trim. She stepped up to the nearest.

"Pardon me," she said, "I'd like to speak to the king and queen."

The guard blinked even more thoroughly than the couple with the hay cart had. With good reason, Moon realized; now she was not only travel-stained and sodden, but dusted with hay as well. She sighed, which seemed to increase the young man's confusion.

"I'll start nearer the beginning," she told him. "I came looking for my teacher, who set off at the end of last autumn to look for the prince. Do you remember a witch, named Alder Owl, from a village two weeks east of here? I think she might have come to the palace to see the king and queen about it."

The guard smiled. Moon thought she wouldn't feel too scornful of a girl who stammered in his presence. "I suppose I could have a message taken to Their Majesties," he said at last. "Someone in the palace may have met your teacher. Hi, Rush!" he called to the guard on the other side of the gate. "This woman is looking for her teacher, a witch who set out to find the prince. Who would she ask, then?"

Rush sauntered over, his cape swinging. He raised his eyebrows at Moon. "Every witch in Hark End has gone hunting the prince at one time or another. How would anyone remember one out of the lot?"

Moon drew herself up very straight, and found she was nearly as tall as he was. She raised only one eyebrow, which she'd always found effective with Fell. "I'm sorry your memory isn't all you might like it to be. Would it help if I pointed out that this witch remains unaccounted for?"

"There aren't any of those. They all came back, cap in hand and dung on their shoes, saying, 'Beg pardon, Lord,' and 'Perishing sorry, Lady.' You could buy and sell the gaggle of them with the brass on my scabbard."

"You," Moon told him sternly, "are of very little use."

"More use than anyone who's sought him so far. If they'd only set my unit to it . . ."

She looked into his hard young face. "You loved him, didn't you?"

His mouth pinched closed, and the hurt in his eyes made him seem for a moment as young as Fell. It held a glass up to her own pain. "Everyone did. He was—is the land's own heart."

"My teacher is like that to me. Please, may I speak with someone?"

The polite guard was looking from one to the other of them, alarmed. Rush turned to him and frowned. "Take her to—merry heavens, I don't know. Try the steward. He fancies he knows everything."

And so the Gate of Birds opened to Moon Very Thin. She followed the polite guard across a paved courtyard held in the wide, high arms of the palace, colonnaded all around and carved with the likenesses of animals and flowers. On every column a torch burned in its iron bracket, hissing in the rain, and lit the courtyard like a stage. It was very beautiful, if a little grim.

The guard waved her through a small iron-clad door into a neat parlor. A fire was lit in the brick hearth and showed her the rugs and hangings, the paneled walls blackened with age. The guard tugged an embroidered pull near the door and turned to her.

"I should get back to the gate. Just tell the steward, Lord Leyan, what you know about your teacher. If there's help for you here, he'll see that you get it."

When he'd gone, she gathered her damp cloak about her and wondered if she ought to sit. Then she heard footsteps, and a door she hadn't noticed opened in the paneling.

A very tall, straight-backed man came through it. His hair was white and thick and brushed his shoulders, where it met a velvet coat faced in creweled satin. He didn't seem to find the sight of her startling, which Moon took as a good sign.

"How may I help you?" he asked.

"Lord Leyan?"

He nodded.

"My name is Moon Very Thin. I've come from the east in search of my teacher, the witch Alder Owl, who set out last autumn to find the prince. I think now . . . I won't find her. But I have to try." To her horror, she felt tears rising in her eyes.

Lord Leyan crossed the room in a long stride and grasped her hands. "My dear, don't cry. I remember your teacher. She was an alarming woman, but that gave us all hope. She has not returned to you, either, then?"

Moon swallowed and shook her head.

"You've traveled a long way. You shall have a bath and a meal and a change of clothes, and I will see if anyone can tell you more about your teacher."

Before Moon was quite certain how it had been managed, she was standing in a handsome dark room with a velvet-hung bed and a fire bigger than the one in the parlor, and a woman with a red face and flyaway hair was pouring cans of water into a bathtub shaped and painted like a swan.

"That's the silliest thing I've ever seen," said Moon in wonder.

The red-faced woman grinned suddenly. "You know, it is. And it may be the lords and ladies think so, too, and are afraid to say."

"One of them must have paid for it once."

"That's so. Well, no one's born with taste. Have your bath, and I'll bring you a change of clothes in a little."

"You needn't do that. I have clean ones in my pack."

"Yes, but have they got lace on them, and a 'broidery flower for every seam? If not, you'd best let me bring these, for word is you eat with the King and Queen."

"I do?" Moon blurted, horrified. "Why?"

"Lord Leyan went to them, and they said send you in. Don't pop your eyes at me, there's no help for it."

Moon scrubbed until she was pink all over, and smelling of violet soap. She washed her hair three times, and trimmed her short nails, and looked in despair at her reflection in the mirror. She didn't think she'd put anyone off dinner, but there was no question that the only thing that stood there was Moon Very Thin, tall and brown and forthright.

"Here, now," said the red-faced woman at the door. "I thought this would look nice, and you wouldn't even quite feel a fool in it. What do you say?"

Draped over her arms she had a plain, high-necked dress of amber linen, and an overgown of russet velvet. The hem and deep collar were embroidered in gold with the platter-heads of yarrow flowers. Moon stared at that, and looked quickly up at the red-faced woman. There was nothing out of the way in her expression.

"It's—it's fine. It's rather much, but . . ."

"But it's the least much that's still enough for dining in the hall. Let's get you dressed."

The woman helped her into it, pulling swaths of lavender-scented fabric over her head. Then she combed out Moon's hair, braided it, and fastened it with a gold pin.

"Good," the red-faced woman said. "You look like you, but dressed up, which is as it should be. I'll show you to the hall."

Moon took a last look at her reflection. She didn't think she looked at all like herself. Dazed, she followed her guide out of the room.

She knew when they'd almost reached their destination. A fragrance rolled out of the hall that reminded Moon she'd missed three meals. At the door, the red-faced woman stopped her.

"You'll do, I think. Still—tell no lies, though you may be told them. Look anyone in the eye, though they might want it otherwise. And take everything offered you with your right hand. It can't hurt." With that the red-faced woman turned and disappeared down the maze of the corridor.

Moon straightened her shoulders and, her stomach pinched with hunger and nerves, stepped into the hall.

She gaped. She couldn't help it, though she'd promised herself she wouldn't. The hall was as high as two rooms, and long and broad as a field of wheat. It had two yawning fireplaces big enough to tether an ox in. Banners hung from every beam, sewn over with beasts and birds and things she couldn't name. There weren't enough candles in all Hark End to light it top to bottom, nor enough wood in the Seawood to heat it, so like the great courtyard it was beautiful and grim.

The tables were set in a U, the high table between the two arms. To her dazzled eye, it seemed every place was taken. It was bad enough to dine with the king and queen. Why hadn't she realized that it would be the court, as well?

At the high table, the king rose smiling. "Our guest!" he called. "Come, there's a place for you beside my lady and me."

Moon felt her face burning as she walked to the high table. The court watched her go; but there were no whispers, no hands raised to shield moving lips. She was grateful, but it was odd.

Her chair was indeed set beside those of the king and queen. The king was white-haired and broad-shouldered, with an open, smiling face and big hands. The queen's hair was white and gold, and her eyes were wide and gray as storms. She smiled, too, but as if the gesture were a sorrow she was loath to share.

"Lord Leyan told us your story," said the queen. "I remember your teacher. Had you been with her long?"

"All my life," Moon replied. Dishes came to roost before her, so she could serve herself: roast meat, salads, breads, compotes, vegetables, sauces, wedges of cheese. She could limit herself to a bite of everything, and still leave the hall achingly full. She kept her left hand clamped between her knees for fear of forgetting and taking something with it. Every dish was good, but not quite as good as she'd thought it looked.

"Then you are a witch as well?" the king asked.

"I don't know. I've been taught by a witch, and learned witches' knowledge. But she taught me gardening and carpentry, too."

"You hope to find her?"

Moon looked at him, and weighed the question seriously for the first time since the Seawood. "I hope I may learn she's been transformed, and that I can change her back. But I think I met her, last night in the wood, and I find it's hard to hope."

"But you want to go on?" the queen pressed her. "What will you do?"

"The only thing I can think of to do is what she set out for: I mean to find your son."

Moon couldn't think why the queen would pale at that.

"Oh, my dear, don't," the king said. "Our son is lost, your teacher is lost—what profit can there be in throwing yourself after them? Rest here, then go home and live. Our son is gone."

It was a fine, rich hall, and he was a fair, kingly man. But it was all dimmed, as if a layer of soot lay over the palace and its occupants.

"What did he look like, the prince?"

The king frowned. It was the queen who drew a locket out of the bodice of her gown, lifted its chain over her head and passed it to Moon. It held, not the costly miniature she'd expected, but a sketch in soft pencil, swiftly done. It was the first informal thing she could recall seeing in the palace.

"He wouldn't sit still to be painted," the queen said wistfully. "One of his friends likes to draw. He gave me that after . . . after my son was gone."

He had been reading, perhaps, when his friend snatched that quiet moment to catch his likeness. The high forehead was propped on a long-fingered hand; the eyes were directed downward, and the eyelids hid them. The nose was straight, and the mouth was long and grave. The hair was barely suggested; light or dark, it fell unruly around the supporting hand. Even setting aside the kindly eye of friendship that had informed the pencil, Moon gave the village girls leave to be silly over this one. She closed the locket and gave it back.

"You can't know what's happened to him. How can you let him go, without knowing?"

"There are many things in the world I will never know," the king said sharply.

"I met a man at the gate who still mourns the prince. He called him the heart of the land. Nothing can live without its heart."

The queen drew a breath and turned her face to her plate, but said nothing.

"Enough," said the king. "If you must search, then you must. But I'll have peace at my table. Here, child, will you pledge it with me?"

Over Moon's right hand, lying on the white cloth, he laid his own, and held his wine cup out to her.

She sat frozen, staring at the chased silver and her own reflection in it. Then she raised her eyes to his and said, "No."

There was a shattering quiet in the hall.

"You will not drink?"

"I will not . . . pledge you peace. There isn't any here, however much anyone may try to hide it. I'm sorry." That, she knew when she'd said it, was true. "Excuse me," she added, and drew her hand out from under the king's, which was large, but soft. "I'm going to bed. I mean to leave early tomorrow."

She rose and walked back down the length of the room, lapped in a different kind of silence.

A servant found her in the corridor and led her to her chamber. There she found her old clothes clean and dry and folded, the fire tended, the bed turned down. The red-faced woman wasn't there. She took off her finery, laid it out smooth on a chair, and put her old nightgown on. Then she went to the glass to unpin and brush her hair.

The pin was in her hand, and she was reaching to set it down, when she saw what it was. A little leaping frog. But now it was gold.

It *was* hers. The kicking legs and goggle eyes, every irregularity—it was her pin. She dashed to the door and flung it open. "Hello?" she called. "Oh, bother!" She stepped back into the room and searched, and finally found the bell pull disguised as a bit of tapestry.

After a few minutes, a girl with black hair and bright eyes came to the door. "Yes, ma'am?"

"The woman who helped me, who drew my bath and brought me clothes. Is she still here?"

The girl looked distressed. "I'm sorry, ma'am. I don't know who waited on you. What did she look like?"

"About my height. With a red face and wild, wispy hair."

The girl stared, and said, "Ma'am—are you sure? That doesn't sound like anyone here."

Moon dropped heavily into the nearest chair. "Why am I not surprised? Thank you very much. I didn't mean to disturb you."

The girl nodded and closed the door behind her. Moon put out the candles, climbed into bed, and lay awake for an uncommonly long time.

In a gray, wet dawn, she dressed and shouldered her pack and by the simple expedient of going down every time she came to a staircase, found a door that led outside. It was a little postern, opening on a kitchen garden and a wash yard fenced in stone. At the side of the path, a man squatted by a wooden hand cart, mending a wheel.

"Here, missy!" he called out, his voice like a spade thrust into gravel. "Hold this axle up, won't you?"

Moon sighed. She wanted to go. She wanted to be moving, because moving would be almost like getting something done. And she wanted to be out of this beautiful place that had lost its heart. She stepped over a spreading clump of rhubarb, knelt, and hoisted the axle.

Whatever had damaged the wheel had made the axle split; the long splinter of wood bit into Moon's right hand. She cried out and snatched that hand away. Blood ran out of the cut on her palm and fell among the rhubarb stems, a few drops. Then it ceased to flow.

Moon looked up, frightened, to the man with the wheel.

It was the man from the hay wagon, white-haired, his eyes as green and gray as sage. He had a ruddy, somber face. Red-faced, like the woman who'd—

The woman who'd helped her last night had been the one from the hay cart. Why hadn't she seen it? But she remembered it now, and the woman's green eyes, and even a fragment of hay caught in the wild hair. Moon sprang up.

The old man caught her hand. "Rhubarb purges, and rhubarb means advice. Turn you back around. Your business is in there." He pointed a red, rough finger at the palace, at the top of the near corner tower. Then he stood, dusted off his trousers, strolled down the path and was gone.

Moon opened her mouth, which she hadn't been able to do until then. She could still feel his hand, warm and callused. She looked down. In the palm he'd held was a sprig of hyssop and a wisp of broom, and a spiraling stem of convolvulus.

Moon bolted back through the postern door and up the first twisting flight of stairs she found, until she ran out of steps. Then she cast furiously about. Which way was that wretched tower? She got her bearings by looking out the corridor windows. It would be that door, she thought. She tried it; it resisted.

He could have kept his posy and given me a key, she thought furiously. Then: *But he did.*

She plucked up the convolvulus, poked it into the keyhole, and said, "Turn away, turn astray, backwards from the turn of day. What iron turned to lock away, herb will turn the other way." Metal grated against metal, and the latch yielded under her hand.

A young man's room, frozen in time. A jerkin of quilted, painted leather dropped on a chair; a case of books, their bindings standing in bright ranks; a wooden flute and a pair of leather gloves lying on an inlaid cedar chest; an unmade bed, the coverlet slid sideways and half pooled on the floor.

More, a room frozen in a tableau of atrocity and accusation. For Moon could feel it, the thing that had been done here, that was still being done because the room had sat undisturbed. Nightshade and thornapple, skullcap, henbane, and fern grown bleached and stunted under stone. Moon recognized their scents and their twisted strength around her, the power of the work they'd made and the shame that kept them secret.

There was a dust of crushed leaf and flower over the door lintel, on the sill of every window, lined like seams in the folds of the bed hangings. Her fingers clenched on the herbs in her hand as rage sprouted up in her and spread.

With broom and hyssop she dashed the dust from the lintel, the windows, the hangings. "Merry or doleful, the last or the first," she chanted as she swung her weapons, spitting each word in fury, "fly and be hunted, or stay and be cursed!"

"*What are you doing?*" said a voice from the door, and Moon spun and raised her posy like a dagger.

The king stood there, his coat awry, his hair uncombed. His face was white as a corpse's, and his eyes were wide as a man's who sees the gallows, and knows the noose is his.

"You did this," Moon breathed; and louder, "You gave him to the King of Stones with your own hand."

"I had to," he whispered. "He made a beggar of me. My son was the forfeit."

"You locked him under the earth. And let my teacher go to her . . . to her *death* to pay your forfeit."

"It was his life or mine!"

"Does your lady wife know what you did?"

"His lady wife helped him to do it," said the queen, stepping forward from the shadows of the hall. She stood tall and her face was quiet, as if she welcomed the noose. "Because he was her love and the other, only her son. Because she feared to lose a queen's power. Because she was a fool, and weak. Then she kept the secret, because her heart was black and broken, and she thought no worse could be done than had been done already."

Moon turned to the king. "Tell me," she commanded.

"I was hunting alone," said the king in a trembling voice. "I roused a boar. I . . . had a young man's pride and an old man's arm, and the boar was too much for me. I lay bleeding and in pain, and the sight nearly gone from my eyes, when I heard footsteps. I called out for help.

" 'You are dying,' he told me, and I denied it, weeping. 'I don't want to die,' I said, over and over. I promised him anything, if he would save my life." The king's voice failed, and stopped.

"Where?" said Moon. "Where did this happen?"

"In the wood under Elder Scarp. Near the waterfall that feeds the stream called the Laughing Girl."

"Point me the way," she ordered.

The sky was hazed white, and the air was hot and still. Moon dashed sweat from her forehead as she walked. She could have demanded a horse, but she had walked the rest of the journey, and this seemed such a little way compared to that. She hoped it would be cooler under the trees.

It wasn't; and the gnats were worse around her face, and the biting flies. Moon swung at them steadily as she clambered over the stones. It seemed a long time before she heard the waterfall, then saw it. She cast about for the clearing, and wondered, were there many? Or only one, and it so small that she could walk past it and never know? The falling water thrummed steadily, like a drum, like a heartbeat.

In a shaft of sun, she saw a bit of creamy white—a flower head, round and flat as a platter, dwarfed with early blooming. She looked up and found that she stood on the edge of a clearing, and was not alone.

He wore armor, dull gray plates worked with fantastic embossing, trimmed in glossy black. He had a gray cloak fastened over that, thrown back off his shoulders, but with the hood up and pulled well forward. Moon could see nothing of his face.

"In the common way of things," he said, in a quiet, carrying voice, "I seek out those I wish to see. I am not used to uninvited guests."

The armor was made of slate and obsidian, because he was the King of Stones.

She couldn't speak. She could command the king of Hark End, but this was a king whose rule did not light on him by an accident of blood or by the acclaim of any mortal thing. This was an embodied power, a still force of awe and terror.

"I've come for a man and his soul," she whispered. "They were wrongly taken."

"I take nothing wrongly. Are you sure?"

She felt heat in her face, then cold at the thought of what she'd said: that she'd accused him. "No," she admitted, the word cracking with her fear. "But that they were wrongly given, I know. He was not theirs to give."

"You speak of the prince of Hark End. They were his parents. Would you let anyone say you could not give away what you had made?"

Moon's lips parted on a word; then she stared in horror. Her mind churned over the logic, followed his question back to its root.

He spoke her thoughts aloud. "You have attended at the death of a child, stilled in the womb to save the mother's life. How is this different?"

"It *is* different!" she cried. "He was a grown man, and what he was was shaped by what he did, what he chose."

"He had his mother's laugh, his grandfather's nose. His father taught him to ride. What part of him was not made by someone else? Tell me, and we will see if I should give that part back."

Moon clutched her fingers over her lips, as if by that she could force herself to think it all through before she spoke. "His father taught him to ride," she repeated. "If the horse refuses to cross a ford, what makes the father use his spurs, and the son dismount and lead it? He has his mother's laugh—but what makes her laugh at one thing, and him at another?"

"What, indeed?" asked the King of Stones. "Well, for argument's sake I'll say his mind is in doubt, and his heart. What of his body?"

"Bodies grow with eating and exercise," Moon replied. This was ground she felt sure of. "Do you think the king and the queen did those for him?"

The King of Stones threw back his cowled head and laughed, a cold ringing sound. It restored Moon to sensible terror. She stepped back, and found herself against a tree trunk.

"And his soul?" said the King of Stones at last.

"That didn't belong to his mother and father," Moon said, barely audible even to her own ears. "If it belonged to anyone but himself, I think you did not win it from Her."

Silence lay for long moments in the clearing. Then he said, "I am well tutored. Yet there was a bargain made, and a work done, and both sides knew what they pledged and what it meant. Under law, the contract was kept."

"That's not true. Out of fear the king promised you anything, but he never meant the life of his son!"

"Then he could have refused me that, and died. He said 'Anything,' and meant it, unto the life of his son, his wife, and all his kingdom."

He had fought her to a standstill with words. But, words used up and useless, she still felt a core of anger in her for what had been done, outrage against a thing she knew, beyond words, was wrong.

So she said aloud, "It's *wrong*. It was a contract that was wrong to make, let alone to keep. I know it."

"What is it," said the King of Stones, "that says so?"

"My judgment says so. My head." Moon swallowed. "My heart."

"Ah. What do I know of your judgment? Is it good?"

She scrubbed her fingers over her face. He had spoken lightly, but Moon knew the question wasn't light at all. She had to speak the truth; she had to decide what the truth was. "It's not perfect," she answered reluctantly. "But yes, I think it's as good as most people's."

"Do you trust it enough to allow it to be tested?"

Moon lifted her head and stared at him in alarm. "What?"

"I will test your judgment. If I find it good, I will let you free the prince of Hark End. If not, I will keep him, and you will take your anger, your outrage, and the knowledge of your failure home to nurture like children all the rest of your life."

"Is that prophecy?" Moon asked hoarsely.

"You may prove it so, if you like. Will you take my test?"

She drew a great, trembling breath. "Yes."

"Come closer, then." With that, he pushed back his hood.

There was no stone helm beneath, or monster head. There was a white-skinned man's face, all bone and sinew and no softness, and long black hair rucked from the hood. The sockets of his eyes were shadowed black, though the light that fell in the clearing should have lit all of his face. Moon looked at him and was more frightened than she would have been by any deformity, for she knew then that none of this—armor, face, eyes—had anything to do with his true shape.

"Before we begin," he said in that soft, cool voice. "There is yet a life you have not asked me for, one I thought you'd beg of me first of all."

Moon's heart plunged, and she closed her eyes. "Alder Owl."

"You cannot win her back. There was no treachery there. She, at least, I took fairly, for she greeted me by name and said I was well met."

"No!" Moon cried.

"She was sick beyond curing, even when she left you. But she asked me to give her wings for one night, so that you would know. I granted it gladly."

She thought she had cried all she could for Alder Owl. But this was the last death, the death of her little foolish hope, and she mourned that and Alder Owl at once with falling, silent tears.

"My test for you, then." He stretched out his hands, his mailed fingers curled over whatever lay in each palm. "You have only to choose," he said. He opened his fingers to reveal two rings, one silver, one gold.

She looked from the rings to his face again, and her expression must have told him something.

"You are a witch," said the King of Stones, gently mocking. "You read symbols and make them, and craft them into nets to catch truth in. This is the meat of your training, to read the true nature of a thing. Here are symbols—choose between them. Pick the truer. Pick the better."

He pressed forward first one hand, then the other. "Silver, or gold? Left or right? Night or day, moon"—she heard him mock her again—"or sun, water or fire, waning or waxing, female or male. Have I forgotten any?"

Moon wiped the tears from her cheeks and frowned down at the rings. They were plain, polished circles of metal, not really meant for finger rings at all. Circles, complete in themselves, unmarred by scratch or tarnish.

Silver, or gold. Mined from the earth, forged in fire, cooled in water, pierced with air. Gold was rarer, silver was harder, but both were pure metals. Should she choose rareness? Hardness? The lighter color? But the flash of either was bright. The color of the moon? But she'd seen the moon, low in the sky, yellow as a peach. And the light from the moon was reflected light from the sun, whose color was yellow although in the sky it was burning white, and whose metal was gold. There was nothing to choose between them.

The blood rushed into her face, and the gauntleted hands and their two rings swam in her vision. It was true. She'd always thought so.

Her eyes sprang up to the face of the King of Stones. "It's a false choice. They're equal."

As she said the words, her heart gave a single terrified leap. She was wrong. She was defeated, and a fool. The King of Stones' fingers closed again over the rings.

"Down that trail to a granite stone, and then between two hazel trees," he said. "You'll find him there."

She was alone in the clearing.

Moon stumbled down the trail, dazed with relief and the release of tension. She found the stone, and the two young hazel trees, slender and leafed out in fragile green, and passed between them.

She plunged immediately into full sunlight and strangeness. Another clearing, carpeted with deep grass and the stars of spring flowers, surrounded by blossoming trees—but trees in blossom didn't also stand heavy with fruit, like a vain child wearing all its trinkets at once. She saw apples, cherries, and pears under their drifts of pale blossom, ripe and without blemish. At the other side of the clearing there was a shelf of stone thrust up out of the grass. On it, as if sleeping, lay a young man, exquisitely dressed.

Golden hair, she thought. *That's why it was drawn in so lightly. Like amber, or honey.* The fair face was very like the sketch she remembered, as was the scholar's hand palm up on the stone beside it. She stepped forward.

Beside the stone, the black branches of a tree lifted, moved away from their neighbors, and the trunk—Not a tree. A stag stepped into the clearing, scattering the apple blossoms with the great span of his antlers. He was black as charcoal, and his antler points were shining black, twelve of them or more. His eyes were large and red.

He snorted and lowered his head, so that she saw him through a forest of polished black dagger points. He tore at the turf with one cloven foot.

I passed his test! she cried to herself. Hadn't she won? Why this? *You'll find him there,* the King of Stones had said. Then her anger sprang up as she remembered what else he'd said: *I will let you free the prince of Hark End.*

What under the wide sky was she supposed to do? Strike the stag dead with her bare hands? Frighten it away with a frown? Turn it into—

She gave a little cry at the thought, and the stag was startled into charging. She leaped behind the slender trunk of a cherry tree. Cloth tore as the stag yanked free of her cloak.

The figure on the shelf of stone hadn't moved. She watched it, knowing her eyes ought to be on the stag, watching for the rise and fall of breath. "Oh, what a *stupid* trick!" she said to the air, and shouted at the stag, "Flower and leaf and stalk to thee, I conjure back what ought to be. Human frame and human mind banish those of hart or hind." Which, when she thought about it, was a silly thing to say, since it certainly wasn't a hind.

He lay prone in the grass, naked, honey hair every which way. His eyes were closed, but his brows pinched together, as if he was fighting his way back from sleep. One sunbrowned long hand curled and straightened. His eyes snapped open, focused on nothing; the fingers curled again; and finally he looked at them, as if he had to force himself to do it, afraid of what he might see. Moon heard the sharp drawing of his breath. On the shelf of stone there was nothing at all.

A movement across the clearing caught Moon's eye and she looked up. Among the trees stood the King of Stones in his gray armor. Sunshine glinted off it and into his unsmiling face, and pierced the shadows of his eye sockets. His eyes, she saw, were green as sage.

The prince had levered himself up onto his elbows. Moon saw the tremors in his arms and across his back. She swept her torn cloak from her shoulders and draped it over him. "Can you speak?" she asked him. She glanced up again. There was no one in the clearing but the two of them.

"I don't—yes," he said, like a whispering crow, and laughed thinly. He held out one spread and shaking hand. "Tell me. You don't see a hoof, do you?"

"No, but you used to have four of them. You're not nearly so impressive in this shape."

He laughed again, from closer to his chest this time. "You haven't seen me hung all over with satin and beads like a dancing elephant."

"Well, thank goodness for that. Can you stand up? Lean on me if you want to, but we should be gone from here."

He clutched her shoulder—the long scholar's fingers were very strong—and struggled to his feet, then drew her cloak more tightly around himself. "Which way?"

Passage through the woods was hard for her, because she knew how hard it was for him, barefoot, disoriented, yanked out of place and time. After one especially hard stumble, he sagged against a tree. "I hope this passes. I can see flashes of this wood in my memory, but as if my eyes were off on either side of my head."

"Memory fades," she said. "Don't worry."

He looked up at her quickly, pain in his face. "Does it?" He shook his head. "I'm sorry—did you tell me your name?"

"No. It's Moon Very Thin."

He asked gravely. "Are you waxing or waning?"

"It depends from moment to moment."

"That makes sense. Will you call me Robin?"

"If you want me to."

"I do, please. I find I'm awfully taken with having a name again."

At last the trees opened out, and in a fold of the green hillside they found a farmstead. A man stood in the farmhouse door watching them come. When they were close enough to make out his balding head and wool coat, he stirred from the door; took three faltering steps into his garden; and shouted and ran toward them. A tall, round woman appeared at the door, twisting her apron. Then she, too, began to run.

The man stopped just short of them, open-mouthed, his face a study in hope, and fear that hope will be yanked away. "Your Highness?"

Robin nodded.

The round woman had come up beside the man. Tears coursed down her face. She said calmly, "Teazle, don't keep 'em standing in the yard. Look like they've been dragged backwards through the blackthorn, both of them, and probably hungry as cats." But she stepped forward and touched one tentative hand to the prince's cheek. "You're back," she whispered.

"I'm back."

They were fed hugely, and Robin was decently clothed in linen and leather belonging to Teazle's eldest son. "We should be going," the prince said at last, regretfully.

"Of course," Teazle agreed. "Oh, they'll be that glad to see you at the palace."

Moon saw the shadow of pain pass quickly over Robin's face again.

They tramped through the new ferns, the setting sun at their backs. "I'd as soon . . ." Robin faltered and began again. "I'd as soon not reach the palace tonight. Do you mind?"

Moon searched his face. "Would you rather be alone?"

"No! I've been alone for—how long? A year? That's enough. Unless you don't want to stay out overnight."

"It would be silly to stop now, just when I'm getting good at it," Moon said cheerfully.

They made camp under the lee of a hill near a creek, as the sky darkened and the stars came out like frost. They didn't need to cook, but Moon built a fire anyway. She was aware of his gaze; she knew when he was watching, and wondered that she felt it so. When it was full dark and Robin lay staring into the flames, Moon said, "You know, then?"

"How I was . . . ? Yes. Just before . . . there was a moment when I knew what had been done, and who'd done it." He laced his brown fingers over his mouth and was silent for a while; then he said, "Would it be better if I didn't go back?"

"You'd do that?"

"If it would be better."

"What would you do instead?"

He sighed. "Go off somewhere and grow apples."

"Well, it wouldn't be better," Moon said desperately. "You have to go back. I don't know what you'll find when you get there, though. I called down curse and banishment on your mother and father, and I don't really know what they'll do about it."

He looked up, the fire bright in his eyes. "You did that? To the king and queen of Hark End?"

"Do you think they didn't deserve it?"

"I wish they didn't deserve it." He closed his eyes and dropped his chin onto his folded hands.

"I think you *are* the heart of the land," Moon said in surprise.

His eyes flew open again. "Who said that?"

"A guard at the front palace gate. He'll probably fall on his knees when he sees you."

"Great grief and ashes," said the prince. "Maybe I can sneak in the back way."

They parted the next day in sight of the walls of Great Hark. "You can't leave me to do this alone," Robin protested.

"How would I help? I know less about it than you do, even if you are a year out of date."

"A lot happens in a year," he said softly.

"And a lot doesn't. You'll be all right. Remember that everyone loves you and needs you. Think about them and you won't worry about you."

"Are you speaking from experience?"

"A little." Moon swallowed the lump in her throat. "But I'm a country witch and my place is in the country. Two weeks to the east by foot, just across the Blacksmith River. If you ever make a King's Progress, stop by for tea."

She turned and strode away before he could say or do anything silly, or she could.

Moon wondered, in the next weeks, how the journey could have seemed so strange. If the Seawood was full of ghosts, none of them belonged to her. The plain of grass was impressive, but just grass, and hot work to cross. In Little Hark she stopped for the night, and the blond boy remembered her.

"Did you find your teacher?" he asked.

"No. She died. But I needed to know that. It wasn't for nothing."

He already knew the prince had come back; everyone knew it, as if the knowledge had blown across the kingdom like milkweed fluff. She didn't mention it.

She came home and began to set things to rights. It didn't take long. The garden wouldn't be much this year, but it would be sufficient; it was full of volunteers from last year's fallen seed. She threw herself into work; it was balm for the heart. She kept her mind on her neighbors' needs, to keep it off her own. And now she knew that her theory was right, that earth and air and fire and water were all a part of each other, all connected, like silver and gold. Like joy and pain.

"You're grown," Tansy Broadwater said to her, but speculatively, as if she meant something other than height, that might not be an unalloyed joy.

The year climbed to Midsummer and sumptuous life. Moon went to the village for the Midsummer's Eve dance and watched the horseplay for an hour before she found herself tramping back up the hill. She felt remarkably old. On Midsummer's Day she put on her apron and went out to dig the weeds from between the flagstones.

She felt the rhythm in the earth before she heard it. Hoofbeats, coming up the hill. She got to her feet.

The horse was chestnut and the rider was honey-haired. He drew rein at the gate and slipped down from the saddle, and looked at her with a question in his eyes. She wasn't quite sure what it was, but she knew it was a question.

She found her voice. "King's Progress?"

"Not a bit." He sounded just as she'd remembered, whenever she hadn't had the sense to make enough noise to drown the memory out. "May I have some tea anyway?"

Her hands were cold, and knotted in her apron. "Mint?"

"That would be nice." He tethered his horse to the fence and came in through the gate.

"How have things turned out?" She breathed deeply and cursed her mouth for being so dry.

"Badly, in the part that couldn't help but be. My parents chose exile. I miss them—or I miss them as they were once. Everything else is doing pretty well. It's always been a nice, sensible kingdom." Now that he was closer, Moon could see his throat move when he swallowed, see his thumb turn and turn at a ring on his middle finger.

"Moon," he said suddenly, softly, as if it were the first word he'd spoken. He plucked something out of the inside of his doublet and held it out to her. "This is for you." He added quickly, in a lighter tone, "You'd be amazed how hard it is to find when you want it. I thought I'd better pick it while I could and give it to you pressed and dried, or I'd be here empty-handed after all."

She stared at the straight green stem, the cluster of inky-blue flowers still full of color, the sweet ghost of vanilla scent. Her fingers closed hard on her apron. "It's heliotrope," she managed to say.

"Yes, I know."

"Do . . . do you know what it means?"

"Yes."

"It means 'devotion.' "

"I know," Robin said. He looked into her eyes, as he had since he'd said her name, but something faltered slightly in his face. "A little pressed and dried, but yours, if you'll have it."

"I'm a country witch," Moon said with more force than she'd planned. "I don't mean to *stop* being one."

Robin smiled a little, an odd sad smile. "I didn't say you ought to. But the flower is yours whether you want it or not. And I wish you'd take it, because my arm's getting tired."

"Oh!" Moon flung her hands out of her apron. "*Oh!* Isn't there a plant in this whole wretched garden that means 'I love you, too'? *Bother!*"

She hurtled into his arms, and he closed them tight around her.

Once upon a time there ruled in the Kingdom of Hark End a king who was young and fair, good and wise, and responsible for the breeding of no fewer than six new varieties of apple. Once upon the same time there was a queen in Hark End who understood the riddle of the rings of silver and gold: that all things are joined together without beginning or end, and that there can be no understanding until all things divided are joined. They didn't live happily ever after, for nothing lives forever; but they lived as long as was right, then passed together into the land where trees bear blossom and fruit both at once, and where the flowers of spring never fade.

TINKER
Jack Cady

Jack Cady has worked as a truck driver, tree high-climber, landscape foreman, auctioneer, and member of the Coast Guard. He currently lives in Washington State, where he teaches at Pacific Lutheran University. Cady's splendid short stories have appeared in venues as diverse as *The Atlantic Monthly*, *The Yale Review*, *Omni*, *Pulphouse*, *The Best American Short Stories*, and *Prime Evil*, gaining him an international following. His books include *The Burning and Other Stories*, *The Well*, and *The Sons of Noah and Other Stories*.

Cady has won the Iowa Prize for Short Fiction, the Atlantic "First" Award, the Washington State Governor's Award, and a fellowship from the National Endowment for the Arts. "Tinker" is an example of Cady at his best: moving, insightful, with magic both subtle and wise. It is reprinted from the Spring 1992 issue of *Glimmer Train* magazine.

—T.W.

There were troubled Augusts once, back when our grandmothers were still alive, and when dog days panted slowly toward busy Septembers. Narrow roads overlaid old Indian trails, cutting through squared-off fields. The roads were white gravel. In midwest August dawns, the roads turned orange. Later in the day, they flowed like strips of light between green and yellow crops. Along these roads the tinker followed his trade.

We would see his wagon a mile off. Children began to holler. Women on the farm, mothers and grandmothers and cousins, exchanged glad looks behind the backs of any men who happened to be around. The tinker was a ladies' man, but not in the usual sense.

This was the time of the Great Depression. Farms were flattened. People were broke. Gasoline was used only for the tractor, or, once a week, taking the Ford to town. In those days horses were not spoiled little darlings. They worked the same as everyone else. Our people lived on hope, religion, the kitchen garden, a few slaughtered swine; and chicken after chicken after chicken. Even now, fifty years later, I cannot look a roasting hen in the eye.

The tinker had a regular route through the county. We saw him twice a year. Most tinkers were older men, but this one was middling young. My mother claimed he was a gypsy, my grandmother claimed him Italian, and the menfolk claimed him an Indian/mulatto who was after someone's white daughter. But, I'd best explain about tinkers. In today's throw-away world they are extinct.

The tinker's wagon was a repair shop on wheels. It resembled a cross-breed between farm wagon and Conestoga, but light enough for hauling by two horses. It carried torches for brazing, patches of sheet metal, patches of copper. It held soles for shoes, and grinders for knives and scissors. It was a-clank with cooking pans hanging along its sides. The tinker repaired worn pots, glued broken china so skillfully one could hardly find the crack, fixed stalled clocks; in fact, repaired anything that required a fine hand. This tinker also repaired worn dreams. That was the seat of his trouble. And ours.

I remember all this, not only through the eyes of a child, but through the eyes of a historian. I sit in my comfortable workroom where carpet is unstained, unstainable, and unremarkable. I look at it and remember wool rugs of a farm house. The rugs carried stains as coherent as a textbook: the darkness of blood when a younger cousin lost a finger in the pulley of a pump; a light space from spilled bleach; or unfaded bright spots beneath chairs—the signs of living, or (as the poet says) "all the appurtenances of home." I type on an old, old typewriter that was made in the '30s. At least that much respect can be shown the story.

When the tinker's wagon appeared on the road it caused a temporary stop in the work. That August when the trouble arose was as tricky as all Augusts. In August the last cut of hay comes in. Farmers gauge the weather sign, cut quickly, watch the horizon for storm as the hay dries. The baler comes through, the men following the tractor and wagon. They buck the bales. In the August when I was nine, the tinker appeared along the dusty road. I was too small to buck hay, was thus driving the tractor.

"Jim," my father said to me, "get the hell up to the house." He stood beside the wagon, shirt sodden with sweat, and sweat darkening the band of his straw hat. My father was a big man with English-blue eyes. He could be kind when he was unworried, but, what with the depression, he had not been unworried for years. My uncle and a cousin stood beside him. My uncle was from my mother's side. He was German, with eyes a thinner blue, and face a little starchy. Another cousin, my eldest, perched on top of the wagon where he stacked bales.

"I'd of thought," my uncle said about the tinker, "that the bastard would have hit jail by now. Or made a little stop out there at the cemetery."

"Bullshit," my eldest cousin said from the top of the load. "He's working. He ain't a tramp." This was a cousin from dad's side. He was known for a smart mouth and radical notions.

"Bullshit back at you," my other cousin said. "Best you can say about him is that he might be a dago." This was a cousin from mom's side, and he was defending his father, who didn't need it.

I climbed from the tractor and headed across twenty acres to the house.

In the days before World War II a boy of nine was not a man, but he was treated as if he soon would be. He had responsibilities, and most boys that age took themselves seriously. If the tinker suddenly decided to rape and pillage there was not a whole lot I could do. That, however, was not the point. The point was that I represented a male presence.

Manhood comes in peculiar ways depending on where you grow. I recall walking across that field of hay stubble in bare feet. No town kid could have done it, although in the small towns boys shed their shoes with the last frost. By August their feet were as tough as mine. The difference was that they had no feel for the land. They did not know that land is supposed to hurt you a little. Weather the same. A farm is real, not pastoral.

An apparition stood at the edge of that twenty-acre hay field. Even today you occasionally see them in the midwest. Solitary black walnuts stand like intricately carved windmills. They spread against the sky, trees spared when the land was cleared. They grow slowly, and spare themselves. No other tree can root within their drip lines. Black walnuts spread poison through the soil.

This tree was a youngster when men and their families forged through the Cumberland Gap, or spread along rivers from a backwoods settlement called Chicago. Now it had a bole thirty feet in circumference. The first branches began at forty feet, and the total height was over a hundred. It ruled the fields, too majestic for human use. It would not serve for a children's swing, or for a hanging tree. Before first snow, when the guns came out for hunting season, we always gathered walnuts beneath spectral branches.

The tinker's wagon pulled into the lane as I passed the back door of the house. My grandmother saw me, looked toward the hayfield, and murmured to herself; probably a verse from Isaiah. At age nine I had small appreciation of women, did not understand that my grandmother was the most beautiful woman I would ever know. She was a storyteller, and she was tall in a time when most women were not. Her white hair fell below her waist when she brushed it. During the day she had it "done up." Her worn housedresses were always pressed by flatirons. Her dresses fell to the tops of her shoes. My grandmother had been a young wife on the Oklahoma frontier when Indians roamed. The depression of the 1880s brought her back to Indiana.

The tinker's horses were wide from summer's roadside grass. One was bay, the other black. Color radiated from the wagon, red, white, and blue paint, green canvas, sun leaping from polished pans which clanked at every jolt in the rutted lane. Sun sparkled and danced against colors. My mother stepped from the house, my least cousin beside her, a girl of fifteen.

Did I understand what was going on? I doubt it, although I surely felt the men's displeasure and the women's pleasure. For my own part, the tinker's visit was exciting. Days on the farm are long. We had a telephone party line, but we had neither radio nor electricity. Townfolk had both.

It was a shy welcome the tinker faced, although he was accustomed to it. Since he moved from farm to farm, he met such welcomes all the time. Families learned how to comfortably handle each other. They had little experience with strangers.

"Missus," the tinker said to my grandmother, "I think of you last night and turn the horses this-a-way." His smile was a generalization among the sun-flashing pans, but he tipped his hat exactly toward my grandmother. His face was dark from either summer or blood. His brown eyes might have been those of a young Mediterranean girl. His eyes held no guile, and his face was—no more, no less—permanently relaxed and happy. In memory he seems a man without needs, an enlightened monk.

Even before he climbed from the wagon my least cousin passed him a dipper of water. Her young breasts moved beneath her housedress, her bobbed hair (which scandalized my grandmother) shone almost golden in sunlight. She had a pretty but puckish face, and lips that sometimes tied themselves with confusion. Although I had little appreciation of women, I was fascinated with what was happening to my cousin. Her body seemed to change every day. No doubt she was self-conscious as she became a woman, but to me she moved with confusing mystery.

"There's marriages all over," the tinker said. "From here to the county line." He drank, then climbed from the wagon. His horses stood placid as a puddle. The tinker not only repaired things, he also served as the county's newspaper. "The Baptists over in Warren bought a bell for the church. You can never tell what a Baptist is going to do." He said this last with a sort of wonder, but with no malice. He passed the dipper back to my least cousin and thanked her.

In the hayfield the men reached the end of a row. The tractor turned, headed back toward the house. I recall noting that another row would make a wagon load. The men would bring the load to the barn. Leaves of the black walnut looked ragged this late in August. The leaves carried no dust because the tree stood tall.

"It sounds like a busy winter," my mother said, and smiled at my least cousin.

"She was raised better," my grandmother said about my mother.

I had not the least notion what was meant. Now, of course, I understand that my mother spoke of the marriages.

"If this isn't the prettiest place on earth, then the Lord is fooling me." The tinker looked across fields toward the hardwood grove. Beyond the grove the river wound among rushes. At this time of year the river ran nearly clear. In spring, or after August storms, it ran brown with rich mud. The tinker looked toward our small farmhouse, then toward the barn. There was no hunger in his eyes, only happiness. He busied himself at repairing dreams.

The Great Depression, in spite of the softening that comes with years, was gray. We were an ambitious people, but ambitions were set aside as we struggled against hard times. Grayness arrived because hard times did not end. Women lost color and men lost creative fire.

The tinker owned only his wagon and team, yet he magically wished for nothing. Because of this he allowed us to see our lives with new eyes. That was at least part of his magic. He did not want what we had, but he showed *us* how to want it. Looking back, I almost understand the other part of his magic.

"There's so much time for thinking," he said to my grandmother. "I wonder after your quilt while I drive." Copper-bottomed pans reflected sun, and the wagon seemed alight with the warmth of mighty candles. The black walnut stood indifferent as a tower. In mid-afternoon it threw a shadow shorter than itself. "Quilts take such a fine hand." The tinker did not say that he also had a fine hand.

"Margaret is growing up," my grandmother said about my least cousin. "She helps. Some day she'll be teaching me."

"She has a delicate way. That's a sign."

My cousin, strong enough to help with the heavy work of slaughtering, looked at her feet and blushed. In the everyday life of the farm my least cousin was no more delicate than a post, but that is not what the tinker meant. "Times are changing, but a lady will always show herself a lady." He turned to my mother, who had just made that unladylike and licentious comment about marriages. "She is also musical?" he asked about my least cousin. At the turn of the century farms had gained a few luxuries. Many farmhouses had pianos, but in the whole county only my mother excelled at music. She had a warm touch better suited for blues than for church. However, in those days we knew nothing about the musical blues.

"It takes a while to learn," my mother said. She did not say that my cousin took little interest. My mother actually blushed. Somehow she had been taken back into the fold of respectability, and the *how* of the matter seemed beyond explanation.

"There's so much to learn," the tinker said to my cousin. "Takes a year, anyway, to rightly do a quilt."

Looking back, I understand that the tinker's magic truly was magic. At least it was magic in any terms we knew then, and certainly in any terms since.

I recall standing there, my bare feet as hard-soled as soil and callus could make them. I recall feeling that mysterious matters lived around me. The values of a farm are stern. I understood clean fence rows and upright dealing. I had been shown no other values. The word 'grace' had never entered my thought beyond its use in sermons.

The tinker's magic was to restore mystery and value to farm-women. No small undertaking.

Imagine a Depression farm. People lived close. A tyranny of custom was our only defense against wide knowledge of each other. When we dressed beside the kitchen woodstove on cold mornings the women dressed first. Then the men entered and dressed while the women went to the parlor. In unheated bedrooms temperatures might fall below zero.

It takes time and privacy to be a lady. The farm offers only hog butchering, kitchen gardens, interminable days of canning, the tedious daily round of cooking and splitting wood and cleaning poultry sheds. Men's work is brutally hard. Women's work begins before dawn and ends with a nightly reading from the Bible.

"I saved back some mending," my grandmother said. "It's only a little."

In those days pots and pans were continually pushed from the hot to the cool side of the stove. Pans wore thin through years. We did not throw away a leaky pan.

I watched the tinker apply the patch, while from the barn came sounds of work as the men began to unload hay. The three women surrounded the tinker. The tinker drilled a clean hole through the leak, snapped on the pan patch, and worked to flatten it on an upright anvil. Deft fingers smoothed that patch into the pan with the skill of a carpenter using a finely set plane. As he worked he spoke about a book of pictures from California. He tsked, then smiled. He mended a boot, and told about a new preacher. The preacher's wife was winning over the congregation, not the preacher. My memory calls back sunlight and quiet, above all, courtesy—an old-fashioned word.

"The sewing machine needs tinkering," my cousin said.

"I'll be but a minute," the tinker told his horses. He followed the three women toward the house. The horses stood almost as solidly as the black walnut. Shade spread dark beneath the wagon. My mother's shoulders did not slump as she walked. My grandmother, always busy, now seemed to stroll. My least cousin, clumsy with her growing up, was lithe in her movement. My heart pounded like rifle shots. I stood knowing I should follow, yet was somehow daunted. Even at age nine I understood that privacy lived in this encounter. A loud curse came from the barn. I looked to see my German cousin leap from the hay wagon and stride toward me.

"Are you ever going to grow up, Jimmy boy?" My cousin passed me, not running, but striding. Over by the barn the other men hesitated, then decided my cousin could handle matters. They returned to work, could not admit the work was hopeless.

Jaws of depression gnawed. No matter how hard men struggled, failure and despair were triumphant. Some years we did not make seed money. The bill for land tax stood dark as that black tree.

The sewing machine sat in a corner of the invaded parlor, and the tinker knelt. He removed a worn sleeve from the treadle. He spoke of a neighbor's daughter, studying at Ball State Teacher's College.

My cousin stood in the doorway. I stood behind him, embarrassed to be there, unable to not be there. The three women watched the tinker. My mother laughed. My grandmother said that college would be good for that particular girl. My least cousin yearned after the tinker's words. To us, college was a grand and remote place. I fidgeted. My grandmother turned, saw us in the doorway.

"Ralph," she said to my cousin, "this is not your place."

I do not know how scorn and sadness can combine in such a low voice. The tinker knelt above his work, but for a moment he fumbled with his wrench. My mother turned. I had never seen such anger from my mother, never saw such anger afterwards. My least cousin blushed and stood silent. The man in the doorway stiffened. He stood rigid as a rifle.

"You'd take away what little joy there is," my grandmother said. "Get about your business." She turned back. My mother looked at me, and I did not understand her quick sadness. Nor, probably, did she.

I sat in the kitchen with Ralph as the tinker finished his work. The man sat with fists closed. His blue eyes turned pale as his face. He fought shame with anger, and while his eyes remained pale his face gradually heated. "We'll see," he kept muttering. "We'll see about this."

That night—with the tinker long departed—marked the crossroads of my growing up. A curious silence lived in kitchen and parlor. We were isolated hearts. My mother avoided speaking with my father. My grandmother murmured to my least cousin, had nothing to say to the men. My least cousin worked in complete silence. Darkness lay across the fields by eight o'clock. Exhausted and sullen men made thin excuses to get out of the house, then made no excuse. They piled in the Ford and left on the road to town. For the first time in memory, I went to bed without hearing my father read a passage from the Bible.

No one spoke because no one knew what to say. A stranger came among us. He wielded the power of appreciation, and the power of unneeding affection.

Night passed. Morning arrived with sullen silence. Haying continued, although on that day the men were dragged-out. We made slow progress. When we went to the house for dinner at noon, the women spoke indifferently. An awful resignation dwelt among the women, a permanent tiredness of spirit. I never again remember spontaneity in that house.

The telephone party line buzzed with news. The tinker's wagon had burned. The tinker was intact. His horses had been unhitched and tied. They were also intact, but the wagon of red and white and blue and green was in ruins . . . .

I wish this story could end here. I would be compelled by its darkness, would feel such sorrow, but would not have to feel the rest. I sit in my comfortable workroom and type on this antique machine that was new when the world went spoiled. The tinker was not a man who would seek revenge. Perhaps he taught what old mystics knew, that wisdom arrives on the breath of inexplicable pain.

We got the hay in, and we had three days of storm. Sunday came with church and Sunday School. Cornfields stood bright, dust gone from leaves washed beneath August thunder. The land expressed grain, but lives turned dull as sermons. We left church and drove the graveled road which lay like a glowing path, but our way led back to the farm.

We were met by sparkles of light dancing among the tattered leaves of that spectral walnut. My mother gasped, remained silent. My grandmother chuckled. My least cousin was so confused she seemed about to weep.

"Get to the house," my uncle said to the women. "I don't want to hear a word." He climbed from the car and stood staring at the walnut. "How in the hell did he do it?"

The tree was alight with polished pans. They hung far out on branches. Pans glowed silver and copper, iron and enamel. No one could climb that tree. Even if a man could, it would be impossible to inch far enough out on the branches.

"He must have nailed boards like steps, then took 'em back down," my English cousin said. "He must of used a pole and hooked that stuff out there. The man is slick." My English cousin, known for radical notions, was not about to defect from us. At the same time he could appreciate what he saw.

"Jim," my father said, "go get the goddamn rifle."

In a sense it was I who defected. Over the next two years I grew closer to my mother and grandmother. My least cousin turned seventeen. She married. The men became silent and critical, but we still worked. Trapped in questions, I became silent. We avoided our confusions.

At the end of two years we lost the farm to taxes. The world started talking about war, but even that most hideous of wars leaves no memory this enduring:

The tinker used piano wire. Bullets only glanced, causing the pans to dance. We shot at the handles, broke a few pans loose. Work called and we worked. The crops came in.

We fired, and fired, and fired; pings, rattles, the sound of bullets. Autumn departed into winter, and shotguns cleared the walnuts. We spoke of cutting the tree, but did not. We fired as new leaves budded in the spring. Guns tore away small branches, and until we lost the farm they tore at my understanding.

My uncle was tight-lipped when we left the farm. My father wept, but my mother did not. I remember the tractor standing silent in the fields, and a few straggling pans hanging in the walnut. I remember our farm truck loaded with household furnishings, and wish that this were all. It is not, however; for what I remember always, can never forget, are two years of wasted ammunition and the sounds of firing, the silhouettes of raised weapons, the rattle of bullets as men sought redemption; through all the seasons shooting guns into that tree.

QUEEQUEG

Craig Curtis

Craig Curtis has published fiction in *The Quarterly*, *The Literary Review*, *The Washington Review*, *The Laurel Review*, *Global Tapestry*, *The New England Review*, *Kansas Quarterly*, and *Quarterly West*. He lives and works as a salesman in the Los Angeles area.

The following is a fantasy tale of delightfully vicious black humor. Anyone who has worked in a corporate environment will understand the protagonist's plight. "Queequeg" comes from *Chicago Review*, Volume 37, #4.

—T.W.

No one liked him. You know how first judgments go. No one wanted to even look at him. He was brought in for dubious reasons. They like to hire on the outside. They like to bring in raw, new blood.

"Hello," he said to me. I had my doubts whether it was English. His bracelets flashed at me. The dark stain of a tattoo hovering over his face had a deleterious effect on the staff—none of whom appreciated the gravity of this situation.

This was an atrocious decision; an insult, to all of us. Our business is products; and selling products. We know what we are doing. We don't need outsiders coming in to spoil accepted patterns of success. We all do our jobs. We make money. But it was a fact now: this savage had been appointed general plant manager. I know the sales department, for one thing, didn't like it. Salesmen are the first to bitch—about anything. This included our sales manager, who should have kept his mouth shut.

Our sales manager should have been the last to complain about a savage. Our sales manager, I should say, has a claw. Rather, a pincher. It's yellow, bright yellow. When he displays it—at his desk—he rolls his sleeve back. He never shows it, with his coat on. He never reveals it to the president of our company—whom I'm convinced has no idea it exists. But it does. He doesn't smoke with it. He lays it out on the desk, and when I walk by, or one of the other salesmen walks by, he lifts it and grabs hold of us. It hurts. It cuts clean through the white sleeve of my work shirt, and holds me fast. I dangle from it until he lets me go.

"That man's a *heathen*," he said that first day. Our sales manager doesn't pull any punches.

As for the buffoon who sits across from me in sales—his name is Vince—he had one word for him: "Weird." Vince is a great *undoer*. The salesman behind the two of us—separated by a half-hearted partition—likes to curl his phone line (all the ripples of it) like a snake. Vince *uncoils* it—daily. Now and then this salesman asks: "Is someone tampering?" He's very naïve. He'll kiss anyone on the butt if he thinks it will get him anywhere. He said (and this was about Queequeg): "There must be some reason they brought him on board." *On board.* As though this is a ship. It isn't.

Immediately the savage took over the vacant office of his predecessor, the office occupied—I don't know when—by our former plant manager, whom no one could remember with any clarity. He hadn't been there long. "Who was *that* in there?" people kept saying. "He was bald, wasn't he?" "No, the man had hair."

Queequeg of course shaved *his*. His skull was the most brutal thing about him. He waltzed into that office, put his harpoon down, and three or four people, on the spot, said: "I'm leaving!"

They didn't. No one means such talk. No one—in his or her right mind—is going anywhere soon. We are professionals. We hang on.

The first general staff meeting was a crack-up. Several of us held our sides. He stood up at the podium and chalkboard, harpoon leaning on the wall behind, and talked basics, like: what we were going to do now, and how we were going to do it—as though we didn't know. He threatened people. He didn't say who. He lifted that spear up and pointed it at an imaginary breast, and just flung it. The steel of it broke the bulletin board on the wall behind us in half. Heads wagged. One older salesman had a heart attack. Two individuals from accounting had to carry him out. At that, Queequeg's smile was enormous—full of bright teeth.

"You damned pig," some of us said, under our breath, because we were scared suddenly—as never before. We didn't know what to do. "Kill him!" someone said. But that was pure jest. No one present had anything to kill him *with*. We are white-collar people; not savages. We wear ties and vests. The fiercest thing we carry is a pen.

This was no picnic. Several of the sales territories were shuffled. Not one of us was happy.

Of course we do have some drop-outs—those who can't, or shouldn't, make it. I am the first to admit this. We have—to name only one—a compulsive favor-doer in sales here. He's always looking for things to do for people. Anything. Like: empty the trash under your desk; take down last month's sales bulletin (which he doesn't chuck, but keeps in his desk; he's got a drawer full of them). He never *sells* anything. But everyone—I don't know why—loves him.

Queequeg called him in one day—not more than a week after the general staff meeting—and cut off his head; cut it cleanly, above the gold chain attached to his crucifix. We found it—the crucifix—hanging from one of Queequeg's ears, which made his strong, bold head lean—at least there were those who thought so. Queequeg shrunk that detached, useless article of anatomy—severed from its body, with that shocked expression still painted in its features, frozen into them—and displayed it in a pickle jar in a slightly green solution.

"I admire the *conviction*," I heard someone say—a squirrel, I should say. Every sales department has a squirrel: someone who justifies everything.

That was not the general feeling most people had about this incident. In fact there were those of us who thought of calling the police. It was no more than talk. You see everyone—in the last analysis—wanted to keep his or her job. The women were just as bad in this respect as the men. In some instances, they were worse. "He's so attractive, even *with* face paint," I heard a youngish woman say. I was stunned by the remark. The savage had caused the death of one man, and put another man in the hospital; and he smelled of body odors and half-dried leather (with the lust of death still in it, the butcher's knife, the murderer's ax), and *fish*. He had to have grown on a diet of salted fish. His breath was nearly intolerable.

"The first person here to surpass his personal sales quota gets the head!" Queequeg said. We marveled at the brazen way he said it. At this he strode out. The head stood—its jar—on top of the stereo amplifier which runs through the plant with speakers everywhere (there is always the sound of music).

But you see I was the first to discover the flaw: a faint harelip. Not much of a harelip. But a harelip. It was there at the beginnings of his words, tainting them with a slight, imperfect maul.

Of course I didn't waste a minute. I started right in on him. You know I had a right to. I was second in dollar receipts for the month. The salesman ahead of me in orders was running scared. This faker, this *savage*, couldn't touch me.

"What's in a harelip," one of the girls in receivables said. She glowed every time she looked at the cannibal. She was the one who liked to get people on the phone and rag on them about payment. She had the power to hold shipments, when her ire was up. Queequeg only fascinated her. "It makes him sexy," she said. She took out her lipstick and spread it thick as butter. All in all, she sparkled more than a chrome fender. When Queequeg stepped inside receivables, the typing speeds doubled at each of the desks. The machines began to inch their way to the steel edges. It was difficult to understand.

But no one is perfect. No one is ever perfectly at ease. Take me. When I first began with the company, I felt small. Yes. Not unnaturally small—just small. I remember a particular sales call—with my new suit and sales book—waiting on the hard oak bench outside the buying office, and looking down at my feet, in their shiny shoes, dangling, hanging over the lip of wood. They didn't touch the floor. It was a pie shop, in a chain of pie shops—a vast chain. Millions had been made on it. Families had become enormously, fabulously wealthy—on pies. I was intrigued. But I did appear somewhat diminutive in the full-length mirror across from me, framed by bronze baking pins beset with red logos.

In fact we had one salesman (another of those types who *didn't*, definitely didn't, fit the mold) who, from the first day, began to get smaller; so much so that by the third week—the week he was fired—I greeted him at his car and looked down to see his knees no higher than the curb and his nose inches from my trousers. I was filled with pity and disgust. "I'm sorry," he said. His carnation had become huge—like a fester—on his lapel, pulling on his flesh and his cloth.

"Can't be helped," I said. I tried to wink. My eyelid stuck.

But you see you grow into things. I grew into this job. Now I tower over the bunch of them, with one exception (whom I intend to best). You never give up trying.

Even so, it is distressful to come home from our office each evening to sleep, and be filled with horrors. Every time I shut my eyes—tired from the day and everything that comes with it—I see it: a head popping through the plastered-over section of wall I put my fist through on one occasion; I see the glasses, the hair, the neck, peeping at me. The apparition says to me: "I'm looking for the cat."

"Fine," I say.

"You *sell*," he says.

"How do you know?" I ask.

"Because I know you inside out," he tells me.

Because I know you inside out. Imagine that. It is not easy being employed. What does an apparition know about being employed? Most people who are out of work never know what it is *to work*. I work for a living. I cannot understand dreams.

Of course with the appearance of Queequeg these nightly visits only increased. The character of these charades changed remarkably with the onset of the savage. For instance: I woke (in what is not really sleep, *natural* sleep) to see Queequeg seated across from me in his office, across the broad walnut of his desk, the slick of its vast surface, vacant of anything but ashtrays and his quiver of arrows, as Q. (Q. is what we called him, after the first month) lectured me on things I already know: details of selling, of convincing. Then he reached across the desk, embraced me, and kissed me on the forehead. "You're a good little boy," he said.

"I'm a *momma's* boy," I retorted. I was infuriated.

At that point, Queequeg turned into an owl and mounted the office window—which is open, in all of these half-dreams—and flew out, eyeing me over the edge of his feathers, until he was a speck no bigger than a roach. I detest such visions.

"It wasn't *your* idea," someone—the name of whom I can't remember—said. This was even before the end of the first fiscal quarter. We were having coffee and sandwiches, watching through the huge glass window that looks down on the production floor, at the people, at the endless rows of moving products and containers. Nothing could be heard because the glass held everything in (I once saw a man, silently and wild-eyed with fear, get himself caught in one of the sprockets on the loading machines; his sleeve was snagged, and the belt lifted him as it moved, choking him by the collar; he turned red like the tattoo on Q.'s face, and when they pulled him free he went stiff as cardboard). "I didn't *say* it was my idea," I said. "But it wasn't *his*, either," I added. "The other one"—and by this I meant his predecessor—"had exactly the same idea."

"But *he*"—Queequeg, Q.—"made it work."

"The cannibal was lucky," I told him.

"I didn't *hear* that," he said. Perhaps that's why I can't remember his name. Our friendship—if it had been that—ended on the remark.

I regret to say the situation deteriorated. The most striking thing, of course, was that I found myself alone when it came to Q. I had been saying things. I was cocky. I could not, you see, accept the fact it was totally his company now, to do with it—

and everyone concerned with it—exactly what he wanted. That malicious brain of his, that hive of misconduct, was on the loose.

There was talk the women employees of this company called Q. at night where he slept—which was a lean-to not more than a mile from the beach (because, he told everyone, he had to *hear* the sea).

He was in by six, then—before any of us. All of us commuted. There was one man (in his forties, possibly older; his face looked like an oatmeal cookie, crumbly at the hairline) who took a bus and then a train, and then walked the last mile on his knees, just for the privilege of working, of making *more*; which he did, though he spent it.

As for the purported calls, I have no way of knowing whether the story was true (it was a fact Q. had the latest in remote phones, with gorgeous hold buttons of solid, invincible plastic); or, if it *was*, whether Q. took any of these ladies up on said offers.

But no one, under any circumstances, got there before the harpoon and the hands which held it.

"How old is Q.?" I asked Grace. Grace is in quality control. Her gold front teeth flashed at me between bites of lipstick the color of unrepentant cinnamon.

"Q. isn't *any* age," she said coolly. I think everyone—Grace included—sensed my inherent antagonism. I was on thin ice. I knew it. "Q. is a Natural Man," she continued. "His roots are not human. He's a wizard."

"A wizard?"

"He's divine."

Divine. That word had begun to circulate, concerning Q. It was quickly becoming truth within the company—within the corporation. It stunned me. Things *were* going better. I knew they were. Some of the changes—in production, in particular—*had* made a difference. But still, I had to consider: how long had it been since these very same people were laughing at the cannibal—this beast? Individuals within the plant were now braceleting their arms with those same colored hoops he had on his. I don't know where they all got them. I suppose they hunted for them. And on a Thursday two men in the engineering section came to work naked from the waist up. I was incredulous. I could not believe my eyes. They said to me—as coolly as Grace: "You're being left behind. You'd better come around."

I went home and I thought I would sleep soundlessly, but this head popped out at me again through the wall and asked me whether I had any sugar.

"I don't!" I said.

"And you *won't*!"

What did he mean by that?

"Q. represents the highest stage in culture," they now said. Where were his detractors now? Production and sales had doubled. The company stock had split. There would be no stopping Q. I think I alone understood that clearly. My sales were excellent. "Q. made that happen," they told me. They were all his partisans now.

But something less tangible and perhaps more real had slipped—had fallen off precipitously. Everyone—and I mean everyone—within a company has a standing; a position. This is not a *position*, as such; whether engineer, or clerk, or president. Rather, a position. You fall into a level on a rung. You clung to it. It is your standing—silent, sure, intact. Only mine wasn't—not any longer. I had done too much talking. I was more or less *insubordinate*. It showed in my face. In my body language. I'd once been listened to. I'd had admirers. There were frowns now for me—or steely indifferences, told in the most simple gestures of disregard.

I thought to myself: there is one truly unbiased individual I can count on. He was cold—I will not deny that. He had been with this company two decades, not less than that. The morning on which I spoke to him—after what was now a regular weekly staff meeting of lances and bludgeons—he was wearing saddleback shoes and a Brooks Bros. suit, a striped tie—narrow as a shaving strap—and cuff links. He was on the window lip, on the seventh floor, arms and legs spread against the sun.

"Reptiles don't warm that fast," his secretary said, squinting at me because my back was turned to the light.

The meeting had adjourned at seven-forty-five. It was now five to eight. I waited until he could move his limbs, and we went down for coffee.

The break room was vacant. I knew I was taking a chance. I had to depend on this man's confidentiality. It was no longer the time for timidity. I could always file unemployment. I didn't need to live in a house. I could walk. I was overweight as it was.

"No," he said. His name is Frank.

"But *you* never liked the man," I said. I didn't dare say cannibal. "And I don't think you like him *now*."

He stared at me. He didn't nod. Then he said: "I can't."

"But you can!" I said.

I tried to tell him we were not people any longer; that we had become savages, and so quickly. There were some rational things about Q. (even I admitted that), but as many *irrational*, to the point of insanity. Three people—to date—had been executed, for failing this or that objective. There was no discussion. The people simply vanished. The monthly reports continued to improve for the company as a whole. More and more individuals reported for work with nothing more on than loincloths. Tattoos had begun to appear. "The man's ruining us," I said.

The gentleman stood, finished the last of his cup, shook my hand, and retreated to his office.

And I knew: it was my fate to act alone. This was a terrible loneliness—worse than the loneliness of working *with* people. *Divine*. That word kept ringing in my head. I couldn't sleep.

He'd slaughtered something. It was difficult to tell—from where I approached— what exactly, he'd killed. I saw whiskers brimming from the blackened hollow of a snout. The blood had coagulated and charred. Q. bent over the fire he'd kindled on the roof. Everything about him was cordoned off. And there were armed guards. The guards followed him wherever he went. They had a shack at the entrance to the company parking lot. They were an independent agency. They answered only to Q. He must have known, then. I had come to him with proof someone in sales was badmouthing him. I had definite proof. He leaned over his kill, pulling the meat from the thigh bones.

"Business has no limits," he said, when he looked up at me.

I stared at him. The guards were milling about the edges of the roof, all looking down—as though danger would come from below. It was winter: cold, bitter winter. His look was only a glance. "Business *has* limits," I said. The butcher knife I'd brought—long and barbarous—cradled in my briefcase. I had only to open it; snap the snaps.

"You aren't like the others," Q. said.

The locks popped.

"No," I said.

"Why can't you be?" he said. His mouth was stuffed with flesh. I could hardly make the words out.

"I refuse."

"Why?"

I struck. And missed.

He sent me roses. I couldn't believe it. I was handcuffed to the bed, in the whiteness of the frigid room. There had been a psychiatrist in already, to map me out, define the parameters of my attempted crime—because, you see, I stuck the knife in the half-cooked carcass turning on the wooden spit. I raised the knife over his head once, held it for a moment—not longer, just that—and plunged it in what he was eating. He didn't look up. Never once.

"Thank you," I wrote on the note which the nurse took to him. I was weak. I was confused.

Later—much later; a month (he hadn't pressed charges)—he called me into his office. My arms—both of which the guards had broken on the spot—were in slings. They'd heal. He wanted—Q. wanted—to talk to me. "Just *talk*," he'd said.

And we did. He sat me down.

"I admire your courage," he said.

"You didn't flinch," I said. "You *knew*."

"Yes I knew," he said.

"Did you know that I wouldn't hit you?"

"No."

That—now that—fascinated me.

"I've a job for you," he said.

"You trust me."

"Yes," he said. That was just the beginning.

ANIMA
M. John Harrison

British writer M. John Harrison is a master of complex tales that hover just at the edge of fantasy, just at the edge of horror. "Anima," from the pages of *Interzone* magazine, published in England, is an intricate, incisive, and ultimately mysterious character study—easily one of the finest stories of the year.

Harrison is best known to fantasy readers for his intoxicating imaginary-world novels *The Pastel City*, *A Storm of Wings*, and the collection *Viriconium Nights*; and to horror readers for a handful of excellent dark fantasy stories. His most recent work is the brilliant contemporary fantasy novel *The Course of the Heart*, and a mainstream novel titled *Climbers*. Harrison lives in London.

—T.W. & E.D.

A week ago last Tuesday I dreamed all night of trying to find out what had happened to the woman I loved. She was a pianist and a writer. We had met in New York when she played a concert of American and British music. She had reminded me how I had once been able to dance. Now, some time later, she had come to Britain to find me. But she could no longer speak, only weep. How had she traveled here? Where did she live? What was she trying to say? It was a dream heavy with sadness and urgency. All avenues of inquiry were blocked. There were people who might know about her, but always some reason why they could not be asked, or would not tell. I walked up and down the streets, examining the goods on the market stalls, my only clue the reissue date of a once-banned medicine.

I never dreamed anything like this until I met Choe Ashton—

Ten past ten on a Saturday night in December, the weekend Bush talked to Gorbachev on the *Maxim Gorki* in half a gale in Valetta Harbour. In the east, governments were going over like tired middleweights—saggy, puzzled, almost apologetic. I sat in the upper rooms of a media drinking club in central London. The occasion was the birthday of a corporate executive called Dawes who sometimes commissioned work from me. Shortly they would be giving him a cake shaped like half a football on which had been iced the words: OVER THE MOON BUT NOT OVER THE HILL!

Meanwhile they were eating pasta.

"Now that's two thousand calories. How much more do you want?"

"So far I've had cheese but not much else, which is interesting—"

"Are we going to get that fettucini we've paid for?"

The women were in TV: the last of the power dressers. The men were in advertising, balding to a pony tail. Men or women, they all had a Range Rover in the car park at Poland Street. They were already thinking of exchanging it for one of the new Mazdas. I moved away from them and went to stare out of the window. The sky over towards Trafalgar Square looked like a thundery summer afternoon. The buildings, side-lit by street lamps, stood out against it, and against one another, like buildings cut from cardboard. I followed an obscure line of neon. A string of fairy lights slanting away along the edge of a roof. Then cars going to and fro down at the junction by St. Martin-in-the-Field, appearing very much smaller than they were. I had been there about a minute when someone came up behind me and said:

"Guess what? I was just in the bog. I switched the hand-drier on and it talked to me. No, come on, it's true! I put my hands under it and it said, 'Choe, I really like drying your hands.' "

I knew his name, and I had seen him around: no more. He was in his forties, short and wiry, full of energy, with the flat-top haircut and earring of a much younger man. His 501s were ripped at the knees. With them he wore a softly tailored French Connection blouson which made his face, reddened as if by some kind of outdoor work, look incongruous and hard.

"Has anything like that ever happened to you? I'm not kidding you, you know. It talked to me!"

I shrugged.

"OK. Give us a fag then, if you don't believe me. Eh?"

He was delighted by my embarrassment.

"I don't smoke," I said.

"Come on," he wheedled. "Every fucker smokes. Dawsie only knows people who smoke. Give us a fag."

I had spent all day feeling as if my eyes were focusing at different lengths. Every so often, things—especially print—swam in a way which suggested that though for one eye the ideal distance was eighteen inches, the other felt happier at twelve. Choe Ashton turned out to be the perfect object for this augmented kind of vision, slipping naturally in and out of view, one part of his personality clear and sharp, the rest vague and impressionistic. What did he do? Whose friend was he? Any attempt to bring the whole of him into view produced a constant sense of strain, as your brain fought to equalize the different focal lengths.

"I'm sick of this," he said. "Let's fuck off to Lisle Street and have a Chinese. Eh?"

He gave me a sly, beautiful smile. An aging boy in a French Connection jacket.

"Come on, you know you want to."

I did. I was bored. As we were leaving, they brought the birthday cake in. People always seem very human on occasions like this. Dawes made several efforts to blow the candles out, to diminishing applause; and ended up pouring wine over them. Then an odd thing happened. The candles, which—blackened, but fizzing and bubbling grossly, dripping thick colored wax down the sides of the football—had seemed to be completely extinguished, began to burn again. Blinking happily around, Dawes had taken the incident as a powerful metaphor for his own vitality, and was already pouring more wine on them.

"Did you see that?" I asked Choe Ashton.

But he was halfway out of the door.

At first we walked rapidly, not talking. Head down, hands rammed into the pockets of his coat. Ashton paused only to glance at the enormous neon currency symbols above the Bureau de Change on Charing Cross Road. "Ah, money!" But as soon as he recognized Ed's Easy Diner, he seemed content to slow down and take his time. It was a warm night for December. Soho was full of the most carefully dressed people. Ashton pulled me towards a group standing outside the Groucho, so that he could admire their louche haircuts and beautifully crumpled chinos. "Can't you feel the light coming off them?" he asked me in a voice loud enough for them to hear. "I just want to bask in it."

For a moment after he had said this, there did seem to be a light round them— like the soft light in a '70s movie, or the kind of watery nimbus you sometimes see when you are peering through a window in the rain. I pulled him away, but he kept yearning back along the pavement towards them, laughing. "I love you!" he called to them despairingly. "I love you!" They moved uncomfortably under his approval, like cattle the other side of a fence.

"The middle classes are always on watch," he complained.

We dodged briefly into a pick-up bar and tried to talk. The only free table was on a kind of mezzanine floor on the way to the ladies' lavatory. Up there you were on a level with the sound system. Drunken girls pushed past, or fell heavily into the table.

"I love them all!" shouted Ashton.

"Pardon?"

"I love them!"

"What, these too?"

"Everything they do is wonderful!"

Actually they just sat under the ads for Jello-shots, Schlitz and Molson's Canadian and drank Lowenbrau: boys in soft three-button shirts and Timberline boots, girls with tailored jackets over white silk trousers. I couldn't see how they had arrived there from Manor House or Finsbury Park, all those dull, broken, littered places on the Piccadilly line; or why. Eventually we got sick of bawling at one another over the music and let it drive us back out into Cambridge Circus.

"I was here this afternoon," he said. "I thought I heard my name called out."

"Someone you knew."

"I couldn't see anyone."

We ended up in one of those Lisle Street restaurants which specialize in degree-zero décor, cheap crockery and grudging service. There were seven tables crammed into an area smaller than a newsagent's shop. The lavatory—with its broken door handle and empty paper roll—was downstairs in the kitchens. Outside it on a hard chair sat a waitress, who stared angrily at you as you went past. They had a payphone:

but if you wanted to use it, or even collect your coat from the coat rack, you had to lean over someone else's dinner. Choe Ashton, delighted, went straight to the crepe paper shrine mounted in the alcove to show me a vase of plastic flowers, a red-and-gold tin censer from which the stubs of old incense sticks protruded like burnt-out fireworks, two boxes of safety matches.

"See this? Make a wish!"

With considerable gentleness he put fresh incense in the censer and struck a match.

"I love these places—" he said.

He sat down and rubbed his hands.

"—but I'm bored with Hot and Sour."

He stared away from the menu and up at the industrial ceiling, which had been lowered with yellow-painted slats. Through them you could still see wires, bitumen, ventilator boxes. A few faded strings ejected from some exhausted Christmas party-popper still hung up there, as if someone had flung noodles about in a claustrophobic fit or paddy.

"Let's have some Bitter and Unfulfilled here!" he called to the waitress. "No. Wait a minute. I want Imitation Pine Board Soup, with a Loon Fung calendar.

"But it has to have copulating pandas on it."

After that we began to drink Tsing Tao beer. Its packaging, he said, the pale grey ground and green, red and gold label, reminded him of something. He arranged several empty cans across the table between us and stared at them thoughtfully for some time, but nothing came of it. I don't remember eating, though we ordered a lot of food. Later he transferred his obsession from the Tsing Tao label to the reflections of the street neon in the mirror behind the bar. SOHO. PEEP SHOW. They were red, greenish-yellow, a cold blue. A strobe flickered inside the door of the peep show. Six people had been in there in two minutes. Two of them had come out again almost immediately. "Fucking hell, sex, eh? Why do we bother?" Ashton looked at me. "I fucking hate it," he said. Suddenly he stood up and addressed the people at the nearer tables. "Anyone who hates sex, stand up!" he tried to persuade them. "Fucking sex." He laughed. "Fucking fucking," he said. "Get it?" The waitresses began to move towards us.

But they had only come to bring the bill and offer him another beer. He smiled at them, moved his hands apart, palms forward, fingers spread.

"No thanks," he said shyly.

"The bill's in Chinese!" he shouted. He brandished it delightedly at the rest of the diners. "Hey!"

I agreed to drive him home. For the first few minutes he showed some interest in my car. At that time I had an Escort RS Turbo. But I didn't drive it fast enough for him, and he was silent again until we were passing The Flying Dutchman in Camberwell. There, he asked in an irritable voice: "Another thing. Why is this pub always in the same place?" He lived on the other side of Peckham, where it nudges up against Dulwich. It took him some time to find the right street. "I've only just moved in." I got him upstairs then consulted my watch. "I think I'd better sleep on your floor," I said. But he had passed out. It seemed like a nice flat, although he hadn't bought much furniture.

I woke late the next morning. Ten o'clock. Sleet was falling. A minicab driver had parked his Renault under the front window, switched its engine off, and turned up Capital Radio so that I could hear clearly a preview of a new track by the Psychedelic Furs. Every thirty seconds he leaned on his horn. At that, the woman who had called him leant out of a fourth floor window in one of the point blocks on the other side of the road and shrieked:

"Cammin dahn!"

Beep.

"Cammin dahn!"

Beep.

"Cammin dahn!"

Beep. Beep. Beep.

"Cammin dahn! Cammin dahn!"

At the back the flat overlooked a row of gardens. They were long and narrow and generally untended; so choked, some of them, with bramble, elder and buddleia stalks, that they reminded you of overgrown lanes between walls of sagging, sugary old brick. In the bleaker ones, you knew, a dog would trot restlessly all day between piles of household or builders' rubbish, under a complex array of washing lines. Choe Ashton's garden had once been kept in better order. There was a patio of black and white flagstones like a chess board, a few roses pruned savagely back to bare earth. The little pond was full of leaves. Suddenly I saw that there was a fox sniffing round the board fence at the bottom of the garden.

At first I thought it was some breed of cat I had never seen before: long-backed, reddish, brindling towards its hindquarters and long tail. It was moving a bit like a cat, sinuously and close to the ground. After a minute or two it found the pond and drank at length, looking up every so often, but too wet and tired, perhaps too ill, to be wary or nervous.

I watched with my heart in my mouth, afraid to move even behind the window in case it saw me and ran off. Choe Ashton came into the room. "Fucking hell," he said. "Are you still here?"

"Sssh. There's a fox in your garden."

He stood beside me. As he watched, the fox moved into the middle of the overgrown lawn, pawing and sniffing at the earth. It yawned. I couldn't see anything there it might eat. I wondered if it might have smelt another fox. It sat down suddenly and stared vaguely into the sleet.

"I can't see anything."

I stared at him.

"Choe, you must be blind—"

He gripped my arm very hard, just above the elbow.

"That hurts," I said.

"I can't fucking *see* any fucking fox," he said quietly.

We stood like that for thirty or forty seconds. In that time the fox went all round the lawn, not moving very fast, then crossed the low brick wall into the next garden, where it vanished among some elders, leafless laburnum bushes and apple trees.

"OK, Choe."

People like Choe are like moths in a restaurant on a summer evening just as it gets dark. They bang from lamp to lamp then streak across the room in long flat wounded trajectories. We make a lot of their confusion but less of their rage. They dash themselves to pieces out of sheer need to be more than they are. It would have been better to leave him alone to do it, but I was already fascinated.

I phoned everyone who had been at the Dawes party. No one knew the whole story. But they all agreed Choe was older than he appeared and, career-wise at least, a bit of a wimp. He was from the north of England. He had taken one of the first really good media degrees—from East Sussex—but never followed it up. He did the odd design job for one of the smaller agencies that operate out of top rooms above Wardour Street. In addition, he had some film work, some advertising work. But who didn't? The interesting thing was how he had filled his time until he appeared in Soho. After East Sussex he had moved back north and taken a job as a scaffolder; then joined a Manchester steeplejacking firm. He had worked in the massive stone quarries around Buxton, and out in the North Sea on the rigs. Returning to London obsessed with motorcycles, he had opened one of the first courier operations of the Thatcher boom. He never kept any job for long. Boredom came too easily to him. Anything hard and dangerous attracted him, and the stories I heard about him, true or not, would have filled a book. He told me some of them himself, later:

Stripping old render near the top of a thirty-story council high-rise in Glasgow, he found himself working from scaffolding fifty feet above a brick-net. These devices— essentially a few square feet of strong plastic netting stretched on a metal frame— are designed to catch dropped tools or bits of falling masonry. With a brick-net, you don't need safety bunting or a spotter on the ground to protect unwary pedestrians. Ashton quickly became obsessed. He thought about the brick-net in his digs at night. (Everyone else was watching *Prisoner in Cell Block H.*) During the day everything that fell seemed to go down into it in slow motion. Things were slow in his life too. One cold windy Monday ten minutes before lunch, he took a sly look sideways at the other jacks working on the scaffolding. Then he screamed and jumped off, turning over twice in the air and landing flat on his back. The breath went out of him—boof! Everything in the net flew up into the air and fell down again on top of him—old mastic tubes, bits of window frame, half bricks.

"I'd forgotten that stuff," he said with a grin.

"Were you injured?"

"I walked a bit stiff that week."

"Was it worth it?"

"It was a fucking trip."

Later, induced by money to take a long-running steelworks job, he decided to commute to Rotherham from London on a Kawasaki 750 racer. Each working week began in the early hours of Monday morning, when, still wobbly from the excesses of the weekend, he pushed this overpowered bright green monster up the motorway at a hundred and fifty miles an hour in the dark. He was never caught, but quite soon he grew bored. So he taught himself to lie along the Kawa with his feet on the back pegs, wedge the throttle open with a broken matchstick so that he could take both hands off the handlebars, and roll a joint in the tiny pocket of still air behind the fairing. At the right speed, he claimed, Kawasaki engineering was good enough to hold the machine on track.

"The idea," he said, "is not to slow down."

I wasn't sure boredom was entirely the issue. Some form of exploration was taking place, as if Choe Ashton wanted to know the real limits of the world, not in the abstract but by experience. I grew used to identifying the common ground of these stories—the point at which they intersected—because there, I believed, I had found Choe's myth of himself, and it was this myth that energized him. I was quite wrong. He was not going to let himself be seen so easily. But that didn't become plain until later. Meanwhile, when I heard him say, "We're sitting on the roof one dinner time, and suddenly I've poured lighter fuel on my overalls and set myself on fire," I would nod sagely and think of Aleister Crowley's friend Russell, discharged from the US Navy after he had shot up forty grains of medical-grade cocaine and tried to set fire to a piece of glass by willpower alone.

"I just did it to see what people would do," Choe said. "They had to beat me out with their hands."

In a broad fake Northern accent he added:

"I'm scared of nowt, me." Then in a more normal voice: "Do you believe that?"

"I think I do," I said, watching with some interest the moth on its flat, savage, wounded trajectory.

He gave me a look of contempt.

This didn't prevent him from flirting all winter, slipping away—but never too far—between the sets of a comically complex personality: always waiting for me to catch up, or catch my breath.

Drunk in bars, he would suggest going to the first night of a photographic exhibition, a new production of Ionesco, ballet at the Royal Opera House: arrive on the night in some immaculate designer two-piece with baggy trousers and immense shoulder pads: and then say—

"I've got the Kawa parked round the corner."

"I'm sure you have, Choe."

"You don't believe I came on it, do you?" And again, appealing to a foyer full of people who had arrived in BMWs:

"This fucker doesn't believe I came on me bike!"

To see how far he would go, I took him to a dance version of *Beauty and the Beast*. He sat there quietly, entranced by the color and movement, quite unconcerned by the awful costumes and Persil white sentimentality, until the interval. Then he said loudly: "It's like the fucking fish tank at the dentist's in here. Look at them!" He meant the audience, which, gorgeously dressed and vaguely smiling, had begun to come and go in the depopulated front stalls like moonlight gourami or neon tetras nosing among the silver bubbles of the oxygenator. Quiet, aimless, decorative, they had come, just like the dancers, to be seen.

"They're a bit more self-conscious than fish, Choe,"

"Are they?"

He stood up.

"Let's go and get some fucking beer. I'm bored with this."

Two or three weeks later, having heard I liked Turgenev, he sent me an expensive old edition of *Sketches from a Hunter's Notebook*, on the front endpapers of which he had written in his careful designer hand:

"Turgenev records how women posted flowers—pressed marguerites and immortelles—to the child-murderer Tropmann in the days before his execution. It was as if Tropmann were going to be 'sent on before.' Each small bouquet or floret was a confused memory of the pre-Christian plea 'Intercede for us' which accompanied the sacrifice of the king or his substitute. But more, it was a special plea: 'Intercede for me.' These notes, with their careful, complex folds, arrived from the suicide provinces—bare, empty coastal towns, agricultural plains, the suburbs of industrial cities. They had been loaded carefully into their envelopes by white hands whose patience was running out between their own fingers like water."

I phoned him up.

"Choe, what a weird quote. Where did you find it?"

"I'm not stupid, you know," he said, and put the phone down. He had written it himself. For two weeks he refused to speak to me, and in the end I won him round only by promising him I would go to the Tate and spend a whole afternoon with the Turners. He shivered his way down to the Embankment from Pimlico tube station to meet me. The sleeves of the French Connection jacket were pushed up to his elbows, to show off slim but powerful forearms tattooed with brilliantly colored peacock feathers which fanned down the muscle to gently clasp his thin wrists.

"Like them? They're new."

"Like what, Choe?"

He laughed. I was learning. Inside the gallery, the Turners deliquesced into light: *Procession of Boats with Distant Smoke*, circa 1845; *The Sun of Venice Going Down to Sea*, 1843. He stood reverentially in front of them for a moment or two. Then the tattooed arms flashed, and he dragged me over to *Pilate Washing his Hands*.

"This fucker though! It can't have been painted by the same man!"

He looked at me almost plaintively.

"Can it?"

Formless, decaying faces. Light somehow dripping itself apart to reveal its own opposite.

"It looks like an Ensor."

"It looks like a fucking Emil Nolde. Let's go to the zoo."

"What?"

He consulted his watch. "There's still plenty of daylight left," he said. "Let's go to the zoo." On the way out he pulled me over to John Singer Sargent's *Carnation, Lily, Lily, Rose*. "Isn't that fucking brilliant?" And, as I turned my head up to the painting, "No, not that, you fucking dickhead, the title. Isn't that the most brilliant title in the world? I always come here to read it."

Regents Park. Winter. Trees like fan coral. Squirrel monkeys with fur a distinct shade of green scatter and run for their houses, squeaking with one high pitched voice. A strange, far-off, ululating call—lyrical but animalistic—goes out from the zoo as if something is signaling. Choe took me straight to its source: lar gibbons. "My favourite fucking animal." These sad, creamy-colored little things, with their dark eyes and curved arthritic hands, live in a long tall cage shaped like a sailing vessel. Inside, concrete blocks and hutches give the effect of deck and bridge fittings. The tallest of these is at the prow, where you can often see one gibbon on its own, crouched staring into the distance past the rhino house.

"Just look at them!" Choe said.

He showed me how they fold up when not in use, the curve of their hands and arms fitting exactly into the curve of their thigh. Knees under their chins they sit hunched in the last bit of winter sun, picking over a pile of lettuce leaves; or swing through the rigging of their vessel with a kind of absent-minded agility. They send out their call, aching and musical. It is raw speech, the speech of desires that can never be fulfilled, only suffered.

"Aren't they perfect?"

We watched them companionably for a few minutes.

"See the way they move?" Choe said suddenly. Then:

"When someone loves you, you feel this whole marvelous confidence in yourself. In your body, I mean."

I said nothing. I couldn't think how the two ideas were linked. He had turned his back on the cage and was staring angrily away into the park, where in the distance some children were running and shouting happily. He was inviting me to laugh at him. When I didn't, he relaxed.

"You feel good in it," he said. "For once it isn't just some bag of shit that carries you around. I—"

"Is that why you're trying to kill yourself, Choe?"

He stared at me.

"For fuck's sake," he said wearily.

Behind us the lar gibbons steered their long strange ship into the wind with an enormous effort of will. A small plaque mounted on the wire netting of the cage explained: "the very loud call is used to tell other gibbons the limit of its territory, especially in the mornings." I thought that was a pity.

In the spring he gave up his job with the agency and went offshore.

"I need some money," he said. "The rigs are the place for that. Besides, I like the helicopter ditching course."

He wanted to take the Kawa round Europe that summer.

"You need dosh to pay the speeding tickets." He thought for a moment. "I like Europe."

And then, as if trying to sum up an entire continent:

"I once jumped over a dog in Switzerland. It was just lying in the middle of the road asleep. I was doing a hundred and ten. Bloke behind me saw it too late and ran it over."

He was away for two or three months, but he hadn't forgotten anything. Whatever it was he wanted me for remained as important to him as it had been when he singled me out at the Dawes party. He came back at the height of summer and knocked at my door in Camden, wearing Levi 620s, brand new 16-hole DMs, a black sleeveless T-shirt which had faded to a perfect fusty green, and a single gold earring. We walked up between the market stalls to Camden Lock, where he sat in the sunshine blinking at the old curved bridge which lifts the towpath over the canal. His arms had been baked brown in Provence and Chamonix, but the peacock feathers still rioted down them, purple, green and electric blue, a surf of eyes; and on his upper left arm one tiny perfect rose had appeared, flushed and pink.

"How was Europe?" I asked him.

"Fucking brilliant," he said absently. "It was great."

"Get many tickets?"

"Too fucking right."

"I like the new tattoo."

"It's good."

We were silent for a bit. Then he said:

"I want to show you something."

"What?"

"It would mean driving up north."

Determined not to make a mistake this time, I said:

"Would two days' time do?"

"Are you sure you want to know this?"

I wasn't sure. But I said yes anyway. In fact it was four or five days before he was free to leave. He wheedled me into letting him drive. A blip in the weather brought strong south-west winds which butted and banged at the RS as he stroked it up the motorway at a steady hundred and twenty. Plumes of spray drifted across the carriageways, so that even the heaviest vehicle, glimpsed briefly through a streaming windscreen, seemed to be moving sideways as well as forwards, caught in some long dreamlike fatal skid. Beyond Nottingham, though, where the road petered out into roadworks, blocked exits and confusing temporary signboards, the cloud thinned suddenly.

"Blue sky!" said Choe, braking heavily to avoid the back of a fleet Cavalier, then dipping briefly into the middle lane to overtake it. Hunched forward over the steering wheel until his face was pressed against the windscreen, he squinted upwards.

"I can see sunshine!"

"Will you watch where you're fucking going?"

He abandoned the motorway and urged the RS into the curving back roads of the White Peak, redlining the rev counter between gear changes, braking only when the bend filled the windscreen with black and white chevrons, pirouetting out along some undrawn line between will and physics. I should have been frightened, but it was full summer, and the rain had brought the flowers out, and all I could see were horses up to their knees in moon-daisies. The verges were fat with clover and cow parsley. The foxgloves were like girls. Thick clusters of creamy flowers weighed down the elders, and wherever I looked there were wild roses the most tremulous pink and white. Every field's edge was banked with red poppies. That would have been enough—fields of red poppies!—but among them, perhaps one to five hundred, one to a thousand, there were sports or hybrids of a completely different color, a dull waxy purple, rather somber but fine.

"How odd! Did you see that, Choe?"

"Don't talk."

After about twenty minutes he stopped the car and switched the engine off.

"This is near enough for now."

We were in a long bleak lay-by somewhere on the A6. The road fell away from us in a gentle curve until it reached the flatter country west and north. Down there

I could see a town—houses for quarry workers, a junction with traffic lights, a tall steel chimney designed to pump hot gases up through the chronic inversion layers of Spring and Autumn.

"When I was a kid," Choe said, "I lived a few miles outside that place." He undid his seatbelt and turned to face me. "What you've got to understand is that it's a fucking dump. It's got that fucking big chimney, and a Sainsburys and a Woolworths, and a fucking bus station." He adjusted the driving mirror so that he could see his own face in it. "I hated that fucking bus station. You know why? Because it was the only way in and out. I went in and out on one of those fucking buses every day for ten years, to take exams, look for jobs, go round the record shop on a wet Saturday afternoon." He pushed the mirror back into its proper place. "Ever spend any time in bus stations?"

"Never."

"I didn't think you had. Let me tell you they're death on a stick. Only people who are socially dead use a bus station."

Everything warm, he said, went on at a distance from people like that. Their lives were at an ebb. At a loss. They had to watch the clean, the happy, the successfully employed, stepping out of new cars and into the lobbies of warm hotels. If the dead had ever been able to do that, they would never be able to do it again. They would never be able to dress out of choice or eat what they would like.

"They're old, or they're bankrupt, or they've just come out of a long-stay mental ward. They're fucked."

All over the north of England they stood around at ten in the evening waiting for the last bus to places called Chinley Cross, or Farfield or Penistone. By day it was worse.

"Because you can see every fucking back-end village you're going through. The bus is fucked, and it never gets up any speed." He appealed to me: "It stinks of diesel and old woollen coats. *And the fuckers who get on are carrying sandwich boxes.*"

I laughed.

"There's nothing intrinsically wrong with a sandwich box," I said.

"Do you want to hear this or not?"

"Sorry, Choe."

"I hated those fucking buses except for one thing—"

He was seventeen or eighteen years old. It was his last summer in the town. By September he would be at East Sussex. He would be free. This only seemed to make him more impatient. Women were everywhere, walking ahead of him on every pavement, packed into the vegetarian coffee-shop at lunchtime, laughing all afternoon on the benches in the new shopping plaza. Plump brown arms, the napes of necks: he could feel their limbs moving beneath the white summer dresses. He didn't want them. At night he fell out with his parents and then went upstairs to masturbate savagely over images of red-haired pre-Raphaelite women he had cut from a book of prints. He hardly understood himself. One afternoon a girl of his own age got on the bus at Stand 18. She was perfectly plain—a bit short and fat, wearing a cardigan of a color he described as "a sort of Huddersfield pink"—until she turned round and he saw that she had the most extraordinary green eyes. "Every different green was in them." They were the green of grass, of laurel leaves, the pale green of a bird's egg. They were the deep blue-green of every sea-cliché he had ever read. "And all at the same time. Not in different lights or on different days. All at the same time." Eyes intelligent, reflective of the light, not human: the eyes of a bird or an animal. They seemed independent of her, as if they saw things on behalf of someone else: as if whatever intelligence inhabited them was quite different from her own. They examined him briefly. In that glance, he believed, "she'd seen everything about me. There was nothing left to know." He was transfixed. If you had ridden that bus as an adult, he said, and seen those eyes, you might have thought that angels travel route X38 to Sheffield in disguise.

"But they don't. They fucking don't."

After that first afternoon she often traveled from Stand 18. He was so astonished by her that when she got off the bus one day at a place called Jumble Wood, he got off too and followed her. A nice middle-class road wound up between bungalows in the sunshine. Above them, on the lip of a short steep gritstone scarp, hung the trees: green and tangled, rather impenetrable. She walked past the houses and he lost sight of her: so he went up to the wood itself. Inside, it was smaller than he had expected, full of a kind of hot stillness. He sat down for a minute or two, tranquilized by the greenish gold light filtering down into the gloom between the oaks; then walked on, to find himself suddenly on the edge of a dry limestone valley. There was a white cliff, fringed with yew and whitebeam. There were grassy banks scattered with ferns and sycamore saplings. At his feet purple vetches twined their tendrils like nylon monofilament round the stems of the moon daisies. He was astonished by the wood avens, pure art nouveau with their complaisantly bowed yellow-brown flowerheads and strange spiky seed cases. He had never seen them before: or the heath spotted orchids, tiny delicate patterns like intaglio on each pale violet petal.

When he looked up again, sunshine was pouring into the narrow valley from its southwestern end, spilling through the translucent leaves of young ash trees, transfiguring the stones and illuminating the grassy slopes *as if from inside*—as if the whole landscape might suddenly split open and pour its own mysterious devouring light back into the world.

"So what did happen, Choe?"

Instead of answering he stared away from me through the windscreen, started the car up, and let it roll gently down the hill, until, on the right, I saw the turning and the sign:

JUMBLE WOOD.

"You decide," he said. "We'll walk up."

I don't know what he wanted me to see, except what he had seen all those years ago. All I found is what he had already described—the wood, smaller than you would expect, full of dust motes suspended in sunshine—and beyond that, on the knife-edge of the geological interface, the curious little limestone valley with its presiding crag like a white church.

"You're going to have to give me a bit more help," I said.

He knelt down.

"See this? Wood avens. I had to look it up in a book."

He picked one and offered it to me.

"It's pretty. Choe, what happened here?"

"Would you believe me if I told you the world really did split open?"

He gazed miserably away from me.

"What?" I said.

"Somehow the light peeled itself open and showed me what was inside. It was her. She walked out of it, with those eyes every green in the world." He laughed. "Would you believe me if I said she was naked, and she stank of sex, and she let me push her down there and then and fuck her in the sunshine? And then somehow she went back into the world and it sealed itself up behind her and I never saw her again?"

"Choe—"

"I was eighteen years old," he said. "It was my first fuck."

He turned away suddenly.

"It was my only fuck," he said. "I've never done it since. Whatever lives here loves us. I know it does. But it only loves us once."

He drove back to London in silence, parked the Escort in Camden and walked off to the tube. I telephoned him daily for two weeks, and then weekly for two months. All I got was his answering machine. In the end I gave up. Someone told me he had moved to Chiswick; someone else that he had left Britain altogether. Then one day in December I got a call from him. He was living in Gravesend.

"All that Jumble Wood stuff," he said. "I made it up. I only told you that to get you going, you know."

I said I would still like to talk.

"Can you get down here?"

I said I could, and we arranged a meeting. He rang to cancel three or four times. Each time it was back on within an hour or two. First I was to meet him at the bar of a pub called the Harbour Lights. Then, if I was bringing a car, at his flat. Finally he agreed to be in the main car park at one o'clock.

I drove down there along the coast road, past the rows of empty caravans, exhausted amusement parks and chemical factories which occupied the low ground between the road and the sea. Wet sleet had fallen on them all that month without once turning into snow. You could hear the women in the supermarkets congratulating themselves on being born on a warm coast, though in fact it was quite raw in the town that afternoon. I found Choe sitting on the wall of the car-park, kicking his feet, his jeans rolled up to show off a pair of paint-splattered workboots. He had shaved his hair off, then let it grow out two or three millimeters so that the bony plates of his skull showed through, aggressive and vulnerable at the same time. He seemed bored and lonely, as if he had been sitting there all morning, his nose running, his face and arms reddening in the wind from the sea.

He jumped off the wall.

"You'll love the Harbour Lights!" he promised, and we began to walk down through the town towards the sea. Quite soon, everything was exciting him again: a girl getting out of a new car; brilliantly colored skateboard components displayed in the window of the Surf Shack; an advertisement for a film he hadn't seen. "See that? Wow!" He waved his arm. "And look at those fucking gannets up there!"

Thinking perhaps that he had thrown them something, the circling birds—they
were actually herring gulls—dipped and veered abruptly in their flight.

"They could wait forever!"

"They're big strong birds," I agreed.

He stared at me.

"I'm fucking scared of them," he said.

"I thought you were scared of nowt."

He laughed.

We had come out on to the sea-front, and there was the Harbour Lights, facing
out across the bay where a handful of wind-surfers bobbed around on a low swell,
their bright sails signaling in acid greens and pinks from a lost summer. "You should
see the pies in here," Choe said delightedly. "There's a kind of black residue in
them. It's the meat."

We went in and sat down.

"Tell me about what you do," he said.

I opened my mouth but he interrupted immediately.

"Look at this place!"

It seemed no different from any other pub on a flat coast, but perhaps that was
what he meant. The brewery had put in an imitation ship's bell; a jukebox played
'60s surfer classics. At one end of the long cavernous bar were a few empty seafood
trays under chipped glass, while at the other the barman was saying to a woman in
a torn fur coat, "You've picked a bad day." He hurried off down to the other end,
where he seemed to fall into a dream. She smiled vaguely after him, then took off
one shoe to examine the heel. A small tan and white dog, driven to hysteria by this
act, rushed barking at her bare foot. The locals laughed and winked at one another.

Choe stared at them with dislike.

"You went along with all this so you'd have something to write," he accused me.

I got my notebook out and put it on the table between us.

"It's a living, Choe."

I went to the bar to get the drinks. "Write something about me then," he said
when I came back. He grinned. "Go on! Now! I bet you can!"

"I don't do portraits, Choe."

The lies liberated from this statement skittered off into infinity like images between
two mirrors. He must have sensed them go, because instead of answering he stood
up and turned his back on me and pretended to look out of the window at the
aimless evolutions of the windsurfers—

They would tack hesitantly towards one another until they had gathered in a slow
drift like a lot of ducks on a pond: then one of them, his sail like neon in the sleety
afternoon light, would shoot out of the mass and fly for quarter of a mile across the
bay in a fast, delirious curve, spray shuddering up around him as he leapt from
wave to wave. During this drive he seemed to have broken free not just from the
other surfers but from Gravesend, winter, everything. Every line of his body tautened
against the pull of the sail—braced feet, bent legs, yellow flotation jacket—was like
an advert for another climate.

Sooner or later, though, the board would swerve, slow down suddenly, subside.
Abandoned by the wind, the bright sail, after hunting about for a second or two in
surprise, sagged and fell into the water like a butterfly into a bath, clinging to a

moment of self-awareness too confused to be of any use. This made Choe Ashton shiver and stare round the bar.

"These fuckers have all committed suicide," he said. His face was so pale I thought he was going to be sick.

"Be fair, Choe," I said cruelly. "You like the pies."

"I won't let you write anything about me."

"How can you stop that, Choe?"

He shrugged.

"I could beat the fuck out of you," he said.

Outside, the tide was coming in resolutely; the light was fading. I went out to the lavatory. Among the stickers on the bar door was one saying, "Prevent Hangovers—Stay Drunk." When I got back the woman at the bar was doing up her coat. "I'd put far too much cayenne in," she told the barman, "but we had to eat it anyway!" The tan and white dog was begging from table to table, and Choe Ashton had gone. I found him outside. Twenty or thirty herring gulls had gathered shrieking above him in the darkening air, and he was throwing stones at them with single-minded ferocity. It was some time before he noticed me. He was panting.

"These fuckers," he said. "They can wait forever." He rubbed the inside of his elbow. "I've hurt my arm."

"They only live a year or two, Choe."

He picked up another stone. The gulls shrieked.

"I only told you that stuff to get you going," he said. "None of it was true. I never even lived there."

I have no idea what happened to Choe Ashton in Jumble Wood. Whatever he says now though, I believe he returns there year after year, probably on the day he took me, the anniversary of his first and perhaps single sexual experience. It is as much an attempt to reassure himself of his own existence as that of the girl he believes came out of the inside of the world. I imagine he stands there all afternoon watching the golden light angle moment to moment across the valley. Seen in the promise of this light, the shadows of the sycamore saplings are full of significance; the little crag resembles a white church. Behind him, on the gritstone side of the geological divide, the wood is hot and tranquil and full of insects. His hand resting on the rough bark of an oak he appeals time and again to whatever lives in that place— "Bring her back. Bring her back to me."—only to be hurt time and again by its lack of response.

I understand that. I understand why he might want to obscure it. From me. From himself. What I don't understand is my own dream.

I've lost no one. My life is perfectly whole. I never dreamed anything like this until I met Choe Ashton. It's since then that I can no longer accept a universe empty of meaning, even if I must put it there myself.

SKIN

Steve Rasnic Tem

In addition to being a writer of fiction, Steve Rasnic Tem is a poet whose work has appeared in *Isaac Asimov's Science Fiction Magazine, Amazing Stories, The Bennington Review, Puerto del Sol,* and in the anthologies *Dragons of Light* and *Blood Is Not Enough*. This short poem first appeared in *Psychos: An Anthology of Psychological Horror in Verse*.

"Skin" is one of a series of approximately eighty poems Tem is writing about different parts of the body.

—E.D.

This costume is what
they know you by,
this disguise
in which you've been upholstered.
Under the skin
the springs are bending
into a pose of comfort
but the stuffing goes rotten
whatever you do. This shroud
keeps the air out
but does not stop the voices
calling your secret name
asking where you've gone
as you in your hiding place
gaze from two rigid holes.

THE HOMUNCULUS:
A Novel in One Chapter

Reginald McKnight

Reginald McKnight is the author of the acclaimed novel *I Get on the Bus,* as well as the collection *Moustapha's Eclipse.* He is the winner of the O. Henry Award, the Kenyon Review New Fiction Prize, the Drue Heinz Prize, and a 1991 National Endowment for the Arts Grant for Literature. McKnight lives in Pittsburgh, Pennsylvania, where he teaches at Carnegie-Mellon University.

"The Homunculus" is a tale both humorous and disturbing in which a writer confronts the devouring power of his imagination. The story comes from McKnight's excellent recent collection, *The Kind of Light That Shines on Texas.*

—T.W.

Many, many years ago there lived a young artist, who, the people said, was full of great potential and great talent. What kind of artist was he? you ask, knowing full well that in our present age almost anyone from a computer programmer to an oil twiller to a grocery boxer is called an artist. Well, my friend, this young man was skilled in many, many things. First of all, he was a marvelous poet. Some say his poetry was on a par with the finest, most well-known poets of that day, though the young man was barely into his twenties when his third book of poetry was published.

He was an adept fiction writer, too. His short stories and novels were the talk of the entire Realm. His saddest stories could squeeze the heart like a great fist. The funniest could rattle the ribs and stop the breath. He wrote with a spare style that somehow cast arabesque shadows in the mind, causing his reading audience to ponder the depths of the soul in all its turns and bends.

It is well known even in our present age that he could sculpt and paint in such a wide array of moods, styles, themes, and patterns that he held the entire art world breathlessly wondering in what untrodden ground he would next place his intrepid, daring feet.

It is also said that he could sing and play lyre, lute, kleetello, guitar, dulcimer, fiddle, cello, and vibraphone. His voice rang with such power and clarity that his audiences (particularly the females) were said to be held in a sort of speechless rapture for days and days after one of his concerts.

He was also very handsome, kind, modest, soft-spoken, gentle, and honest. He respected his elders, was generous to his peers, fatherly to the young. He gave alms to the poor, cheer to the sullen, wisdom to the foolish, attention to the marginal.

But he was not happy.

You ask, my friend, why this wonderful soul, this light of the world, this one, who, as our people say, so clearly showed the "thumbprint of the Old One" was not happy? No one knew. Not even the young artist himself really knew, or at least he was unwilling to say. Those of a spiritual inclination said that it was his karma. That he was born an artistic genius on a plane in which he could neither quite fully express himself nor be completely understood. Those of a more skeptical persuasion—there were a handful—said that it was because of a deeply embedded but well-hidden vanity, and a lust for absolute power. They said that all he created, either consciously or unconsciously, he created to subjugate the minds and hearts of his audience and ultimately to make them his slaves.

But others said—though none had ever heard him confess this—that it was because he could not have the love of one woman: Nohla, the beautiful daughter of the kindly, humble miller, Rafkhan. They said that the two were in love for only one year, though in secret (Rafkhan had great hopes that Nohla would one day become a surgeon, and he would sooner lose his right hand than see his child's future fuddled by love), but then, quite suddenly, Nohla, either because she saw something in the young artist that was akin to what his detractors, those few skeptics, saw, or because she became convinced her father was right, ended the affair. All that we can say is that she carried some deep, unfathomable discomfiture in her bosom that told her she could no longer be with this man, and so she shattered his young heart.

Whatever the reasons, the young man stopped creating and entertaining before the year was over. He seldom left his home after a while, but sat inside for weeks and months on end, brooding and pacing. He let his beard grow long, let his countenance sour, and ate little. It has been said that his servants heard him sing from time to time, but only to himself, almost in a whisper, in a cracked, atonal voice. He admitted very few friends: his brother, Rhoe the Mighty, still, statistically, the greatest treadleback in the history of our national sport, and his close friend and neighbor, Azzizan. Neither Rhoe nor Azzizan could bear to see their young loved one in such pain and grief. But when they would ask him, "What ails ye, brother?" "What grinds thee, friend?," all that he is said to have answered was, "Me? I'm just thinking. Just thinking, that's all." Then one day, after an evening of putting mouth to ear and ear to mouth in an alehouse not far from the young artist's house, Rhoe and Azzizan decided they should persuade the young man to take a journey. After several weeks they succeeded.

The young artist took only a fortnight preparing for the journey, traveling throughout the Greater Realm to say good-bye to all his friends and patrons. Then, at last, he set sail for what legend calls the Land of Light and Dark. He was at sea for some three months, and during the entire journey kept himself in his cabin in much the same way he had kept to himself in his home. It was a journey without incident, for the most part. The crew on the ship were of the usual rambunctious sort, and often kept the young man awake nights with their perpetual revelry, pranks, and boisterous, bold talk about what they would do once putting down in the Land of Light and Dark.

The Land, as you know, is no more. It was swallowed by our oceans uncountable years ago. Our archaeologists have recovered, what? a few buttons, a chalice or two, a bronze slingshot? We know so little of the physical place. All we have are these stories, and who knows precisely how true they are. The Land is now a place more of mystery and legend than of history and fact. In it, we are told, were five of the eight known mysteries of the Ur-Realm. It was known to be a land of both blood-freezing violence and beauty so profound that it is said the Old One actually slept there. With its winged people with the skin of polished obsidian who spoke only in proverbs, its diamond white rivers that cut through soil so rich that the meanest, bitterest seed would sprout into waxy green leaves and pulpy fruit, with its dramatic waterfalls, its infinite canyons, its smoke blue mountains, its caverns of gold and jade, its many curiously constructed beasts, who, it is said, spoke the language of the winged people, the young artist told himself that no other land could bring out in him what had been so deeply buried.

The first several months in this strange land went well for the young artist. He made many friends, ate strange and delightful foods, swam the diamond waters, drank sweet teas that made him dream of Nohla. He shaved off his beard and dressed in the fine, bright clothing of the obsidian people. He learned some of their language, which inspired in him sage thought. He let them carry him aloft and show him the world as only birds could see it. Things went well for him. His heart grew big again. And one morning he awoke in a creative flame. He began to write!

It had been so long since he had written anything that he took the cautious road and began keeping a journal. In it he wrote of everything he was seeing and doing and feeling. He devoted just as much time to describing, in detail, all the strange fruits and vegetables there as he did to describing the people and the geography. He also wrote of the things in his heart, of his dissatisfaction with his past work, his weaknesses as a human being, and his great love for Nohla.

His writing, steady, furious, impassioned, came to take up more and more of his time. He seldom ventured outside his house, and he spent less and less time with his friends. And on three occasions his friend N'Tho, a good man, a tall, intelligent man who'd saved him from the grip of a waterfall he'd ventured too close to in his first week in the country, rapped on his door and asked him, would he not care for a slice of yellow sunshine, a bowl of friendship, and a cup of laughter. And each time the young artist would smile and thank him, but say no. "Your land has . . . has, uh, set me afire, and the smithy's best work is at noon." And N'Tho would turn and leave, saying, "Is it true that when the bird finishes its nest it no longer cares whether the grass grows?"

"No, no, good friend," would be the reply, "but the, uh, whispers of the heart are greater than the screams of the flesh." And one, two, three times did he close the door on the retreating back of N'Tho.

It wasn't long before he was virtually friendless, before, as we say in the southern region, his kitchen grew quiet. But he never noticed. His work had reached such a feverish intensity that not even he realized for the longest time that his journal had become first a novel, then a poem, then a prayer, than a chant, then a one-act play, an opera—it actually made sound!—a painting, a sculpture—and then— wonder of wonders—the thing became flesh! A miniature version of himself!

Of course, finally he did notice himself, but it did take a while, for his work still compelled him, devoured him, you might say, and—quite naturally—his mind was rather distracted. But one day as he scribbled and chiseled and stitched upon the . . . text . . . we shall call it, he began to notice that his fingers were clutching his own throat, in a manner of speaking, and his thumbs were shaping his own, well . . . it wasn't a sentence anymore, he had to admit to himself. It wasn't a canvas or clay, it was—"My chin!" he said aloud. "Blessed Old One, I—"

" 'Bout time you noticed, homes."

"You're me—"

"Uh-huh—"

"A little version of—"

" 'At's right."

"Oh my."

He silently disrobed, put out his candle, and went to sleep. When he awoke the next morning, his mind felt clear, and he chuckled, thinking to himself that perhaps he had been working too hard. He decided to get up, wash, have a large breakfast, and spend the day visiting his friends. But as he reached for his robes he saw his little self sitting on the edge of his writing desk, eating a page of his journal. "What are you doing?" he demanded.

The homunculus shot his black beady gaze at his maker. "You mean what am *I* doing?" he said.

"Who are you? What are you? Where did you come—"

"What it look like I'm doing, fool?"

"That's my journal! Stop that, you—"

"But I'ma tell you something, brother. You got to cut down on the salt. See, when you bending over your work, hacking away like you do, you be sweating all *over* these pages. But other than that they pretty good." The young artist looked at the little creature, and he could not help but be torn between a number of emotions: anger, fear, astonishment, and, perhaps most discomforting of all, admiration, for the little man was perfect in every way that the eyes could discern. Black eyes and black hair, white teeth, sharp jawbones, powerful arms, long fingers, seamless skin, a spine as straight as a shaft of light. He was magnificent, and were it not for the little man's crude language, and most especially, were it not for the fact that the little one was eating his journal by the fistful, the artist would have liked to sit the chap on his knee and study him. But the very fact that the homunculus *was* eating his journal kept all action at bay, impelled the cycle of these emotions.

Finally, however, as the little man reached for the third of the eight-hundred-eighty-eight-page manuscript, the young artist possessed himself enough to clutch the finger-sized arm of this literary gourmand. "Do you mind?" the young man said.

The homunculus looked him up and down. He arched an eyebrow. "Yes I do, man. Lemme go."

"You're making a mess of my journal."

"Well I ad*mit* I ain't got good table manners, but I'ma still eat this thing."

"Like Hatsax you will!" And the young artist grabbed the pitcher near his bed and smashed it down where the homunculus stood. But as you might guess, it was in vain, for the creature had disappeared.

The young artist spent the better part of the day overturning his rooms in search of the creature's hole or portal or whatever it might be the thing had come through. He ordered his servants to keep the place clean and to make sure that the doors remained shut and that the window screens were kept in place. Nevertheless, he found nothing. Exhausted, stiff with anger, he gathered himself enough to brew a cup of tea and sit down to write. He wanted to rewrite those first two pages of his journal. But this was a problem because the last several months of work had flown with such momentum that there had simply been no time for him to stop and reread what he'd written. He'd no idea where to begin. "I remember something about fruits and vegetables . . . and people, yes, people with wings, and Nora, my love." Nora? he thought. No, it was Noah, or Nova, or . . . Really he was not sure, and it occurred to him that he was too long out of touch with those things that had moved him, lo those months ago, to journey to this land and rediscover his creative embers. "Yes," he said, "first thing tomorrow I will visit my old friends the What's-Their-Names and that nice tall fellow whose life I saved when he ventured too close to the falls, and I'll see those people and talk to them or something. Perhaps they can explain this nonsense." He drank one last cup of tea and went to bed.

A warm yellow light leaked into his bedroom and crept up his sheets. He opened his eyes, then aimed his hearing at what he'd dreamed was the sound of frying fish. He sniffed the air, half expecting his nose to fill with the sweet smell of ocean pod or peacefish or tin-shells. But he could smell nothing. And the frying sound, he discovered, was not the sound of fresh fish bubbling in hot oil but the sound of crackling paper. "It's back," he hissed.

The little artist licked a finger, then licked another. "Morning, blood. Thought you wasn't never gonna get up."

The young artist hurled the sheet off his legs and sprang to his feet. "What are you doing to me?"

"Is you stupid? Take a scope at y'self, boy. I'm here 'cause you here. But yo, what kinda ink you use on page eight, homely? It's giving me serious gastronomics."

As though he were alone, the young man snapped his fingers, and said, "It's the tea! Of course, the tea! Oh, Blessed the Old One be! That's it, yes, that's it and I swear it off forever." He snatched up his clothes and dressed himself on the way out of the room, thinking these thoughts: "What I do first, you see, is go see my friends and have them over to my place. If they see no Little Me—and they won't—I'll know for certain that it was the tea I've been drinking, not to mention the strain of working, the poor diet, the dearth of sunshine and exercise and fresh air. Oh my dear friends, oh my dear Nolna, you shall soon have me again."

The poor boy. Had he paid closer mind to the culture of the Land of Light and Dark, he would have known that to refuse a slice of yellow sunshine, a bowl of friendship, and a cup of laughter three consecutive times, without indicating to the friend that he should return before the new moon, is to flatly refuse the friendship forever and always; he would probably, at the very least, have invited N'Tho in for a minute or two. Too bad he did not. For that whole morning, door after door pushed at the heels of the young artist, until it became clear to him that he had somehow become anathema to the winged people. He walked home with stooped shoulders. "Well," he said to himself, "at least I've still got Nonah." But it soon occurred to him that he could not conjure an image of her face, and as he turned the knob of his door he finally admitted to himself that he couldn't remember her name. "But it must be in my journal," he thought, and dashed to his studio. He found his little self, with a round, full stomach and closed eyes, snoozing atop his much-reduced manuscript. "You little spawn of Hatsax! You Old-forsaken pup of a scuttlerat. You oily-lipped, foul, cretinous do—"

The little one shot up from his supine position and backed himself against the wall. "Yo, man, ice'n up yourself. You buggin, homeboy." But the young artist would have no more. He grabbed his letter opener and lunged at the little beast. Of course, he missed. "Look, man," the homunculus said, scrambling atop a lamp, "chill. All that salt you done layed down on them pages gonna kill me before you do. Your stuff's getting harder to eat every five minutes. I'ma be honest with you, man. Page sixty-three I simply could not get past my soup coolers."

The young artist hadn't realized he'd dropped the letter opener till he heard it clatter to the floor. "You've eaten sixty-two pages?"

"Sixty-five if you don't count page sixty-three. Th'ew that one away." The homunculus reached into his pocket, pulled out a tiny pipe, a tiny book of matches, lit the pipe, took a long deep puff, blew the smoke in the young artist's face, shook out the match, and squinted one black eye at his maker. "So, what you writing about, boy?" he said.

"You mean you don't even know?"

The little one slipped the matchbook back into his pocket, shuffled his feet a bit, and said, "Well, not really, but I am what I eat, I guess you could say."

The artist dropped into a chair and hung his head low. What was the use of fighting? he thought. He was clearly insane. His friends had abandoned him; it was probably too late to begin reading his work now, for if he could not remember his old love's name or the color of her hair or the shape of her smile, what was the use in fighting? This little version of himself, whether he be real or illusory, was, it seemed, all he had. The two of them sat till the sun began to cast its orange light in through the southern windows of his studio. The only sound that could be heard was the hiss and burble of the little one's pipe. Suddenly, the homunculus spoke. "Tell me something, Skippy," he said. "Whycome you never stopped to read what you wrote?"

The artist shrugged and sighed. "I don't know, exactly. Fear, perhaps? It's everything I've ever wanted to do, I've ever wanted to say. It's my whole life. It's about my lovely What's-Her-Name. It's . . . rather it could be—*could* have been, anyway, the greatest work ever created. Old One! There is something wonderful about it. And . . . and even if no one had ever liked it, why, even if no one had ever even read it, I know in my heart that it's changed me. It's done something to me. How all this has happened—how it resulted in you, I mean—I don't know, but I have just known it was a great work. So great, perhaps, that I knew that even I wouldn't be able to understand it." He let his head fall to the back of his chair, but kept his eyes on the little one. The little one sucked on his pipe, grimacing every now and then, but let several minutes go by before he said, "You hongry?"

"No."

"I'm hongry. You mind?"

The artist shrugged. The homunculus chuckled softly, took the pipe from his mouth, and knocked out the ashes on the artist's desk. "Yep," he said. "Look like to me this great work a yours is just about finito, buddy-bud. Ain' no sense in letting it go to waste. Sure you don't mind?"

The young man made no reply.

"So," said the homunculus, "you writing this here thing for the love of some woman, huh?" And then he turned to, gobbling, smacking, chewing with great heat. "Well," said the young artist, in a voice that could have been no more hollow had he spoken into a bucket while standing in the middle of a prayer chamber. "Well," said he, "at first I didn't think so. I never admitted it to myself, but the more I wrote the more it seemed so. But then the work itself became the thing. And I—" Out the corner of his eye he noted the flurry of movement as the little one fed himself. The leaves of the manuscript flew in a haze of motion, and the arms and hands of the homunculus appeared to multiply by twos and fours, so frenetically did he propel them. And by increments the little thing began to grow. At two hundred twenty-two pages he'd doubled in size, at four hundred forty-four he'd quadrupled. By now he was half the size of his maker. But the artist began to notice something more unsettling than this: The little man looked enormously uncomfortable; his arms seemed to move by themselves; every dozen pages or so he would feverishly glance up at his maker. His eyes seemed to say, stop me, why don't you! He looked nauseous with panic, but still he ate in a hail of movement. Finally, he was swallowing the eight hundred eighty-eighth page. He looked precisely, exactly, undeniably like his maker, inch for inch, whisker for whisker. The only differences between the two men were that one sat in a chair, the other on the desk, and one looked astonished and bemused, the other queasy and gray. The queasy one said, through trembling lips, "Y-you better read this motherfuh-fuh, man, 'cause—" Too late. He folded over as if cut in two, and vomited the entire manuscript, unchewed, unwrinkled, unripped, unsoggy, with the force of an unknotted water balloon. And he shrunk at a rate faster than he'd grown. And he disappeared in a puff of blue smoke. And he didn't come back.

The young artist began reading what he'd written almost immediately. Including page sixty-three. He never gave his double another thought. He read unceasingly for eight days and eight nights, one hundred eleven pages per day. When he finished, he floated the eight hundred eighty-eighth page onto the floor and sobbed till his temples pounded and his throat clamped nearly shut. He had taken no food and water for a week and a day, and, of course, fell gravely ill. He plunged into a well of sleep. A great fever swept through him, so great it was that it touched off a tremendous fire in his rooms, a fire which neither burned him nor even woke him. But all his work was lost.

On the ninth day he awoke and found his rooms whole, and cleaner than they had been in months. The doctor, whom his servants had called eight days before, felt his forehead, shook his hand, and wished him well. His chambermaid brought him a hearty meal of rice and sauce, fruit and vegetables. The next morning he made arrangements to return home. He packed all his possessions but searched in vain for his work. He moved the furniture this way and that way, but could find nothing.

He returned to the Realm and rented a small room near the Central Square. And he learned that during the one thousand seven hundred seventy-six days he had been gone, it had come to pass that his work was no longer regarded as the great thing it once had been. Other talented young artists had replaced him in the hearts of the people. But this did not perturb him. He had read his work, and he knew.

He spent the rest of his days working with Rafkhan the miller (whose daughter, they say, became a great impresario somewhere in the Outer Realm; Rafkhan never spoke her name from the day she left, so it never was remembered to the artist). He listened to the music of singers and composers, and studied, with admiration, the literature of the most popular writers and poets of the day. He visited museums. He bought inexpensive art, when he could, and decorated his room nicely. He married a young woman who had never heard of him. He raised seven sons and daughters. He took hardly any salt at all in his food.

He died at the age of one hundred sixteen, neither a happy man nor a sad man.

THE ANNUNCIATION

Cristina Peri Rossi

Cristina Peri Rossi was born in Montevideo in 1941 and studied literature at the University of Montevideo. Because of her resistance to the military takeover of Uruguay, she was forced to flee to Barcelona, Spain, in 1972, where she still resides. Rossi's published work includes collections of short stories, journalistic essays, and poems, including *Indicios pánicos*; *La rebelión de los ninos*; and *El museo de los esfuerzos inútiles*. An English translation of her novel *The Ship's Fool* was published in London in 1989.

In the following story (translated from the Spanish by Mary Jane Tracy) the fantastic and the miraculous remain in the eye of the beholder. Like many of her tales, it speaks to the political events of her native land without ever confronting them directly. Rather, she lets the Story speak, directly to the heart.

—T.W.

The Virgin Mary appeared while I was collecting stones from the water. I collect the big stones, not the little ones. She seemed to come from the sea, although I'm not really sure because the water is everywhere you look, and I was stooped over, my head down, collecting stones. I lift them out of the water, pick out the best, carry them in my arms and take them up to shore. At first I didn't think it was the Virgin.

That morning it was gray and lead-colored like the sea.

I had seen her only once before, in church, when we took her out for a procession. I never thought I'd see her walking down the beach with those special colored eyes and that sadness over the death of her son. I couldn't imagine it because I'm always alone and because she didn't have her crown, that Virgin's crown, but there she was, softly stamping down the sand under her feet. But then, I didn't doubt it for an instant. There's never anyone on this beach, hidden away as it is and somewhat far from the rest of the land. It's so remote, isolated, and only has the sea for company. I'm always alone, collecting stones. At first my hands freeze and my fingers slip; my fingers that want to grab onto the stones and hunt them as if they were sea animals. Whale stones, mountains from the sea. Straight ahead, down below, and to both sides, all you see is water, green and blue water, yellowish water, and enormous rocks stuck there like boats run aground. I plunge my hands in, and

66

my fingers slip from the wet surfaces of the stones. The color of the stones changes
when you take them out of the water. Sometimes they are full of moss and lichens,
full of seaweed tangled up with sea urchins. But when your hands get used to it,
they move through the water like fish. Then I rest them on the dark surface of a
stone, take it between my fingers, and bring it up. Once the stones are hoisted up,
I carry them to shore.

*We got here ten days ago, and since then we haven't seen anyone. Nobody has
seen us.*

The fishermen's boats are tossed on the sand, abandoned. There are wildflowers
growing up around the spongy boards of one of them, green stems and a white
crown among the damp and splintered planks. It's dying slowly. It's dying, falling
apart, lying there on the sand. A seagull flies overhead, its wings forming a cross,
its chest dark, and it comes down lightly. It perches on the boat's useless oar, which
is stuck, shaft first, into the sand. It used to be that when the fishermen went out
to sea, in each boat there was a big lamp up front like an eye that lit up underwater
secrets, the private life of the water and its fish, a round eye without lids, with a
powerful and serene gaze. The fishermen used to clean it, scrub it, adjust its light,
watch over it. Now their lamps rest caked with rust and drip their menstrual blood
on to the sand.

Just a little boy who plays in the water and collects stones.

Sometimes a ship goes by in the distance. The sand invades the shore and climbs
over the empty boats. I collect stones and carry them away from the water so that
when the waves lick up the shore they don't find them. I work like this all morning.
I often get tired of carting stones. My fingers are cold and cramping, the air is green,
the trees roar with the wind, the waves howl, and I can tell there is some disturbance;
the atmosphere, the elements are preparing something, something is developing in
the sea's womb. But when I look at the water and see so many stones beneath, I go
back to my work right away without getting distracted, without stopping because
there are so many more at the bottom. The water goes through my legs when I
squat down, the water and some small fish, silvery, agile and uneasy. I don't know
if they see me. I've never known what or how fish see, nor where they are looking,
with those big, staring eyes. I don't know if they look through the water, if their
glances are scattered among the stones and the seaweed at the bottom. I was never
a fish. I didn't have fins on my side, I wasn't born in the sea, I didn't eat seaweed.

In such a lonely place.

There are stones of many colors, I'd say of all the known colors and of some
others that only come from the sea and from living in the sea among lichens and
plants. She didn't wear a crown; she was walking slowly, floating over the sand.

*As if he weren't alone, as if the water, the stones, and the sound of the wind were
his companions. Totally absorbed in his work and somehow understanding the
harmony of the universe. He found his role, his function in this routine task, and he
took it on with dignity and respect, with conviction. Only the gulls have been able
to see us.*

I collect stones every day, even if it rains or is windy. Sometimes the sea is calm
when I go in, calm and still like an elephant lying on its side sleeping. The boats
don't move, and their masts look like crosses. The water then is very heavy, as if it
were made of stone. It's solid water, water made of cement. Nothing moves on its

surface, nothing moves below. The sea's activity stops; it becomes dense and all water looks the same: heavy. Motionless, it marks everything with its peace; even the birds seem to fly more slowly so as not to disturb it. Other times, the wind blows hard and the gulls can't fly. They stay a long time hanging in the air, their wings tensed and open, unfolded, but unable to go forward. They cry and don't move, as if a string kept them prisoners. And the sea is full of waves, waves that disappear in the misty atmosphere. Then the boats get nervous and try to flee from the storm and find refuge in the beach huts; there are some that are so eager to get away that they pull on their ropes until they cut loose, and once freed, get silly, like wanton and wild girls, going this way and that, losing their way, bumping up against each other and against the rocks, hitting their hips on the stones. The wind roars, the waves splash over the wall, the red buoys sink in this turbulent sea, and after an instant pop up again, keeping their heads up as if they were shipwrecked and trying with all their might to keep afloat until someone rescues them. The sea roars and everything seems like it's just about to break: the gray and mauve sky into thunder and lightning, the gulls' tense wings, the little stone and wooden pier, the boats' ropes, the lanterns and masts that list from one side to another.

How has he ended up here? Who could have brought him?

There are white statues under the sea. I've seen them: sculptured images of women, sometimes missing an arm, sometimes a leg, others an entire head. They are not always there; they aren't always visible. Sometimes the colors of the sea cover them up totally; at other times its the long string of seaweed and its inhabitants, the sea urchins, that hide their presence. Driven so deeply into the bottom of the sea, they could be mistaken for it, if the bottom were white, if it had a woman's hips. They never come to the surface. No current lifts them up, places them on a water pedestal. No force from the bottom of the sea hoists them, raises them like a banner. They don't come up to look at the sky or to lie down in the sand like bathers. There is nothing that makes them want to leave the water. They don't dream about the air or touching land. Sunk into the bottom of the sea, sometimes they let a leg or white arm be seen, and they hide their figures, their delicate hands, their tilted necks. They hide their secrets, aloof, among the folds of their gowns, and the oblivious fish pass by, touching them lightly, nibbling their breasts, licking their white necks. They are totally different from the mutilated bodies that the sea sometimes brings up from the depths of war and throws on to shore, with their panic-stricken eyes and hair streaked with seaweed. Decent people, silently and without getting involved, gather them up—they don't have teeth, ears, fingers, hands—and bury them up in the mountain. Unhappy people hide them in silence, studding the forest and fouling the land with their bodies.

How has he ended up here? Who could have brought him?

I was picking up a stone when I saw her coming from far away. Then I didn't know who was coming. The morning was green and the sea was murky. I only saw a gray figure that was coming with the wind. The stone was heavy, and I had to hold it with both hands. I stole it from the bottom of the sea when it was still golden; the air immediately darkened it and the water had taken little bites out of its surface, like so many eyes that now looked at me. I put it on the sand, far away from the sea's incessant drilling and layering, and I went back to shore, not without first looking at the gray figure that was coming with the wind and slowly getting closer.

"Who is the boy?"

"He comes and goes from the water as if the sea were his domain. As if only he reigned over the entire area. But humbly. Like a worker. Concentrating hard on his tasks. Without stopping, I think he never rests.

That morning everything was green, gray and green like under the water, like the color of the fish parading among the stones.

I couldn't turn back then because he had seen me. Anyway he was very caught up in his work of carrying stones.

I went back and forth. Back and forth. There were a lot of stones on the bottom; the bottom is always full of stones and seaweed. She was slowly coming closer. Like the waves, like the wind, she was coming closer, crunching the sand under her feet. She walked slowly without moving her arms, and it seemed that her legs were barely moving. I don't know if she came out of the water or where she came from because I was very busy with the stones, which were giving me a lot to do. I didn't look anywhere but straight ahead. I didn't look back or off to one side.

I was going to keep on my way, happy that I had not done anything to arouse his interest, when suddenly he looked straight at me, as if he recognized me, as if he had seen me before. He drove his eyes right into me and slowly, very slowly, as if he were identifying me feature by feature, as if his memory were bringing back marks, fingerprints, he straightened up right in front of me, now completely sure.

I was going to keep at my work; I was going to go back to the water and bend down to get another stone when I saw her. I looked at her from up close and I recognized her. I was fixed to the spot.

I hesitated a second.

He was in front of me.

I thought about running away. Fleeing.

It's not every day you see the Virgin coming out of the water. It's not every day she comes walking down the beach. She didn't seem to be wet, and her clothes were completely dry. She had eyes the color of the sea just like I'd seen at church one time when they put her out in public and took her on a procession through the town. We children and the old people carried her around like a trophy from the sea, as if she were a gigantic exotic fish that was going to feed us all year long. We took her out of church and carried her through the town's cobbled streets, and everyone came out to look at her. The windows were opened and women and children threw flowers at her, old people left their beds to see her, and men who were standing at the bar turned around, put their drinks aside, and respectfully doffed their hats to greet her. Throughout the entire procession, I was afraid that she'd fall off her pedestal—the streets were cobbled after all—and roll on the ground, and that her black mourning cape would get all dirty and she'd lose the beautiful handkerchief that she held in her hands for drying her eyes at the death of her son. I was on the edge the whole time, watching her step by step, out of fear that she'd stumble and fall and that her delicate porcelain hands would get broken and that she'd lose her crown, and that tears would flood her eyes.

One time when we caught a very big fish, there was a holiday and procession and everybody came out to look at it. At night they put candles all around it, and some people made bonfires on the beach. All night the whales snored on the high seas.

And instead of running away, I ran toward her and once I was close, I bowed. I bowed formally for a moment. She looked at me calmly; then I raised my head and saw that her eyes were the color of water. I remembered those eyes well from the day of the procession, sad and undefinably tender eyes, the eyes of a woman whose son has been killed and who feels so much pain that she doesn't think about vengeance because her sadness is so great that it brings out more love than anger. That woman's son had been killed—his body was probably still floating in the water and one of these days would appear on shore, his throat cut and an eye gouged out, full of seaweed and lichens, full of mud—and now she was walking down the beach. You could tell she was suffering from her eyes although she looked serene enough. I handed her a fishbone cup to hold the water from her eyes, in case she wanted to cry. It was really a bowl made from a very big fish, just the right size to hold sea water, fruit juices, women's tears. It's also useful to dig in the sand, to make holes. She looked at the cup and took it into her hands. Bone gets white with time, white and dry, with little black holes. She seemed to like her present, but she didn't cry right away. She held it in her hands a long time, and she looked at herself in it as if it were a mirror. Right away, I set out to clean the sand so she could sit down. I picked a square space, sheltered from the sea and the wind, protected by some wild rush. The dunes there are as high as mountains, and they almost hide the woods. The mounds are so hard and compact that nothing can sweep them away, not a whipping wind, not even a drifting sea. I cleaned the space with wicker rods, taking off the ants, insects, pieces of wood, shells, and all the other things the sea had left behind. I swept the surface with great care and, stooped over, I smoothed it with my hands in order to have it flat and smooth, comfortable to sit on.

I was surprised and didn't know what to do. He didn't ask any questions. He didn't say a word. Right away he brought me a bone cup, and he started to clean the sand behind a dune, taking off all its dirt and impurities. I looked right and left, looking for a way to disappear.

Then I invited her to sit down. I invited her to sit down with a gesture; I put out my right arm so she could hold on to it and slowly bend over, taking a seat on the throne of clean sand that was nearby. She looked tired and who knows where she came from, following the shoreline, suffering, suffering, following the shore. Along the way, she had lost her crown or they had taken it from her, just like they killed her son. She had also lost that handkerchief that she always used to have in her hands to dry her tears, and the little light dress that covered her body was clearly not enough to keep out the cold. I invited her to sit down because she seemed tired, and the wind was blowing. At any moment, the tide would begin to come in, but she would be protected there.

The enormous beach that we had all thought deserted lay as far as the eye could see. I wasn't familiar with this mountain; I didn't know where the sea ended. I could only turn back, exhausted and cold, turn back, but he would have seen me again in this vast empty space if I had decided to turn back. Then he probably would have asked me questions. I was vaguely unsettled as if waiting for a premonition. The gray and mauve sky suddenly opened up, making way for a round sun, the color of death and shining like metal. The outline of a distant forest, completely enveloped in mist, seemed to be suspended between the sea and the sky, as if it were ascending into the heavens. The air was damp, palpable, full of the tension of an upcoming storm. The sound of the water breaking and the wind blowing seemed to me like the death throes of some gigantic marine animal hidden among the waves. Everywhere there seemed to be a revelation in the making.

Once she sat down, I gestured for her to wait and I ran off to the mountain to look for pine boughs, wild flowers and poppies. I know the mountain well, but I was so nervous and excited that I lost time going around in circles, dead ends that didn't take me anywhere. Like puppies that jump up into the air, turn about, and go back and forth like crazy when they see their master, I got lost among paths full of plants. I hurt my hands, grabbed flowers and boughs without thinking, pulled up roots, crushed stalks on account of my nerves, and squashed the ivy as I walked. My ears were attuned to the sound of the tide as it came in, they heard its ascent, its growth; I couldn't see it, but I could hear it. Like two enemies that know each other well, I lay in wait, and it was ready to take advantage of my smallest slip.

I ran down the mountain with my arms full of pine boughs and wild flowers, so fast that I lost some on the way. She was there, sitting in the square of sand I made for her, protected from the sea, the wind, and from the ants, melancholy, looking without seeing, and the breeze shook her fragile dress as if it were a sail. One by one, I placed the aromatic boughs at her feet, in a circle, taking care that they didn't touch her dress. There were gray boughs partly covered with lichen and with lighter covered bark; if you scratch them a little, right away the pine's true skin would appear, green and resinous. There were dry sticks, crackling with pointed ends, that are used to build a fire in winter. I thought that this smell would maybe help her bear her sadness. She didn't look at me; she looked far away, and the water in her eyes was as deep as a day of fog and storms. There were some little pine nuts, just come out, very tight on the bough, with a hard shell and bright color. And there were white starling nests among the pine boughs, soft and silky like cotton balls. They were lightly woven nests that the birds embroidered with care; I thought that their softness and smooth surface would provide her with some nice sensations, welcoming and warm. Surrounded by boughs and plants, wild flowers and rush, she looked like a mountain virgin who had come down to the beach to look at the sea for a moment.

Right away I went to look for the piece of wood in the shape of a wolf that the water had dragged up the day before. Sometimes the water does this: brings things then leaves them on the shore and goes away as if it had traveled so far, as if it had walked days and nights just to bring that one thing, just to nudge up onto the sand those things it has collected on its journey. They are the sea's humble gifts; after thinking for hours and hours, after going back and forth from the depths to the surface, it hurls up a dead fish, a rotted piece of wood, a handful of seaweed or an open and empty shell. They are its wet, humble tributes. It had brought the piece of wood the day before; I found it not far from there, on the shore, wet from the waves, and I took it out of the water. That was hard because it had absorbed a lot of water and had become heavy. It was the shape and color of a sea wolf, so I grabbed it again by the head and dragged it over the beach to place it beside the Virgin. I left it next to her, but facing the sea so it wouldn't miss the world from which it came, in which it had been born and lived. He lay down to rest, tame, but he kept his head erect, overseeing the coast and its dangers. Watched over by the sea wolf like this, her throne seemed less forsaken, her realm more guarded.

Surrounded by pine boughs, reeds, and flowers, having the stately figure of the wolf in front of her, she seemed more like the Virgin that I had seen that time in church, dressed in a black robe and carried around on a moveable pedestal. As I did then, I gave her lots of white flowers, yellow flowers, lilac and celestial blue flowers picked on the mountain. I hurried down the mountain and placed them, one by one, on her dress. Sometimes she looked back—her dead son—and her eyes were infinitely sad. With a gesture, I showed her that the mountain was full of flowers, that there were many more, but that I couldn't bring them all; I had other things to do for her. The tide advanced, serious, step by step, and each time it got closer to us. It left its damp stain on the ground, a little bit of foam floated by and later left, innocently, as if it hadn't moved forward, as if it wanted to hide its progress. I looked at the sea and then looked at her. There was considerable distance separating them, but I started to build a small sand wall anyway, to keep the odd stream of water from wetting her feet. I am very fast when I work, and I'm used to fighting the sea. I quickly built a sand barrier, a moist sea wall a few centimeters high that would act as a fortress against the water's penetration. I made it this size so she could look over it at the sea without having to get up or even raise her head.

On the other hand, the sea could see her only with great difficulty.

He brought me small gifts. Things from the sea and forest. I don't know why he did it, but I thought I couldn't stop him. Whatever it was that he imagined, I didn't understand. His gestures were full of kindness and appreciation, and I was too tired to reject these gifts no matter how crazy they were. Although numb with cold, tired and without energy, I thought that I couldn't spend much more time there. Clearly it was dangerous to stay out in the open, defenseless on the enormous beach, exposed. As dangerous was it to turn back, have the boy look for me and go around shouting to find me, alerting everyone to my presence. I stayed still, without knowing what to do, without deciding, letting myself be more tired than cautious. Meanwhile, he kept coming and going, bringing little presents with each trip.

I went to look for an old oar half buried in the sand. It had stayed sunken there, part of the remains of a fishing boat—eaten by the salt, dampness, and water—whose broken skeleton served some birds as a stronghold. I had sometimes played inside the boat, full of stagnant water. I had touched its wooden planks, its crossed masts, felt its surfaces, skimmed its hollows. And the oar was hidden in the sand, sticking out its widest end, useless and full of holes. I brandished it in the air like a sword, shaking off all the sand that had stuck on it and, whirling it above my head, I ran along the deserted beach until I came to the dune where the Virgin was resting. I was very happy when I offered it to her, showing her what to do with it. First, I made all the gestures necessary to row. Then with rapid movements, I showed her how it could be used, if necessary, as a defensive weapon. She didn't pay much attention to my lessons. She was worried and looked behind her constantly. I left the oar at her side, like a queen's sceptre. I remembered the hole in the rock where I was saving things that I rescued from the sea. I was happy to have been collecting things every day so that I could now go find them and give them to her. She didn't say anything, but she waited. Just like a sailor who returns from each one of his trips loaded with presents and happy to be home; just as he affectionately and smugly displays his cloth from China, textiles from Holland, and jewels from Egypt; I too came and went, fervently, happy to go, happy to return. But her sad eyes looked backward, without seeing. The whole time I was afraid she would fall. They picked us, the old and the children, to carry her, to bring her through the crowds, to guide her through the town. It was my job to push the pedestal from one side. We left the church enveloped in a majestic silence, fitting for a procession. The old men and women went up ahead; we children followed.

We were hidden for ten days without anyone seeing us, without one of us being recognized. Only a little boy found one of us walking on the beach.

Stumbling, we pushed the cart, which was hitting against the cobbled street and shaking. She was in mourning, wearing a long black velvet robe that hung from her head to her feet because they had killed her son. And she was very sad, a great sorrow came through her wet eyes, the color of water. The robe was black and soft, a very deep black, very moving. I touched just the edge of her robe and trembled. Now she wasn't dressed in mourning, surely because a lot of time had passed since her son's death, but the sorrow didn't change. Now she wasn't dressed in black, but she suffered just the same. And her hands—the hands that showed were very slender and very white—under the black velvet robe held a lace handkerchief, surely to dry the tears when all the water she carried in her eyes overflowed at her son's death. The robe had a golden border, a small design in thread that I couldn't bring myself to touch. She still hadn't cried because the handkerchief was dry, but her expression was that of someone who would start crying at any moment, not screaming like the women of the town when they cry, but sadly and gently because the weeping from discovering that they've killed her only son is not one of shouting; it's one of deep sorrow. All the torches were lit when we set off from the church. And the old people's faces were full of wrinkles that got deeper in the candlelight. I was afraid that she would fall walking through the cobbled streets.

"She can fall," I said to one of the townsmen who was pushing along with me.

"If we walk carefully, she won't fall," he replied, but I didn't feel reassured.

If one of the others, for instance, were just a little less careful, she could fall to the ground instantly and hurt herself and dirty her robe and lose her beautiful handkerchief and scratch her hands. It was easier for us to protect her from the soldiers (from those soldiers who had killed her son) than to keep her from falling.

"Someone might be careless," I told him, nervously.

"She won't fall," he answered. "All of us together will support her."

I had saved many things in the hole: old rusty fish hooks that still kept their sharp points, menacing creatures; parts of line that had fallen off fishing rods; pieces of net that used to trap fishes and had become moldy; huge shells to hear the sea when you're far away and can't see it; a gigantic fishbone whitened by the sun; a burro's jaw; many pieces of sea glass, multicolored and polished by the water; tree bark with lichens still clinging to them; ropes from the boats; sailor's knots; big twisted nails; and a dark wooden box that floated in from a sunken ship. I stuck my hand into the hole and took out everything, one by one. I ran with my hands full to where she was—looking backwards—and I kept putting things in her lap. The tide kept coming in, each time a little bit closer, licking the edge of the sand wall. I drove the fishbone into the top of the wall-like watch tower, a silent warning beacon, a light in the night that tells the traveller of a nearby danger: a sandbank or a sunken ship. I spread the piece of net at her feet, a majestic carpet for her to walk on; it was a smooth and delicate net, and with it, I outlined a map of the country where we would have liked to live, before the war. I planted the sea glass all around her like towers, like so many bishops and pawns, a purple horse head, a steel sword, a golden lantern, a mistletoe cathedral, an emerald fish eye. I placed the knots next to her hair so that it would not blow away, to fasten it to the sand if it wanted to run, if it wanted to go away to cry out its grief somewhere else. And I fastened the ropes around her waist, to tie her up like the boats are tied to the pier against the wind and the swaying tide. Surrounded by so many trophies, she seemed to be a water virgin, a marine statue, the figurehead of a ship I had seen once in a Maritime Museum. I had made a crown out of a long tendril of vines and placed it on her head; it was dark with very green leaves growing out of each side of a supple stem. Slowly, ceremoniously, I put it on her head. Now she seemed just right, finished and perfect, like the Virgin in church. Some bright wet seaweed on her dress became her robe.

He came and went, from the sea to shore, from shore to me, but always distant, never coming too close to me. A bird flew over, and he threw a stone at it. Harsh, he frightened away the ants and the mollusks. Cautious, he watched over the advancing tide and was always moving, very busy, bringing things.

Then I heard a noise. A different noise that didn't come from the sea or the sand. I know beach noises well, the noises of the birds, of rough sea, of underground currents. I know the noise of the faraway wind and of clouds charged with electricity. I heard a noise, and I got up immediately. I looked from one side of the beach to the other. The tide, coming up, was licking the edge of the sand wall that I had made. The fishbone, erect as a lighthouse, was aiming at the gruff sky. The tide, going back, was leaving seaweed on the shore. And the sea wolf, lying down with its head raised, was watching, expectantly, close to us.

I had to make a decision. Speak to him or flee, return to the place I had come from, even at the risk of his following me, even at the risk of his starting out on my same path.

The noise came from the mountain, and neither the trees nor the wind made it, neither the birds nor the branches caused it; it was much more muffled and metallic sounding, it was a human noise. I got to my feet and on guard; she kept sitting, looking backward.

"Where are the men who killed her son?" I had asked when we took the Virgin from the church.

"I don't know," my friend answered. "Pay attention to pushing the cart."

Most likely now they are looking for her. All this time I had been playing without realizing that they were probably closing in. I know the sounds of the sea and the mountain well. I know when it sounds like a storm is brewing, when the wind is coming up and when the fish are snoring. They crucified him, after making him drag a heavy cross for the entire way, they made fun of his pain. And they wouldn't hesitate to do it again if they found her. And now the tide was climbing up the wall, licking the fishbone.

Then I heard a noise: Not just one, but one that lasted a long time and was followed by others. A noise that filled me with fear and anxiety. I am not familiar with the noises of the mountain or of the sea. I always lived in the city.

They were advancing, without doubt. They were advancing through the mountain, and they had the resolute steps of men who are armed and ready for anything.

The steps of Roman soldiers, with their heavy swords, and their crowns of thorns and their summary judgments, and their slow crucifixions.

The gulls were crying, and the sea was getting higher. So too the wind blowing among the pines was making the branches rattle and I heard sounds of something breaking. I heard wood groaning and stones hammering.

I ran to the top of the mountain and saw them coming. They had pistols and guns.

Then I decided and started to run back in the direction I came from. I started to run, and I stepped on the flowers. I heard the crackling of the shells, and a piece of glass stuck into my foot. I started to run without looking behind me, suspicious of the sound of the sea, the sound of the wind, and the shrieking of the birds.

They had pistols and guns, dogs, knives, and lanterns. From the top of the mountain, I saw them coming. There were many Roman soldiers and their officials, their hirelings, their vassels and servants.

I ran without thinking, I ran without knowing, I ran between the water, the birds, and the wind. Then I saw him. He was holding some big wooden oars which he spun around his head to frighten the soldiers. He probably took them by surprise, protected by the afternoon shadows. He knocked down two or three in this way, running with the oars in his hands and spinning them around in a circle, like a windmill's vanes. At first he probably caused confusion. It was dark, and he was very agile; he moved around very quickly from one place to another, without letting go of the oars.

I ran without thinking, I ran without knowing, I ran between the water, the birds, and the wind to stop them.

But then I didn't see anything more. I had to turn around to keep running. Until I recognized the sound of shots. The only sound you hear in the city.

THE BONE WOMAN
Charles de Lint

Canadian author Charles de Lint is both prolific and versatile; his long list of publications includes works of adult fantasy, fiction, horror (under the pseudonym Samuel M. Key), children's fiction, poetry, and critical nonfiction. He is best known, however, as a pioneer of Urban Fantasy, bringing myth and folklore motifs into a modern-day urban context. *Spiritwalk* and *Dreams Underfoot* are his most recent books in this vein. Other recent works include *The Little Country, Into the Green,* and *Broceliande* (in collaboration with British artist Brian Froud).

Each year at Christmastime de Lint publishes an original story (or collection of poems) in a limited-edition chapbook form through Triskell Press. These small, magical booklets are sent to family, friends, and colleagues; the latest of these, "The Bone Woman," has found its way into this volume.

—T.W.

No one really stops to think of Ellie Spink, and why should they?

She's no one.

She has nothing.

Homely as a child, all that the passing of years did was add to her unattractiveness. Face like a horse, jaw long and square, forehead broad; limpid eyes set bird-wide on either side of a gargantuan nose; hair a nondescript brown, greasy and matted, stuffed up under a woolen toque lined with a patchwork of metal foil scavenged from discarded cigarette packages. The angularity of her slight frame doesn't get its volume from her meager diet, but from the multiple layers of clothing she wears.

Raised in foster homes, she's been used, but she's never experienced a kiss. Institutionalized for most of her adult life, she's been medicated, but never treated. Pass her on the street and your gaze slides right on by, never pausing to register the difference between the old woman huddled in the doorway and a bag of garbage.

Old woman? Though she doesn't know it, Monday, two weeks past, was her thirty-seventh birthday. She looks twice her age.

There's no point in trying to talk to her. Usually no one's home. When there is, the words spill out in a disjointed mumble, a rambling, one-sided dialogue itemizing a litany of misperceived conspiracies and ills that soon leave you feeling as confused as she herself must be.

Normal conversation is impossible and not many bother to try it. The exceptions are few: The odd pitying passerby. A concerned social worker, fresh out of college and new to the streets. Maybe one of the other street people who happens to stumble into her particular haunts.

They talk and she listens or she doesn't—she never makes any sort of a relevant response, so who can tell? Few push the matter. Fewer still, however well-intentioned, have the stamina to make the attempt to do so more than once or twice. It's easier to just walk away; to bury your guilt, or laugh off her confused ranting as the excessive rhetoric it can only be.

I've done it myself.

I used to try to talk to her when I first started seeing her around, but I didn't get far. Angel told me a little about her, but even knowing her name and some of her history didn't help.

"Hey, Ellie. How're you doing?"

Pale eyes, almost translucent, turn towards me, set so far apart it's as though she can only see me with one eye at a time.

"They should test for aliens," she tells me. "You know, like in the Olympics."

"Aliens?"

"I mean, who cares who killed Kennedy? Dead's dead, right?"

"What's Kennedy got to do with aliens?"

"I don't even know why they took down the Berlin wall. What about the one in China? Shouldn't they have worked on that one first?"

It's like trying to have a conversation with a game of Trivial Pursuit that specializes in information garnered from supermarket tabloids. After awhile I'd just pack an extra sandwich whenever I was busking in her neighbourhood. I'd sit beside her, share my lunch and let her talk if she wanted to, but I wouldn't say all that much myself.

That all changed the day I saw her with the Bone Woman.

I didn't call her the Bone Woman at first; the adjective that came more immediately to mind was fat. She couldn't have been much more than five-foot-one, but she had to weigh in at two-fifty, leaving me with the impression that she was wider than she was tall. But she was light on her feet—peculiarly graceful for all her squat bulk.

She had a round face like a full moon, framed by thick black hair that hung in two long braids to her waist. Her eyes were small, almost lost in that expanse of face, and so dark they seemed all pupil. She went barefoot in a shapeless black dress, her only accessory an equally shapeless shoulder-bag made of some kind of animal skin and festooned with dangling thongs from which hung various feathers, beads, bottle-caps and other found objects.

I paused at the far end of the street when I saw the two of them together. I had a sandwich for Ellie in my knapsack, but I hesitated in approaching them. They seemed deep in conversation, real conversation, give and take, and Ellie was— knitting? Talking *and* knitting? The pair of them looked like a couple of old gossips, sitting on the back porch of their building. The sight of Ellie acting so normal was something I didn't want to interrupt.

I sat down on a nearby stoop and watched until Ellie put away her knitting and stood up. She looked down at her companion with an expression in her features that I'd never seen before. It was awareness, I realized. She was completely *here* for a change.

As she came up the street, I stood up and called a greeting to her, but by the time she reached me she wore her usually vacuous expression.

"It's the newspapers," she told me. "They use radiation to print them and that's what makes the news seem so bad."

Before I could take the sandwich I'd brought her out of my knapsack, she'd shuffled off, around the corner, and was gone. I glanced back down the street to where the fat woman was still sitting, and decided to find Ellie later. Right now I wanted to know what the woman had done to get such a positive reaction out of Ellie.

When I approached, the fat woman was sifting through the refuse where the two of them had been sitting. As I watched, she picked up a good-sized bone. What kind, I don't know, but it was as long as my forearm and as big around as the neck of my fiddle. Brushing dirt and a sticky candy-wrapper from it, she gave it a quick polish on the sleeve of her dress and stuffed it away in her shoulder-bag. Then she looked up at me.

My question died stillborn in my throat under the sudden scrutiny of those small dark eyes. She looked right through me—not the drifting, unfocused gaze of so many of the street people, but a cold far-off seeing that weighed my presence, dismissed it, and gazed farther off at something far more important.

I stood back as she rose easily to her feet. That was when I realized how graceful she was. She moved down the sidewalk as daintily as a doe, as though her bulk was filled with helium, rather than flesh, and weighed nothing. I watched her until she reached the far end of the street, turned her own corner and then, just like Ellie, was gone as well.

I ended up giving Ellie's sandwich to Johnny Rew, an old wino who's taught me a fiddle tune or two, the odd time I've run into him sober.

I started to see the Bone Woman everywhere after that day. I wasn't sure if she was just new to town, or if it was one of those cases where you see something or someone you've never noticed before and after that you see them all the time. Everybody I talked to about her seemed to know her, but no one was quite sure how long she'd been in the city, or where she lived, or even her name. I still wasn't calling her the Bone Woman, though I knew by then that bones were all she collected. Old bones, found bones, rattling around together in her shoulder-bag until she went off at the end of the day and showed up the next morning, ready to start filling her bag again.

When she wasn't hunting bones, she spent her time with the street's worst cases—people like Ellie that no one else could talk to. She'd get them making things—little pictures or carvings or beadwork, keeping their hands busy. And talking. Someone like Ellie still made no sense to anybody else, but you could tell when she was with the Bone Woman that they were sharing a real dialogue. Which was a good thing, I suppose, but I couldn't shake the feeling that there was something more going on, something if not exactly sinister, then still strange.

It was the bones, I suppose. There were so many. How could she keep finding them the way she did? And what did she do with them?

My brother Christy collects urban legends, the way the Bone Woman collects her bones, rooting them out where you'd never think they could be. But when I told him about her, he just shrugged.

"Who knows why any of them do anything?" he said.

Christy doesn't live on the streets, for all that he haunts them. He's just an observer—always has been, ever since we were kids. To him, the street people can be pretty well evenly divided between the sad cases and the crazies. Their stories are too human for him.

"Some of these are big," I told him. "The size of a human thighbone."

"So point her out to the cops."

"And tell them what?"

A smile touched his lips with just enough superiority in it to get under my skin. He's always been able to do that. Usually, it makes me do something I regret later which I sometimes think is half his intention. It's not that he wants to see me hurt. It's just part and parcel of that air of authority that all older siblings seem to wear. You know, a raised eyebrow, a way of smiling that says "you have so much to learn, little brother."

"If you really want to know what she does with those bones," he said, "why don't you follow her home and find out?"

"Maybe I will."

It turned out that the Bone Woman had a squat on the roof of an abandoned factory building in the Tombs. She'd built herself some kind of a shed up there—just a leaning, ramshackle affair of cast-off lumber and sheet metal, but it kept out the weather and could easily be heated with a woodstove in the spring and fall. Come winter, she'd need warmer quarters, but the snows were still a month or so away.

I followed her home one afternoon, then came back the next day when she was out to finally put to rest my fear about these bones she was collecting. The thought that had stuck in my mind was that she was taking something away from the street people like Ellie, people who were already at the bottom rung and deserved to be helped, or at least just left alone. I'd gotten this weird idea that the bones were tied up with the last remnants of vitality that someone like Ellie might have, and the Bone Woman was stealing it from them.

What I found was more innocuous, and at the same time creepier, than I'd expected.

The inside of her squat was littered with bones and wire and dog-shaped skeletons that appeared to be made from the two. Bones held in place by wire, half-connected ribs and skulls and limbs. A pack of bone dogs. Some of the figures were almost complete, others were merely suggestions, but everywhere I looked, the half-finished wire-and-bone skeletons sat or stood or hung suspended from the ceiling. There had to be more than a dozen in various states of creation.

I stood in the doorway, not willing to venture any further, and just stared at them all. I don't know how long I was there, but finally I turned away and made my way back down through the abandoned building and out onto the street.

So now I knew what she did with the bones. But it didn't tell me how she could find so many of them. Surely that many stray dogs didn't die, their bones scattered the length and breadth of the city like so much autumn residue?

Amy and I had a gig opening for the Kelledys that night. It didn't take me long to set up. I just adjusted my microphone, laid out my fiddle and whistles on a small table to one side, and then kicked my heels while Amy fussed with her pipes and the complicated tangle of electronics that she used to amplify them.

I've heard it said that all Uillean pipers are a little crazy—that they have to be to play an instrument that looks more like what you'd find in the back of a plumber's truck than an instrument—but I think of them as perfectionists. Every one I've ever met spends more time fiddling with their reeds and adjusting the tuning of their various chanters, drones and regulators than would seem humanly possible.

Amy's no exception. After awhile I left her there on the stage, with her red hair falling in her face as she poked and prodded at a new reed she'd made for one of her drones, and wandered into the back where the Kelledys were making their own preparations for the show which consisted of drinking tea and looking beatific. At least that's the way I always think of the two of them. I don't think I've ever met calmer people.

Jilly likes to think of them as mysterious, attributing all kinds of fairy-tale traits to them. Meran, she's convinced, with the green highlights in her nut-brown hair and her wise brown eyes, is definitely dryad material—the spirit of an oak tree come to life—while Cerin is some sort of wizard figure, a combination of adept and bard. I think the idea amuses them and they play it up to Jilly. Nothing you can put your finger on, but they seem to get a kick out of spinning a mysterious air about themselves whenever she's around.

I'm far more practical than Jilly—actually, just about anybody's more practical than Jilly, God bless her, but that's another story. I think if you find yourself using the word magic to describe the Kelledys, what you're really talking about is their musical talent. They may seem preternaturally calm off-stage, but as soon as they begin to play, that calmness is transformed into a bonfire of energy. There's enchantment then, burning on stage, but it comes from their instrumental skill.

"Geordie," Meran said after I'd paced back and forth for a few minutes. "You look a little edgy. Have some tea."

I had to smile. If the Kelledys had originated from some mysterious elsewhere, then I'd lean more towards them having come from a fiddle tune than Jilly's fairy tales. "When sick is it tea you want?" I said, quoting the title of an old Irish jig that we all knew in common.

Meran returned my smile. "It can't hurt. Here," she added, rummaging around in a bag that was lying by her chair. "Let me see if I have something that'll ease your nervousness."

"I'm not nervous."

"No, of course not," Cerin put in. "Geordie just likes to pace, don't you?"

He was smiling as he spoke, but without a hint of Christy's sometimes annoying demeanor.

"No, really. It's just . . . ."

"Just what?" Meran asked as my voice trailed off.

Well, here was the perfect opportunity to put Jilly's theories to the test, I decided. If the Kelledys were in fact as fey as she made them out to be, then they'd be able to explain this business with the bones, wouldn't they?

So I told them about the fat woman and her bones and what I'd found in her squat. They listened with far more reasonableness than I would have if someone had been telling the story to me—especially when I went on to explain the weird feeling I'd been getting from the whole business.

"It's giving me the creeps," I said, finishing up, "and I can't even say why."

"*La Huesera*", Cerin said when I was done.

Meran nodded. "The Bone Woman," she said, translating it for me. "It does sound like her."

"So you know her."

"No," Meran said. "It just reminds us of a story we heard when we were playing in Phoenix a few years ago. There was a young Apache man opening for us and he and I started comparing flutes. We got on to one of the Native courting flutes which used to be made from human bone and somehow from there he started telling me about a legend they have in the Southwest about this old fat woman who wanders through the mountains and *arroyos*, collecting bones from the desert that she brings back to her cave."

"What does she collect them for?"

"To preserve the things that are in danger of being lost to the world," Cerin said. "I don't get it."

"I'm not sure of the exact details," Cerin went on, "but it had something to do with the spirits of endangered species."

"Giving them a new life," Meran said.

"Or a second chance."

"But there's no desert around here," I said. "What would this Bone Woman being doing up here?"

Meran smiled. "I remember John saying that she's been seen as often riding shotgun in an eighteen-wheeler as walking down a dry wash."

"And besides," Cerin added. "Any place is a desert when there's more going on underground than on the surface."

That described Newford perfectly. And who lived a more hidden life than the street people? They were right in front of us every day, but most people didn't even see them anymore. And who was more deserving of a second chance than someone like Ellie who'd never even gotten a fair first chance?

"Too many of us live desert lives," Cerin said, and I knew just what he meant.

The gig went well. I was a little bemused, but I didn't make any major mistakes. Amy complained that her regulators had sounded too buzzy in the monitors, but that was just Amy. They'd sounded great to me, their counterpointing chords giving the tunes a real punch whenever they came in.

The Kelledys' set was pure magic. Amy and I watched them from the stage wings and felt higher as they took their final bow than we had when the applause had been directed at us.

I begged off getting together with them after the show, regretfully pleading tired-ness. I *was* tired, but leaving the theatre, I headed for an abandoned factory in the Tombs instead of home. When I got up on the roof of the building, the moon was full. It looked like a saucer of buttery gold, bathing everything in a warm yellow light. I heard a soft voice on the far side of the roof near the Bone Woman's squat. It wasn't exactly singing, but not chanting either. A murmuring, sliding sound that raised the hairs at the nape of my neck.

I walked a little nearer, staying in the shadows of the cornices, until I could see the Bone Woman. I paused then, laying my fiddlecase quietly on the roof and sliding down so that I was sitting with my back against the cornice.

The Bone Woman had one of her skeleton sculptures set out in front of her and she was singing over it. The dog shape was complete now, all the bones wired in place and gleaming in the moonlight. I couldn't make out the words of her song. Either there were none, or she was using a language I'd never heard before. As I watched, she stood, raising her arms up above the wired skeleton, and her voice grew louder.

The scene was peaceful—soothing, in the same way that the Kelledys' company could be—but eerie as well. The Bone Woman's voice had the cadence of one of the medicine chants I'd heard at a powwow up on the Kickaha Reservation—the same nasal tones and ringing quality. But that powwow hadn't prepared me for what came next.

At first I wasn't sure that I was really seeing it. The empty spaces between the skeleton's bones seemed to gather volume and fill out, as though flesh were forming on the bones. Then there was fur, highlit by the moonlight, and I couldn't deny it any more. I saw a bewhiskered muzzle lift skyward, ears twitch, a tail curl up, thick-haired and strong. The powerful chest began to move rhythmically, at first in time to the Bone Woman's song, then breathing of its own accord.

The Bone Woman hadn't been making dogs in her squat, I realized as I watched the miraculous change occur. She'd been making wolves.

The newly-animated creature's eyes snapped open and it leapt up, running to the edge of the roof. There it stood with its forelegs on the cornice. Arching its neck, the wolf pointed its nose at the moon and howled.

I sat there, already stunned, but the transformation still wasn't complete. As the wolf howled, it began to change again. Fur to human skin. Lupine shape, to that of a young woman. Howl to merry laughter. And as she turned, I recognized her features.

"Ellie," I breathed.

She still had the same horsey-features, the same skinny body, all bones and angles, but she was beautiful. She blazed with the fire of a spirit that had never been hurt, never been abused, never been degraded. She gave me a radiant smile and then leapt from the edge of the roof.

I held my breath, but she didn't fall. She walked out across the city's skyline, out across the urban desert of rooftops and chimneys, off and away, running now, laughter trailing behind her until she was swallowed by the horizon.

I stared out at the night sky long after she had disappeared, then slowly stood up and walked across the roof to where the Bone Woman was sitting outside the door of her squat. She tracked my approach, but there was neither welcome nor dismissal in those small dark eyes. It was like the first time I'd come up to her; as far as she was concerned, I wasn't there at all.

"How did you do that?" I asked.

She looked through, past me.

"Can you teach me that song? I want to help, too."

Still no response.

"Why won't you *talk* to me?"

Finally her gaze focused on me.

"You don't have their need," she said.

Her voice was thick with an accent I couldn't place. Once again, she ignored me. The pinpoints of black that passed for eyes in that round moon face looked away into a place where I didn't belong.

Finally, I did the only thing left for me to do. I collected my fiddlecase and went on home.

Some things haven't changed. Ellie's still living on the streets and I still share my lunch with her when I'm down in her part of town. There's nothing the Bone Woman can do to change what this life has done to the Ellie Spinks of the world.

But what I saw that night gives me hope for the next turn of the wheel. I know now that no matter how downtrodden someone like Ellie might be, at least somewhere a piece of her is running free. Somewhere that wild and innocent part of her spirit is being preserved with those of the wolf and the rattlesnake and all the other creatures whose spirit-bones *La Huesera* collects from the desert—deserts natural, and of our own making.

Spirit-bones. Collected and preserved, nurtured in the belly of the Bone Woman's song, until we learn to welcome them upon their terms, rather than our own.

The idea of La Huesera *comes from the folklore of the American Southwest. My thanks to Clarissa Pinkola Estés for making me aware of the tale.*

THE STORY OF
THE ELDEST PRINCESS

A. S. Byatt

British writer A. S. Byatt is the author of several critically acclaimed works, including *Shadow of a Sun, The Game, The Virgin in the Garden, Still Life,* and *Sugar and Other Stories.* Her extraordinary novel *Possession,* a fascinating literary mystery about the lives of imaginary Victorian poets, won the 1990 Booker Prize, and I cannot recommend it too highly.

"The Story of the Eldest Princess" is a wise and wonderful original fairy tale. It comes from a delightful British collection of contemporary adult fairy tales titled *Caught in a Story.*

—T.W.

Once upon a time, in a kingdom between the sea and the mountains, between the forest and the desert, there lived a King and Queen with three daughters. The eldest daughter was pale and quiet, the second daughter was brown and active, and the third was one of those Sabbath daughters who are bonny and bright and good and gay, of whom everything and nothing was expected.

When the eldest Princess was born, the sky was a speedwell blue, covered with very large, lazy, sheep-curly white clouds. When the second Princess was born, there were grey and creamy mares' tails streaming at great speed across the blue. And when the third Princess was born, the sky was a perfectly clear plane of sky-blue, with not a cloud to be seen, so that you might think the blue was spangled with sun-gold, though this was an illusion.

By the time they were young women, things had changed greatly. When they were infants, there were a series of stormy sunsets tinged with sea-green, and seaweed-green. Later there were, as well as the sunsets, dawns, where the sky was mackerel-puckered and underwater-dappled with lime-green and bottle-green and other greens too, malachite and jade. And when they were moody girls the green colors flecked and streaked the blue and the grey all day long, ranging from bronze-greens through emerald to palest opal-greens, with hints of fire. In the early days the people stood in the streets and fields with their mouths open, and said oh, and ah, in tones of admiration and wonder. Then one day a small girl said to her mother that there had been no blue at all for three days now, and she wanted to see blue again. And her mother told her to be sensible and patient and it would blow over, and in about a month the sky was blue, or mostly blue, but only for a few days, and streaked, ominously, the people now felt, with aquamarine. And the blue days were further and further apart, and the greens were more and more varied, until a time when it became quite clear that the fundamental color of the sky was no longer what they still called sky-blue, but a new sky-green, a pale flat green somewhere between the colors which had once been apple and grass and fern. But of course apple and grass and fern looked very different against this new light, and something very odd and dimming happened to lemons and oranges, and something more savage and hectic to poppies and pomegranates and ripe chillies.

The people, who had at first been entranced, became restive, and, as people will, blamed the King and the Queen for the disappearance of the blue sky. They sent deputations to ask for its return, and they met and muttered in angry knots in the Palace Square. The royal couple consulted each other, and assured each other that they were blameless of greening, but they were uneasy, as it is deep in human nature to suppose human beings, oneself or others, to be responsible for whatever happens. So they consulted the chief ministers, the priests, and a representative sample of generals, witches and wizards. The ministers said nothing could be done, though a contingency-fund might usefully be set up for when a course of action became clear. The priests counseled patience and self-denial, as a general sanative measure, abstention from lentils, and the consumption of more lettuce. The generals supposed it might help to attack their neighbors to the East, since it was useful to have someone else to blame, and the marches and battles would distract the people.

The witches and wizards on the whole favored a Quest. One rather powerful and generally taciturn wizard, who had interfered very little, but always successfully, in affairs of State, came out of his cavern, and said that someone must be sent along the Road through the Forest across the Desert and into the Mountains, to fetch back the single silver bird and her nest of ash-branches. The bird, he added, was kept in the walled garden of the Old Man of the Mountains, where she sipped from the crystal fountain of life, and was guarded by a thicket of thorns—poisonous thorns—and an interlaced ring of venomous fiery snakes. He believed that advice could be sought along the way about how to elude their vigilance, but the only advice he could give was to keep to the Road, and stray neither in the Forest, nor in the Desert, nor in the rocky paths, and always to be courteous. Then he went back to his cavern.

The King and Queen called together the Council of State, which consisted of themselves, their daughters, the chief minister and an old duchess, to decide what to do. The Minister advised the Quest, since that was a positive action, which would please the people, and not disrupt the state. The second Princess said she would go of course, and the old duchess went to sleep. The King said he thought it should be done in an orderly manner, and he rather believed that the eldest Princess should go, since she was the first, and could best remember the blue sky. Quite why that mattered so much, no one knew, but it seemed to, and the eldest Princess said she was quite happy to set out that day, if that was what the council believed was the right thing to do.

So she set out. They gave her a sword, and an inexhaustible water-bottle someone had brought back from another Quest, and a package of bread and quails' eggs and lettuce and pomegranates, which did not last very long. They all gathered at the city gate to wish her well, and a trumpeter blew a clear, silver sound into the emptiness ahead, and a minister produced a map of the Road, with one or two sketchy patches, especially in the Desert, where its undeviating track tended to be swallowed by sandstorms.

The eldest Princess traveled quickly enough along the Road. Once or twice she thought she saw an old woman ahead of her, but this figure vanished at certain bends and slopes of the path, and did not reappear for some time, and then only briefly, so that it was never clear to the Princess whether there was one, or a succession of old women. In any case, if they were indeed, or she was indeed, an old woman, or old women, she, or they were always very far ahead, and traveling extremely fast.

The Forest stretched along the Road. Pale green glades along its edges, deeper rides, and dark tangled patches beyond these. The Princess could hear but not see, birds calling and clattering and croaking in the trees. And occasional butterflies sailed briefly out of the glades towards the Road, busy small scarlet ones, lazily swooping midnight blue ones, and once, a hand-sized transparent one, a shimmering film of wings with two golden eyes in the center of the lower wing. This creature hovered over the Road, and seemed to follow the Princess for several minutes, but without ever crossing some invisible barrier between Forest and Road. When it dipped and turned back into the dappled light of the trees the Princess wanted to go after it, to walk on the grass and moss, and knew she must not. She felt a little hungry by now, although she had the inexhaustible water-bottle.

She began to think. She was by nature a reading, not a traveling princess. This meant both that she enjoyed her new striding solitude in the fresh air, and that she had read a great many stories in her spare time, including several stories about princes and princesses who set out on Quests. What they all had in common, she thought to herself, was a pattern in which the two elder sisters, or brothers, set out very confidently, failed in one way or another, and were turned to stone, or imprisoned in vaults, or cast into magic sleep, until rescued by the third royal person, who did everything well, restored the first and the second, and fulfilled the Quest.

She thought she would not like to waste seven years of her brief life as a statue or prisoner if it could be avoided.

She thought that of course she could be very vigilant, and very courteous to all passers-by—most eldest princess's failings were failings of courtesy or over-confidence.

There was nobody on the Road to whom she could be courteous, except the old woman, or women, bundling along from time to time a long way ahead.

She thought, I am in a pattern I know, and I suspect I have no power to break it, and I am going to meet a test and fail it, and spend seven years as a stone.

This distressed her so much that she sat down on a convenient large stone at the side of the road and began to weep.

The stone seemed to speak to her in a thin, creaking, dry sort of voice. "Let me out," it said. "I cannot get out." It sounded irritable and angry.

The Princess jumped up. "Who are you?" she cried. "Where are you?"

"I am trapped under this stone," buzzed the voice. "I cannot get out. Roll away the stone."

The Princess put her hands gingerly to the stone and pushed. Pinned underneath it in a hollow of the ground was a very large and dusty scorpion, waving angry pincers, and somewhat crushed in the tail.

"Did you speak?"

"Indeed I did. I was screaming. It took you an age to hear me. Your predecessor on this Road sat down just here rather heavily when I was cooling myself in this good crack, and pinched my tail, as you see."

"I am glad to have been able to help," said the Princess, keeping a safe distance.

The Scorpion did not answer, as it was trying to raise itself and move forwards. It seemed to move with pain, arching its body and collapsing again, buzzing crossly to itself.

"Can I help?" asked the Princess.

"I do not suppose you are skilled in healing wounds such as mine. You could lift me to the edge of the Forest where I might be in the path of someone who can heal me, if she ever passes this way again. I suppose *you* are tearing blindly along the Road, like all the rest."

"I am on a Quest, to find the single silver bird in her nest of ash-branches."

"You could put me on a large dock-leaf, and get on your way, then. I expect you are in a hurry."

The Princess looked about for a dock-leaf, wondering whether this irascible creature was her first test, which she was about to fail. She wiped up another tear, and plucked a particularly tough leaf, that was growing conveniently in reach of the Road.

"Good," said the fierce little beast, rearing up and waving its legs. "Quick now, I dislike this hole extremely. Why have you been crying?"

"Because I am not the princess who succeeds, but one of the two who fail and I don't see any way out. You won't force me to be discourteous to you, though I have remarked that your own manners are far from perfect, in that you have yet to thank me for moving the stone, and you order me here and there without saying "please," or considering that humans don't like picking up scorpions."

She pushed the leaf towards it as she spoke, and assisted it onto it with a twig, as delicately as she could, though it wriggled and snapped furiously as she did. She put it down in the grass at the edge of the Forest.

"Most scorpions," it observed, "have better things to do than sting at random. If creatures like you stamp on us, then of course we retaliate. Also, if we find ourselves boxed in and afraid. But mostly we have better things to do." It appeared to reflect for a moment. "*If* our tails are not crushed," it added on a dejected note.

"Who is it," the Princess enquired courteously, "who you think can help you?"

"Oh, she is a very wise woman, who lives at the other side of the Forest. She would know what to do, but she rarely leaves home and why should she? She has everything she might want, where she is. If you were going *that* way, of course, you could carry me a little, until I am recovered. But you are rushing headlong along the Road. Good-bye."

The Princess was rushing nowhere; she was standing very still and thinking. She said:

"I know that story too. I carry you, and ask you, but will you not sting me? And you say, no, it is not in my interest to sting you. And when we are going along, you sting me, although we shall both suffer. And I ask, why did you do that? And you answer—it is my nature."

"You are a very learned young woman, and if we *were* traveling together you could no doubt tell me many instructive stories. I might also point out that I *cannot* sting you—my sting is disabled by the accident to my tail. You may still find me repugnant. Your species usually does. And in any case, you are going along this road, deviating neither to right nor left. Good-bye."

The Princess looked at the Scorpion. Under the dust it was a glistening blue-black, with long arms, fine legs and complex segments like a jet necklace. Its claws made a crescent before its head. It was not possible to meet its eye, which was disconcerting.

"I think you are very handsome."

"Of course I am. I am quick and elegant and versatile and delightfully intricate. I am surprised, however, that you can see it."

The Princess listened only distractedly to this last remark. She was thinking hard. She said, mostly to herself:

"I *could* just walk out of this inconvenient story and go my own way. I *could* just leave the Road and look for my own adventures in the Forest. It would make no difference to the Quest. I should have failed if I left the Road and then the next could set off. Unless of course I got turned into stone for leaving the Road."

"I shouldn't think so," said the Scorpion. "And you could be very helpful to *me*, if you chose, and I know quite a few stories too, and helping other creatures is always a good idea, according to them."

The Princess looked into the Forest. Under the green sky its green branches swayed and rustled in a beckoning way. Its mossy floor was soft and tempting after the dust and grit of the Road. The Princess bent down and lifted up the Scorpion on its leaf and put it carefully into the basket which had contained her food. Then, with a little rebellious skip and jump, she left the Road, and set out into the trees. The Scorpion said she should go south-west, and that if she was hungry it knew where there was a thicket of brambles with early blackberries and a tree-trunk with some mushrooms, so they went in search of those, and the Princess made her mouth black without *quite* assuaging her hunger.

They traveled on, and they traveled on, in a green-arched shade, with the butterflies crowding round the Princess's head and resting on her hair and shoulders. Then they came to a shady clearing, full of grassy stumps and old dry roots, beneath one of which the Princess's keen eye detected a kind of struggling and turbulence in the sand. She stopped to see what it was, and heard a little throaty voice huskily repeating:

"Water. Oh, please, water, if you can hear me, water."

Something encrusted with sand was crawling and flopping over the wiry roots, four helpless legs and a fat little belly. The Princess got down on her knees, ignoring the angry hissing of the Scorpion. Two liquid black eyes peered at her out of the sandy knobs, and a wide mouth opened tremulously and croaked "Water" at her. The Princess brought out her inexhaustible water-bottle and dropped drops into the mouth and washed away the crust of sand, revealing a large and warty green and golden toad, with an unusual fleshy crest on its head. It puffed out its throat and held up its little fingers and toes to the stream of water. As the sand flowed away, it could be seen that there was a large bloody gash on the toad's head.

"Oh, you are hurt," cried the Princess.

"I was caught," said the Toad, "by a Man who had been told that I carry a jewel of great value in my head. So he decided to cut it out. But that is only a story, of course, a human story told by creatures who like sticking colored stones on their heads and skins, and all I am is flesh and blood. Fortunately for me, my skin is mildly poisonous to Men, so his fingers began to itch and puff up, and I was able to wriggle so hard that he dropped and lost me. But I do not think that I have the strength to make my way back to the person who could heal me."

"We are traveling in her direction," said the Scorpion. "You may travel with us if you care to. You could travel in this Princess's luncheon-basket, which is empty."

"I will come gladly," said the Toad. "But she must not suppose I shall turn into a handsome Prince, or any such nonsense. I am a handsome Toad, or would be, if I had not been hacked at. A handsome Toad is what I shall remain."

The Princess helped it, with a stick, to hop into her lunch-basket, and continued on through the Forest, in the direction indicated by the Scorpion. They went deeper and darker into the trees, and began to lose sense of there being paths leading anywhere. The Princess was a little tired, but the creatures kept urging her on, to go on as far as possible before night fell. In the growing gloom she almost put her foot on what looked like a ball of thread, blowing out in the roots of some thorny bushes.

The Princess stopped and bent down. *Something* was hopelessly entangled in fine black cotton, dragging itself and the knots that trapped it along in the dust. She knelt on the Forest floor and peered, and saw that it was a giant insect, with its legs and its wing-cases and its belly pulled apart by the snarled threads. The Princess, palace-bred, had never seen such a beast.

"It is a Cockroach," observed the Scorpion. "I thought cockroaches were too clever and tough to get into this sort of mess."

"Those threads are a trap set by the Fowler for singing birds," observed the Toad. "But he has only caught a giant Cockroach."

The Princess disentangled some of the trailing ends, but some of the knots cut into the very substance of the creature, and she feared to damage it further. It settled stoically in the dust and let her move it. It did not speak. The Princess said:

"You had better come with us. We appear to be traveling towards someone who can heal you."

The Cockroach gave a little shudder. The Princess picked it up, and placed it in the basket with the Scorpion and the Toad, who moved away from it fastidiously. It sat, inert, in its cocoon of black thread and said nothing.

They traveled in this way for several days, deeper into the Forest. The creatures told the Princess where to find a variety of nuts, and herbs, and berries, and wild mushrooms she would never have found for herself. Once, a long way off, they heard what seemed to be a merry human whistling, mixed with bird cries. The Princess was disposed to turn in its direction, but the Scorpion said that the whistler was the Fowler, and his calls were designed to entice unwary birds to fly into his invisible nets and to choke there. The Princess, although she was not a bird, was filled with unreasoning fear at this picture, and followed the Scorpion's instructions to creep away, deeper into the thornbushes. On another occasion, again at a distance, she heard the high, throaty sound of a horn, which reminded her of the hunting-parties in the Royal Parks, when the young courtiers would bring down deer and hares and flying fowl with their arrows, and the pretty maidens would clap their hands and exclaim. Again she thought of turning in the direction of the sound, and again, the creatures dissuaded her. For the poor Toad, when he heard the note of the horn, went sludge-grey with fear, and began to quake in the basket.

"That is the Hunter," he said, "who cut at my crest with his hunting-knife, who travels through the wood with cold corpses of birds and beasts strung together and cast over his shoulder, who will aim at a bright eye in a bush for pure fun, and quench it in blood. You must keep away from him." So the Princess plunged deeper still into the thornbushes, though they were tugging at her hair and ripping her dress and scratching her pretty arms and neck.

And one day at noon the Princess heard a loud, clear voice, singing in a clearing, and, peering through a thornbush, saw a tall, brown-skinned man, naked to the waist, with black curly hair, leaning on a long axe, and singing:

> Come live with me and be my love
> And share my house and share my bed
> And you may sing from dawn to dark
> And churn the cream and bake the bread
> And lie at night in my strong arms
> Beneath a soft goosefeather spread.

The Princess was about to come out of hiding—he had such a cheery smile, and such handsome shoulders—when a dry little voice in her basket, a voice like curling wood-shavings rustling, added these lines:

> And you may scour and sweep and scrub
> With bleeding hands and arms like lead
> And I will beat your back, and drive
> My knotty fists against your head
> And sing again to other girls
> To take your place, when you are dead.

"Did you speak?" the Princess asked the Cockroach in a whisper. And it rustled back:

"I have lived in his house, which is a filthy place and full of empty beer-casks and broken bottles. He has five young wives buried in the garden, whom he attacked in his drunken rage. He doesn't kill them, he weeps drunken tears for them, but they lose their will to live. Keep away from the Woodcutter, if you value your life."

The Princess found this hard to believe of the Woodcutter, who seemed so lively and wholesome. She even thought that it was in the creatures' interest to prevent her from lingering with other humans, but nevertheless their warning spoke to something in her that wanted to travel onwards, so she crept quietly away again, and the Woodcutter never knew she had heard his song, or seen him standing there, looking so handsome, leaning on his axe.

They went on, and they went on, deeper into the Forest, and the Princess began to hunger most terribly for bread and butter, touched perhaps by the Woodcutter's Song. The berries she ate tasted more and more watery and were harder and harder to find as the Forest grew denser. The Cockroach seemed inanimate, perhaps exhausted by its effort at speech. The Princess felt bound to hurry, in case its life was in danger, and the other creatures complained from time to time of her clumsiness. Then, one evening, at the moment when the sky was taking on its deepest version of the pine-green that had succeeded dark indigo, the Scorpion begged her to stop and settle down for the night, for its tail ached intolerably. And the Toad added its croaking voice, and begged for more water to be poured over it. The Princess stopped and washed the Toad, and arranged a new leaf for the Scorpion, and said:

"Sometimes I think we shall wander like this, apparently going somewhere, in fact going nowhere, for the rest of our days."

"In which case," rasped the Scorpion, "mine will not be very long, I fear."

"I have tried to help," said the Princess. "But perhaps I should never have left the Road."

And then the flaky voice was heard again.

"If you go on, and turn left, and turn left again, you will see. If you go on now."

So the Princess took up the basket, and put her sandals back on her swollen feet, and went on, and left, and left again. And she saw, through the bushes, a dancing light, very yellow, very warm. And she went on, and saw, at a great distance, at the end of a path knotted with roots and spattered with sharp stones, a window between branches, in which a candle burned steadily. And although she had never in her cossetted life traveled far in the dark, she knew she was seeing, with a huge sense of hope, and warmth and relief, and a minor frisson of fear, what countless benighted travelers had seen before her—though against midnight blue, not midnight-green— and she felt at one with all those lost homecomers and shelter-seekers.

"It is not the Woodcutter's cottage?" she asked the Cockroach. And it answered, sighing, "No, no, it is the Last House, it is where we are going."

And the Princess went on, running, and stumbling, and hopping, and scurrying, and by and by reached the little house, which was made of mossy stone, with a slate roof over low eaves and a solid wooden door above a white step. There was a good crisp smell of woodsmoke from the chimney. The Princess was suddenly afraid—she had got used to solitude and contriving and going on—but she knocked quickly, and waited.

The door was opened by an old woman, dressed in a serviceable grey dress, with a sharp face covered with intricate fine lines like a spider's web woven of her history, which was both resolute, thoughtful, and smiling. She had sharp green eyes under hooded, purple lids, and a plaited crown of wonderful shining hair, iron-grey, silver and bright white woven together. When she opened the door the Princess almost fainted for the wonderful smell of baking bread that came out, mingled with other delicious smells, baked apples with cinnamon, strawberry tart, just-burned sugar.

"We have been waiting for you," said the Old Woman. "We put the candle in the window for you every night for the last week."

She took the Princess's basket, and led her in. There was a good log fire in the chimney, with a bed of scarlet ash, and there was a long white wooden table, and there were chairs painted in dark bright colors, and everywhere there were eyes, catching the light, blinking and shining. Eyes on the mantelpiece, in the clock, behind the plates on the shelves, jet-black eyes, glass-green eyes, huge yellow eyes, amber eyes, even rose-pink eyes. And what the Princess had taken to be an intricate colored carpet rustled and moved and shone with eyes, and revealed itself to be a mass of shifting creatures, snakes and grasshoppers, beetles and bumblebees, mice and voles and owlets and bats, a weasel and a few praying mantises. There were larger creatures too—cats and rats and badgers and kittens and a white goat. There was a low, peaceful, lively squeaking and scratching of tiny voices, welcoming and exclaiming. In one corner was a spindle and in another was a loom, and the old lady had just put aside a complicated shawl she was crocheting from a rainbow-colored basket of scraps of wool.

"One of you needs food," said the Old Woman, "and three of you need healing."

So the Princess sat down to good soup, and fresh bread, and fruit tart with clotted cream and a mug of sharp cider, and the Old Woman put the creatures on the table, and healed them in her way. Her way was to make them tell the story of their hurts, and as they told, she applied ointments and drops with tiny feathery brushes and little bone pins, uncurling and splinting the Scorpion's tail as it rasped out the tale of its injuries, swabbing and stitching the Toad's wounded head with what looked like cobweb threads, and unknotting the threads that entwined the Cockroach with almost invisible hooks and tweezers. Then she asked the Princess for her story, which the Princess told as best she could, living again the moment when she realized she was doomed to fail, imitating the Scorpion's rasp, and the Toad's croaking glup, and the husky whisper of the Cockroach. She brought the dangers of the Forest into the warm fireside, and all the creatures shuddered at the thought of the Hunter's arrow, the Fowler's snare and the Woodman's axe. And the Princess, telling the story, felt pure pleasure in getting it right, making it just so, finding the right word, and even—she went so far—the right gesture to throw shadow-branches and shadow-figures across the flickering firelight and the yellow pool of candlelight on the wall. And when she had finished there was all kinds of applause, harmonious wing-scraping, and claw-tapping, and rustling and chirruping.

"You are a born storyteller," said the old lady. "You had the sense to see you were caught in a story, and the sense to see that you could change it to another one. And the special wisdom to recognize that you are under a curse—which is also a blessing—which makes the story more interesting to you than the things that make it up. There are young women who would never have listened to the creatures' tales about the Woodman, but insisted on finding out for themselves. And maybe they would have been wise and maybe they would have been foolish: that is *their* story. But you listened to the Cockroach and stepped aside and came here, where we collect stories and spin stories and mend what we can and investigate what we can't, and live quietly without striving to change the world. We have no story of our own here, we are free, as old women are free, who don't have to worry about princes or kingdoms, but dance alone and take an interest in the creatures."

"But—" said the Princess, and stopped.

"But?"

"But the sky is still green and I have failed, and I told the story to suit myself."

"The green is a very beautiful color, or a very beautiful range of colors, I think," said the old lady. "Here, it gives us pleasure. We write songs about greenness and make tapestries with skies of every possible green. It adds to the beauty of the newt and the lizard. The Cockroach finds it restful. Why should things be as they always were?"

The Princess did not know, but felt unhappy. And the creatures crowded round to console her, and persuade her to live quietly in the little house, which was what she wanted to do, for she felt she had come home to where she was free. But she was worried about the sky and the other princesses. Then the Cockroach chirped to the old lady:

"Tell us the rest of the story, tell us the end of the story, of the story the Princess left."

He was feeling decidedly better already, his segments were eased, and he could bend almost voluptuously.

"Well," said the old lady, "this is the story of the eldest Princess. But, as you percipiently observe, you can't have the story of the eldest, without the stories of the next two, so I will tell you those stories, or possible stories, for many things may and do happen, stories change themselves, and these stories are not histories and have not happened. So you may believe my brief stories about the middle one and the youngest or not, as you choose."

"I always believe stories whilst they are being told," said the Cockroach.

"You are a wise creature," said the Old Woman. "That is what stories are for. And after, we shall see what we shall see." So she told

The brief story of the second Princess

When the second Princess realized that the first was not returning, she too set out, and met identical problems and pleasures, and sat down on the same stone, and realized that she was caught in the same story. But being a determined young woman she decided to outwit the story, and went on, and after many adventures was able to snatch the single silver bird in her nest of branches and return in triumph to her father's palace. And the old wizard told her that she must light the branches and burn the bird, and although she felt very uneasy about this she was determined to do as she should, so she lit the fire. And the nest and the bird were consumed, and a new glorious bird flew up from the conflagration, and swept the sky with its flaming tail, and everything was blue, as it had once been. And the Princess became Queen when her parents died, and ruled the people wisely, although they grumbled incessantly because they missed the variety of soft and sharp greens they had once been able to see.

The brief story of the third Princess

As for the third Princess, when the bird flamed across the sky, she went into the orchard and thought, I have no need to go on a Quest. I have nothing I must do, I can do what I like. I have no story. And she felt giddy with the empty space around her, a not entirely pleasant feeling. And a frisky little wind got up and ruffled her hair and her petticoats and blew bits of blossom all over the blue sky. And the Princess had the idea that she was tossed and blown like the petals of the cherry-trees. Then she saw an old woman, with a basket, at the gate of the orchard. So she walked towards her and when she got there, the Old Woman told her, straight out,

"You are unhappy because you have nothing to do."

So the Princess saw that this was a wise old woman, and answered politely that this was indeed the case.

"I might help," said the Old Woman. "Or I might not. You may look in my basket."

In the basket were a magic glass which would show the Princess her true love, wherever he was, whatever he was doing, and a magic loom, that made tapestries that would live on the walls of the palace chambers as though they were thickets of singing birds, and Forest rides leading to the edge of vision.

"Or I could give you a thread," said the Old Woman, as the Princess hesitated, for she did not want to see her true love, not yet, not just yet, he was the *end* of stories not begun, and she did not want to make magic Forests, she wanted to see real ones. So she watched the old lady pick up from the grass the end of what appeared to be one of those long, trailing gossamer threads left by baby spiders traveling on the air in the early dawn. But it was as strong as linen thread, and as fine as silk, and when the Old Woman gave it a little tug it tugged tight and could be seen to run away, out of the orchard, over the meadow, into the woods and out of sight.

"You gather it in," said the Old Woman, "and see where it takes you."

The thread glittered and twisted, and the Princess began to roll it neatly in, and took a few steps along it, and gathered it, and rolled it into a ball, and followed it, out of the orchard, across the meadow, and into the woods, and . . . but that is another story.

"Tell me one thing," said the eldest Princess to the Old Woman, when they had all applauded her story. The moon shone in an emerald sky, and all the creatures drowsed and rustled. "Tell me one thing. Was that you, ahead of me in the road, in such a hurry?"

"There is always an old woman ahead of you on a journey, and there is always an old woman behind you too, and they are not always the same, they may be fearful or kindly, dangerous or delightful, as the road shifts, and you speed along it. Certainly I was ahead of you, and behind you too, but not only I, and not only as I am now."

"I am happy to be here with you as you are now."

"Then that is a good place to go to sleep, and stop telling stories until the morning, which will bring its own changes."

So they went to bed, and slept until the sun streaked the apple-green horizon with grassy-golden light.

CALCUTTA, LORD OF NERVES
Poppy Z. Brite

Poppy Z. Brite has lived all over the American South and has worked as a gourmet candy maker, an artist's model, a cook, and an exotic dancer. Her work began to appear in the horror small press while she was still in her teens, and she has rapidly become an important writer of horror fiction with stories in *Borderlands*, *Women of Darkness*, and *Dead End: City Limits*. Her first novel, *Lost Souls*, was published last year to great acclaim, and her new novel, *Drawing Blood*, is scheduled for this coming November.

Not since Dan Simmons wrote *Song of Kali* has anyone used the setting of India as effectively as Brite does in this story. Mysterious and fetid, it seems the perfect environment in which to set a tale of zombies—a hell on earth.

—E.D.

I was born in a North Calcutta hospital in the heart of an Indian midnight just before the beginning of the monsoon season. The air hung heavy as wet velvet over the Hooghly River, offshoot of the holy Ganga, and the stumps of banyan trees on the Upper Chitpur Road were flecked with dots of phosphorus like the ghosts of flames. I was as dark as the new moon in the sky, and I cried very little. I feel as if I remember this, because this is the way it must have been.

My mother died in labor, and later that night the hospital burned to the ground. (I have no reason to connect the two incidents; then again, I have no reason not to. Perhaps a desire to live burned on in my mother's heart. Perhaps the flames were fanned by her hatred for me, the insignificant mewling infant that had killed her.) A nurse carried me out of the roaring husk of the building and laid me in my father's arms. He cradled me, numb with grief.

My father was American. He had come to Calcutta five years earlier, on business. There he had fallen in love with my mother and, like a man who will not pluck a flower from its garden, he could not bear to see her removed from the hot, lush, squalid city that had spawned her. It was part of her exotica. So my father stayed in Calcutta. Now his flower was gone. He pressed his thin chapped lips to the satin of my hair. I remember opening my eyes—they felt tight and shiny, parched by the flames—and looking up at the column of smoke that roiled into the sky, a night sky blasted cloudy pink like a sky full of blood and milk.

There would be no milk for me, only chemical-tasting drops of formula from a plastic nipple. The morgue was in the basement of the hospital and did not burn. My mother lay on a metal table, a hospital gown stiff with her dying sweat pulled up over her red-smeared crotch and thighs. Her eyes stared up through the blackened skeleton of the hospital, up to the milky bloody sky, and ash filtered down to mask her pupils.

My father and I left for America before the monsoon came. Without my mother Calcutta was a pestilential hell-hole, a vast cremation grounds, or so my father thought. In America he could send me to school and movies, ball games and Boy Scouts, secure in the knowledge that someone else would take care of me or I would take care of myself. There were no *thuggees* to rob me and cut my throat, no *goondas* who would snatch me and sell my bones for fertilizer. There were no cows to infect the streets with their steaming sacred piss. My father could give me over to the comparative wholesomeness of American life, leaving himself free to sit in his darkened bedroom and drink whiskey until his long sensitive nose floated hazily in front of his face and the sabre edge of his grief began to dull. He was the sort of man who has only one love in his lifetime, and knows with the sick fervor of a fatalist that this love will be taken from him someday, and is hardly surprised when it happens.

When he was drunk he would talk about Calcutta. My little American mind rejected the place—I was in love with air-conditioning, hamburgers and pizza, the free and undiscriminating love that was lavished upon me every time I twisted the TV dial—but somewhere in my Indian heart I longed for it. When I turned eighteen and my father finally failed to wake up from one of his drunken stupors, I returned to the city of my bloody birth as soon as I had the plane fare in my hand.

Calcutta, you will say. What a place to have been when the dead began to walk.

And I reply, what better place to be? What better place than a city where five million people look as if they are already dead—might as well be dead—and another five million wish they were?

I have a friend named Devi, a prostitute who began her work at the age of fifteen from a tarpaper shack on Sudder Street. Sudder is the Bourbon Street of Calcutta, but there is far less of the carnival there, and no one wears a mask on Sudder Street because disguises are useless when shame is irrelevant. Devi works the big hotels now, selling American tourists or British expatriates or German businessmen a taste of exotic Bengal spice. She is gaunt and beautiful and hard as nails. Devi says the world is a whore, too, and Calcutta is the pussy of the world. The world squats and spreads its legs, and Calcutta is the dank sex you see revealed there, wet and fragrant with a thousand odors both delicious and foul. A source of lushest pleasure, a breeding ground for every conceivable disease.

The pussy of the world. It is all right with me. I like pussy, and I love my squalid city.

The dead like pussy too. If they are able to catch a woman and disable her enough so that she cannot resist, you will see the lucky ones burrowing in between her legs as happily as the most avid lover. They do not have to come up for air. I have seen them eat all the way up into the body cavity. The internal female organs seem to be a great delicacy, and why not? They are the caviar of the human body. It is a sobering thing to come across a woman sprawled in the gutter with her intestines sliding from the shredded ruin of her womb, but you do not react. You do not distract the dead from their repast. They are slow and stupid, but that is all the more reason for you to be smart and quick and quiet. They will do the same thing to a man—chew off the soft penis and scrotal sac like choice morsels of squid, leaving only a red raw hole. But you can sidle by while they are feeding and they will not notice you. I do not try to hide from them. I walk the streets and look; that is all I do anymore. I am fascinated. This is not horror, this is simply more of Calcutta.

First I would sleep late, through the sultry morning into the heat of the afternoon. I had a room in one of the decrepit marble palaces of the old city. Devi visited me here often, but on a typical morning I woke alone, clad only in twisted bedsheets and a luxurious patina of sweat. Sun came through the window and fell in bright bars across the floor. I felt safe in my second-story room as long as I kept the door locked. The dead were seldom able to navigate stairs, and they could not manage the sustained cooperative effort to break down a locked door. They were no threat to me. They fed upon those who had given up, those too traumatized to keep running: the senile, abandoned old, the catatonic young women who sat in gutters cradling babies that had died during the night. These were easy prey.

The walls of my room were painted a bright coral and the sills and door were aqua. The colors caught the sun and made the day seem cheerful despite the heat that shimmered outside. I went downstairs, crossed the empty courtyard with its dry marble fountain, and went out into the street. This area was barren in the heat, painfully bright, with parched weeds lining the road and an occasional smear of cow dung decorating the gutter. By nightfall both weeds and dung might be gone. Children collected cow shit and patted it into cakes held together with straw, which could be sold as fuel for cooking fires.

I headed toward Chowringhee Road, the broad main thoroughfare of the city. Halfway up my street, hunched under the awning of a mattress factory, I saw one of the catatonic young mothers. The dead had found her too. They had already taken the baby from her arms and eaten through the soft part at the top of the skull. Vacuous bloody faces rose and dipped. Curds of tender brain fell from slack mouths. The mother sat on the curb nearby, her arms cradling nothing. She wore a filthy green sari that was ripped across the chest. The woman's breasts protruded heavily, swollen with milk. When the dead finished with her baby they would start on her, and she would make no resistance. I had seen it before. I knew how the milk would spurt and then gush as they tore into her breasts. I knew how hungrily they would lap up the twin rivers of blood and milk.

Above their bobbing heads, the tin awning dripped long ropy strands of cotton. Cotton hung from the roof in dirty clumps, caught in the corners of the doorway like spiderweb. Someone's radio blared faintly in another part of the building, tuned to an English-language Christian broadcast. A gospel hymn assured Calcutta that its dead in Christ would rise. I moved on toward Chowringhee.

Most of the streets in the city are positively cluttered with buildings. Buildings are packed in cheek-by-jowl, helter-skelter, like books of different sizes jammed into a rickety bookcase. Buildings even sag over the street so that all you see overhead is a narrow strip of sky crisscrossed by miles of clotheslines. The flapping silks and cottons are very bright against the sodden, dirty sky. But there are certain vantage points where the city opens up and all at once you have a panoramic view of Calcutta. You see a long muddy hillside that has become home to a *bustee*, thousands and thousands of slum dwellings where tiny fires are tended through the night. The dead come often to these slums of tin and cardboard, but the people do not leave the *bustee*—where would they go? Or you see a wasteland of disused factories, empty warehouses, blackened smokestacks jutting into a rust-colored sky. Or a flash of the Hooghly River, steel-gray in its shroud of mist, spanned by the intricate girder-and-wirescape of the Howrah Bridge.

Just now I was walking opposite the river. The waterfront was not considered a safe place because of the danger from drowning victims. Thousands each year took the long plunge off the bridge, and thousands more simply waded into the water. It is easy to commit suicide at a riverfront because despair collects in the water vapor. This is part of the reason for the tangible cloud of despair that hangs over Calcutta along with its veil of humidity.

Now the suicides and the drowned street children were coming out of the river. At any moment the water might regurgitate one, and you would hear him scrabbling up the bank. If he had been in the water long enough he might tear himself to spongy gobbets on the stones and broken bricks that littered the waterfront; all that remained would be a trace of foul brown odor, like the smell of mud from the deep part of the river.

Police—especially the Sikhs, who are said to be more violent than Hindus—had been taking the dead up on the bridge to shoot them. Even from far away I could see spray-patterns of red on the drab girders. Alternately they set the dead alight with gasoline and threw them over the railing into the river. At night it was not uncommon to see several writhing shapes caught in the downstream current, the fiery symmetry of their heads and arms and legs making them into five-pointed human stars.

I stopped at a spice vendor's stand to buy a bunch of red chrysanthemums and a handful of saffron. The saffron I had him wrap in a twist of scarlet silk. "It is a beautiful day," I said to him in Bengali. He stared at me, half amused, half appalled. "A beautiful day for what?"

True Hindu faith calls upon the believer to view all things as equally sacred. There is nothing profane—no dirty dog picking through the ash bin at a cremation ground, no stinking gangrenous stump thrust into your face by a beggar who seems to hold you personally responsible for all his woes. These things are as sacred as feasting day at the holiest temple. But even for the most devout Hindus it has been difficult to see these walking dead as sacred. They are empty humans. That is the truly horrifying thing about them, more than their vacuous hunger for living flesh, more than the blood caked under their nails or the shreds of flesh caught between their teeth. They are soulless; there is nothing in their eyes; the sounds they make— their farts, their grunts and mewls of hunger—are purely reflexive. The Hindu, who has been taught to believe in the soul of everything, has a particular horror of these drained human vessels. But in Calcutta life goes on. The shops are still open. The confusion of traffic still inches its way up Chowringhee. No one sees any alternatives.

Soon I arrived at what was almost invariably my day's first stop. I would often walk twenty or thirty miles in a day—I had strong shoes and nothing to occupy my time except walking and looking. But I always began at the Kalighat, temple of the Goddess.

There are a million names for her, a million vivid descriptions: Kali the Terrible, Kali the Ferocious, skull-necklace, destroyer of men, eater of souls. But to me she was Mother Kali, the only one of the vast and colorful pantheon of Hindu gods that stirred my imagination and lifted my heart. She was the Destroyer, but all final refuge was found in her. She was the goddess of the age. She could bleed and burn and still rise again, very awake, beautifully terrible.

I ducked under the garlands of marigolds and strands of temple bells strung across the door, and I entered the temple of Kali. After the constant clamor of the street, the silence inside the temple was deafening. I fancied I could hear the small noises of my body echoing back to me from the ceiling far above. The sweet opium glaze of incense curled around my head. I approached the idol of Kali, the *jagrata*. Her gimlet eyes watched me as I came closer.

She was tall, gaunter and more brazenly naked than my friend Devi even at her best moments. Her breasts were tipped with blood—at least I always imagined them so—and her two sharp fangs and the long streamer of a tongue that uncurled from her open mouth were the color of blood too. Her hair whipped about her head and her eyes were wild, but the third crescent eye in the center of her forehead was merciful; it saw and accepted all. The necklace of skulls circled the graceful stem of her neck, adorned the sculpted hollow of her throat. Her four arms were so sinuous that if you looked away even for an instant, they seemed to sway. In her four hands she held a noose of rope, a skull-staff, a shining sword, and a gaping, very dead-looking severed head. A silver bowl sat at the foot of the statue just beneath the head, where the blood from the neck would drip. Sometimes this was filled with goat's or sheep's blood as an offering. The bowl was full today. In these times the blood might well be human, though there was no putrid smell to indicate it had come from one of the dead.

I laid my chrysanthemums and saffron at Kali's feet. Among the other offerings, mostly sweets and bundles of spice, I saw a few strange objects. A fingerbone. A shrivelled mushroom of flesh that turned out upon closer inspection to be an ear. These were offerings for special protection, mostly wrested from the dead. But who was to say that a few devotees had not lopped off their own ears or finger joints to coax a boon from Kali? Sometimes when I had forgotten to bring an offering, I cut my wrist with a razor blade and let a few drops of my blood fall at the idol's feet.

I heard a shout from outside and turned my head for a moment. When I looked back, the four arms seemed to have woven themselves into a new pattern, the long tongue seemed to loll farther from the scarlet mouth. And—this was a frequent fantasy of mine—the wide hips now seemed to tilt forward, affording me a glimpse of the sweet and terrible petalled cleft between the thighs of the goddess.

I smiled up at the lovely sly face. "If only I had a tongue as long as yours, Mother," I murmured, "I would kneel before you and lick the folds of your holy pussy until you screamed with joy." The toothy grin seemed to grow wider, more lascivious. I imagined much in the presence of Kali.

Outside in the temple yard I saw the source of the shout I had heard. There is a stone block upon which the animals brought to Kali, mostly baby goats, are be-headed by the priests. A gang of roughly dressed men had captured a dead girl and were bashing her head in on the sacrificial block. Their arms rose and fell, ropy muscles flexing. They clutched sharp stones and bits of brick in their scrawny hands. The girl's half-pulped head still lashed back and forth. The lower jaw still snapped, though the teeth and bone were splintered. Foul thin blood coursed down and mingled with the rich animal blood in the earth beneath the block. The girl was nude, filthy with her own gore and waste. The flaccid breasts hung as if sucked dry of meat. The belly was burst open with gases. One of the men thrust a stick into the ruined gouge between the girl's legs and leaned on it with all his weight.

Only in extensive stages of decay can the dead be told from the lepers. The dead are greater in number now, and even the lepers look human when compared to the dead. But that is only if you get close enough to look into the eyes. The faces in various stages of wet and dry rot, the raw ends of bones rubbing through skin like moldy cheesecloth, the cancerous domes of the skulls are the same. After a certain point lepers could no longer stay alive begging in the streets, for most people would now flee in terror at the sight of a rotting face. As a result the lepers were dying, then coming back, and the two races mingled like some obscene parody of incest. Perhaps they actually could breed. The dead could obviously eat and digest, and seemed to excrete at random like everyone else in Calcutta, but I supposed no one knew whether they could ejaculate or conceive.

A stupid idea, really. A dead womb would rot to pieces around a fetus before it could come halfway to term; a dead scrotal sac would be far too cold a cradle for living seed. But no one seemed to know anything about the biology of the dead. The newspapers were hysterical, printing picture upon picture of random slaughter by dead and living alike. Radio stations had either gone off the air or were broadcasting endless religious exhortations that ran together in one long keening whine, the edges of Muslim, Hindu, Christian doctrine beginning to fray and blur.

No one in India could say for sure what made the dead walk. The latest theory I had heard was something about a genetically engineered microbe that had been designed to feed on plastic: a microbe that would save the world from its own waste. But the microbe had mutated and was now eating and "replicating" human cells, causing basic bodily functions to reactivate. It did not much matter whether this was true. Calcutta was a city relatively unsurprised to see its dead rise and walk and feed upon it. It had seen them doing so for a hundred years.

All the rest of the lengthening day I walked through the city. I saw no more dead except a cluster far away at the end of a blocked street, in the last rags of bloody light, fighting each other over the bloated carcass of a sacred cow.

My favorite place at sunset is by the river where I can see the Howrah Bridge. The Hooghly is painfully beautiful in the light of the setting sun. The last rays melt onto the water like hot *ghee*, turning the river from steel to khaki to nearly golden, a blazing ribbon of light. The bridge rises black and skeletal into the fading orange sky. Tonight an occasional skirl of bright flowers and still-glowing greasy embers floated by, the last earthly traces of bodies cremated farther up the river. Above the bridge were the burning *ghats* where families lined up to incinerate their dead and cast the ashes into the holy river. Cremation is done more efficiently these days, or at least more hurriedly. People can reconcile in their hearts their fear of strangers' dead, but they do not want to see their own dead rise.

I walked along the river for a while. The wind off the water carried the scent of burning meat. When I was well away from the bridge, I wandered back into the maze of narrow streets and alleyways that lead toward the docks in the far southern end of the city. People were already beginning to settle in for the night, though here a bedroom might mean your own packing crate or your own square of sidewalk. Fires glowed in nooks and corners. A warm breeze still blew off the river and sighed its way through the winding streets. It seemed very late now. As I made my way from corner to corner, through intermittent pools of light and much longer patches of darkness, I heard small bells jingling to the rhythm of my footsteps. The brass bells of rickshaw men, ringing to tell me they were there in case I wished for a ride. But I could see none of the men. The effect was eerie, as if I were walking alone down an empty nighttime street being serenaded by ghostly bells. The feeling soon passed. You are never truly alone in Calcutta.

A thin hand slid out of the darkness as I passed. Looking into the doorway it came from, I could barely make out five gaunt faces, five forms huddled against the night. I dropped several coins into the hand and it slid out of sight again. I am seldom begged from. I look neither rich nor poor, but I have a talent for making myself all but invisible. People look past me, sometimes right through me. I don't mind; I see more things that way. But when I am begged from I always give. With my handful of coins, all five of them might have a bowl of rice and lentils tomorrow.

A bowl of rice and lentils in the morning, a drink of water from a broken standpipe at night.

It seemed to me that the dead were among the best-fed citizens of Calcutta.

Now I crossed a series of narrow streets and was surprised to find myself coming up behind the Kalighat. The side streets are so haphazardly arranged that you are constantly finding yourself in places you had no idea you were even near. I had been to the Kalighat hundreds of times, but I had never approached it from this direction. The temple was dark and still. I had not been here at this hour before, did not even know whether the priests were still here or if one could enter so late. But as I walked closer I saw a little door standing open at the back. The entrance used by the priests, perhaps. Something flickered from within: a candle, a tiny mirror sewn on a robe, the smoldering end of a stick of incense.

I slipped around the side of the temple and stood at the door for a moment. A flight of stone steps led up into the darkness of the temple. The Kalighat at night, deserted, might have been an unpleasant prospect to some. The thought of facing the fierce idol alone in the gloom might have made some turn away from those steps. I began to climb them.

The smell reached me before I ascended halfway. To spend a day walking through Calcutta is to be assailed by thousands of odors both pleasant and foul: the savor of spices frying in *ghee*, the stink of shit and urine and garbage, the sick-sweet scent of the little white flowers called *mogra* that are sold in garlands and that make me think of the gardenia perfume American undertakers use to mask the smell of their corpses.

Almost everyone in Calcutta is scrupulously clean in person, even the very poor. They will leave their trash and their spit everywhere, but many of them wash their bodies twice a day. Still, everyone sweats under the sodden veil of heat, and at midday any public place will be redolent with the smell of human perspiration, a delicate tang like the mingled juices of lemons and onions. But lingering in the stairwell was an odor stronger and more foul than any I had encountered today. It was deep and brown and moist; it curled at the edges like a mushroom beginning to dry. It was the perfume of mortal corruption. It was the smell of rotting flesh.

Then I came up into the temple, and I saw them.

The large central room was lit only with candles that flickered in a restless draft, first this way, then that. In the dimness the worshippers looked no different from any other supplicants at the feet of Kali. But as my eyes grew accustomed to the candlelight, details resolved themselves. The withered hands, the ruined faces. The burst body cavities where ropy organs could be seen trailing down behind the cagework of ribs.

The offerings they had brought.

By day Kali grinned down upon an array of blossoms and sweetmeats lovingly arranged at the foot of her pedestal. The array spread there now seemed more suited to the goddess. I saw human heads balanced on raw stumps of necks, eyes turned up to crescents of silver-white. I saw gobbets of meat that might have been torn from a belly or a thigh. I saw severed hands like pale lotus flowers, the fingers like petals opening silently in the night.

Most of all, piled on every side of the altar, I saw bones. Bones picked so clean that they gleamed in the candlelight. Bones with smears of meat and long snotty runners of fat still attached. Skinny arm-bones, clubby leg-bones, the pretzel of a pelvis, the beadwork of a spine. The delicate bones of children. The crumbling ivory bones of the old. The bones of those who could not run.

These things the dead brought to their goddess. She had been their goddess all along, and they her acolytes.

Kali's smile was hungrier than ever. The tongue lolled like a wet red streamer from the open mouth. The eyes were blazing black holes in the gaunt and terrible face. If she had stepped down from her pedestal and approached me now, if she had reached for me with those sinuous arms, I might not have been able to fall to my knees before her. I might have run. There are beauties too terrible to be borne.

Slowly the dead began to turn toward me. Their faces lifted and the rotting cavities of their nostrils caught my scent. Their eyes shone iridescent. Faint starry light shimmered in the empty spaces of their bodies. They were like cutouts in the fabric of reality, like conduits to a blank universe. The void where Kali ruled and the only comfort was in death.

They did not approach me. They stood holding their precious offerings and they looked at me—those of them that still had eyes—or they looked through me. At that moment I felt more than invisible. I felt empty enough to belong among these human shells.

A ripple seemed to pass through them. Then—in the uncertain candlelight, in the light that shimmered from the bodies of the dead—Kali did move.

The twitch of a finger, the deft turn of a wrist—at first it was so slight as to be nearly imperceptible. But then her lips split into an impossibly wide, toothy grin and the tip of her long tongue curled. She rotated her hips and swung her left leg high into the air. The foot that had trod on millions of corpses made a pointe as delicate as a prima ballerina's. The movement spread her sex wide open.

But it was not the petalled mandala-like cleft I had imagined kissing earlier. The pussy of the goddess was an enormous deep red hole that seemed to lead down to the center of the world. It was a gash in the universe, it was rimmed in blood and ash. Two of her four hands beckoned toward it, inviting me in. I could have thrust my head into it, then my shoulders. I could have crawled all the way into that wet crimson eternity, and kept crawling forever.

Then I did run. Before I had even decided to flee I found myself falling down the stone staircase, cracking my head and my knee on the risers. At the bottom I was up and running before I could register the pain. I told myself that I thought the dead would come after me. I do not know what I truly feared was at my back. At times I thought I was running not away from something, but toward it.

I ran all night. When my legs grew too tired to carry me I would board a bus. Once I crossed the bridge and found myself in Howrah, the even poorer suburb on the other side of the Hooghly. I stumbled through desolate streets for an hour or more before doubling back and crossing over into Calcutta again. Once I stopped to ask for a drink of water from a man who carried two cans of it slung on a long stick across his shoulders. He would not let me drink from his tin cup, but poured a little water into my cupped hands. In his face I saw the mingled pity and disgust with which one might look upon a drunk or a beggar. I was a well-dressed beggar, to be sure, but he saw the fear in my eyes.

In the last hour of the night I found myself wandering through a wasteland of factories and warehouses, of smokestacks and rusty corrugated tin gates, of broken windows. There seemed to be thousands of broken windows. After a while I realized I was on the Upper Chitpur Road. I walked for a while in the watery light that fills the sky before dawn. Eventually I left the road and staggered through the wasteland. Not until I saw its girders rising around me like the charred bones of a prehistoric animal did I realize I was in the ruins of the hospital where I had been born.

The hole of the basement had filled up with broken glass and crumbling metal, twenty years' worth of cinders and weeds, all washed innocent in the light of the breaking dawn. Where the building had stood there was only a vast depression in the ground, five or six feet deep. I slid down the shallow embankment, rolled, and came to rest in the ashes. They were infinitely soft; they cradled me. I felt as safe as an embryo. I let the sunrise bathe me. Perhaps I had climbed into the gory chasm between Kali's legs after all, and found my way out again.

Calcutta is cleansed each morning by the dawn. If only the sun rose a thousand times a day, the city would always be clean.

Ashes drifted over me, smudged my hands gray, flecked my lips. I lay safe in the womb of my city, called by its poets Lord of Nerves, city of joy, the pussy of the world. I felt as if I lay among the dead. I was that safe from them: I knew their goddess, I shared their many homes. As the sun came up over the mud and glory of Calcutta, the sky was so full of smoky clouds and pale pink light that it seemed, to my eyes, to burn.

IN THE LOOKING GLASS, LIFE IS DEATH

Jessica Amanda Salmonson

Jessica Amanda Salmonson lives in Seattle, Washington. She has published five fantasy novels and numerous short stories and poems. Her most recent novel, *Anthony Shriek*, is her first horror novel. She is well regarded as an editor for her work on the magazines *Fantasy Macabre, Fantasy and Terror,* and the award-winning anthologies *What Did Miss Darrington See?* and *Amazons!* "In the Looking Glass, Life Is Death" shows off Salmonson's baroque style with grace. It is from the magazine *Deathrealm.*

—E.D.

> "*Alice in a chalice,*
> *Very fine, very fair . . ."*
> —Corinne Roosevelt Robinson, 1930

Alice in a chalice
I drink thee with my lips, my eyes,
Dreaming till forever dies
'Midst the roots of trees.

Alice without malice
Living in a palace
Full of cosmic fallacies, tries
To be all pleasantries.

Alice out of balance
I catch thee with my arms, my knees
Through the looking glass are we,
The ghost of you, the ghost of me,
Reenacting tragedies.

Alice, never callous,
Naytheless destroys the seas,
Dreaming till forever dies
Beneath the golden skies.

THE PARAKEET AND THE CAT

Scott Bradfield

Scott Bradfield was born in California in 1955. He taught for five years at the University of California, where he received his doctorate in American Literature, and presently he teaches English at the University of Connecticut. His dazzling first novel, *The History of Luminous Motion*, was published in 1989; his short fiction has been collected in the volume *Dream of the Wolf*.

The following ascerbic parable of "The Parakeet and the Cat" is reprinted from *Conjunctions*, the literary magazine of Bard College.

—T.W.

"Being yourself is never a very easy row to hoe," Sid said, nibbling sourly at a bit of unidentifiable root or mulch. "Being the only stray parakeet in a drab world filled with cackling hive-minded pigeons, sparrows, black crows and pheromone-splashed finches can be a pretty dismal experience indeed. Especially if you're all alone. Especially if you're at all like me, and inclined to be pretty morose at the drop of a hat *anyway*."

Without a doubt, winter was the hardest season. In winter, even the leaves abandoned you, while all the anxious birds you were just getting to know on the high wires departed precipitously for warm, ancestral climes—places with mythic, irreproachable names like Capistrano, Szechwan, São Paulo, Bengal. Other birds never told you where they were going, how long it took to get there, or even invited you along for the ride. They seemed to think that if *they* had a perfectly nice location picked out for the off-season, *every*body did.

"It's sort of like being all dressed up with no place to go," Sid told the ducks at his local pond. "I mean, my hormones have shifted into superdrive. My blood's beating with procreation and heat. And not only can't I find any girl parakeets, I can't even find the goddamn continent of Australia." The ducks were an addled, pudgy lot, filled with ambitionless quacks and broad steamy flatulence, fattened by white breads and popcorn dispensed by local children and senior citizens. They sat and jiggled their rumps in sparse blue patches of the partially frozen pond. Snow was everywhere. Winter was pretty indisputable now.

"God*damn* it's cold," the ducks honked and chattered. "Jesus fucking Christ it's *cold* cold cold. We're freezing our collective little butts off out here."

Ducks might be self-involved, Sid thought, but they were still a lot better than no company at all. If you kept close to ducks, you might pick up stray bits of cracker or information now and again, or be alerted by the emergency squawks that proclaimed wolf-peer or weasel-crouch. The winter world was a hazardous and forlorn place, and you could use all the friends you could get. Buses and planes and whirling frisbees and crackling power cables, children with rocks and slingshots and BB guns and pocketknives. The wide world was filled with angular objects that were always rushing toward you without any regard for personal space or decorum. Not to mention the ruder angularities of solitude and exile. Not to mention hunger, sadness, constitutional ennui or even just the bloody weather.

Sid had possessed a home of his own once. A tidy gilded cage with newsprinted linoleum, plastic ladders, bells on wires, bright sexy mirrors and occasional leafy treats of damp lettuce and hard, biteable carrot. Beyond the cage, as ominous as history, stretched a lofty universe of massive walls and furniture and convergent ceilings inhabited by gargantuan creatures with glistening forests of hair and long fat fingers. These gargantuan creatures were always poking these fat fingers at you, and making you sit on them. They whistled and kissed, or made tisky chittering noises, as if *they* were really the parakeets and you too damn stupid to tell otherwise.

"You think you're Mister Big Shot when you've got it all," Sid told the ducks, who were nibbling a waterproof, oily substance into their feathers with irritable little huffs and snaps. "Food, water, a warm place to go to the bathroom—that's all you care about. You happily climb the plastic ladder, or happily ping the bell, or happily chat yourself up in the flashing happy mirror all day long and everybody's happy, because that's what you're sup*posed* to do, that's the life you're sup*posed* to live. Happy happy happy days, all the happy goddamn day long, happy little morons just pissing your happy lives away in some stupid cage. I mean, you *think* you're living your own life and all, but you're not *really*. You're just living the life that's expected from you. That's why you're in a cage, after all. That's why you're getting all that free food."

Sometimes, when Sid was feeling especially bitter and over-reflective, he paced back and forth on a sturdy branch that overlooked the most duck-populous rim of pond. He took quick bites out of the twigs and leaves and flung them hastily over one shoulder, like forsaken illusions. "Then one day you get sick, just a little head cold, and *you're* not worried. But the gargantuan people outside aren't so optimistic, and want to know what happens to you *then*? Want to know where this happy little free ride takes you for a happy spin *now*? Into the trash can, that's where. Right into the smelly old happy trash basket, whether you like it or not."

When Sid stood at the farthest, thinnest extreme of branch, he could feel the faint vegetable pulse of the tree between his toes, he could see the widest horizons of frosty blue pond and white winter sky. "Boy, I'll remember *that* day as long as I live. I'm totally headachy and miserable. I'm coughing up phlegm like it's going out of style. I'm feeling too weak to keep my perch, see, so I drop down to the bottom of the cage for a few succinct winks. I guess while I was sleeping, the gargantuan people gave the cage a few exploratory thumps—I think I remember that much. But I was too tired to react. I just wanted to take this long nap at the bottom of the cage, and the very next thing I know, *bingo*! I'm digging my way out of a newspaper-padded shoe box in the trash can outdoors. I'm sick as a dog. I'm so pissed off I can't see straight. I mean, suddenly there's all this *space* everywhere, loads and loads of *space*, fat and white and dense with dimensions I've never noticed before. The always. The indescribable. The *everything*. I just wandered and wandered, and before long I stumble across you guys, and this nice blue pond you've got for yourselves. The rest, as they say, is history."

Though the ducks might sit and listen to Sid for a while, absently preening one another and snapping at fleas, eventually they grew impatient and irascible. They got up and waddled about self-importantly.

"He's *such* a bore," the ducks complained loudly, flapping in Sid's general direction. "Talk talk talk—*that's* all he does. And want to know how often the subject of ducks comes up? Zero times, that's how many. In fact, we're beginning to suspect this guy doesn't have any interesting duck stories to tell *whatsoever*!"

Being as the odds against his ever running across a female of his own species were something like thirteen trillion to one, spring didn't offer much promise for Sid. This made winters especially hard, especially while the snow fell and icy winds knocked you about. Spring was the sort of dream you had to dream *with* somebody, and Sid was beginning to feel this particular dream was one he would never successfully dream at all.

"Have you even *seen* any girl parakeets?" Sid asked whenever he encountered random sparrows or blackbirds. Usually they were strays who had suffered recent illnesses or injuries, their eyes clarified by wild, dispirited memories of flocks that had long abandoned them. "I mean, they don't even have to be that cute or anything—I don't mind. And if you haven't seen any girl parakeets, how about Australia? It's like this really big vast yellow place—a continent-sized island, in fact. I don't think it's the sort of place you'd ever forget about once you'd seen it. *I* never saw it, and I dream about it every night."

Sid's dreams of Australia were filled with bounding orange prehistoric-looking creatures and black, canny aborigines who hurled hatcheted boomerangs and fired poison darts from blowguns. Brilliant clouds of parakeets swarmed in the bright sky, crying out Sid's name, wheeling and singing songs about an ever-imminent spring which would surely last forever. Whenever Sid awoke on his cold branch he could still hear those distant parakeets singing. Then he took one glance around the frigid, lens-like pond he knew. It was only the routine squawking of ducks. Ducks and ducks and ducks of them.

"Look at Screwy!" they cried (for the ducks were eternally ragging one another, like old maiden sisters). "He's trying to eat another gum wrapper!"

"And look—here comes Big Bubba Duck. And boy, does he ever look pissed off at Harriet!"

Raging with secret, genetic industry, Sid spent entire days chewing things up. Branches and leaves and nuts, punching through their knotty, fibrous tissues with his sharp hooked beak.

"This is what I do," Sid told the ducks, flinging bits of wood and pulp everywhere like a miniature buzz saw. "I'm a wood borer. I bore wood." When Sid wasn't talking to the ducks, he was tearing everything within reach into splintery little pieces. Day after day, hour after hour, sometimes even late into the night when he couldn't sleep.

"I'm a wood borer," Sid proclaimed edgily, his eyes wide with something like panic. "Wood boring just happens to be one of those things I do really, really well."

One day, after a particularly dense snowfall, a cat arrived at the pond, bringing with it a murky, hematic odor of cynicism and unease.

"Hey there, you guys," the cat said, maintaining a polite distance. The cat was gray, and sat itself smugly on a large gray rock. "Boy, are you ever an attractive-looking bunch of ducks! Seriously, I'm really impressed. I never even suspected ducks *came* as good-looking as you guys, or halfway near as intelligent, either. I guess that just goes to show me, doesn't it? I guess that just goes to show that I don't know that much about ducks after all."

At first, the ducks glided off warily into the cold trembling pond, pretending not to be bothered, but never taking their eyes off the cat for one moment, either.

"I'll tell you something, guys," the cat continued, in a voice as gentle and intrepid as desire. "I just came from the city, and you don't have any idea how lucky you've got it out here. What a nightmare. What a cesspool of smog and urine and crime and poverty they've constructed for themselves in the city, boy. Dog eat dog, cat eat cat, cars running *every*body over without so much as a hi or a how-de-do. Bang crash roar crash bang—I've had enough city life to last me a few thousand centuries or so. Which brings me, of course, to why I've decided to move out here to the woods with you guys. Fresh air, sunshine, plenty of exercise. And of course a *strictly* monitored vegetarian diet from now on. I'm taking charge of my life, boy, and taking it on the road. Call me an outlaw, if you wish; call me a rebel. But I'm tired of living the life society *tells* me to live. I'm finally going to live *my* life for *my* self, thank you very much. Come hell or high water."

While his smooth voice wetly purred, the cat licked his stubby, retractile claws and groomed his long twitchy whiskers, as if dressing himself for church. Then, giving the ducks a last fond look over his shoulder, he rested his head on the large gray rock and fell indefensibly asleep.

"Frankly, I don't think you ducks are exactly the brightest flock of fowl I've ever come across in my rude travels," Sid said, perched high atop a thin, buoyant willow. "We're talking a fat gray cat now, and that means cat with a capital C A T, and I can't believe I'm having to actually spell it *out* to you guys. Cats are what you call notoriously fond of fowl, fowl being you ducks and me both. We're like this cat's dream of a main meal, and I don't care what he says about wildlife solidarity, or karma, or pantheism, or even free will. That cat wants to eat us alive. He wants to chew our flesh and rip our blood vessels into stringy pasta. But he wants to play with us first. He wants to tease us and cut us and watch us die slow. That's because *he's* a cat, and *we're* what you call fowl. Am I going too fast for you guys or what?"

With the arrival of the cat's sedulous gray voice, a cloud of drift and complacency began to descend over the tiny duck pond. The ducks took longer naps on the bank, and didn't squawk so much, or flap, or flirt, or battle. They wandered off aimlessly into the high reeds and bushes, snapping up bits of worm and seed, cuddling with their ducklings and gazing up at the slow riot of white, hypnotic clouds and mist. It was as if everyone had suddenly ceased dreaming all at once, Sid thought. It was as if expectation didn't persist here anymore, or incandescence, or passion, or blood. Across the pond's cold glaring logic, the only heat was the large gray cat's heat, the only voice was the large gray cat's voice, the only burn and lungy whisper and modular red pulse was the cat's, the cat's, the cat's, the cat's.

"*Carpe diem,*" the cat said. "Seize the day, live for the moment, enjoy it all while you still can. As long as you've got your health, you've got *everything.*" When the cat wasn't sleeping, he was speaking his low voice across the pond, a voice which the steely surface of water seemed to reflect and amplify, like light or temperature. "Sleep and eat and make love and party, party, party till the cows come home. Why live for tomorrow when tomorrow may never come? History, genetics, philosophy, evolution, teleology and math—that's the world of the city, pals. That's the world of machinery, concrete, hypermarts, petroleum and death. We, on the other hand, are in and of nature. We make our own rules, define our own characters and attitudes and laws. You may be ducks, and I may be a cat, but that doesn't mean we can't also be really good friends. I'm actually a pretty thoughtful and sincere individual—once you get to know me, that is. Everybody likes me, everybody trusts me. Everybody perhaps with the exception of my little pal, the parakeet. Isn't that right?" the cat said, peering up into the acute angles of sunlight that intersected the jostling willow like spiritual traffic. "Isn't that right, little pal?"

That's right, Sid thought firmly to himself, refusing to allow the cat even a glance or a whisper. He didn't want to grant the cat any responses that could be woven into luminous spells of innuendo, gossip and misdirection. He didn't want his best thoughts and intentions to be mistranslated into catlike purposes.

And just to clarify the matter a little more precisely, Sid thought, I don't happen to trust you one single little bit.

"Did anybody ever tell you that you have really beautiful plumage?" the cat said, and began licking his knobby paws again, his thick tongue snagging every so often against a stray indication of claw.

I know, Sid thought, staring off resolutely at a distant mountain. My plumage is quite exceptionally beautiful indeed.

Just about the time of the first slow thaw, Sid went for a flight around the pond and discovered the partially devoured remains of a duck concealed behind a copse of blueberries. Flies converged there, and an odor of bad meat and disintegration. Initially Sid felt a moment of giddy, electric self-displacement, as if suddenly confronted by his own reflection in some twisted mirror. The sky seemed closer, the wind harder, the ice colder. Then, with an involuntary jolt of panic, Sid leapt flying into the brilliant white sky.

"It was Screwy," Sid told the other ducks back at the pond. "And just the way I always said it would be. Lungs, kidneys, liver, brains—that cat even chewed the spleen out of him. We got to stick together, now. We got to keep alert, assign guard duties and group leaders. We got to remain calm and, *what*ever happens, stay the hell out of the high brush. Women—keep your ducklings in line. Guys—sharpen your bills against that sandy rock over there. This is war, this is Jericho, this is the Final Battle. Evil has come to our pond, and it's snoozing away on that big gray rock over there. Evil has come to our pond in the form of a cat, and that cat wants *all* of us for its next breakfast."

"Evil?" the cat sighed, reaching out with its front paws for a hard, slow stretch. "Isn't that a bit much, really? Aren't we all part of the same food chain, aren't we all equal in the eyes of Mother Nature? Don't go getting all moralistic on me, Mr. Parakeet. Ducks die in this hasty world of ours, and so do cats—that's the law of flesh. And Screwy, if you remember, was not a particularly astute duck. If you stop and think about it for one moment, you might realize that Screwy could have been eaten by just about *any*body. So don't go blaming me because of my species, pal. My species may be feline, but my heart is true, and I only wish all of you—ducks and parakeets alike—nothing but the best health, the longest lives, the happiest dreams. And now, if you don't mind," the cat said, resting his chin on his paws, "I think I'll get back to my own happy dreams for a while."

"Quack quack," said the addled ducks, milling about in a dispirited feathery batch. "Screwy is no longer a duck, the cat is no longer a cat. Parakeets and cats disregard ducks altogether, and only talk about abstractions like Evil and Law and Society and War. This is a little too complicated. This is a little too obtuse. Let's do like the cat does, and take ourselves a nice long nap. Let's all take a nap and dream of fat, meaty flies in our mouths, and a world filled with nothing but other happy, happy ducks."

Sid began keeping meticulous census on the extinguishing flock. Fifty-seven, fifty-six, fifty-four, forty. Thirty-nine, thirty-seven, thirty-one, twenty-five. He couldn't always locate them after they disappeared, but he could quickly sense the general attitude of cool and unworried disaffection that possessed the pond's addled survivors like some sort of inoculation. The survivors rarely looked at one another anymore, or exhibited any signs of affection. They allowed their ducklings to wander off unprotected into the high brush, they didn't eat as much as usual, they grew thin, spotty and slightly diarrheic. Sometimes they slept, or drifted aimlessly on the thawing pond among wide broken platforms of ice, or just strolled aimlessly in circles on the bank, snapping at indistinguishable pebbles and insects. It was as if the ducks had surrendered to a force far greater than themselves, a force which permitted them to nap, disregard, wander, delude, demagnify and concede. The world's escalating reality was making the ducks more and more conjectural and abstract. Soon the bank and brush surrounding the pond were littered with splintery duck bones, broken duck bills and moist forlorn puddles of bloody duck feathers.

"They don't listen to a word I say," Sid complained to himself out loud. "It's like I'm talking to myself. It's like we don't even speak the same language anymore."

"They do what nature tells them," the cat said wisely, sharpening his claws against the base of Sid's willow. "That's why they're at peace with themselves, that's why they can sleep and nap and rest. They realize that the universe is just this big blazing oven, burning entire planets for fuel, driving into the long black spaces all alone without any proper destination in mind. Ducks aren't smart enough to trouble themselves with things like morality or justice—and that's where they're one up on you and me. Heaven's a dream they'll dream *after* this life, and not before. Why don't you try it yourself, pal? Why don't you just take it easy and go with the flow? We all die, we all suffer, none of our dreams hold. It's not necessarily bad, or evil, or tragic, or sad. Just look around you—the ice sparkles, the bare trees sway. Winter's a pretty beautiful season, if you give it half a chance. As long as you've got a nice thick coat to keep you warm."

Every night, Sid grew feverish with bad dreams and black reflections. He tried to stay awake and watch the cat, who never seemed to abandon the perimeter of gray rock. He could see the cat's luminous green eyes in the darkness, eyes that watched him while he drifted away into near-deliriums, lulled by the cat's ceaseless gray voice.

"Come down out of the tree," the cat whispered. "Come down and take a bath in the pond. It's not so painful once you know, it's not so scary once you're taken by its teeth. It can even be a very sensual experience, or at least so I've heard. You won't be lonely anymore. You won't suffer. You won't live dreams that always disappoint, you won't feel hope that always flees, you won't know love that always lies."

Sid began to lose his formidable appetite; he stopped trying to rally the ducks into assuming tactical deployments and responsibilities; he even stopped boring wood. He sat in the high willow all day long simply trying to stay awake, drifting into reveries and naps, awakening with a galvanic thrill whenever he smelled the cat in the tree and looked down.

"I just thought I'd come up and visit for a little while," the cat said, attached to the willow's trunk by four alert paws. "Do you mind if I come up just a little further? Oh, okay. But maybe later? Maybe later in the week?" And then, with a casual glance over his shoulder, the cat retreated backwards down the trunk of the tree again, his long tail twitching, his fat rump writhing with a slow, almost erotic beat.

What *could* you count on in life? Sid wondered. Loneliness, predation, crepuscular scurryings, agony and death and the cold comfort of abstractions? The ducks in the pond continued to dwindle and nap. Twenty-three, nineteen, eighteen, twelve. Winter, Sid thought. Cold and very white.

"What's it all about?" Sid asked himself out loud, half asleep, nearly submerged by his own watery dejection. "What's it all mean?"

"Nothing," the cat whispered. "Or at least nothing that matters."

"Who really cares?" Sid asked. "Who's there to hold you in the night, or hear you cry? Who's there to tell you it'll all be better in the morning?"

"Nobody," the cat whispered. "Nobody, nowhere."

"Why's it worth doing, then? Why should I struggle? Why should I even try anymore?"

"You shouldn't," the cat whispered, out there in the darkness. "You shouldn't struggle, you shouldn't try. Just come down out of the tree, pal. Come down here with me and *I'll* take care of you. We're similar sorts of people, you and me. We're different from everybody else. *We* belong *together*."

At night now Sid could hear the cat boldly taking the ducks and unashamedly eating them. The ducks hardly made any fuss at all anymore, or emitted any sounds. There was just the rushed guttural purr of the cat, and the wet sound of meat in his throat.

Night and annihilation were everywhere. All day long the fat gray cat slept on the large gray rock.

* * *

Sid knew he couldn't last; he knew he'd have to surrender eventually.

"First rule: I don't want to be cut," Sid said. "I don't want to be bitten, or tortured, or flayed. I want to go with dignity. Then, afterwards, I don't care what happens. That's just my material substance, that's not my *me*. But I know I can't do it alone. I'm too scared. I know I'll chicken out at the last moment. That's why I need *you*."

"Don't be frightened," the cat said, gazing placidly at Sid in the high branches. "Of course I'll do anything *I* can to help."

They embarked one morning after a cold rain. The high dark clouds were just beginning to break apart. On the bank, a small remaining band of thin, desultory ducks slept together fitfully in the shadow of the large gray rock, wheezing and dreaming. First, the cat waded alone into the pond and winced.

"The water's pretty cold," the cat said. "But I've got a nice thick coat, so I don't mind."

As the cat began to paddle, Sid leapt weakly from the willow and landed on the cat's fat behind.

"I want to go out there," Sid said. "To the island."

The island contained a few leafless trees and one broken, abandoned children's fortress cobbled together with planks of wood and old orange crates. Everything seemed misty and uncertain to Sid that morning. He had not slept properly in weeks. He couldn't keep his meals down. He knew what he had to do, but he didn't feel any desperation about it, or sadness, or urgency. He simply knew he was too tired to go on living with the way things were. He had to get it over with while he still had the strength.

"Anywhere you'd like," the cat said agreeably, looking at Sid over his shoulder, his body coiled and alert beneath the water like an assumption.

"I always thought drowning was the best way to go," Sid said distantly, watching the island approach, counting his reflections in the rippled water. "I always thought it would be just like falling asleep."

"I'm sure it's very peaceful," the cat said. "I mean, but in the long run, of course, it doesn't really matter *how* you go, does it?" The cat's eyes were sly half-crescents, void and messageless, like signals from outer space. "It just matters *that* you go, and with as little pain as possible—that's *my* philosophy. I mean, the only people death really affects are the loved ones left behind—and you're not exactly leaving the world very crowded in *those* departments, pal. Or are you?"

"No," Sid said. "I guess not."

"Death's pretty much overrated, when you get right down to it," the cat said, his voice expanding across the pond with a curt gray clarity. "I don't think death's any more inscrutable than life, really. It's not destination, or conclusion, or loss. I think of it more as translation—a reintegration of the furious self into the selfless, eternally mundane process of *living*, grinding on and on and on. Not truth. Not justice. Not morality or law. And certainly not individuals like us, pal. Individuals don't mean very much compared to the eternal burning engines of the night. Space and plane-tary explosions and famine and floods and madness and war. I guess I'm what you'd have to call a pantheistic sort of cat, being as I believe—oh my."

They were only a few yards from the brink of the island, and the cat had come to an abrupt halt in the water.

"What's that?"

There was something brittle about the cat's voice now, something tentative and uncatlike.

"What's what?" Sid asked and, with a succinct flurry of wings, transferred himself to a gnarl of a drifting branch.

The cat was squinting with concentration, his chin partially submerged beneath the lid of water. "I seem to have one of my feet caught in something."

"Reach down with your other foot," Sid said. Sid was feeling dreamy and sad. Nothing broke the corrugated surface of the pond except the earnest, conspiratorial figures of parakeet and cat.

"Yes," the cat said. "If I just . . . Oh, that's not it. Now I've got my other foot caught, too."

"They're what the ducks call slipweeds," Sid said, "because they never give you the slip. I realize it doesn't make sense calling them slipweeds—but then, go figure ducks. I don't know if you've noticed, but ducks never swim near this island. Ducks keep to the other side of the pond entirely."

"Oh my," the cat said. The cat's eyes were suddenly wider. He spat out trickles of water that rilled into his mouth. "This is a bit dire, isn't it?"

"Maybe for you," Sid said.

"Listen," the cat said, "maybe if you came over here a little closer . . ."

"Fat chance," Sid said. "A snowball's chance in hell."

"You don't like me very much, do you?" The cat was beginning to struggle and kick a little, like a fish on a line. "I think you're being very unfair. For a cat, you know, I'm actually a pretty nice guy."

"I'm sure you are," Sid said, his own voice enveloping him like a dream. He was trying to keep his eyes open. He was trying not to fall asleep. "I'm sure you're a perfect saint—for a cat, that is."

"Oh hell," the cat said, and then, with a sudden twist and a plash, his round black snout vanished beneath the surface of water like a midnight vision overcome by harsh, irrefutable sunlight.

Sid was too exhausted to fly. He floated on the knobby branch for hours, hearing the secret rhythm of waves, the moist interior warmth of planets, pausing occasionally to take a sweet sip of water, or ponder his own imponderable reflection in the brightly lidded pond.

"Maybe the cat was right about destinations," Sid thought, drifting in and out of sleep as the branch rocked, rocked him. "Maybe, in fact, destinations are places we never get to. Love, home, safety, death. Heaven and marriage and family and hell. Maybe they're just notions of permanence we've invented in order to protect ourselves from the general impermanence of life itself. Maybe the universe *is* an oven. Maybe life really *is* without meaning. But maybe, just *maybe*, these aren't reasons to give up life, but only reasons to enjoy and appreciate it more. Maybe we don't ever get anywhere, or find what we want, or know anything utterly. But maybe that means we can stop punishing ourselves so much, too. Just getting up every day and doing the best job we can—maybe *that's* the most we can ever expect from life. Doing the best job we can every day, and then being kind to ourselves afterwards."

By the time Sid's branch reached shore it was late afternoon, and Sid took himself a little bath. He nibbled damp neglected crumbs from the sand, and felt a tiny kernel of strength blossom in his heart and face. Everything about the waning sunlight seemed slightly richer, warmer, bluer and more real than it had that morning. In the shade of the large gray rock, even the frazzled ducks were beginning to stir a little. Sid couldn't help feeling momentarily pleased with himself.

"Hey, cat!" Sid called out over his shoulder, brushing the water from his wings with a little swagger.

As if in response, a few trembling bubbles surfaced from the blue pond.

"Screw you, *pal!*" Sid said, and then, just as suddenly, he realized.

Completely out of the blue, Spring had begun.

GLORY

Nicholas Royle

Nicholas Royle was born in 1963 in South Manchester, England, and now lives in London. Since 1984, he has published about fifty stories, which have appeared in *Interzone, Dark Voices, Obsessions, The Year's Best Horror Stories*, and a variety of other publications. He has also edited the original anthologies *Darklands* and *Darklands 2*.

"Glory" is reprinted from the anthology *Narrow Houses*, a volume that explores the theme of superstition. Royle's story is rich in detail and skillfully keeps the reader off balance throughout this descent into horror.

—E.D.

The photographs are supposed to be ready within the hour, but when I go to get them the man says there was a fault with the machine and I should come back at five.

As I leave work and walk towards the booth in the tube station I think about what happened at the wedding and what the photos will show. Will they show "a" or "b"? Quickening my step I worry that if I choose "a," "b" might happen. I can't be sure, though. Nor can I be confident that "a" will happen if I choose "b." It's just as well that on this occasion I don't have to choose.

I wait in the bottleneck at the entrance to Green Park tube, part of a large crowd of commuters and tourists. If I could be one of them I wouldn't have to worry about the photos, nor about what I saw at the wedding. Or *thought* I saw. Thinking about it now twenty-four hours later it seems fantastic. Maybe I shouldn't have had that third pint—certainly not with me having to drive back. The photos will prove I was just seeing things.

But the screams seemed so *real*.

Bob and Sonja have asked me to take photographs at their wedding, just informal shots while the professionals take care of the line-ups and groups. I don't mind because it'll give me something to do. Usually I just stand around feeling awkward and avoiding eye contact. I always try to dress smartly yet comfortably but suspect they may be incompatible in my case.

A telephoto lens is perfect for these occasions. You can hang around at the back and pick people out of groups without them being aware of it. I often say the best photographs are unposed. So I lay my small telephoto in the canvas bag alongside the camera and collect the films from the fridge, where they have been stored.

I never really look forward to weddings. I can never relax at them. I've been looking forward to Bob and Sonja's even less because I know Thacker will be there. At school he was the sort of bastard who used to grass to the teachers ("I think you ought to have a look in Morris's locker, sir, he's got a whole stack of them. Disgusting, they are.") *and* sneak behind the bike sheds or into the back room of the chippy for a cigarette. No one dared grass on him, though, partly because he had a protector in the form of Fry, a huge, psychotic boy with a disagreeable habit of cracking his knuckles as he looked at you, and partly because his father was head of geography.

At first I thought it might be interesting to see how much Thacker had changed in seven years. Then I remembered the acidic taste of humiliation and the burning sensation in the corners of my eyes when he caught sight of me reading from a crib in the German mock A-level exam. I suppose I should have put all that behind me, but I can feel it as clearly now as I did then in that oak-paneled exam room. I never knew if he told anyone about it, but the thought that we shared a secret was more upsetting than him grassing on me. I'm as scared of him now as I always was.

I only agreed to go because I knew how upset Bob and Sonja would be if I wasn't there. And being on photo duty will give me something to take my mind off Thacker.

The old Escort starts first time. The canvas bag is on the back seat. I check the clock and see that it's only ten minutes later than I intended to set off. I don't know how busy it will be on the motorway, so I'm leaving with plenty of time to spare.

The motorway isn't too bad and I cruise below 70. Not out of respect for the law but because if I take the old thing any higher, parts start to vibrate and appear more independent of each other than allows me to be comfortable. As I edge farther north I seem to be leaving the bright weather behind. I hope it won't rain, mainly for Bob and Sonja's sakes. Before leaving the motorway I pull off into a service area and sit in the car for ten minutes in the middle of the carpark. I tell myself that this is the freedom I enjoy as a single man—the freedom to sit in a carpark for ten minutes without having to explain it to anyone—and it feels like the emptiest, most futile gesture I've ever made to try and convince myself I'm content on my own.

I get out of the car and stroll over to use the toilet. I inspect the video games and walk around the shop without making any purchases. Back at the car I check the camera equipment to see that I have got everything. I appear to have.

On my way out of the services I pass a hitchhiker. I used to have to do that, I remind myself, but I'm already accelerating to rejoin the motorway by the time I draw level. I make a hand signal to him through the windscreen intended to convey my apologies. But his features snarl up as if he's misinterpreted my action. I immediately feel foolish and guilty.

I have to keep stopping once I've left the motorway and the A-roads to consult the map hand-drawn by Sonja's mother that came with my invite.

Negotiating an incongruous one-way system in the village, I spot a church spire rising above the trees and start to look for a parking space. The first opportunity presents itself outside a pub a few hundred yards away. I park and sit in the car for a moment contemplating the wedding. And Thacker. There is a knot of tension in my stomach.

I straighten my tie and climb out of the car, reaching for the canvas bag. I walk round to the church and take up a position at the top of the path near the main doors. I'm half an hour early.

The first people to arrive are dressed in jeans and white trainers so that I know they are not guests but bellringers. I keep my camera lowered. The vicar is identifiable by his white collar. I don't photograph him either. There is a quiet spell, then a young woman appears suddenly before me on the path. "Hello," I say, determined to seize the moment and fulfil my duty. "Would you mind if I get a picture of you? I'm supposed to take informal shots of people as they arrive. Do you mind?" She starts to protest but with a flicker of a smile so I guess it's all right to proceed. I focus quickly, tell her to smile again and press the shutter. "Thanks," I say.

"You're welcome," the young woman says in a Black Country accent. "But what I was trying to tell you is I'm not attending this wedding. I'm taking a shortcut to another one." She giggles and walks off with a rolling gait, leaving me feeling sheepish. I believe I'm blushing but as there is no one to see, it doesn't matter. I think of the rock that falls in the desert: if there's no one there to see it, does it still fall?

Before long, genuine guests begin arriving. Owing to their average age and the fact that I recognize none of them, I realize they must be Bob's or Sonja's relatives. With my long lens I can get them as they climb out of their cars and come up the path. One or two see what I am doing and smile diffidently. One lady wearing a hat like a fruit bowl shields her face with her hand and mutters to her companion. I don't want to upset anyone but I'm doing what I've been asked to do.

I recognize Bob's friends Dave and Kathy. Dave is carrying their little girl, Glory. Unable to have children of their own they adopted Glory. So I heard from Bob; this is the first time I have seen the little girl. She is a beauty, loose blond curls, shining blue eyes and healthy pink cheeks. There is something else in her face that I can't isolate, something that appears beyond her years and knowledge; maybe it is just intelligence. Anyway, I've got a job to do. Glory is the only one who knows what I'm doing and looks in my direction, but as I raise the camera and press the shutter an elderly relative passes between me and my subject.

I take the camera away from my face to look at her but she has turned away and Dave and Kathy are crossing the threshold into the church.

There are lots of people coming up the path. Obviously more relatives or family friends, and behind them is a group of Bob's football mates: blokes he knew on his course at college and still goes to matches with at the weekend. I've never met them but I recognize them from the way Bob has described them to me. Three of them stride forward together and a little way behind follows a fourth, whom I recognise as Jonesy, with his girlfriend. He looks as if he would rather not have to hang back.

Then my stomach goes as cold as ice because behind that couple are Thacker and a woman. He looks the same except for his center parting, which has become a victim of hairline recession but doesn't make him any less threatening. He looks as uncomfortable in a suit as he always did in school uniform. The woman with him looks pinched and pained in a blue dress she's worn to a dozen weddings.

Camera raised, I click off picture after picture of them. He hasn't seen me. The camera is a good mask.

I wait until the last minute then slip inside and sit down on the pew nearest to the door. The service is bearable. No more. I am glad it doesn't go on any longer than it does. I'm outside and in position behind a privet bush seconds after the bride and groom have made their exit. They stand in front of the main doors for a photo opportunity and I snap those taking pictures of the happy couple. I see Thacker and the woman with him come out and I crouch a little lower. It occurs to me that if I continue being careful I might manage to avoid them altogether.

I take pictures until Bob and Sonja have climbed into their hired vintage Rolls and are driven away. Then I hang back until Thacker has disappeared.

Bob and I were never really friends at school—we got to know each other properly at college—which goes some way towards explaining how Thacker and I both got invited to the wedding. They got on all right at school and I think there's some vague family connection which meant he had to be asked. I don't really want to go into it too deeply in case Bob reveals that they have become great mates.

The drive from the church to the hotel takes about twenty minutes. All the way I'm holding back tears. Holding them back because I'm frightened that if I give way to them, they might never stop.

I turn off the main road into a lane which the sign says will bend this way and that for two miles.

I am sorely tempted to bunk off and explain later to Bob and Sonja that I couldn't bear to be around Thacker because he unsettled me too much. But my foot stays on the accelerator and I know I'm almost there.

He caught me out once in the West Basement toilets. I thought I was alone down there and I was considering a theory which had occurred to me. All the locks in West Basement were broken and I was trying to decide whether or not to push open a cubicle door which was ajar. If it was ajar there was no way of knowing if there was someone in there or not, except by trying the door. I was thinking that if I left the door there would be no one inside, but if I tried to open it there would be someone. It seemed as if I could affect whether there was someone there or not by choosing whether to open or leave the door.

I can remember very clearly the sounds of West Basement: water dripping from old taps and shower heads, hissing cisterns and the quiet rumble of boys' feet as they ran along the corridor above my head. While I was dithering in front of the door, actually touching it with my fingers and wondering if that touch was the moment of creation, a foreign sound intruded. It sounded like the turning of pages, the closing of a cover, then more rustling and a terribly sudden chain flush. Before I had a chance to do more than look guilty, a cubicle several doors down opened and Thacker came out. He was holding an A4 folder in his hand, which seemed like a strange thing to take into the toilet. He wasn't the sort to be so keen to get his homework done. What else would he conceal in an A4 folder?

"What are you doing, Morris?" he asked me slyly. My hand was still stretched out towards the cubicle door.

"I'm just going to the bog," I said with a degree of defiance. Unwisely sarcastic, I added, "Is that all right?"

He retorted, "Going for a wank, are you, you little twat?"

It was familiar language but down in West Basement alone with Thacker it made my stomach contort. I pushed hurriedly at the door and got a shock when it hit against something inside and an unknown voice snapped, "Fuck off! I'm in here."

As I fled Thacker's taunts echoed off the cold stone walls: "What are you, Morris, a puff? Gay boy, gay boy!" He thought I had known there was someone in there and was trying to see in or go in and join whoever it was. Thacker wasn't the kind of boy you could explain the truth to so I never bothered to try.

The hotel is one of those big old places you find on the outskirts of Midlands villages that could look quite impressive if it wasn't for the British theme park mentality, which seems to affect hoteliers as severely as it afflicts the Department of the Environment. There are imitation tapestries depicting battle scenes and hunts, flock wallpaper and velvet lampshades. I accept a glass of sherry and brandish my camera with my other hand. Determined not to mingle, in case some social osmosis brings me into contact with Thacker, I cross the room and go outside through the French windows. A number of guests are already standing about on the lawns and occupying the white plastic tables, no doubt the very same tables on which King Charles II rested his weary head after fleeing the Battle of Worcester and before nipping into the Heritage Bar for a swift half.

At the other end of the lawn I can see Thacker has introduced himself to Jonesy. Their two partners stand sideways on to each other looking at the grass. I focus and snap the four of them.

The professional photographer arrives and sets up his stall, then his assistant shepherds everyone into the right groups. There seem to be endless permutations of Bob's family and Sonja's family, Bob's close family, Sonja's friends and distant family, and so on. I get a few good pictures of people watching other people, mainly profiles. Bob's footballing mates are standing together in a group and from their expressions and gestures I can tell they are discussing a game. They're good for a couple of shots, then I have to change the film.

Dave and Kathy stand close to the French windows and Dave watches Glory closely as she runs round in circles on the lawn. When a little boy approaches her she eyes him suspiciously. She puts one finger in her mouth and sways from side to side and that sees him off. With a little jump and flap of her skirt she raises a delighted smile on Dave's worried face.

There's an awkward moment when I have to pose in the same group as Thacker. I'm now a couple of inches taller than he is so I'm standing in the back row while he's just three along in front of me. I pray he won't turn round and when he does I bury my face in my handkerchief. I don't even know if he knows I'm at the wedding. It's quite possible he wouldn't remember me, so I don't know why I'm getting in such a state about him.

In the hotel's Boscobel Banquet Suite I find myself next to Dave and Kathy, and Glory.

"It's a lovely name," I say rather unimaginatively.

Kathy beams at me and Dave tousles Glory's hair. She shifts about on her chair and demands to be fed. Dave cuts up her food and feeds it to her. When she picks up a knife Dave's hand shoots out quick as a flash to retrieve it from her, concern creasing his brows. It moves me to see how much he cares. His obvious love for her awakes strong paternal feelings in me. There's no reason why I shouldn't have such feelings, even though I'm unlikely ever to realize them. Dave and Kathy are nice people and fairly easy to talk to, but I'm glad when the meal is over. I always get into a tangle with too much cutlery and often when the dessert comes I find I've already used my dessert spoon and I have to wield a huge fish fork against a harmless bowl of trifle.

Back in the Heritage Bar the serious drinking now begins. I hang back while at the front of the queue Thacker gets himself a pint of lager and a half in a straight glass for his partner. They move outside. When it's my turn I get a half and take a few sips before putting it down on a table and stepping out through the French windows. Most people are on the lawn again but they're making considerably more noise than before the meal. I pop back inside to finish my drink and get another. It'll be at least a couple of hours before I have to drive, so I get a pint.

As I'm walking away I notice Thacker stepping up to the bar. Still he appears not to have seen me. Outside, groups of friends and relatives are taking more pictures of each other. By now I'm quite getting into it. Avoiding Thacker seems like a game at which I'm excelling. I sink half my pint and stand the glass on one of the historic plastic tables. Dave and Kathy are standing on the lawn a few yards away. Glory is running around apparently not in the slightest bit tired. A woman in a turquoise dress and black hat calls to Kathy. She wants them to get into a picture with a number of other friends. I drink another mouthful of beer and kneel down to take my own picture of the group. Dave is still trying to catch Glory and get her to stand still. Her curls bounce up and down as she dodges his grasp and she bubbles with laughter.

A curious and unsettling impression strikes me as I raise the camera to my eye and look through the viewfinder. Glory seems to vanish out of frame and her laughter reaches such a pitch it almost becomes a scream. Immediately I drop the camera from my eye and she pops out from behind Dave's legs giggling.

Maybe I'm drinking too fast.

At last Dave grabs her and holds her in front of him at the edge of the group. The woman in the turquoise dress is pointing her camera at the group and stepping backwards, obviously striving not to cut off their feet. I raise mine again and hear another sound like a scream as I click the shutter release. It must be a bird. Also, Glory must have managed to slip out of Dave's hands and between someone's legs because I'm sure she wasn't in the shot. But now she's back again. What a handful she must be for Dave and Kathy, but what a joy. I feel a pang for her which must be my paternal instinct again.

The turquoise-dress woman is joining the group and a young man with a ponytail is trotting out to take a picture for himself. I'm going to take another as well. I focus again and shoot. As soon as I've done so I realize that once again Glory disappeared while I was taking the picture. And I thought I noticed something else: a white shape against the lawn behind the group. But when I look now there's nothing there. The ponytail man is taking another, so I raise my own apparatus once more.

Glory is not standing between Dave's legs as she was just a second ago.

I distinctly hear a scream.

And there's a white shape in the picture behind the group.

I press the shutter and lower the camera.

Glory has reappeared.

I'm drinking too fast. I need to clear my head. When I had wine at dinner I didn't think that I might want a beer later. I shouldn't be mixing them. I stand up and my head swims. As it clears I see Thacker standing near the French windows and looking straight at me. His partner stands a few feet behind him, looking bored. I feel the blood drain from my face. Why on earth did he bring her, whoever she is? I can't stare him out; he makes me too uneasy. I pick up my beer glass in mock bravado and drain it, then turn and walk away from the hotel towards the far end of the lawn.

I saw Thacker in West Basement a second time. I'd been changing after playing five-a-side at lunchtime, and was just leaving West Basement when I heard a series of unusual sounds coming from one of the cubicles: scuffling noises and panting and my first thought was that someone was being beaten up. By nature I'm a coward but I can't pass by if I think someone's being hurt.

My second thought, however, was quite different.

Either way, there were two boys in one cubicle and that wasn't right. If I opened the door I would find one alternative. If I walked away it would be the other. By choosing to open the door or walk away I determined what actually was taking place, and what had been taking place even before I became aware of it. I was affecting reality backwards in time.

Such was my conviction.

If I walked away, it would have been a fight. And if I pushed open the door it would be the other thing. I couldn't walk away because I couldn't carry the guilt of leaving someone to get hurt. So I had to open the door.

Inside the cubicle were Thacker and a boy I vaguely knew from the lower sixth called Benns. Thacker was sitting down on the toilet seat fully dressed. Benns was standing with his trousers round his ankles. He stared at me in shock. Thacker had obviously been brought up to believe it was rude to talk with your mouth full: he gave me a long silent look that struck me as conspiratorial.

He knew I wouldn't tell anyone.

He knew that I couldn't.

In many ways it would be like grassing on myself.

It is precisely because of the secrets we share that I fear Thacker so much. However intensely I may dislike him, he is an inseparable part of me.

The way he looked at me following Glory's apparently mischievous disappearing act made me feel sick to my stomach. He knows better than I what is going on, but he makes me a party to it. When I look back he is drinking. The group is still assembled and Glory is running in and out of people's legs. I look through the viewfinder. The telephoto lens draws the group closer to me but I can't see Glory. A bird screams overhead. Above Dave's right shoulder against a grassy bank in front of the hotel is the white shape, an irregular oblong. It must be a piece of fluff caught inside the lens and magnified. But there's something about it that disturbs me. As soon as I take the picture and lower the camera Glory reappears. Dave scoops her up in his arms and throws a concerned, almost accusatory look in my direction.

Unwilling to accept what seems to be happening I try again with the camera.

No Glory.

White oblong in the background.

A scream.

That's me finished. No more photographs.

I sit in the Heritage Bar for half an hour and down another pint. At the far end of the bar Thacker is doing the same. I notice Dave and Kathy making for the exit, Dave holding Glory's little hand, then I see Bob coming towards me. I realize I've hardly spoken to him and Sonja.

"How are you? Where've you been?" Bob asks me.

"Taking pictures," I say. "How does it feel then?"

Bob shrugged and grinned. Out of the corner of my eye I notice Thacker leaving, followed by the woman he came with.

"What's the time, Bob?" I ask, looking at his watch. "I must go. It'll be dark."

"Are you all right to drive?" Bob asks, clearly worried I may have had too much to drink.

"I'm fine. Give us a ring."

As I'm crossing the carpark towards my Escort I see Thacker just leaning into his Sierra. When he winks at me I stop in my tracks, instantly sobered up. I run to my car, past Kathy who is searching for her car keys while Dave calls out to Glory to stop dawdling because it's time to go home. She strays a couple of yards and Dave reaches for her, but I'm into second gear and out of the carpark before Thacker has coordinated his actions well enough to engage first and loose the clutch. I don't want to be around when his drunken wheelspin goes out of control.

I've got the photos now. I didn't open them on the tube. I didn't dare in case I overreacted to what I feared they might show. I waited till I got home. Then I looked at them.

Glory doesn't appear in a single one. You can't even see the hem of her skirt disappearing behind someone's trouser leg. She's not even in the one I took of Dave and Kathy and her on their way into the church. It was one of Sonja's uncles who stepped in front of Dave just as I clicked the shutter.

Looking at the photographs I can hear the screams again. They're as lifelike now as they were then. With trembling hands I pour a drink to try and calm my nerves.

It's the white oblong shape that's reduced me to this state, more than the fact of Glory's vanishing. In the background of every shot that should have featured Glory I have found the white shape. Its definition is clearer on the glossy prints than it was through my lens. The white shape is a child's coffin.

Now the phone is ringing and I feel sick with remorse.

MURDER MYSTERIES
Neil Gaiman

Neil Gaiman has recently emigrated from his native England to the United States. He is best known for his continuing work on the *Sandman* series of graphic novels, including the World Fantasy award-winning *Midsummer's Night Dream* issue. He is currently working on a new series for the Vertigo imprint of DC, *Death*, and the limited series *Sweeney Todd* with Michael Zulli. Gaiman is also the co-author with Terry Pratchett of the comic novel *Good Omens*. He has written only a few short stories. They have been published in *Fantasy Tales* and in the anthologies *More Tales from the Forbidden Planet* and *Snow White, Blood Red*.

"Murder Mysteries" was first published in the *Midnight Graffiti* anthology. It's a subtle and ultimately terrifying story of predestination, murder, and vengeance.

—E.D.

The Fourth Angel says:

> *Of this order I am made one,*
> *From Mankind to guard this place*
> *That through their Guilt they have forgone,*
> *For they have forfeited His Grace;*
> *Therefore all this must they shun*
> *Or else my Sword they shall embrace*
> *And myself will be their Foe*
> *To flame them in the Face.*

Chester Mystery Cycle: *The Creation, and Adam and Eve.* Circa 1461.

This is true.

Ten years ago, give or take a year, I found myself on an enforced stopover in Los Angeles, a long way from home. It was December, and the California weather was warm and pleasant. England, however, was in the grip of fogs and snow storms, and no planes were landing there. Each day I'd phone the airport, and each day I'd be told to wait another day.

This had gone on for almost a week.

I was barely out of my teens. Looking around today at the parts of my life left over from those days, I feel uncomfortable, as if I've received a gift, unasked, from another person: a house, a wife, children, a vocation. Nothing to do with me, I could say, innocently. If it's true that every seven years each cell in your body dies and is replaced, then I have truly inherited my life from a dead man; and the misdeeds of those times have been forgiven, and are buried with his bones.

I was in Los Angeles. Yes.

On the sixth day I received a message from an old sort-of-girlfriend from Seattle: she was in LA too, and she had heard I was around on the friends-of-friends network. Would I come over?

I left a message on her machine. Sure.

That evening: a small blonde woman approached me, as I came out of the place I was staying. It was already dark.

She stared at me, as if she were trying to match me to a description, and then, hesitantly, she said my name.

"That's me. Are you Tink's friend?"

"Yeah. Car's out back. C'mon: she's really looking forward to seeing you."

The woman's car was one of the huge old boat-like jobs you only ever seem to see in California. It smelled of cracked and flaking leather upholstery. We drove out from wherever we were to wherever we were going.

Los Angeles was at that time a complete mystery to me; and I cannot say I understand it much better now. I understand London, and New York, and Paris: you can walk around them, get a sense of what's where in just a morning of wandering. Maybe catch the subway. But Los Angeles is about cars. Back then I didn't drive at all; even today I will not drive in America. Memories of LA for me are linked by rides in other people's cars, with no sense there of the shape of the city, of the relationships between the people and the place. The regularity of the roads, the repetition of structure and form, mean that when I try to remember it as an entity all I have is the boundless profusion of tiny lights I saw one night on my first trip to the city, from the hill of Griffith Park. It was one of the most beautiful things I had ever seen, from that distance.

"See that building?" said my blonde driver, Tink's friend. It was a red-brick art deco house, charming and quite ugly.

"Yes."

"Built in the 1930s," she said, with respect and pride.

I said something polite, trying to comprehend a city inside which fifty years could be considered a long time.

"Tink's real excited. When she heard you were in town. She was so excited."

"I'm looking forward to seeing her again."

Tink's real name was Tinkerbell Richmond. No lie.

She was staying with friends in a small apartment clump, somewhere an hour's drive from downtown LA.

What you need to know about Tink: she was ten years older than me, in her early thirties; she had glossy black hair and red, puzzled lips, and very white skin, like Snow White in the fairy stories; the first time I met her I thought she was the most beautiful woman in the world.

Tink had been married for a while at some point in her life, and had a five-year-old daughter called Susan. I had never met Susan—when Tink had been in England, Susan had been staying on in Seattle, with her father.

People named Tinkerbell name their daughters Susan.

Memory is the great deceiver. Perhaps there are some individuals whose memories act like tape recordings, daily records of their lives complete in every detail, but I am not one of them. My memory is a patchwork of occurrences, of discontinuous events roughly sewn together: the parts I remember, I remember precisely, whilst other sections seem to have vanished completely.

I do not remember arriving at Tink's house, nor where her flatmate went.

What I remember next is sitting in Tink's lounge, with the lights low; the two of us next to each other, on the sofa.

We made small talk. It had been perhaps a year since we had seen one another. But a twenty-one-year-old boy has little to say to a thirty-two-year-old woman, and soon, having nothing in common, I pulled her to me.

She snuggled close with a kind of sigh, and presented her lips to be kissed. In the half-light her lips were black. We kissed for a little, and I stroked her breasts through her blouse, on the couch; and then she said:

"We can't fuck. I'm on my period."

"Fine."

"I can give you a blow job, if you'd like."

I nodded assent, and she unzipped my jeans, and lowered her head to my lap.

After I had come, she got up and ran into the kitchen. I heard her spitting into the sink, and the sound of running water: I remember wondering why she did it, if she hated the taste that much.

Then she returned and we sat next to each other on the couch.

"Susan's upstairs, asleep," said Tink. "She's all I live for. Would you like to see her?"

"I don't mind."

We went upstairs. Tink led me into a darkened bedroom. There were child-scrawl pictures all over the walls—wax-crayoned drawings of winged fairies and little palaces—and a small, fair-haired girl was asleep in the bed.

"She's very beautiful," said Tink, and kissed me. Her lips were still slightly sticky. "She takes after her father."

We went downstairs. We had nothing else to say, nothing else to do. Tink turned on the main light. For the first time I noticed tiny crow's-feet at the corners of her eyes, incongruous on her perfect, Barbie-doll face.

"I love you," she said.

"Thank you."

"Would you like a ride back?"

"If you don't mind leaving Susan alone . . . ?"

She shrugged, and I pulled her to me for the last time.

At night, Los Angeles is all lights. And shadows.

A blank, here, in my mind. I simply don't remember what happened next. She must have driven me back to the place where I was staying—how else would I have gotten there? I do not even remember kissing her good-bye. Perhaps I simply waited on the sidewalk and watched her drive away.

Perhaps.

I do know, however, that once I reached the place I was staying I just stood there, unable to go inside, to wash and then to sleep, unwilling to do anything else.

I was not hungry. I did not want alcohol. I did not want to read, or talk. I was scared of walking too far, in case I became lost, bedeviled by the repeating motifs of Los Angeles, spun around and sucked in so I could never find my way home again. Central Los Angeles sometimes seems to me to be nothing more than a pattern—like a set of repeating blocks: a gas station, a few homes, a mini-mall (donuts, photo developers, laundromats, fast-foods), and repeat until hypnotized; and the tiny changes in the mini-malls and the houses only serve to reinforce the structure.

I thought of Tink's lips. Then I fumbled in a pocket of my jacket, and pulled out a packet of cigarettes.

I lit one, inhaled, blew blue smoke into the warm night air.

There was a stunted palm tree growing outside the place I was staying, and I resolved to walk for a way, keeping the tree in sight, to smoke my cigarette, perhaps even to think; but I felt too drained to think. I felt very sexless, and very alone.

A block or so down the road there was a bench, and when I reached it I sat down. I threw the stub of the cigarette onto the pavement, hard, and watched it shower orange sparks.

Someone said, "I'll buy a cigarette off you, pal. Here."

A hand, in front of my face, holding a quarter. I looked up.

He did not look old, although I would not have been prepared to say how old he was. Late thirties, perhaps. Mid forties. He wore a long, shabby coat, colorless under the yellow street lamps, and his eyes were dark.

"Here. A quarter. That's a good price."

I shook my head, pulled out the packet of Marlboros, offered him one. "Keep your money. It's free. Have it."

He took the cigarette. I passed him a book of matches (it advertised a telephone sex line; I remember that), and he lit the cigarette. He offered me the matches back, and I shook my head. "Keep them. I always wind up accumulating books of matches in America."

"Uh huh." He sat next to me, and smoked his cigarette. When he had smoked it halfway down, he tapped the lighted end off on the concrete, stubbed out the glow, and placed the butt of the cigarette behind his ear.

"I don't smoke much," he said. "Seems a pity to waste it, though."

A car careened down the road, veering from one side to the other. There were four young men in the car: the two in the front were both pulling at the wheel, and laughing. The windows were wound down, and I could hear their laughter, and the two in the back seat ("*Gaary, you asshole! What the fuck are you onnn, mannnn?*"), and the pulsing beat of a rock song. Not a song I recognized. The car looped around a corner, out of sight.

Soon the sounds were gone, too.

"I owe you," said the man on the bench.

"Sorry?"

"I owe you something. For the cigarette. And the matches. You wouldn't take the money. I owe you."

I shrugged, embarrassed. "Really, it's just a cigarette. I figure, if I give people cigarettes, then if ever I'm out, maybe people will give me cigarettes." I laughed, to show I didn't really mean it, although I did. "Don't worry about it."

"Mm. You want to hear a story? True story? Stories always used to be good payment. These days . . ." he shrugged ". . . not so much."

I sat back on the bench, and the night was warm, and I looked at my watch: it was almost one in the morning. In England a freezing new day would already have begun: a work-day would be starting for those who could beat the snow and get into work; another handful of old people, and those without homes, would have died, in the night, from the cold.

"Sure," I said to the man. "Sure. Tell me a story."

He coughed, grinned white teeth—a flash in the darkness—and he began.

"First thing I remember was the Word. And the Word was God. Sometimes, when I get *really* down, I remember the sound of the Word in my head, shaping me, forming me, giving me life.

"The Word gave me a body, gave me eyes. And I opened my eyes, and I saw the light of the Silver City.

"I was in a room—a silver room—and there wasn't anything in it except me. In front of me was a window, that went from floor to ceiling, open to the sky, and through the window I could see the spires of the City, and at the edge of the City, the Dark.

"I don't know how long I waited there. I wasn't impatient or anything, though. I remember that. It was like I was waiting until I was called; and I knew that some time I would be called. And if I had to wait until the end of everything, and never be called, why, that was fine too. But I'd be called, I was certain of that. And then I'd know my name, and my function.

"Through the window I could see silver spires, and in many of the other spires were windows; and in the windows I could see others like me. That was how I knew what I looked like.

"You wouldn't think it of me, seeing me now, but I was beautiful. I've come down in the world a way since then.

"I was taller then, and I had wings.

"They were huge and powerful wings, with feathers the color of mother-of-pearl. They came out from just between my shoulder blades. They were so good. My wings.

"Sometimes I'd see others like me, the ones who'd left their rooms, who were already fulfilling their duties. I'd watch them soar through the sky from spire to spire, performing errands I could barely imagine.

"The sky above the City was a wonderful thing. It was always light, although lit by no sun—lit, perhaps, by the City itself: but the quality of light was forever changing. Now pewter-colored light, then brass, then a gentle gold, or a soft and quiet amethyst . . ."

The man stopped talking. He looked at me, his head on one side. There was a glitter in his eyes that scared me. "You know what amethyst is? A kind of purple stone?"

I nodded.

My crotch felt uncomfortable.

It occurred to me then that the man might not be mad; I found this far more disquieting than the alternative.

The man began talking once more. "I don't know how long it was that I waited, in my room. But time didn't mean anything. Not back then. We had all the time in the world.

"The next thing that happened to me, was when the Angel Lucifer came to my cell. He was taller than me, and his wings were imposing, his plumage perfect. He had skin the color of sea mist, and curly silver hair, and these wonderful gray eyes . . .

"I say *he*, but you should understand that none of us had any sex, to speak of." He gestured towards his lap. "Smooth and empty. Nothing there. You know.

"Lucifer shone. I mean it—he glowed from inside. All angels do. They're lit up from within, and in my cell the Angel Lucifer burned like a lightning storm.

"He looked at me. And he named me.

" 'You are Raguel,' he said. 'The Vengeance of the Lord.'

"I bowed my head, because I knew it was true. That was my name. That was my function.

" 'There has been a . . . a wrong thing,' he said. 'The first of its kind. You are needed.'

"He turned and pushed himself into space, and I followed him, flew behind him across the Silver City, to the outskirts, where the City stops and the Darkness begins; and it was there, under a vast silver spire, that we descended to the street, and I saw the dead angel.

"The body lay, crumpled and broken, on the silver sidewalk. Its wings were crushed underneath it and a few loose feathers had already blown into the silver gutter.

"The body was almost dark. Now and again a light would flash inside it, an occasional flicker of cold fire in the chest, or in the eyes, or in the sexless groin, as the last of the glow of life left it forever.

"Blood pooled in rubies on its chest and stained its white wing-feathers crimson. It was very beautiful, even in death.

"It would have broken your heart.

"Lucifer spoke to me, then. 'You must find who was responsible for this, and how; and take the Vengeance of the Name on whoever caused this thing to happen.'

"He really didn't have to say anything. I knew that already. The hunt, and the retribution: it was what I was created for, in the Beginning; it was what I *was*.

" 'I have work to attend to,' said the Angel Lucifer.

"He flapped his wings, once, hard, and rose upwards; the gust of wind sent the dead angel's loose feathers blowing across the street.

"I leaned down to examine the body. All luminescence had by now left it. It was a dark thing; a parody of an angel. It had a perfect, sexless face, framed by silver hair. One of the eyelids was open, revealing a placid gray eye; the other was closed. There were no nipples on the chest and only smoothness between the legs.

"I lifted the body up.

"The back of the angel was a mess. The wings were broken and twisted; the back of the head stove in; there was a floppiness to the corpse that made me think its spine had been broken as well. The back of the angel was all blood.

"The only blood on its front was in the chest area. I probed it with my forefinger, and it entered the body without difficulty.

"He fell, I thought. And he was dead before he fell.

"And I looked up at the windows that ranked the street. I stared across the Silver City. *You did this, I thought. I will find you, whoever you are. And I will take the Lord's vengeance upon you."*

The man took the cigarette stub from behind his ear, lit it with a match. Briefly I smelled the ashtray smell of a dead cigarette, acrid and harsh; then he pulled down to the unburnt tobacco, exhaled blue smoke into the night air.

"The angel who had first discovered the body was called Phanuel.

"I spoke to him in the Hall of Being. That was the spire beside which the dead angel lay. In the Hall hung the . . . the blueprints, maybe, for what was going to be . . . all this." He gestured with the hand that held the stubby cigarette, pointing to the night sky and the parked cars and the world. "You know. The universe.

"Phanuel was the senior designer; working under him were a multitude of angels laboring on the details of the Creation. I watched him from the floor of the hall. He hung in the air below the Plan, and angels flew down to him, waiting politely in turn as they asked him questions, checked things with him, invited comment on their work. Eventually he left them, and descended to the floor.

" 'You are Raguel,' he said. His voice was high, and fussy. 'What need have you of me?'

" 'You found the body?'

" 'Poor Carasel? Indeed I did. I was leaving the Hall—there are a number of concepts we are currently constructing, and I wished to ponder one of them, *Regret* by name. I was planning to get a little distance from the City—to fly above it, I mean, not to go into the Dark outside, I wouldn't do that, although there has been some loose talk amongst . . . but, yes. I was going to rise, and contemplate.

" 'I left the Hall, and . . . ' he broke off. He was small, for an angel. His light was muted, but his eyes were vivid and bright. I mean really bright. 'Poor Carasel. How could he *do* that to himself? How?'

" 'You think his destruction was self-inflicted?'

"He seemed puzzled—surprised that there could be any other explanation. 'But of course. Carasel was working under me, developing a number of concepts that shall be intrinsic to the Universe, when its Name shall be spoken. His group did a remarkable job on some of the real basics—*Dimension* was one, and *Sleep* another. There were others.

" 'Wonderful work. Some of his suggestions regarding the use of individual viewpoints to define dimensions were truly ingenious.

" 'Anyway. He had begun work on a new project. It's one of the really major ones—the ones that I would usually handle, or possibly even Zephkiel,' he glanced upward. 'But Carasel had done such sterling work. And his last project was *so* remarkable. Something apparently quite trivial, that he and Saraquael elevated into . . . ' he shrugged. 'But that is unimportant. It was *this* project that forced him into non-being. But none of us could ever have foreseen . . .'

" 'What was his current project?'

"Phanuel stared at me. 'I'm not sure I ought to tell you. All the new concepts are considered sensitive, until we get them into the final form in which they will be Spoken.'

"I felt myself transforming. I am not sure how I can explain it to you, but suddenly I wasn't me—I was something larger. I was transfigured: I was my function.

"Phanuel was unable to meet my gaze.

" 'I am Raguel, who is the Vengeance of the Lord,' I told him. 'I serve the Name directly. It is my mission to discover the nature of this deed, and to take the Name's vengeance on those responsible. My questions are to be answered.'

"The little angel trembled, and he talked fast.

" 'Carasel and his partner were researching *Death*. Cessation of life. An end to physical, animated existence. They were putting it all together. But Carasel always went too far into his work—we had a terrible time with him when he was designing *Agitation*. That was when he was working on Emotions . . . '

" 'You think Carasel died to—to research the phenomenon?'

" 'Or because it intrigued him. Or because he followed his research just too far. Yes.' Phanuel flexed his fingers, stared at me with those brightly shining eyes. 'I trust that you will repeat none of this to any unauthorized persons, Raguel.'

" 'What did you do when you found the body?'

" 'I came out of the Hall, as I said, and there was Carasel on the sidewalk, staring up. I asked him what he was doing and he did not reply. Then I noticed the inner fluid, and that Carasel seemed unable, rather than unwilling to talk to me.

" 'I was scared. I did not know what to do.

" 'The Angel Lucifer came up behind me. He asked me if there was some kind of problem. I told him. I showed him the body. And then . . . then his Aspect came upon him, and he communed with The Name. He burned so bright.

" 'Then he said he had to fetch the one whose function embraced events like this, and he left—to seek you, I imagine.

" 'As Carasel's death was now being dealt with, and his fate was no real concern of mine, I returned to work, having gained a new—and I suspect, quite valuable—perspective on the mechanics of *Regret*.

" 'I am considering taking *Death* away from the Carasel and Saraquael partnership. I may reassign it to Zephkiel, my senior partner, if he is willing to take it on. He excels on contemplative projects.'

"By now there was a line of angels waiting to talk to Phanuel. I felt I had almost all I was going to get from him.

" 'Who did Carasel work with? Who would have been the last to see him alive?'

" 'You could talk to Saraquael, I suppose—he was his partner, after all. Now, if you'll excuse me . . . '

"He returned to his swarm of aides: advising, correcting, suggesting, forbidding." The man paused.

The street was quiet, now; I remember the low whisper of his voice, the buzz of a cricket somewhere. A small animal—a cat perhaps, or something more exotic, a raccoon, or even a jackal—darted from shadow to shadow among the parked cars on the opposite side of the street.

"Saraquael was in the highest of the mezzanine galleries that ringed the Hall of Being. As I said, the Universe was in the middle of the Hall, and it glinted and sparkled and shone. Went up quite a way, too. . ."

"The Universe you mention, it was, what, a diagram?" I asked, interrupting for the first time.

"Not really. Kind of. Sorta. It was a blueprint: but it was full-sized, and it hung in the Hall, and all these angels went around and fiddled with it all the time. Doing stuff with *Gravity*, and *Music* and *Klar* and whatever. It wasn't really the universe, not yet. It would be, when it was finished, and it was time for it to be properly Named."

"But . . ." I grasped for words to express my confusion. The man interrupted me.

"Don't worry about it. Think of it as a model, if that makes it easier for you. Or a map. Or a—what's the word? Prototype. Yeah. A Model T Ford universe." He grinned. "You got to understand, a lot of the stuff I'm telling you, I'm translating already; putting it in a form you can understand. Otherwise I couldn't tell the story at all. You want to hear it?"

"Yes." I didn't care if it was true or not; it was a story I needed to hear all the way through to the end.

"Good. So shut up and listen.

"So I met Saraquael, in the topmost gallery. There was no one else about—just him, and some papers, and some small, glowing models.

" 'I've come about Carasel,' I told him.

"He looked at me. 'Carasel isn't here at this time,' he said. 'I expect him to return shortly.'

"I shook my head.

" 'Carasel won't be coming back. He's stopped existing as a spiritual entity,' I said.

"His light paled, and his eyes opened very wide. 'He's dead?'

" 'That's what I said. Do you have any ideas about how it happened?'

" 'I . . . this is so sudden. I mean, he'd been talking about . . . but I had no idea that he would . . . '

" 'Take it slowly.'

"Saraquael nodded.

"He stood up and walked to the window. There was no view of the Silver City from his window—just a reflected glow from the City and the sky behind us, hanging in the air, and beyond that, the Dark. The wind from the Dark gently caressed Saraquael's hair as he spoke. I stared at his back.

" 'Carasel is . . . no, was. That's right, isn't it? *Was*. He was always so involved. And so creative. But it was never enough for him. He always wanted to understand everything—to experience what he was working on. He was never content to just create it—to understand it intellectually. He wanted *all* of it.

" 'That wasn't a problem before, when we were working on properties of matter. But when we began to design some of the Named emotions . . . he got too involved with his work.

" 'And our latest project was *Death*. It's one of the hard ones—one of the big ones, too, I suspect. Possibly it may even become the attribute that's going to define the Creation for the Created: if not for *Death*, they'd be content to simply exist, but with *Death*, well, their lives will have meaning—a boundary beyond which the living cannot cross . . . '

" 'So you think he killed himself?'

" 'I know he did,' said Saraquael. I walked to the window, and looked out. Far below, a *long* way, I could see a tiny white dot. That was Carasel's body. I'd have to arrange for someone to take care of it. I wondered what we would do with it; but there would be someone who would know, whose function was the removal of unwanted things. It was not my function. I knew that.

" 'How?'

"He shrugged. 'I know. Recently he'd begun asking questions—questions about *Death*. How we could know whether or not it was right to make this thing, to set the rules, if we were not going to experience it ourselves. He kept talking about it.'

" 'Didn't you wonder about this?'

"Saraquael turned, for the first time, to look at me. 'No. That *is* our function—to discuss, to improvise, to aid the Creation and the Created. We sort it out now, so that when it all Begins, it'll run like clockwork. Right now we're working on Death. So obviously that's what we look at. The physical aspect; the emotional aspect; the philosophical aspect . . .

" 'And the *patterns*. Carasel had the notion that what we do here in the Hall of Being creates patterns. That there are structures and shapes appropriate to beings and events that, once begun, must continue until they reach their end. For us, perhaps, as well as for them. Conceivably he felt this was one of his patterns.

" 'Did you know Carasel well?'

" 'As well as any of us know each other. We saw each other here; we worked side by side. At certain times I would retire to my cell, across the City. Sometimes he would do the same.'

" 'Tell me about Phanuel.'

"His mouth crooked into a smile. 'He's officious. Doesn't do much—farms everything out, and takes all the credit.' He lowered his voice, although there was no other soul in the gallery. 'To hear him talk, you'd think that *Love* was all his own work. But to his credit he does make sure the work gets done. Zephkiel's the real thinker of the two senior designers, but he doesn't come here. He stays back in his cell in the City, and contemplates; resolves problems from a distance. If you need to speak to Zephkiel, you go to Phanuel, and Phanuel relays your questions to Zephkiel . . . '

"I cut him short. 'How about Lucifer? Tell me about him.'

" 'Lucifer? The Captain of the Host? He doesn't work here . . . He has visited the Hall a couple of times, though—inspecting the Creation. They say he reports directly to the Name. I have never spoken to him.'

" 'Did he know Carasel?'

" 'I doubt it. As I said, he has only been here twice. I have seen him on other occasions, though. Through here.' He flicked a wingtip, indicating the world outside the window. 'In flight.'

" 'Where to?'

"Saraquael seemed to be about to say something, then he changed his mind. 'I don't know.'

"I looked out of the window, at the Darkness outside the Silver City.

" 'I may want to talk with you some more, later,' I told Saraquael.

" 'Very good.' I turned to go. 'Sir? Do you know if they will be assigning me another partner? For *Death*?'

" 'No,' I told him. 'I'm afraid I don't.'

"In the center of the Silver City was a park—a place of recreation and rest. I found the Angel Lucifer there, beside a river. He was just standing, watching the water flow.

" 'Lucifer?'

"He inclined his head. 'Raguel. Are you making progress?'

" 'I don't know. Maybe. I need to ask you a few questions. Do you mind?'

" 'Not at all.'

" 'How did you come upon the body?'

" 'I didn't. Not exactly. I saw Phanuel, standing in the street. He looked distressed. I inquired whether there was something wrong, and he showed me the dead angel. And I fetched you.'

" 'I see.'

"He leaned down, let one hand enter the cold water of the river. The water splashed and rilled around it. 'Is that all?'

" 'Not quite. What were you doing in that part of the City?'

" 'I don't see what business that is of yours.'

" 'It is my business, Lucifer. What were you doing there?'

" 'I was . . . walking. I do that sometimes. Just walk, and think. And try to understand.' He shrugged.

" 'You walk on the edge of the City?'

"A beat, then, 'Yes.'

" 'That's all I want to know. For now.'

" 'Who else have you talked to?'

" 'Carasel's boss, and his partner. They both feel that he killed himself—ended his own life.'

" 'Who else are you going to talk to?'

"I looked up. The spires of the City of the Angels towered above us. 'Maybe everyone.'

" 'All of them?'

" 'If I need to. It's my function. I cannot rest until I understand what happened, and until the Vengeance of the Name has been taken on whoever was responsible. But I'll tell you something I *do* know.'

" 'What would that be?' Drops of water fell like diamonds from the Angel Lucifer's perfect fingers.

" 'Carasel did not kill himself.'

" 'How do you know that?'

" 'I am Vengeance. If Carasel had died by his own hand,' I explained to the Captain of the Heavenly Host, 'there would have been no call for me. Would there?'

"He did not reply.

"I flew upwards, into the light of the eternal morning.

"You got another cigarette on you?"

I fumbled out the red and white packet, handed him a cigarette.

"Obliged.

"Zephkiel's cell was larger than mine.

"It wasn't a place for waiting. It was a place to live, and work, and *be*. It was lined with books, and scrolls, and papers, and there were images and representations on the walls: pictures. I'd never seen a picture before.

"In the center of the room was a large chair, and Zephkiel sat there, his eyes closed, his head back.

"As I approached him he opened his eyes.

"They burned no brighter than the eyes of any of the other angels I had seen, but somehow, they seemed to have seen more. It was something about the way he looked. I'm not sure I can explain it. And he had no wings.

" 'Welcome, Raguel,' he said. He sounded tired.

" 'You are Zephkiel?' I don't know why I asked him that. I mean, I knew who people were. It's part of my function, I guess. Recognition. I know who *you* are.

" 'Indeed. You are staring, Raguel. I have no wings, it is true, but then, my function does not call for me to leave this cell. I remain here, and I ponder. Phanuel reports back to me, brings me the new things, for my opinion. He brings me the problems, and I think about them, and occasionally I make myself useful by making some small suggestions. That is my function. As yours is vengeance.'

" 'Yes.'

" 'You are here about the death of the Angel Carasel?'

" 'Yes.'

" 'I did not kill him.'

"When he said it, I knew it was true.

" 'Do you know who did?'

" 'That is *your* function, is it not? To discover who killed the poor thing, and to take the Vengeance of the Name upon him.'

" 'Yes.'

"He nodded.

" 'What do you want to know?'

"I paused, reflecting on what I had heard that day. 'Do you know what Lucifer was doing in that part of the City, before the body was found?'

"The old angel stared at me. 'I can hazard a guess.'

" 'Yes?'

" 'He was walking in the Dark.'

"I nodded. I had a shape in my mind, now. Something I could almost grasp. I asked the last question: 'What can you tell me about *Love?*'

"And he told me. And I thought I had it all.

"I returned to the place where Carasel's body had been. The remains had been removed, the blood had been cleaned away, the stray feathers collected and disposed of. There was nothing on the silver sidewalk to indicate it had ever been there. But I knew where it had been.

"I ascended on my wings, flew upwards until I neared the top of the spire of the Hall of Being. There was a window there, and I entered.

"Saraquael was working there, putting a wingless mannikin into a small box. On one side of the box was a representation of a small brown creature, with eight legs. On the other was a representation of a white blossom.

" 'Saraquael?'

" 'Hm? Oh, it's you. Hello. Look at this: if you were to die, and to be, let us say, put into the earth in a box, which would you want laid on top of you—a spider, here, or a lily, here?'

" 'The lily, I suppose.'

" 'Yes, that's what I think, too. But *why*? I wish . . .' He raised a hand to his chin, stared down at the two models, put first one on top of the box then the other, experimentally. 'There's so much to do, Raguel. So much to get right. And we only get one chance at it, you know. There'll just be one universe—we can't keep trying until we get it right. I wish I understood why all this was so important to Him . . . '

" 'Do you know where Zephkiel's cell is?' I asked him.

" 'Yes. I mean, I've never been there. But I know where it is.'

" 'Good. Go there. He'll be expecting you. I will meet you there.'

"He shook his head. 'I have work to do. I can't just . . . '

"I felt my function come upon me. I looked down at him, and I said, 'You will be there. Go now.'

"He said nothing. He backed away from me, toward the window, staring at me; then he turned, and flapped his wings, and I was alone.

"I walked to the central well of the Hall, and let myself fall, tumbling down through the model of the universe: it glittered around me, unfamiliar colors and shapes seething and writhing without meaning.

"As I approached the bottom, I beat my wings, slowing my descent, and stepped lightly onto the silver floor. Phanuel stood between two angels, who were both trying to claim his attention.

" 'I don't care how aesthetically pleasing it would be,' he was explaining to one of them. 'We simply cannot put it in the center. Background radiation would prevent any possible life-forms from even getting a foothold; and anyway, it's too unstable.'

"He turned to the other. 'Okay, let's see it. Hmm. So *that's Green*, is it? It's not exactly how I'd imagined it, but. Mm. Leave it with me. I'll get back to you.' He took a paper from the angel, folded it over decisively.

"He turned to me. His manner was brusque, and dismissive. 'Yes?'

" 'I need to talk to you.'

" 'Mm? Well, make it quick. I have much to do. If this is about Carasel's death, I have told you all I know.'

" 'It is about Carasel's death. But I will not speak to you now. Not here. Go to Zephkiel's cell: he is expecting you. I will meet you there.'

"He seemed about to say something, but he only nodded, walked toward the door.

"I turned to go, when something occurred to me. I stopped the angel who had the *Green*. 'Tell me something.'

" 'If I can, sir.'

" 'That thing.' I pointed to the Universe. 'What's it going to be *for*?'

" 'For? Why, it is the Universe.'

" 'I know what it's called. But what purpose will it serve?'

"He frowned. 'It is part of the plan. The Name wishes it; He requires *such and such*, to *these* dimensions, and having *such and such* properties and ingredients. It is our function to bring it into existence, according to His wishes. I am sure *He* knows its function, but He has not revealed it to me.' His tone was one of gentle rebuke.

"I nodded, and left that place.

"High above the City a phalanx of angels wheeled and circled and dove. Each held a flaming sword that trailed a streak of burning brightness behind it, dazzling the eye. They moved in unison through the salmon-pink sky. They were very beautiful. It was—you know on summer evenings, when you get whole flocks of birds performing their dances in the sky? Weaving and circling and clustering and breaking apart again, so just as you think you understand the pattern, you realize you don't, and you never will? It was like that, only better.

"Above me was the sky. Below me, the shining City. My home. And outside the City, the Dark.

"Lucifer hovered a little below the Host, watching their maneuvers.

" 'Lucifer?'

" 'Yes, Raguel? Have you discovered your malefactor?'

" 'I think so. Will you accompany me to Zephkiel's cell? There are others waiting for us there, and I will explain everything.'

"He paused. Then, 'Certainly.'

"He raised his perfect face to the angels, now performing a slow revolution in the sky, each moving through the air keeping perfect pace with the next, none of them ever touching. 'Azazel!'

"An angel broke from the circle; the others adjusted almost imperceptibly to his disappearance, filling the space, so you could no longer see where he had been.

" 'I have to leave. You are in command, Azazel. Keep them drilling. They still have much to perfect.'

" 'Yes, sir.'

"Azazel hovered where Lucifer had been, staring up at the flock of angels, and Lucifer and I descended towards the city.

" 'He's my second-in-command,' said Lucifer. 'Bright. Enthusiastic. Azazel would follow you anywhere.'

" 'What are you training them for?'

" 'War.'

" 'With whom?'

" 'How do you mean?'

" 'Who are they going to fight? Who else *is* there?'

"He looked at me; his eyes were clear, and honest. 'I do not know. But He has Named us to be His army. So we will be perfect. For Him. The Name is infallible and all-just, and all-wise, Raguel. It cannot be otherwise, no matter what—' He broke off, and looked away.

" 'You were going to say?'

" 'It is of no importance.'

" 'Ah.'

"We did not talk for the rest of the descent to Zephkiel's cell."

I looked at my watch: it was almost three. A chill breeze had begun to blow down the LA street, and I shivered. The man noticed, and he paused in his story. "You okay?" he asked.

"I'm fine. Please carry on. I'm fascinated."

He nodded.

"They were waiting for us in Zephkiel's cell: Phanuel, Saraquael, and Zephkiel. Zephkiel was sitting in his chair. Lucifer took up a position beside the window.

"I walked to the center of the room, and I began.

" 'I thank you all for coming here. You know who I am; you know my function. I am the Vengeance of the Name: the arm of the Lord. I am Raguel.

" 'The angel Carasel is dead. It was given to me to find out why he died, who killed him. This I have done. Now, the Angel Carasel was a designer in the Hall of Being. He was very good, or so I am told . . .

" 'Lucifer. Tell me what you were doing, before you came upon Phanuel, and the body.'

" 'I have told you already. I was walking.'

" 'Where were you walking?'

" 'I do not see what business that is of yours.'

" '*Tell me.*'

"He paused. He was taller than any of us; tall, and proud. 'Very well. I was walking in the Dark. I have been walking in the Darkness for some time now. It helps me to gain a perspective on the City—being outside it. I see how fair it is, how perfect. There is nothing more enchanting than our home. Nothing more complete. Nowhere else that anyone would want to be.'

" 'And what do you do in the Dark, Lucifer?'

"He stared at me. 'I walk. And . . . There are voices, in the Dark. I listen to the voices. They promise me things, ask me questions, whisper and plead. And I ignore them. I steel myself and I gaze at the City. It is the only way I have of testing myself—putting myself to any kind of trial. I am the Captain of the Host; I am the first among the Angels, and I must prove myself.'

"I nodded. 'Why did you not tell me this before?'

"He looked down. 'Because I am the only angel who walks in the Dark. Because I do not want others to walk in the Dark: I am strong enough to challenge the voices, to test myself. Others are not so strong. Others might stumble, or fall.'

" 'Thank you, Lucifer. That is all, for now.' I turned to the next angel. 'Phanuel. How long have you been taking credit for Carasel's work?'

"His mouth opened, but no sound came out.

" '*Well?*'

" 'I . . . I would not take credit for another's work.'

" 'But you did take credit for *Love*?'

"He blinked. 'Yes. I did.'

" 'Would you care to explain to us all what *Love* is?' I asked.

"He glanced around uncomfortably. 'It's a feeling of deep affection and attraction for another being, often combined with passion or desire—a need to be with another.' He spoke dryly, didactically, as if he were reciting a mathematical formula. 'The feeling that we have for the Name, for our Creator—that is *Love*. . . amongst other things. *Love* will be an impulse that will inspire and ruin in equal measure . . . We are'—he paused, then began once more—'we are very proud of it.'

"He was mouthing the words. He no longer seemed to hold any hope that we would believe them.

" 'Who did the majority of the work on *Love*? No, don't answer. Let me ask the others first. Zephkiel? When Phanuel passed the details on *Love* to you for approval, who did he tell you was responsible for it?'

"The wingless angel smiled gently. 'He told me it was his project.'

" 'Thank you, sir. Now, Saraquael: whose was *Love?*'

" 'Mine. Mine and Carasel's. Perhaps more his than mine, but we worked on it together.'

" 'You knew that Phanuel was claiming the credit for it?'

" '. . . yes.'

" 'And you permitted this?'

" 'He—he promised us that he would give us a good project of our own to follow. He promised that if we said nothing we would be given more big projects—and he was true to his word. He gave us *Death*.'

"I turned back to Phanuel. 'Well?'

" 'It is true that I claimed that *Love* was mine.'

" 'But it was Carasel's. And Saraquael's.'

" 'Yes.'

" 'Their last project—before *Death?*'

" 'Yes.'

" 'That is all.'

"I walked over to the window, looked out at the silver spires, looked at the dark. And I began to speak.

" 'Carasel was a remarkable designer. If he had one failing, it was that he threw himself too deeply into his work.' I turned back to them. The angel Saraquael was shivering, and lights were flickering beneath his skin. 'Saraquael? Who did Carasel love? Who was his lover?'

He stared at the floor. Then he stared up, proudly, aggressively. And he smiled.

" 'I was.'

" 'Do you want to tell me about it?'

" 'No.' A shrug. 'But I suppose I must. Very well, then.

" 'We worked together. And when we began to work on *Love*. . . we became lovers. It was his idea. We would go back to his cell, whenever we could snatch the time. There we touched each other, held each other, whispered endearments and protestations of eternal devotion. His welfare mattered more to me than my own. I existed for him. When I was alone I would repeat his name to myself, and think of nothing but him.

" 'When I was with him . . . ' He paused. He looked down. '. . . nothing else mattered.'

"I walked to where Saraquael stood; lifted his chin with my hand, stared into his gray eyes. 'Then why did you kill him?'

" 'Because he would no longer love me. When we started to work on *Death* he—he lost interest. He was no longer mine. He belonged to *Death*. And if I could not have him, then his new lover was welcome to him. I could not bear his presence—I could not endure to have him near me and to know that he felt nothing for me. That was what hurt the most. I thought . . . I hoped . . . that if he was gone then I would no longer care for him—that the pain would stop.

" 'So I killed him; I stabbed him, and I threw his body from our window in the Hall of Being. But the pain has *not* stopped.' It was almost a wail.

"Saraquael reached up, removed my hand from his chin. 'Now what?'

"I felt my aspect begin to come upon me; felt my function possess me. I was no longer an individual—I was the Vengeance of the Lord.

"I moved close to Saraquael, and embraced him. I pressed my lips to his, forced my tongue into his mouth. We kissed. He closed his eyes.

"I felt it well up within me then: a burning, a brightness. From the corner of my eyes, I could see Lucifer and Phanuel averting their faces from my light; I could feel Zephkiel's stare. And my light became brighter and brighter, until it erupted—from my eyes, from my chest, from my fingers, from my lips: a white, searing fire.

"The white flames consumed Saraquael slowly, and he clung to me as he burned.

"Soon there was nothing left of him. Nothing at all.

"I felt the flame leave me. I returned to myself once more.

"Phanuel was sobbing. Lucifer was pale. Zephkiel sat in his chair, quietly watching me.

"I turned to Phanuel and Lucifer. 'You have seen the Vengeance of the Lord,' I told them. 'Let it act as a warning to you both.'

"Phanuel nodded. 'It has. Oh, it has. I—I will be on my way, sir. I will return to my appointed post. If that is all right with you?'

" 'Go.'

"He stumbled to the window, and plunged into the light, his wings beating furiously.

"Lucifer walked over to the place on the silver floor where Saraquael had once stood. He knelt, stared desperately at the floor as if he were trying to find some remnant of the angel I had destroyed: a fragment of ash, or bone, or charred feather; but there was nothing to find. Then he looked up at me.

" 'That was not right,' he said. 'That was not just.' He was crying; wet tears ran down his face. Perhaps Saraquael was the first to love, but Lucifer was the first to shed tears. I will never forget that.

"I stared at him, impassively. 'It was justice. He killed another. He was killed in his turn. You called me to my function, and I performed it.'

" 'But . . . he *loved*. He should have been forgiven. He should have been helped. He should not have been destroyed like that. That was *wrong*.'

" 'It was His will.'

"Lucifer stood. 'Then perhaps His will is unjust. Perhaps the voices in the Darkness speak truly after all. How *can* this be right?'

" 'It is right. It is His will. I merely performed my function.'

"He wiped away the tears with the back of his hand. 'No,' he said, flatly. He shook his head, slowly, from side to side. Then he said, 'I must think on this. I will go now.'

"He walked to the window, stepped into the sky, and he was gone.

"Zephkiel and I were alone in his cell. I went over to his chair. He nodded at me. 'You have performed your function well, Raguel. Shouldn't you return to your cell, to wait until you are next needed?' "

The man on the bench turned toward me: his eyes sought mine. Until now it had seemed—for most of his narrative—that he was scarcely aware of me; he had stared ahead of himself, whispered his tale in little better than a monotone. Now it felt as if he had discovered me, and that he spoke to me alone, rather than to the air, or the City of Los Angeles. And he said:

"I knew that he was right. But I *couldn't* have left then—not even if I had wanted to. My aspect had not entirely left me; my function was not completely fulfilled. And then it fell into place; I saw the whole picture. And like Lucifer, I knelt. I touched my forehead to the silver floor. 'No, Lord,' I said. 'Not yet.'

"Zephkiel rose from his chair. 'Get up. It is not fitting for one angel to act in this way to another. It is not right. Get up!'

"I shook my head. 'Father, You are no angel,' I whispered.

"Zephkiel said nothing. For a moment my heart misgave within me. I was afraid. 'Father, I was charged to discover who was responsible for Carasel's death. And I do know.'

" 'You have taken your vengeance, Raguel.'

" '*Your* vengeance, Lord.'

"And then He sighed, and sat down once more. 'Ah, little Raguel. The problem with creating things is that they perform so much better than one had ever planned. Shall I ask how you recognized me?'

" 'I . . . I am not certain, Lord. You have no wings. You wait at the center of the City, supervising the Creation directly. When I destroyed Saraquael, You did not look away. You know too many things. You . . . ' I paused, and thought. 'No, I do not know how I know. As You say, You have created me well. But I only understood who You were and the meaning of the drama we had enacted here for You, when I saw Lucifer leave.'

" 'What did you understand, child?'

" 'Who killed Carasel. Or at least, who was pulling the strings: For example, *who* arranged for Carasel and Saraquael to work together on *Love*, knowing Carasel's tendency to involve himself too deeply in his work?'

"He was speaking to me gently, almost teasingly, as an adult would pretend to make conversation with a tiny child. 'Why should anyone have "pulled the strings," Raguel?'

" 'Because nothing occurs without reason; and all the reasons are Yours. You set Saraquael up: yes, he killed Carasel. But he killed Carasel so that *I* could destroy *him*.'

" 'And were you wrong to destroy him?'

"I looked into His old, old eyes. 'It was my function. But I do not think it was just. I think perhaps it was needed that I destroy Saraquael, in order to demonstrate to Lucifer the Injustice of the Lord.'

"He smiled, then. 'And whatever reason would I have for doing that?'

" 'I . . . I do not know. I do not understand—no more than I understand why You created the Dark, or the voices in the Darkness. But You did. You caused all this to occur.'

"He nodded. 'Yes. I did. Lucifer must brood on the unfairness of Saraquael's destruction. And that—amongst other things—will precipitate him into certain actions. Poor sweet Lucifer. His way will be the hardest of all my children; for there is a part he must play in the drama that is to come, and it is a grand role.'

"I remained kneeling in front of the Creator of All Things.

" 'What will you do now, Raguel?' he asked me.

" 'I must return to my cell. My function is now fulfilled. I have taken vengeance, and I have revealed the perpetrator. That is enough. But—Lord?'

" 'Yes, child.'

" 'I feel dirty. I feel tarnished. I feel befouled. Perhaps it is true that all that happens is in accordance with Your will, and thus it is good. But sometimes You leave blood on Your instruments.'

"He nodded, as if He agreed with me. 'If you wish, Raguel, you may forget all this. All that has happened this day.' And then He said, 'However, you will not be able to speak of this to any other angels, whether you choose to remember it or not.'

" 'I will remember it.'

" 'It is your choice. But sometimes you will find it is easier by far not to remember. Forgetfulness can sometimes bring freedom, of a sort. Now, if you do not mind,' He reached down, took a file from a stack on the floor, opened it, 'there is work I should be getting on with.'

"I stood up and walked to the window. I hoped He would call me back, explain every detail of His plan to me, somehow make it all better. But He said nothing, and I left His Presence without ever looking back."

The man was silent, then. And he remained silent—I couldn't even hear him breathing—for so long that I began to get nervous, thinking that perhaps he had fallen asleep, or died.

Then he stood up.

"There you go, pal. That's your story. Do you think it was worth a couple of cigarettes and a book of matches?" He asked the question as if it was important to him, without irony.

"Yes," I told him. "Yes. It was. But what happened next? How did you . . . I mean, if . . ." I trailed off.

It was dark on the street, now, at the edge of daybreak. One by one the streetlights had begun to flicker out, and he was silhouetted against the glow of the dawn sky. He thrust his hands into his pockets. "What happened? I left home, and I lost my way, and these days home's a long way back. Sometimes you do things you regret, but there's nothing you can do about them. Times change. Doors close behind you. You move on. You know?

"Eventually I wound up here. They used to say no one's ever originally from LA. True as Hell in my case."

And then, before I could understand what he was doing, he leaned down and kissed me, gently, on the cheek. His stubble was rough and prickly, but his breath was surprisingly sweet. He whispered into my ear: "I never fell. I don't care what they say. I'm still doing my job, as I see it."

My cheek burned where his lips had touched it.

He straightened up. "But I still want to go home."

The man walked away down the darkened street, and I sat on the bench and watched him go. I felt like he had taken something from me, although I could no longer remember what. And I felt like something had been left in its place—absolution, perhaps, or innocence, although of what, or from what, I could no longer say. An image from somewhere: a scribbled drawing, of two angels in flight above a perfect city; and over the image a child's perfect handprint, which stains the white paper blood-red. It came into my head unbidden, and I no longer know what it meant.

I stood up.

It was too dark to see the face of my watch, but I knew I would get no sleep that day. I walked back to the place I was staying, to the house by the stunted palm tree, to wash myself, and to wait. I thought about angels, and about Tink; and I wondered whether love and death truly went hand in hand.

The next day the planes to England were flying again.

I felt strange—lack of sleep had forced me into that miserable state in which everything seems flat and of equal importance; when nothing matters, and in which reality seems scraped thin and threadbare. The taxi journey to the airport was a nightmare. I was hot, and tired, and testy. I wore a T-shirt in the LA heat; my coat was packed at the bottom of my luggage, where it had been for the entire stay.

The airplane was crowded, but I didn't care.

The stewardess walked down the aisle with a rack of newspapers, the *Herald Tribune, USA Today,* and the *LA Times.* I took a copy of the *Times,* but the words left my head as my eyes scanned over them. Nothing that I read remained with me. No, I lie: somewhere in the back of the paper was a report of a triple murder: two women, and a small child. No names were given, and I do not know why the report should have registered as it did.

Soon I fell asleep. I dreamed about fucking Tink, while blood ran sluggishly from her closed eyes and lips. The blood was cold and viscous and clammy, and I awoke chilled by the plane's air-conditioning, with an unpleasant taste in my mouth. My tongue and lips were dry. I looked out of the scratched oval window, stared down at the clouds, and it occurred to me then (not for the first time) that the clouds were in actuality another land, where everyone knew just what they were looking for and how to get back where they started from.

Staring down at the clouds is one of the things I have always liked best about flying. That, and the proximity one feels to one's death.

I wrapped myself in the thin aircraft blanket, and slept some more, but if further dreams came then they made no impression upon me.

A blizzard blew up shortly after the plane landed in England, knocking out the airport's power supply. I was alone in an airport elevator at the time, and it went dark and jammed between floors. A dim emergency light flickered on. I pressed the crimson alarm button until the batteries ran down and it ceased to sound; then I shivered in my LA T-shirt, in the corner of my little silver room. I watched my breath steam in the air, and I hugged myself for warmth.

There wasn't anything in there except me; but even so, I felt safe, and secure. Soon someone would come and force open the doors. Eventually somebody would let me out; and I knew that I would soon be home.

HUNGRY

Steve Rasnic Tem

Steve Rasnic Tem is a prolific and talented short story writer and poet. He has sold more than 170 short stories to publications of the mystery, horror, science fiction, and western genres. Most recently, his short fiction has appeared in *Best New Horror 2*, *Dark at Heart*, *Snow White, Blood Red*, and *The Year's Best Fantasy and Horror: Fifth Annual Collection*. His short fiction has been nominated for the Bram Stoker Award, the British Fantasy Award, and the World Fantasy Award, winning the British Fantasy Award in 1988 for his story "Leaks." A collection of his stories, *Dark Shapes in the Road*, has recently been published by the French publisher Denoël. In addition to the two stories reprinted in this volume, I also recommend his *Decoded Mirrors: 3 Tales After Lovecraft* from Necronomicon Press.

"Hungry" is one of several stories in *The Year's Best Fantasy and Horror: Sixth Annual Collection* about familial relationships: the strains, jealousies, and loyalties. But even more so, this visceral, wrenching tale is about unconditional love—a mother's love. It was first published in *Borderlands 3*.

—E.D.

Mama?

Vivian Sparks took her hands out of the soapy water and stared into the frosted kitchen window. There was a face in the ice and fog, but she wasn't sure which of her dead children it was. Amy or Henry, maybe—they'd had the smallest heads, like early potatoes, and about that same color. Those hadn't been their real names, of course. Ray always felt it was wrong to name a stillborn, so they didn't get a name writ down on paper, but still she had named every one of them in her heart: Amy, Henry, Becky, Sue Ann, and Patricia, after her mother. Patricia had been the smallest, not even full-made really, like part of her had been left behind in the dark somewhere. Ray had wanted Patricia took right away and buried on the back hill, he'd been so mad about the way she came out. But the midwife had helped Vivian bathe the poor little thing and wrap her up, and she'd looked so much like a dead kitten or a calf that it made it a whole lot worse than the others, so dark and wet and wrinkled that Vivian almost regretted not letting Ray do what he'd wanted.

Mama . . .

But it wasn't the dead ones, not this time. A mother knows the voice of her child, and Vivian Sparks felt ashamed to have denied it. It felt bad, always hearing the dead ones and never expecting the one she'd have given up anything for, no matter what Ray said. Ray wouldn't have let her adopt him, if it hadn't been for those stillborns, but she would have done it on her own if she had to, even if she'd had ten other children to care for. It was her own darling Jimmie Lee out there in the cold foggy morning. It had to be.

Vivian opened the back door and looked out onto the bare dirt yard that led uphill to the lopsided gray barn. Ray's lantern flickered in there where he was checking on the cows. She couldn't see much else because of the dark, and the fog. It was still trying real hard to be Spring here in late March—she'd caught a whiff of lilac breeze yesterday afternoon—but it worried her that the hard frost was going to put an end to that early flowering before she'd see any blossoms. That was always a bad sign when the lilacs came out too soon and the ice killed the hope of them.

"Mama, it's me."

Vivian reached up and touched her throat, trying to help a good swallow along. Suddenly her throat felt as if it were full of food, and she just couldn't get it all down. Ray said it was because of Jimmie Lee, her problem with eating, said it had been like that for her ever since Jimmie Lee came into their lives. "You don't eat right no more. I guess you can't," he said over and over, the way he repeated something to death when he had a mad feeling about it. "Can't say that I even blame you—it's understandable. Watchin' him go at it, it'd put anybody off their food. That's why I never watched."

She guessed there was truth in what he said, but she didn't like to think about it that way. What she liked to think was that it was all her feelings for Jimmie Lee coming up into her throat when she'd looked at him, or now when she thought about him, all the sadness and the love that made it hard for her to breathe, much less eat. And the memory of him touching her on her throat, gazing at her mouth the night before he left home to join that awful show. That was another reason for her to be touching her throat now, in that same place.

"Mama, I come back to visit."

Vivian could hardly speak. Maybe the love in her throat was so big it was closing up her windpipe. "Come on, come . . . on, honey. Been a long time."

Past the east fence she could see the darkness gray a little and move away. She started to walk over but a simple yet awful sound—a young man clearing his throat—stopped her. She clutched the huge lump in her throat. It was warm, as if it might burn her fingers.

"Mama, I ate something off the road a while back. I just gotta get rid of it, then I'll come up where you can see me."

She turned her back to him even though it would have been much too dark to see what he was about to do. But after watching him a thousand times when he was little she felt like he was a grown boy now, and deserved some show of respect, and she wasn't sure but maybe this was one way to do it. At the same time she knew her turning away wasn't at all being the good mama, either. She didn't want to see it anymore. She didn't feel like she should have to.

Back in the darkness there was a sound like damp skin stretching, splitting, some awful coughs and gurglings like her son's throat was turning itself inside out (dear God it's got worse!) and then a loud, mushy thump.

A few minutes later she could hear him walking up behind her. "I'm sorry, Mama." His voice was hoarse, like he'd been crying. He used to cry all the time when he was little, complaining all the time about being so hungry, and never getting full no matter how much she fed him, how much Ray let her feed him, or how ever much Jimmie Lee ate on his own to try to fill that awful hunger. His nose would run and his eyes would look all raw and scraped and he'd stop trying to keep himself clean. Vivian took a handkerchief out of her front apron pocket now and turned around to give it to him.

"Thanks, Mama. I'll get good and clean for you, just for you." The young man standing in front of her, saying just what he used to say to her when he was a little boy and had made himself such an awful mess, was taller, surely, and had little scraggly patches of beard here and there where once had been unnaturally pink skin, but other than that he still seemed the pale, skinny little boy who had left her years ago. His chin was covered with thick, soupy slobber which he wiped off with the handkerchief. She didn't mind—that had always been her job, to provide the handkerchiefs, the towels, waiting patiently while he cleaned himself up, directing him now and then to a missed spot or two. Ray had never been able to stand even that little bit of clean up; he'd always just left the room.

"My goodness!" She made herself sound impressed, although what she was really feeling was relieved, and desperate to hug him to her. "My handsome older son."

Jimmie Lee grinned then, showing teeth even worse than she remembered. She could see that at least he'd been able to get some dental work done, but it looked like the fillings and braces had been filed, points added here and there to make him look more like a silly machine, some big city kitchen gadget of some kind. She wondered if it really helped him get the food down or if it was all just for some sideshow or movie work he'd been doing. He'd written her once about one of the movies—"Flesh Eaters From Beyond Mars," or some such silliness. He'd said in the letter that the movie people liked him because he saved them money on special effects, but she'd never really understood what any of that was about.

Other than the metal in his mouth her sweet boy hadn't changed much. Certainly he couldn't weigh much more now than when he'd left her: his body straight up and down like a sleeve with no hips or shoulders to speak of, but his neck about twice as wide as it should be, and faintly ringed, like a snake's belly. Set atop that stout neck was the largest jaw she'd ever seen—it hung out like the bird bath on top the pedestal she had out in the front flower bed. His mouth was wider than normal, she guessed, but had never seemed as big as it should be for that size jaw. His lips were almost blue, and cracked, and there were a bunch more splits in the skin at the corners of his mouth. Because of all the stretching his skin had to do there hair growth had always been spotty. She'd tried to get him to use lotions and oils, but like most children he just forgot all the time. So she'd always rub some into his face every night, being especially careful around the mouth and chin. She wondered if he knew somebody now who cared enough to do that for him.

His eyes were the wide eyes of a lost child's, but then they always had been. Jimmie Lee now was just a larger version of the poor baby that had been born in a backwoods barn and just left there eighteen years before. No one else had wanted the funny-looking child but Vivian had known from the very first moment she saw him that this was her son, and would be forever. Even Ray, for all his puffin' and embarrassment about the boy, had resented it when one of the neighbors suggested that maybe they shouldn't keep him. This was his son, even though sometimes he sorely couldn't stand being around him.

And then Jimmie Lee had gone out into the world, maybe to find his "real" mother, or maybe to find whatever it was he was hungry for. She didn't know, and was afraid then, and was afraid now, to ask. All she'd had to remember him by was this awful swelling in her throat every time she thought of him, and every time she struggled to eat or drink something. But nobody'd ever told her that life was fair to mothers.

"Did you ever find her, son?"

"Who, Mama?"

"Why, the one who gave birth to you. The one who just left you here all them years ago." She tried to keep the bitterness out of her voice, but the vein went too wide and deep to hide.

His throat gurgled and a raw smell escaped. She started to turn away, but he held out his hand to stop her. "It's okay, mama. I still got it under control. I'm a lot more careful about how and when I eat now. Something I learned on the road, having to be around other people." He looked at her. She waited. "I never found her, Mama. Guess I didn't try much after the beginning. I guess I was a little afraid of what she'd look like."

"You stayin' long?"

"I can't. I finally figured out it's best I be around folks who don't know me so well. But I just had to see you again, and smell you, and listen to you talk. I had to."

Her throat filled and she had to force it back down so that she could speak again. "You best get inside now, have something to . . ." She looked away from his nervous, hungry face, to where he'd come from in the dark beyond the fence, now turning gray so fast she could see a little bit of what he'd left there: great big mounds of meat still steaming in the cold, their hides partly dissolved away, large hunks of their manes missing, the meat turned to something like jelly, their teeth protruding from lipless mouths. A couple of Winn Gibson's prize mares, she suspected. Well, she guessed Ray was just going to have to deal with Winnie on that one, like he had all those times before. She sighed. "Guess you'd best just get inside . . ."

Jimmie Lee held up the brightly-colored, tattered poster beside his face. "It don't look much like me, I reckon, but the owner said they had to exaggerate a little bit to draw a crowd. He said people expected it like that, so that it wasn't lyin' exactly. They called me the Snake Boy." The poster showed a giant snake with her son's lost baby eyes on it, its huge mouth gaped open and an elephant disappearing inside. Lined up into the distance were chickens, bears, and a horse with a huge belly, all with worried looks on their faces.

"That's very nice, son," Vivian said quietly.

"But I only stayed there a few months. I didn't much like people lookin' at me like that, you know, mama?"

"I know, sweetheart."

"It was like the way people used to stare at me around here, only worse. Worse 'cause they were strangers, I guess. I never did like strangers watchin' me while I was eatin'."

"It certainly is impolite," she said. "People shouldn't stare at other people while they're eating. You can hardly digest your food that way." She raised her hand to her throat.

"So that's why I left the show. I did odd jobs after that, until I got to do those movies I wrote you about. And once for a few months I had me a dandy of a job in one of those meat-packing plants. It was late at night, and I had the place all to myself. It was great."

"I'm sure it was, Jimmie Lee."

"But the owner of the sideshow, he really could entertain you. That was a good part of it, mama—it weren't all bad. He'd crack all these jokes when he introduced me, and then he'd make more of 'em while I did my 'act,' but all I did was sit up on that stage and eat. But he'd say these things and all the people would laugh and I reckon that's a real good thing. He was real funny, mama, you shoulda seen. You'd a laughed till you cried, I bet."

"I bet I would that, honey."

"We had ourselves enough show 'round here to last us a lifetime, I reckon."

Vivian clutched at her apron. She hadn't heard him come in. She twisted in her chair in time to see Ray throw down his old coat and go stomping off to the bathroom to wash up.

"I guess daddy still don't want me around here." Jimmy Lee sat still with his legs spread, long nervous hands dangling and twisting between his knees.

"Your daddy just gets tired, honey. We all get tired now and then."

She could hear her husband splashing in the water, then hands slapping it onto his face. Jimmie Lee's eyes were large and white in the dimly-lit room. When he was small his eyes always looked like that. Before they discovered the hunger he had, Ray used to joke that Jimmie Lee's eyes were bigger than his mouth. "I get tired, too," Jimmie Lee said. "And, Mama, I still get so hungry."

Vivian couldn't move. She stared at her son with tears in her eyes. "I love you, honey. I just keep loving you and loving you."

"I know, Mama. But it's like the love goes inside me and gets lost and then it just isn't there anymore. Like I eat the love, Mama. And then I'm still hungry."

Ray came back into the room and flopped down into his recliner. He sighed and looked directly at Jimmie Lee. "Well, son, you're lookin' . . . better. Better than the last time I seen you. That's good to see. You doin' a job now? You find yourself somethin' you can do?"

Jimmie Lee leaned forward and tried to smile. But the cracks in his lips and around his mouth bent and twisted the smile. Vivian started crying softly to herself and Ray looked at her with what she thought was an unusual sadness on the face of this man she'd known almost all her life. Then Jimmie Lee must have known something was wrong, because it looked as if he were trying to pull the smile back in, and it just made it worse.

"I left that show, Papa. I know that'll please you. Made a couple of movies. And I did some real work, too, like at a packing plant, and once I spent almost a year at this junkyard outside Charlotte . . ."

"Junk yard? You learn the junk business? Now that can be a good trade for a young man. There's always goin' to be junk lyin' around."

Jimmie Lee looked down at his feet. "Well, papa, there was pieces the man couldn't sell, and they were just sittin' around his yard, takin' up too much space he said, and he couldn't get rid of them . . ."

His father interrupted. "You're talkin' about the eatin' now, and I ain't gonna talk about the eatin'."

"But, Papa, eatin' metal junk, specially cars, why that's become almost like a regular thing in some places. They put it in the papers, and sometimes it even gets on the TV. Some fella'll eat a big Buick, or an old Ford Mustang . . ."

His father leaned forward out of his recliner and stared hard at Jimmie Lee. "We don't talk about the eatin' in this house. Look how you've gone and upset your mother."

Vivian sat rock-still in her chair, her eyes closed and mouth open, crying without sound.

"Vivian, why don't you go on out to the hen house and get the boy some fresh eggs? The boy always liked fresh eggs."

She stared at him, her eyes sharp and red. "Wh-what?"

"Papa, I don't need eggs . . ."

"Sure you do. Vivian, go get the boy some eggs. He used to eat a dozen of 'em at a time, from what I remember. Shell and all. But at least it was real food. Go on now."

Vivian stood stiffly, and left the room. She went out through the back door and around the side toward the hen house. But when she passed near the open window of the living room she stopped, because she could hear her husband and her son talking inside. And she knew what they would be talking about—she knew what Ray would be saying to Jimmie Lee. She crept closer, and stood just under the lilac bush by the window, where she could see their faces, and the feelings painted there.

Ray started talking low and firm. "Now it's good to see you, I mean that, son. I know I ain't always been as soft as I should of when you were at home, but I been thinkin' about you every day since you left us. You been sorely missed—you sure have—and not just by your Mama." He leaned back and sighed. "But your Mama's sick, boy, real sick, and I just don't know if she can stand watchin' what you go through, havin' it be like it was before."

"Mama? What's wrong with her? Tell me . . ."

"Well, she never did eat all that well, and I reckon we all know the reason for that." Jimmie Lee looked down at his stomach and away. Vivian held her throat and struggled not to make a sound. "But that don't matter so much now. It weakened her, and she's had pneumonia so many times over the years she damn near coughed her lungs out. But she's got the cancer now, and it's clean through her, Doc Jennings says, and she can't have long to go."

Jimmie Lee's face was sheened with sweat. That's what he did, instead of crying. His body never had let him cry.

"Even less, I reckon, if you stay around, son."

Jimmie Lee stood up. "I understand, Papa. I appreciate you levelin' with me."

"You're a good son, Jimmie Lee."

Vivian rushed down to the hen house and grabbed what she could, then ran back into the house and into the living room, out of breath, a scarf full of eggs hugged to her bosom. Jimmie Lee was still standing, but had already started for the door. She looked at her husband, then at Jimmie Lee. "You're leavin'," she said flatly. The eggs tumbled out of her arms and splattered across the braided rug.

"I gotta check some things out down at the pasture," his father said, getting up. He pulled on his sweater, started to leave, then walked over to Jimmie Lee and gave him a quick hug.

After her husband left the house Vivian still stood there among the broken eggs, looking at Jimmie Lee as if she were memorizing him, or trying to puzzle him out. Jimmie Lee bent over and started picking up the egg shells. "Leave those alone," she said softly. He straightened back up and looked down at her, his thin lips twitching, the scars around his mouth wrinkling like worms moving across his face. "He told you, didn't he?" she said. "He told you all of it."

Jimmie Lee nodded. "I better go, Mama."

"You come here, baby." She held out her arms to him and when he wouldn't come any closer she walked over to him and attached her frail body to his. "You're not leavin' me this time."

"Mama, please. I gotta go."

"No, sir."

"Mama, I'm hungry." And he tried to push her body away.

She pressed closer, and raised her hand to his lips. "I know, baby." And pulled his thin, cracked lips apart with her fingers. And put her fingers inside her baby's mouth, then put her hand inside, then both hands. As if out of his control, his huge jaw dislocated, his pliant facial muscles stretched. He tried to pull back, to make his mouth let go of her, but she wouldn't have any of that. "No, child. Just take it, child." His mouth wouldn't let go, and as her head disappeared inside him he heard her say again, "I'm not leaving you."

For the first time in his life, what he ate, all that he ate, became nourishment, and remained inside him.

PLAYING WITH

M. R. Scofidio

Marnie Scofidio grew up in Buffalo, New York, worked in Los Angeles as a blues singer, and now lives in England. She loves ghost stories and has been heavily influenced by the work of M. R. James. Her short fiction has been published in *The Bone Marrow Review* and *Heliocentric-Net*.

"Playing With" is reprinted from *The Urbanite*'s "party" issue. It starts off as a tart depiction of mores and shifting relationships in the late twentieth century. . . but ultimately develops into something much darker.

—E.D.

The evening had begun to sour when Vi demanded they play a party game.

The soap actor spoke through a half-chewed bit of cocktail sausage. "Oh, Christ, whatever for? Aren't you all bored to death as it is? Come out to the garden with me, darling, I'll show you a party game you won't forget for a while."

Scots bastard, Hugh thought, sulking over a canned Club cocktail. He'd just about managed one hand up Tamsin's black silk pencil skirt when Vi had come storming into the dining room, scrounging for a cigarette. The rest of the party soon followed, in the time-honored tradition of parties. Go looking for attention, everyone ignores you; wander off for a bit of reflection on your own, or to watch the submarine races, and the whole damn world wanders off after you. This room had quickly grown just as smoky as the kitchen and sitting room were, and even noisier. The hostess probably would have preferred her guests stay out of her expensively furnished dining room, but wasn't there to protest. Rumor had it she was nicely occupied in one of the upstairs bedrooms.

The actor threw Tamsin a stage wink. Hugh couldn't believe her falling for it; she smiled as though the big fake had presented her with the most precious of jewels. He suffered the death of his erection, but not much, for Hugh was drunker than he'd realized and besides, it was only a small erection.

A man dressed for the evening in a pink, turquoise and black polyester track suit asked his companion if she had seen Jenny in her new beer commercial. The woman, whose upper head was shaved, the lower strands of hair having been tortured into several spikes hung with tiny paper replicas of flags of the world, replied, No, but it seemed that since Jenny had acquired a very minor role in a Beeb One comedy, her personality traits were rapidly progressing from merely annoying to positively insufferable.

"Why must you share your predilection for lung cancer with me?" Hugh asked no one in particular, not really expecting an answer in the din of people all talking just to hear the sound of their own voices.

Vi said very loudly, "All I really wanted, Tam, dear, was a bit of privacy so we could talk. Who are all these fucking people?"

Tamsin giggled as the actor poured wine in her glass.

"I know how to get rid of everybody. Let's play party games!"

Hugh tried to maneuver himself over to the fridge wherein lay canned cocktails stacked to heaven, this without touching his ex-wife.

"That sounds marvelous. What kind of party games?"

"You would say that, you tart. When I'm trying to get *rid* of everybody."

"Don't listen to a word Vi's saying. She's out of her mind on drink and pills, has been for years." This from a tall man in a wrinkled brown suit, whose beard grew in several different directions and colors.

"What time is it? Are we too late for the pub?"

Hugh was well aware Vi wasn't at all interested in having Tamsin to herself for a chat. The buddy-buddy thing was an act. She had just figured out that Hugh wanted Tamsin, and how she could cock it up for him; appearing in the dining room looking for cigarettes, that greased-back Edinburgh hambone in tow. Since their divorce last spring, Vi managed to put all her energies into finding ways of thwarting his desires, ruining his uncertain attempts at starting new relationships, reminding him during late-night phone calls of his inability to get himself off the dole and into a job again. He hated answering the phone at night but he hated the new silence in the house even more. He was very weak, he knew, but all he could do was wish things were different, and mere wishing never worked on anything. How often he had sincerely wished Vivien dead. She still held his three piece suit firmly in her grasping little hand, if no longer for pleasure. This she reminded him of now with a malevolent little smile she threw at him, over her shoulder.

"Yes, a party game is definitely in order. See, now it's working! The room's only half as full as it was."

"Because this is the most boring party anyone's been to in London all year," said the actor, blowing kisses towards Tamsin's breasts. "What party game are we going to play?"

Hugh snapped the ring off of a fresh canned cocktail with a great and deliberate violence. "Why not Charades, or Go Piss Up A Rope?"

"Don't bother to say anything if you're just having a go, Hugh," said Vi. "I want real suggestions. Nothing obscure or American. You remember Hugh's from California," she announced to the room at large, as if it were a disease.

"Look," said a very slight man in spectacles and a Harley-Davidson motorcycle jacket, "this whole area is supposed to be built over plague sites. Why don't we have a séance?"

"Bril-liant," said Vi.

"And you could write a story about it, Nigel."

"I don't write ghost stories, I write splatterpunk fantasy."

"Well, anyway, we can't have a séance because no one here knows how," said the man with the beard. "It's supposed to be quite dangerous unless you have an experienced medium running things."

"Rot," said Nigel. He reminded Hugh of a worm inside a big shiny black apple skin, with studs on it. "All you need is a round table, and a candle, and some people to form a circle. Really, John."

"Would our hostess mind?"

"Who cares?" The actress named Jenny cradled a marble lighter in fluid hands. A tiny blue flame clicked up, illuminating her features and the angle of the cigarette as her mouth twisted its tip down into the fire, reflecting tiny dots of fire in her darkened eyes.

"Jenny, you've become insufferable since you've started working again."

"You just wish you were, Nigel. Working, that is. At anything."

Wrong thing to say to a writer, Hugh thought, watching Nigel's shoulders stiffen.

"I don't know if any spirits would want to come to our séance, with all this carping going on," said Tamsin softly. Hugh tried to catch her eye again, without success. Earlier, she'd been eager enough to run off with him, talking quietly and then later ardently returning his kiss in a darkened hallway, tongue swift and teasing, tender breasts arching into his hands. Now she seemed to not want to know. It was a shame, for they were so much alike, sensitive, interested in the same things, art and wildlife and jazz.

He was beginning to get used to it, this far-reaching influence of his ex-wife on his existence. In Wood Green Shopping City, at parties given by mutual friends, even going to the sweet shop up the street to buy an Evening Standard—she always seemed to be there, with her crude jokes and painfully loud voice, like a curse. So here he was still wishing there were something he could do to be rid of her, but not having the least idea what. Except to maybe blot her out of his thoughts with alcohol. And to go on wishing, wishing healthy Vi would just turn around and drop dead.

"Right. Everybody around the table. Who's going to find us a candle?"

"There must be candles, probably in that cupboard. Hugh, you have a look, go on now, there's a lovely man."

Why don't you do it yourself, he said. But only in his head. He found himself mechanically moving toward the shelves of china and crystal. The sound of trembling valuables shimmered on the air as he jiggled the drawers out, one by one. God how he hated that woman he had married.

"Are there any rules to this?"

"Of course there're rules, you idiot. Haven't you ever watched a horror movie in your life?" Vi's laughter prevented her remark from becoming an insult. "You have to have a medium; you have to have all the lights turned off—and you have to not break the circle you've made with your hands before the spirits have finished speaking."

"What a load of old wank."

"What if we need to use the loo?"

"Go pee now. I don't want you spoiling my game."

Hugh sat back in his chair, looking at Vi through narrowed eyes. In the soft light of the candle flame he could see reminders of why he had fallen in love with her:

her gleaming dark helmet of hair, the grace of her movements, her sexual exuberance. He opened his eyes wide. He made himself look at the pouches of fat beginning to lodge around her jaw and chin, fleshing out her cheeks where the skin had started to roughen and pock; he saw how her hair had dulled, and her eyes had faded, lacking focus now even though she was sober. Her cigarette jutted from her frown, stray ash skittering across the polished surface of their hostess' mahogany table.

They ringed themselves around it, clasping hands. Hugh found himself opposite Tamsin. The actor's hand came from behind her neck to settle comfortably in the nest of her fingers. Vi appointed herself medium. She raised her arms dramatically, the hands she gripped following into the air, perhaps against their will—but everyone was taking Vi's dictum quite seriously and would not break the circle, even though the only spirits present now swirled over the bottom of Hugh's cocktail can.

"Eenie-meenie, chilly-beanie, the spirits are about to speak!"

"Very funny, Hugh. Do you mind?"

"What happens next, Vi?"

"We close our eyes, and wait."

For the first time Hugh noticed the grandfather clock next to the dish cupboard, and that it ticked, for in the ensuing silence its ticking was monstrously loud. He was having a hard time sitting straight in his chair, and now that they were all holding hands there was a niggling but insistent itch plaguing his nose, and he badly wanted a cigarette.

"Aren't we supposed to ask questions?"

"Shhhhh."

"No, I mean really. I mean, how are we supposed to raise any ghosts of whatever unless we ask them is anybody there, that sort of thing?"

"Raise spirits. Oi! That's a laugh. Old Vi can barely raise herself out of bed in the morning."

There was a skitter of laughter around the table. Then Tamsin spoke, very softly. "I don't like this much. Maybe we should stop."

"IS ANYBODY THERE?" Vi bellowed, ignoring her. "Is . . . there . . . anybody . . . in the room?"

"Best not to wake the dead," intoned Nigel, in his very best Hammer voice.

Vi snapped, "We *must* know if anybody is there!"

There was someone's sharp intake of breath as the candle flame shot straight up, then wavered, elongating itself, a slender pillar of fire rising slowly towards the ceiling. Hugh had just opened his eyes preparatory to standing up to leave but then he saw Vi's shut eyes through the flame, her mouth working soundlessly, and he sat back in his chair, fascinated. Now there was a voice that seemed to come from somewhere under the table, weak and thin and high, *she's very good at this and I never even knew*, but the voice began to grow stronger as the flame rose higher; and faintly, as though very far away, there was the steady insistent ringing of a bell. The hand on his right dug its nails into his skin, almost causing him to yelp. Now there were words. One word. He thought it was *burn*, said over over and over again, a mumbled sobbing chant. Then the voice broke, falling, distorting like the voice does on a record stopped mid-revolution with a clumsy finger, its tones dropping to an unnatural deepness and Hugh had known Vi sixteen years and he knew she was not capable of this and his hair stood straight up on his head as the voice cried, "Burnt in the streets, burnt, the whole pile, you cannot breathe clean air for the ashes of the dead floating in it. Shall London ever smell sweet again? Ay, burn burn burn."

Hugh saw the candle flame bend and stream towards Vi, entering her open mouth. She sat motionless as fire illuminated her face from within, tiny spurts of yellow sparking her nostrils, red flushing her skin like blood rising inside her skull; fire twisted out of her ears, encircling her neck, sheeting her entire body so that she sat motionless in the flame's burning heart.

Jenny began to whimper. Hugh hushed her sharply. "Not now."

Everyone stared as Vi's mouth opened; her tongue, yellow and unburnt, licked red teeth. "Burn burn burn," said the voice, its bass music intertwined with the faint ringing of the bell. The medium's lips did not move.

"Stop it," someone said. "Stop it, Vi, please. Someone stop her."

"*It's not Vi.*"

No it's not, thought Hugh, and we mustn't break the circle. Vi sat with her eyes closed, a human torch, the inhuman voice issuing, horrible and thin, from her open mouth. He never knew what he was doing until he was already out of his chair and the force of his movement had freed his hands from the others' with a sweaty, smacking sound as he cried out, "We must know: *is there anybody there?*"

He saw the people on either side of him as though they were something he was dreaming; he saw their hands fall back onto the polished round surface of the table, and he staggered back when Vi's eyes snapped open and looked straight, accusingly at him. But the look lasted only for the briefest of moments. She burst into real flame before anything else could happen. He felt heat blazing on his face and his ex-wife's screams were nearly intolerable as she burnt alive in front of all of them, unable to move herself as though she had been tied to that chair, and though they tried they couldn't put the fire out. It burnt with a bright and steady glow until there was nothing left but a few blackened bones, and a terrible reeking smell that the hostess was never again able to get out of her house.

HUMAN REMAINS

Edward Bryant

A native of Wyoming who currently lives in Denver, Colorado, Edward Bryant is an award-winning short story writer whose work has been collected in *Cinnabar* and *Particle Theory*. His most recent book is the short novel *Fetish*, and he is currently working on a story collection titled *Ed Gein's America*.

"Human Remains" comes from Bryant's new small-press collection, *Darker Passions*. Like much of his recent fiction, it combines a perceptive use of one of America's media obsessions (in this case, serial killers) with his usual fine rendering of female characters to create an odd and very disturbing "what if?" story.

—E.D.

Vicky first thought a little girl had lost the doll in the women's room just off the main lobby of the West Denver Inn. It was a Barbie, just like she remembered from years before. The doll was straight and pink and impossibly proportioned. It lay on the dull white tile beneath the tampon machine. Vicky had heard the clatter as she passed on her way to the sink. Perhaps she had brushed it off, somehow, with an unwary elbow.

Something wasn't right. The doll did *not* look at all as she remembered.

Vicky set her black patent-leather purse on the faux marble counter by the sinks, switched the soft leather briefcase to her left hand, and knelt. She saw that the doll was tightly bound with monofilament. Tough, nearly transparent fishing line wound around the doll, binding the ankles, the arms at the waist, the chest, the shoulders, the throat, even around the head, taut across the parted lips. The line wound so tight, plastic bulged slightly around the loops. The bindings actually cut into the doll's unreal skin.

She gingerly extended the fingers of her right hand and touched Barbie's shoulder. Cold. *Had* a little girl lost this here? Vicky forced herself to pick up the doll. Had one of the other women out in the restaurant bar left this? She brought the doll close to her face. Was that a glisten of something red at the corner of Barbie's lips? The fishing line caught and reflected the harsh overhead light. No, there was no blood. It was only a trick of the light.

Vicky wondered at the obvious strength of the line. If it could do this to the durable synthetics of the doll, what would it do to a caught fish? She had a feeling it would take superhuman—super . . . what *was* the word for fish?—strength to break these bonds.

Caught would be caught.

She saw no knots where the line ends connected. And maybe there was no need to find them. No point. Trapped. Caught for good. Vicky wound her fingers around the Barbie and turned toward the restroom door. Suddenly she wanted to leave the sharp light and the harsh, astringent odor of disinfectant.

She noticed nothing now save the doll's seeming to become warmer. Lose heat, gain heat. Barbie was taking heat from Vicky's grip, her skin, her body, her living, pumping blood.

As she swung the door inward with her left hand, Vicky thrust the doll into her briefcase. Now she had a secret. It was a long time since she had had a *new* secret.

This weekend, she had a sudden feeling, it was important to keep a secret or two ready and waiting. Something chilling and exciting rippled through her.

When she'd left the table, her companions had been talking about politics local to Colorado, Utah, Oregon, Washington, presidential campaigns, ballot initiatives to alter the whole tone and conduct of capital punishment. Now the other four women were talking about shoes.

Vicky smiled and sat down. Her half-empty supper dishes had been removed. From her side of the table, she could look out the wide expanse of restaurant window, down across the Platte River valley, off to the east across the glittering October skyline of Denver. Above the lights, a nearly full moon had risen. It was another week until Halloween. Trails of fast-moving lights limned the freeway below.

Dixie, the Oregon blonde Vicky already thought of as the wannabe, was saying, "Listen, tomorrow's Saturday, there's gotta be a *lot* of fall shoe sales at the malls."

Sonya and Kate, the dark-haired sisters from Utah, looked at each other and laughed. Kate said, "Listen, we've got malls in Salt Lake."

"If we want to shop for pumps or ogle Birkenstocks, we'll just crank up the Shoe Channel on cable later tonight in the room." That was Sonya, the elder sister by maybe two years.

Vicky scooted her chair forward and took a sip of coffee. It had cooled to room temperature. Entropy. She remembered the word from a magazine article in her gynecologist's waiting room. "Southwest Plaza has 27 different shoe stores," she said absently.

"You counted?" said Carol Anne. She was conspicuously younger than the other women at the table. Vicky wondered about that but had stopped short of asking directly. "I shop there too, but I never counted all the shoe stores."

Vicky shrugged. "Anyhow, you can't try them on on the Shoe Channel."

"I bet Mrs. Marcos watches," said Dixie. "Is there really a Shoe Channel? We don't get that on cable in Eugene."

The supper crowd was beginning to thin out. Vicky realized that most of the faces were women she had seen, and some she had talked to, earlier in the afternoon, when everyone had arrived at the hotel.

"Okay, I'm not going to argue," said Dixie, smiling. She, Vicky already had noted, laughed a lot. "Tomorrow's another day. How about tonight? Are we all going to go out somewhere? I know you two sisters have got a car. Is there a Chippendale's in Denver? Carol Anne? You look hip and you *live* here."

"Beats me," said Carol Anne. "I'm out west in Golden. That's the suburbs. No stud dancers out there." She seemed to be blushing a little.

Dixie looked at Vicky. Vicky realized she was hugging the soft briefcase with the bound Barbie doll. She could feel its hardness through the leather. "Don't look at me," Vicky said. "I haven't been to a place like that since—" A chill ran through her belly and up her spine. She felt her shoulders twitch involuntarily. *Since the ride.*

A man walked up to the table. Vicky at first thought it was the waiter, and then realized that he was another diner. She recognized him as the guy who had been sitting with a woman, probably his wife, at the next table. He was a florid man, perhaps in his fifties, in a dark gray suit. His blue eyes were small and piercing. He had a gray mustache.

He stared down at them. Vicky thought Dixie was going to say something.

"Listen," said the man, looking quickly from face to face. "I was talking to the manager. He's a friend of mine and he told me what you're all doing. I gotta tell you something. I think you're all a bunch of sick fucks." He turned on his heel and walked away. His wife quickly got up from their table and followed her husband toward the door. She had averted her eyes, Vicky noticed, from the whole exchange.

The five women at the table stared at each other. Sonya turned and looked after the retreating figures of the man and his wife. She looked angry enough to spit, but said nothing. Kate shook her head.

"Yeah," said Dixie, "me too. What a jerk."

Carol Anne looked as if she might cry.

Vicky hugged the doll in the briefcase even tighter, then took a few deep breaths and relaxed her grip. She reached over the tabletop and touched Carol Anne's hand, wanting to comfort her, reassure her.

The waiter picked that moment to return to ask if anyone wanted more coffee.

They tacitly agreed not to keep talking about the business-suited man with the silent wife. The enthusiasm for male dancers had dwindled. Dixie started talking about movies. Sonya mentioned that the front desk rented VCRs to guests. "Do any of you have the tape?" she said. "The Dobson tape? $29.95 before it got discounted at K-Mart?"

"I looked at it once," said Dixie. "All that bullshit about booze and porn."

"I—" Carol Anne started to say something but stopped. She looked to be in her early twenties. Very pretty, Vicky thought. Long brown hair styled back across her shoulders. Maybe like my daughter would have looked if I'd ever had one.

"You were saying?" Dixie said encouragingly.

An alarm sounded in Vicky's brain. Don't push her, she thought. Maybe she really doesn't want to talk.

Carol Anne said, "I watched it, oh, maybe a hundred times." The rest of the women stared.

"Why?" Vicky almost breathed rather than said the words aloud. Obsessed, she thought. And so, *so* young.

The younger woman looked down at her lap. "I thought maybe there would be . . . a clue. Something. Anything." She drifted off into silence.

Vicky knew the others wanted to ask, *what clue*? What are you looking for? No one said anything at all. But lord, they wanted to. *Obsessed*.

And then there was another new presence at the table. It was a young man in a busboy's jacket with brown corduroy trousers. "Bobby" was stitched over his heart. He looked from one face to the next. His eyes, Vicky thought, looked far older than his fresh face.

" 'Scuse me, ladies," he said, "did one of you forget—"

Vicky's hand was already unconsciously reaching for the black purse.

Which wasn't there on the corner of the table where it should have been.

"—your bag?" He raised his hand and there was Vicky's black purse.

"It's mine." She reached and took it from him.

"You left it in the ladies' room," said Bobby. "You gotta watch that around here. This is the city." He caught her eye. His gaze lingered. Boldly.

Vicky touched the leather with her fingertips. This was mildly disorienting. "Thanks," she said. "I appreciate it. Thank you very much."

"Don't think nothing of it," said Bobby. He made a vague waving gesture with his left hand. "No harm done." He bobbed his head as if embarrassed, caught Vicky's eye again for just a moment, then turned and walked back toward the kitchen.

Vicky stared. Had the young man smiled? She thought she'd seen a fleeting twist of his lips as he turned. Had he just flirted with her? Returning lost items would be a great way to meet women. *Flirt*. She hadn't thought about that word in a long time.

And then she thought of something else. Could lost items be used as bait? But who was fishing?

"Vicky?" Dixie was saying. "Hello, Earth to Vicky? You there, girl?"

Vicky started, realized she was shaking a little, tried to breathe regularly. "I'm here. I guess I was just thinking about how terrible it would have been to lose this," she said, cradling the purse in her hand.

"Cancelling the cards would be a royal pain," said Kate, the younger sister.

"Never mind the cards," said Dixie. "I'd be worried some wacko'd track me down from the driver's license and show up on my doorstep."

"Isn't that a little paranoid?" Kate said.

Her big sister smiled faintly. "Aren't we all probably just a little paranoid?"

As it turned out, no one went anywhere. The five of them stayed until first the restaurant kitchen, then the bar closed. They talked. Lord, how they talked, Vicky thought.

They talked about that fatal, climactic morning in January, those few years before. Sixteen minutes past seven, EDT.

It was like, where were you when President Kennedy was shot? When John Lennon died? When the Challenger exploded. What were you doing at 7:16 in the morning, January 24, 1989? Listening to a radio. Watching television. Praying his appeals would be turned down.

"I slept through it," said Dixie. "I'd been watching on CNN most of the night. I went to sleep. I couldn't help it."

"Let me tell you something," said Kate. She glanced at Sonya. "My sister and me, we know a woman whose daughter was killed. But she was also against capital punishment. She wrote letters and made a thousand phone calls trying to stop the execution."

Sonya looked off toward the dark space above the bar. "What can you say? She was entitled. She was wrong, but she was entitled." Her voice dropped off. She said something else and Vicky thought it was something like, "Burn him. Burn them all."

There was muted laughter at the table behind them. But none at Vicky's. They talked more about the execution.

"I'll tell you something *really* interesting," said Dixie, "though the rest of you may already know this." She shrugged. "I didn't. I just found out. There was a guard who looked real close at the executioner. The guy with the hand on the switch was all covered up, with a black hood and all, you know, just like in a horror movie? Anyhow, the guard says the guy's eyelashes were incredible. Thick and long, he said. He thought maybe the executioner was a woman."

They all thought about that for a moment. "No reason why she couldn't have been," said Sonya. "Poetic justice."

"How would she get the assignment?" said Carol Anne.

No one had a good answer.

"Maybe it was just a job," said Kate. "They all drew cards, maybe. The officials, I mean. The queen of spades or something meant pull the switch. I would have done it."

"I would have too," said Sonya. "Under the hood, I think I'd have smiled." Her teeth clicked together. "I'd have laughed."

Dixie nodded. Vicky and Carol Anne said nothing.

The already low lights in the bar flickered momentarily and everyone jumped.

They had never met one another before today. Perhaps they would never meet again. But the five of them had, Vicky thought to herself, an incredibly strong bond tying them together. Or more precisely, maybe, they just had something lucky in common.

Sonya and Kate talked about living in Midvale, a little Utah community south of Salt Lake City. In 1974, in October, when Sonya had been 19 and Kate 17, they had been driving home from an Osmonds concert in Salt Lake. One minute the Chevy had been running fine, the next, it was making grinding noises, and the next, it was coasting off on the shoulder on I-15, just past the exit for Taylorsville.

"It was bizarre," said Sonya. "here we were on an Interstate, and it was only about midnight, and nobody would stop. It was like we were invisible."

And that was when the handsome stranger wheeled his Volkswagen off the highway and pulled in behind them. It was too dark to tell what color the VW was, but the teenagers could see his face in the domelight. He offered to give Sonya a ride into Midvale, but suggested Kate stay with the Chevy to keep an eye on things.

"We said no deal," said Kate. "We both would go into Midvale, or none of us would."

The stranger put his fingers around Sonya's wrist as though to drag her into the Volkswagen. Kate held up a tire iron she had picked up from the Chevy's floor. And that was it. The stranger let go, apologized like a gentleman, spun out on the gravel and disappeared into the Utah night.

"He killed a girl from Midvale," said Sonya. "We knew her. We didn't know her well, but after they finally found her bones, we went to the funeral and cried."

Dixie's was a lower-key story, as Vicky had suspected.

"It was 1975," said Dixie. "I was a blonde then, just like now, and I know what you're thinking. Well, he killed two blondes. He wanted brunettes, but he'd settle. He wasn't that predictable."

Vicky was glad she hadn't said anything earlier. She'd known about the blonde victims. She simply, for whatever reason, had been suspicious of Dixie's attitude.

"I was picking up some stuff for my mom at Safeway," Dixie continued. "In Eugene. I remember coming up to my car with a bag of groceries in each arm, thinking about saying a dirty word because I couldn't reach the key in my jeans without either putting a bag down or else risking scattering apples and lima beans across half the lot. Anyhow, just as I got up to the car, there was this good-looking guy—I mean, he looked way out of place in the Safeway lot—with his arm in a sling. I was concentrating on getting hold of my key, so I didn't pay much attention to what he was saying at first, but like I said, he was pretty cute, so I didn't ignore him completely. He wanted help getting the tire changed on his Volks, he said. Not much help, just having me jump up and down on the spider to loosen the nuts." Dixie grinned. "I thought I'd be a Girl Scout, so I went over a few steps, still with the bags in my arms, and sure enough, there was the VW. It was a metallic brown Beetle, but I couldn't see any flat tire. It was about then I heard my mom's voice telling me about talking to strangers, so I said to him there was a Texaco station with a mechanic just about four blocks down Willamette, and he should get some help there."

"That was it?" said Sonya. "He didn't try to grab you?"

"He was a perfect gentleman," said Dixie dryly. "Didn't say another word. Just thanked me, turned around and started walking down the street. I got in my mom's car and left. That was that."

Then they asked Carol Anne for her story, but the young woman demurred. "I'm really tired." They looked at her. "I mean, I don't want to talk about any of this right now," she said. "I guess I'm having a little trouble just listening to what all of you are saying."

"So why are you here?" said Dixie.

"Give her a break," said Vicky quickly. She's just a kid. That's what she didn't say. It would just have triggered more questions. She made a sudden decision to get Carol Anne off the hook. "Anyway, I'm all psyched to play confessional."

"Okay," said Kate.

Dixie glanced at Carol Anne, then looked back to Vicky and nodded. "Then it's your turn."

"I was hitchhiking," said Vicky. "It was April 1975 and the school year was winding down." I just flunked out, she thought, and then wondered why she just didn't admit it. Maybe she did have a little pride left. "I was in Grand Junction, over on the western slope. I had the cash, but decided to catch a ride back to Denver just for the hell of it." For the adventure, she thought. Right. The adventure. Hanging around the club where they'd let her dance topless for tips.

"I waited a while out on the east edge of town. It was morning and there seemed to be a lot more people driving west into the Junction. Finally I got a ride. I think you know who picked me up."

Slow, serious nods from Kate and Sonya. Dixie's mouth twitched. Carol Anne just looked back soberly.

"He was the most charming man I'd ever met," said Vicky. And still is, she thought. "We drove for almost an hour before anything happened." She fell silent.

"So?" Dixie prompted.

"He pulled off on a dirt road. He said there was something wrong with the engine. It sounded like something you'd hear from some highschool jock taking the good girl in class out to lover's lane."

"And?" said Kate.

Vicky took a long breath. "He tried to rape me. He had a knife and some handcuffs. When he tried to force the cuffs on my wrist nearest him, I bit him hard on his hand. I was able to get the door open, and then I was out of there." It wasn't rape, she thought. It was mutual seduction. She'd never seen the knife, though the cuffs were real enough. But her moment of panic had come at the point of orgasm when his strong fingers had tightened around her throat. At that moment, she had . . . flinched. Chickened out, she sometimes told herself in the blackest of moods. At any rate, she had kicked free of the stranger. "I ran into the scrub trees where I knew he couldn't drive a car, and then I hid. After dark, I still waited until the moon rose and set, and then I walked back to the highway. I was lucky. The first car that stopped was a state trooper. I don't think I would have gotten in a car with anyone else that night."

Sonya and Dixie and Kate all nodded. Wisely. Then Dixie started to turn toward Carol Anne again.

Vicky said, "Sorry to break this up, but it's getting late and I'm exhausted. We'll all have the chance to talk tomorrow." She glanced pointedly at Carol Anne. The younger woman got the hint.

"I'm going to call it a night too," she said. "Tomorrow," she said to Dixie. "I promise."

The sisters from Utah decided to stay a while longer and finish their soda waters, though the ice was long since melted. Dixie headed for the elevator.

Carol Anne said to Vicky, "I want to get some fresh air before bed. There's a kind of mezzanine outside, up over the parking lot and the valley. You want to come along?"

Vicky hesitated, then nodded.

"What time is it?" said Carol Anne. They passed through the bar exit. The bartender locked the door behind them.

"I don't have a watch on," said Vicky.

"It's two-thirty," said a voice in the dimly lit hallway.

Vicky recoiled, then peered forward. "You," she said. "The guy who brought back my purse. Bobby."

"Bobby Cowell," he said. "At your service, ma'am." There was something in his tone that was not deferential at all. "Always at your service."

"Thanks again, Bobby," Vicky said. She realized Carol Anne had retreated a step.

"Did you count the cash?" said Bobby, stepping closer. He had a musky scent.

"I trust you," said Vicky. And she did. Sometimes she surprised herself.

Bobby must have realized that. He nodded slowly. "If there's anything I can do for you while you're here, anything at all . . ." The man's voice was carefully modulated, sincere.

"Thanks again." Vicky led Carol Anne past Bobby Cowell.

The man faded into the hallway. "I'd like to get to know you," he called low after them.

Vicky walked faster.

"I think he likes you," said Carol Anne.

"He's more your age," said Vicky. But she knew she did not completely mean that with sincerity. "Attractive guy." She had seen his type before. Oh, yes.

Carol Anne laughed. Vicky couldn't recall having heard her laugh aloud. "He looks like a Young Republican." She paused. "And he probably drives a bronze VW." Carol Anne laughed again, but this time the sound was hollow.

The two women stood against the railing overlooking the Platte Valley. Traffic below them on I-25 was minimal. To the south they could see the bright arc lamps of some sort of highway maintenance. Vicky could feel heat radiating from Carol Anne's side.

"You know, I keep wondering about something," said Carol Anne.

"What's that?" Vicky found her eyes attracted to the red aircraft warning lights blinking on the skyscrapers less than a mile away.

"This is really petty and my soul'll probably burn in hell just for thinking it."

"Let's hear it." Vicky's attention snapped back to the woman next to her.

"My dad told me once that he figured maybe a million people went to Woodstock."

"That may be a little exaggerated," said Vicky.

"No, I mean, a lot of people were so in love with the idea of having been there, but even if they didn't go, they *said* they did. Maybe they even *thought* they did."

"So are you talking about this event here?" said Vicky. "I think everybody here believes she went through whatever she went through." She suddenly started to feel the fatigue of the night for real. Her head was buzzing.

"I guess—well, okay," said Carol Anne.

"Let me suggest something even more troubling," said Vicky. In the darkness, she saw the pale oval of Carol Anne's face turn toward her. "You know about astronaut syndrome?"

"No," said Carol Anne, sounding puzzled.

"People used to go to the moon," said Vicky. "Men did, anyway. I read an article once, where they interviewed guys who walked on the moon. You know something, it was the biggest, most exciting, most important thing that ever happened to them."

"So?" said Carol Anne, apparently not getting the point.

"So they had to come back to earth. So they had to spend the rest of their lives doing things that were incredibly less exciting and important. Politics and selling insurance and writing books were nothing like walking on the moon."

Carol Anne was silent for a while. "So everyone here, I mean, all the women who came in for this gathering thing, they walked on the moon?"

"They all lived," said Vicky. "They survived. Nothing as exciting will ever happen to them again."

"What about you?" said Carol Anne. She clapped her hand over her mouth as if suddenly trying to stop the words.

"I fit the pattern," said Vicky, trying to smile and soften the words. "I've gone through a lot of men, a lot of jobs, a husband, more men, more dead-end jobs. Nothing so powerful has ever happened to me again." She thought, it sounds like a religious experience. *And maybe it is.*

Carol Anne issued something that sounded a little like a sigh, a little bit of a sob.

"Now," said Vicky. "What about you? You're too young for the moon. You know it and I know it. We've been talking about *them*. Now there's just me, and just you. And you've heard about me." Well, most of it, she thought.

Carol Anne reached out blindly and took Vicky's hand. She held it tightly. She seemed to be trying to say something. It wasn't working.

"Calm down," said Vicky. "It's all right." She took the younger woman in her arms. "It's all right," she repeated.

"I never knew him," said Carol Anne, her words muffled against Vicky's shoulder. "Not directly. But I think he killed my mother." She started to cry. Vicky rocked her gently, let her work it out.

"We don't know for sure," Carol Anne said finally. "My dad and I, we just don't know. They never found any remains. I was five back in 1975. My mom was really young when she had me. You know something? My birthday is January 24. And for nineteen years I didn't know what the significance was going to be. In 1989 on my birthday, I only got one present. The execution." She smiled mirthlessly. "Before that. 1975. It was earlier in the winter than when you got away from him. We lived in Vail. We found my mom's car in the public parking lot. It was unlocked and the police said later someone had pulled the coil wire. They said there was no sign of violence. She just vanished. We never saw her again." Carol Anne started again to cry. "She didn't run away, like some people said. He got her. And there are no remains."

After a while, Vicky pulled a clean tissue from her purse. "So why are you here?"

There was a very long silence, after which Carol Anne blew her nose noisily. "I thought maybe something someone might say would give me a clue. About my mother. I've read everything. I've seen all the tapes. Over and over. I just want to know, more than anything else, what happened."

No, thought Vicky, I don't think you do. She knew what would happen when she said it, but she said it anyway. "Your mother's dead, Carol Anne. I'm sorry. I'm very sorry. But you know it."

Carol Anne sobbed for a very long time. She took a fresh tissue from Vicky. "I know it. I know that. I just want to know more. How it happened. Who—"

"It's enough to accept that she's gone," said Vicky. "Maybe someday you'll find out more." She hesitated. "I hope you do."

"I'm 22," said Carol Anne. "My whole life's revolved around this for seventeen years."

"Do you have . . . someone?"

"My father died five years ago. I don't have a boyfriend if that's what you mean." Her voice was mournful. "I guess I don't have much of a life at all."

I'm glad you said it, Vicky thought. "You will," she said aloud. "But you've got to leave all this old baggage. You can't forget it, but you can allow it to fade. Your dues are paid. Believe it." Just say good-bye, she thought. Good night for good, and make it stick. She reached out again for Carol Anne's hand. And then she packed the young woman off to bed. At the door of Carol Anne's room, Vicky said, "I'll see you in the morning. Try to get some sleep."

Carol Anne looked like she was trying to smile bravely. Then she shut the door. Vicky heard the chain lock rattle into place.

Her own room was down a floor and at the opposite end of the wing. The windows overlooked the parking lot. If she craned her neck, Vicky could see the downtown office towers with their cycling crimson aircraft beacons.

She didn't turn on the lights when she entered the room. Vicky lay down on the bed still dressed, the purse and briefcase nestled up against her like kittens. She stared up into the darkness as though she could still see stars. The bright, winking stars of western slope Colorado. The star patterns of 1975. She wondered if she went to the window and looked down, whether she would see moonlight glinting off the shell-like curve of a hunched VW. Bobby's VW? There was something about his name that tickled at the edge of her attention, something she couldn't quite remember.

She found her fingers, as though of their own volition, opening the briefcase and taking out the tightly bound Barbie doll. Vicky couldn't see it, but she could feel the taut loops of monofilament cutting into the vinyl dollflesh. She clutched the talisman and smiled invisibly.

Some men, Vicky thought, would only send flowers.

But then, as the darkness seeped through every pore, every orifice of her body, filling her with night and grief, she thought of Carol Anne and began to cry. Vicky had not cried in all too long. Not in seventeen years, to be exact.

Seventeen years without a life. Seventeen years looking.

At least, she thought, Carol Anne is young. She can go away from this weekend and re-create her life. She doesn't have to be empty.

And what about me? Vicky thought, before clamping down savagely on self-pity.

What, indeed. Seventeen years before. It was perhaps the next-to-biggest event of her life. The most important was still to come. Perhaps. It had been on its way since 1975. And had been derailed in January 1989. No, that's not it either, she thought, feeling the long-time confusion. All I want is to walk on the moon again.

Vicky cried herself to sleep.

She knew she was dreaming, but that did not diminish the effects.

She still lay in her bed, but now it was larger than she could envision and softer than she could hope. She lay bound tightly, so tightly she could not move.

But the thing about helplessness was, she no longer had to take responsibility for anything at all. Almost cocooned in monofilament, she could feel the line cut into her skin, deep into her flesh, thin incisions of pain that burned like lasers.

The pain, she realized, was a mercy compared to the years of numbness. The bindings that restrained her body also retained her heat, and now that heat built and built and suffused her from the core of her flesh to the outer layers of skin.

Blood ran from the corner of her mouth, where the line dug so tight, she could not extend her tongue to lick it away. But some ran back inside anyway. Her blood was warm and slick and salty.

She moaned and moved as best she could inside her bonds. It was almost enough.

Vicky awoke confused, staring in disorientation at the bedside clock. She guessed it was still an hour before dawn. She had not slept for long. But she wanted to stretch, and so she did so. Her body felt alive. More, it felt . . . she searched for an apt word . . . hopeful.

Then she turned her head and recoiled back against the pillow. Bobby Cowell stood at the foot of her bed. His left hand swung back and forth slowly. Something metallic glittered. A pass-key. Vicky tried to speak.

He had been watching her sleep.

He had watched her dream.

"There's just something about you," he said softly. He smiled in the dim light, teeth showing white.

There was no conscious planning. She swung her legs off the bed, hearing the briefcase slide to the carpet, then sat up and took a deep breath or two to counter the sudden vertigo. After a few seconds, she got up and hesitated.

She could lunge for the phone. Or the door. She saw no weapon in evidence other than the key.

"I know who you are," said Bobby. "I know everything you want." He stepped back away from the door. She could flee.

"What do *you* want?" Vicky said.

"To take you for a ride. It's still a beautiful night. We'll go up into the mountains."

It was so much like a dream. She didn't remember to bring a coat, but the late, late night didn't seem to be all that cold, so it didn't matter.

At the bottom of the fire-stair well, she waited for him. "I figured you'd come," he said softly, taking her arm.

"I will," said Vicky. Was she still sleeping? All in motion only slightly slower than reality.

They exited the stairwell. "I have my car out in the lot," said Bobby.

Vicky nodded and put her free hand over his fingers on her arm. "I figured that," she said. His fingers were warm. The excitement inside her was cold. She looked up and saw the distant, sinking moon.

They passed the mezzanine and turned toward the steps leading down to the parking lot. Vicky hesitated a split second, stared back over Bobby's shoulder, hesitated a little longer.

At the other end of the platform, Carol Anne stood, leaning away from the city, staring back at them. Her expression altered mercurially. Vicky didn't think Bobby had seen Carol Anne watching them. Maybe she'd see Carol Anne in the morning. Maybe not.

"Come on," said Vicky, turning back to the steps. And at the beginning of the final descent to the outside world, she thought about the last enigmatic expression on Carol Anne's face. Wistful?

She hoped—wished desperately—it was only that.

IT COMES AND GOES

Robert Silverberg

Robert Silverberg has written science fiction, horror, fantasy, historical, and erotic literature as well as nonfiction books on science, history, and archaeology. He has won five Nebula Awards and four Hugo Awards. His many novels include *Dying Inside, The Book of Skulls, Born with the Dead, Tom O'Bedlam, Lord Valentine's Castle, The Face of the Waters*, and most recently, *Kingdoms of the Wall*. His collections of short fiction include *The Conglomeroid Cocktail Party, Majipoor Chronicles*, and *The Collected Stories of Robert Silverberg Volume 1: Secret Sharers*. He has also edited many fine anthologies, including *New Dimensions* and currently (with Karen Haber) the *Universe* series, which was edited for many years by the late Terry Carr.

Silverberg rarely writes traditional horror (an exception might be "Warm Man"), but much of his work contains horrific elements, even the science fiction.

Silverberg's sharp, uncluttered prose style fits "It Comes and Goes" perfectly. The story, first published in *Playboy* magazine, it is not overtly horrific, yet it leaves a residue of disquiet.

—E.D. & T.W.

The house comes and goes, comes and goes, and no one seems to know or to care. It's that kind of neighborhood. You keep your head down; you take notice only of the things relevant to your personal welfare; you screen out everything else as irrelevant or meaningless or potentially threatening.

It's a very ordinary house, 30 or 40 years old, a cheap, one-story white-stucco job on a corner lot, maybe six rooms: green shutters on the windows, a scruffy lawn, a narrow, badly paved path running from the street to the front steps. There's a screen door in front of the regular one. To the right and left of the doorway is some unkempt shrubbery, with odds and ends of rusting junk scattered around it—a garbage can, an old barbecue outfit, stuff like that.

All the houses around here look much the same; there isn't a lot of architectural variety in this neighborhood. Just rows of ordinary little houses, adding up to an ordinary kind of place, neither a slum nor anything desirable; aging houses inhabited by stranded people who can't move up and who are settled enough so that they've stopped slipping down. Even the street names are stereotyped small-town standards, instantly forgettable: Maple, Oak, Spruce, Pine. It's hard to tell one street from another, and usually, there's no reason you should. You're able to recognize your own, and the others—except for Walnut, where the shops are—are just for filler. I know how to get from my place to the white house with the screen door—turn right, down to the corner and right again, diagonal left across the street—but even now, I couldn't tell you whether it's on Spruce corner of Oak or Pine corner of Maple. I just know how to get there.

The house will stay here for five or six days at a time and then, one morning, I'll come out and the lot will be vacant, and so it remains for ten days or two weeks. And then there it is again. You'd think people would notice that, you'd think they'd talk; but they're all keeping their heads down, I guess. I keep my head down, too, but I can't help noticing things. In that sense, I don't belong in this part of town. In most other senses, I guess I do, because, after all, this is where I am.

The first time I saw the house was on a drizzly Monday morning on the cusp of winter and spring. I remember that it was a Monday because people were going to work and I wasn't, and that was still a new concept for me. I remember that it was on the cusp of winter and spring because there were still some curling trails of dirty snow on the north side of the street, left over from an early-March storm, but the forsythia and crocuses were blooming in the gardens on the south side. I was walking down to the grocery on Walnut Street to pick up the morning paper. Daily walking, rain or shine, is very important to me; it's part of my recovery regimen, and I was going for the paper because I was still into studying the help-wanted ads at that time. As I made my way down Spruce Street (or maybe it was Pine Street), some movement in a doorway across the way caught my eye, and I glanced up and over.

A flash of flesh it was.

A woman, turning in the doorway.

A *naked* woman, so it seemed. I had just a quick side glimpse, fuzzed and blurred by the screen door and the gray light of the cloudy morning, but I was sure I saw gleaming golden flesh: a bare shoulder, a sinuous hip, a long stretch of haunch and thigh and butt and calf, maybe a bit of bright pubic fleece also. And then she was gone, leaving incandescent tracks on my mind.

I stopped right on a dime and stood staring toward the darkness of the doorway, waiting to see if she'd reappear. Hoping that she would. Praying that she would, actually. It wasn't because I was in such desperate need of a free show but because I wanted her to have been real. Not simply a hallucination. I was clean that morning and had been for a month and a half, ever since the seventh of February, and I didn't want to think that I was still having hallucinations.

The doorway stayed dark. She didn't reappear.

Of course not. She couldn't reappear, because she had never been there in the first place. What I had seen had been an illusion. How could she possibly have been real? Real women around here don't flash their bare butts in front of doorways at nine in the morning on cold drizzly days, and they don't have hips and thighs and legs like that.

But I let myself off the hook. After all, I was clean. Why borrow trouble? It had been a trick of the light, I told myself. Or maybe, *maybe*, a curious fluke of my overwrought mind. An odd mental prank. But, in any case, nothing to take seriously, nothing symptomatic of significant cerebral decline or collapse.

I went on down to the Walnut Street grocery and bought that morning's *Post-Star* and looked through the classified ads for the one that said:

IF YOU ARE AN INTELLIGENT, CAPABLE, HARD-WORKING HUMAN BEING WHO
HAS GONE THROUGH A BAD TIME BUT IS NOW IN RECOVERY AND LOOKING TO
MAKE A COMEBACK IN THE GREAT GAME OF LIFE, WE HAVE JUST THE JOB FOR
YOU.

It wasn't there. Somehow, it never was.

On my way home, I thought I'd give the white house on the corner a lot a second glance, just in case something else of interest was showing. The house wasn't there, either.

My name is Tom and I am chemically dependent.

My name is Tom and I am chemically dependent.

My name is Tom and I am chemically dependent.

I tell you that three times because what I tell you three times is true. If anything at all is true about me, that much is. It is also true that I am 40 years old, that I have had successful careers in advertising, public relations, mail-order promotion and several other word-oriented professions. Each of those successful careers came to an unsuccessful end. I have written three novels and a bunch of short stories, too. And, between the ages of 29 and 39, I consumed a quantity of cocaine, marijuana, acid, uppers, downers, reds, whites, purples and assorted other items of the underground pharmacopoeia that normal people would find hard to believe. I used some things that normal people have never heard of, too. I suppose I would have gone on to other drugs not yet invented, once they became available, because there was always some new kind of high to seek, or some new sort of low to avoid, et cetera, et cetera, and the way to do it, I had learned, was through chemistry. On my 40th birthday, I finally took the necessary step, which was to admit that drugs were a monster too strong for me to grapple with and that my life had become unmanageable. And that I was willing to turn to a Power that is stronger than I am, stronger even than the drug monster, and humbly ask that power to restore me to sanity and to help me defend myself against my enemy.

I live now in a small, furnished room in a small town so dull you can't remember the names of the streets. I belong to the program and I go to meeting three or four times a week and I tell people whose surnames I don't know about my faults (which I freely admit) and my virtues (which I do have), and about my one great weakness. Then they tell me about theirs.

My name is Tom and I am chemically dependent.

I've been doing pretty well since the seventh of February.

Hallucinations were one thing I didn't need in this time of recovery. I had already had my share.

I didn't realize at that point that the house had vanished. People don't customarily think in terms of houses vanishing, not if their heads are screwed on right, and, as I have just pointed out, I had a vested interest in believing that, as of the seventh of February, my head was screwed on right and it was going to stay that way.

No, what I thought was simply that I must have gone to the grocery by way of one street and come home by way of another. Since I was clean and had been so for a month and a half, there was no other rational explanation.

I went home and made some phone calls to potential employers, with the usual result. I watched some television. If you've never stayed home on a weekday morning, you can't imagine what television is like at that time of day, most of it. After a while, I found myself tuning to the home shopping channel for the sheer excitement of it.

I thought about the flash of flesh in the screen doorway.

I thought about the effect that a nice little line of white powder laid out on a mirror would create in me, too. You don't ever stop thinking about things like that, the look of mirrors and the technique of creating little white lines on them and the taste you get in your nostrils and the effect that the substance has. Especially the effect of the substance. You don't banish that from your mind, quite the contrary, and when you aren't thinking about the taste in your nostrils or the effect of the substance, you're thinking about weird peripheral things, like the shape of the mirror. Believe me, you are.

It rained for three or four days, miserable, nonstop rain, and I didn't do much of anything. Then finally I went outdoors again, a right and a right and look across to the left, and there was the white house, bright in the spring sunshine. Very casually, I glanced over at it. No flashes of flesh this time.

I saw something much stranger, though. A rolled-up copy of the morning paper was lying on the lawn of a house with brown shingles next door. A dog was sniffing around it, a goofy-faced nondescript white mutt with long legs and a black head. Abruptly, the dog scooped up the paper in its jaws, as dogs will do, and turned and trotted around to the front of the white house.

The screen door opened a little way. I didn't see anybody opening it. It remained ajar. The wooden door behind it seemed to be open, also.

The dog stood there, looking around, shaking its head from side to side. It seemed bewildered. As I watched, it dropped the paper and began to pant, its tongue hanging out as if this were the middle of July and not the end of March. Then it picked up the paper again, bending for it in an oddly rigid, robotic way. It raised its head and turned and stared right at me, almost as if it were asking me to help it. Its eyes were glassy and its ears were standing up and twitching. Its back was arched like a cat's. Its tail rose straight up behind it. I heard low rusty-sounding growls.

Then, abruptly, it visibly relaxed. It lowered its ears and a look of something like relief came into its eyes and its posture again became that of a good old droopy dog. It wriggled its shoulders almost playfully. Wagged its tail. And went galloping through the screen door, bounding and prancing in that dumb way dogs have, holding the newspaper high. The door closed behind it.

I stayed around for a while. The door stayed closed. The dog didn't come out.

I wondered which I would rather believe: that I had seen a door open itself and let a dog in or that I had *imagined* I had seen a door open itself and let a dog in?

*   *   *

Then there was the cat event. This was a day or two later.

The cat was a lop-eared ginger tom. I had seen it around before. I like cats. I liked this one especially. He was a survivor, a street-smart guy. I hoped to learn a thing or two from him.

He was on the lawn of the white house. The screen door was ajar again. The cat was staring toward it and he looked absolutely *outraged*.

His fur was standing out half a mile and his tail was lashing like a whip and his ears were flattened back against his head. He was hissing and growling at the same time, and the growl was that eerie, banshee moan that reminds you what jungle creatures cats still are. He was quivering as if he had electrodes in him. I saw muscles violently rippling along his flanks and great convulsive shivers running the length of his spine.

"Hey, easy does it, fellow!" I told the cat. "What's the matter? What's the matter, guy?"

What was the matter was that his legs seemed to want to move toward the house and his brain didn't. He was struggling every step of the way. The house was *calling* him, I thought suddenly, astonishing myself with the idea. As it had called the dog. You call a dog long enough and eventually its instincts take command and he comes, whether it feels like it or not. But you can't make a cat do a fucking thing against its will, not without a struggle. There was a struggle going on now. I stood there and watched it and I felt real uneasiness.

The cat lost.

He fought with truly desperate fury, but he kept moving closer to the door all the same. He managed to hold back for a moment just as he reached the first step, and I thought he was going to succeed in breaking loose from whatever was pulling him. But then his muscles stopped quivering, his fur went back to where it belonged and his whole body slackened perceptibly; and he crept across the threshold in a pathetic, beaten-looking way.

At my meeting that night I wanted to ask the others if they knew anything about the white house with the screen door. They had all grown up in this place; I had lived here only a couple of months. Maybe the white house had a reputation for weirdness. But I wasn't sure which street it was on, and a round-faced man named Eddie had had a close escape from some sinsemilla after an ugly fight with his wife and needed to talk about that. When that was over, we all sat around the table and discussed the high school basketball play-offs. High school basketball is a big thing in this part of the state. Somehow, I couldn't bring myself to say, "Do you mind if I change the subject, fellows? Because I saw a house a few blocks from here gobble up a dog and then a cat like it was a roach motel." They'd think I had slipped into abusing illicit substances again and they'd rally round like crazy to help me get steady once more.

I went back there a few days later and couldn't find the house. Just an empty lot with grizzled brown, late-winter grass, no paved pathway, no steps, no garbage can, nothing. This time, I knew I hadn't accidentally gone up some other street. The house next to the white house was still there, the brown-shingled one where the dog had found the newspaper. But the white house was gone.

What the hell? A house that comes and goes?

Sweat came flooding out all over me. Was it possible to have hallucinations in such convincing detail when I had been clean for a couple of months? When you're using, you tend to hallucinate, because the heavy user tends to get about six hours of sleep a week—not a night, but a week—and the sleeplessness goes to work on you sooner or later, and you start seeing bugs on the wall, rats on the floor, people who aren't there watching you through a spy hole in the ceiling that also isn't there. But I was getting plenty of sleep these days, and even so, look what was happening. First I was frightened and then I was angry. I didn't deserve this. If the house weren't a hallucination, and I didn't seriously think it was, then what was it? I was working hard at putting my life back together and I was entitled to have reality stay real around me.

Easy, I thought. Easy. You're not entitled to anything, fellow. But you'll be OK, so long as you recognize that nobody requires you to be able to explain mysteries beyond your understanding. Just go easy, take things as they come, and stay cool, stay cool, stay cool.

The house came back four days later.

I still couldn't bring myself to talk about it at meetings, even though that probably would have been a good idea. I had no problem at all with admitting publicly that I was a drug abuser, far from it. At least not in a room filled with others of my kind. But standing up and telling everyone that I was crazy was something else entirely.

Things got even more bizarre. One afternoon, I was out in front of the house and a kid's tricycle came rolling down the street all by itself, as though pulled by an invisible cord. It rolled right past me and turned the corner and I watched it traverse the path and *go up the steps* of the white house and disappear inside. Some sort of magnetic pull? Radio waves?

Half a minute later, the owner of the tricycle came huffing along, a chubby boy of about five, in blue leggings. "My bike!" he was yelling. "My bike!" I imagined him running up the path and disappearing into the house, too, like the dog, the cat and the tricycle. I couldn't let that happen. But I couldn't just grab him and hold him, either, not in an era when a grown man who simply smiles at a kid in the street is likely to get booked. So, I did the next best thing and planted myself at the head of the path leading across the white house's lawn. The kid banged into my shins and fell down. I looked up the block and saw a woman coming, his aunt, maybe, or his grandmother. It seemed safe to help the kid up, so I did. Then I smiled at her and said, "He really ought to look where he's going."

"My bike!" the boy wailed. "Where's my *bike?*"

The woman looked at me and said, "Did you see someone take the child's tricycle?"

"Afraid I can't say, ma'am," I replied, shrugging my most amiable shrug. "I was coming around the corner, and there was the boy running full tilt into me. But I didn't see any tricycle." What else was I going to tell her? *I saw it go up the steps and into the house by itself?*

She gave me a troubled glance. But obviously I didn't have the tricycle in my coat pocket and I guess I don't look like the sort of man who specializes in stealing things from little children.

A dog. A cat. A tricycle.

I turned and walked away. Up Maple to Juniper, and down Juniper to Beech, and left on Beech onto Chestnut. Or maybe it was up Oak to Sycamore and then on to Locust and Hickory. Maple, Oak, Chestnut, Hickory—what difference did it make? They were all alike.

I doubled back eventually and got to the house just in time to see a boy of about 14 wearing a green-and-yellow jersey come trotting down the street, tossing a football from hand to hand. As he went past the white house, the screen door swung open and the inner door swung back and the kid halted, turned and very neatly threw the football through, a nice high, tight arc.

The doors closed.

The kid stood stock-still in the street, staring at his hand as if he had never seen it before. He looked stunned.

Then, after a moment, he broke out of his stasis and started up the path to the house. I wanted to call out to him to keep away, but I couldn't get any sound out and I wasn't sure what I could say to him, anyway.

He rang the doorbell. Waited.

I held my breath.

The door started to open again. Trying to warn him, I managed to make a little scratchy, choking sort of sound.

But the kid didn't go in. He stood for a moment, peering inside and then he turned and ran, across the lawn, over the hedges and down the street.

What had he seen?

I ran after him. "Hey, kid! Kid, wait!"

He was going so fast, I couldn't believe it. I was a pretty good runner in my time, too. But my time was some time ago.

Instead of going to the meeting that night, I went to scout out the house. Under cover of darkness, I crept around it in the shrubbery like your basic Peeping Tom, trying to peer through the windows.

Was I scared? Utterly shitless, yes. Wouldn't you be?

Did I want a hit? Don't be naïve. I *always* want a hit, and not just one. I certainly wanted a good jolt right now. It would give me fantastic energy, it would give me sublime confidence, it would give me the unshakable savoir-faire of Sherlock Holmes himself. But I wouldn't have stopped at one little line. My name is Tom and I am chemically dependent.

What did I see? I saw a woman, very likely the same one I had caught that quick glimpse of in the doorway that first drizzly Monday morning. I got only quick glimpses now. She was moving around from room to room, so that I didn't have a chance to see her clearly, but what I saw was plenty impressive. Tall, blonde, sleek—that much was certain. She wore a floor-length red robe made of some glossy, metallic fabric that fell about her in a kind of liquid shimmer. Her movements were graceful and elegant. There didn't seem to be anything in the way of furniture inside, just some cartons and crates, which she was carrying back and forth. Stranger and stranger. I didn't see the cat or the dog or the tricycle.

I scrabbled around from window to window for maybe half an hour, hoping for a good look at her. I was moving with what I thought was real skill, keeping low, staying down behind the lilacs or whatever, rising cautiously toward window-sill level for each quick peek. I suppose I might have been visible from the street, but the night was moonless and people don't generally go out strolling around here after dark.

There didn't appear to be anyone else in the house. And for about 15 minutes, I didn't see her, either. Maybe she was in the shower, maybe she had gone to bed. I was tempted to ring the bell. But what for? What would I say to her if she answered? What was I doing here in the first place?

I crept backward through the shrubbery, thinking it was time to leave. And, then, there she was, framed in a window, looking straight out at me.

Smiling. Beckoning.

Come hither, Tommy boy.

I thought about the cat. I thought about the dog. I began to shake.

Like the kid with the football, I turned and ran, desperately sprinting through the quiet streets in an overwhelming excess of unreasoning terror.

I was getting to the point where I thought it might be calming to have a little hit. In the old days, the first line always settled me down. It lifted the burden, it soothed the pain, it answered the questions. It made laying out a second line very easy. The second suggested the third, the third required the fourth, the fourth demanded the fifth—and so on, all day and all night without hindrance, chasing that wondrous high that never really comes back again, right on to pallor, indifference, insomnia, vomiting, weight loss, falling hair, bleeding nostrils, sunken eyeballs, palpitations, paranoia, outpourings of gibberish, empty bank accounts, hallucinations, impotence, the shakes, the shivers, the queebles, the collywobbles and all the rest.

I didn't go for the hit. I went to a meeting instead, jittery and perplexed. I said I was wrestling with a mystery. I didn't say what it was. Let them fill in the blanks, anything they felt like. Even without the details, they'd know something of what I was going through.

They, too, were wrestling with mysteries. Otherwise, what were they doing there?

The house was gone for two weeks. I checked for it every day. Spring had arrived in full force before it returned. Trees turned green, plants were blooming, the air grew warm and soft.

The woman was back, too, the blonde. I never failed to see her now, every time I went by, and I went by every day. It was as if she knew I was coming. Sometimes she was at the window, but usually she was standing just inside the screen door. Some days she dressed in the red slinky robe, some days in a green one. She had a few other outfits, too, all of them classy but somewhat oddly designed—shoulders too wide, the cut too narrow. Once—incredibly, unforgettably—she came to the door in nothing at all but her own sleek skin and stood for a moment on splendid display, framed perfectly in the doorway, sunlight glinting off her lovely body.

She was always smiling. She must have known I was the one who had been peeping that night and it didn't seem to bother her. The look on her face said, *Let's get to know each other a little better, shall we?* Always that warm, beckoning smile. Sometimes, she'd give me a little come-on-in flick of her finger tips.

Not on your life, sister. Not on your life.

But I couldn't stop coming by. The house, the woman, the mystery—all pulled me like a magnet.

By now, I had two theories. The simple one was that she was lonely, horny, bored, looking for distraction. Maybe it excited her to be playing these games with me. In this quiet little town, where the chief cause of death surely must be boredom, she liked to live dangerously.

Too simple, much too simple. Why would a woman who looked like she did be living a lonely, horny life? Why would she be in this kind of town in the first place? The theory didn't account for the comings and goings of the house. Or for what I had seen happen to the cat, the dog, the tricycle, the boy with the football. The dog had returned—the day I was given the full frontal show, it was sitting on the step just below the screen door, next to an old orange mug that someone had left sitting there—but it never went more than a couple of yards from the house, and it moved in a weird, lobotomized way. There had been no further signs of the cat or the tricycle.

Which led to my other theory, the roach motel theory.

The house comes from the future, I told myself. They're studying the late 20th Century and they want to collect artifacts. So every now and then, they send this time machine disguised as a little white-stucco house here, and it scoops up toys, pets, newspapers, whatever it can grab. Most likely, they aren't really looking for cats or dogs, but they takes what they gets. And now they're trying to catch an actual live 20th Century man. Trolling for him the way you'd troll for catfish, except that you'd use a beautiful woman—sometimes naked—as the bait.

A crazy idea? Sure. But I couldn't come up with a saner one.

Ten days into spring and the house was gone again. When it came back about a week later, the woman didn't seem to be with it. They were giving her some time off, maybe. They still seemed interested in luring me inside. I'd come by and take up my position by the curb, and the door would quietly swing open, though no one was visible inside. And it would stay open, waiting for me to traipse up the walk and go in.

It was a temptation. I felt it pulling on me harder and harder every day, as my own here-and-now, real-life, everyday options looked bleaker and bleaker. I wasn't finding a new job. I wasn't making useful contacts. My money, not much to begin with, was running out. All I had was the program and the people who were part of it here, and though they were fine enough people, they weren't the kind I could get really close to in any way not having to do with the program.

So why not go up that path and into the house? Even if they were to sweep me up and take me off to the year 2999, and even if I were never heard from again, what would I have to lose? A drab life in a furnished room in a nowhere town, living on the last of my dwindling savings, while I dreamed of white powder and purple pills and went to meetings at which a bunch of victims of the same miserable malady struggled constantly to keep their leaky boats from sinking? Wherever I would go would be better than that. Perhaps incredibly better.

But, of course, I didn't *know* that the shining visitors from the future would sweep me off to an astounding new existence in the year 2999. That was only my own nutty guess, my wild fantasy. Anything at all might happen to me if I passed through that doorway. Anything. It was a kind of Russian roulette, and I didn't even know the odds against me.

One day, I taped a piece of paper to a rubber ball from the five-and-dime and tossed it through the opened door. On it I had written these questions:

WHO ARE YOU?

WHERE ARE YOU FROM?

WHAT ARE YOU LOOKING FOR?

DO YOU WANT ME?

WHAT'S IN IT FOR ME?

WILL YOU HARM ME?

I waited for an answering note to come bouncing out. But none ever did.

The house went away. The house came back. The woman still wasn't there. Nobody else seemed to be, either. But the door swung open expectantly for me, seemingly of its own accord. I would stand and stare, making no move, and after a time, it would close again.

I bought another ball and threw another message through the door.

SEND ME THE GIRL AGAIN, THE BLONDE

ONE. I WANT TO TALK TO HER.

The house went away again and stayed away a long while—nearly a month this time—so that I began to think it would never come back (and then that it had actually never been there at all). There were days when I didn't even bother to walk past the vacant lot where I had seen it.

Then I did, and it was there, and the woman was in the doorway smiling, and she said, "Come on in and visit me, sailor?"

She was wearing something gauzy and she was leaning against the doorframe with her hand on her hip. Her voice was a soft, throaty contralto. It all felt like a scene out of a Forties movie. Maybe it was; maybe they had been studying up.

"First, you tell me who you are, all right? And where you come from."

"Don't you want to have a good time with me, pal?"

Damn right I do. I felt it in my groin, my pounding chest, my knees.

I moistened my lips. I thought of the way the house had reeled in that angry, snarling cat. How it had pulled that tricycle up the stairs. I felt it pulling on me. But I must have more ability to fight back than a cat. Or a tricycle.

I said, "There's a lot I need to know first."

"Come on in and I'll tell you everything." Softly. Huskily. Irresistibly. *Almost* irresistibly.

"Tell me first. Come out here and talk to me."

She winked and shook her head. "Here's looking at *you*, kid." Studying old movies, all right. She closed the door in my face.

What they hammer into you in the program is that you may think you're pretty tough, but in fact, when you've added up all the debts and credits, the truth is you aren't as strong as you like to pretend you are. You're too weak not to reach for some sort of drug when you feel a little edgy or a little low; it's only after you admit how weak you are and turn elsewhere for help that you can begin to find the strength you need.

I had found that strength. I hadn't done any sort of stuff on the seventh of February, or the eighth or the ninth. One day at a time, I wasn't doing any drugs, and by now that one day at a time added up to four months and 11 days, and when tomorrow came around I would add another day to the string, and I was beginning to feel fairly confident I could keep going that way for the rest of my life.

But the house was something else again. I was starting to see it as a magic gateway to God knows where, just as drugs had once been for me. It came and went, and the woman smiled and beckoned and offered throaty invitations, and I recognized that I had let myself become obsessed with it and couldn't keep away from it, and the next time the house came back there was a good chance that I'd go sauntering up the path and through the door.

Which was crazy.

I hadn't put myself through this whole ordeal of recovery just for the sake of waltzing through a different magic gateway, had I? Especially when I didn't have the slightest idea of what might lie on the far side.

I thought about it and thought about it and thought about it and decided that the safest and smartest thing to do was to get out of here. I would move to some other town that didn't have houses that came and went, or languid, naked blondes standing in doorways inviting me to step inside. So one drowsy July morning I bought a bus ticket to a town 40 miles from where I'd been living. It was about the same size and had a similar name and looked just about as dull; and on the street behind the lone movie theater I found a house that had a FURNISHED ROOM sign stuck in its lawn and rented a place very much like the one I had (except that the rent was ten dollars more a month). Then I went around to the local program headquarters—I had already checked with my own to make sure they had one here, you can bet on that—and picked up the schedule of meeting hours.

Done. Safe. A clean break.

I'd never see that white house again.

I'd never see *her* again.

I'd never face that mysterious doorway and never feel the pull it exerted.

And, as I told myself all that, the pain of irrevocable loss rose up inside me and hit me from within, and I thought I was going to fall down.

I was in the bus depot then, waiting to catch the bus going back, so I could pack my suitcase and settle things with my landlady and say goodbye to my friends, such as they were, in the program. I looked around and there she was, standing stark-naked in the doorway of the baggage room, smiling at me in that beckoning way of hers.

Not really. It was a different woman, and she wasn't blonde, and she was wearing a bus-company uniform, and she wasn't even looking at me.

I knew that, actually. I wasn't hallucinating. But I had *wanted* her to be the other one so badly that I imagined that I saw her. And I realized how deep the obsession had become.

I must have seen her 50 times during the ride back. Waving at me from the head of a country lane as the bus flashed by. Smiling at me from a bicycle going the other way. Riding in the back of a pickup truck bouncing along in front of us. Standing by the side of the road trying to hitch a ride. Her image haunted me wherever I looked. I sat there shivering and sweating, seeing her beckoning in the doorway and watching that door closing and closing and closing again in my mind.

It was evening by the time the bus reached town. The wise thing would have been to take a shower and go to a meeting, but I went to the house instead, and there was someone standing outside, staring at the screen door.

He was about my age, a short guy with a good gut and tousled, reddish hair just beginning to fade into gray. He looked vaguely familiar. I wondered if I had seen him at a meeting once or twice, perhaps. As I came by, he threw me an uneasy, guilty glance, as if he were up to something. His eyes were a pale blue, very bloodshot.

I went past him about ten paces, paused there, turned around.

"You waiting for someone?" I asked.

"I might be."

"Someone who lives in there?"

"What's that to you?"

"I was just wondering," I said, "if you could tell me who lives in that house."

He shrugged as if he hadn't quite heard me. The blue eyes turned chilly. I wanted to pick him up and throw him into the next county. The way he was looking at me, he probably felt the same way about me.

I said, "A woman lives there, right?"

"Fuck off, will you?"

"A blonde woman?"

"Fuck off, I said."

Neither of us moved.

"Sometimes I come by here and I see a blonde woman in the window, or standing in the doorway," I went on. "I wonder if you've seen her sometimes, too."

He didn't say anything. His eyes flickered almost involuntarily toward the house.

I followed the motion and there she was, visible through the window with the green shutters to the right of the door. She was wearing one of her misty wraps, and her hair was shining like spun gold. She smiled. Gestured with a quick movement of her head.

Come on inside, why don't you?

I almost did. Another five seconds, another three, and I would have trotted down that narrow, paved pathway as obediently as the dog that had the newspaper in his mouth. But I didn't. I was still afraid of what might lie beyond. I froze in my tracks; and then the redheaded man started to move. He went past me and up the path. Like a sleepwalker, like a zombie.

"Hey—wait——"

I caught him by the arm. He swung around, furious, and we struggled for a moment and then he broke loose and clamped both his hands on my shoulders and pushed me with tremendous force into the shrubbery. I tripped over one of the pieces of odd metal junk that were always lying around near the door, and went sprawling on my face. When I got myself disentangled, it was just in time to see the redheaded man wrench the screen door open and run inside.

I heard the inner door slam.

And then the house disappeared.

It vanished like a pricked bubble, taking the shrubbery with it, the garbage cans and other junk as well, and I found myself kneeling on weeds in the midst of a vacant lot, trembling as if I had just had a stroke. After a moment or two, I got shakily to my feet and walked over to the place where the house had been. Nothing. Nothing. No trace. Gone as if it had never been there at all.

A couple of days later, I moved back to my old place. There didn't seem much risk anymore, and I missed the place, the town, the guys at the meeting. It's been months now, and no house. I rarely skip a day, going by the lot, but it remains empty. The memory of it, of *her*, haunts me. I look for the redheaded man, too, but I've never seen him. I described him once at a meeting and someone said, "Yeah, sounds like Ricky. He used to live around here." Where was he now? Nobody had any idea. Neither do I.

Another time, I got brave enough to ask some of them if they had ever heard about a little white house that, well, sort of comes and goes. "Comes and goes?" they said. "What the hell does that mean?" I let the question drop.

I have a feeling that it was all some kind of a test, and I may have flunked it. I don't mean that I've missed out on a terrific woman. She was only the bait; I know better than to think that she was real or that she ever could have been available for me if she were. But that sense of a new start—of another life, however weird, beyond the horizon—forever lost to me now, that's what I'm talking about. And the pain runs deep.

But there's always a second chance, isn't there? They tell you that in the program, and I believe it. I have to. From time to time, I've left notes in the empty lot:

> WHEN YOU COME BACK NEXT TIME,
> DON'T LEAVE WITHOUT ME.
> I'M READY NOW. I'M SURE OF IT.

The house comes and goes, that I know. It's gone now, but it'll come again. I'm here. I'm watching. I'm waiting.

THE BEWITCHED BURR

Grozdana Olujic

Grozdana Olujic has published four novels in England and in the United States, as well as a collection of fairy tales, *Rose of Mother-of-Pearl*, the title story of which appeared in an illustrated English translation. Her fairy tales have been recorded, filmed, animated, and translated into more than a dozen languages.

"The Bewitched Burr" is one of several short, wry fantasy tales written by Olujic and translated from the Serbo-Croatian by Jascha Kessler and the author. The ongoing troubles in Olujic's homeland give this little original fairy tale a particularly sharp bite.

—T.W.

When the deviltries of Devilkin finally got to be too much for even his own mother, the High Council decreed that he must be sent away to bedevil folk in the Upper World. They said, "Let him make them miserable until he grows a bit older and quieter—he's already raised enough hell here in Hell!"

But Devilkin wasn't willing to forsake the fun he was having with his good old friends. Whatever could there be for him to do on Earth, for heaven's sake! Men would know what he was as soon as they laid eyes on his horns and his curly little tail. They'd skin him alive and pack him off back home. Let them send someone else to the Upper World. The little one tucked his tail in and hid himself away in the darkest corner of Hell. But who can conceal himself from the Boss Devil?

"Come out of there, or I'll pull your ears off!" thundered the Head of the Underworld, the oldest and dingiest devil of all. "Look at this brave critter—some hero he is, running away!" the old devil laughed, his belly bouncing.

Devilkin went stiff as stone as the Head Devil patted his cheek and said, "Take this burr with you. Anyone you touch with it will instantly grow a tail and horns, for this burr is bewitched. Soon there'll be so many horned and tailed people that nobody will even notice you. Skip along now!" The Boss Devil placed the bewitched burr on Devilkin's palm and warned him to watch out: If the burr touched someone who cared for another's good more than his own, it would turn into a rose. All horns and tails would vanish, and Devilkin would have to run for it as fast as he could, or they'd surely flay him right there. But, not to worry, chortled the Boss Devil, "One's own skin is nearest and dearest to men and devils alike!" and waved

181

his hand. Before you could even wink, Devilkin popped out on the busiest street in the city.

Right away he threw the burr at the first man passing by, and a huge tail adorned him. Another got a tail, and horns too. Oh, oh, oh! People hooted with laughter. "Hoo ha ha! Look at your horns!" one fellow yelled at his friend. "What great big horns you have! Oh, hee hee hee . . . !"

"You'd better take a look at your own fat tail!" sneered the second, slapping his friend's face, as he grabbed at his horns. Slap, smack! Biff, bam! And they began to fight, while a bunch of idlers gathered around them. "Hit him! What are you waiting for!" they guffawed, and egged them on.

"The Boss was right!" thought Devilkin. "These Upper Worlders are no better than we are!"

"Bing! Bang! Bing!" Devilkin hurled his burr here and there. Oh my, how the town quaked. Neighbor assaulted neighbor, son struck father, husband beat wife. "Me oh my," sighed Devilkin with pleasure, "if my folks could only get an eyeful of this!"

No one went to work. Instead, people were setting fire to their neighbors' homes. Quicker than you could clap your hands, the first house exploded in flames. Then the first street was burning. Fires crackled and roared everywhere. The Mayor was horrified: What was to be done? If this went on, there soon would be no city left!

The Council of Sages convened. Nothing came of that. "Maybe old Tataga could tell us what to do," someone said, remembering the oldest citizen of them all, who'd outlived six kings and seven wars—or was it six wars and seven kings? "She knows the language of the birds and the grass."

The old woman only shook her head. "For this you need another tongue altogether!"

Wilder and wilder, the strange dance whirled on. Devilkin would toss the burr, and people would shove each other at it, giggling with glee. "Watch this!" shouted a horned fellow going by while madly riding a tailed man, as the tailed fellow twisted his tormentor's horns and yelled, "Who do you think you are to snigger at me!" The tailed man punched out the horned man, and got pummeled right back.

"The Boss sure was telling it true," Devilkin grinned: "Everyone's own skin is nearest and dearest of all!" People tore at one another: they broke each other's noses and cracked each other's heads. Hospitals overflowed with the injured. Yet they went right on fighting.

"This is some sort of plague!" an old woman muttered, as the burr flashed about the city like wildfire. No wonder neighbor gave neighbor a wide berth. Yet the toll of wounded grew ever greater. What could anyone do? Finally, it occurred to some that their troubles were all the fault of that flying burr. But no one was bold enough to try catching it, and certainly they all were much too cowardly to try to scotch it. People ran about helter-skelter, all the while telling themselves, "Maybe it won't hit me!"

Like a great golden bee, the burr buzzed around town. Whiz! it flew. Zing! it hit. Housewives stopped cooking and washing. Teachers shut their schools up tight—but they sprouted horns anyway. Bakers refused to bake bread. Hunger and filth spread like autumn fog. Who paid any attention to Old Tataga when she warned that dirt would bring disease? Who cared anything for tomorrow? Garbage lay heaped knee-high. But no one would lend a hand to cart it away.

Horns? Tails? Nonsense! Travelers hearing the tale from far off laughed. But as soon as some of them saw the miserable city, they began to avoid it. Tataga was right. Even the wild geese had no chance to fly away south: the town was caught by the plague. Streets and boroughs were dying out. Hatred alone lived there. Horns and tails abominated each other. But they loathed those without tails and horns even more. Their eyes would glint with glee as they caught and pushed new wretches at the burr.

Devilkin jumped for joy. If only his brothers could see this! Whee! Heigh ho! How happy they'd be! Hip, hop, hip! hopped Devilkin, as the town emptied. Here and there an occasional homeless person waded through refuse, hunting for something to eat. "Boy, the Old One sure had it wrong when he told me someone might spoil the magic!" Devilkin thought.

Just then a little girl carrying her baby brother stepped from a dilapidated shack. Devilkin took one look at her and burst out laughing so hard the tears streamed down his cheeks. The little girl was lame, and a hunchback to boot. Devilkin stared at her and thought, "I'll bet she's stepped out to find a scrap of food."

Limping comically, the little girl struggled through the garbage, hugging her baby brother to her. *Zing!* the burr went whizzing at her. The little girl stood stock still, frozen with fear. "Oh Mamma," she cried, "now I'll have horns too!" Instantly the idea came into her head: she could avoid the burr by holding the baby out in front of her! But she was even more appalled by that thought. For the lovely baby was so innocent. "I'm the one who ought to catch the plague!" the little girl sighed, and thrust her little brother behind her. The burr flew right at her chest.

"Can this be?" Devilkin could not believe his eyes when he saw the burr bump into the hunchback girl . . . and turn into a golden rose. "Oh my!"

Before you could have clapped your hands, the hump had dwindled away, the twisted legs grown straight. "What is this? Am I dreaming?" Devilkin rubbed his eyes. Instead of a crippled little hunchback creature, before him stood a lovely girl holding a rose in her hand. She lifted it to her face and then held it out to the first person who came along for him to smell.

Devilkin groaned, "What the devil! Where's his tail?"

The news of this magic blew through the town faster than the wind. One after another, horned and tailed citizens marched into the tumbledown shack—and stepped out again with neither horns nor a tail.

What more is left to tell you?

When twilight came, there was but one little person with horns and a tail standing in the middle of the town square. Then he vanished into thin air. The rose disappeared too. Except that the perfume of the rose lingered around the girl for a little while longer. Then it too faded away.

SWIMMING LESSON

Charlotte Watson Sherman

Charlotte Watson Sherman has published prose and poetry in magazines including *Obsidian*, *The Black Scholar*, *CALYX Journal*, *Painted Bride Quarterly* and *Ikon*; and in the collections *Memories and Visions*, *Gathering Ground*, and *When I Am Old I Shall Wear Purple*. She has won a Seattle Arts Commission grant for her work, and the King County Arts Commission Fiction Award. Sherman lives in Seattle with her husband and two children where she works as a mental health specialist and has been the Outreach Coordinator for Seattle Rape Relief.

"Swimming Lesson" is a gentle tale of American Magical Realism, reprinted from Sherman's recent collection, *Killing Color*, published by Calyx Books in Oregon. "Swimming Lesson" and the other memorable, beautifully crafted stories in *Killing Color* are highly recommended.

—T.W.

I like to sit on this big old mossy pillow and lay my head back on one of them twisted red oak roots that look like arms comin up outta the ground, arms that feel like the satin of Aunt Leatha's skin when she stoops down to gather me up and swing me round, and I lay in the roots like I'm layin in my mama's lap, listenin to her hum them old old songs, sound like folks bottled up with sorrow so sweet it turn to sugar.

This tree's right next to the old black pond where sometimes we get out in the water that covers our skinny arms with sparklin oil and we splash and kick and laugh.

I member the day somebody got the crazy idea to throw Neethie in the water and try to make her swim, and we all knew it was the wrong thing to do and didn't think bout what grown folks always say bout if you know better do better. We didn't think bout that when we was way out in all that green by the black water neath that big old red sun, but we shoulda, like I told everybody what would listen later. But nobody listened, not Egghead Sammy Ray Yarbrough, not even C.C. Beauregard whose daddy runs the funeral parlor and everybody is scairt of him cause he might get mad and get his daddy to come for ya in the middle of the night and put ya in that old hearse look like a big fat shiny beetle and take ya to the funeral parlor and put ya in a casket. So nobody, not me, not Elmo, not Ruby, not nobody said a word when Egghead Sammy Ray Yarbrough and C.C. Beauregard decided they was gonna make Neethie swim.

Now, anybody got half a piece of sense know Neethie can't swim, don't like the water, can't even walk right on land on accounta one leg bein shorter than the other and don't nobody usually say nothin bout it one way or nuther cause that just the way she come into the world, lookin kinda like a crookedy upsidedown wishbone. But some folks be laughin bout that big-sole shoe she gotta wear on her short leg so she don't walk lopsided. But she still limp a little even with that big shoe on. I like Neethie even though she do live in the Bible most of the time.

Mama always say ain't nothin wrong with Neethie livin in the Bible and wrinkle up her face and tell me I need to live in it too and ask me don't I want to enter the Golden Gates of Righteousness? I say I only wanna enter the golden arches of that shiny new hamburger stand they got there in Jackson and she won't even let me do that.

But we probably wouldn'ta thought to put Neethie in the water if Ruby hadn'ta been talkin bout how Jesus could walk on water. C.C. Beauregard said: No he can't, can't nobody walk on water. But I told em what my playuncle Eaton told me bout the slaves in the old days who left beatins and hoein and cotton and cleanin and set out cross the fields and headed north where they thought they could be free, and how some of em come to that yellow river that flow not too far from here and thought they had come to the end of they journey cause they couldn't swim and didn't know what all was in that water. Then they'd stoop at the edge and wet they faces and start moanin pieces of words they member from when we was all free, sound like: *hmmhmm o-o o-o-o-o mlongo*. And the wind would start to blow and the trees on the edge of the riverbank would start to sway and the air would feel like how my mama say it feel sometime when Reverend Samuel hit a high note in the middle of his preachin, and the women start to tremble and the deacons start to shake and everybody's eyes start to water with tears rollin down. That's how my playuncle Eaton say it feel when the runaways bent down at the edge of the yellow river thinkin bout freedom and how they couldn't swim and hummin: *mlongo mlongo hmmhmmhmmhmm o-o*. They knew they couldn't turn back so they kept on hummin that song and then they feet sank in the red mud at the edge of the river and come up covered with green sprouts climbin on they ankles and circlin round and tiny wings grew from each ankle and started flappin back and forth and back and forth, gentle at first and then faster and faster. And they could feel the cold of them chains deep in the wet earth and the wings beatin harder and then they took a step into the yellow water but they first foot didn't go down. It stayed right on top of the waves, and they put they other foot in the water and the same thing happened, it didn't go down, and they look over they shoulder for they last look at the land that tried to turn em into mules. They know they wouldn't never turn back, so they kept on walkin and the tiny wings kept beatin and they glided on cross the yellow river and only got the bottom of they pants and dresses wet.

But then Sammy Ray Yarbrough, whose head's big as a jug of water, broke in with his silly self and said, "Can't no slaves or nobody else walk cross no water, not even with wings on they back," and he don't believe Jesus did it neither. Ruby said she's gone tell his mama he said that, so he said o.k., if Neethie can walk on water, then anybody can cause Neethie was the closest thing to Jesus any of us knew bout. C.C. Beauregard said he'd go and get Neethie and bring her to the pond.

Now me and Ruby and Elmo tried to shift round and act like we wasn't scairt, but I knew we all musta been thinkin bout the whuppin we was gonna get when our mamas found out we'd pushed Neethie in the water, specially since she had a short leg and had to wear that big old shoe. I wasn't sure but it sound to me like this was cruelty and mama always say cruelty's one of the worst things in the world. Anyway, after a little while here come C.C. Beauregard holding Neethie by the hand and pullin her through bushes the color of bloodstone.

Soon as they got up to where we was standin near the edge of the pond Elmo started cryin, but didn't nobody pay him no mind cause Elmo always start cryin whenever somethin's bout to happen, good or bad. Mama say that boy just like to cry.

But when C.C. Beauregard brought Neethie to the edge of the pond I could feel tears wellin up in my own eyes, cause I knew it was gonna be one of them whuppins what hurts for a long, long time, probably one with a switch, cause Neethie was dressed up in a white ruffly dress that looked like it was for Sunday school, had her hair curled all over her head and had on some black patent leather buckle up shoes that was shinin like a mirror. I could see the trees and the sun when I looked down in them shoes.

Now Neethie's eyes was full of all of that kindness from livin in the Bible. And folks never made much over her short leg in front of her. She looked like some kind of brown angel standin there by the pond holdin C.C. Beauregard's hand.

"See, I told you I'd tell you what I brought you to the pond for, didn't I?" C.C. Beauregard asked.

"Uh huh," said Neethie.

Nobody else said a mumblin word. It was pretty quiet cept for the crickets whistlin and a few birds talkin in the trees and frogs croakin. We wasn't gonna say nothin and I was hopin Neethie have sense enough to turn round and go on back home, but C.C. Beauregard told her he was gonna teach her how to swim so she could come out and play with us at the pond every day steada goin and sittin up with the Bible and all them old folks all the time. Then he asked her wouldn't she like that?

"Uh huh," Neethie said.

So then C.C. Beauregard told her the onliest way for him to teach her how to swim was for him to see if her body was heavy in the water and the only way he could tell that was if she stepped out on that log and walked clear back to us. Egghead Sammy Ray Yarbrough'd found a short log and pushed it up to the edge of the pond where it lay in the water lookin like a big fat link sausage.

Neethie said, "You want me to walk out on that log and walk back on the water like Jesus?"

And C.C. Beauregard said, "Yeah, I want you to walk back just like Jesus."

Well, what he go and say that for? I didn't know whether to laugh or cry so I just started hummin that sound my playuncle Eaton told me was magic: *mlongo mlongo hmmhmmhmm o-o.*

Neethie started to get out on the log and Elmo started to holler. Ruby started cryin real soft-like where you almost couldn't hear her, what with Elmo's screamin and the wind whistlin in the trees.

C. C. Beauregard said, "Neethie, you think you better take that big shoe off?"

Neethie didn't say nothin, just looked kinda sweet and pitiful with her big black eyes lookin out on the water.

Now we all knew she couldn't swim a lick so if she fell in, there was gonna be hell to pay as my daddy say when I'm in double trouble. My legs started to itch and I could already feel that switch, but I just kept on singin: *hmmhmmhmm o-o mlongo*. When Neethie was at the end of the log, she dropped her head back and looked up into the sky and said, "I believe." That was it. Just "I believe," and me and Ruby and Elmo with his cryin self all held hands and stood in a kinda circle at the end of the log, and C.C. Beauregard and Egghead Sammy Ray Yarbrough started movin back to the trees slow and easy. And then Neethie turned round and looked at C.C. Beauregard and asked, "You ready?" And that crazy boy just looked at Neethie with his eyes poppin out and didn't say nothin. So me and Ruby started singin them old magic words and Elmo was so scairt he stopped cryin and started singin em too: *mlongo mlongo hmmhmmhmm o-o*. The words that was old magic went deep inside Neethie, deep inside, and Neethie stepped off the log into the air and put her foot down on that black water and she stayed up even with that big shoe on. Me and Ruby and Elmo squeezed our hands tighter and pressed our eyes shut, and sang the words louder and louder: *mlongo mlongo hmmhmmhmm o-o*. And the words pulled Neethie on cross the water and when we opened our eyes, Neethie was standin right there with us, her smile big as Egghead Sammy Ray Yarbrough's head, cept he wasn't there to see it.

Well, I thought that woulda fixed C.C. Beauregard and Egghead Sammy Ray Yarbrough good, but they didn't even get to see Neethie walk on water cause they slipped through the trees and run off soon as she stepped off the log.

We told Neethie it was good they was gone, cause they probably wouldn'ta knowed what they was lookin at anyway.

Then Ruby said, "Let's go over to the Sunflower Ice Cream Shop and get us some sodas to celebrate."

"Celebrate what?" Neethie asked.

"Us all not gettin the whuppin of our lives," I said, and naturally Elmo started cryin.

MEMORIES OF THE FLYING BALL BIKE SHOP

Garry Kilworth

British author Garry Kilworth has published more than a dozen novels for adults and for children, as well as numerous excellent short stories collected in *The Songbirds of Pain, In the Hollow of the Deep-Sea Wave, Dark Hills, Hollow Clocks,* and *In the Country of Tattooed Men*. He is the winner of the 1991 World Fantasy Award for the story "The Ragthorn" (co-written with Robert Holdstock and reprinted in last year's volume of *The Year's Best Fantasy and Horror*).

Kilworth's semipermanent home is in rural Essex, but he grew up in the Middle East and has traveled and lived abroad for most of his life. For a number of years he has resided in Hong Kong, which has provided the setting for the following poignant tale.

—T.W.

The old Chinese gentleman was sitting cross-legged in the shadow of an alley. He was smoking a long bamboo pipe, which he cradled in the crook of his elbow. I had noticed him as we climbed the temple steps, and the image stayed with me as we wandered through the Buddhist-Tao shrine to Wong Tai Sin, a shepherd boy who had seen visions.

It was so hot the flagstones pulsed beneath our feet, but despite that David was impressed with the temple. We waded through the red-and-gold litter which covered the forecourt, the dead joss sticks cracking underfoot. Cantonese worshippers were present in their hundreds, murmuring orisons, rattling their cans of fortune sticks. Wong Tai Sin is no showcase for tourists, but a working temple in the middle of a high rise public housing estate. Bamboo poles covered in freshly washed clothes overhung the ornate roof, and dripped upon its emerald tiles.

The air was heavy with incense, dense enough to drug the crickets into silence. We ambled up and down stone staircases, admiring carvings the significance of which was lost in generations of western nescience, and gazed self-consciously at the worshippers on their knees as they shook their fortune sticks and prayed for lucky numbers to fall to the flagstones.

We left the temple with our ignorance almost intact.

The old man was still there, incongruous amongst the other clean-shaven Hong

Kong men, with their carefully acquired sophistication, hurrying by his squatting form.

He had a wispy Manchu beard, long grey locks, and dark eyes set in a pomelo-skin face. A sleeveless vest hung from bony shoulders, and canvas trousers covered legs that terminated in an enormous pair of bare feet. The bamboo pipe he was smoking was about fifty centimeters long, three centimeters in diameter, with a large watercooled bowl at one end, and a stem the size of a drinking straw at the other. He had the stem in his lipless mouth, inhaling the smoke.

There was a fruit stall owner, a man I had spoken to on occasion, on the pavement nearby. I told David to wait by the taxi stand and went over to the vendor. We usually spoke to each other in a mixture of Cantonese and English, neither of us being fluent in the foreign language. He was fascinated by my red hair, inherited from my Scottish Highland ancestors.

"*Jo san*," I said, greeting him, "*leung goh ping gwoh, m'goi.*"

I had to shout to make myself heard above the incredibly loud clattering coming from behind him, where sat three thin men and a stout lady, slamming down mah jong tiles as if trying to drive them through the formica table top.

He nodded, wrapped two apples in a piece of newspaper, and asked me for two dollars.

Paying him, I said, "That man, smoking. Opium?"

He looked where I was pointing, smiled, and shook his head vigorously.

"Not smoke opium. No, no. *Sik yin* enemy."

I stared at the old gentleman, puffing earnestly away, seeming to suck down the shadows of the alley along with the smoke.

"*Sik yin dik yan-aa?*" I said, wanting to make sure I had heard him properly. "Smoke *enemy?*"

"*Hai.* Magic smoke-pipe," he grinned. "*Magic,* you know? Very old *sik yin-* pipe."

Gradually I learned that the aged smoker had written down the name of a man he hated, on "dragon" paper, had torn it to shreds, and was inhaling it with his tobacco. Once he had smoked the name of his enemy, had the hated foe inside him, he would come to *know* the man.

The idea was of course, that when you knew the hated enemy—and by *know*, the Chinese mean to understand completely—you could predict any moves he might make against you. You would have a psychological advantage over him, be able to forestall his attacks, form countermoves against him. His strategy, his tactics, would be yours to thwart. He would be able to do nothing which you would not foresee.

"I think . . ." I began to say, but David interrupted me with a shout of, "I've got a taxi, *come* on!", so I bid the stall owner a hasty good-bye, and ran for the waiting vehicle. We leapt out into the fierce flow of Hong Kong traffic, and I put the incident aside until I had more time to think about it.

That evening, over dinner at the Great Shanghai Restaurant in Tsimshatsui, I complained bitterly to David about John Chang.

"He's making my life here a misery," I said. "I find myself battling with a man who seems to despise me."

David was a photographer who had worked with me on my old Birmingham paper. He had since moved into the big time, with one of the nationals in London, while I had run away to a Hong Kong English language newspaper, after an affaire had suffered a greenstick fracture which was obviously never going to heal.

David fiddled with his chopsticks, holding them too low down the shafts to get any sort of control over them. He chased an elusive peppered prawn around the dish. It could have still been alive, the way it evaded the pincers.

"You always get people like that, on any paper, Sean—you know that. Politicians, roughriders, ambitious bastards, you can't escape them just by coming east. Some people get their kicks out of stomping on their subordinates. What is he, anyway? Senior Editor?"

David finally speared the prawn with a single chopstick and looked around him defiantly at the Cantonese diners before popping it into his mouth.

"He's got a lot of power. He could get me thrown out, just like that."

"Well, suck up to the bastard. They like that sort of thing, don't they? The Chinese? Especially from European *gwailos* like you. Take him out to lunch, tell him he's a great guy and you're proud to be working with him—no, *for* him. Tell him the Far East is wonderful, you love Hong Kong, you want to make good here, make your home here. Tell the bastard anything, if it gets him off your back. Forget all that shit about crawling. That's for school kids who think that there's some kind of virtue in swimming against the tide. You've got to make a go of it, and this bloke, what's his name? Chang? If he's making your life hell, then neutralize the sod. Not many people can resist flattery, even when they recognize what it is—hookers use it all the time—'you big strong man, you make fantastic lovey, I never have man like you before.' Codswallop. *You* know it, *they* know it, but it *still* makes you feel good, doesn't it? Speaking of hookers, when are you going to take me down the Wanch . . . ?"

He was talking about Wan Chai, the red light district, which I knew I would have to point him towards one evening of his holiday. David liked his sex casual and stringless, despite all the evil drums in such a lifestyle these days. I needed emotion with my lovemaking, not cheap scent and garlic breath.

I lay in bed that night, thinking about what David had said. Maybe the fault did lie with me? Maybe I was putting out the wrong signals and John Chang thought I did not like him, had not liked him from our first meeting? Some men had sensitive antennae, picked up these vibrations before the signaller knew himself what messages he intended to transmit.

No, I was sure that wasn't it. I had gone out of my way to be friendly with John Chang. I had arrived in Hong Kong, eager to get to know the local people, and had seen John Chang as a person to whom I would have liked to get close. But from the beginning he had come down hard on me, on my work, on everything I did. I had been singled out for victimization, and he piled adverse criticism on my head whenever he got the chance.

However, I was willing to admit that I was not the easiest of employees to get along with, from a social point of view.

John Chang had a happy marriage. I had never met his wife, but she phoned him at the office quite often, and the tone and manner of the conversation indicated a strong loving relationship. This caused me to be envious of him. I once dreamed of having such a relationship with Nickie, and had failed to make it work. I still loved her, of course, and on days I missed her most I was testy and irritable with everyone, including John Chang.

I fell asleep thinking that perhaps I was more than partly to blame for John Chang's attitude toward me. I vowed to try to improve things, once my vacation was over and I was back at work.

There was a cricket making insistent noises, somewhere in the bedroom. It took several sleep-drugged minutes for me to realize that it was the phone chirruping. David? Had he gone down the Wanch and got himself into trouble?

"Hello, Sean Fraser . . ."

"Fraser?" John Chang's clipped accent. "Get down to the office. We need you on a story."

I sat up in bed.

"I'm on vacation. I've got a guest here, dammit!"

"Sorry, can't help that. Tim Lee's gone sick. He was covering the Governor's annual speech. You'll have to do it."

The line went dead. He had replaced the receiver.

I slammed the phone down and seethed for a few minutes, before getting out of bed to have a shower and get dressed. David was still asleep on the living room couch when I went through to the kitchen. I woke him and told him what had happened, apologized, and said I would see him that evening.

"Don't worry about me, mate. I can sort myself out. It's that bastard of a boss *you* want to sort out."

Once I had covered the usual bland yearly speech presented by the British Governor of Hong Kong—written by a committee into a meaningless string of words—John Chang wanted me to visit a fireman who lived in the Lok Fu district. The man had been partially blinded six weeks previously while fighting a fire in Chung King Mansions, a notorious giant slum where holidaying backpackers found relatively cheap accommodation in an impossibly expensive city.

"It's five o'clock," I protested to Chang, "and I have a guest to look after."

He regarded me stonefaced.

"You're a reporter. You don't work office hours."

"I'm on bloody holiday."

"That's tough. You cover this, *then* you're on vacation—unless I need you again. If you want to work for someone else, that's fine too. Understand me?" He stared hard at me, probably hoping I would throw his job in his face. I was not about to do that.

I said coldly, "I understand."

I rang David and said I would be home about nine o'clock. I advised him to go out and eat, because I was going to grab some fast food on my way to Lok Fu. He seemed happy enough, and told me not to worry, but that wasn't the point. The point was that I was close to strangling John Chang with my bare hands.

I saw the young fireman. He seemed philosophical about his accident, though to me his disability pension seemed incredibly small. His wife was working as a bank clerk and now he could look after their two infants, instead of sending them to the grandparents for the weekdays. He could still see a little, and as he pointed out, government apartments, like most private apartments in Hong Kong, were so small it had only taken him a short while to get a mental picture of his home.

During the interview the fireman pressed brandies upon me, as is the custom amongst the Hong Kong Chinese. By the time I left him, I was quietly drunk. I caught a taxi. The driver took me through Wong Tai Sin, and I passed the temple David and I had visited the previous evening. On impulse I told the driver to stop and paid him off.

The old man was still there, at the opening to the alley. He was sitting on a small stool, staring dispassionately at passersby with his rheumy eyes. The pipe was lying on a piece of dirty newspaper, just behind him. I stumbled over to him, trying to hide my state of inebriation.

I pointed to the pipe.

"*Ngoh, sik yin-aa?*" I said, asking to smoke it.

Cantonese is a tonal language, the same words meaning many different things, and by the way he looked at me I knew I had got my tones wrong. I had probably said something like "Me fat brickhead" or something even more incomprehensible.

"*M'maai,*" he said emphatically in Cantonese, thinking I wanted to buy the pipe and informing me that it was not for sale.

I persisted, and by degrees, got him to understand that I only wanted to smoke it. I told him I had an enemy, a man I hated. I said I wished "to know" this man, and would pay him for the use of his magic pipe. He smiled at me, his face a tight mass of contour lines.

"*Yi sap man,*" he agreed, asking me for twenty dollars. It was a very small sum for gaining power over the man that was making my life a misery.

I tore off a margin piece of newspaper and wrote JOHN CHANG on it, but the old man brushed this aside. He produced a thin strip of red-and-gold paper covered on one side with Chinese characters and indicated that I should write the name on the back of it. When I had done so, he tore it into tiny pieces. I could see the muscles working in wrists as thin as broom handles, as his long-nailed fingers worked first at this, then at tamping down the paper shreds and tobacco in the pipe bowl.

He handed the musty-smelling instrument to me and I hesitated. It looked filthy. Did I really want that thing in my mouth? I had visions of the stem crawling with tuberculosis bacilli from the spittle of a thousand previous smokers. But then there was a flame at the bowl, and I was sucking away, finding the tobacco surprisingly smooth.

I could see the dark smoke rising from the rubbish burning cauldrons of Wong Tai Sin Temple, and as I puffed away on the ancient bamboo pipe, an intense feeling of well-being crept over me. I began to suspect the tobacco. Was it indeed free of opium? Had I been conned, by the fruit seller and the old man both? Maybe the old man was the fruit stall owner's father? It didn't seem to matter. I liked the pair of them. They were wonderful people. Even John Chang seemed a nice man, at that moment in time.

When the holiday was over, David left Hong Kong, and I returned to work. John Chang was in a foul mood the morning I arrived, and was screaming at a young girl for spilling a few drops of coffee on the floor. A woman reporter caught my eyes and made a face which said, "Stay out of his way if you can."

The warning came too late.

"You," snapped John Chang, as I passed him. "That fireman story was bloody useless. You didn't capture the personal side *at all*."

"I thought I did," I said stiffly.

"What you think is of no interest to me. I asked you to concentrate on the man and his family, and you bring in all that rubbish about government pensions."

"I thought it needed saying."

He gave me a look of disgust and waved me away as if I were some coolie who was irritating, but not worth chastising further. I felt my blood rise and I took a step toward him, but Sally, the woman reporter, grabbed my arm. She held me there until John Chang had left the room.

I turned, the fury dissipating, and said, "Thanks."

She gave me a little smile.

"You would only be giving him the excuse he needs," she said in her soft Asiatic accent. Peter Smith, another reporter, said, "Too bloody right, mate. Don't give him the satisfaction."

"He looked as if he could have killed that girl," I said to Sally, a little later. "All over a few spots of coffee."

"It was her perfume. For some reason that brand drives him crazy. I used to wear it myself, but not any more. Not since I realized what it does to his temper . . ."

Understand the one you hate.

I had to admit my temporary drunken hopes for a magical insight into John Chang had failed. There was no magic on the modern streets of Hong Kong. An antique pipe, nicotined a dirty yellow, stained black with tobacco juice, dottle clinging to the bowl, was nothing more than what it was—a lump of wood. Had I really believed it would help me?

I guess a desperate man will believe anything, even that he will some day manage to forget a woman he loves: will wake up one morning free of her image, the sound of her voice in his head gone, her smell removed from his olfactory memory. Memory sometimes works to its own secret rules and is not always subject to the will of its owner.

Memories can be cruel servants.

I began to have strange dreams, even while awake, of a woman I did not know. She was small, slim and dark, with a familiar voice. We were very intimate with one another. I pictured her in a kitchen, her hands flying around a wok, producing aromas that drove my gastric juices crazy. I saw her brown eyes, peering into mine from behind candles like white bars, over a dining-room table made of Chinese rosewood. There was love in those eyes. We drank a wine which was familiar to my brain but not to my tongue. She chattered to me, pleasantly, in Cantonese. I understood every word she said.

These pictures, images, dreams, began to frighten me a little, not because they were unpleasant, but because they felt comfortable. They worried me with their coziness. I wondered whether they were some kind of replacement for the memories that I was attempting to unload: the result of a compensatory mental illness. Perhaps I was trying to fill emotional gaps with strange fantasies of a Chinese woman.

I began to look for her in the street.

There were other, more disconcerting thoughts, which meant very little to me. Scenes, cameos, flashes of familiar happenings that meant nothing to me emotionally. I pictured myself going into stores and shops I did not recognize, for articles I had never even considered buying. There was an ambivalence to my feelings during these scenes. I saw myself buying an antique porcelain bowl, the design of which I instinctively and intensely disliked. Yet I purchased it with loving care and a knowledge of ceramics I had not previously been aware of possessing. In another scene, I went into a bakery and bought some Chinese moon cakes, a highly sweetened, dense foodstuff which most *gwailos* avoid, and I was no exception.

I was sure I was going quite mad.

John Chang kept me busy, hating him. He did not let up on me for one moment during the sweltering summer months, when the wealthy fled to cooler climes and school teachers blessed the long vacations they got during the season when Hell relocated to the Hong Kong streets.

During this humid period the Chinese lady with the loving eyes continued to haunt me. I would languish at my desk after work, reluctant to leave the air conditioned building, picturing myself making love with this woman in a bed with satin sheets, surrounded by unfamiliar furniture. It seemed right. Everything about it seemed right, except when I questioned it with some other part of my mind, the part firmly based in the logic that said *you do not know this woman*. It was true. I had never met anyone like her, yet she looked at me as if I were hers, and some unquestioning area of my mind, less concerned with what I *knew*, and content to be satisfied with what I *felt*, told me yes, this had happened, this was a proper interpretation of my experiences.

I began to read about schizophrenia, wondering whether I was one of those people who have more than one personality, but the books that I read did not seem to match what was happening to me. I balked when it came to seeing a therapist. I was afraid there was something quite seriously wrong with me.

In October, some people organized a junk trip to Lamma Island, the waterfront of which is lined with excellent fish restaurants. Sally asked me if I was going and I said I might as well. Most of the newspaper's employees would be there, and a few of the employers as well. The weather had turned pleasantly hot, had left the dehumanizing summer humidity behind in September. It promised to be a good evening.

There were rumors that John Chang would be going, but that did not deter me. I wondered if I could get drunk enough to tell him what I thought of him.

I was one of the last to jump aboard the junk, which then pulled out into the busy harbor. I stared at the millions of lights off to port: Causeway Bay, Wan Chai and Central, resplendent during the dark hours. A beer was thrust into my hand. I drank it from the can and looked around me. Sally was there. She waved. Peter Smith stood in animated conversation with another of our colleagues, his legs astride to combat the rolling motion of the craft in the choppy harbor waters. Then I noticed John Chang, sour-faced, standing by the rail.

Beside him was a lady I had never seen before, not in the flesh, but a woman with whom I had made love, in my head, a thousand times. My heart began to race and I felt myself going hot and cold, alternately, wondering whether I should try to hide somewhere until the evening was over. If she sees me, I thought, she's bound to recognize me as the one . . .

Then I pulled myself up short. One *what*? What had I done to her? Nothing. Not a blessed thing. So where did these pictures come from that had invaded my head? The best way to find out was to talk to her. I tried to catch her eyes, hoping she would come over to me without bringing John Chang.

Eventually I captured her attention and she looked startled. Did she know me after all? Was I indeed living some kind of Jekyll and Hyde existence? It was only after a few minutes that I understood she was not staring into my face at all: it was my red hair that had her attention. Then she realized she was being rude and averted her gaze, but Chang had caught us looking at each other and motioned for her to cross the deck with him. Before I could turn away, he was standing in front of me, gesturing towards the woman at his side.

"I don't believe you've met my wife, have you Fraser?"

She spoke in a gentle tone, admonishing him.

"John, Mr. Fraser must have a first name?"

He looked a little disconcerted.

"Yes, of course," he said stiffly. "Sean. Sean Fraser. Scottish I think."

"My ancestors were," I blurted, "but we've lived south of the border for two generations. The red hair, you know, is proof of my Celtic origins. I'm still a Scot, in spirit."

I shook her hand, acutely embarrassed by the fact that I knew what she looked like naked, lying on the bed, waiting for me to press myself against her. *John Chang's wife.* There were two small brown moles under her left breast. There were stretch marks around her abdomen.

I felt the silkiness of her palm, knowing that soft touch. I remembered the time she had whispered urgent nonsense into my ear, the first time our orgasms had coincided exactly, a miracle of biology which had left us breathless for several minutes afterwards, when we had both laughed with the utter joy of the occasion.

Staring into her eyes, I knew that if there was a memory of such happenings, they did not include *me*. What I saw there was a terrible sadness, held in check by a great strength. Alice Chang was one of those splendid people who find a natural balance within themselves. When a negative aspect of life causes them to lose equilibrium, a positive one rises from within their spirit, to meet it, cancel it out.

"I'm very pleased to meet you, Alice," I said.

"Oh, you know my name." She laughed. "I thought John tried to keep me a secret. Do you know this is the first time he has allowed me to meet his colleagues?"

I looked quickly at John Chang, and then said, "I'm afraid I've heard him speaking to you on the phone. The office has good acoustics. I don't eavesdrop intentionally."

"I'm sure you don't," she said, and then he steered her away, towards one of the directors, leaving me sweating, holding onto the rail for support. Not because of the rocking motion of the boat, but because my legs felt weak.

*   *   *

The following weekend I took a boat trip to Lantau Island and sat at a beach restaurant, staring at the sea and sand. I needed a peaceful place to think. Hong Kong's national anthem, the music of road drills, pile drivers, traffic, buzz saws, metal grinders *et al.* was not conducive to reflective thought.

There were evergreens along the shoreline of Silvermine Bay, decorated with hundreds of tattered kites. The children used the beach to fly their toys, which eventually got caught in the branches of the large conifers, and remained there. The brightly-colored paper diamonds gave the firs the appearance of Christmas trees. Around the trunks of the kite-snatchers were dozens of bicycles, chained to each other for security, left there by adolescents now sprawled on the sands.

I had managed to engineer one more chat with Alice Chang, before the end of that evening on Lamma, and spoke about the antique porcelain bowl, describing it. I had to lie to her, telling her that John had spoken to me about it, seemed proud to be its owner.

"Oh, yes. He loves ceramics, you know. It's his one expensive hobby."

I knew now I was experiencing John Chang's memories.

It was nothing to do with me. I had not made love to Alice Chang, but I carried John Chang's memories of such occasions, those that he wished to recall, and some he did not. It was a disturbing ordeal. There was a grim recollection of being hit a glancing blow by a truck, when he was small, and another when he was falsely accused of stealing from his school friends. I was gradually getting "to know" my Chinese boss and there were some dark areas in there which terrified me. I woke up at night, sweating, wondering where the fear was coming from, what was causing the desire to scream.

The night after the junk trip, I had spoken to Sally.

"How many kids has John Chang got?" I asked her casually.

She shook her head.

"None, so far as I know. Why do you ask?"

"Oh, no reason. I met his wife, last night. I thought she mentioned something about a child, but I couldn't be sure. I suppose I must have been mistaken."

Sally said, "I'm positive you are."

I drank steadily, as I tried to puzzle through my jumbled memories of his early marriage, and my eyes kept being drawn towards the bicycles, chained to the tree trunks. I struggled with a black beast of a memory, which was utterly reluctant to emerge from a hole it had dug itself.

A *bicycle*.

This was the key, but something prevented me from opening the lock. There was the idea that a bicycle was a detested thing, a deadly, ugly machine that should be outlawed, banned from use. *People who sell bicycles should be prosecuted, imprisoned, hung by the neck . . .*

That was very strong, *very* strong.

One of the kids from the beach came and unlocked her bike, climbed into the saddle, and rode away along the path. I experienced a forceful desire to scream at her, tell her to get off, return the machine to the salesman.

Where?

A shop sign popped into my head, which read: THE FLYING BALL CYCLE CO.

Then that dark cloud extended itself from the back of my brain, blacking out anything that might have followed.

Back at the flat I received a surprise telephone call from England. From Nickie. She asked me how I was. Did I like the Far East? Yes, she was fine. She was seeing one or two people (she didn't call them men) and things were absolutely fine.

Her voice was recognizably thin and tight, even over the phone. There was great anger there, pressing against her desire to sound casual. I noticed that it was 3 o'clock in the morning, her time, and I guessed she had been unable to sleep, obsessed with relentlessly reviewing the bitter times, furious with herself for failing to retaliate strongly, when something hurtful had been said, wishing she could raise the subject again, but this time be the one to wield the knife, cut the deepest.

I knew how she felt, having gone through the same cycle, many nights. We had both fired words, intended to wound, but we both remembered only being hit.

I told her I was having some trouble with one of my bosses. She sympathized coldly, but what she had really called about was the fact that I still had two of her favorite poetry books. She would like them back again, please, the Hughes and the Rilke.

Oh, those, yes, but three o'clock in the morning?—she really must want them badly, I said. I told her I remembered seeing them, just before leaving England for Hong Kong, but could not put my hand on them at this time. Could she call again later, when I had done some more unpacking?

No, she couldn't. I had been in Hong Kong for nearly a year. Hadn't I unpacked my things *yet*?

Her words became more shrill as the anger seeped through like a gas, altering the pitch of her voice.

When I did manage to unpack, could I please post them back to her? Yes, she was aware they were only paperbacks and could be replaced, but she didn't see why she should buy new copies when she already owned some—good-bye.

The emptiness that filled the room, after she had put down the phone, would have held galaxies.

I tried not to hate her, but I couldn't help it. She was there, I was here. Thousands of miles apart.

I picked up the Rilke, from the bedside table, open at *Orpheus, Eurydice, Hermes*. It was pencil marked in the margins, with her comments on the text. It was her handwriting I had been reading, not Rilke's poem. The flourishes were part of her, of the woman I had loved, and I had been sentimentalizing, as well as studying them for some small insight into her soul. I wanted to understand her, the secret of her self, in order to discover *why*. Why had it gone wrong?

The terrible ache in me could not be filled by love, so I filled it with hate instead. I wanted to kill her, for leaving me, for causing me so much emotional agony. I wanted to love her. I wanted her to love me. I hated her.

On Monday afternoon, I cornered Peter Smith. I recalled that he used to cover cycling stories for the paper. At one time his speech had been full of jargon—

accushift drivetrains, Dia-Compe XCU brakes, oversized headsets, Shimano de-railleurs. The language of the initiated, for the enthusiasts.

"You're a bike fanatic," I said. "You cycle in New Territories, don't you?"

"Not so much now," he patted a growing paunch, "but I used to. Why, you looking for a sport to keep you fit?"

"No, I came across this guy who kept raving about the Flying Ball Bike Shop. Know it?"

Smith laughed.

"My boy, that shop is a legend amongst cyclists. You can write to the owner of the Flying Ball from any corner of the earth, and he'll airmail the part you need and tell you to pay him when you eventually pass through Hong Kong."

"Why *Flying Ball?* Is that some kind of cog or wheel bearing invented specifically for push bikes?"

Smith shook his head.

"I asked the owner once. He told me the shop had been named by his grandfather, and he forgot to ask the old man what it meant. The secret's gone with grandpa's polished bones to a hillside grave overlooking water. Part of the legend now."

"Where is it? The shop, I mean."

"Tung Choi Street, in the heart of Mong Kok," he said, "now buzz off, I've got a column to write."

I went back to my desk. A few moments later I experienced a sharp memory pang and looked up to see the office girl placing a polystyrene cup of steaming brown liquid on my desk top. She smiled and nodded, moving on to Sally's desk. I could smell her perfume. It was the same one she had been wearing the day John Chang had bawled at her.

It was twilight when I reached Tung Choi Street. Mong Kok is in the Guinness Book of Records as the most densely populated area on the face of the earth. It is teeming with life, overspilling, like an ants' nest in a time of danger. It is rundown, sleazy, but energetic, effervescent. Decaying tenements with weed-ridden walls overhang garage-sized factory-shops where men in dirty T-shirts hammer out metal parts for everything and anything: stove pipes, watering cans, kitchen utensils, car exhausts, rat cages, butter pats, fish tanks, containers, and so on. What you can't buy ready-made to fit, you can have knocked up within minutes.

Over the course of the day, the factory-shops vomit their wares slowly out across the greasy pavement, into the road. The vendors of fruit and iced drinks fill in the spaces between. Through this jungle of metal, wood, and plastic plough the taxis and trucks, while the pedestrians manage as best they can to hop over, climb, circumnavigate. Business is conducted to a cacophony caused by hammers, drills, saws, car horns. It can have a rhythm if you have a broad musical tolerance and allow it flexibility.

THE FLYING BALL CYCLE CO.

I found the shop after two minutes' walking.

I stood on the opposite side of the road, the two-way flow of life between me and this unimposing little bike shop, and I remembered. It hit me with a force that almost had me reeling backwards, into the arms of the shopkeeper amongst whose goods I was standing. The dark area lifted from my brain, and the tragedy was like an awful light, shining through to my consciousness. The emotional pain revealed by this brightness, so long covered and now unveiled, was appalling.

And this was not my agony, but *his*.

I turned and stumbled away from the scene, making for the nearest telephone. When I found one, I dialed John Chang's home number. It had all come together the moment I laid eyes on the Flying Ball: the hate John Chang bore towards me; the unexplained stretch marks on Alice Chang's abdomen; the blankness in his eyes, the sadness in hers.

"Mrs. Chang? This is Sean Fraser. We met on the junk—yes, the other night. I wonder if you could ask John to meet me, in the coffee shop by Star Ferry? Yes, that's the one. Can you say it's very important. It's about your son, Michael . . . Yes, I know, I know, but I have to talk to him just the same. Thanks."

I put down the receiver and hailed a taxi.

I was on my second cup of coffee when he arrived. He looked ashen and for once his façade of grim self-assurance was missing. I ordered him a cup of coffee and when it arrived, put some brandy in it from a half-bottle I had bought on the way. He stared at the drink, his lean face grey, his lips colorless.

"What's all this about?" he said. The words were delivered belligerently, but there was an underlying anxiousness to the tone. "Why did you ask me to come here, Fraser?"

He hadn't touched his coffee, and I pushed it towards him.

"I know about Michael," I said.

His eyes registered some pain.

"I know how he died."

"What business is it of yours?" he said in a low voice. "How dare you? You're interfering in my family affairs. You leave my family alone."

"I'm not interested in your family. I'm interested in the way you treat *me*. Since I've been in Hong Kong, you've made my life hell. I didn't bring your family into the office, *you* did. You're punishing me for something you won't even allow yourself to think about. You've blocked it out and the guilt you feel is causing you to hurt other people, especially redheaded *gwailos*.

"I've been the target for your suppressed anger, your bottled grief, for as long as I can stand. It's got to stop, John. I'm not responsible for Michael's death, and you know it, really. I just happen to be a European with red hair. I wasn't even in Hong Kong when that driver took your son's life . . ."

"Shut up!" he shouted, causing heads to turn and look, then turn back again quickly. His face was blotched now with fury, and he was gripping the cup of coffee as if he intended to hurl it into my face.

"This is what happened, John," I said quietly, ignoring his outburst. "It was Christmas, and, being a Christian, you celebrated the birth of Christ in the way that *gwailo* Christians do. You bought presents for your wife and twelve-year-old son. You gave your wife some perfume, a brand you won't allow her to use now because it reminds you of that terrible time, and you asked your son what he would like most in the world . . ."

There were tears coming down John Chang's face now, and he stumbled to his feet and went through the door. I left ten dollars on the table and followed him.

He was standing against the harbor wall, looking down into the water, still crying. I moved up next to him.

"He said he wanted a bicycle, didn't he, John? One of those new mountain bikes, with eighteen, twenty gears. You took Michael down to Mong Kok, to the Flying Ball Bike Shop, and you bought him what he wanted because you were a loving father, and you wanted to please him. He then begged to be allowed to ride it home, but you were concerned, you said no, repeatedly, until he burst into tears—and finally, you relented.

"You said he could ride it home, if he was very, very careful, and you followed behind him in the car."

I paused for a moment and put my arm around his shoulders.

"The car that overtook you, halfway home, was driven by a red-haired foreigner, a *gwailo*, and he hit Michael as he swerved in front of you to avoid an oncoming truck. The bike itself was run over. It crumpled, like paper, and lay obscenely twisted beside your son's body. You stopped, but the other driver didn't. He sped away while you cradled Michael's limp body in your arms, screaming for an ambulance, a doctor.

"They never caught the hit-and-run driver, and you've never forgiven yourself. You still want him, don't you, that murdering red-headed *gwailo*, the man who killed your son? You want to punish him, desperately, and maybe some of that terrible guilt you feel might go away."

He turned his tear-streaked face toward me, looked into my eyes, seeking a comfort I couldn't really give him.

I said gently, "That wasn't me, John. You know it wasn't me."

"I know," he said. "I know, I know. I'm so sorry."

He fell forward, into my arms, and we hugged each other, for a brief while. Then we became embarrassed simultaneously, and let go. He went back to leaning on the wall, but though the pain was still evident, his sobbing had ceased.

Finally he turned, asked the obvious question: how did I know so much detail about Michael's death? It had happened many years ago.

Rather than go into the business with the pipe, I told him I had been to Wong Tai Sin, to a clairvoyant, and the man had looked into John's past for me.

"It cost me a lot of money," I said, to make it sound more authentic. If there's one thing that Hong Kongers believe in, it's the authority money has to make the impossible possible. John Chang did not laugh at this explanation or call me a liar. A little brush with the West does not wipe out five thousand years of Chinese belief in the supernatural.

Then he went home, to his wife, leaving me to stare at the waters of the fragrant harbor and think about my own feelings of love and hate. *Understand the man you hate.* How can you hate a man you understand? I began to realize what the old man with his magic pipe was selling. Not power over one's enemy. Love. That's what he had for sale. His was a place where you could look at hate, understand it enough to be able to turn it into love.

I knew something else. Now that I had confronted John, now that we understood one another, the memories of his past would cease to bother me. The pipe had done its work.

*   *   *

The following week, one evening when a rain as fine as Irish drizzle had come and gone, leaving a fresh scent to the air, I took a taxi to Wong Tai Sin Temple. The old man was still there, sitting at the entrance to the alley, his pipe by his side.

I went up to him and gave him twenty dollars, and he smiled and silently handed me the pipe and a piece of red-and-gold paper decorated with Chinese characters.

On the back of the paper I wrote the name of a person I loved and hated—NICHOLA BLACKWOOD—and tore it into tiny pieces, hoping that distance was no barrier to magic.

BATS

Diane de Avalle-Arce

Diane de Avalle-Arce lives and writes novels at the edge of Los Padres National Forest, describing herself as a refugee from the twentieth century. "Bats" is a rich and subtle tale of Magical Realism set in Guanajuato, Mexico. It is reprinted from the August issue of *Isaac Asimov's Science Fiction Magazine*—a venue that may surprise readers unfamiliar with the magazine and its commitment to publishing fantasy and Magical Realist fiction in addition to its staple science fiction fare.

For readers interested in further Magical Realist works with a Mexican/American flavor, Kathleen Alcalá's collection *Mrs. Vargas and the Dead Naturalist*, published by Calyx Books in 1992, is also recommended, as well as Leslie Marmon Silko's latest novel, *Almanac of the Dead*.

—T.W.

It was the old and cruel custom of the shoeshine boys of Guanajuato, when they had no pressing matters on hand, to catch a bat and make it smoke. You nail the bat to a board fence, by each wing, and put a lit cigarette in the mouth as it opens in a soundless shriek. The tip of the cigarette glows and smoke curls out of the bat's nostrils, as though it were enjoying a gringo's *rubio* tobacco.

This is no longer done, by order of Manuel Aceves, chief among the shoeshine boys of the barrio of San Martin. Rose, the lady who wore white gloves, had something to do with it, and so (though he never made the connection) did Dr. Murphy, a prominent physician in the American colony. Rufina, who keeps the Bar Zotzil on top of La Valenciana, might claim some credit, but she and the grey cat have enough to do without concerning themselves about such things.

It was and is the custom for the gringos to emerge from their pink villas on the outskirts of Guanajuato just before sundown, and drive up to La Valenciana for their evening drink. They admire the view and complain about the laundress and the lack of parts for their cars. This being the hour when the hand is more willing to reach into the pocket and extend a bill, not waiting for change, Manuel Aceves with his shoeshine kit was accustomed to climb the stone steps zig-zagging up the hill to the mine, cutting the loops of the road between nopales and yucca.

The evening of his revelation, he was late; it was nearly dark, and the ground was cold in the shadow of the hill, although the sun behind the mountain gilded the twin towers of the church of La Valenciana. Manuel usually pretended he was the Emperor Moctezuma climbing the Great Temple of the Sun—though he is all four quarterings Chichimeca of Guanajuato and proud of it—but this evening he forgot the Emperor Moctezuma, watching the bats leaving the church.

They came out in a thin spiral, like smoke rising from a small fire, then in a twisted column, a pillar growing upward, larger at the top like a funnel, spinning faster and faster. The funnel danced back and forth as the wind pushed it, until the bats streamed out eastward in a cloud, passing over his head. He heard the hissing of hundreds of thousands of little wings, making a downdraft of warm ammoniac air around him. Still the bats poured out, the long cloud like the plumed serpent Quetzalcoatl, while the sky behind the mountain turned from gold to red to the clear cold green that precedes the deep indigo of night.

Already the church looked a horned bulky animal asleep, and the Cafe Zotzil crouched at its foot like a smaller animal with open glowing eyes, when Manuel Aceves humped his shoeshine box into the bar. The place was almost full, with only Rufina to run back and forth with drinks, while the grey cat minded the bar under the grinning mask of Zotzil the Bat God.

Manuel ordered a Coca-Cola, and Rufina threw a dishrag at him and said she hoped that Zotzil would eat him.

"Come, Rufina," he said, "the old gods are dead. The Spaniards killed them. Then we Chichimecas killed the Spaniards, until we got tired of it, and when we wish, we will kill the gringos, too."

"Throw yourself in the well," responded Rufina, loading her tray.

The Bar Zotzil was the old well-house of La Valenciana mine, when the mine had produced silver enough to build and decorate a hundred churches a year. Those times were long gone. The mine was sealed and the church empty, but the well was still there: a hole five meters wide in the floor, with a railing. Green water rushed past the hole, over a pale sand bottom. There were no fish, but the grey cat watched the water just in case, and the gringos threw cigarette butts in it.

Manuel shrugged and made a face at Rufina's back, then composed his smooth copper mask for business. Dr. Murphy first. Grey laceless shoes with tassels on them, grey pants and jacket, grey hair, grey face with purple veins. Dr. Murphy drank whiskey in the Bar Zotzil from sundown until the bar closed, although he slept much of the time. Manuel flashed his smile and said, "Shine? Shine?" Without waiting for the answer, he went to work with his rags.

Before he'd finished, *la señora* Carol sat down at the table. A pink lady, hair like a cornfield in stubble. Manuel had once thought of charging her extra because her feet were so long. Her shoes were pink lizards, which gave him pause for thought. Rummaging through his box, he listened to the conversation; Manuel understood more English than he let on.

They talked about the restoration of the church, which *la señora* Carol said was a project close to her heart. Manuel did not think gringos had hearts, not like people had. Restoring the church was not close to Manuel's heart, but if more tourists came to the area because of it, he wanted their business. On the other hand, if the Minister of Culture came to declare the church a Historical Monument, beggars and shoeshine boys and women selling lace tablecloths from baskets would be banished. So he listened carefully. *La señora* Carol wanted Dr. Murphy to contribute to the fund for illuminating the church.

"To shine like a good deed in a naughty world?" said Dr. Murphy. "It's a robber baron's bad conscience construed in masonry. That's all it amounts to. Leave it to the bats."

"Ugh," said the lady, fanning herself with a paper napkin. "I can't *bear* bats. The illumination should get rid of them if it does nothing else. Do you think the Board of Health would bear part of the cost?"

"Why?" said Dr. Murphy. He finished his whiskey. "If they ask me, I'll tell 'em more people die in a year of church-picnic potato-salad than of bat-related disease in a century."

"You can't be serious. What about *vampire* bats, which I hope those aren't? Don't the cattle ranchers—"

"If the cow had the choice of providing *you* with a steak dinner, or a *bat* with an ounce of blood, she'd choose to accommodate the bat! Rufina! Another of these. Why, the bat's saliva is an anti-coagulant with antibiotic properties, she'd be none the worse. Whereas the *steak*—"

"Phillip, you do have the oddest take on things! I hope you're not going to set yourself up against the whole North American community *just* when we're doing something that will really make a difference!"

Manuel finished the shoes with his brightest smile and held out his dirty hand, which *la señora* Carol pretended not to see. Dr. Murphy gave him a five-hundred-peso bill and said to keep the change, which would have been better if it were not a one-hundred-peso bill with false corners pasted on it. Manuel sincerely hoped he gave money like that to *la señora* Carol for her restoration fund.

He looked around for more customers, but it was a bad evening for shoes; in dry weather, the dust of the brown hills does not cling to the mirror-surface of shoes shined by Manuel the previous evening. Helping himself to a Coke behind Rufina's back, he settled on his heels in a corner.

" 'Oh, fat white woman whom nobody loves, why do you walk through the fields in gloves?' " said Dr. Murphy through his teeth in a funny way.

Rose—the gringa round like a squash or a real person, instead of chili-shaped like the other gringos—came in like a cow with staggers and dropped into a chair. She was as red as her namesake, and pressed both her gloved hands against her breastbone; slowly, she turned white as trout-bellies.

The other gringos didn't like Rose because she lived in the town, over the shop that sells silver and turquoise birds, and gave pesos to street children and told them to go to school.

"Have a glass of water—where are your *pills*, for God's sake?"

Rose shook her head. She took a fish head out of a plastic bag and put it under her chair for the grey cat. "I can't, I told you—I can't take the pills. If I take them, I can't sleep."

"Your blood pressure is literally killing you," Dr. Murphy snapped. The grey hand trembled with the glass. "I can't understand how you've survived *this* long."

La señora Carol changed the subject, because gringos don't believe in death. They never take food to the *ánimas* for the Day of the Dead, *never*. Manuel knew.

"Do you know you've come just in time to see the illumination of La Valenciana? Any minute now they'll turn on the lights!"

Rose looked even sicker. "Tonight?" she said in a thread of a voice. "I thought it was next month?"

"Oh, the mayor and the American consul, and just possibly the Minister of Culture, will come next month, for the dedication of the plaque crediting the American colony. But the outside illumination is ready. It'll be wonderful, just you wait and see."

But Rose was up and blundering into the rail of the well. She grasped it and looked around. Manuel, with an eye to opportunity, was at her elbow in a moment.

She flinched, then leaned on the hard dirty little arm. "You're Manuel, aren't you? I have a job for you, if you won't be afraid."

"I, afraid? Manuel Aceves is pure Chichimeca, and the meanest shoeshine boy in barrio San Martin!"

"I thought so," said Rose.

Rufina appeared. "Does the *señora* wish to lie down?"

"No," said Rose. "Manuel and I are going to the church now."

"It will be locked, *señora*. The workmen are all gone."

"That's all right," said Rose, taking a big iron key out of her bag.

Manuel, piloting the lady out of the Bar Zotzil, was not surprised that she had a key to the church. If you pay enough, you can have the key to anything you want. But why? There was nothing of value in La Valenciana. Or *was* there? Did the gringa know of hidden treasure under the altar? Who knew what the old Spaniards might have hidden in the church, under tons of bat guano in the belfries? Manuel's step quickened.

Outside the yellow fan of light from the doorway, it was dark as Rufina's braid, although the stars blazed long trails overhead.

"The side door," said Rose. "This one."

Inside the church, it was dark as a mine. Only the high altar glinted gold from the windows, a blind naked cherub with yellow curls here, the halo of a saint there. But Rose seemed to know her way, unsteady but determined, and Manuel half-followed and half-supported her up a winding stair behind the stone baptistry. They went up and up, and Manuel realized they must be climbing the west tower.

At the top there was a door, unlocked, and Rose pushed it open. Her breathing was shallow and rapid, but Manuel held his breath, looking for the treasure. There would be gold, and silver, and emeralds, and rubies, and pearls! He would take it and buy the whole city of Guanajuato, like a plate of glazed salt-clay food for the Day of the Dead: the Market and the Fort with the Mummies; the streets full of businessmen in suits the color of flour; the taxis and buses and the cars of the gringos; the policemen and their carbines; schools and banks and bars, and houses where the women wore paint and laughed so loud you could hear them all over the barrio.

But he could see nothing in the tower but the grey rectangle of the louvers, though he knew they must be under the bell-mouths, huge and black. He smelled cold bronze, and dust, ammonia, the plastic coverings of new electrical wires. Rose tripped on something and her full weight on his shoulder made him stagger. She rummaged in her bag.

"Thank you, Manuel. You can go now. Here's a hundred *pesos*." She snapped on a little flashlight with a cloth tied over the glass. Huge flickering shadows sprang up on the walls, two figures drawn up to dizzy height, crossed by black bars of beams, blurry with cobwebs and inches of dust. There were footprints in the dust on the floor as if it were sand, workmen's boots, Rose's shoes with heels, Manuel's bare feet, rat-paws, and some marks that were none of these.

Rose sat down cross-legged, with a gasp. "Can't you find your way out, Manuel? I don't need any more help now."

"I want to stay, *señora*, truly." For Manuel was Chichimeca of Guanajuato, and any treasure there might be was his as much as anyone's.

"All right, if you won't be frightened."

Manuel, *frightened?* Never since he could remember.

Rose was speaking in a low voice, he did not know whether to herself or to him, making no move toward where treasure might be hidden. He could see no sign of it.

"The lights," she said. "They've put floodlights all over, and opened the louvers. It will be light day and night. You won't stay here, Jimmy; you can't. This will be the last time. Jimmy?"

Manuel, squatting on his heels, watching, wondered if she might be wandering in her wits, for she had drunk no whisky nor even beer at the Bar Zotzil. She took off her gloves and pushed up the yellow sleeve of her blouse. She stretched out the left arm, trembling, with the back of the hand resting on the floor. And such an arm: pale as melon, mottled with red and violet, the blue veins twisting the bone from which the flesh hung slack.

She whistled. It was a high thin sound, as to a very small dog. Manuel followed her eyes and saw a bat, not hanging but right side up, crouched in the angle of a rafter. The flashlight beam showed its pug-dog face with ears pricked, wings like an umbrella half-unfolded. The mouth opened candy-pink, but what struck Manuel most was the unblinking black eyes that didn't reflect like an animal's at night.

"Here, Jimmy," whispered Rose, and the bat dropped to the floor in a brief flutter of membrane-wings as wide as Manuel's forearm was long.

He almost thought he heard it answer, like a feather in his ear. He was so afraid he crossed himself, as he had not done since his mother died, but it was no good, a bat that lived in the bells of a church must have no fear of anything.

The bat hitched itself along the floor on its rat-feet, helping with the long wing-thumbs. Manuel did not move, and every detail printed itself on his memory, like a painting on glass. The bat looked at him, looked into his eyes as no animal could do, nor any rich person in a cafe, and saw *him*, Manuel Aceves as he was, and opened its mouth. It had tiny sharp teeth, like thorns.

"Hold still," whispered Rose. "He's nervous of you."

And Manuel held still as though a spell were on him, because here was the Bat God Zotzil in the tower of the church of La Valenciana, and he had never believed in either of them.

The bat came with its humping gait, and climbed onto Rose's fingers. The hand lay quiet but the blue veins quivered and rolled over each other. The bat nuzzled her wrist, here and there, and held to it. Rose breathed, low and steady, many times, as it sucked the vein.

At last she put out her other hand, and, with her finger, stroked the bat, like Rufina stroking her cat when she was in a good mood. The bat arched its head back, and Manuel saw a mark like ink on Rose's wrist. It didn't bleed.

"This is Jimmy," she said. "Several of them will come, but he's the only one I can pet. See if he'll let you."

And then Manuel proved he was who he was. He stretched out his own dark paw and touched the bat, like warm silk, like the finest glove leather, and felt its heart beating, and heard Rose's harsh breathing and his own in the moment before the floodlights went on, brighter than day.

No one noticed their return to the Cafe Zotzil but Rufina, because all the gringos were admiring the illuminated façade of La Valenciana—except Dr. Murphy, who was asleep in his chair with his head on the table. Manuel removed some hundreds of thousands of *pesos* from his pocket and from the handbag of *la señora* Carol, under the indifferent gaze of the grey cat, and slipped down the hill in the darkness.

There was after all no treasure, and Rose was right that the bats would never come back to La Valenciana. She died some weeks later of a heart attack in the rooms over the shop that sold silver and turquoise birds. Manuel was sorry. By then he was no longer a shoeshine boy, but a boarder in the school of the Aescolapian Brothers, because a man of power, a man who has touched the heart of the world and seen it is far, far bigger than Guanajuato, must have the education to rise above the barrio San Martin.

ORIGAMI MOUNTAIN
Nancy Farmer

Nancy Farmer grew up in Yuma, Arizona, and lived in Zimbabwe for seventeen years before returning to the United States. She currently lives in Menlo Park, California, and writes full-time. In 1988 she was the Writers of the Future Gold Award–winner for her first published story, "The Mirror." Her first novel, written for children, *Do You Know Me?*, has just been published, and she is working on *The Ear, the Eye, and the Arm*, a novel that makes use of her knowledge of the Shona tribe of Zimbabwe; she hopes this book will be the African equivalent of *The Lord of the Rings*. She was a recipient of a National Endowment for the Arts grant in 1992.

"Origami Mountain" is a very Japanese story that gets its versimilitude from Farmer's immersion in the culture of her Japanese college roommate. On the surface "Origami Mountain" is a mystery—a rich industrialist disappears—but beyond that the story reveals a great deal about Japanese cultural attitudes and about the uneasy relationship between the haves and have-nots. It is reprinted from *The Magazine of Fantasy & Science Fiction*.

—E.D.

When Jiro Tanaka did not come home from work, his wife, Miya, assumed he was at a nightclub. Even when he did not arrive by midnight, she sighed and went around their mansion in Pacific Heights. She checked the windows, the burglar alarm, and the children's bedrooms. Then she lay in bed and listened for the sound of his feet on the floor.

The Tanaka house had been built with wooden floors that squeaked when anything larger than a mouse ran over them. They were called *nightingale floors*, a feature of old Japanese castles, where it was a matter of life and death to know when someone was creeping up on you. Dr. Tanaka had imported an architect from Japan to build them.

Miya wondered which nightclub he was in. He would be surrounded by his favorite employees. They would laugh at all his jokes and get drunk before he did. At the end of the night, Jiro would be left alone with his helpless and stupefied workers. The more disgusting they were, the more powerful he would feel, which was how it should be: he was the boss.

Or perhaps he was at an obscene movie. He liked pornography, especially the kind where the women were tied up and tortured. It wasn't enjoyable for him to bring home a video because Miya didn't react. She sat, stony-faced, showing neither pleasure nor distress. It was better to take a fresh-faced employee who would trip over his shoelaces if a woman smiled at him. Like Jimmy.

Miya felt sorry for Jimmy. He was as close to a farm boy as you could find in someone with a Ph.D. in physics. Jimmy came from Okinawa, a mark against him because Jiro was prejudiced against people from Okinawa. They had big heads, he said, big hands and curly hair. They were like oxen. Jimmy had a wide, innocent face and freckles, as well as a friendly, open attitude. Jiro did not trust spontaneously friendly people.

He would have taken Jimmy to an obscene movie, and perhaps others to watch the fun. Miya felt sorry for him, but there was nothing she could do about it. She couldn't even protect herself.

When Jiro had not appeared by breakfast, another possibility occurred to her: he had a mistress. This did not upset her. She hoped he had, because he would spend all his time with her. No doubt he'd gone straight from his assignation to the office. Miya woke the children up, bathed and fed them. They spent a pleasant day in Origami Park, and when they got home, Jiro wasn't there.

With one thing and another, a week passed before Miya thought to report it to the police.

"A whole week!" yelled Homer, slamming down the receiver. "The head of one of the biggest companies in San Francisco goes missing a week before anyone reports it."

His partner, Stewart, opened a new file on the Mac and entered Jiro Tanaka's name. "Anybody miss him at work?"

"Yeah, they knew he was gone," said Homer. "The work went on without him. Japanese factories are like that. Someone drops dead, and the next person in line takes his place."

"What do they make?" Stewart spun the cylinder in his revolver, a habit that intrigued Homer. He thought of it as the policeman's prayer wheel.

"What *don't* they make?" he said. "Every kind of chemical, but they're best known for Yum Powder."

Stewart whistled. "Didn't they get the pants sued off them for that?"

"Still in court. And likely to stay there for the next hundred years. Can't prove a thing."

"Except that one hundred thousand babies dropped about twenty I.Q. points eating it," said Stewart.

"Babies Cry for Yum Powder," said Homer. "How can you prove a twenty-point I.Q. drop? Anyhow, our problem is to find this benefactor of mankind and return him to his grieving employees."

"Haven't we got more important things to do?"

"Would you rather be breaking into a crack house in Oakland?"

"No," admitted Stewart.

"Besides, the chief says to give this case our best. Tanaka donated about a million to certain city officials."

"Ah," said Stewart.

They made a strange-looking pair. Stewart was a barrel-chested white man of about two hundred pounds. In a swim suit, he looked as though he were wearing a fur coat, but even in uniform the hair crept down the back of his hands and up his neck. He had short, bandy legs, but he could move like an express train when he had to.

Homer, on the other hand, was just over the minimum height and weight limit for a police officer. He looked like a black business executive. His shoes were always polished, and the cuticles trimmed from his nails. But if you asked a crook which policeman he would rather be left alone with, he always chose the bigger man.

They stood outside the hulking mansion in Pacific Heights. "Look at the security," said Stewart. Cameras scanned them from a high wall; floodlights pointed in at the garden. He rang the bell.

"Please show I.D.," said a voice from behind the gate. The officers held their wallets up to the camera. The bolts drew back, and a gardener peered at them. "Down!" he shouted. For an instant the policemen thought he meant them, but snarls erupted as the man dragged a pair of pit bulls from the path and clicked chains on their collars. Stewart's hand strayed to his can of Mace. Homer looked bland, as he always did when most dangerous.

"Very sorry," the gardener apologized. "I should have locked them up before you arrived."

They followed him to the house, where a small, middle-aged woman waited. "Mrs. Tanaka?" said Homer.

"Thank you for coming," she said. She took them on a tour of the house as she talked about her husband. Homer and Stewart followed in the hope of uncovering a lead.

"These floors need an oil job," remarked Stewart as squeaks rippled through the wood.

Mrs. Tanaka giggled, and explained about nightingale floors.

"Did your husband have a lot of enemies?" said Homer. Mrs. Tanaka giggled again, a sound, he thought, that could get irritating. She didn't answer the question, however. They came to the master bedroom, and Homer halted abruptly at the door. Stewart swallowed hard. There, on a shelf, was a row of the most grotesque Black Sambo dolls Homer had ever seen. There were at least ten, with goggly eyes and fat, rubbery lips.

Mrs. Tanaka noticed Homer's stare. "Aren't they cute?" she said. "Jiro buys them in Japan. One of them even talks. Would you like to hear it?"

"No," said Homer in a strangled voice. They went on, with the woman chattering about Jiro's habits, but in fact saying nothing about where he might be. They came to a recreation room, and she clapped her hands at two children, a boy and a girl, who were jumping on an expensive sofa in front of a TV.

They thrust power gloves at the screen and shrieked with excitement. "Please get down," Mrs. Tanaka said. The children slid to the floor and sat there, quivering like a pair of cats in a room full of mice.

"Can we go to Origami Park?" said the boy. "We're bored."

"After the officers have gone," said Mrs. Tanaka.

"Are you cops?" said the boy. Homer nodded. "Oh boy, have you killed anyone? Let me see the guns."

"We're Peace Officers," explained Stewart. "We don't kill people. You may not see the guns."

"They're phonies," the boy told his sister, and they went back to Nintendo.

The policemen found out nothing from Mrs. Tanaka or the gardener. Stewart drove to the factory. "Nice dolls," he said, while having a *mano-a-mano* with a cable car on one of San Francisco's steepest streets.

"Remind me to show you my collection of honkie dolls. Don't play chicken with cable cars. They always win." Homer slid down in the seat so he would not have to see the inflamed face of the cable car driver as they shot past. "I don't think Jiro Tanaka ran away. He has everything he could want right here."

"Maybe it was the lawsuit over Yum Powder," grunted Stewart, bumping across the trolley tracks on Market Street. "What exactly did it do?"

"Made everything taste *wonderful*. It was a super brain stimulant."

"Like monosodium glutamate?"

"Much better. The food didn't even have to be good to begin with. Manufacturers could use it on dog shit, and probably did."

"How did it get past the Food and Drug people?" Stewart rolled into the wasted streets of the Mission District. Suddenly it was as though they weren't in the same town. They found themselves in a sinkhole so depressing, you'd have to kick in a window to keep from thinking about suicide.

"It passed the tests," said Homer. "This is one armpit of a neighborhood." He rolled up his window. "The additive was too expensive to produce, though, so Tanaka used a genetically altered bacterium to make huge quantities of it. There was a contaminant. Jesus, is that the factory?"

They came around a corner to a dead-end street. Ahead was the Jigoku Chemical Works. Gray and windowless, it sat like a giant turd on a concrete serving dish.

"Holy Moly, I thought Japanese were fanatics about beauty," said Stewart.

"Doesn't look like it," said Homer. The men were silent as they drove to the iron doors. More cameras, more clanking of chains. The air smelled—Homer wasn't sure *what* it smelled like, but it made the skin on his neck creep. The gate went up, and they drove in. The bottom level was a parking lot. A guard led them to an elevator. At each floor the elevator paused, and they looked out on industrial scenes that came out of Dante.

Huge pipes snaked around boilers; vats bubbled, steam hissed, and the noise was constant, shrill, and deafening. And behind it all was the strange smell, like hot, raw meat, or maybe the mouth of a predatory beast.

"You like working here?" Homer asked the guard.

"Of course! Jigoku is the greatest company in the world. Biggest per capita production, lowest overhead. We Jigoku employees take pride in bringing better living to people everywhere."

"Just thought I'd ask," said Homer. He thought he was going to vomit if he didn't get fresh air soon, but fortunately, the top floor was offices, and the smell was weaker. They were ushered into a small room.

"Air's better," sighed Homer. "How do they get a flower to survive here?" He nodded at a flower arrangement on a low table.

"Fake," said Stewart, feeling the petals.

"By the time the day's over, I'm not gonna have any illusions left. Do you think they have plastic-flower-arranging classes?"

"And tea-bag ceremonies," said Stewart.

Their hysterical laughter was interrupted by a young man in a lab coat. "So happy you like our factory," he said. Homer did a double take. Yes, the man had freckles.

"Jimmy Tsuga," he said, extending a hand. Homer had the impression that, not long ago, Jimmy Tsuga had been up to his ankles in cow shit. All he needed to complete the hayseed image was a sprig of buckwheat between his front teeth.

"Have you found anything out about our director?" said Jimmy.

"We're making inquiries," Homer said. "Can you tell me why no one reported his absence for a week?"

"We thought he was taking a vacation."

"Does the director always take vacations without telling anyone?"

Jimmy ducked his head and giggled, exactly like Mrs. Tanaka. Homer was fascinated. "There's a film festival in town," the scientist managed to say.

"Film festival?" said Stewart, genuinely puzzled.

Jimmy's embarrassment deepened. "*Erotic* film festival." The two policeman stared at him, but he didn't elaborate.

"This goes on all day?" said Homer gently.

"All night. During the day"—Jimmy paused to gather his inner resources—"he rests up."

"*Where* does he rest up?"

"Various places," said Jimmy vaguely.

"Dr. Tsuga," said Homer in a calm voice that made Stewart, who knew him, tense up. "A very important man is missing. He is a multimillionaire. He has great political influence. He is the kingpin of a worldwide chemical industry, but nobody seems to miss him for an entire week. Nobody has any idea of his habits or where he might be. You know what this smells like to me, Dr. Tsuga? It smells like murder, and one of the first things an investigator looks for is who benefits from it. Who gets to inherit the directorship of Jigoku Chemical Works if Jiro Tanaka is dead?"

"Me," said Jimmy.

"I thought so. Now, for all I know, Jiro Tanaka has been cooked up in one of those boilers we passed on the way up here. The smell is bad enough, but before we get into the ins and outs of dismantling this place to look for bone fragments, do you have any idea where Dr. Tanaka might be resting up from his midnight beaver shows?"

The effect of this statement was extraordinary. Jimmy turned so pale, the freckles stood out like inkblots. He opened his mouth, but no sound came out. For a moment, Homer thought he was going to confess, but such things happened only to Perry Mason. After a few moments, Jimmy said, "Origami Park."

"That's the second time I've heard that mentioned today. Is it reasonable for a man to spend a whole week in a park? Or is it something like Disneyland?"

"You could spend a lifetime in Origami," said Jimmy. "But it's not a theme park. It's—" He struggled to find the words. "You see, most of our employees come from

Japan. We have an arrangement with other companies to rotate their workers here. It gives them a chance to learn English and to see another country."

"It also means you don't have to pay them much," said Homer.

"That's true," admitted Jimmy. "The point I'm making is, quite often they're disappointed. Housing is difficult, customs are strange, and the workplace is not . . . attractive."

"You could say that," said Stewart.

"We Japanese need beauty," went on Jimmy in a rush, as though he were afraid he would lose his nerve if he paused. "Everywhere, even in the poorest house, there's a scroll or a flower, something a person can look at to feel uplifted. But here"—he swept out his arm to include the whole factory—"it's like Hell. Noise, ugliness, stench. It drives people crazy. They commit suicide. You have no idea how many people we lost when this place first opened. The factories in Japan complained, and I argued with Dr. Tanaka to please, please put in a garden and control the noise, but he said this was the most efficient factory in the world. We weren't allowed to change a single bolt or put up a picture—" He stopped, breathing heavily. Homer and Stewart didn't say a word. They knew they would get better results by waiting.

"Finally," said Jimmy after he had calmed down, "the companies in Japan refused to send more workers, so he built Origami Park."

"Which is beautiful," said Homer softly.

"Yes! It's like a piece of Japan. No matter what terrible things happen, you can go there and be healed."

"You're homesick, aren't you?" said Homer.

Jimmy said nothing, but stared at the plastic flower arrangement. Suddenly he ripped it out and threw it on the floor. "I'll give you a pass to Origami Park. You can't get in otherwise."

He led them down the stairs rather than using the elevator, so they could get a better look at the factory. "What *is* that smell?" said Stewart.

"Yum Powder."

"*Yum Powder?*"

"Dr. Tanaka thought we should keep making it."

"But it's banned."

"Not in Africa. Anyhow, we aren't making it anymore. I'm having the vats cleaned, which is why there's still a slight smell. You should have been here last week." He waved them out. Homer and Stewart paused to let a van ease onto the concrete wasteland surrounding Jigoku Chemical Works.

"Go ahead," said Homer.

"Wait." Stewart pointed at a group of men working on the far side of the wasteland. The sound of jackhammers floated back to them. "They're taking up the concrete."

"That was a nursery truck that just went up there," said Homer.

They watched as small trees were unloaded. The workers stopped drilling and went over to admire them. "They seem pretty sure Dr. Tanaka isn't coming back," said Stewart at last.

"Yes," said Homer. They drove on in silence while Homer rustled a newspaper until he found what he was looking for. *"Kingdom of Snuff Film Festival,"* he read. *"Midnight shows. Just like the real thing: See beautiful, bosomy women beg for their lives. Scenes of medieval torture. Screams of agony. No mercy shown. Just like the real thing.* Jesus, is this legal?"

"You're the cop," said Stewart.

"What kind of rock did this Tanaka crawl out from under?"

"You're still mad about the Sambo dolls."

"Shit, no. We're talking major evil here: a factory so terrible, people kill themselves rather than work in it; baby poison shipped to Third World countries. No wonder someone offed him."

"We don't know that," said Stewart.

"Well, I can tell you, if he isn't dead, *I'm* gonna off him."

"Way to go, Peace Officer," said Stewart. They crossed the Bay Bridge and worked their way through the Berkeley Hills. On the other side lay a park. You needed a pass to enter it. It was so secret, Homer bet not even the neighbors knew it was there. It certainly wasn't on the map. They drove up one of those long, golden California hills and parked in front of a high wall.

"Pretty well hidden," said Stewart. "How big would you say this place is?"

"Five acres? Ten? I don't know. I'm not a farm boy." Homer went to the gate, but it opened before he could ring the bell.

"Dr. Tsuga told me to expect you," said an old man in a gray kimono. He looked about eighty years old, but he moved with surprising briskness. The policemen followed him in. And then stopped.

And stared.

They looked for a long time, unable to speak. The scene that stretched out before them seemed to go on forever. There were hills and lakes, pines and maples, among which small houses were hidden. They were made of ribs of dark wood and paper panels: Japanese houses. The trees were Japanese, and so were the rocks. Probably the smell was, too. Homer couldn't identify it, but it was nice. The ground below was covered with a rolling mat of thick and springy green.

"Moss," said the old man. "We have four hundred varieties of moss in here, imported from Kyoto. Some people come just to look at that."

They followed him in a dream. Each corner revealed more corners; each path branched off to others. Bridges crossed noisy streams; strange birds called from the trees, threading their cries among the hollow rattle of bamboo wind chimes. And there was a wind, although the air outside had been perfectly still.

But the thing that drew their eyes, and as quickly dropped them by the sheer size and impossibility of it, was the mountain.

It rose in a graceful arc high above the groves of maple and pine. The lower slopes were dark basalt, but the top—Homer had to rub his eyes —was snow-tipped. There was only one kind of mountain that had such perfect, classical lines: a volcano.

"Origami Mountain," said the old gardener in a quiet voice.

"How—," began Homer, but he couldn't go on. There was no logical explanation. How could a five-acre park have a whole *mountain* in it, as well as forests, lakes, and houses?

"Gardening is a very old art in Japan," said the old man in answer to his unspoken question. "We are a small island and have many people, yet everyone wants to experience nature. It was absolutely necessary to develop Origami gardening."

He led them to an inn, where a pretty young girl ducked her head and brought them tea and cakes. "Originally, Westerners thought origami applied to paper folding. You take a large sheet of paper—" He signaled to the girl, and she brought him some. "You fold it here, here, and *here*, and suddenly you have a crane." He held it up. "Or a basket or a flower. But all the while, it is really a large piece of paper. Origami gardening goes the other way. A very small piece of land is *unfolded* until it contains all the natural beauty in the world. There aren't many men who know how to do this. We were lucky to get Mr. Fukuda."

Homer found his voice at last. "Mr. Fukuda did this?"

"Yes." The old man bit into what looked like a lump of Play-Doh. "You sip the tea, which is bitter, and taste the sweetened rice cake," he explained. "It's supposed to show you the inherent bitterness and sweetness of life."

"Where is Mr. Fukuda?" said Homer, refusing to get sidetracked.

"He's working on another park."

Homer sighed. "Have you seen Dr. Tanaka in the past week?"

"Of course."

The two policemen straightened up. Here at last was something to work on. They waited. "Would you care to tell us about it?" said Stewart.

"He came a week ago," said the gardener. "About dusk, which is when most people visit. He walked up there." He pointed at the serene, snow-tipped mountain.

"Was anyone with him?"

"Many people. Origami Mountain is very popular. Dr. Tanaka was with his factory workers. They started about dusk and came back after the moon rose. It's very nice to watch the moon rise from up there, and we provide paper lanterns at the top so visitors can find their way down."

"When they returned," said Homer patiently, "was Dr. Tanaka with them?"

"No," said the gardener.

"Well, what happened to him?" Homer was having difficulty keeping his voice down.

"Stayed up there, I imagine." The old man sipped his tea tranquilly, as though he hadn't dropped a bombshell on the two policemen.

"I think we have to look. Thank you for the tea," said Homer.

"Don't mention it," said the old gardener.

They followed the trail, curving around, but slowly working their way up. "It's five miles up this fucking mountain," puffed Stewart. "How the hell did they fit it in here?"

"Don't ask me. I can't even figure out my mileage," said Homer, equally tired. But he was fueled with a kind of anger. Damn these Japanese with their boxes within boxes. He felt as though they were playing with him, deliberately leaving clues for their own ends. Well, he would follow them out. He'd get to the center of their goddamn maze and find out what their game was.

They came around a boulder and almost fell into the crater. "Jesus H. Christ," said Stewart, swaying and hanging on to the boulder. They looked down into a pit of bubbling lava. Heat painted their faces with sweat. The reek of sulfur made them gasp.

"He came up with his faithful employees, but he didn't come down," said Homer.

"God," said Stewart, turning away from the searing heat.

They went down in silence. By the time they were at the bottom, it was dusk. People had come into the garden, many people: the workers of Jigoku Chemical Works. Families walked in quiet groups. Father, mother, and dull-eyed children. They weren't at all like the children of Jiro Tanaka.

"He gave Yum Powder to his employees," said Jimmy Tsuga, making the policemen jump. He was seated on a rock by the entrance. "They were his guinea pigs."

The old gardener sat next to him, a lump in the dusk not unlike one of the craggy rocks. "You should have stayed up there," he said. "Moonrise is late, but starlight is also very nice."

"Where is Mr. Fukuda?" said Homer.

"Making another park. We got a bargain this time, a whole square mile."

Homer paused cautiously. "Where?"

"Near Detroit. The land was going cheap."

The policemen looked at the two Japanese, sitting peacefully in the shadows. Behind him a breeze stirred, laden with the scent of unknown flowers and a hint of ice. "You could fit a whole country in that," he said at last.

"You could," said Jimmy Tsuga, and smiling, he opened the gate and showed the officers out.

RUBY LAUGHTER, TEARS OF PEARL

James Powell

The acclaimed mystery writer James Powell is becoming a regular in *The Year's Best Fantasy and Horror* volumes. His offbeat police-procedural-circus-story "A Dirge for Clowntown" was included in our third annual volume and also won the *Ellery Queen's Mystery Magazine* readers' poll as the best short story of the year. We reprinted his black humor Christmas tale "Santa's Way" in last year's volume.

"Ruby Laughter, Tears of Pearl" comes, like the previous stories, from *Ellery Queen's*. It is a delightful, luminous fairy tale reminiscent of the timeless, magical stories of G. K. Chesterton and James Thurber.

Enjoy.

—T.W.

On the day Princess Nicolodia was born the King ordered his brother-in-law to stand in the town square, blowing his bugle and handing out slices of bread and butter to the population. The King regretted that he couldn't do more but his was a poor kingdom. In fact, his subjects were slightly better off than he was. At least they could till their fields or tend their shops. But the King was expected to do nothing all day except practice good posture and solemnity. On top of that, he had to live in a drafty palace with a thatched roof and supply his own throne. The King often thought of throwing the whole thing over. But small and poor though the Kingdom was, it had been in his family for a long time. So he stayed, rather hoping the people liked it that way. And they rather did. It was nice having a king of their own, particularly one who never taxed them or sent them off to war. Besides, they knew that if this king went away another people's king would come and rule over them.

The people turned out for Princess Nicolodia's christening party armed with covered dishes, for they took pride in the fact that they never put the King out of pocket for ruling over them. For his part, the King smiled proudly at the baby, kissed his wife, the Queen, drank his share of cider, and danced in his wooden way with any woman who asked him. But all the while he kept an eye peeled for the fairy godmother who serviced the royal families locally. She liked to make her entrance in a flash of blue light, gift in hand. The King prayed it would be a silver christening mug that he could sell on the sly and have indoor plumbing installed in the palace. He feared it would be matching luggage.

But when the last of the fireworks had echoed from the hills, the fairy godmother still hadn't appeared. Hiding his disappointment, the King shook hands with the departing guests. Then he and his wife finished off what remained of the desserts and retired. Sometime after midnight they were awakened by a flash of blue light. There stood the fairy godmother, her pointed hat and the hoops of her hoopskirt askew, waving a leather, three-ring pocket organizer. "I had you people down for next week," she admitted sheepishly. "To make amends I guess I'll have to give Nicolodia the Biggie."

The King nodded, as if that was the most natural thing in the world. The Queen asked, "What's the Biggie?"

"You'll find out come her twelfth birthday," replied the fairy godmother. "Let's just say it's a gift so precious we only get one to give away." She waved the pocket organizer over the baby's crib. "There," she sighed. "Now I'm a lame-duck fairy godmother. When word gets out people will be taking their business elsewhere in droves."

"Suppose we just keep this our little secret?" suggested the King.

The fairy godmother flashed him a grateful smile, waved the pocket organizer again, and disappeared.

When Princess Nicolodia's twelfth birthday finally came around the kingdom had fallen on hard times. First a fungus called tapioca slime destroyed the turnip crop. Then a disease called turnip foot struck the tapioca trees. The tired, careworn faces of the people as they arrived for her birthday party touched the Princess's heart and she began to cry. To everyone's astonishment, her tears turned to pearls as they hit the ground. Now the people's gift was a house sparrow they had painted scarlet and edged its wings in gold, hoping the Princess would believe it was a Carpathian nightingale. The bird made Nicolodia laugh with delight, and when she did, rubies fell from her lips.

The amazed King assigned his brother-in-law the job of following the Princess about with a basket and picking up the pearls and rubies. Then he sat down with the royal councilors to decide what was to be done. The Sticks, as the conservative councilors came to be called, advised filling the royal coffers by giving the Princess daily beatings. The Feathers, or liberals, suggested regular tickling. But the King refused, saying, "Let her live a normal life, laughing when she's happy, crying when she's sad. Surely there's enough joy and sorrow in this life for our little kingdom's needs."

In fact, when news of the phenomenal Princess spread abroad Moody's rating service classified the kingdom Triple A, allowing the King to embark on an ambitious program of public works by borrowing money on anticipated joy and sorrow. He cobbled the streets and established an agricultural college with a special mandate to find a cure for tapioca slime and turnip foot.

As Princess Nicolodia approached marriageable age the sons of the neighboring kings began mooning around. Soon you couldn't throw a rock at the palace porch without drawing royal blood. For her part, the Princess found all this princely attention unsettling and couldn't look out the front window without getting the hiccups.

One day some sharp-eyed strangers calling themselves aluminum-siding salesmen rode into town. That night, while the King's brother-in-law slept curled up around his blunderbuss on the floor outside the Princess's bedroom door, the strangers slipped in by the window and kidnaped her.

The next morning the frantic King tracked the kidnapers' hoofprints out to the great crossroads on the edge of town where they took the turning that led to Bad Wolfstein. That walled city atop a peak in the Slag Mountains was home to the most rapacious people in all creation. City ordinances forbade street signs and public clocks so the natives could sell visitors directions and the time of day. It was the kind of place where people were supposed to be paying you a compliment if they stole your hat. And the sticky-fingered leader of this grasping community was Mr. Many-Pockets himself, His Honor Mayor Avaricious O'Greedy.

When the King told his people where the Princess had been taken they vowed to storm the city and rescue her. But he advised against it. Bad Wolfstein thrived on besieging armies. During the day, secure behind their walls, they would bundle up the arrows shot into the city for resale back to the enemy. At night, particularly just after the besiegers had a payday or received parcels from home, the Bad Wolfsteiners would slip out on crepe soles and steal anything in the enemy camp that wasn't nailed down. When winter came they prospered by selling the besiegers blankets and firewood. By spring the same army that had advanced up the mountain with bright battle flags and shining armor would creep back down again barefoot, bankrupt, and in burlap rags. "No," said the King, "I must put on the royal thinking cap and find some clever plan to rescue the Princess." To devote himself entirely to this purpose he appointed his brother-in-law king *pro tem.*

For the next few days the people watched the King walking about scratching his head. Then one afternoon they saw him stop in his tracks and pound a fist in the palm of his hand. After that he could only be seen early mornings coming back from the newsstand studying the *Wall Street Journal.* For the rest of the day he locked himself up in the music conservatory, an old armory whose walls the Queen had decorated with musical instruments. Soon the most ear-splitting caterwaul was coming from that end of the palace, as if every musical instrument had been rolled into one and then tormented with a sharp stick to the accompaniment of an interminable metallic clatter. This was followed by several weeks of screams and terrible noises like someone retching on a large tongue depressor.

Meanwhile the kingdom had fallen on hard financial times. The cobblestone supplier, faced with a long overdue account, came around with a crew to dig up the streets. The King might have soft-soaped the man out of it. But all his brother-in-law could think to do was bob and weave and challenge him to a fistfight, which he lost. The kingdom felt the humiliation deeply and stayed indoors until the cobbles had been carted away.

Finally the King announced he was ready to go to Bad Wolfstein and rescue his daughter. And he sent word to the porch crowd offering to put in a good word for any prince who joined him. But they declined, citing rude cabbies, the crosstown traffic, parking, and the high prices of everything. Only a young student named Swineherd stepped forward. Swineherd had fallen in love with the Princess, who'd been in his animal psychology class. But he'd never declared his love. How could a penniless commoner aspire to the hand of a princess with tears of pearl and ruby laughter?

So the King kissed the Queen goodbye. Then he and Swineherd loaded up the palace handcart with mysterious boxes and packages and set off. They hadn't gone far when they met a young boy named Jack leading a cow. Jack was on his way to be swindled at the Bad Wolfstein cattle market. Now the King happened to be carrying some magic beans dreamed up by the research and development boys at the agricultural college. When he suggested trading the magic beans for Jack's cow, the young boy agreed and turned homeward, delighted to save the shoe leather.

As the King and Swineherd continued on their way, the young man told his tragic story. One year his father, a forward-looking pig farmer, decided to get top dollar for his animals by herding them fifty miles to the railhead for shipment out East. The morning of the pig drive he'd opened the farmyard gate and, standing in his stirrups, he'd waved his broad-brimmed hat and called out, "Pigs yo-o!" In a shot, two thousand pigs were off and running every which way. Many reached the forest where the giant swill-berries grew. Enough found their way into neighborhood cook pots to make the air smell of pork and sauerkraut for weeks. Swineherd had come to agricultural college seeking the answer to the question his father, now a broken man, kept muttering to himself: "If we can't herd them, why in hell do they call us swineherds?" As Swineherd's story ended, the turrets of Bad Wolfstein were rising in the distance.

At the city gate the King and his young companion found that admission cost one chicken per person. The tollbooth man took the cow and gave them three chickens change. They were soon pushing the handcart down narrow, crooked streets through surly, jostling crowds.

"We'll never find her in a place like this," despaired Swineherd.

"Sure we will," said the King. "Trust me. I've thought this whole thing out."

Soon a hard rain began to fall. At the next tavern the King went inside and spoke to the owner. Then he and Swineherd pushed the handcart around to the back. "Figuring they'd be short on entertainers by now, I offered to be tonight's floor show," explained the King. "It'll get us our supper and a dry place to sleep." Then he took a concertina, a ukulele, two tambourines, a set of cymbals, and a harmonica out of the handcart, attaching them about his person with ingenious straps, harnesses, and rigs. The concertina, for example, he buckled between his knees. The cymbals he wore like a hat and clashed by means of springs and a pull chain.

"Can I be your assistant?" asked Swineherd, who was anxious to see the show.

"One-man bands don't have assistants," replied the King, strapping on a pair of roller skates. "Your job will come soon enough. For now just guard the chickens."

The King glided through the back door and into the smoky spotlight. The half-empty barroom greeted him with that particular groan reserved for one-man bands who tap dance on roller skates. But the King, knowing cutthroats and brigands were a sentimental lot, had tailored his act accordingly, ending with a sing-along including numbers like "Bad Wolfstein Must Be Heaven For My Mother Came From There" and "Carry Me Back to Old Bad Wolfstein (That's Where the Rotters and the Cons and Traitors Go)" that left the crying barflies clapping for more. As he skated from the floor it occurred to the King that he was probably the first of his line to sweat. Supper was thin soup and sour beer. But the next night a packed house and thunderous applause earned a thicker soup and a modest chablis.

Just as the food arrived, a short man in a shiny suit slid into the booth with the King and Swineherd and introduced himself as Max, a theatrical agent. "Caught your act," he said. "Not bad. Too good for this dump. Sign with me and I'll get you two weeks at the Plaza." When the King agreed, Max called for another spoon, ate ten percent of their soup, and hurried off about his business.

So the act opened at the Plaza. The next day, as the King read the sterling review in the *Morning Bugle*'s "Man About Bad Wolfstein" column, Swineherd sighed and said, "I wonder what Nicolodia's doing right now."

"Crying, I should think," said the King, turning the paper to the financial section. "Pearl values started on the skids about the time she was kidnaped. Now they're in a real tailspin. You can't even give pearls away." He gave the young man a comforting look. "I know all this waiting around's hard to take. But my plan's working. Didn't you see who caught the act last night? The big guy in the fake beard at the corner table."

"The one who stole the ashtray when he left?"

The King nodded. "O'Greedy himself."

"I don't get it."

"I said entertainers were in short supply," the King reminded him. "Doesn't that tell you something?"

Just then Max hurried in and asked the King, "Hey, can you do funny?"

"Can I ever," said the King.

"So here's the deal," said Max. "A certain party needs to be cheered up and kept that way. It's big bucks if we can do the job. On the down side, if we fail, I lose a client." To make his meaning clear Max chopped off an invisible head with the edge of his hand.

A carriage was waiting for them after the midnight show. The King rode in silence, sitting there in his one-man band outfit, staring into the darkness. Earlier he had instructed Swineherd to do all the talking. He had also ordered him to wear roller skates, too, and not to forget the chickens. The trip took them up and up many a steep street until they reached one that dead-ended at an old abandoned coopers' warehouse where wooden barrels had once been stored. At their knock the warehouse door opened and the King stepped through. But when Swineherd tried to follow he was grabbed by the shirt and lifted off his feet. A giant of a man with a battered head and ears and nose to match examined him by torchlight. "Now just who the hell are you?" he demanded in a cutthroat voice.

"I'm his assistant," gasped Swineherd.

The man tightened his grip a couple of turns and hissed, "One-man bands don't have assistants."

"He's been sick."

The man's mouth moved as though chewing over Swineherd's words. Then he demanded, "Why the chickens?"

"For the big finale," said Swineherd.

The man hurled Swineherd into the arms of the four burly ruffians guarding the King. Decked out in knives, swords, peg legs, eye-patches, and an occasional hook for a hand, this sinister crew frisked the new arrivals for weapons, then seized them by the elbows and rolled them up a series of ramps until they reached the fifth floor. More armed men joined them along the way, until their escort grew to twenty. The King smiled reassurances at his worried young companion as they were pushed into a large, windowless, high-ceilinged room lit and warmed by a small brazier in the middle of the floor. There, tied to a chair next to the fire, was the King's weeping daughter. As his eyes adapted to the gloom he saw the floor lay thick with pearls. In one corner, beside a burlap sack half filled with pearls, stood a broom and a dustpan, as if someone had tired of sweeping them up. In fact, the walls were stacked ceiling high with sacks of unmarketable pearls.

"If there's no profit in sorrow, we must try laughter," said the Mayor of Bad Wolfstein, who was sitting over to one side with an executioner's axe across his knees. O'Greedy was still wearing the full black beard of the night before, perhaps as protection against the chill in the air. "Of course, it's a no-lose situation for me," he continued. "Make the young lady laugh and I grow richer. Fail and I get to chop off your head. No big thrill, you say. True, but a damn cheap one. And I'm fond of cheap." O'Greedy signaled for more torches for the performance.

As the room filled with light, the Princess recognized her father and laughed with joy, adding rubies to the pearls at her feet. An amazed O'Greedy looked from the precious stones to the King and Swineherd and his jaw fell even more. The two unarmed men who stood before him a moment ago were now holding swords.

The King cocked his head apologetically while he gave his chest a dyspeptic rap with his fist. Yes, the one-man band who tap danced on roller skates had also mastered the ancient art of sword swallowing. Before the Mayor could sound the alarm, the King placed four roller-skate wheels in the middle of the man's chest and toppled him over backwards. O'Greedy's men laughed from the doorway, thinking it part of the act. They grinned as the King skated backwards in a circle around the room playing "Happy Days Are Here Again" on tambourine, harmonica, cymbals, and concertina, while behind his back he beat out the rhythm with his sharp sword on the bags of pearls along the walls. But when they saw Swineherd cut Nicolodia's bonds, O'Greedy's men rushed into the room just in time to be upended by the gush of pearls across the floor.

As the Mayor and his henchmen struggled to regain their footing and pearls hissed out onto the floor, the lower sacks sagged, setting those above to teetering. The King and Swineherd quickly skated the Princess out of the room and bolted the door behind them. At the top of the ramp the King introduced his daughter to Swineherd and explained why the young man had come. Then the King ordered her to hold the chickens and, turning his back, he tucked her knees under his arms while the young man grabbed her around the waist from behind. Then, bending at the knees like skiers, the two men went rolling downward with the Princess between them, picking up speed as each floor flashed by. But when they hit the top of the final ramp the King saw the doorkeeper. The man must have heard them coming. There he was planted sideways in the open doorway with a large club on his shoulder and his hindquarters wagging like Mudville's Casey, daring the human contraption on wheels to try to get by him. Suddenly the man's smile vanished, he dropped the club and vanished out the door. The King glanced back over his shoulder and uttered a royal curse. Rushing down the ramp close behind them was a three-foot-high wall of pearls. On top of it, riding the door to the fifth-floor room like a surfboard, was O'Greedy, his beard flowing out behind him, waving the executioner's axe.

The King, the Princess, and Swineherd passed through the open door and went careening down the steep cobblestone street in the moonlight. Behind them they heard the roar as the pearly mass burst through the warehouse door and came rolling after them, O'Greedy, door, and all. The King had anticipated the possibility of pursuit but nothing like this. All he could do was crouch more to reduce the drag. Down, down they went at a dizzying clip with the nacreous death at their heels until, at last, they reached the lower town on whose leveler streets the rushing tide of pearls started to lose momentum. So did the roller skates. But not O'Greedy. He shot ahead of the ebbing pearls, riding the door across the slick cobbles and coming on fast. Ahead the King could see the torches marking the city gate. Would they reach it in time? And even if they did, would that be enough to save them? "Skate, man! Skate like hell!" he shouted back at Swineherd. But they couldn't outrace O'Greedy. The man was breathing down Swineherd's neck. As they reached the gate the Mayor raised the executioner's axe.

"Quick, the chickens!" ordered the King as they entered the tollbooth's exact-change lane. His daughter tossed the chickens into the toll hopper. O'Greedy was right behind and halfway into his downswing with the axe when the tolltaker, not recognizing who was behind the fake beard, reached out an arm that stopped the Mayor dead in his tracks to demand another chicken.

A moment later something woke the children in the lower town and drew them to their bedroom windows. When they saw the streets shining with pearls in the moonlight, they rubbed their eyes in wonderment and called their parents. The parents came grumpily and, being up-to-date on such matters, went back to bed, scoffing, "Pearls, only pearls. There's no profit in pearls." But the children stayed at the window with their cheeks in their hands until the sun rose and the street cleaners came to wash the pearls away. But the children would never forget those pearls in the moonlight nor cease to marvel that something with no profit in it could be so beautiful.

As for Princess Nicolodia and Swineherd, they married, built a home, and started to raise a family. Happiness was the general state of affairs and the rubies fell thick and fast. They kept enough for their own modest needs and gave the rest to the King. Soon the town had been recobbled, the agricultural college expanded, and thanks to Moody's reinstated Triple A rating, an irrigation system constructed that brought water to every field in the kingdom. The King had just started drawing up plans for a convention center when oversupply kicked the bottom out of the ruby market.

One night at the dinner table as she passed her preoccupied husband the turnips, the Queen said, "A penny for your thoughts."

"I was just wondering what I'm going to tell the cobblestone man this time," said the King.

As he spoke his brother-in-law came in and, apologizing for being late, sat down and said, "Hey, leave the cobblestone man to me."

"How so?" asked the King.

"Remember back there when Nicolodia was having all those hiccups?" said his brother-in-law as he unfolded his napkin. "Didn't I ever show you those weird little things that popped out with every hic? The tiny rectangles with connected dots and lines on them? Well, I looked those little buggers up one way and down the other. Damned if I could figure out what they were for. So I said to myself, Brother-in-law, you're just going to have to build a machine these doohickeys'll fit into. And I did. It turned out to be a computer. They're computer chips."

"Ah," said the King, as though that was the most natural thing in the world.

"What's a computer?" asked the Queen.

"Damned if I know," said the brother-in-law. "Nobody'd ever built one before. But our worries are over. I got some Japanese businessmen talking big bucks."

The King smiled and cocked his head. Life was certainly strange. There was no profit in pearls or rubies or in joy or sorrow, for that matter. But hiccups, it looked like hiccups were a different story.

I SING OF A MAIDEN
Judith Tarr

Judith Tarr is the author of numerous lyrical fantasy and intelligent historical novels, including *A Wind in Cairo*, *Ars Magica*, *The Dagger and the Cross*, and most recently, *Lord of the Two Lands*. Until recently a teacher of classics and creative writing at Wesleyan University in Connecticut, Tarr has joined the exodus of writers and book people to Tucson, Arizona, where she trains her Lippizan horse and writes full-time.

Tarr has a degree in classics from England's Cambridge University and a Ph.D. in medieval studies from Yale University. Both of these disciplines' influences are evident in the following tender fantasy tale from the holiday anthology *The Magic of Christmas*.

—T.W.

Quiet.

A cold that not quite touched the bone.

Light soft through the fretwork of stone so old and so worn with the touch of hand and body and the moving air that they seemed as fragile as carvings in snow. Stars on the vaulting within the chapel, in a sky faded to dusk from midnight, but the gilding bright still, each star in its ring of fallow gold, close enough, almost, for one to touch; almost to hold in the hand.

Somewhere a child was singing, high and impossibly sweet.

> *I sing of a maiden that is makeless:*
> *King of all kings to her son she ches. . . .*

I sat just out of the, light, listening. I was alone, but not lonely. I had myself for company, and a pad on which I had been sketching the pillars that surrounded the chapel: each different, each with its own character, but all together holding up the enormous weight of the cathedral. It was solid over me. Comforting.

The thread of singing faded. The quiet was deeper after, so deep that I heard my own heart beating. My feet were cold. I was hungry. Elizabeth would have tea when I came back, scones and jam and cream and chatter. She never understood what I saw in quiet, least of all in the Undercroft—the crypt, she called it, with a shudder for effect.

Not that it was quiet I loved, so much as timelessness. If I could be alone, and feet and voices and clatter and trampling shut away above, I could just be, and be out of time. No questions. No histories. I had enough of both, where I came from. Here I wanted to be still.

One of the shadows moved. I frowned at it. This was hardly my place, let alone my cathedral, but I had been happy with my solitude.

It was only one of the priests. I was on nodding terms with most of them, but this one I hadn't seen before. He seemed startled to see me. I nodded, a bit frostily. He didn't nod back. I looked pointedly down at my sketchpad. When I looked up he was gone.

He had spoiled my mood. I gathered my things together and braced to face the world above, and Elizabeth.

"Shortish man?" she asked me round a mouthful of scone. "Fairish? Going bald on top? And not Father Dunstan? But you know him, you met when you first came, and he wanted to talk about transubstantiation, and you were really rather rude."

"I don't discuss theology with strangers," I said. She knew that perfectly well. "No, I know who that is. This was someone else. Maybe he's new; or here for the season."

"Perhaps," said Elizabeth, but darkly. Elizabeth knows everything and everyone, in and out of Canterbury. I expected that she would have his entire life's history by morning, with references, and signed by the archbishop himself. Elizabeth is a far better historian than I. Thorough; and completely without scruples.

I told her so. She sniffed. "And what would I do, tramping about and digging up old bones? I've enough to do here with looking after you."

Like a hen with one chick, I was careful not to say. Elizabeth takes in guests and makes them family, will they or nill they, but they were thin on the ground this year and this season: the grey shank of December and every sensible pilgrim safe at home where he belonged, waiting for April and its famous showers. In April I would be home again, writing the book I was supposed to be researching here—though germinating was a better word for it. Burying it deep and refusing to think about it, and letting it grow on its own.

"Have another scone, do," said Elizabeth, used by now to my silences. "You know they don't keep."

Elizabeth had told me that they were thinking of building a new altar in the cathedral: in the corner everyone comes to and pauses at, where Thomas Becket was murdered. It was just itself now, a stretch of pavement worn smooth, a few words set in the wall, the name and the date and what was done there, and if you turned one way you went out into the cloister, but if you turned the other you found the steps leading up, and the tombs that flanked the choir. Someone was always shrieking at the old bishop in his finery on top, and the rotting corpse carved so carefully below; or calling to someone else to see Henry IV, and was it Part One or Part Two; or galloping off across the cathedral to see the dead prince with his armor hung above his tomb. Thomas, of course, was gone, tomb and bones and gold and jewels and pilgrims and all. Cromwell saw to that. Cromwell is the Devil in English cathedrals; everything lost or broken is Cromwell's fault.

Thomas at least was someone else's fault. Four knights, and a king who wanted him got rid of. A clot of people had just gone through with one of the guides, and I'd had the story all over again, Murder in the Cathedral, but here, and—if I tilted my mind just so—now. Shut out the hereandnow with its noises and sillinesses, postcards on sale in the nave and schoolchildren running wild in the chapels. Forget the cathedral that they built on top of the cathedral, turn Bell Harry Tower, all the exuberant height of him, to air and nothing, go back before High Gothic into low rounded Romanesque; and then, for broad daylight, make it night, set knights in the shadows, the gleam of a sword, the chink of mail under the surcoat; a monk cowering, just there, and milord archbishop coming out to his prayers, no suspicion of murder or mayhem—a sword rising—a voice—

The wall was cold against my back, even through my coat. This time I'd seen it almost clear. Almost, even, smelled it: unwashed bodies, blood, iron, and something cold, that maybe was murder.

He was there again. Staring again. Jolting me out of my mood. Standing up, I was almost as tall as he was. He was younger than I'd thought, and he seemed to be trying to grow a beard, or else he'd forgotten to shave that morning. He looked less startled than he had before. I half expected him to ask me if I was ill.

He didn't say anything. Without really knowing why, I tried a smile. After a bit he smiled back.

The voice was singing as it had before, from everywhere and nowhere.

> *He came all so still where his mother was,*
> *As dew in April that falleth on the grass. . . .*

I turned to see where it was coming from. There was no one in sight. One of the children must have got into the choir, and his keeper gone running to stop him. I was sorry. He had a better voice than most of the choristers.

The priest, when I turned back, was gone. Shy, I thought. Or glad of an excuse to escape. People never properly understood why I had to do my time-traveling in broad daylight, let alone in public. Not that it was anything I could help, sometimes, when I was in the throes of something new; even something so new it had no name yet, just was.

I came out of the cathedral into sunlight that was surprising, even knowing it had been there, turning all the windows to floods of jeweled light. It was cold for England, like the New England I came from, and everyone was out in it, jostling one another along the walks and clumping under the gate of the close. The streets beyond were full of them. The shops were all lit with lights, a bit wan in the sun, and twinings of holly and ivy, balsam and fir, round the edges of windows and doors. When the doors opened I heard snatches of music, tinny with distance.

> *The holly and the ivy,*
> *When they are both full grown:*

Of all the trees that are in the wood,
The holly bears the crown.

Pagan enough for a Christian holiday. It made me smile. Elizabeth had put up holly on the mantel, and had brought out the box of ornaments for the tree she insisted we would have, and the Pudding—just so she said it: the Pudding, with a capital—was made and wrapped away in the pantry to age, and she had ordered the goose for a proper Dickensian feast. I wondered if I would have dreams, the night before Christmas, Past and Present and To Come, and a rebuke for having my holiday alone on the other side of the water, and not in my family's bosom. Being alone and happy was a much worse sin than time-traveling in public. Time-traveling was merely eccentric. Happy solitude was unthinkable.

Old Canterbury is big as medieval towns go, but that's small still inside the newer city. Even now I was surprised to see how soon I came to the wall. I stopped as I always did, to lay a hand on it: rounded flints, translucent blue-grey and chalky white. They were cold today in spite of the sun, with winter in them, but if I had had steel, I could have struck fire. I went up into a shock of sudden wind. Cars roared on the road below, where the moat was once, whipping round and past the station. I leaned on a crenel. A dog ran past me, with a child in yelling pursuit. Over beyond them the ruined castle stood on its mound. Precious little of it was left; it had been little enough when it stood.

It was all one. Cars and railroads, children and dogs, old castle and old walls and young-old cathedral standing over them all. Like the song of the Maiden: the words were ancient, but the music was a hundred years old, if that; and yet they went together.

"The Worm Ouroboros," I said, "that biteth his own tail."

I would get a book out of this, one way and another. Lectures, too. Classes. Wherewithal for traveling in time. Scientists were going about it all wrong, putting numbers on it, measuring it. They would do better to ask a Zen Master. Or a dotty American writer lady on the wall in Canterbury, grinning at the wind.

He came all so still where his mother lay,
As dew in April that falleth on the spray.

"Why April?" I asked.

There was no one to answer. And no one to sing, either; not out here, not so clear.

St. Augustine's abbey lay in ruins around me. I stood by the grave of a Saxon king, though maybe his bones were long gone; his ghost was, for all I knew, but if I closed my eyes I could hear the monks moving in the cloister and chanting in the choir.

This was too clear to be imagination, even as vivid as mine was, but too odd to be anything but a trick of the ear.

"April for spring," said someone behind me. Or I thought he said. His accent was very strange; thick as any Yorkshireman's, but crisper, with something almost familiar about the vowels. "April for the green things growing, and the new world springing."

"But we sing it in December," I said.

"Holly is green beneath the snow," he said, "and ivy."

I turned to see the priest from the cathedral. He was wrapped in a dark cape, with what looked like fur around the edges, and he was smiling at me. But when he looked around, his smile died. "It's all gone," he said.

I shouldn't have laughed. It was too much like the scholar, seeing Athens for the first time in his old age, and appalled because it was in ruins.

"Henry did that," I said to the priest, "though sometimes they blame it on Cromwell."

"Henry?" the priest asked. "But—" He closed his eyes. I thought he was going to faint; I reached to catch if he went over.

He slipped away before I could touch him. I was dizzy myself. Seeing for a moment, hearing, feeling the walls around me, the monks in their day's round, the ordered commotion of a great abbey.

"Our Henry would never break this place," said the priest.

I stared at him. If I made my eyes wide, the dizziness stopped, for a while. "Who are you?" I asked suddenly.

"My father named me Thomas," he said, "but they call me Mad Tom, and Thomas the Alchemist, though what I would want with Hermes when I have Aristotle and Aquinas, none of them can say."

"My mother named me Madeleine," I said, "and that's cross enough to bear, if I hadn't been an oddity, too." I squinted. It made me dizzier, but he barely blurred. "You are a figment of my imagination."

He looked down at himself. He was not, after all, bald on top. He was tonsured. I had known it, of course. I was even giving him a properly antique accent, though my ingenuity failed when it came to giving him the vocabulary.

"I'm only what I am," he said.

"You're not there," I said. "You didn't walk out of—what? Fifteen-something? I imagined every bit of you."

"I dreamed you, I think," he said, "and ruins—there's a black dream for a black winter."

"You don't exist," I said. And swung out my hand to prove it.

It met air. He was gone. It was cold in the ruined abbey, by the old king's grave. From the look of the sky, it was going to rain.

I knew I should tell Elizabeth that there was no such priest as I'd described; she hated to hunt and find no quarry, and here I'd sent her after a ghost. But when it came time to tell her, over the chop and the nice bit of sweet, as she put it, that constituted supper, I said nothing after all. It was embarrassing, for one thing. For another, I was not quite willing to let him go. I'd never had a hallucination so real before, real enough to talk to.

Writers will tell you that their characters talk to them. And so they do. Incessantly. But even the most insistent of characters seldom stands up in front of his author, as solid as herself, and real right down to the razor's nick on his chin. I hadn't been glad when my hand passed through air. I'd been bitterly sorry.

And suppose, I thought. Suppose . . .

*   *   *

I should have known what good it would do to try calling him up. Characters haunt you without mercy, or they shut themselves up in a hard cold block and refuse to come out for any bribery. When I tried to write this one down, he fell flat as cardboard. When I drew him, he stretched into a cartoon. When I stood in the ruined abbey and imagined him with every vein a-pop, he didn't even flicker into being. He was not *my* character. I had no story in which he fit, except the one I lived in.

Suppose he was, then. Suppose he was real.

If time were as fluid as that—if I could imagine, but what I imagined could be— why shouldn't he have walked out of it? He dreamed, he'd all but said. He was dreaming me.

In Chartres there is a circle on the floor, a maze set in the stone. They say that if you walk in on the solstice day, and come to the middle, time stops. Now and then are one. And where the sun's ray falls through the rose window's center, just there, you can reach through. You can touch.

Canterbury is a maze of its own. The city is a circle, and the streets tangle in it, and the cathedral sits in the center. I, sitting under it, under the stars in Our Lady's chapel, had no sun to show me the way, but the candles were bright enough. I hadn't thought till I came there, that it was the solstice. I wasn't thinking that anything would come of it. I wanted the quiet, that was all.

> *He came all so still to his mother's bower,*
> *As dew in April that falleth on the flower.*

I looked at the figure by the altar. "Were you trying to call me up?" I asked.

At the same time he said, "Did you summon me?"

I shook my head. He shook his. I didn't leave my chair, though it was a beastly thing: one of those wooden folding monstrosities that churches issue as a penance. He didn't leave the altar. He might have been taking sanctuary on it.

"It's the song," I said. "It's the key. But if you aren't singing it . . ."

"I wished to see," he said. "But I've spoken no spells. I'm no magus; no alchemist, either. I read, you see. And think. Thinking's a sin, I'm told."

"So it is." I shifted in the chair. My tailbone was aching. "Maybe you thought yourself right into ghosthood."

He crossed himself. He was hundreds of years dead, if he'd ever lived at all, but I couldn't help it; I thought of him as young, and younger every time I saw him. "I am no dead man," he said sharply, almost angrily. "Are you a dead woman?"

"Not that I've noticed," I said.

"So," he said. He sat down on the altar step. His shoes, I noticed, were quite in period. Fifteenth century, the historian in me said. They needed mending. He had lice, very likely, and bathed in summer if at all. His teeth were dreadful.

He was quite beautiful, if he was real, and sitting there, and talking to me.

I should be asking him questions. Discovering truths scholars dreamed of. Finding answers to questions, solving mysteries, being the historian I pretended to be.

I said, "I read a story once. Of lonely people, and traveling in time, and finding a place where everyone can be content. It was France, I think. Villon was dead."

He didn't ask me who that was. "I'm not lonely. I like to be alone. It's peaceful. It lets me work."

"It gives me leave to pray," he said, "and think. I'm made for the cloister, maybe; but I do love to walk the roads, and go on journeys for my lord archbishop, and be a pilgrim. One day I'll go to Jerusalem."

"I've been," I said.

His eyes lit up. His breath came out in a long sigh. "Tell me!"

I told him. Then he told me of walking from Canterbury to Dover, and taking ship across the Channel, and walking down through France to Chartres. He shivered. "That is no Christian place," he said, "however holy the church that stands on it."

"Did you walk the labyrinth?" I asked.

His answer was slow. "Yes. I saw nothing. I was mazed, no more, from walking round and round."

"I was sick and had to leave," I said. "Maybe it worked after all, and I never knew it."

"Maybe God willed that we meet, however strange the meeting." He wrapped his arm about his knees. "Need there be a reason in it?"

"Well," I said. "No." I stood up. He didn't move as I came closer. He looked as solid as the cathedral, and as real. "Do you know when I am?" I asked him.

"Not past," he said, "but to be." He wasn't afraid. He wasn't an innocent, either. People grew up faster where he was, and grew up harder. "You could be a demon," he said, "but were you that, this place would never hold you."

"You're very calm about it."

"I've thought on it," he said, "and prayed. I'd talk to my confessor, but he'd not understand. He's a good man, Father Dickon. But narrow. He'd say that we were never meant to see but what our eyes can see, or know but what the simplest man can know."

"So much for theology," I said.

He laughed. "So women dispute in the schools. And do stags swim in the sea, and fish fly?"

"Men fly," I said, "and women, too. We've walked on the moon."

He didn't believe me. "And my abbey is a ruin," he said when he'd finished laughing at me. "That's grief. But this still stands. This is the same." His eyes took in the chapel, and the crypt beyond it. "The world is still as it was, and as it always shall be."

"It does change," I said. "Some things are worse. Some are much better."

"It's the world still," he said, "and God is king of it."

Who was I to question faith? Or, for that matter, to touch a ghost. This time it was I who left him. I wasn't thinking while I did it, or wondering why. I wanted to be away, alone. I wanted to think. Prayer wasn't in me; we'd lost that. Or I had.

Elizabeth had the radio on, turned up high and bellowing out choruses. I came in in a thunder of *Hallelujahs*, through a fog of cloves and cinnamon: she'd been doing the pies, and singing with the choir. We'd have a dozen for dinner, come Christmas Day, and the weather was turning cold; snow, maybe, the radio said when the last *Hallelujah* was over.

"Snow at Christmas," said Elizabeth. "Imagine that."

I captured a bowl and a knife, and started to peel apples. "We have snow most years, at home," I said. "It doesn't feel like Christmas without it."

The radio was singing in German.

> Es ist ein' Ros entsprungen,
> Auf einer Würzel zart. . . .

" 'Lo, how a rose e'er blooming, From tender stem hath sprung.' " Elizabeth had a lovely voice, thin but clear. A little like the voice that sang me out of time. She attacked a round of dough with the roller, odd punctuation to so tender a song.

"Christmas songs are always about spring," I said, "and flowers."

"There are winter ones, too," said Elizabeth. "All the Noëls. And 'Silent Night.' "

"And 'Good King Wenceslas.' " I cut an apple in half, and then in quarters, and cored it. "He wasn't good at all, you know. He was an appalling despot."

"It's a lovely song," Elizabeth said.

I cut the apple in careful slices. One tempted me. I ate it. It was sweet: English apples are, not like American apples, which are more sour than not. "That's it, isn't it? It's not what he was, but how he's remembered. Would it be different if you could talk to him?"

"He's dead," said Elizabeth. "And good riddance if he was a bad king."

"Somewhere he's not dead. Somewhere he's alive."

"In hell, no doubt," Elizabeth said. She scooped up apples and began to fill the crust.

"Still," I said. "What if he were?"

"Are you going to write a book about him?"

I looked at the apple in my fingers, and at Elizabeth. I sighed. "I don't suppose I could talk you into putting cinnamon in this?"

"That's heretical," she said.

"American," I said.

"Didn't I just say so?"

I peeled the apple. She made the pie without cinnamon, but then she made another one with: orthodoxy and heresy, side by side. She didn't ask me again about the book. I didn't know that I was writing one. Living one, maybe. And trying too hard. Forgetting how to be, and be quiet, and let it come as it would.

The best gifts are the ones that came unasked for. Real or imagined, Thomas was that: a gift. A reward for my silence, or a rebuke for my solitude—did it matter which? I wanted to see him again. I didn't want to ask him anything, or to know anything but that he was there. A serious failing in a scholar, but I couldn't help it. It wasn't what he knew that mattered. It was that he was.

Nights are long in England, in the dark of the year. They fall early, and they fall deep. The night before Christmas was grey and raw, with an iron tang that promised snow. By the time we'd brought in the tree and set it up, the first flakes were falling. When the lights were on and lit, it was falling hard, and yet it fell in silence except for the whining of the wind. The radio was excited, and scared, too. England has grown out of the habit of snow. I was glad that our dozen guests would come in by train, come morning, or could walk in from the town.

The roads wouldn't be passable, I didn't think, if the snow went on as it had begun.

All that evening the carolers came and went, making the rounds of the town. We had sweets for them, and hot rum, and mulled wine—hippocras, I called it, and Elizabeth wanted to know what was hypocritical about good burgundy. She forgave me for laughing, eventually.

Near midnight we wrapped ourselves up and put on our wellies in proper English style, and went to the cathedral. The snow blinded us; the wind whipped us raw. We pressed through it, laughing at it. This night of all nights, it was right and proper.

The cathedral blazed with light, throbbed with music. The choir was in the stalls, the nave full almost to bursting. We found a place well to the side, near Becket's deathplace. I felt no death there tonight. We were a little out of the light, but the singing was clear, filling the high vaulted space.

> *Rejoice! Rejoice! Emmanuel*
> *Shall come to thee, O Israel.*

Elizabeth leaned away from me, exchanging greetings with a woman whom I vaguely recognized. I, on the end, could be by myself and simply listen. I was warm, even with snow melting on my hat and trying to run down my neck. The light was soft here, pale gold. All the crowds of people were only, like the snow and the wind, as they ought to be. So had they been for a thousand years and half a thousand more, more or less, since this faith came to Britain. And maybe before in this holy place, but for another child, and for another Lady, maiden-mother-crone, woman and goddess. Her chapel was under my feet. They were singing of her now. *Nova, nova, 'Ave' fit ex Eva!* And, softer:

> *Mother and maiden, was never none but she;*
> *Well might such a Lady God's mother be.*

The light was no dimmer, the air no colder, but the walls around me were narrower, the tower lower, the press of people closer. I was on my feet. I'm not tall, but I was tall here, as women went.

I was here, and I was there in the higher, brighter, newer-older place, I was in both worlds at once, both times. Sitting next to Elizabeth, hearing the mass as the Church of England sang it. Standing among faces I did not know, hearing the older chants, the music of Rome as yet unchallenged. And standing, sitting, kneeling through a whirl of memory-made-real, back and back and back, down to the beginning, and cold earth underfoot and cold sky overhead and the priestess singing of another faith altogether.

Someone stirred on my left hand. Someone breathed, drawn in sharp. I reeled dizzily in one time of the many, steadying my eyes on Thomas's face. I was still aware, as dim as the edge of a dream, that I sat beside Elizabeth. And stood beside him, close enough to touch.

And knowing. That was the last of the song, the hymn of the Maiden. Its round was done. Its magic was ended.

The woman next to me, who wore a stranger's face, shifted her weight. She jostled me. I almost fell. She had touched me. I was here. It was real. My nose told me. We had forgotten what the human animal was like, we fanatics of soap and the bath.

It didn't matter. I was *here*. The light was all candlelight. The faces were faces out of a book of hours, or from a tapestry.

Thomas stared at me. His face was full of wonder; but full of sadness, too. Was he sorry he had dreamed me into being?

"No," he said when I said it. Stretching out his hand. I stretched mine to meet it. The closer they came, the slower they moved.

I was not thinking of realities. There were times for that. For recalling when this was, what plagues were in it, what hope there could be for a woman out of time, or for a priest with, it seemed, a gift for calling up demons. I was here. I had done what I had always dreamed of doing: made all times one, and stepped out of my own, and seen another world.

Our hands met. His was warm and strong, and rougher than I had expected. Maybe mine was as odd to him, and yet as familiar. Would he have expected claws after all, or a cloven hoof?

"Stay," he said suddenly. "Stay with me."

I looked at him. "What would I do here?"

"Be," he said.

"Is it so simple?"

He shrugged. It was an eloquent gesture; hardly English at all. English as I knew it. "God sent you to me. Surely He wills you to stay."

"Or," I said, "maybe not God, but another Lady altogether."

"Aye," he said, "well. And doesn't He always listen to His mother?"

The procession was coming down the aisle in a cloud of light and frankincense, the prelates in their vestments, the acolytes in their lace and sackcloth, the princes in their finery. I should crane, I should stare; I should struggle to see faces that no one living had seen.

No one living when I was born.

My eyes stayed on Thomas, seeing the rest about the edges. There was no blurring in it, no shadow of a world that would be. I was here entirely, body and mind.

And yet.

My fingers tightened on his; then pulled free. "You were a gift," I said, "and welcome beyond measure. But you belong here, and I belong there. This time can't hold us both, except for this hour, on this night when all times meet."

"If you will not stay here, then I shall go there," he said. "I should like to see what the world is, so far away from this."

"What would you do there?"

"Be." He laughed at my expression. "Will you take me to Jerusalem?"

"I can't—"

He had my hand again, holding fast. The heat of his wanting was fierce enough to burn.

"Why?" I asked him.

"For that it is a gift. For that I prayed, and you answered my prayer. For that it can be, and I would have it."

"You'll hate it," I said. "You'll be all out of time."

He shook his head. Wise, innocent, stubborn boy. I was dizzy. Slipping. Struggling to pull free. Or maybe to hold fast.

The choir—his choir—raised bright voices up to heaven.

> *Dum puella fecundatur, O, O:*
> *Eia! Eia! Nova gaudia!*

Their singing blurred and shrank and faded, and flooded back in a measure wholly new.

> *Joy to the world! The Lord is come.*
> *Let earth receive her king. . . .*

I was not thinking of kings. I was thinking of explanations. I could not say that I cared, much. The hand in mine was as warm and strong as ever, and barely a tremor in it. His eyes were enormous, taking it all in, drinking it deep.

There were explanations, of course. And complications. We got round them, one way and another, Elizabeth and Thomas and I. Elizabeth never did need to know how the poor man had lost his passport, or why he came in fancy dress, and not a penny to his name. Sometimes I thought that she knew everything, and only pretended to believe the story we told. She was happy enough, God knew, to see me with a friend, as she put it, however odd he was.

But all of that came later. First there was Christmas day, and snow if not quite up to the rafters then deep enough to wonder at, and a dozen of us to dinner, and one for whom all this world was new. True Thomas, I thought, Thomas out of world and time, secure in his Lady's hand.

"Don't question," he said, precisely when I forget: the wine had been good, the wassail plentiful, and we were all singing between tree and fire, and the snow still falling outside.

I glared at him. "I was happy," I said, "alone."

"So was I," he said. "Before."

"You're a priest," I said.

He shook his head, tonsure and all; and we'd spun a wild tale to explain that, and they'd believed it, because we dared them to. "Minor orders, only, and at my family's bidding. My true love was a book and a dream. Now look!" His hand swept the room. "More books here than I've seen in my lord archbishop's own library, and you call them few, and paltry. More world than I could have imagined, and more wonders in it, and all for my tasting."

"Some, you won't like," I said. But it was hard to stay sour with him grinning at me. The bath had been a battle and a half. The dentist, next. And a doctor. And . . .

He didn't care. Why should I? Gifts were for giving, I'd always been taught. And for accepting.

*   *   *

The snow fell, soft and deep. The guests left by ones and twos, except the one who would stay, tucked up in the second-best room. Quiet fell. No voice sang in it. No voice needed to. That song was done, that silence filled; that gift given, in the end and in the beginning, out of life and out of time, and into both again.

Worm that biteth his own tail.

Et in saecula saeculorum.

So mote it be.

ALSO STARRING
Cliff Burns

Cliff Burns is a young writer who lives in the Canadian Arctic. He has published more than seventy short stories in small press magazines, including *EOTU*, *The Silver Web*, and *Midnight Graffiti*.

"Also Starring" is a brief offbeat tale of modern urban life that comes from the Canadian speculative fiction anthology *Tesseracts* (Volume IV).

—T.W.

At precisely 11:00 A.M. (PDT) a man who looked like Harry Dean Stanton entered a Savings and Loan on Wilshire, waved a pistol at a cashier and demanded money, as much as she could stuff in the brown paper bag he gave her. Once this was done he backed toward the door, saluted jauntily to the closed-circuit cameras mounted overhead and made his escape.

The staff film buff immediately identified him. The cops who responded to the alarm were skeptical. Still, they did some checking and learned that the actor was on location, costarring in the new David Lynch film which was wrapping up six weeks of shooting in Gainesville, Florida. The plot of the movie was not immediately known but when pressed the publicist admitted that Stanton played the role of a depraved armed robber. All agreed that it was an interesting coincidence.

Less than a week later a Wilford Brimley look-alike held up a jewelry store. It was strictly a smash and grab job but it was carried out with homespun perfection. Someone recognized him from his cereal commercials. The actor was briefly detained but his manager and a photographer provided convincing alibis.

It was clear that a pattern was developing. A man impersonating fine character actors was on a crime spree. A team of detectives was assigned to the case which was given top priority by their superiors. A spokesperson promised quick results.

The police gained the complete cooperation of the Screen Actors' Guild and its counterparts. They investigated dozens of disgruntled actors, professional makeup people and wannabees. Acting on a tip, they staked out Paramount Pictures.

Two days later Maureen Stapleton knocked over a 7-Eleven.

The city was in an uproar. Edward Herrmann and Joe Pesci were accosted on the street. Both had to be hospitalized for their injuries. It was reported that Michael J. Pollard had gone into hiding for his own protection.

The major studios hired extra security personnel. New copyright laws were enacted which made the impersonation of famous figures punishable by hefty fines and jail terms. Several distraught drag queens committed suicide. Rich Little declared personal bankruptcy.

Then, a break.

A man reportedly a dead ringer for Ned Beatty was seen loitering outside an exclusive men's clothing store in Bel Air. A swarm of police officers converged on the scene, cordoned off several city blocks. The real Mr. Beatty was located in San Francisco.

The imposter somehow became alerted to the presence of police, dashed across the street and disappeared into a throng of curious onlookers. Unfortunately he emerged as Charlotte Rampling, accent and all. He was ordered to halt and was shot several times while attempting to remove something—later identified as a compact—from a small, stylish purse.

As the imposter lay dying, ringed by police and bystanders, there were no clever parting words, no glib one-liners like "top of the world, ma!" or even "the horror, the horror."

Many marveled at how he stayed in character to the very end, batting those lovely lashes, pursing those thin, sensuous lips and expiring with grace and aplomb.

Like Charlotte would have.

ON EDGE

Christopher Fowler

Christopher Fowler lives in London and runs a film promotional company and a movie development company. He has published three novels, *Roofworld*, *Rune*, and *Red Bride* and has recently finished a fourth, *Darkest Day*. He is also the author of three story collections, *City Jitters*, *City Jitters 2*, and *The Bureau of Lost Souls*.

A warning: Visit your dentist *before* you read "On Edge." This is probably the most unpleasant story in this volume. William Goldman's novel *Marathon Man* and its movie version have nothing on the following twisted little piece of horror, which originally appeared in *Dark Voices 4*.

—E.D.

A brazil nut, thought Thurlow, of all the damned things. That'll teach me. He leaned back tentatively in the plastic chair and studied the posters which had been taped to the walls around him.

CONFIDENTIAL HIV TESTING.

UNWANTED PREGNANCIES.

MIND THAT CHILD HE MAY BE DEAF.

He thought; no wonder people avoid coming here. Sitting in the waiting room gave you a chance to consider your fate at leisure. He checked his watch, then listened. From behind a distant door came the whine of an electric drill. Determined to blot the sound from his brain, he checked through the magazines on the table before him. Inevitably there were two battered copies of *The Tattler*, some ancient issues of *Punch* and a magazine called *British Interiors*. With the drill howling faintly at the back of his brain, he flicked idly through the lifestyle magazine. A pied-à-terre in Kensington decorated in onyx and gold. A Berkshire retreat with a marble bas-relief in the kitchen depicting scenes from *The Aeneid*. The people who lived in these places were presumably drug barons. Surely their children occasionally knocked over the bundles of artfully arranged dried flowers, or vanished into priest's holes to be lost within the walls?

As he threw the magazine down in disgust the drill squealed at a higher pitch, suggesting that greater force had been used to penetrate some resistant obstacle.

A damned brazil nut. Next time he'd use the crackers instead of his teeth. God, it hurt! The entire molar had split in half. Torn skin, blood all over the place. He was sure there was still a piece of nutshell lodged between the gum and the tooth, somewhere deep near the nerve. The pain speared through his jaw like a white-hot knife every time he moved his head.

The receptionist—her name was something common that he never quite caught—had sighed when she saw him approach. She had studied her appointment book with a doubtful shake of her head. He had been forced to point out that, as a private patient, his needs surely took precedence over others. After all, what else was the system for? He had been coming here regularly for many years. Or to put it more accurately, he had arranged appointments in this manner whenever there was a problem with his teeth. Apparently Dr. Samuelson was away on a seminar in Florida, so he'd be seeing someone new, and he might have to wait a while. With the pain in his tooth driving him crazy, Thurlow didn't mind waiting at all.

There were two other people in the room. He could tell the private patient at a glance. The woman opposite, foreign-looking, too-black hair, too much gold, obviously had money. The skinny teenaged girl in jeans and a T-shirt had Council House written all over her. Thurlow sniffed, and the knife rocketed up into his skull, causing him to clutch at his head. When the pain had subsided once more to a persistent dull throb, he examined his watch again. He'd been sitting here for nearly forty minutes! This was ridiculous! He rose from his seat and opened the door which led to the reception desk. Finding no one there, he turned into the white tiled corridor beyond. Somebody would have to see him if he kicked up a fuss.

In the first room he reached, an overweight woman was pinned on her back with her legs thrown either side of the couch while the dentist hunched over her, reaching into her mouth like a man attempting to retrieve keys from a drain. In the second room he discovered the source of the drilling. Here, an exhausted teenaged man gripped the armrests of the chair with bony white knuckles while his dentist checked the end of the drill and drove it back into his mouth, metal grinding into enamel with the wincing squeal of a fork on a dry plate.

"You're not supposed to be back here, you know."

Thurlow turned around and found a lean young man in a white coat looking crossly at him.

"I've been waiting for nearly an hour," said Thurlow, feeling he had earned the exaggeration.

"And you are . . . ?"

"Mr. Thurlow. Broken tooth. I was eating a brazil nut . . ."

"Let's not discuss it in the corridor. You'd better come in."

Thurlow would have been annoyed by the brusqueness of the dentist's manner had he not heard the upper class inflections in his voice, and noted the smart knot of his university tie. At least this way he would be dealt with by a professional.

Thurlow entered the room, removed his jacket, then waited by the red plastic couch while the dentist made an entry in his computer.

"I normally have Dr. Samuelson," he explained, looking about.

"Well, he's not here, he's . . ."

"I know. Florida. All right for some. You're new, I suppose. You're very young."

"Everyone looks young when you start getting older, Mr. Thurlow. I'm Dr. Matthews." He continued tapping the keyboard, then raised his eyes to the screen. "You haven't had a check-up for well over a year."

"Not for a check-up, no," said Thurlow, climbing onto the couch.

"I had a thing, a lump." He waggled his fingers at his cheek. "I thought it was a cyst."

"When was the appointment?" Matthews was clearly unable to find the reference on his screen.

"I didn't have one. Anyway, it wasn't a cyst. It was a spot."

"And the time before that?"

"I lost a filling. Ginger nuts. Same thing the year before that. Peppermints."

"So you haven't seen the hygienist for a while?"

"And I don't need to see one now," said Thurlow. "They always try to fob you off with dental floss and sticks with rubber prongs on. What is this anyway, going on about the check-ups? Are you on commission?"

Dr. Matthews ignored his remark and approached the couch. As Thurlow made himself comfortable, the dentist slipped a paper bib around his neck and fastened it.

"Don't you have an assistant?"

"I used to have one, but she didn't like my methods so I murdered her," said Matthews. "Ha ha." He adjusted the chair from a control pad by his foot, then switched on the water-rinse pump.

"I always like to make jokes. It takes the edge off. Mouth open, please." He swung a tray of dental tools over Thurlow's chest. Thurlow opened wide, and the light from the dentist's pencil torch filled his vision. He watched as the hooked probe went in, tapping along the left side of his molars, and glimpsed the little circular mirror at the corner of his vision. Saliva quickly began to build in his mouth. The tapping continued. He knew he would have to swallow soon. Quickly sensing his unease, Matthews placed a spit-pump in the corner of his mouth. It made a loud draining sound, like water going down a sink.

Suddenly Thurlow felt the sharp point of the probe touch down on the bare nerve in his split tooth. It was as if an electric current had been passed through his head. If it had remained in contact for a second longer he would have screamed and bit the tool clean in half. Matthews observed the sudden twitch of his patient's body and quickly withdrew the instrument.

"I think we can safely say that we've located the problem area," he said dryly, shining the torch around, then lowering the large overhead light. "That's pretty nasty. Wouldn't be so bad if it was an incisor. It's split all the way from the crown to the root. The gum is starting to swell and redden, so I imagine it's infected. I'll have to cut part of it away."

Thurlow pulled the spit-pump from his mouth. "I don't want to hear the details," he said, "It's making me sick." He replaced the pump and lay back, closing his eyes.

"Fine. I'll give you a jab and we'll get started." Matthews prepared a syringe, removed the plastic cap from the tip and cleared the air from the needle. Then he inserted it into the fleshy lower part of Thurlow's left gum. There was a tiny pop of flesh as the skin surface was broken and the cool metal slipped into his jaw, centimeter by centimeter. Thurlow felt the numbing fluid flood through his mouth, slowly removing all sensation from his infected tooth.

"As you're squeamish, I'll give you an additional Valium shot. Then I can work on without upsetting you." He rolled back Thurlow's shirt sleeve and inserted a second syringe, emptying it slowly. "It's funny when you think of it," he said, watching the calibrations on the side of the tube. "Considering all the food that has to be cut and crushed by your deciduous and permanent canines, incisors and molars, it's a miracle there's anything left in your mouth at all. Of course, humans have comparatively tiny teeth. It's a sign of our superiority over the animals."

Thurlow finally began to relax. Was it the drug that was making him feel so safe and comfortable in Matthews's hands, or merely the dentist's air of confident authority? He hummed softly as he worked, laying out instruments in familiar order while he waited for the drugs to take effect. A feeling of well-being crept over Thurlow. His arms and legs had grown too heavy for him to move. His heart was beating more slowly in his chest. The lower half of his face was completely numb. Suspended between sleep and wakefulness, he tried to identify the tune that Matthew was humming, but concentration slipped away.

The dentist had placed two other metal instruments in his mouth; when did he do that? One was definitely there to hold his jaws apart. Although the overhead light was back-reflected and diffuse, it shone through Thurlow's eyelids with a warm red glow. There was a metallic clatter on the tray.

"I'm going to cut away part of the damaged gum tissue now," said Matthews. Hadn't he demanded to be spared the details? The long-nosed scissors glinted against the light, then vanished into his mouth, to clip through flesh and gristle. His mind drifted, trying not to think of the excavation progressing below.

"I don't think there'll be enough left to cap," said Matthews. "The one next to it is cracked pretty badly, too. What the hell was in that nut?"

When the drill started, Thurlow opened his eyes once more. Time seemed to have lapsed, for now there seemed to be several more instruments in his mouth. The drill howled on, the acrid smell of burning bone filling his nostrils. However, thanks to the effect of the Valium dose, he remained unconcerned. The drill was removed, and Matthews's fingers probed the spot. There was a sharp crack, and he held up the offending tooth for Thurlow to see, first one half, then the other.

"You want this as a souvenir? I thought not. Now, to do this properly I should really clear out your root canal and drive a metal post into the gum," he said. "But that's a long, painful process. Let's see what how we can work around it without tearing your entire jaw off. Ha ha."

The drill started up again and entered his mouth. Thurlow could not tell which of his teeth it was touching, but by the familiar burning smell he guessed it was drilling deep into the enamel of a molar.

"That's better," said Matthews. "I can see daylight through the hole. Now that we have room to maneuver, let's bring in the big guns." He produced a large semicircular metal clip and attached it to the side of Thurlow's lower lip. A new instrument appeared before the light, a large curved razor blade with a serrated tip, like a cheese grater with teeth. The dentist placed it in his mouth and began drawing it across the stump of the damaged molar. The rasping vibrated through Thurlow's head, back and forth, back and forth, until he began to wonder if it would ever stop.

"This is no good, no good at all." He withdrew the instrument, checked the blunted tip and tossed it onto the tray in disgust. "I need something else. Something modern, something—technological." He vanished from view, and Thurlow heard him thumping around at the side of the room. "One day," he called, "all dentistry will be performed by laser. Just think of the fun we'll have then!" He returned with a large piece of electrical equipment that boasted a red flashing LED on top. Matthews's grinning face suddenly filled his vision.

"You're a very lucky man," he said. "Not many people get to have *this* baby in their mouths." He patted the side of the machine, from which extended a ribbed metal tube with a tiny rotating steel saw. When he flicked it on, the noise was so great that he had to shout. "You see, the main part of the tooth is made of a substance called dentine, but below the gumline it becomes bonelike cement, which is softer . . ."

He missed the next part as the saw entered his mouth and connected with tooth enamel. One of the pipes wedged between his lower incisors was spraying water onto the operating zone while another was noisily sucking up saliva. His mouth had become a hardhat area. Suddenly something wet and warm began to pour down his throat. Matthews turned off the saw and hastily withdrew it.

"Darn," he said loudly, "that's my fault, not watching what I'm doing. I've been a little tense lately."

He reached behind him and grabbed up a wad of tissue, which he stuffed into Thurlow's mouth and padded at the operation site, only to withdraw it red, filled and dripping. "Sorry about that, I was busy thinking about something else. Good job I'm not a crane driver, I'd be dropping girders all over the place."

Now there seemed to be something lodged in Thurlow's esophagus. Through the anesthetic he began to experience a stinging sensation. Bile rose in his throat as he started to gag.

"Wait, wait, I know what that is." Matthews reached in his gloved hand and withdrew something, throwing it onto the tray. "You've been a brave boy. A hundred years ago this would have been a horribly painful experience, performed without an anesthetic, but thanks to modern techniques I'll have you finished in just a few more hours. Ha ha. Just kidding."

He reached back to the tray and produced another steel frame, this one constructed like the filament wire in a light bulb. Carefully unscrewing it, he arranged the contraption at the side of his patient's mouth. Thurlow was starting to feel less calm. Perhaps the Valium was wearing off. Suppose his sensations returned in the middle of the drilling? Yes, he could definitely feel his jaw now. A dull pain had begun to throb at the base of his nose. The dentist was stirring something in a small plastic dish when he saw Thurlow shifting in his chair.

"Looks like I didn't give you a large enough dose," he said, concerned. He removed the plastic cap from another syringe and jabbed it into Thurlow's arm.

"There," he said, cheerfully depressing the plunger. "Drug cocktail happy hour! You want a little umbrella in this one?"

Thurlow stared back at him with narrowed eyes, unamused. Matthews grew serious. "Don't worry, when you wake up I'll have finished. I think you've been through enough for one day, so I'm giving you a temporary filling for now, and we'll do that root canal on your next appointment."

As he began to spoon the cement into Thurlow's mouth on the end of a rubber spatula, Thurlow felt himself drifting off into an ethereal state of semiwakefulness.

While he floated in this hazy dream-state, his imagination unfettered itself, strange visions uncoiling before him in rolling prisms of light. The humming of the dentist became a distant litany, a warm and familiar soundtrack, like the worksong of a seamstress. Colors blended into one another, bitter scents of jasmine and disinfectant. He was home and safe, a child again. Then these half-formed memories were replaced by the growing clarity of the present, and he realized that he was surfacing back to reality.

"Oh, good," said Matthews as his eyes flickered open. "Back in the land of the living. For a minute I thought I'd overdosed you. Ha ha. We're just waiting for the last part to dry." He reached into Thurlow's mouth and probed around with a steel scraper, scratching away the last of the filler. Thurlow suddenly became aware of the restraining strap fixed across his lap, holding him in place. How long had that been there?

"You know, we had a nasty case of 'tooth squeeze' in here last week, ever hear of that? Of course, you can't answer with all this junk in your mouth, can you? He was an airline pilot. His plane depressurized, and it turned out he had an air bubble trapped beneath a filling. When the cabin atmosphere decreased, the air expanded. His tooth literally blew up in his mouth. Bits were embedded in his tongue. What a mess." Matthews peered into his mouth, one eye screwed tight. "It happens to deep sea divers, too, only their teeth implode. And I've seen worse. There was one patient, a kid who rollerskated into a drinking fountain . . ." As he checked his handiwork he mercifully lost his train of thought. "Well, that last batch seems to have done the trick." The sensation was slowly returning to Thurlow's face. Something was very sore, very sore indeed. He raised his hands, hoping to see if he could locate the source of the pain, but Matthews swatted them down. "Don't touch anything for a while. You must give it a chance to set. I still have some finishing off to do."

The pain was increasing with every passing second. It was starting to hurt very badly, far worse than when he had arrived for treatment. Something had gone wrong, he was sure of it. He could only breathe through his nose, and then with difficulty. He tried to speak, but no sound came out. When he tried to pull himself upright, Matthews's arm came around the chair and pushed him back down. Now the dentist stepped fully into his view. Thurlow gasped.

It looked as if someone had exploded a blood transfusion bag in front of him. He was dripping crimson from head to foot. It was splashed across his chest and stomach, draining from his plastic apron to form a spreading pool between his feet. The white tiled floor was slick with blood. Streaks marred the walls in sweeping arcs, like rampant nosebleeds. Thurlow's head reeled back against the rest. What in God's name had happened? Pain and panic overwhelmed him as his hands clawed the air and he fought to stand, chromatic sparkles scattering before his eyes. The soporific drugs were still in his system, affecting his vision. "You shouldn't be up and about yet," said Matthews. "I've not finished."

"You're no dentist," Thurlow tried to say, the white-hot knives shrieking through his brain, but his words came out as a series of hysterical rasps.

The dentist seemed to understand him. "You're right, you're right, I'm no dentist." He shrugged, his hands held out. So sue me. "I always wanted to be one but I couldn't get my certificate. I just can't pass exams. I get angry too easily. Still, it's a vocation with me, a calling. I know what I'm doing is right. I'm simply ahead of my time. Let's finish up here."

He thrust his hand into his patient's mouth and made a tightening motion. A starburst of pain detonated between Thurlow's eyes. The dentist held his head back against the rest while he pulled at something. There was a *ting* of metal, and he extracted a twisted spring. On one end a small silver screw was embedded in a bloody scrap of bright red gum.

"You don't need this bit," said Matthews jovially. He picked up a Phillips screwdriver and inserted it in Thurlow's mouth, ratcheting away happily, as if he was fixing a car. "I like to think of this as homeopathic medicine," he explained, "except that I'm more of an artist. I went to art school but I didn't pass the exam because—you guessed it—" he nodded his head dumbly, *silly old me*, "I got angry again. They took me out of circulation for a while." He removed the screwdriver and wiped it on his apron, then peered inside Thurlow's aching mouth with a benign smile. "Still, every once in a while I like to try out a few of my ideas. I choose a town and I search through the Yellow Pages, then I visit all the private dentists that are listed. Sometimes I find one with a vacant operating room, and then I just wait for custom. I carry the part, you see, white coat, smart tie, good speaking voice. Biros in the top pocket." He pointed to his jacket. "And I keep the door locked while I work. No one ever tries to stop me, and nothing would ever come out in the papers if they did, because private dentists are too scared of losing their customers. You'd never think it could be that simple, would you?"

He went to the desk beside the operating chair and detached a large circular mirror. "Let's face it, when was the last time you asked to see a dentist's credentials? It's not like the police. Now, let's see how you turned out."

Thurlow could barely breathe through the ever-increasing pain, but as the dentist tilted the mirror in his direction, the next sight that met his eyes almost threw him into a faint.

"Good, isn't it?" said Matthews. "Art in dentistry."

Thurlow's face was unrecognizable. His lips had been cut and peeled back in fleshy strips, then pinned to his cheeks with steel pins. Most of his teeth had been filed into angular shapes, some pointed, others merely slanting. His upper gums had been opened to expose the pale bone beneath. A number of screws had been driven into his flayed jaw, and were attached by cables. The last two inches of his tongue—the lump he had felt in his throat—were missing completely. He watched as the leaking stump jerked obscenely back and forth like a severed snake. Around his mouth a contraption of polished steel had been fitted to function as an insane brace, a complex network of wires and springs, cogs and filaments. The skin beneath his eyes had turned black with the pummeling his mouth had taken.

"I know what you're thinking," whispered Matthews. "It's special, but not spectacular. You haven't seen the best bit yet. This isn't merely art, it's—kinetic dental futurism. Watch."

Matthews reached up and turned a tiny silver handle on the left of Thurlow's jaw. The springs and wires pulled taut. The cogs turned. Thurlow's mouth grimaced and winked, the flaps of his lips contorting back and forth as his face was twisted into a series of wide-mouthed grins and tight, sour frowns. On a separate spring, the end of his tongue flickered in and out of his own ear. The pain was unbearable. Fresh wounds tore in his gums and cheeks as the mechanism yanked his mouth into an absurd rictus of a laugh. Matthews released his grip on the silver handle and smiled, pleased with himself.

"Is there somebody in there?" The receptionist was calling through the door.

"This stuff won't catch on for years yet," said the dentist, ignoring the rattling doorknob behind him. He tilted the mirror from side to side before Thurlow's horrified face. Finally, he set the mirror down and released the restraining strap from the operating couch. Blinkered by the heavy steel contraption that had been screwed into his jaw, Thurlow was barely able to stand. As he tipped his head forward the weight pulled him further, and blood began to pour from his mouth. He wanted to scream, but he knew it would hurt too much to pull open his jaws without the help of the contraption. The receptionist began to bang on the door.

"Don't worry," said the dentist with a reassuring smile. "It'll seem strange at first, but you'll gradually get used to it. I'm sure all my patients do eventually." He turned around and looked out of the window. "That's the beauty of these old buildings; there's always a fire escape."

He unclipped the security catch on the casement and pushed it open, raising his legs and sliding them through the gap. Blood smeared from his saturated trousers onto the white sill. "I nearly forgot," he called back as Thurlow blundered blindly into the door, spraying it with his blood. "Whatever you do—for God's sake—don't forget to floss."

His laughter echoed hard in Thurlow's ears as a descending crimson mist replaced his tortured sight.

MARTYRDOM
Joyce Carol Oates

I consistently find that the most successful short story writers are those who cross the genre boundaries, consciously or not. Joyce Carol Oates, best known for her literary fiction, has also been building a reputation for herself as a writer of psychological suspense novels under the pseudonym Rosamund Smith. Her short fiction appears regularly in venues as diverse as *Playboy*, *Omni*, *The New Yorker*, *TriQuarterly*, and *Raritan*, and in horror anthologies as well as in mainstream collections. Oates is the author of more than twenty novels and many volumes of short stories, poems, essays, and plays. In 1970 she received the National Book Award for her novel *them*, and she has twice been the recipient of the O. Henry Award for Continuing Achievement. Her most recent novel, *Black Water*, was a nominee for the National Book Award.

"Martyrdom," from the anthology *MetaHorror*, is more raw than most of Oates's psychological horror. It juxtaposes two lives in a slightly skewed but unfortunately plausible North America (possibly the same world as "Family," which appeared in our third annual collection).

—E.D.

1

A sleek tiny baby he was, palpitating with life and appetite as he emerged out of his mother's birth canal, and perfectly formed: twenty miniature pink toes intact, and the near-microscopic nails already sharp; pink-whorled tiny ears; the tiny nose quivering, already vigilant against danger. The eyes were relatively weak, in the service of detecting motion rather than figures, textures, or subtleties of color. (In fact, he may have been color blind. And since this deficiency was never to be pointed out to him, he was arguably "blind" in a secondary, metaphysical sense.) His baby's jaws, lower and upper, were hinged with muscle, and unexpectedly strong. And the miniature teeth set in those jaws—needle-sharp, and perfectly formed. (More of these teeth, soon.) And the quizzical curve of the tail, pink, hairless, thin as a mere thread. And the whiskers, no more than a tenth of an inch long, yet quivering, and stiff too, like the bristles of a tiny tiny brush.

2

What a beautiful baby *she* was, Babygirl the loving parents called her, conceived in the heat of the most tender yet the most erotic love, fated to be smothered with love, devoured with love, an American Babygirl placed with reverent fingers in her incubator. Periwinkle blue eyes, fair silk-soft blond hair, perfect rosebud lips, tiny pug nose, uniform smoothness of the Caucasian skin. A call went out to nursing mothers in ghetto neighborhoods requesting milk from their sweet heavy balloon-breasts, mother's milk for pay, since Babygirl's own mother failed to provide milk of the required richness. Her incubator filtered our contaminated air and pumped pure oxygen into her lungs. She had no reason to wail like other infants, whose sorrow is so audible and distracting. In her incubator air humid and warm as a tropical rain forest Babygirl thrived, glowed, prospered, *grew*.

3

And how *he* grew, though nameless even to his mother! How *he* doubled, trebled, quadrupled *his* weight, within days! Amid a swarm of siblings he fended his way, shrewd and driven, ravenous with hunger. Whether he was in the habit of gnawing ceaselessly during his waking hours, not only edible materials but such seemingly inedible materials as paper, wood, bone, metal of certain types and degrees of thinness, etc., because he was ravenously hungry or because he simply liked to gnaw, who can say? It is a fact that his incisors grew at the rate of between four and five inches a year, so he had to grind them down to prevent their pushing up into his brain and killing him. Granted the higher cognitive powers generated by the cerebral cortex, he might have speculated upon his generic predicament: is such behavior voluntary, or involuntary; where survival is an issue, what *is* compulsion; under the spell of Nature, who can behave *unnaturally*?

4

Babygirl never tormented herself with such questions. In her glass-topped incubator she grew ounce by ounce, pound by pound, feeding, dozing, feeding, dozing—no time at all before her dimpled knees pressed against the glass, her breath misted the glass opaque. Her parents were beginning to be troubled by her rapid growth, yet proud too of her rosy female beauty, small pointed breasts, curving hips, dimpled belly and buttocks and crisp cinnamon-colored pubic hair, lovely thick-lashed eyes with no pupil. Babygirl had a bad habit of sucking her thumb so they painted her thumb with a foul-tasting fluorescent-orange iodine mixture and observed with satisfaction how she spat, and gagged, and writhed in misery, tasting it. One mild April day, a winey-red trail of clotted blood was detected in the incubator, issuing from between Babygirl's plump thighs, we were all quite astonished and disapproving but what's to be done? Babygirl's father said, Nature cannot be overcome, nor even postponed.

5

So many brothers and sisters he had, an alley awash with their wriggling bodies, a warehouse cellar writhing and squeaking with them, he sensed himself multiplied endlessly in the world, thus not likely to die *out*. For of all creaturely fears it is believed the greatest is the fear of, not merely dying, but dying *out*. Hundreds of thousands of brothers and sisters related to him by blood which was a solace, yes but also a source of infinite anxiety for all were ravenous with hunger, the *squeak! squeak! squeak!* of hunger multiplied beyond accounting. He learned, on his frantic clicking toenails, to scramble up sheer verticals, to run to the limits of his endurance, to tear out the throats of his enemies, to leap, to fly—to throw himself, for instance, as far as eleven feet into space, from one city rooftop to an adjacent rooftop—thus thwarting his pursuers. He learned to devour, when necessary, the living palpitating flesh of prey while on the run. The *snap!* of bones radiated pleasure through his jaws, his small brain thrummed with happiness. He never slept. His heartbeat was fever-rapid at all times. He knew not to back himself into a corner, nor to hide in any space from which there was no way out. He was going to live forever!—then one day his enemies set a trap for him, the crudest sort of trap, and sniffing and squeaking and quivering with hunger he lunged for the moldy bread-bait and a spring was triggered and a bar slammed down across the nape of his neck snapping the delicate vertebrae and near severing his poor astonished head.

6

They lied to her, telling her it was just a birthday party—for the family. First came the ritual bath, then the anointing of the flesh, the shaving and plucking of certain undesirable hairs, the curling and crimping of certain desirable hairs, she fasted for forty-eight hours, she was made to gorge herself for forty-eight hours, they scrubbed her tender flesh with a wire brush, they rubbed pungent herbs into the wounds, the little clitoris was sliced off and tossed to the clucking hens in the yard, the now-shaven labia were sewed shut, the gushing blood was collected in a golden chalice, her buckteeth were forcibly straightened with a pliers, her big hooked nose was broken by a quick skilled blow from the palm of a hand, the bone and cartilage grew back into more desirable contours, then came the girdle-brassiere to cinch in Babygirl's pudgy twenty-eight-inch waist to a more desirable seventeen-inch-waist, so her creamy hips and thighs billowed out, so her gorgeous balloon-breasts billowed out, her innards were squeezed up into her chest cavity, she had difficulty breathing at first, and moist pink-tinted bubbles issued from her lips, then she got the knack of it, reveling in her classic "hour-glass" figure and new-found power over men's inflammable imaginations. Her dress was something fetching and antique, unless it was something sly and silky-slinky, a provocative bustline, a snug-fitting skirt, she was charmingly hobbled as she walked her dimpled knees chafing together and her slender ankles quivering with the strain, she wore a black lace garter belt holding up her gossamer-transparent silk stockings with straight black seams, in her spike-heeled pointed-toed white satin shoes she winced a bit initially until she got the knack and very soon she got the knack, the shameless slut. Giggling and brushing and making little fluttery motions with her hands, wriggling her fat ass, her nipples hard and erect as peanuts inside the sequined bosom of her dress, her eyes glistened like doll's eyes of the kind that shut when the doll's head is thrust back, the periwinkle-blue had no pupils to distract, Babygirl was not one of those bitches always thinking plotting calculating how to take advantage of some poor jerk, she came from finer stock, you could check her pedigree, there were numerals tattooed into her flesh (the inside of the left thigh), she could be neither lost nor mislaid, nor could the cunt run away, and lose herself in America the way so many have done, you read about it all the time. They misted her in the most exquisite perfume—one whiff of it, if you were a man, a normal man, there's a fever in your blood only one act can satisfy, they passed out copies of the examining physician's report, she *was* clean of all disease venereal or otherwise, she *was* a virgin, no doubt of that though tripping in her high heels and grinning and blushing peering through her fingers at her suitors she sometimes gave the wrong impression, poor Babygirl: those lush crimson lips of such fleshy contours they suggested, even to the most gentlemanly and austere among us, the fleshy vaginal labia.

7

Filthy vermin! obscene little beast! they were furious at him for *being* as if, incarnated thus, he'd chosen his species, and took a cruel pleasure in carrying the seeds of typhus in his guts, bubonic plague virus in his saliva, poisons of all kinds in his excrement. They wanted him dead, they wanted all of his kind extinct, nothing less would satisfy them firing idle shots at the town dump as, squeaking in terror, he darted from one hiding place to another, reeking garbage exploding beside him as the bullets struck, they blamed him for the *snap!* of poultry bones in predators' jaws, they had no evidence but they blamed him for a litter of piglets devoured alive, and what happened to that baby in the ground-floor apartment on Eleventh Street left unattended for twenty minutes when its mother slipped out to buy cigarettes and milk at the 7-Eleven store a block away—*Oh my God! Oh oh oh don't tell me, I don't want to know*—and a fire that started and blazed out of control in the middle of a frigid January night because insulation around some electrical wires had been gnawed through, but how was that his fault, how *his*, where was the proof amidst hundreds of thousands of his siblings, each possessed by a voracious hunger and a ceaseless need to gnaw? Pursuing him with rocks, a gang of children, whooping and yodeling across the rooftops injuring him as in desperation he scrambled up the side of a brick wall, yes but he managed to escape even as his toenails failed him and he slipped, fell—fell sickeningly into space—down an air-shaft—five storeys—to the ground below—high-pitched squeaky shrieks as he fell—plummeted downward thrashing and spiraling in midair, red eyes alight in terror for such creatures know terror though they do not know the word "terror," they embody terror, that's to say em*body* it, though every cell in his body strained to live, every luminous particle of his being craved immortality, even as you and me. (Of the suffering of living things through the millennia, it is wisest not to think, Darwin advises.) So he fell off the edge of the roof, down the airshaft, the equivalent of approximately one hundred seventy times his size measured from nose to rump (but excluding his tail which, uncurled, straight and stiff, is longer than his length— eight inches!) so we were watching smiling in the knowledge that the dirty little bugger would be squashed flat, thus imagine our indignation and outrage to see him land on his feet! a tiny bit shaken, but uninjured! untouched! a fall that would have broken every bone in our goddam bodies and *he* shakes his whiskers and furls up his tail and scampers away! And the rancid night parted like black water to shield him.

8

It was the National Guard Armory, rented for the night at discount price, a slow season, and in the cavernous smoke-filled gallery fresh-groomed men sat attentive in rows of seats, their faces indistinct as dream-faces, their eyes vague and soft as molluscs focussed on Babygirl, fingers fat as cigars poking in their crotches, genitalia heavy as giant purplish-ripe figs straining at the fabric of their trousers. Yes but these are carefully screened and selected gentlemen. Yes but these are serious fellows. Most of them pointedly ignore the vendors hawking their wares in the Armory, now's hardly the time for beer, Coke, hotdogs, caramel corn, the men's eyes are hotly fixed on Babygirl my God get a load of *that*. To find a worthy wife in today's world is no simple task. An old-fashioned girl is the object of our yearning, the girl that married old dead dad is our ideal, but where is she to be found?—in today's debased world. So Babygirl tossed her shimmering cinnamon curls and prettily pouted, revealed her dazzling white smile, in a breathy singsong she recited the sweet iambic verse she had composed for this very occasion. So Babygirl twirled her gem-studded baton. Flung her baton spinning up into the rafters of the Armory where at the apogee of its flight it seemed for a magic instant to pause, then tumbled back down into Babygirl's outstretched fingers—the rows of staring seats burst into spontaneous applause. So Babygirl curtsied, blushed, ducked her head, paused to straighten the seams of her stockings, adjusted an earring, adjusted her girdle that cut so deeply into the flesh of her thighs there would be angry red indentations there for days, Babygirl giggled and blew kisses, her lovely skin all aglow, as the auctioneer strutted about hamming it up with his hand-held microphone, Georgie Bick's his name, cocky and paunchy in his tux with the red cummerbund. Hey whooee do I hear 5,000, do I hear 8,000, gimme 10–, 10–, 10,000, in a weird high-pitched incantatory voice so mesmerizing that bidding begins at once, a Japanese gentleman signaling a bid by touching his left earlobe, a swarthy turbaned gentleman signaling with a movement of his dark-glittering eyes, Hey whooee do I hear 15,000, do I hear 20,000, do I hear 25–, 25–, 25,000, thus a handsome moustached Teutonic gentleman cannot resist Yes, a Mediterranean gentleman, a gentleman with a shaved blunt head, a gentleman from Texas, a heavyset perspiring gentleman rubbing at the tip of his flushed pug nose, Do I hear 30,000, do I hear 35,000, do I hear 50,000, winking and nudging Babygirl, urging her to the edge of the platform, C'mon sweetie now's not the time for shyness, c'mon honey we all know why you're here tonight don't be coy you cunt, clumsy cow-cunt, gentlemen observe those dugs, those udders, and there's *udder* attractions too, hardee-har-har! And from up in the balcony, unobserved till now, a handsome white-haired gentleman signals with his white-gloved hand Yes.

9

He was battle-weary, covered in scabs, maggot-festering little wounds stippling his body, his once-proud tail was gangrenous, the tip rotted away, yet he remained stoic and uncomplaining gnawing through wood, through paper, through insulation, through thin sheets of metal, eating with his old appetite, the ecstasy of jaws, teeth, intestines, anus, if the time allotted to him were infinite as his hunger it's certain he *would* gnaw his way through the entire world and excrete it behind him in piles of moist dark dense little turds. But Nature prescribes otherwise: the species into which he was born grants on the average only twelve months of survival—if things go well. And this May morning things are decidedly not going well here on the fourth floor of the partly empty ancient brick building on Sullivan Street housing on its first floor the Metropole Bakery, most acclaimed of local bakeries, "Wedding Cakes Our Specialty Since 1949," he has nested in a nook in a wall, he has been nibbling nervously on a piece of something theoretically edible (the hardened flattened remains of a sibling struck by a vehicle in the street, pounded into two dimensions by subsequent vehicles) sniffing and blinking in an agony of appetite: on the fourth floor, with his many thousands of fellows, since, it's one of Nature's quiddities, when BROWN and BLACK species occupy a single premise, BROWN (being larger and more aggressive) inhabit the lower levels while BLACK (shier, more philosophical) are relegated to the upper levels where food foraging is more difficult. So he's eating, or trying to eat, when there's a sound as of silk being torn, and a furry body comes flying at him, snarling, incisors longer and more deadly than his own, claws, hind legs pummeling like rotor blades, every flea and tick on his terror-struck little body is alert, every cell of his being cries out to be spared, but Sheba with her furry moon face has no mercy, she's a beautiful silver tabby much adored by her owners for her warm affectionate purring ways but here on this May morning in the ancient brick building housing the Metropole Bakery she is in a frenzy to kill, to tear with her jaws, to eat, the two of them locked in the most intimate of embraces, yowling, shrieking, he'd go for her jugular vein but, shrewd Sheba, she has already gone for his jugular vein, they are rolling crazily together in the filth, not just Sheba's terrible teeth but her maniac hind legs are killing him; yes but he's putting up a damned good fight yes he has ripped a triangular patch of flesh out of her ear, yes but it's too late, yes you can see that Sheba's greater weight will win the day, even as he squeaks and bites in self-defense Sheba has torn out his throat, she has in fact disemboweled him, his hapless guts in slimy ribbons now tangled in her feet, what a din! what a yowling! you'd think somebody was being killed! and he's dying, and she begins to devour him, warm-gushing blood is best, twitchy striated muscle is best, pretty Sheba shuts her jaws on his knobby little head and crushes his skull, his brains inside his skull, and he goes *out*. Just goes *out*. And the greedy tabby (who isn't even hungry: her owners keep her sleek and well fed, of course) eats him where they've landed, snaps his bones, chews his gristle, swallows his scaly tail in sections, his dainty pink-whorled ears, his rheumy eyes, his bristly whiskers, as well as his luscious meat. And afterward washes herself, to rid herself of his very memory.

10

Except: wakened rudely from her post-prandial nap by a sickish stirring in her guts, poor Sheba is suddenly wracked by vomiting, finds herself reeling ungracefully and puking on the stairs, descending to the rear of the Metropole Bakery, mewing plaintively but no one hears as, teetering on a rafter above one of the giant vats of vanilla cake batter, poor Sheba heaves out her guts, that's to say *him*, the numerous fragments and shreds of *him*: a convulsive gagging and choking that concludes with the puking-up of his whiskers, which are now broken into half- and quarter-inch pieces. Poor puss!—runs home meek and plaintive and her adoring mistress picks her up, cuddles, scolds, Sheba where have you *been*! And Sheba's supper comes early that evening.

11

Madly in love, Mr. X is the most devoted of suitors. And then the most besotted of bridegrooms. Covering Babygirl's pink-flushed face with kisses, hugging her so tight she cries *Oh!* and all of the wedding company, her own daddy in particular, laugh in delight. Mr. X is a dignified handsome older gentleman. He's the salt of the earth. He leads Babygirl out onto the polished dance floor as the band plays "I Love You Truly" and how elegantly he dances, how masterfully he leads his bride, blood-red carnation in his lapel, chips of dry ice in his eyes, wide fixed grinning-white dentures, how graceful the couple's dips and bends, Babygirl in a breathtakingly beautiful antique wedding gown worn by her mother, her grandmother, and her great-grandmother in their times, an heirloom wedding ring as well, lilies of the valley braided in the bride's cinnamon curls, Babygirl laughs showing the cherry-pink interior of her mouth, she squeals *Oh!* as her new husband draws her to his bosom, kisses her full on the lips. His big strong fingers stroke her shoulders, breasts, rump. There are champagne toasts, there are gay drunken speeches lasting well into the evening. The Archbishop himself intones a blessing. Babygirl on Mr. X's knee being fed strawberries and wedding cake by her bridegroom, and feeding her bridegroom strawberries and wedding cake in turn, each sucking the other's fingers, amid kisses and laughter. Chewing her wedding cake Babygirl is disconcerted to discover something tough, sinewy, bristly in it, like gristle, or fragments of bone, or tiny bits of wire, but she is too well-bred and embarrassed to spit the foreign substance, if it is a foreign substance, out: discreetly pushes it with her tongue to the side of her mouth, behind her molars, for safe-keeping. For his part, Mr. X, a gentleman, washes his mouthfuls of wedding cake down with champagne, swallows everything without blinking an eye. This is the happiest day of my life he whispers into Babygirl's pink-whorled ear.

12

It was an experiment in behavioral psychology, in the phenomenon of conditioning, to be published in *Scientific American*, and there to cause quite a stir, but naturally *he* wasn't informed, poor miserable bugger, nor did he give consent. Semi-starved in his wire mesh cage, compulsively gnawing on his own hind legs, he quickly learned to *react* to the slightest gesture on the part of his torturers, his monitored heartbeat raced in panic, his jaundiced eyeballs careened in their sockets, a meta-physical malaise permeated his soul like sulphur dioxide, after only a few hours. Yet his torturers persisted for there were dozens of graphs and charts to be filled out; dozens of young assistants involved in the experiment. In the gauging of "terror" in dumb beasts of his species they shocked him with increasing severity until virtual puffs of smoke issued from the top of his head, they singed his fur with burning needles, poked burning needles into his tender anus, lowered his cage over a Bunsen burner, wiped their eyes laughing at his antics, shaking and rattling his cage, spinning his cage at a velocity of ninety miles an hour, they marveled at how he was conditioned to respond not just to their gestures but to their words as if he could understand them and then, most amazing of all,—this would be the crux of the controversial article in *Scientific American*—after forty-eight hours he began to react unerringly to the mere *thought* that the torture would be resumed. (Provided the experimentors consciously "thought" their thoughts inside the laboratory, not outside.) A remarkable scientific discovery!—unfortunately, after his death, never once to be duplicated. Thus utterly worthless as science and a bit of a joke in experimental psychology circles.

13

How Mr. X adored his Babygirl!—lovingly bathing her in her fragrant bubble bath, brushing and combing her long wavy-curly cinnamon hair that fell to her hips, cooing to her, poking his tongue in her, bringing her breakfast in bed after a fevered night of marital love, insisting upon shaving, with his own straight razor, the peachy-fuzzy down that covered her lovely body, and the stiff "unsightly" hairs of underarms, legs, and crotch. Weeks, months. Until one night his penis failed him and he realized he was frankly bored with Babygirl's dimpled buttocks and navel, her wide-open periwinkle-blue eyes, the flattering *Oh!* of her pursed rosebud lips. He realized that her flat nasal voice grated against his sensitive nerves, her habits disgusted him, several times he caught her scratching her fat behind when she believed herself unobserved, she was not so fastidious as to refrain from picking her nose, frequently the bathroom stank of flatulence and excrement after she emerged from it, her menstrual blood stained the white linen heirloom sheets, her kinky hairs collected in drains, her early-morning breath was rancid as the inside of his own oldest shoes, she gazed at him with big mournful questioning cow-eyes, Oh what is wrong dearest, oh! don't you love me any longer? What did I *do*! lowering her bulk onto his knees, sliding her pudgy arms around his neck, exhaling her meaty breath in his face, so, cruelly, he parted his knees and Babygirl fell with a graceless thud to the floor. As she stared at him speechless in astonishment and hurt he struck her with the backside of his hand, bloodying her nose, Oh you will, bitch, will you! he grunted, will you! Eh!

14

Mating, and mating. Mating. A frenzy of mating. In the prime of his maleness he fathered dozens, hundreds, thousands of offspring, now they're scurrying and squeaking everywhere, little buggers everywhere underfoot, nudging him aside as he feeds, ganging up on him, yes a veritable gang of them, how quickly babies grow up, it's amazing how quickly babies grow up, one day an inch long, the next day two inches long, the next day four inches long, those tiny perfect toes, claws, ears, whiskers, graceful curved tails, incisors, ravenous appetite *And the horror of it washed over me suddenly: I cannot die, I am multiplied to infinity.* It was not his fault! His enemies are even now setting out dollops of powdery-pasty poison, to rid the neighborhood of him and his offspring, but it was not his fault! A fever overtook him, him and certain of his sisters, almost daily it seemed, yes daily, maybe hourly, no time to rest, no time for contemplation, a two-inch thing, a sort of a knob of flesh, a rod, hot and stiff with blood, piston-quick, tireless, unfurling itself out of the soft sac between his hind legs, yes and he was powerless to resist, it was more urgent even than gnawing, more excruciatingly pleasurable, *he* was but an appendage! thus innocent! But his enemies, plotting against him, don't give a damn, they're cruel and cold-blooded setting out dollops of this most delicious poison, sugary, pasty, bread-moldy, delicious beyond reckoning, he should know better (shouldn't he?) but he's unable to resist, pushing his way into the sea of squeaking quivering young ones, seething sea, dark waves, wave upon wave eating in a delirium of appetite, a single feeding organism you might think, it's a diabolical poison however that doesn't kill these poor buggers on the premises but induces violent thirst in them thus shortly after feeding he and his thousands of sons and daughters are rushing out of the building, in a panic to find water, to drink water, to alleviate this terrible thirst, they're drawn to the dockside, to the river, there are screams as people see them emerge, the dark wave of them, glittering eyes, whiskers, pink near-hairless tails, they take no notice of anyone or anything in their need to get to water, there in the river a number of them drown, others drink and drink and drink until, as planned, their poor bodies bloat, and swell, and *burst*. And city sanitation workers wearing gas masks complain bitterly as they shovel the corpses, small mountains of corpses, into a procession of dumpster trucks, then they hose down the sidewalks, streets, docks. At a fertilizer plant he and his progeny will be mashed down, ground to gritty powder and sold for commercial/residential use. No mention of the poison of course.

15

Grown increasingly and mysteriously insensitive to his wife's feelings, Mr. X, within their first year of marriage, began to bring home "business associates" (as he called them) to ogle Babygirl, to peek at her in her bath, to whisper licentious remarks in her ears, to touch, fondle, *molest*—as Mr. X, often smoking a cigar, calmly watched! At first Babygirl was too astonished to comprehend, then she burst into tears of indignation and hurt, then she pleaded with the brute to be spared, then she flew into a tantrum tossing silky garments and such into a suitcase, then she was lying in a puddle on the bathroom floor, nights and days passed in a delirium, her keeper fed her grudgingly and at irregular intervals, there were promises of sunshine, greenery, Christmas gifts, promises made and withheld, then one day a masked figure appeared in the doorway, in leather military regalia, gloved hands on his hips, brass-studded belt, holster and pistol riding his hip, gleaming black leather boots the toes of which Babygirl eagerly kissed, groveling before him, twining her long curly-cinnamon hair around his ankles. Begging, Have mercy! don't hurt me! I am yours! in sickness and in health as I gave my vow to God! And assuming the masked man was in fact Mr. X (for wasn't this a reasonable assumption, in these circumstances?) Babygirl willingly accompanied him to the master bedroom, to the antique brass four-postered bed, and did not resist his wheezing, straining, protracted and painful lovemaking, if such an act can be called lovemaking, the insult of it! the pain of it! and not till the end, when the masked figure triumphantly removed his mask, did Babygirl discover that he was a stranger—and that Mr. X himself was standing at the foot of the bed, smoking a cigar, calmly observing. In the confusion of all that followed, weeks, months, there came a succession of "business associates," never the same man twice, as Mr. X grew systematically crueler, hardly a gentleman any longer, forcing upon his wife as she lay trussed and helpless in their marriage bed a man with fingernails filed razor-sharp who lacerated her tender flesh, a man with a glittering scaly skin, a man with a turkey's wattles, a man with an ear partly missing, a man with a stark-bald head and cadaverous smile, a man with infected draining sores like exotic tattoos stippling his body, and poor Babygirl was whipped for disobedience, Babygirl was burnt with cigars, Babygirl was slapped, kicked, pummelled, near-suffocated and near-strangled and near-drowned, she screamed into her saliva-soaked gag, she thrashed, convulsed, bled in sticky skeins most distasteful to Mr. X who then punished her additionally, as a husband will do, by withholding his affection.

16

So light-headed with hunger was he, hiding in terror from his enemies beneath a pile of bricks, he began to gnaw at his own tail—timidly at first, then more avidly, with appetite, unable to stop, his poor skinny tail, his twenty pink toes and pads, his hind legs, choice loins and chops and giblets and breast and pancreas and brains and all, at last his bones are picked clean, the startling symmetry and beauty of the skeleton revealed, now he's sleepy, contented and sleepy, washes himself with fastidious little scrubbing motions of his paws then curls up in the warm September sun to nap. A sigh ripples through him: exquisite peace.

17

Except: two gangling neighborhood boys creep up on him dozing atop his favorite brick, capture him in a net and toss him squeaking in terror into a cardboard box, slam down the lid that's pocked with air holes, he's delivered by bicycle to a gentleman with neatly combed white hair and a cultivated voice who pays the boys $5 each for him, observes him crouched in a corner of the box rubbing his hands delightedly together chuckling softly, Well! you're a rough-looking fella aren't you! To his considerable surprise, the white-haired gentleman feeds him; holds him up, though not unkindly, by the scruff of his neck, to examine him, the sleek perfectly-formed parts of him, the rakish incisors most particularly. Breathing audibly, murmuring, with excited satisfaction. Yes. I believe you will do, old boy.

18

No longer allowed out of the house, often confined to the bedroom suite on the second floor, poor Babygirl nonetheless managed to adjust to the altered circumstances of her life with commendable fortitude and good humor. Spending most of her days lying languorously in bed, doing her nails, devouring gourmet chocolates brought her by one or another of Mr. X's business associates, sometimes, in a romantic mood, by the unpredictable Mr. X himself, she watched television (the evangelical preachers were her favorites), complained to herself in the way of housewives in America, tended to her wounds, clipped recipes from magazines, gossiped over the telephone with her female friends, shopped by catalogue, read her Bible, grew heavier, sullen, apprehensive of the future, plucked her eyebrows, rubbed fragrant creams into her skin, kept an optimistic attitude, made an effort. Of the disturbing direction in which her marriage was moving she tried not to think for Babygirl was not the kind of wife to whine, whimper, nag, not Babygirl so imagine her surprise and horror when, one night, Mr. X arrived home and ran upstairs to the bedroom in which, that day, she'd been confined, tied to the four brass posts of the marital bed by white silken cords, and in triumph threw open his camel's hair coat, See what I've brought for you, my dear! unzipping his trousers with trembling fingers and as Babygirl stared incredulous out *he* leapt—squeaking, red-eyed, teeth bared and glistening with froth, stiff curved tail erect. Babygirl's screams were heartrending.

19

Mr. X and his (male) companions observed with scientific detachment the relationship between Babygirl and He (as, in codified shorthand, they referred to him): how, initially, the pair resisted each other most strenuously, even hysterically, Babygirl shrieking even through the gag stuffed in her mouth as He was netted in the bed with her, such a struggle, such acrobatics, He squeaking in animal panic edged with indignant rage, biting, clawing, fighting as if for His very life, and Babygirl, despite her flaccid muscles and her seemingly indolent ways, putting up a fight as if for *her* very life! And this went on for hours, for an entire night, and the night following, and the night following that. And there was never anything so remarkable on Burlingame Way, the attractive residential street where Mr. X made his home.

20

He did not want this, no certainly he did not want this, resisting with all the strength of his furry little being, as, with gloved hands, Mr. X forced him *there*—poor Babygirl spread-eagled and helpless bleeding from a thousand welts and lacerations made by his claws and teeth and why was he being forced snout-first, and then head-first, then his shoulders, his sleek muscular length, why *there*—in *there*—so he choked, near-suffocated, used his teeth to tear a way free for himself yet even as he did so Mr. X with hands trembling in excitement, as his companions, gathered round the bed, watched in awe pushed him in farther, and then *farther*—into the blood-hot pulsing toughly elastic tunnel between poor Babygirl's fatty thighs—and still *farther* until only the sleek-furry end of his rump and his trailing hind legs and, of course, the eight-inch pink tail were visible. His panicked gnawing of the fleshy walls that so tightly confined him released small geysers of blood that nearly drowned him, and the involuntary spasms of clenching of poor Babygirl's pelvic muscles nearly crushed him, thus how the struggle would have ended, if both he and Babygirl had not lost consciousness at the same instant, is problematic. Even Mr. X and his companions, virtually beside themselves in unholy arousal, were relieved that, for that night, the *agon* had ceased.

21

As, at her martyrdom, at the stake in Rouen, as the flames licked mindlessly ever higher and higher to consume her, to turn her to ashes, Jeanne d'Arc is reported to have cried out "Jesu! Jesu! Jesu!" in a voice of rapture.

22

And who would clean up the mess. And who, with a migraine, sanitary pad soaked between her chafed thighs, she's fearful of seeing her swollen jaw, blackened eye in any mirrored surface weeping quietly to herself, padding gingerly about in her bedroom slippers, mock-Japanese quilted housecoat. The only consolation is at least there's a t.v. in most of the rooms so, even when the vacuum is roaring, she isn't alone: there's Reverend Tim, there's Brother Jessie, there's Sweet Alabam' MacGowan. A consolation at least. For, not only did Babygirl suffer such insult and ignominy at the hands of the very man who, of all the world, was most responsible for her emotional well-being, not only was she groggy in the aftermath of only dimly remembered physical trauma, running the risk, as she sensed, of infection, sterility, and a recrudescence of her old female maladies,—not only this but she was obliged to clean up the mess next morning, who else. Laundering the sheets, blood-stained sheets are no joke. On her hands and knees trying (with minimal success) to remove the stains from the carpet. Vacuum the carpet. And the dirt-bag is full and there's a problem putting in a new dirt-bag, there always is. Faint-headed, wracked several times with white-hot bolts of pain so she had to sit, catch her breath. And the pad between her legs soaked hard in blackish blood like blood-sausage. And the steel wool disintegrating in her fingers as gamely she tries to scour the casserole dish clean, dissolves in tears, Oh! where has love gone! so one evening he surprises her, in that melancholy repose, the children are in on it too, what's today but Babygirl's birthday and she'd tormented herself thinking no one would remember but as they sweep into the restaurant, the Gondola that's one of the few good Italian restaurants in the city where you can order pizza too, the staff is waiting, Happy Birthday! balloons, half-chiding there's a chorus, Did you think we'd forgotten? and Babygirl orders a sloe gin fizz which goes straight to her head and she giggles and suppresses a tiny belch patting her fingers to her mouth, later her husband is scolding one of the boys but *she's* going to steer clear of the conflict, goes to the powder room, checks her makeup in the rose-lit flattering mirrors seeing yes, thank God the bruise under her left eye is fading, then she takes care to affix squares of toilet paper to the toilet seat to prevent picking up an infectious disease, since AIDS Babygirl is even more methodical, then she's sitting on the toilet her mind for a moment blissful and empty until, turning her head, just happening to turn her head, though probably she sensed its presence, she sees, not six inches away, on the slightly grimy sill of a frosted-glass window, the red-blinking eyes of a large rodent, oh dear God is it a rat, these eyes fixed upon *hers*, her heart gives a violent kick and nearly *stops*. Poor Babygirl's screams penetrate every wall of the building.

THE SECOND BAKERY ATTACK
Haruki Murakami

Haruki Murakami was born in Kobe, Japan, in 1949. He studied Greek Drama and managed a jazz bar in Tokyo before turning to writing full-time. Murakami presently lives in Rome, Italy.

Murakami is the author of A Wild Sheep Chase (winner of Japan's Noma Literary Award), Hard-Boiled Wonderland and the End of the World (Winner of the Tanizaki Prize), Dance, Dance, Dance, and Norwegian Wood, an international best-seller. He had also translated novels by F. Scott Fitzgerald, John Irving, Paul Theroux, and Raymond Carver into Japanese. His New Yorker story "TV People" was reprinted in the fourth annual volume of The Year's Best Fantasy and Horror.

The following wry and surrealistic tale, translated from the Japanese by Jay Rubin, comes from the January issue of Playboy.

—T.W.

I'm still not sure I made the right choice when I told my wife about the bakery attack. But then, it might not have been a question of right and wrong. Which is to say that wrong choices can produce right results, and vice versa. I myself have adopted the position that, in fact, *we never choose anything at all*. Things happen. Or not.

If you look at it this way, *it just so happens* that I told my wife about the bakery attack. I hadn't been planning to bring it up—I had forgotten all about it—but it wasn't one of those now-that-you-mention-it kind of things, either.

What reminded me of the bakery attack was an unbearable hunger. It hit just before two o'clock in the morning. We ate a light supper at six, crawled into bed at nine-thirty and went to sleep. For some reason, we woke up at exactly the same moment. A few minutes later, the pangs struck with the force of the tornado in The Wizard of Oz. These were tremendous, overpowering hunger pangs.

Our refrigerator contained not a single item that could be technically categorized as food. We had a bottle of French dressing, six cans of beer, two shriveled onions, a stick of butter and a box of refrigerator deodorizers. With only two weeks of married life behind us, we had yet to establish a precise conjugal understanding with regard to the rules of dietary behavior. Let alone anything else.

I had a job in a law firm at the time, and she was doing secretarial work at a design school. I was either 28 or 29—why can't I remember the exact year we married?—and she was two years and eight months younger. Groceries were the last things on our minds.

We both felt too hungry to go back to sleep, but it hurt just to lie there. On the other hand, we were also too hungry to do anything useful. We got out of bed and drifted into the kitchen, ending up across the table from each other. What could have caused such violent hunger pangs?

We took turns opening the refrigerator door and hoping, but no matter how many times we looked inside, the contents never changed. Beer and onions and butter and dressing and deodorizer. It might have been possible to sauté the onions in the butter, but there was no chance those two shriveled onions could fill our empty stomachs. Onions are meant to be eaten with other things. They're not the kind of food you use to satisfy an appetite.

"Would madame care for French dressing sautéed in deodorizer?"

I expected her to ignore my attempt at humor, and she did. "Let's get in the car and look for an all-night restaurant," I said. "There must be one on the highway."

She rejected that suggestion. "We can't. You're not supposed to go out to eat after midnight." She was old-fashioned that way.

I breathed once and said, "I guess not."

Whenever my wife expressed such an opinion (or thesis) back then, it reverberated in my ears with the authority of a revelation. Maybe that's what happens with newlyweds, I don't know. But when she said this to me, I began to think that this was a special hunger, not one that could be satisfied through the mere expedient of taking it to an all-night restaurant on the highway.

A special kind of hunger. And what might that be? I can present it here in the form of a cinematic image.

One, I am in a little boat, floating on a quiet sea. *Two*, I look down and, in the water, I see the peak of a volcano thrusting up from the ocean floor. *Three*, the peak seems pretty close to the water's surface, but just how close, I cannot tell. *Four*, this is because the hypertransparency of the water interferes with the perception of distance.

This is a fairly accurate description of the image that arose in my mind between the time my wife said she refused to go to an all-night restaurant and I agreed with my "I guess not." Not being Sigmund Freud, I was, of course, unable to analyze with any precision what this image signified, but I knew intuitively that it was a revelation. Which is why—the almost grotesque intensity of my hunger notwithstanding—I all but automatically agreed with her thesis (or declaration).

We did the only thing we could do: opened the beer. It was a lot better than eating those onions. She didn't like beer much, so we divided the cans, two for her, four for me. While I was drinking the first one, she searched the kitchen shelves like a squirrel in November. Eventually, she turned up four butter cookies. They were leftovers, soft and soggy, but we each ate two, savoring every morsel.

It was no use. Upon this hunger of ours, as vast and boundless as the Sinai Peninsula, the butter cookies and beer left not a mark.

Time oozed through the dark like a lead weight in a fish's gut. I read the print on the aluminum beer cans. I stared at my watch. I looked at the refrigerator door.

I turned the pages of yesterday's paper. I used the edge of a postcard to scrape together the cookie crumbs on the table top.

"I've never been this hungry in my whole life," she said. "I wonder if it has anything to do with being married."

"Maybe," I said. "Or maybe not."

While she hunted for more fragments of food, I leaned over the edge of my boat and looked down at the peak of the underwater volcano. The clarity of the ocean water all around the boat gave me an unsettled feeling, as if a hollow had opened somewhere behind my solar plexus—a hermetically sealed cavern that had neither entrance nor exit. Something about this weird sense of absence—this sense of the existential reality of nonexistence—resembled the paralyzing fear you might feel when you climb to the top of a steeple. This connection between hunger and acrophobia was a discovery for me.

Which is when it occurred to me that I had once before had this same kind of experience. My stomach had been just as empty then. . . . When? . . . Oh, sure, that was—

"The time of the bakery attack," I heard myself saying.

"The bakery attack? What are you talking about?"

And so it started.

"I once attacked a bakery. Long time ago. Not a big bakery. Not famous. The bread was nothing special. Not bad, either. One of those ordinary little neighborhood bakeries right in the middle of a block of shops. Some old guy ran it who did everything himself. Baked in the morning, and when he sold out, he closed up for the day."

"If you were going to attack a bakery, why that one?"

"Well, there was no point in attacking a big bakery. All we wanted was bread, not money. We were attackers, not robbers."

"We? Who's we?"

"My best friend back then. Ten years ago. We were so broke we couldn't buy toothpaste. Never had enough food. We did some pretty awful things to get our hands on food. The bakery attack was one."

"I don't get it." She looked hard at me. Her eyes could have been searching for a faded star in the morning sky. "Why didn't you get a job? You could have worked after school. That would have been easier than attacking bakeries."

"We didn't want to work. We were absolutely clear on that."

"Well, you're working now, aren't you?"

I nodded and sucked some more beer. Then I rubbed my eyes. A kind of beery mud had oozed into my brain and was struggling with my hunger pangs.

"Times change. People change," I said. "Let's go back to bed. We've got to get up early."

"I'm not sleepy. I want you to tell me about the bakery attack."

"There's nothing to tell. No action. No excitement."

"Was it a success?"

I gave up on sleep and ripped open another can of beer. Once she gets interested in a story, she has to hear it all the way through. That's just the way she is.

"Well, it was kind of a success. And kind of not. We got what we wanted. But, as a holdup, it didn't work. The baker gave us the bread before we could take it from him."

"Free?"

"Not exactly, no. That's the hard part." I shook my head. "The baker was a classical-music freak, and when we got there, he was listening to an album of Wagner overtures. So he made us a deal. If we would listen to the record all the way through, we could take as much bread as we liked. I talked it over with my buddy and we figured OK. It wouldn't be work in the purest sense of the word, and it wouldn't hurt anybody. So we put our knives back into our bag, pulled up a couple of chairs and listened to the overtures to *Tannhäuser* and *The Flying Dutchman*."

"And after that, you got your bread?"

"Right. Most of what he had in the shop. Stuffed it into our bag and took it home. Kept us fed for maybe four or five days." I took another sip. Like soundless waves from an undersea earthquake, my sleepiness gave my boat a long, slow rocking.

"Of course, we accomplished our mission. We got the bread. But you couldn't say we had committed a crime. It was more of an exchange. We listened to Wagner with him and, in return, we got our bread. Legally speaking, it was more like a commercial transaction."

"But listening to Wagner is not work," she said.

"Oh, no, absolutely not. If the baker had insisted that we wash his dishes or clean his windows or something, we would have turned him down. But he didn't. All he wanted from us was to listen to his Wagner LP from beginning to end. Nobody could have anticipated that. I mean—Wagner? It was like the baker put a curse on us. Now that I think of it, we should have refused. We should have threatened him with our knives and taken the damn bread. Then there wouldn't have been any problem."

"You had a problem?"

I rubbed my eyes again.

"Sort of. Nothing you could put your finger on. But things started to change after that. It was kind of a turning point. Like, I went back to the university, and I graduated, and I started working for the firm and studying for the bar exam, and I met you and got married. I never did anything like that again. No more bakery attacks."

"That's it?"

"Yup, that's all there was to it." I drank the last of the beer. Now all six cans were gone. Six pull-tabs lay in the ashtray, like scales from a mermaid.

Of course, it wasn't true that nothing had happened as a result of the bakery attack. There were plenty of things that you could easily have put your finger on, but I didn't want to talk about them with her.

"So, this friend of yours, what's he doing now?"

"I have no idea. Something happened, some nothing kind of thing, and we stopped hanging around together. I haven't seen him since. I don't know what he's doing."

For a while, she didn't speak. She probably sensed that I wasn't telling her the whole story. But she wasn't ready to press me on it.

"Still," she said, "that's why you two broke up, isn't it? The bakery attack was the direct cause."

"Maybe so. I guess it was more intense than either of us realized. We talked about the relationship of bread to Wagner for days after that. We kept asking ourselves if we had made the right choice. We couldn't decide. Of course, if you look at it sensibly, we *did* make the right choice. Nobody got hurt. Everybody got what he wanted. The baker—I still can't figure out why he did what he did—but, anyway, he succeeded with his Wagner propaganda. And we succeeded in stuffing our faces with bread.

"But even so, we had this feeling that we had made a terrible mistake. And somehow, this mistake has just stayed there, unresolved, casting a dark shadow on our lives. That's why I used the word curse. It's true. It was like a curse."

"Do you think you still have it?"

I took the six pull-tabs from the ashtray and arranged them into an aluminum ring the size of a bracelet.

"Who knows? I don't know. I bet the world is full of curses. It's hard to tell which curse makes any one thing go wrong."

"That's not true." She looked right at me. "You can tell, if you think about it. And unless you, yourself, personally break the curse, it'll stick with you like a toothache. It'll torture you till you die. And not just you. Me, too."

"You?"

"Well, I'm your best friend now, aren't I? Why do you think we're both so hungry? I never, ever, once in my life felt a hunger like this until I married you. Don't you think it's abnormal? Your curse is working on me, too."

I nodded. Then I broke up the ring of pull-tabs and put them into the ashtray again. I didn't know if she was right, but I did feel she was on to something.

The feeling of starvation was back, stronger than ever, and it was giving me a deep headache. Every twinge of my stomach was being transmitted to the core of my head by a clutch cable, as if my insides were equipped with all kinds of complicated machinery.

I took another look at my undersea volcano. The water was even clearer than before—much clearer. Unless you looked closely, you might not even notice it was there. It felt as though the boat were floating in mid-air, with absolutely nothing to support it. I could see every little pebble on the bottom. All I had to do was reach out and touch them.

"We've been living together for only two weeks," she said, "but all this time I've been feeling some kind of weird presence." She looked directly into my eyes and brought her hands together on the table top, her fingers interlocking. "Of course, I didn't know it was a curse until now. This explains everything. You're under a curse."

"What kind of presence?"

"Like there's this heavy, dusty curtain that hasn't been washed for years, hanging down from the ceiling."

"Maybe it's not a curse. Maybe it's just me," I said, and smiled.

She did not smile.

"No, it's not you," she said.

"OK, suppose you're right. Suppose it is a curse. What can I do about it?"

"Attack another bakery. Right away. Now. It's the only way."

"Now?"

"Yes. Now. While you're still hungry. You have to finish what you left unfinished."

"But it's the middle of the night. Would a bakery be open now?"

"We'll find one. Tokyo's a big city. There must be at least one all-night bakery."

We got into my old Corolla and started drifting around the streets of Tokyo at 2:30 A.M., looking for a bakery. There we were, me clutching the steering wheel, her in the navigator's seat, the two of us scanning the street like hungry eagles in search of prey. Stretched out on the back seat, long and stiff as a dead fish, was a Remington automatic shotgun. Its shells rustled dryly in the pocket of my wife's windbreaker. We had two black ski masks in the glove compartment. Why my wife owned a shotgun, I had no idea. Or ski masks. Neither of us had ever skied. But she didn't explain and I didn't ask. Married life is weird, I felt.

Impeccably equipped, we were nevertheless unable to find an all-night bakery. I drove through the empty streets, from Yoyogi to Shinjuku, on to Yotsuya and Akasaka, Aoyama, Hiroo, Roppongi, Daikanyama and Shibuya. Late-night Tokyo had all kinds of people and shops, but no bakeries.

Twice we encountered patrol cars. One was huddled at the side of the road, trying to look inconspicuous. The other slowly overtook us and crept past, finally moving off into the distance. Both times I grew damp under the arms, but my wife's concentration never faltered. She was looking for that bakery. Every time she shifted the angle of her body, the shotgun shells in her pocket rustled like buckwheat husks in an old-fashioned pillow.

"Let's forget it," I said. "There aren't any bakeries open at this time of night. You've got to plan for this kind of thing, or else——"

"Stop the car!"

I slammed on the brakes.

"This is the place," she said.

The shops along the street had their shutters rolled down, forming dark, silent walls on either side. A barbershop sign hung in the dark like a twisted, chilling glass eye. There was a bright McDonald's hamburger sign some two hundred yards ahead, but nothing else.

"I don't see any bakery," I said.

Without a word, she opened the glove compartment and pulled out a roll of cloth-backed tape. Holding this, she stepped out of the car. I got out my side. Kneeling at the front end, she tore off a length of tape and covered the numbers on the license plate. Then she went around to the back and did the same. There was a practiced efficiency to her movements. I stood on the curb staring at her.

"We're going to take that McDonald's," she said, as coolly as if she were announcing what we would have for dinner.

"McDonald's is not a bakery," I pointed out to her.

"It's *like* a bakery," she said. "Sometimes you have to compromise. Let's go."

I drove to McDonald's and parked in the lot. She handed me the blanket-wrapped shotgun.

"I've never fired a gun in my life," I protested.

"You don't have to fire it. Just hold it. OK? Do as I say. We walk right in and as they say 'Welcome to McDonald's,' we slip on our masks. Got that?"

"Sure, but——"

"Then you shove the gun in their faces and make all the workers and customers get together. Fast. I'll do the rest."

"But——"

"How many hamburgers do you think we'll need? Thirty?"

"I guess so." With a sigh, I took the shotgun and rolled back the blanket a little. The thing was as heavy as a sandbag and as black as a dark night.

"Do we really have to do this?" I asked, half to her and half to myself.

"Of course we do."

Wearing a McDonald's hat, the girl behind the counter flashed me a McDonald's smile and said, "Welcome to McDonald's." I hadn't thought that girls would work at McDonald's late at night, so the sight of her confused me for a second. But only for a second. I caught myself and pulled on the mask. Confronted with this suddenly masked duo, the girl gaped at us.

Obviously, the McDonald's hospitality manual said nothing about how to deal with a situation like this. She had been starting to form the phrase that comes after "Welcome to McDonald's," but her mouth seemed to stiffen and the words wouldn't come out. Even so, like a crescent moon in the dawn sky, the hint of a professional smile lingered at the edges of her lips.

As quickly as I could manage, I unwrapped the shotgun and aimed it in the direction of the tables, but the only customers there were a young couple—students, probably—face down on the plastic table, sound asleep. Their two heads and two strawberry-milk-shake cups were aligned on the table like an avant-garde sculpture. They slept the sleep of the dead. They didn't look likely to obstruct our operation, so I swung my shotgun back toward the counter.

All together, there were three McDonald's workers: the girl at the counter, the manager—a guy with a pale, egg-shaped face, probably in his late 20s—and a student type in the kitchen, a thin shadow of a guy with nothing on his face that you could read as an expression. They stood together behind the register, staring into the muzzle of my shotgun like tourists peering down an Incan well. No one screamed and no one made a threatening move. The gun was so heavy I had to rest the barrel on top of the cash register, my finger on the trigger.

"I'll give you the money," said the manager, his voice hoarse. "They collected it at eleven, so we don't have too much, but you can have everything. We're insured."

"Lower the front shutter and turn off the sign," said my wife.

"Wait a minute," said the manager. "I can't do that. I'll be held responsible if I close up without permission."

My wife repeated her order, slowly. He seemed torn.

"You'd better do what she says," I warned him.

He looked at the muzzle of the gun atop the register, then at my wife and then back at the gun. He finally resigned himself to the inevitable. He turned off the sign and hit a switch on an electrical panel that lowered the shutter. I kept my eye on him, worried that he might hit a burglar alarm, but, apparently, McDonald's restaurants don't have burglar alarms. Maybe it had never occurred to anybody to attack one.

The front shutter made a huge racket when it closed, like an empty bucket being smashed with a baseball bat, but the couple sleeping at the table was still out cold. Talk about a sound sleep: I hadn't seen anything like that in years.

"Thirty Big Macs. For takeout," said my wife.

"Let me just give you the money," pleaded the manager. "I'll give you more than you need. You can go buy food somewhere else. This is going to mess up my accounts and——"

"You'd better do what she says," I said again.

The three of them went into the kitchen area together and started making 30 Big Macs. The student grilled the burgers, the manager put them in buns and the girl wrapped them up. Nobody said a word.

I leaned against a big refrigerator, aiming the gun toward the griddle. The meat patties were lined up on the griddle, like brown polka dots, sizzling. The sweet smell of grilling meat burrowed into every pore of my body like a swarm of microscopic bugs, dissolving into my blood and circulating to the farthest corners, then massing together inside my hermetically sealed hunger cavern, clinging to its pink walls.

A pile of white-wrapped burgers was growing nearby. I wanted to grab one and tear into it, but I couldn't be sure that such an act would be consistent with our objective. I had to wait. In the hot kitchen area, I started sweating under my ski mask.

The McDonald's people sneaked glances at the muzzle of the shotgun. I scratched my ears with the little finger of my left hand. My ears always get itchy when I'm nervous. Jabbing my finger into an ear through the wool, I was making the gun barrel wobble up and down, which seemed to bother them. It couldn't have gone off accidentally because I had the safety on, but they didn't know that and I wasn't about to tell them.

My wife counted the finished hamburgers and put them into two small shopping bags, 15 burgers to a bag.

"Why do you have to do this?" the girl asked me. "Why don't you just take the money and buy something you like? What's the good of eating thirty Big Macs?"

I shook my head.

My wife explained, "We're sorry, really. But there weren't any bakeries open. If there had been, we would have attacked a bakery."

That seemed to satisfy them. At least they didn't ask any more questions. Then my wife ordered two large Cokes from the girl and paid for them.

"We're stealing bread, nothing else," she said. The girl responded with a complicated head movement, sort of like nodding and sort of like shaking. She was probably trying to do both at the same time. I thought I had some idea how she felt.

My wife then pulled a ball of twine from her pocket—she came equipped—and tied the three to a post as expertly as if she were sewing on buttons. She asked if the cord hurt, or if anyone wanted to go to the toilet, but no one said a word. I wrapped the gun in the blanket, she picked up the shopping bags and out we went. The customers at the table were still asleep, like a couple of deep-sea fish. What would it have taken to rouse them from a sleep so deep?

We drove for half an hour, found an empty parking lot by a building and pulled in. There we ate hamburgers and drank our Cokes. I sent six Big Macs down to the cavern of my stomach, and she ate four. That left 20 Big Macs in the back seat. Our hunger—that hunger that had felt as if it could go on forever—vanished as the dawn was breaking. The first light of the sun dyed the building's filthy walls purple and made a gigantic SONY BETA ad tower glow with painful intensity. Soon the whine of highway-truck tires was joined by the chirping of birds. The American Armed Forces radio was playing cowboy music. We shared a cigarette. Afterward, she rested her head on my shoulder.

"Still, was it really necessary for us to do this?" I asked.

"Of course it was!" With one deep sigh, she fell asleep against me. She felt as soft and as light as a kitten.

Alone now, I leaned over the edge of my boat and looked down to the bottom of the sea. The volcano was gone. The water's calm surface reflected the blue of the sky. Little waves—like silk pajamas fluttering in a breeze—lapped against the side of the boat. There was nothing else.

I stretched out in the bottom of the boat and closed my eyes, waiting for the rising tide to carry me where I belonged.

A LITTLE NIGHT MUSIC

Lucius Shepard

Lucius Shepard is going to be considered one of the major American writers of this decade. He has already made a considerable reputation for himself in the fields of science fiction and the fantastic during the 1980s. He won the John W. Campbell Award in 1985 for Best New Writer, and no year since has gone by without his work appearing on the final ballot for at least one major award. In 1987 he received the Nebula Award for his landmark novella "R & R" and in 1988 and 1992 he picked up World Fantasy Awards for his short story collections *The Jaguar Hunter* and *The Ends of the Earth*, respectively. His latest books are the novella *Kalimantan* and the vampire novel *The Golden*.

"A Little Night Music," originally published in *Omni*, is a bitter little horror story. Shepard maintains remarkable control over difficult material from the story's memorable opening line through the gradual emotional deterioration of the narrator.

—E.D.

Dead men can't play jazz.

That's the truth I learned last night at the world premiere performance of the quartet known as Afterlife at Manhattan's Village Vanguard.

Whether or not they can play, period, that's another matter, but it wasn't jazz I heard at the Vanguard, it was something bluer and colder, something with notes made from centuries-old Arctic ice and stones that never saw the light of day, something uncoiling after a long black sleep and tasting dirt in its mouth, something that wasn't the product of creative impulse but of need.

But the bottom line is, it was worth hearing.

As to the morality involved, well, I'll leave that up to you, because that's the real bottom line, isn't it, music lovers? Do you like it enough and will you pay enough to keep the question of morality a hot topic on the Donahue show and out of the courts? Those of you who listened to the simulcast over WBAI have probably already formulated an opinion. The rest of you will have to wait for the CD.

I won't waste your time by talking about the technology. If you don't understand it by now, after all the television specials and the (ohmygod-pleasenotanother) in-depth discussions between your local blow-dried news creep and their pet science fiction hack, you must not want to understand it. Nor am I going to wax profound and speculate on just how much of a man is left after reanimation. The only ones who know that aren't able to tell us, because it seems the speech center just doesn't thrive on narcosis. Nor does any fraction of sensibility that cares to communicate itself. In fact, very little seems to thrive on narcosis aside from the desire . . . no, like I said, the *need* to play music.

And for reasons that God or someone only knows, the *ability* to play music where none existed before.

That may be hard to swallow, I realize, but I'm here to tell you, no matter how weird it sounds, it appears to be true.

For the first time in memory, there was a curtain across the Vanguard's stage. I suppose there's some awkwardness involved in bringing the musicians out. Before the curtain was opened, William Dexter, the genius behind this whole deal, a little bald man with a hearing aid in each ear and the affable, simple face of someone who kids call by his first name, came out and said a few words about the need for drastic solutions to the problems of war and pollution, for a redefinition of our goals and values. Things could not go on as they had been. The words seemed somewhat out of context, though they're always nice to hear. Finally he introduced the quartet. As introductions go, this was a telegram.

"The music you're about to hear," William Dexter said flatly, without the least hint of hype or hyperventilation, "is going to change your lives."

And there they were.

Right on the same stage where Coltrane turned a love supreme into a song, where Miles singed us with the hateful beauty of needles and knives and Watts on fire, where Mingus went crazy in 7/4 time, where Ornette made Kansas City R&B into the art of noise, and a thousand lesser geniuses dreamed and almost died and were changed before our eyes from men into moments so powerful that guys like me can make a living writing about them for people like you who just want to hear that what they felt when they were listening was real.

Two white men, one black, one Hispanic, the racial quota of an all-American TV show, marooned on a radiant island painted by a blue-white spot. All wearing sunglasses.

Ray-Bans, I think.

Wonder if they'll get a commercial.

The piano player was young and skinny, just a kid, with the long brown hair of a rock star and sunglasses that held gleams as shiny and cold as the black surface of his Baldwin. The Hispanic guy on bass couldn't have been more than eighteen, and the horn player, the black man, he was about twenty-five, the oldest. The drummer, a shadow with a crew cut and a pale brow, I couldn't see him clearly but I could tell he was young, too.

Too young, you'd think, to have much to say.

But then maybe time goes by more slowly and wisdom accretes with every measure . . . in the afterlife.

No apparent signal passed between them, yet as one they began to play.

Goodrick reached for his tape recorder, thinking he should listen to the set again before getting into the music, but then he realized that another listen was unnecessary—he could still hear every blessed note. The ocean of dark chords on the piano opening over a snaky, slithering hiss of cymbals and a cluttered rumble plucked from the double bass, and then that sinuous alto line, like snake-charmer music rising out of a storm of thunderheads and scuttling claws, all fusing into a signature as plaintive and familiar and elusive as a muezzin's call. Christ, it stuck with you like a jingle for Burger King . . . though nothing about it was simple. It seemed to have the freedom of jazz, yet at the same time it had the feel of heavy, ritual music.

Weird shit.

And it sure as hell stuck with you.

He got up from the desk, grabbed his drink and walked over to the window. The nearby buildings ordered the black sky, ranks of tombstones inscribed with a writing of rectangular stars, geometric constellations, and linear rivers of light below, flowing along consecutive chasms through the high country of Manhattan. Usually the view soothed him and turned his thoughts to pleasurable agendas, as if height itself were a form of assurance, an emblematic potency that freed you from anxiety. But tonight he remained unaffected. The sky and the city seemed to have lost their scope and grandeur, to have become merely an adjunct to his living room.

He cast about the apartment, looking for the clock. Couldn't locate it for a second among a chaos of sticks of gleaming chrome, shining black floors, framed prints, and the black plush coffins of the sofas. He'd never put it together before, but the place looked like a cross between a Nautilus gym and a goddamn mortuary. Rachel's taste could use a little modification.

Two-thirty A.M. . . . Damn!

Where the hell was she?

She usually gave him time alone after a show to write his column. Went and had a drink with friends.

Three hours, though.

Maybe she'd found a special friend. Maybe that was the reason she had missed the show tonight. If that was the case, she'd been with the bastard for . . . what? Almost seven hours now. Screwing her brains out in some midtown hotel.

Bitch! He'd settle her hash when she got home.

Whoa, big fella, he said to himself. Get real. Rachel would be much cooler than that . . . make that, *had been* much cooler. Her affairs were state of the art, so quietly and elegantly handled that he had been able to perfect denial. This wasn't her style. And even if she were to throw it in his face, he wouldn't do a thing to her. Oh, he'd want to, he'd want to bash her goddamned head in. But he would just sit there and smile and buy her bullshit explanation.

Love, he guessed you'd call it, the kind of love that will accept any insult, any injury . . . though it might be more accurate to call it pussywhipped. There were times he didn't think he could take it anymore. Times like now when his head felt full of lightning, on the verge of exploding and setting everything around him on fire. But he always managed to contain his anger and swallow his pride, to grin and bear it, to settle for the specious currency of her lovemaking, the price she paid to live high and do what she wanted.

Jesus, he felt strange. Too many pops at the Vanguard, that was likely the problem. But maybe he was coming down with something.

He laughed.

Like maybe middle age? Like the married-to-a-chick-fifteen-years-younger-paranoid flu?

Still, he had felt better in his time. No real symptoms, just out of sorts, sluggish, dulled, some trouble concentrating.

Finish the column, he said to himself, just finish the damn thing, take two aspirin and fall out. Deal with Rachel in the morning.

Right.

Deal with her.

Bring her breakfast in bed, ask how she was feeling, and what was she doing later?

God, he loved her!

Loves her not. Loves. Loves her not.

He tore off a last mental petal and tossed the stem away. Then he returned to the desk and typed a few lines about the music onto the computer and sat considering the screen. After a moment he began to type again.

> Plenty of blind men have played the Vanguard, and plenty of men have played there who've had other reasons to hide their eyes, working behind some miracle of modern chemistry that made them sensitive to light. I've never wanted to see their eyes—the fact that they were hidden told me all I need to know about them. But tonight I wanted to see. I wanted to know what the quartet was seeing, what lay behind those sunglasses starred from the white spot. Shadows, it's said. But what sort of shadows? Shades of gray, like dogs see? Are we shadows to them, or do they see shadows where we see none? I thought if I could look into their eyes, I'd understand what caused the alto to sound like a reedy alarm being given against a crawl of background radiation, why one moment it conjured images of static red flashes amid black mountains moving, and the next brought to mind a livid blue streak pulsing in a serene darkness, a mineral moon in a granite sky.
>
> Despite the compelling quality of the music, I couldn't set aside my curiosity and simply listen. What was I listening to, after all? A clever parlor trick? Sleight of hand on a metaphysical level? Were these guys really playing Death's Top Forty, or had Mr. William Dexter managed to chump the whole world and program four stiffs to make certain muscular reactions to subliminal stimuli?

The funny thing was, Goodrick thought, now he couldn't stop listening to the damn music. In fact, certain phrases were becoming so insistent, circling round and round inside his head, he was having difficulty thinking rationally. He switched the radio on, wanting to hear something else, to get a perspective on the column.

No chance.

Afterlife was playing on the radio, too.

He was stunned, imagining some bizarre *Twilight Zone* circumstance, but then realized that the radio was tuned to WBAI. They must be replaying the simulcast. Pretty unusual for them to devote so much air to one story. Still, it wasn't everyday the dead came back to life and played song stylings for your listening pleasure.

He recognized the passage.

They must have just have started the replay. Shit, the boys hadn't even gotten warmed up yet.

Heh, heh.

He followed the serpentine track of the alto cutting across the rumble and clutter of the chords and fills behind it, a bright ribbon of sound etched through thunder and power and darkness.

A moment later he looked at the clock and was startled to discover that the moment had lasted twenty minutes.

Well, so he was a little spaced, so what? He was entitled. He'd had a hard wife . . . life. Wife. The knifing word he'd wed, the dull flesh, the syrupy blood, the pouty breasts, the painted face he'd thought was pretty. The dead music woman, the woman whose voice caused cancer, whose kisses left damp mildewed stains, whose . . .

His heart beat flabbily, his hands were cramped, his fingertips were numb, and his thoughts were a whining, glowing crack opening in a smoky sky like slow lightning. Feeling a dark red emotion too contemplative to be anger, he typed a single paragraph and then stopped to read what he had written.

> The thing about this music is, it just feels right. It's not art, it's not beauty, it's a meter reading on the state of the soul, of the world. It's the bottom line of all time. A registering of creepy fundamentals, the rendering into music of the crummiest truth, the statement of some meager final toler- ance, a universal alpha wave, God's EKG, the least possible music, the absolute minimum of sound, all that's left to say, to be, for them, for us . . . maybe that's why it feels so damn right. It creates an option to suicide, a place where there is no great trouble, only a trickle of blood through stony flesh and the crackle of a base electric message across the brain.

Well, he thought, now there's a waste of a paragraph. Put that into the column, and he'd be looking for work with a weekly shopping guide. Hey, who knows, it might not be so bad, writing about fabric bargains and turkey raffles and swap meets. Might put him back in touch with his roots.

He essayed a laugh and produced a gulping noise.

Damn, he felt lousy.

Not lousy, really, just . . . just sort of nothing. Like there was nothing in his head except the music. Music and black dead air. Dead life.

Dead love.

He typed a few more lines.

> Maybe Dexter was right, maybe this music *will* change your life. It sure as hell seems to have changed mine. I feel like shit, my lady's out with some dirtball lowlife and all I can muster by way of a reaction is mild pique. That's a goddamn change, sure enough. I mean, maybe the effect

of Afterlife's music is to reduce the emotional volatility of our kind, to diminish us to the level of the stiffs who play it. That might explain Dexter's peace-and-love rap, put it into a cautionary context. People who feel like I do wouldn't have the energy for war, for polluting, for much of anything. They'd probably sit around most of the time, trying to think something, hoping for food to walk in the door . . .

Jesus, what if the music actually did buzz you like that? Tripped some chemical switch and slowly shut you down, brain cell by brain cell, until you were about three degrees below normal and as lively as a hibernating bear. What if that were true, and right this second it was being broadcast all over hell on WBAI?

This is crazy, man, he told himself, this is truly whacko.

But what if Dexter's hearing aids had been ear plugs, what if the son of a bitch hadn't listened to the music himself? Maybe that speech of his had been more than cautionary. What if he knew how the music would affect the audience, what if he was after turning half of everybody into zombies all in the name of a better world?

And what would be so wrong with that?

Not a thing.

Cleaner air, less war, more food to go around . . . just stack the dim bulbs in warehouses and let them vegetate, while everyone else cleaned up the mess.

Not a thing wrong with it . . . as long as you weren't in the half that had listened to the music.

The light was beginning to hurt his eyes. He switched off the lamp and sat in the darkness, staring at the glowing screen. He glanced out the window. Since last he'd looked, it appeared that about three-quarters of the lights in the adjoining buildings had been darkened, making it appear that the remaining lights were some sort of weird code, spelling out a message of golden squares against a black page. He had a crawly feeling along his spine, imagining thousands of other Manhattan nighthawks growing slow and cold and sensitive to light, sitting in their dark rooms, while a whining alto serpent stung them in the brain.

The idea was ludicrous—Dexter had just been shooting off his mouth, firing off more white liberal bullshit. He was no mad scientist, no deviant little monster with a master plan.

Still, Goodrick didn't feel much like laughing.

Maybe, he thought, he should call the police . . . call someone.

But then he'd have to get up, dial the phone, talk, and it was so much more pleasant just to sit here and listen to the background static of the universe, to the sad song of a next-to-nothing life.

He remembered how peaceful Afterlife had been, the piano man's pale hands flowing over the keys, like white animals gliding, making a rippling track, and the horn man's eyes rolled up, showing all white under the sunglasses, turned inward toward some pacific vision, and the bass man, fingers blurring on the strings, but his head fallen back, gaping, his eyes on the ceiling, as if keeping track of the stars.

This was really happening, he thought, he believed it was happening, he knew it, and yet he couldn't rouse himself to panic. His hands flexed on the arms of the chair, and he swallowed, and he listened. More lights were switched off in the adjoining towers. This was really fucking happening . . . and he wasn't afraid. As a matter of fact, he was beginning to enjoy the feeling. Like a little vacation. Just turn down the volume and response, sit back and let the ol' brain start to mellow like aging cheese.

Wonder what Rachel would have to say?

Why, she'd be delighted! She hadn't heard the music, after all, and she'd be happy as a goddamn clam to be one of the quick, to have him sit there and fester while she brought over strangers and let them pork her on the living room carpet. I mean, he wouldn't have any objection, right? Maybe dead guys liked to watch. Maybe . . . His hands started itching, smudged with city dirt. He decided that he had to wash them. It would be a chore, but he figured he'd have to move sometime. Couldn't just sit there and shit himself.

With a mighty effort, feeling like he weighed five hundred pounds, he heaved up to his feet and shuffled toward the bathroom. It took him what seemed a couple of minutes to reach it, to fumble for the wall switch and flick it on. The light almost blinded him, and he reeled back against the wall, shading his eyes. Glints and gleams shattering off porcelain, chrome fixtures, and tiles, a shrapnel of light blowing toward his retinas. "Aw, Jesus, " he said. "Jesus!" Then he caught sight of himself in the mirror. Pasty skin, liverish, too-red lips, bruised-looking circles around his eyes. Mr. Zombie, he said to himself, is attired in a charcoal gray suit with Mediterranean lapels by Calvin Swine, his silk rep tie is by Necktie Party, his coral shirt is made of silk and pigeon blood, his shoes are actually layers of filthy dead skin wrinkled into an alligator pattern, and his accessories are by Mr. Mort U. Ary.

At last he managed to look away.

He turned on the faucet. Music ran out along with the bright water, and when he stuck his hands under the flow, he couldn't feel the cold water, just the gloomy notation spidering across his skin.

He jerked his hands back and stared at them, watched them dripping glittering bits of alto and drum, bass and piano. After a moment he switched off the light and stood in the cool, blessed dark, listening to the alto playing in the distance, luring his thoughts down and down into a golden crooked tunnel leading nowhere.

One thing he had to admit, having your vitality turned down to the bottom notch gave you perspective on the whole vital world. Take Rachel, now. She'd come in any minute, all bright and smiling, switching her ass, she'd toss her purse and coat somewhere, give him a perky kiss, ask how the column was going . . . and all the while her sexual engine would be cooling, ticking away the last degrees of heat like how a car engine ticks in the silence of a garage, some vile juice leaking from her. He could see it clearly, the entire spectrum of her deceit, see it without feeling either helpless rage or frustration, but rather registering it as an untenable state of affairs. Something would have to be done. That was obvious. It was surprising he'd never come to that conclusion before . . . or maybe not so surprising. He'd been too agitated, too emotional. Now . . . now change was possible. He would have to talk to Rachel, to work things out differently.

Actually, he thought, a talk wouldn't be necessary.

Just a little listening experience, and she'd get with the program.

He hated to leave the soothing darkness of the bathroom, but he felt he should finish the column . . . just to tie up loose ends. He went back into the living room and sat in front of the computer. WBAI had finished replaying the simulcast. He must have been in the john a long time. He switched off the radio so he could hear the music in his head.

I'm sitting here listening to a little night music, a reedy little whisper of melody leaking out a crack in death's door, and you know, even though I can't hear or think of much of anything except that shivery sliver of sound, it's become more a virtue than a hindrance, it's beginning to order the world in an entirely new way. I don't have to explain it to those of you who are hearing it with me, but for the rest of you, let me shed some light on the experience. One sees . . . clearly, I suppose, is the word, yet that doesn't cover it. One is freed from the tangles of inhibition, volatile emotion, and thus can perceive how easy it is to change one's life, and finally, one understands that with a very few changes one can achieve a state of calm perfection. A snip here, a tuck taken there, another snip-snip, and suddenly it becomes apparent that there is nothing left to do, absolutely nothing, and one has achieved utter harmony with one's environment.

The screen was glowing too brightly to look at. Goodrick dimmed it. Even the darkness, he realized, had its own peculiar radiance. B-zarre. He drew a deep breath . . . or rather tried to, but his chest didn't move. Cool, he thought, very cool. No moving parts. Just solid calm, white, white calm in a black, black shell, and a little bit of fixing up remaining to do. He was almost there.

Wherever *there* was.

A cool alto trickle of pleasure through the rumble of nights.

I cannot recommend the experience too highly. After all, there's almost no overhead, no troublesome desires, no ugly moods, no loathesome habits . . .

A click—the front door opening, a sound that seemed to increase the brightness in the room. Footsteps, and then Rachel's voice.

"Wade?"

He could feel her. Hot, sticky, soft. He could feel the suety weights of her breasts, the torsion of her hips, the flexing of live sinews, like music of a kind, a lewd concerto of vitality and deceit.

"There you are!" she said brightly, a streak of hot sound, and came up behind him. She leaned down, hands on his shoulders, and kissed his cheek, a serpent of brown hair coiling across his neck and onto his chest. He could hardly smell her perfume, just a hint of it. Perfect. She drenched herself in the stuff, and usually he had big trouble breathing around her, choking on the flowery reek.

"How's the column going?" she asked, moving away.

He cut his eyes toward her. That teardrop ass sheathed in silk, that mind like a sewer running with black bile, that heart like a pound of red raw poisoned hamburger. Those cute little puppies bounding along in front.

He remembered how she'd used to wear her hair up, wear aprons, just like ol'

Wilma Flintstone, how he'd come home and pretend to be an adulterous Barney Rubble.

How they'd laughed.

Yabba dabba doo.

And now the fevered temperature of her soiled flesh brightened everything. Even the air was shining. The shadows were black glares.

"Fine," he said. "Almost finished."

> . . . only infinite slow minutes, slow thoughts like curls of smoke, only time, only a flicker of presence, only perfect music that does not exist like smoke . . .

"So how was the Vanguard?"

He chuckled. "Didn't you catch it on the radio?"

A pause. "No, I was busy."

Busy, uh-huh.

Hips thrusting up from a rumpled sheet, sleek with sweat, mouth full of tongue, breasts rolling fatly, big ass flattening.

"It was good for me," he said.

A nervous giggle.

"Very good," he said. "The best ever."

He examined his feelings. All in order, all under control . . . what there was of them. A few splinters of despair, a fragment of anger, some shards of love. Not enough to matter, not enough to impair judgment.

"Are you okay? You sound funny."

"I'm fine," he said, feeling a creepy, secretive tingle of delight. "Want to hear the Vanguard set? I taped it."

"Sure . . . but aren't you sleepy? I can hear it tomorrow."

"I'm fine."

He switched on the recorder. The computer screen was blazing like a white sun.

> . . . the crackling of a black storm, the red thread of a fire on a distant ridge, the whole world irradiated by a mystic vibration, the quickened inches of the flesh becoming cool and easy, the White Nile of the calmed mind flowing everywhere . . .

"Like it?" he asked.

She had walked over to the window and was standing facing it, gazing out at the city.

"It's . . . curious," she said. "I don't know if I like it, but it's effective."

Was that a hint of entranced dullness in her voice? Or was it merely distraction? Open those ears wide, baby, and let that ol' black magic take over.

> . . . just listen, just let it flow in, let it fill the empty spaces in your brain with muttering, cluttering bassy blunders and a crooked wire of brassy red snake fluid, let it cozy around and coil up inside your skull, because it's

all you know, America, and all you fucking need to know, Keatsian beauty
and truth wrapped up in a freaky little melody . . .

The column just couldn't hold his interest. Who the hell was going to read it,
anyway? His place was with Rachel, helping her through the rough spots of the
transition, the confusion, the unsettled feelings. With difficulty, he got to his feet
and walked over to Rachel. Put his hands on her hips. She tensed, then relaxed
against him. Then she tensed again. He looked out over the top of her head at
Manhattan. Only a few lights showing. The message growing simpler and simpler.
Dot, dot, dot. Stop. Dot, dot. Stop.
   Stop.
   "Can we talk, Wade?"
   "Listen to the music, baby."
   "No . . . really. We have to talk!"
She tried to pull away from him, but he held her, his fingers hooked on her
hipbones.
   "It'll keep 'til morning," he said.
   "I don't think so." She turned to face him, fixed him with her intricate green
eyes. "I've been putting this off too long already." Her mouth opened, as if she
were going to speak, but then she looked away. "I'm so sorry," she said after a
considerable pause.
   He knew what was coming, and he didn't want to hear it. Couldn't she just wait?
In a few minutes she'd begin to understand, to know what he knew. Christ, couldn't
she wait?
   "Listen," he said. "Okay? Listen to the music and then we'll talk."
   "God, Wade! What is it with you and this dumb music?"
   She started to flounce off, but he caught her by the arm.
   "If you give it a chance, you'll see what I mean," he said. "But it takes a while.
You have to give it time."
   "What are you talking about?"
   "The music . . . it's really something. It does something."
   "Oh, God, Wade! This is important!"
   She fought against his grip.
   "I know," he said, "I know it is. But just do this first. Do it for me."
   "All right, all right! If it'll make you happy." She heaved a sigh, made a visible
effort at focusing on the music, her head tipped to the side . . . but only for a
couple of seconds.
   "I can't listen," she said. "There's too much on my mind."
   "You're not trying."
   "Oh, Wade," she said, her chin quivering, a catch in her voice. "I've been trying,
I really have. You don't know. Please! Let's just sit down and . . ." She let out
another sigh. "Please. I need to talk with you."
   He had to calm her, to let his calm generate and flow inside her. He put a hand
on the back of her neck, forced her head down onto his shoulder. She struggled,
but he kept up a firm pressure.
   "Let me go, damn it!" she said, her voice muffled. "Let me go!" Then, after a
moment: "You're smothering me."

He let her lift her head.

"What's wrong with you, Wade?"

There was confusion and fright in her face, and he wanted to soothe her, to take away all her anxieties.

"Nothing's wrong," he said with the sedated piety of a priest. "I just want you to listen. Tomorrow morning we . . ."

"I don't want to listen. Can't you understand that? I don't. Want. To listen. Now let me go."

"I'm doing this for you, baby."

"For me? Are you nuts? Let me go!"

"I can't, baby. I just can't."

She tried to twist free again, but he refused to release her.

"All right, all right! I was trying to avoid a scene, but if that's how you want it!" She tossed back her hair, glared at him defiantly. "I'm leaving . . ."

He couldn't let her say it and spoil the evening, he couldn't let her disrupt the healing process. Without anger, without bitterness, but rather with the precision and control of someone trimming a hedge, he backhanded her, nailed her flush on the jaw with all his strength, snapping her head about. She went hard against the thick window glass, the back of her skull impacting with a sharp crack, and then she slumped to the floor, her head twisted at an improbable angle.

Snip, snip.

He stood waiting for grief and fear to flood in, but he felt only a wave of serenity as palpable as a stream of cool water, as a cool golden passage on a distant horn.

Snip.

The shape of his life was perfected.

Rachel's, too.

Lying there, pale, lips parted, face rapt and slack, drained of lust and emotions, she was beautiful. A trickle of blood eeled from her hairline, and Goodrick realized that the pattern it made echoed the alto line exactly, that the music was leaking from her, signalling the minimal continuance of her life. She wasn't dead, she had merely suffered a necessary reduction. He sensed the edgy crackle of her thoughts, like the intermittent popping of a fire gone to embers.

"It's okay, baby. It's okay." He put an arm under her back and lifted her, supporting her about the waist. Then he hauled her over to the sofa. He helped her to sit, and sat beside her, an arm about her shoulders. Her head lolled heavily against his, the softness of her breast pressed into his arm. He could hear the music coming from her, along with the electric wrack and tumble of her thoughts. They had never been closer than they were right now, he thought. Like a couple of high school kids on a couch date. Leaning together, hearing the same music, hearts still, minds tuned to the same wavelength.

He wanted to say something, to tell her how much he loved her, but found that he could no longer speak, his throat muscles slack and useless.

Well, that was okay.

Rachel knew how he felt, anyway.

But if he could speak, he'd tell her that he'd always known they could work things out, that though they'd had their problems, they were made for each other . . .

Hey, Wilma, he'd say, yabba dabba doo.

And then they would begin to explore this new and calmer life, this purity of music and brightness.

A little too much brightness, if you asked him.

The light was growing incandescent, as if having your life ultimately simplified admitted you to a dimension of blazing whiteness. It was streaming up from everything, from the radio, the television, from Rachel's parted lips, from every surface, whitening the air, the night, whiting out hope, truth, beauty, sadness, joy, leaving room for nothing except the music, which was swelling in volume, stifling thought, becoming a kind of thirsting presence inside him. It was sort of too bad, he said to himself, that things had to be like this, that they couldn't have made it in the usual way, but then he guessed it was all for the best, that this way at least there was no chance of screwing anything up.

Jesus, the goddamn light was killing his eyes!

Might have known, he thought, there'd be some fly in the ointment, that perfection didn't measure up to its rep.

He held onto Rachel tightly, whispering endearments, saying, "Baby, it'll be okay in a minute, just lie back, just take it easy," trying to reassure her, to help her through this part of things. He could tell the light was bothering her as well by the way she buried her face in the crook of his neck.

If this shit kept up, he thought, he was going to have to buy them both some sunglasses.

TOM AND JERRY VISIT ENGLAND

Jo Shapcott

Jo Shapcott lives in London and has twice won Britain's National Poetry Competition. Her first book, *Electroplating the Baby*, won the Commonwealth Prize. Her book of poems, *Phrase Book*, has recently been published.

The following is one of my favorite treasures culled from a year of hunting through obscure sources for possible selections for this volume. (My thanks to editorial assistant Brian McDonald for his help in locating this one.) This quirky, charming poem comes from the Spring 1992 issue of *The Southern Review*.

—T.W.

Oh boy, I thought. A chance
to visit England and Oh boy here, out
of nowhere, a voice to describe it. Reader,
I dreamt of coming back to tell you about marching
round the Tower of London, in a beefeater suit,
swishing my axe at Jerry, belting after him
into the Bloody Tower, my back legs
circling like windmills in a gale,
and the ravens flapping around our heads.
You would hear it all: tea with the Queen
at Buckingham Palace and me scattering
the cucumber sandwiches at the sight
of Jerry by the silver salver. I couldn't wait
for the gorgeous tableau: Queenie with her mouth
in a little shocked screaming shape, her crown
gone crooked as she stood cringing on the throne
with her skirts up round her knees, and Jerry
down there laughing by the footstool.
I would be a concertina zigzag by that time
with a bone china cup stuffed in my face
and a floral teapot shoved on my head so hard

my brains would form a spout and a handle
when it cracked and dropped off.

I can't get this new voice to explain to you
the ecstasy in the body when you fling
yourself into such mayhem, opening yourself
to any shape at all and able to throw out
stars of pain for everyone to see.

But reader, the visit wasn't like that.
I ended up in a poem and it made me uneasy.
Cats prefer skulking and sulking
in the dark, we prefer mystery
and slinking. This is even true of me
with my stupid human face opening
into only two or three stupid expressions:
cunning, surprise, and maybe rage.
And I couldn't find Jerry.

"Where's the mouse?" I found myself tripping
over commas and colons hard like diamonds, looking
for him. "Where's the mouse?" I kept asking,
"Where's the mouse?" I banged full face into a query—
and ended up with my front shaped
like a question mark for hours. That was scary:
I usually pop right back into myself in seconds.
So I hesitated for once before flinging myself
down the bumpy staircase where all the lines ended.
I went on my rear and at the bottom you would have seen me,
end up, bristling with splinters, and nose down
snuffling for any trace of mouse smell.
Reader, it was my first tragic movie:
I couldn't find the mouse.

THE SLUICE

Stephen Gallagher

Stephen Gallagher was born in Salford, Lancashire, in 1954. He made his first professional sale in 1978 and turned full-time free-lance in 1980. His novels include *Chimera, Valley of Lights, Oktober, Down River, The Boat House,* and *Rain.* His most recent novel is *Nightmare, with Angel.* He also has nine radio plays to his credit and three television plays. His short stories have appeared in *Shadows, Winter Chills, Night Visions 8, Fantasy & Science Fiction,* and *The Year's Best Fantasy and Horror: Fifth Annual Collection.*

"The Sluice" is from *Narrow Houses,* an original anthology about superstition. Where do superstitions come from? I'd guess that many develop directly or indirectly out of the universal human terror of death and dying. But what happens when a person doesn't understand the concept of death? How does he deal with the disappearance of a loved one? Gallagher shows us one possibility.

—E.D.

It was a sunny if none-too-warm Saturday afternoon in spring; not a bad day for a trip out, compared to some I've handled. The party consisted of six of our residents along with two volunteer student workers, with me along to drive the minibus and hold the spending money. We all had a song on the way down. Well, you might call it a song, but Michael kept messing it up by hooting like a seal.

Attendance wasn't exactly heavy when we got there, and we parked with no problem. Every year the local arts center would hold its Third World Fair in aid of overseas charities, and every year almost nobody came. From our point of view it made for an ideal outing—no crowds, no pressure, none of the opposition that we'd experienced from some of the store managers in the middle of town—and for the couple of hours of pleasure that it gave, it was well worth the trouble of keeping everybody rounded up and together.

"Come on," I said as everybody fussed and clambered their way out of the bus. "Xanadu beckons."

What the arts center people had done was to set out stalls and tables in the grounds of their converted church in the manner of an old-fashioned village fête, except that instead of cakes and knitwear it was all banana bread and handmade leather goods. The day's raffle prizes were . . . well, I stared at some of them for nearly ten minutes, on and off, and I still couldn't tell you *what* they were. All I know is that they were handcrafted in some village somewhere and they had straw sticking out of them. I was letting the volunteers do most of the running around; they'd already started to work out who to watch and who they'd be most likely to lose. Sarah and Rosalie and Martin were never any problem, they followed when you called them and stayed put when told. David, on the other hand, had a tendency to lag behind and involve shopkeepers or stallholders in an intense and one-sided conversation. His torrent of words never had any coherence to it at all; there wasn't an ounce of harm in him, but it could worry some people.

"How's it going so far?" I said to Lambert, one of the student volunteers who'd been with us for less than a week. Lambert was his first name. I know, I thought the same thing the first time I heard it.

"I was thinking I'd need a chair and a whip to keep this bunch in order," he said, ushering David along to catch up with the rest of the party over at the tombola stall. "But I reckon I'd have more use for a sheepdog and a whistle."

I went along with them and handed out spending money for tombola tickets and the like, and while all of that was going on I checked out some of the nearby stalls for second-hand books. All I saw was the usual kind of thing, girls' pony annuals side-by-side with the Wireless Operator's Handbook for 1954; so when everybody had bought and checked their tickets and nobody had won anything, I rejoined the party and announced that it was time for tea and cake inside. The two student helpers looked relieved at the prospect, which only showed how much they had to learn.

"Okay, Big Nurse," Michael said, tugging his forelock. "You're all right by me."

They all moved off toward the church building and left me standing there with the woman who was in charge of the stall. She was young and pale and smiling in spite of an obvious bad cold which gave a red tip to her nose. She wore a big overcoat and a woolen beret. She sniffled into a tissue and then said, "How many's in the party? Is it seven?"

"Six," I said.

"Where are they all from?"

"The Whittington Hospital. All long-stay residents."

"Is that place still open? I'd heard they were closing it down."

"They're working on it," I said. "But there's still a few of us left."

She was rummaging in one of the cardboard boxes behind the table. She said, "Are you *sure* it's not seven?"

"You're counting Lambert," I said. "He's one of the helpers."

"Here, then," she said, bringing a polythene packet out of the box. "Tell them these are consolation prizes. One each."

"Thanks," I said, studying the packet for a few moments before asking, as tactfully as I could, "Uh . . . what are they?"

"Guatemalan Worry Dolls," she said. "They come in packets of six. They're supposed to have special properties, I don't know what they are. But there's a leaflet inside explaining what to do with them."

I thanked her again, and then went on into the old church. The tearoom was set in a corner of what had once been the nave. Everybody around the table was shouting their order at Sue, the other student volunteer, and then promptly changing his or her mind on hearing what someone else was having. Except for Michael, who was saying that he wanted a pint of lager.

"Now listen here, Michael," I said, squeezing my way through to the table. "We're on holy ground now. And you *know* that God frowns on lager louts."

We got them all sorted out with hot tea and Cokes and cherry cake, and then I produced the little Worry Dolls and had Sue hand them out while I read the printed leaflet aloud. Then I saw that Sue had one doll left over and I looked to see who was missing; it was Martin, who'd been taken to the toilet by Lambert and who was only now returning.

"Here you go, Martin," I said. "There's one for you, too. It's kind of ugly, I'm sorry. But they're all pretty much the same."

He took it and held it in his big fist, and he looked at it with a pleased kind of wonder like King Kong getting his first close-up squint at Fay Wray. Except that this doll was nothing much to get excited about. Barely more than the size of one joint of my little finger, it was unfinished-looking and bald on one side. It had stumpy little drawn-on fingers, no feet, and tiny nailheads for its eyes. Its clothing was a shapeless scrap of material tied around it with cotton.

"It doesn't matter," Martin said. "It's the one I wanted anyway."

When Martin had come to us, he'd been the middle-aged child of two devoted but increasingly desperate and infirm old people. They'd given over their entire adult lives to his care without a word of complaint, but they were starting to have to face the fact that nobody lives forever and that Martin seemed likely to outlast the two of them. He'd come to us as a day resident at first, and then we'd introduced a few overnight stays building right up to a full week. We called this his summer holiday. He'd moved in for good toward the end of the previous year.

I can remember the day. I can with most of them, there's always something that sticks in your mind when it comes to the big goodbye. Roscoe had led Martin away to what he'd already come to think of as his own room, and his parents had stayed down in the entrance hall. Whittington was a big old Victorian place, what had once been called an asylum, and the entrance hall was all marble and fluted columns and a big oak staircase. Right in the middle of all this architecture, Martin's parents had seemed shrunken and sad. They'd had sick, nervous smiles on their faces, and for a while they hadn't moved. Then Martin's father had said quietly, "Come on, Mother," and they'd turned to go home alone. The next morning, Martin had risen early and packed his bag all ready for leaving. Roscoe, who was the only member of the nursing staff who'd been there for longer than me, had sat him on the bed and carefully explained the situation.

That, as I recall, was the only time that he ever became really emotional. For the rest of the time, he fitted in well.

After the outing, I drove us all back. Everybody sang, and Michael hooted until everybody else turned on him, after which he kept up a morose silence for the rest of the journey. There was a cheer as we turned in through the open gateway to Whittington, and there was still another half-mile to go. The place must have been something to see, once. In fact it still was, although it was no longer the town-in-miniature that it had been in earlier years. Most of the buildings stood empty, the hospital having been closed down one section at a time with the eventual aim of selling it off complete. We drove past the house in the grounds where I'd lived when I'd first come to work here. It had been boarded up, like almost everything else.

At lights-out that night I looked in on Martin, who was already in his pajamas and sitting on his bed.

"Teeth?" I said.

"I've done them," he said.

"You know what happens if you don't."

"They all fall out," he said.

I don't think that the Guatemalan doll had been out of his hand since the moment I'd given it to him. He was studying it now. He'd missed the reading of the leaflet and so I said, "Did anybody explain to you how that's supposed to work?"

He shook his head.

"It's called a worry doll," I said. "You keep it under your pillow, and while you sleep it takes all of your worries away."

He studied the doll with renewed interest for a moment. Then he said, "What does it do with them?"

"For that," I said, "you'll have to ask someone more qualified than me."

"Roscoe?" he said.

"Well, you can try him."

Martin liked Roscoe, I knew, in spite of the fact that Roscoe had been getting a little testy of late. Liked him better than he did me, I reckoned. He studied the doll for a moment longer and then he said, "I haven't got any worries, anyway." Then he set it on the bedside table and climbed in under the covers.

"Do you want to read?" I said as he settled down.

But he shook his head, and then reached up for the pull-cord to switch off the light.

"Hey," I said. "Give me chance to get out."

And Martin grinned and pulled the cord, and then I had to pretend to bump into all the furniture on the way back to the door, which always got a laugh.

No worries.

Well, it was probably true. For all its institutionalized nature, his was a protected life. His mother had died before that first winter was over; we were having some trouble trying to get a suit to fit him for the funeral when we heard that Martin's sister, who hadn't paid him a single visit since he'd joined us, had decided that his attendance wouldn't be a good idea. So, no funeral. His father had come over, and we'd left them alone together for most of an afternoon . . . and afterwards, as before, Martin would sometimes let slip something to indicate that he hadn't entirely taken the new situation on board. He'd talk about seeing his mother the next time that she came. Or of growing lavender for her, whose scent she'd always favored. Sometimes, we'd gently remind him.

But a lot of the time, we'd let it pass.

I more or less forgot about the dolls after that. So did everybody, apart from Martin. David had lost his the same day, while most of the others had gone into drawers or keepsake boxes. Martin made a small display case for his out of leftover picture-frame wood, and he kept it on his bedside table. It was a neatly made little box with a glass front, but then he was pretty meticulous; good at framing, good with plants . . . those big hands of his were capable of a surprising delicacy.

We had a workshop. It was one of my areas of supervision; I kept the key, and I was responsible for safety and keeping check on all the tools. Like everything else, it was bigger than it needed to be. It ran the full length of one side of the residence block, with my little cohort of workers tapping and cutting and gluing down at one end. Roscoe would join me there sometimes, and we'd talk shop over coffee. Roscoe had charge of the greenhouse and conservatory, and could leave his people unsupervised for a while. But the workshop had drills and blades and presses and a guillotine, so I had to be there all the time.

"Sandra was down in town last night," Roscoe was telling me one morning. Sandra was a likable woman in her mid-forties who worked in our admin office. "She said that she'd seen old Tom Lewin outside the Black Horse asking people for money. He'd no coat and he looked as if he hadn't had a wash or a shave in a week. If that's a return to the community, I'm Howard the Duck."

Tom Lewin was about sixty, and had spent about two-thirds of his life in various institutions. Most of us doubted that there had ever been anything much wrong with him back at the beginning. I said, "Wasn't he supposed to have moved to one of the halfway houses?"

"Well," Roscoe said, gesturing at the length of the workshop with his coffee mug, "look at the size of this place. You can't run it down to nothing and expect the halfway houses to cope. And the bed and breakfast landlords couldn't give a toss, for them it's just bodies in beds and a giro every week."

"*That's* the business we should be in."

"Well," Roscoe said gloomily, "I can tell you, if it goes on like this I'm going to be looking for some other line. I'm too young to retire and too old to retrain, so where the fuck does that leave me?"

He went away looking bleak and unsettled. I know that the uncertainty of our future had been playing on his mind for some time. He was a hell of a nurse—I've never seen anybody better for talking-down a patient in a suicidal mood—but I never could have described Roscoe himself as a calm person.

And if that assessment needed any confirmation, I got it just a couple of weeks later.

David came looking for me, and caught up with me in the corridor. He was in quite a state of agitation which, of course, made it even harder for him to make himself understood.

I said, "David, calm down," but of course he didn't. There's nothing more frustrating than having a clear head and no way of communicating what's in it. I said, "Don't get all worked-up, just show me what you mean."

So he led me downstairs and out of the building, talking in a torrent all the time. I had no idea where he was taking me. I've already explained that Whittington was a huge place; there had been a time when it had been almost self-sufficient with a working farm within its boundaries and, going back to more than a century ago, its own railway link with the nearest town. We'd covered a couple of hundred yards out along the front of the main building before I'd realized with certainty that he was leading me past the conservatory and toward the Sluice.

The big door was open, and I could hear the echoes of shouting inside. I started to run. It was Roscoe's voice.

Martin came out of the door at quite a speed. He was wearing his gardening apron, and his big hands were pressed hard over his ears almost as if his head were threatening to explode. I tried to stop him, well aware that it would be like trying to stop a speeding train. I caught his arm and swung him around and shouted his name to get his attention.

"Martin!" I said. "Martin, listen to me, listen to what I'm saying! Breathe deeply, slow down! Are you hurt? Is someone else hurt?"

Some of the other members of staff were arriving by now. Martin was pale and panting, and he stared at me as I tried to calm him. I looked to one of the other nurses and said, "Walk him inside. I'll try to find out what's wrong."

The nurse and one of the helpers took Martin and walked him, trembling now, back toward the main building. Lambert had joined us, and he nervously followed me into the Sluice.

The Sluice was our nickname for it. Actually it was the old Whittington mortuary, disused for nearly ten years and one of the few buildings on-site that was scheduled for demolition. Some of the fittings were still inside, but these days any Whittington dead were taken directly to the main mortuary in town. Whittington dead were no rarity. A core of elderly patients remained as the place was being run down, and many of them would see their lives out here. Only eighteen weeks before I'd lost somebody from my own ward—although not, I'm grateful to say, while I was on shift—in a suicide from a second-floor window.

With Lambert on my heels I went through into the main room, and there I found Roscoe.

The former mortuary suite was still all-white, although penetrating damp had begun to flake the paint away in patches on the upper walls. The roof above consisted of one huge skylight in glass and cast iron, flooding the place with soft daylight. Everything in here seemed to glow, as if seen through a tank of cold water. The back rooms of the place had been pressed into use as a furniture store—or furniture dump, I should more accurately say. As for the rest of it, what with the glass and the daylight and the constant temperature, Roscoe had seized upon it as a propagating room for his seedlings, and he'd beaten the opposition who'd wanted it for an art studio. Incongruous, I know. But only to some.

He had soil trays everywhere, all of them labeled and dated. There were empty cupboards, many of them with their doors open. And there was the Sluice itself—the big postmortem table with its sloping drain channels and brass taps to give a constant flow of running water across it. It was dusty now, the brasswork turning green. Roscoe was leaning over this, head-down, the stance of a man who'd just thrown up over a ship's rail.

"Oh, God," he said wearily. "What have I done?"

I looked at Lambert. He was wide-eyed and slightly open-mouthed, like a small child in some kind of apprehensive state. I caught his eye, and nodded for him to go.

He went.

I looked at Roscoe and said, "I don't know what you've done. You try telling me."

"We were making up the plant trays for the centenary display," he said, "and everything was going fine. Then I noticed that Martin had picked out the lavender and he was putting the tray to one side. And I knew why because we've had the same conversation at least once every bloody week for the past six months."

I didn't have to ask, because I could guess. The lavender was for his mother.

"Well," Roscoe went on, "I just went pop. I was talking about her going to heaven and he was shouting about her coming back again. And the next thing I know is, I'm telling him exactly what dead means and I'm showing him the table to prove it. I told him that nobody, but nobody ever comes back and it's about time he accepted it. If we'd still had stiffs in here I'd probably have been whipping off the sheets to show him the postmortem scars. What the hell was I thinking of?"

I said, "You blew up, that's all."

"Yeah," Roscoe agreed hollowly.

"It doesn't have to go any further than this. But you'll have to be the one to square it with Martin."

He looked up at me then. His eyes were watery and grief-stricken.

"If I can," he said.

I looked in on Martin at lights-out that night. Someone had been with him for all the rest of the day. The Ventolin inhaler for his asthma was on his bedside table, but apparently he hadn't needed it.

I said, "Are you all right?"

He nodded. He was sitting on the bed in his pyjamas, and he seemed pretty subdued.

I said, "Roscoe's here, he wants to say something to you. He won't come in if you don't want him to, but . . . I think you ought to let him. Will you do that?"

He nodded again. Roscoe, who'd been waiting and listening outside, hesitantly moved into the doorway.

"Martin says all right," I told him, saying it more loudly than I needed to because I was mainly saying it for Martin to hear. Martin didn't look directly at him and Roscoe didn't step over the threshold, so that he stayed mostly a silhouette against the outside corridor lighting.

Roscoe said, "I apologize for what I did. I shouldn't have done it. And I'm sorry for what I said about your mother. I know you loved her and I know she loved you. We'll keep the plants and we'll . . . take them to the cemetery for her. We can put them in together."

Martin spoke.

He said, "You pushed me and I hadn't done anything."

In a way, I was relieved. It was better than silent resentment. Roscoe said, "I'm sorry for that, too." And then there was a long pause and then, because there didn't seem to be anything more that he could say, he said, "Well . . . goodnight."

"Goodnight," Martin said, and Roscoe hesitated for a moment longer and then he left.

I checked the cartridge on the inhaler, and when I spotted the Worry Doll in its case I picked it up and said, "Hey, remember this? Remember how it works?" Martin looked. "Take it out and pop it under your pillow and see what happens."

For a moment I thought he was just going to look away without interest. But then he took the box and started to fumble it open.

I was relieved. It was like that first step of the injured. As he carefully lifted his pillow and laid the Worry Doll on the bolster underneath, I was thinking what a great idea of mine this had been. A pit for his nightmares, into which they could vanish. . . .

Well. It had seemed that way, at the time.

My shift pattern changed at the end of the week, and it was some days before I was able to catch Martin alone. He was down in the lounge in one of the threadbare chairs by the bookshelves. Most of the books were pretty threadbare, too. He could read, but sometimes he just liked to sit and turn the pages.

"Hey, Martin," I said. "How are you doing?"

He looked up. "I'm all right."

"Friends with Roscoe yet? I know it's important to him."

"I've forgiven him," he said. "I know he's sorry." And then he said, confidingly, "I get bad dreams, now, you know."

I reached to pull up a chair. "Do you want to talk about them?"

"No need," he said. "The dolly takes them all away."

And that was all he would say.

I don't know if it was just my imagination, but that summer seemed to mark a number of changes in Martin. He appeared to grow older and grayer, and no longer to be the big child that he'd once seemed. It was strange to see him with his father after that, their ages completely at odds with their frozen-in-time relationship. The old man wasn't getting down to us more often than once a month by then; he'd moved in to live with his married daughter and her family out on the coast, and it was over an hour's car journey each way, and the old man himself didn't drive any more. He had to rely on his son-in-law for transport. Martin's sister still hadn't been near the place.

At the end of one visit, the old man took me aside and said to me, "I'm glad Martin's so happy here. I couldn't have hoped for anything better."

I said, "He's got no shortage of friends. Everybody likes him."

"Only," he said, "we always worried about what would happen." He was holding on to my arm, partly to keep my attention and partly to keep himself steady; he'd changed, too, almost as if you could see the life slowly draining out of him as its end came nearer. You see it a lot in my line. It gets so that you know, and it isn't even remarkable. He went on, "Usually with children you do your best for them, and then you watch them take over until they can manage on their own. You always worry about them, but at least you know they don't need you quite the same . . . it's like you've had your turn in the saddle, and it's their turn now. They take all the weight, and you kind of feel that your job's done. Only with Martin, it never could be."

"I know what you mean," I said, and I started to walk him down toward the waiting car. "You've got nothing to worry about. We'll look after him."

"Mother used to fret, so. About us both dying and leaving him in a world where nobody wanted him. But here . . . the way he talks about everybody . . . it's like he's got a whole new family."

I got a look at the son-in-law then. He was sitting in the car with the radio on, and he didn't even glance out. He looked bored. I went back inside and joined Martin at the window where, without being aware that he was doing it, he waved goodbye to his daddy for the very last time.

Here's what happened.

Exactly one month later, Martin was sitting downstairs waiting for his visit and I was up in the ward filling in timesheets when I got a message to go to the office and take a phone call.

It was the son-in-law. He told me that the old man had suffered a stroke the previous night, and that he was in the local infirmary now and wasn't expected to last the weekend. His daughter was with him and she specifically didn't want Martin to be there. For Martin's own sake, of course.

You can imagine what I thought of this.

"What's the matter?" I said. "What are you saying?"

"Just that it's a sensitive time for her. She's been through a lot in this past couple of years."

I said, "It wouldn't be that she's afraid of people seeing him and knowing that he's her brother, would it?"

"That's totally uncalled-for," he protested, but I'd barely started on him yet.

"This is his father we're talking about," I said. "He's not some unwanted family pet, you know . . ."

But the son-in-law had already hung up.

I went down to Martin. He was still in the entrance hall, watching the driveway for cars. I said, "Come on, Martin, your dad's not so well today. We're going to go and see him."

I grabbed him and dragged him out to where my old banger was parked. I hadn't been off the site in a couple of days so it took a while to get started, and then we set out toward the coast. Martin asked no questions, but sat in silence. I was angry. I'd seen this kind of thing so many times before, and today I'd seen it once too often. Martin had been denied his grief once, and it was about to happen again; anybody could see that he was closer to his parents than his sister had ever been . . . but now here she was, reappearing at the end of their lives when they'd least control, fixing the situation according to how she wanted to see it.

Pushing Martin out, in a phrase.

They'd no record at Reception, but they asked me to wait. I left Martin sitting with the Accident and Emergency cases and set off to do some scouting. On the next floor I caught up with a nursing Sister and said, "Does Carol Chester still work on one of the wards around here?"

"She left to have a baby last year," the nursing Sister said. "If she comes back at all, it'll be around March."

"Look," I said, "perhaps you can help me. I trained with Carol, I'm a charge nurse over at Whittington. One of my patients had a relative admitted last night, and your front desk doesn't know what it's up to."

"That's usual," she said. "Just step in the office."

Less than five minutes later I was in Men's Medical, looking at an empty bed. The bed linen was in a bag beside it, awaiting collection.

It had all been for nothing. We were too late, and the old man was gone. I turned to leave.

On the way past the ward office, I saw her coming out. Martin's sister, I could guess it from what little resemblance there was. And there's something about the set of people's faces after a certain age, they tell a story about the owner that can differ from what they'd like you to believe. What I saw here was not simply a woman who had present cause to be unhappy. What I saw was a woman who wouldn't ever be at ease in her life, but who would never quite be able to understand why.

I could have been really sharp. I could. I said, "Mrs. Wilson?"

She looked at me. "Yes?"

"I'm very sorry," I said.

She nodded, and went on by.

I went back down into the Receiving area. Martin was still in the same seat, and he was watching all around him with wary curiosity. The place was pretty full, but there were two or three empty places on either side of him. He looked up at me, and my expression must have told him everything.

"It's all over, Martin," I said.

"Daddy's in heaven?" he said.

I could only nod.

And then I said, "Let's go home."

Before we set out, I phoned ahead so the others would know. It was late in the afternoon by the time we got back, and as we were walking up the steps to the entrance door I said to Martin, "Do you want someone to sleep in your room with you tonight? It may not be a bad idea."

"I want Michael to stay," he said.

"I was thinking more of one of the staff. I'll stay with you, if you like."

"Michael," he said.

I looked at him as we were going in through the big double-doors. He hadn't said much at all during the journey. I could remember how he'd been after the news of his mother's death, and this was quite different. Then he'd been like a child, uncertain of what to feel but picking up his cues from everyone else— reflecting their solemnity like a mirror, and sometimes forgetting himself and letting a grin break through. Now there was a kind of gravity about him; the problem I feared was that, because of how he was, his mind could be like a locked room where he sat in the darkness alone.

I wished he could have seen his father. I'd seen dead so many times, and I knew that the only big surprise in it was that it was nothing special. What Roscoe's remorse couldn't undo was that Martin had been pushed face-first into only half of the story with the horrifying paraphernalia of the Sluice; he'd been brought to know of the terrors of death but not the simple, material banality of dead. He knew nothing of that; and it's the things of which we know least that tend to scare us most.

Michael was asked and agreed, and a second bed was moved into Martin's room and made up. Michael wouldn't have anything to worry about, because Martin would be sedated. Roscoe would be around for most of the night, and he'd keep an eye on everything.

Shortly after midnight, there was a hammering at my door.

This was when I lived in one of the self-contained staff apartments in the West Wing. After the first house I'd bought a place in the village less than a mile down the road, but when we'd sold up after the separation I'd moved back onto the site. But that's a whole different story.

I was still up and about. I'd been reading. I went to the door, and there stood Michael—pajamas, slippers, and that was it. He was shivering. I got him an overcoat and he told me that Martin, despite the sedation, was up and out of his room.

Roscoe, it seemed, was not to be found. And Martin seemed to be upset.

We headed back to the ward, through corridors that could still seem endless at this hour of the night. I didn't see Roscoe. Martin's bed was empty, his covers flung back and his pillow thrown to the floor. When I came back out into the passageway, some of the other residents had begun to emerge and were looking puzzled.

"It's all right," I told them, "there's no problem. It's all being dealt with. Everybody back to bed."

Then I saw it.

They talk about your blood running cold. Well, mine did. I waited until everybody including Michael had gone back to their beds, and then I switched on the main corridor lights.

What I'd seen was now confirmed as a single, bloody handprint on the corridor wall. And there were more of them further along, and in one place a little spray-pattern of blood on the wall and on the floor . . . and hair. Bunches of the stuff, pulled out like feathers. And at the top of the fire stairs at the corridor's end, a torn piece of scalp of about two square inches with hair growing out of it like turf out of wet rubber.

I switched on the main stairway lights and hurried down. At the second turn, I could see somebody's feet by the ground-floor fire doors and I recognized Roscoe's shabby old trainers. As I descended I had this terrible image of Martin dragging Roscoe down the corridor, gripping him with those strong hands and holding him in a staggering headlock while plucking his head like a chicken. . . .

But no. Roscoe groaned as I turned him over and I saw a darkening bruise in the middle of his brow which made it look as if he'd been smacked headfirst into a wall, but he was otherwise whole.

I said, "What happened here?"

"Martin was trying to get into the Sluice," he said, rubbing his temples and trying to blink his eyes into focus. "He was in quite a state, he could hardly breathe. I tried to bring him back, and he fought me all the way and then did this." He winced. "Then I think he took the fire extinguisher off the wall and went back."

The Sluice?

I ran the distance over the darkened ground. The door to the Sluice stood open, and was surrounded by snow. But the snow was an illusion, actually foam sprayed about by the erupting fire extinguisher that Martin had used to batter in the lock. The cylinder now lay to one side, its gases all spent.

I couldn't imagine what Martin could have expected to find here. Or perhaps I could, but didn't want to acknowledge it. The Sluice had probably now been planted in his mind forever as the gateway to the dead. I went in with caution, remembering Roscoe on the stairs. I switched on the lights.

"Oh, my God," said Roscoe sadly, from behind me.

About twenty soil trays had been swept onto the floor. Some had broken, all had spilled. Martin was up on the old postmortem sluice table, lying on his side and curled into a ball. One hand was up before his face, and held tightly in it was the Worry Doll. The doll's sightless eyes stared at Martin, but Martin's eyes were closed and couldn't stare back. He'd ripped out almost half of his own hair and, grotesquely, each of them—Martin and the doll—now mirrored the other. The side of his scalp was a bloody mess and I could actually see a gleam of bone in one place, but already the blood was drying out. I worked my hand in between his neck and his shoulder and felt for a pulse, but there was nothing.

I get bad dreams . . . the dolly takes them all away.

A pit for his nightmares. But any pit can overflow and spill back at us, if pushed beyond its capacity. I'd tried to banish his bad dreams; but perhaps I'd simply given them a place to gather and intensify. And when the dolly had finally failed and turned it all back at him, he'd run before the nightmares until he'd reached this place. The gateway. The way to those he loved. In the Sluice he'd crawled into the lap of death, and there he'd closed his eyes and gone to sleep.

I looked at his face again. He was smiling.

But I could never know why.

It was as I turned to leave, thinking of the immediate calls that would have to be made and the arrangements that would have to be set in motion, that I could swear I caught a scent of something. Not of the damp, or of the dust, or even of the mildewed stuffing in the old furniture outside.

None of the seedlings was yet in flower, but there was a springtime aroma.

An impossible presence.

A scent . . . almost of lavender.

RATBIRD
Brian W. Aldiss

British writer Brian W. Aldiss is best known as the Hugo and Nebula Award–winning author
of literary, experimental science fiction novels and stories (such as *Barefoot in the Head* and
The Saliva Tree). Closely identified with the influential New Wave movement of the 1960s,
he is also regarded as an important anthologist and critic—all of which leads people to forget
that he has written works in a fantastic vein, such as his gorgeous epic *The Malacia Tapestry*.

The following story straddles such genre divisions—it's part SF, part fantasy, part fable,
and part myth. It comes from Britain's revived *New Worlds* magazine, in a special issue
edited by Michael Moorcock.

—T.W.

> . . . To warn and warn: that one night, never more
> To light and warm us, down will sink the lurid sun
> Beneath the sea, and none
> Shall see us more upon this passionate shore.

The disintegration of the old world? Easy. I'll manage it. Everything will end not
with a bang but a whisper—a whisper of last words. Words. So it began. So it will
end. When I grow up.

Here I lie on this crimson equatorial shore, far from where the great electronic
city dissolves itself under its own photochemical smogs.

Here I lie, about to tell you the legend of the Other Side. Also about to go on a
journey of self-discovery which must bring me back to my beginnings. As sure as I
have tusks, this is ontology on the hoof.

So to begin with what's overhead. The sun disputes its rights to rule in the sky
above. Every day it loses the struggle, every morning it begins the dispute over
again. Brave, never-disheartened sun!

I lie under the great sea almond tree which sprouts from the sand, looking up
into its branches where light and shade dispute their rival territories. This is called
beauty. Light and shade cohabit like life and death, the one more vivid for the
dread presence of the other.

In my hand I clutch—

. . . But the great grave ocean comes climbing up the beach. There's another eternal dispute. The ocean changes its colors as it sweeps towards where I lie. Horizon purple, mid-sea blue, shore-sea green, lastly golden. Undeterred by however many failures, the waves again attempt to wet my feet. Brave, remorseless sea!

(What should a legend contain? Should it be of happiness or of sorrow? Or should it permit them to be in—that word again—dispute?)

—What I clutch in my hand is a fruit of the sea almond. It's not large, it's of a suitable nut shape, it's covered with a fine but coarse fiber, like pubic hair. In fact, the nut resembles a girl's pudendum. Else why clutch it? Is that not where all stories lie, in the dumb dell of the pudendum? The generative power of the story lies with the organ of generation—and veneration.

Let me assure you, for it's all part of the legend, at the miracle of my birth I came forth when summoned by my father. He tapped. I emerged. A star burned on my forehead. I'm unique. You believe you are unique? But no, I am unique. In their careless journeys across the worlds, the gods create myriads of everything, of almond trees, of waves, of days, of people. But there's only one Dishayloo, with no navel and a star on his forehead.

So my journey and tale are about to commence. Knowing as much, my friends, who sit or stand with me under the tree, stare out to sea in silence. They think about destiny, oysters, or sex. I have on my T-shirt which says "Perestroika Hots Fax."

A distant land. That's what's needed. I've met old men who never went to sea. They speak like spiders and don't know it. They have lost something and don't know what they have lost. Like all young men I must make a journey. The dispute between light and shade must be carried elsewhere, waves must be surmounted, pudenda must open with smiles of welcome, fate must be challenged. Before the world disappears.

We all must change our lives.

So I rise and go along the blazing beach to the jetty, to see Old Man Monsoon. They call him Monsoon. His real name has been forgotten in these parts, funny old garbled Christian that he is. He can predict the exact hour the rains will come. And many more things.

Once Monsoon was called Krishna. Once he visited the Other Side, as I will relate.

He saw me coming and stood up in his boat. He's a good story-teller. He says, "What is the human race," (looking obliquely at my tusks as he speaks) "but a fantastic tale?" Told, he might add, with a welter of cliché and a weight of subordinate clauses, while we await a punchline.

The friends accompany me to the jetty. At first in a bunch, then stringing out, some hastening, some loitering, though the distance is short. So with life.

Monsoon and I shake hands. He wears nothing but a pair of shorts. He is burnt almost black. His withered skin mummifies him, though those old Golconda eyes are golden-black still. People say of Monsoon that he has a fortune buried in a burnt out refrigerator on one of the many little islands standing knee-deep in the sea. I don't believe that. Well, I do, but only in the way you can believe and not believe simultaneously. Like Rolex watches from a different time zone.

He shows yellow teeth between grey lips and says in a voice from which all color has faded, "Isn't there enough trouble in the world without youngsters like you joining in?"

Grey lips, yellow teeth, yet a colorless voice . . . Well, let us not linger over these human paradoxes.

I make up something by way of reply. "I've lost my shadow, Monsoon, and must find it if I have to go to the end of the Earth. Perhaps you can foretell when the end of the Earth will be?"

He points to the puddle of dark at my feet, giggling, raising an eyebrow to my friends for support.

"That's not *my* shadow," I tell him. "I borrowed this one off a pal who wants it back by nightfall. He has to wear it at his mother's wedding."

When I have climbed into the boat, Monsoon starts the engine with one tug of the starter rope. It's like hauling at a dog's lead. The hound wakes, growls, shakes itself, and with a show of haste begins to pull us towards the four corners of the great morning.

The craft creaks and murmurs to itself, in dispute with the waters beneath its hull. And the sweet sound of the waves plays against old board. The ocean, some idiot said, is God's smile.

Monsoon picks up my thought and distorts it. "You smile like a little god, Dishayloo, with that star on your brow. Why always so happy?"

I gaze back at my friends ashore. They shrink as they wave. Everything grows smaller. Hasten, hasten, Dishayloo, before the globe itself shrinks to nothing!

"The smile's so as not to infect others with sorrow. It's therapy—a big hospitable hospital. Antidote to the misery virus. Did you ever hear tell of the great white philosopher Bertram Russell?"

The Golconda eyes are on the horizon to which our boat is hounding us, but Monsoon's never at a loss for an answer. "Yes, yes, of course. He was a friend of mine. He and I used to sail together to the Spice Islands to trade in vitamin pills and conch shells. I made a loss but Bertra Muscle became a rupee millionaire. These days, he lives in Singapore in a palace of unimaginable concrete and grandeur."

Now the friends form no more than a frieze, spread thin along the shore, like bread on a lake of butter. Soon, soon, the dazzle has erased them. My memory does the same. Sorry, one and all, but the legend has begun.

Talk's still needed, of course, so I say, "This was a different man, Pappy. The guy I mean said . . ."

But those words too were forgotten.

". . . Why should I recall what he said? Are we no better than snails, to carry round with us a whole house of past circumstance?"

My hands were trailing in the water. Prose was not my main concern. Monsoon picked up on that.

"Pah. 'House of past circumstance . . .' What are you, a poet or something? Something or nothing? The Lord Jesus had a better idea. He knew nothing dies. Even when he snuffed it on Mount Cavalry, he knew he would live again."

"Easy trick if you're the son of God."

The Golconda gold eyes flared at me. "He was a bloke in a million. Go anywhere, do anything."

" 'Have mission, will travel.' " All the time the dear water like progress under the prow.

"Born in India, I believe, sailed in Noah's boat because there was no room at the Indus." His face had taken on the expression of imbecile beatitude the religious sometimes adopt. "Jesus was poor, like me. He couldn't pay Noah one cent for the trip. Noah was a hard man. He gave him a broom and told him to go and sweep the animal turds off the deck."

"What happened?"

"Jesus swept."

Cloud castles stood separately on the horizon, bulbous, like idols awaiting worship.

Something about moving over a smooth sea prompted Monsoon to chatter. I scarcely listened as he continued his thumbnail portrait of Jesus.

"He wasn't exactly a winner but he was honest and decent in every way. Or so the scriptures tell us. And a good hand with a parable."

The little boat was in the lap of the ocean. The shoreline behind was indistinct; it could have meant anything—like a parable. Ahead, two small humps of islands lay stunned with light. I began to feel the charge of distance, its persuasive power.

Perhaps the islands were like humpbacked whales. But the world's old. Everything has already been compared with everything else.

The old man said, "You'll soon have left us. We'll be no more in your mind, and will die a little because of it. So I'll tell you a story—a parable, perhaps—suitable for your life journey."

And he began the tale of the ratbird.

Monsoon spoke in more than one voice. I abridge the tale here, there being only so many hours in a day. Also I've removed his further references to Jesus, diluting it. Same tale, different teller, only coconut milk added.

There was this white man—well, two white men if you include Herbert—whom Monsoon knew as a boy, before he was Monsoon. This white man—well, he and Herbert—arrived at this port in Borneo where Boy Monsoon lived in a thatched hut with Balbindor.

Like many whites, Frederic Sigmoid was crazed by the mere notion of jungle. He believed jungles were somewhere you went for revelation. In his vain way, he placed the same faith in jungles that earlier whites had put in cathedrals or steam ships. But Frederic Sigmoid—Doctor Sigmoid—was rich. He could afford to be crazy.

Back in Europe, Sigmoid had cured people by his own process, following the teaching of a mystic called Ouspensky and adding a series of physical pressures called reflexology. Now here he was in Simanggang with his mosquito nets, journals, chronometers, compasses, barometer, medicine cabinet, guns, and one offspring, out to cure himself or discover a New Way of Thought, whichever would cause most trouble in a world already tormented by too much belief. Seek and ye shall find. Find and ye shall probably regret.

With Sigmoid was his pale son, Herbert. Monsoon and his adoptive father, Balbindor, were hired to escort the two Sigmoids into the interior of Borneo. Into the largely unexplored Hose Range, and an area called the Bukit Tengah, where lived a number of rare and uncollected species, including the ratbird—happy until this juncture in their uncollected state. Animal and insect: all congratulated themselves on failing to make some Cambridge encyclopedia.

Balbindor was a coastal Malay of the Iban tribe. However, he had been into the interior once before, in the service of two Dutch explorers who, in the manner of all Dutch explorers, had died strange deaths: though not before they had communicated to civilization a mysterious message: "Wallace and Darwin did not know it, but there are alternatives." Balbindor, four-foot-six high, brought the word hot-foot back to the coast.

Sigmoid was keener on alternatives than his son Herbert. Confidence men always have an eye for extra exits. Thirteen days into the rainforest, led by Balbindor and sonlet, and the doctor remained more determined than his offspring. The night before they reached the tributary of the Baleh river they sought, Balbindor overheard a significant exchange between father and son.

Herbert complained of heat and hardship, declaring that what he longed for most in the world was a marble bathroom with warm scented water and soft towels. To which his father rejoined that Herbert was a gross materialist. Going further, Sigmoid retreated into one of his annoying fits of purity, declaring, "To achieve godliness, my boy, you must give up all possessions . . ."

Herbert replied bitterly, "I'm your one possession you'll never give up."

Had this been a scene in a movie, it would have been followed by pistol shots and, no doubt, the entry of a deadly snake into the Sigmoid tent. However, the story is now Balbindor's. He shall tell it in his own excruciating words. And Balbindor, never having seen any movie, with the solitary exception of *The Sound of Music* (to which he gave three stars), lacked a sense of drama. Father and son, he reported, kissed each other as usual and went to sleep in their separate bivouacs.

If my story, then I tell. Not some other guy. Many error in all story belong other guy. I Iban man, real name no Balbindor. I no see *Sound Music* ever. Only see trailer one time, maybe two. Julie Andrews good lady, I marry. My kid I take on no call Monsoon. Monsoon late name. Kid, he come from India. I take on. I no call Monsoon, I call Krishna. My son they die logging camp, all same place, three time. Too much drink. I very sad, adopt Krishna. He my son, good boy. Special golden eye. I like, OK.

This Doctor Sigmoid and he son Herbert very trouble on journey. We go on Baleh river, boat swim good. All time, Herbert he complain. White men no sweat pure, too many clothe. No take off clothe. Then boat swim up tributary Puteh, no swim good. Water he go way under boat. Mud he come, stop boat.

We hide boat, go on feet in jungle. Very much complain Herbert and father he both. They no understand jungle. They no eat insect. Insect eat them.

Jungle many tree, many many tree. Some tree good, some tree bad, some tree never mind. I tell number tree. Tamarind tree, he fruit bitter, quench throat thirst. Help every day. Sigmoid no like, fear poison. I no speak him. All same jungle olive, good tree. We drink pitcher plant, all same like monkey.

Monkey they good guide. Krishna and me we do like monkey. Understand jungle. Wake early, when first light in jungle. Deer trail fresh, maybe catch deer along blowpipe. Monkey wake early, eat, sing, along branches. Sigmoids no like wake early. Day cool. I like wake early, make Sigmoids rise up. Go quiet. Creep along, maybe catch kill snake for pot.

Many ant in Hose Range, big, little, many color. All go different way. I speak ant, ant speak me. Go this way, go that. Every leaf he fall, he mean a something. I understand. I plenty savvy in jungle.

One week, two week, three week, we walk in jungle, sometime up, sometime down. For Sigmoids, very hard to go. Both smell bad. Too much breath. No control. Dutch men control of breath good. Herbert he very scare. No like jungle, all same long time. No good man, swear me. I understand. Herbert he no think I understand.

Three week, get very near area Bukit Tengah. Now all path go up, need more care. Many cliff, many rock. One fall, maybe finish. Waterfall, he pour bad water. I know smell bad water nose belong me. Krishna and two bearer and I, we no drink bad water. Come from Other Side. I tell Sigmoids no drink water come Other Side. They no care, no understand, they drink bad waterfall water plenty. Take on bad spirit. I understand. I shout much, Krishna he cry all same long time. Herbert he shout me, try hit little Krishna.

I tell Herbert, "You drink water belong Other Side. Now you got bad spirit. You no get back Europe. You finish man."

Herbert no savvy. He plenty sick. I see him bad spirit. It suck him soul. Now I plenty scare.

Every day more slow. Other Side he come near. Bearer man they two, they no like go more far. I hear what they speak together. I savvy what Orang Asli speak, I tell Dr. Sigmoid. He swear. No please me. Both Sigmoids have fever. Black in face, very strange. Smell bad more.

Big storm come over from Other Side, maybe hope drive us away. Thunder he flatten ears, lightning he blind eyes, rain he lash flesh, wind he freeze skin. We hide away under raintree, very fear. Night it come, big wizard, I no understand. Too black. In night bearer they go, I no hear. Two bearer they run off. Steal supply. I very sad I no hear. In morning dawnlight I say to doctor sorry. Bearer they scare, go back wife. Doctor he swear again. I say, no good swear. Who hear swear with good nature? Best leave alone, keep silent. He no like. Make bad face.

Day after storm, we come Other Side. I see how monkey they no go Other Side. Different monkey on Other Side, speak different language. Different tree, grow other different leaf. Fruit they different, no wise eat. Insect different.

Also one more bad thing. I see men belong Other Side in jungle. They move like ghost but I see. Krishna he see, he point. Plenty eye in jungle belong Other Side. No like. Other Side men they much difference. How they think different, no good.

I see, I understand, Krishna he understand. I no make Sigmoids understand.

"Geology," I explain Sigmoids. I speak they language good. "He change. Different earth begin now since many many old time. All thing different, different time. Different inside time. Womb bring forth different thing. Bad go there, no go. Only look one day."

"Balls," he say.

I sick with him doctor. I make speak, "I keep my ball belong me. You go, and Herbert. I no go one more pace. Krishna, he no go one more pace."

Herbert he bring out gun. I very fear. I know him mad with bad spirit. I say him, "Two piece Dutch man they come here. Pretty soon they finish. Why you no sense? Come back home along me, Krishna."

He get more mad.

I was really disgusted with this idiot native Balbindor or whatever his name was. Here we were. At great expense to ourselves, father and I had finally arrived on the very threshold of Bukit Tengah, the Middle Mountain, and this difficult little man and his black kid were refusing to proceed.

It just was not rational. But you don't expect rationality from such people. These natives are riddled with superstition.

Also, I blamed him for the way the bearers had deserted us. We had quite an argument. I was trembling violently from head to foot. Most unpleasant.

I want to say this, too, about the whole incident. Balbindor treated father and me all along as complete fools. We could grasp that he was trying to tell us we had arrived at some sort of geological shift, much like the Wallace Discontinuity east of Bali, where two tectonic plates meet and flora and fauna are different on the two opposed sides. We knew that better than he did, having researched the matter in books before the expedition, but saw no reason to be superstitious about it.

We had also observed that there were those on the other side of the divide who were watching us. Father and I were going to go in there whether or not Balbindor and his son accompanied us. We saw the necessity to make an immediate impression on the new tribe, since we would be dealing with them soon enough.

That was why I shot Balbindor on the spot. It was mainly to introduce ourselves.

Little Krishna ran off into the jungle. Perhaps the little idiot thought I was going to shoot him as well. I suppose I might have done. I was pretty steamed up.

"Put your revolver away, you fool," Father said. That was all the thanks I got from him. When has he ever been grateful?

We had no idea what to do with Balbindor's corpse. Eventually we dragged it to the waterfall and flung it in. We slept by the waterfall that night and next morning, at our leisure, crossed the divide into the Other Side (the silly name had stuck).

For two days we traveled through dense alien jungle. We were aware that there were men among the thickets following us, but it was the monkeys who caused us most trouble. They were no bigger than leaf monkeys, but had black caps and a line of black fur about the eyes, giving them an oddly human look. Father trapped one with the old Malayan gourd trick, and discovered it to have only four toes on each foot and four fingers on each hand. We came at last to a clearing brought about by a massive outcrop of rock. Here we rested, both of us being overcome by fevers. We could see the barbaric scenery about us, the tumbled mass of vegetation, with every tree weighted down by chains of epiphytes and climbers. Above them loomed densely clad peaks of mountains, often as not shrouded by swift moving cloud.

These clouds took on startling devilish shapes, progressing towards us. It may have been the fever which caused this uncomfortable illusion.

Days must have passed in illness. I cannot say how strange it was, how peculiarly dead I felt, when I awoke to find myself at a distance from my father. Dreadful sensations of isolation overcame me. Moreover, I was walking about. My feet seemed not to touch the ground.

I discovered that I could not get near my father. Whenever I seemed to advance towards him, my steps deviated in some way. It was as if I suffered from an optical illusion so strong that it consumed my other senses. I could do no more than prowl about him.

Father was sitting cross-legged by the remains of a fire on which he had roasted the leg of a small deer. Its remains lay by him. He was talking to a small wizened man with long hair and a curved bone through his cheeks which made him appear tusked. The face of this man was painted white. For some reason, I felt terrified of him, yet what chiefly seemed to scare me was a minor eccentricity of garb: the man wore nothing but an elaborate scarf or band or belt of fabric about his middle. No attempt had been made to cover his genitals, which were painted white like his face.

Prowling in a circular fashion seemed all I was capable of, so I continuously circled the spot. Although I called to my father, he took no notice, appearing totally absorbed in his conversation with the white-faced man. I now noted that the latter had on each hand only three fingers and a thumb, and only four toes on each foot, in the manner of the monkeys we had come across in another existence.

I was filled with such great uneasiness and hatred that I chattered and jibbered and made myself horrible.

Again and again I attempted to advance towards my father. Only now did I realize that I loved this man to whose power I had been subject all my life. Yet he would not—or perhaps could not—take the slightest notice of me. I set up a great screaming to attract his attention. Still he would not hear.

Father, Father, I called to you all my life! Perhaps you never ever heard, so wrapped up were you in your own dreams and ambitions. Now for this last time, I beg you to attend to your poor Herbert.

I know you have your own story. Allow me mine, for pity's sake!

It would be true to say without exaggeration that throughout my mature life, in my quest to transform humanity, I had been in search of Mr. White Face, as I thought of him. (He refused to tell his name. That would have given me power over him.) I have a firm belief in transcendental power, unlike poor Herbert.

White Face materialized out of thin air when I was drinking at a pool. There on my hands and knees, by gosh! I looked up—he was standing nearby, large as life. Naked except for the band round his belly; yet something about him marked him immediately as a singular character. (A flair for judging character is one of my more useful talents.)

A remarkable feature of White Face's physiognomy was a pair of small tusks (six inches long) piercing the cheeks and curving outwards. My knowledge of anatomy suggested they were rooted in the maxilla. They gave my new acquaintance a somewhat belligerent aspect, you may be sure!

Already he has told me much. We have spent two whole days from sun-up till sun-down in rapt conversation. His thought processes are entirely different from mine. Yet we have much in common. He is the wise man of his people as I, in

Europe, am of mine. Grubby little man he may be—he shits in my presence without embarrassment—yet in his thought I perceive he is fastidious. I can probably adapt some of his ideas.

Much that he says about divisions in the human psyche is reflected in pale form in the Hindu sacred books of the Upanishads (which is hardly surprising, since White Face claims that all the world's knowledge of itself emanated from "the Other Side" during the ice age before last, when Other Siders went out like missionaries over the globe, reaching as far as Hindustan).

What I do find difficult to swallow—we argued long about this—is some strange belief of his that the world is immaterial and that humanity (if I have it correctly) is no more than a kind of metaphysical construct projected by nature and relying on *words* rather than *flesh* for its continued existence. Perhaps I've misunderstood the old boy. I'm still slightly feverish. Or he's mad as a hatter.

Only knowledge is precious, he says. And knowledge is perpetually being lost. The world from which I come is in crisis. It is losing its instinctual knowledge. Instinctual knowledge is leaking away under the impact of continual urbanization. That, I believe. It is not in conflict with my own doctrines. He thinks our world will shortly die.

Then the Other Side will recolonize the world with new plants and animals—and understanding. (His kind of understanding, of course.) He wants to convince me to become his disciple, to go forth and encourage the world-death to come swiftly. By the third day of our discussion, I begin more and more to comprehend how desirable it is that the civilization to which I belong should be utterly destroyed. Yet still I hesitate. We drink some of his potent *boka* and rest from intellectual debate.

I ask, How are things so different here?

In answer, he shows me a ratbird.

Some distance from the rock on which we sat in conference—conferring about the future of the world, if that doesn't sound too pompous—an angsana stood, a large tropical tree, its branches full of birds to which I paid no attention. Birds have never been one of my major interests, I need hardly say.

Mr. White Face began a kind of twittering whistle, a finger planted in each corner of his lips. Almost immediately, the birds in the angsana responded by flying out in a flock, showing what I took to be anxiety by sinking to the ground and then rapidly rising again. Each time they sank down, they clustered closely, finally expelling one of their number, who fluttered to the ground and began—as if under compulsion—to walk, or rather scuttle, towards us; whereupon the other birds fled into the shelter of their tree.

As the bird came nearer, White Face changed his tune. The bird crawled between us and lay down at our feet in an unbird-like manner.

I saw that its anatomy was unbird-like. Its two pink legs ended in four toes, all pointing forward with only a suggestion of balancing heel. Wings and body were covered in grey fur. And the face was that of a rodent. In some ways it resembled a flying fox, common throughout Malaysia, in some ways it resembled a rat; but its easy flight and way of walking proclaimed it a bird.

And now that I looked again at Mr. White Face, I saw that beneath his paint, his face had some of the configurations of a rat, with sharp little jaws and pointed nose, not at all like the inhabitants of Sarawak, a blunt-faced company, with which I was acquainted.

Obeying his instruction, I proffered my hand, open palms upwards, towards the animal. The ratbird climbed on and began to preen its fur unconcernedly.

Nobody will blame me if I say that in the circumstances I became very uneasy. It seemed to me that in Mr. White Face I had stumbled upon an evolutionary path paralleling—rivaling—our accepted one; that this path sprang from a small ground mammal (possibly tusked) very different from the arboreal tarsier-like creature from which homo sapiens has developed. I was face to face with . . . *homo rodens* . . . Over millions of years, its physical and mental processes had continued in its own course, parallel to but alien from ours. Indeed, perhaps inimical to ours, in view of the long-standing hostility between man and rat.

Rising to my feet, I flicked the ratbird into the air. It looped the loop. Instead of flying off, it settled at my feet.

I found I was unable to walk about. My legs would not move. Some magic had trapped me. At this unhappy moment, I recalled that mysterious sentence, "Wallace and Darwin did not know it, but there are alternatives." The alternative had been revealed to me; with magnificent hardihood, I had ventured into the Other Side; was I to suffer the fate of the two Dutch explorers?

Mr. White Face continued to sit crossed-legged, gazing up at me, his tusked countenance quite inscrutable. I saw the world through glass. It was unmoving. I felt extremely provoked. Perhaps the argumentative Balbindor had been correct in saying I should not have drunk from the waterfall springing from the Other Side. It had left me in White Face's power.

And I was uncomfortably aware of the spirit of Herbert. After the foolish lad had died of his fevers—unable to pull through illness like me with my superior physique—his spirit had been powerless to escape. It circled me now, yowling and screaming in a noxious way. I tried to ignore it. But how to escape my predicament?

I stared down at the white face of the ratman. Then, from my days as a chemist, I remembered a formula for bleach. Perhaps the magic of science would overcome this detestable witchcraft (or whatever it was that held me in thrall).

As loudly as I could, I recited the formula by which bleach is produced when chlorine reacts with sodium hydroxide solution:

"$Cl_2(g) + 2NaOH(aq) \rightarrow NaCl(aq) + NaClO(aq) + H_2O(l)$."

Even as I chanted, I felt power return to my muscles. The great tousled world about me began to stir with life again. I was free. Thanks to bleach and a Western education—and of course an excellent memory.

I kicked at the ratbird, which fluttered off.

"I don't care for your kind of hospitality," I told White Face.

"Well, you have passed my test," he said. "You are no weakling and your words are strong. To each of us there are two compartments which form our inner workings. One part is blind, one part sees. Most of our ordinary lives are governed by the part that sees, which is capable of performing ordinary tasks. That part is like a living thing which emerges from an egg. But there is the other part, which is blind and never emerges from the egg. It knows only what is unknown. It acts in time of trouble. You understand?"

"You perhaps speak in parable form of two divisions of the brain. If so, then I believe I understand you." (I did not think it politic to express my reservations.)

He gave a short dry laugh, exposing sharp teeth. "Oh, we like to believe we understand! Suppose we have never understood one single thing of the world about us and inside us? Suppose we have lived in utter darkness and only believed that darkness was light?"

"All things may be supposed. So what then?"

He said, "Then on the day that light dawns, it will be to you as if a sudden incomprehensible darkness descends."

After this horrifying statement he made a beckoning gesture and began running.

Since he made swiftly towards the forest, I had not much option but to follow. But his words had chilled me. Suppose indeed that we were hedged in by limitations of comprehension we could not comprehend? The ratbird had already shaken many of my convictions regarding life on earth and how it had evolved.

Mr. White Face's mode of progression through the forest was at odds with my previous guide, Balbindor, and his method of procedure; but then, the trees, the very trees we passed through, were different. Their bark, if bark it was, possessed a highly reflective surface, so that to move forward was to be accompanied by a multitudinous army of distortions of oneself. (In this hallucinatory company, it was impossible not to feel ill at ease. Jumpy, in a word.)

I did not understand how it was possible to find one's way in such a jungle. White Face was presumably trusting to his second compartment, "the part that never hatched," to see him along his course.

In which case, the blind thing was unexpectedly reliable. After two days of arduous travel, we came to a dark-flowing river. On the far side of it stood a village of longhouses, much like the ones we had left back on the coast, except that these were entered by round doors instead of the normal rectangular ones.

Uncomfortable as I was in White Face's company, there was comfort in the sense of arrival. I was possessed of a lively curiosity to investigate this kampong of the Other Side—that lively curiosity which has carried me so successfully through life.

One factor still contributed to my unease. The ghost of my son pursued me yet, his translucent image being reflected from the trunk of every tree, so that it sometimes appeared ahead of me as well as on every side. Herbert waved and screamed in the dreariest manner imaginable (uncanny, yet nevertheless slightly reminiscent of his behavior throughout his life).

"We shall cross the river," White Face announced, putting two skinny fingers into the corners of his mouth and whistling to announce our presence.

"Will Herbert cross with us?" I asked, I trust without revealing my nervousness.

He dismissed the very idea. "Ghosts cannot cross moving water. Only if they are ghosts of men with wooden legs."

After White Face had signaled to some men on the opposite bank, a narrow dugout canoe was paddled across to collect us. By the time we landed at a rickety jetty, a number of inhabitants had gathered, standing cautiously back to observe us with their heads thrust forward as if they were short sighted.

All of them had tusks. Some tusks were large and curled, or adorned with leaves. I could not fail to see that all, men, women and children, wore nothing in the tropical heat but a band—in the case of the women this was quite ornate—around their middles, leaving everything else uncovered. The breasts of the women were small, and no more developed than those of the men. (The women also had tusks, so that I wondered if they were used for offense or defense. Presumably the missionary position in coitus would have its dangers. One might be stabbed *in medias res*.)

They were in general a strange lot, with sharp beaky faces quite unlike the Malays to whom I was accustomed. In their movements was something restless. A kind of rictus was common. I saw that here was opportunity for anthropological study which, when reported abroad, could but add to my fame. I wanted a look in a mouth to see where those tusks were anchored.

White Face addressed some of the men in a fast flowing and high-pitched language. They made respectful way for him, as he led me through the village to a longhouse standing apart from the others.

"This is my home and you are welcome," he said. "Here you may rest and recover from your fever. The spirit of your son will not harm you."

To my dismay, I found that the bleach formula had left my mind and would not be recalled. Did this mean I was still under his spell? So it was with reluctance that I climbed the ramp leading into the longhouse with its two great tusks over the circular entrance.

Inside, I was barely able to stand upright at the highest point, for I was head and shoulders taller than my sinister host; and it did not escape my notice that the roof at its highest point was infested with cobwebs, in the corners of which sat large square spiders. Also, when he gestured to me to sit down on the mats which covered the floor, I could not but observe two fairly fresh (tuskless) skulls above the door by which we had entered. Catching my glance, Mr. White Face asked, "Do you speak Dutch?"

"Do they—now?" I asked, with sarcasm.

But he had a response. "On the night of the full moon they do speak. I cannot silence them. You shall hear them by and by, and become familiar with the eloquence of death."

We then engaged in philosophical discourse, while a servant woman, cringing as she served us, brought a dark drink like tea in earthenware bowls which fitted neatly between Mr. White Face's tusks.

After two hours of conversation, during which he questioned me closely concerning Ouspensky, he apologized that his wife (he used a different word) was not present. It appeared that she was about to deliver a son.

I congratulated him.

"I have twelve sons already," he said. "Though this one is special, as you may see. A miraculous son who will further our most powerful ambitions, a wizard of words. So it is written . . . Now let us discuss how the end, closure, and abridgment of your world may be brought about, since we are in agreement that such an objective is desirable."

Although I was less ready than before to agree that such an objective was desirable, I nevertheless found myself entering into his plans. (The dark drink had its effect.) The plans were—to me at least—elaborate and confusing. But the horrifying gist of his argument was that homo sapiens might be extinguished by *pantun*. I understood that *pantun* was a form of Malayan poetry, and could not grasp how this might annihilate anything; but, as he continued, I began to see—or I thought in that dazed state I saw—that he believed all human perceptions to be governed by words, and, indeed, distorted and ultimately betrayed by words. "Betrayed" was the word he used. This, he said, was the weakness of homo sapiens: words had weakened the contract with nature that guaranteed mankind's existence. (All our spiritual ills were evidence of this deteriorating state of affairs.)

There were ways by which all homo sapiens could be reduced—abridged—into a story, a kind of poem. Those who live by the word die by the word. So he said. We could end as a line of *pantun*.

I cannot reduce this plan of his into clear words. It was not delivered to me in clear words, but in some sort of squeaky Other Side music with which he aided my understanding. All I can say is that there in that creepy hut, I came to believe it was perfectly easy to turn the whole story of the world I knew into a world of story.

As we were getting into the how of it—and drinking more of that dark liquid—the servant hurried in with an apology and squeaked something. White Face rose.

"Come with me," he said. "My wife (he used the different word) is about to bring forth the thirteenth son."

"Will she mind my presence?"

"Not at all. Indeed, your presence is essential. Without your presence, you can have no absence, isn't that so?" (Whatever that meant. If that is truly what he said.)

In we went, into curtained-off quarters at the far end of the longhouse. All misty with scented things burning and jangling instruments being played by two long-tusked men.

His wife lay on the floor on a mat, attended by the servant girl. Her stomach did not appear extended. She was entirely naked, no embroidered band round her middle. For the first time, I saw—with what sense of shock I cannot explain—*that she had no navel*. Nor was this some kind of unique aberration. The servant girl—perhaps in honor of the occasion—was also nude and without the customary middle band. She also had no navel. I was struck as by an obscenity, and unprepared for what followed. (Tusks I could take; lack of navel implied a different universe of being.)

"Now the birth begins," said Mr. White Face, as his wife lifted one leg, "and you will find all will go according to plan. The story of your species will become a kind of Möbius strip, but at least you will have had a role in it, Dr. Sigmoid."

He had never used my name previously. I knew myself in his power; as never before I felt myself powerless, a thin benaveled creature without understanding. I had believed these strange people of the Other Side to be distant descendants of a kind of rodent ancestor. But that was a scientific illusion built on evolutionary terminology. The truth was different, more difficult, less palatable. As the woman lifted her leg, an egg emerged from her womb.

An egg not of shell like a bird's: leathery, rather like a turtle's. An egg! A veritable egg, ostrich sized.

A terrible rushing noise beset me. The longhouse flew away. I was surrounded by bright sunlight, yet in total darkness, as foretold. Even worse—far worse—I was not I. The terror of wonderment, real understanding, had changed all. Only the egg remained.

With a sense of destiny, I leaned forward and tapped upon it with an invisible finger. It split.

*   *   *

At the miracle of my birth, I came forth when my father summoned me. A star was set upon my forehead. I am unique. The gods that make their careless journeys across the world, playing with science or magic as they will, create thousands of everything, of sea almonds, of waves, of days—of words. Yet there is only one Dishayloo. No navel, and a star in the middle of his forehead.

Born to shine in a world of story.

THE SAILOR WHO SAILED AFTER THE SUN

Gene Wolfe

Gene Wolfe is one of the most gifted and respected writers in the fantasy field, owing to such extraordinary works as *The Book of the New Sun*, *The Devil in a Forest*, and *Castleview*. His latest collection, *Storeys from the Old Hotel*, is highly recommended, and a new novel, *Nightside the Long Sun*, has just been published. Wolfe has received the World Fantasy Award, the John W. Campbell Memorial Award, and the Nebula Award. He and his wife live outside of Chicago, Illinois.

"The Sailor Who Sailed After the Sun" is an entertaining and evocative fable reprinted from the small-press anthology *Grails: Quests, Visitations and Other Occurrences*, published in Atlanta, Georgia, by Unnameable Press.

—T.W.

> But if the great sun move not of himself;
> *but is an errand boy in heaven . . .*
> —Melville

In the good days now lost, when cranky, old-fashioned people still wore three-cornered hats and knee breeches, a lanky farm boy with hair like tow walked to New Bedford with all his possessions tied up in a red-and-white kerchief. Reuben was his name. He gawked at the high wooden houses so close together (for he had never seen the like), at the horses and the wagons, and at all people—hundreds of men and dozens of women all shoulder-to-shoulder and pushing one another up and down the streets. Most of all, he gawked at the towering ship in the harbor; and when, after an hour or so, a big man with a bushy black beard asked whether he was looking for work, he nodded readily, and followed the big man (who was the chief mate) aboard, and signed a paper.

Next morning the third mate, a man no older than Reuben himself, escorted Reuben to a chandler's, where he bought two pairs of white duck trousers, three striped shirts, a hammock, a pea-jacket, a seabag, and some other things, the cost of everything to be deducted from his pay. And on the day after that, the ship set sail.

Of its passage 'round the Horn to the great whaling grounds of the Southeast

Pacific, I shall say little, save that it was very hard indeed. There were storms and more storms; nor were they the right sort of storms, which blow one in the direction in which one wishes to go. These were emphatically storms of the wrong sort. They blew the ship back into the Atlantic time after time; and Reuben believed that was what made them storms of the wrong sort until one blew the man who slung his hammock aft of Reuben's own from the mizzen yard and into the churning waters of the West Scotia Basin. The man who had slung his hammock aft of Reuben's had been the only man aboard with whom Reuben had forged the beginnings of a friendship, and the emptiness of that hammock, as it swung back and forth with the labored pitching of the ship, weighed heavily against him until it was taken down.

At last the storms relented. From open boats tossed and rolled in frigid seas, they took two right whales (which are whales of the right sort) and one sperm whale (which is not). There is no more onerous work done at sea than the butchering and rendering of whales. It is without danger and thus without excitement; nor does it involve monotony of the sort that frees the sailor's mind to go elsewhere. It means working twelve hours a day in a cold, cramped, and reeking factory in which one also lives, and everything—men, clothes, hammocks, blankets, decks, bulkheads, masts, spars, rigging, and sails—gets intolerably greasy.

One dark day when the ice wind from the south punished the ship worse even than usual, and patches of freezing fog raced like great cold ghosts across the black swell, and the old, gray-bearded captain rubbed his greasy eyeglasses upon the sleeve of his greasy blue greatcoat and cursed, and five minutes afterward rubbed them there again, and cursed again, they were stove by a great sperm whale the color of coffee rich with cream. For a moment only they saw him, his great head dashing aside the waves, and the wrecks of two harpoons behind his eye, and the round, pale scars (like so many bubbles in the coffee) two feet across left by the suckers of giant squid.

He vanished and struck. The whole ship shivered and rolled.

In an instant everything seemed to have gone wrong.

In the next it appeared that everything was as right as it had ever been, four-square and shipshape, after all; and that the crash and shock and splintered planks had been an evil dream.

Yet they were stove, nevertheless. The ship was taking green water forward, and all the pumps together could not keep pace with it. They plugged the hole as well as they could with caps and coats and an old foresail, and when, after three days that even the big, black-bearded mate called hellish, they reached calmer waters, they passed lines under the bow, and hauled into place (there in the darkness below the waterline) a great square of doubled sailcloth like a bandage.

After that they sailed for nearly a month with the pumps going night and day, through waters ever bluer and warmer, until they reached a green island with a white, sloping beach. Whether it lay among those lands first explored by Captain Cook, or on the edge of the Indies, or somewhere east of Africa, Reuben did not know and could not discover. Some mentioned the Friendly Islands; some spoke of the Cocos, some of the Maldives, and still others of Ile de France or Madagascar. It is probable, indeed, that no one knew except the captain, and perhaps even he did not know.

Wherever it was, it seemed a kindly sort of place to poor Reuben. There, through long, sunny days and moonlit nights, they lightened the ship as much as possible, until it rode as high in the water as a puffin, and at high tide warped it as near the beach as they could get it, and at low tide rolled it on its side to get at the stove-in planking.

One day, when the work was nearly done and his watch dismissed, Reuben wandered farther inland than he usually ventured. There was a spring there, he knew, for he had fetched water from it; he thought that he recalled the way, and he longed for a drink from its cool, clear, upwelling pool. But most of all (if the truth be told) he wished to become lost—to be lost and left behind on that island, which was the finest place that he had ever known save his mother's lap.

And so of course he *was* lost, for people who wish to be lost always get their way. He found a spring that might (or might not) have been the one he recalled. He drank from it, and lay down beside it and slept; and when he woke, a large gray monkey had climbed down out of a banyan tree and thrust a long, careful gray hand into his pocket, and was looking at his clasp knife.

"That's mine," Reuben said, sitting up.

The monkey nodded solemnly, and as much as said, "I know."

But here I have to explain all the ways in which this monkey talked, because you think that monkeys do not often do it. Mostly, at first, he talked with his face and eyes and head, looking away or looking up, grinning or pulling down the corners of his mouth. Later he talked with his hands as well, just as I do. And subsequently he came to make actual sounds, grunting like the mate or sighing like the captain, and pushing his lips in or out. All this until eventually—and long before he had finished talking with Reuben—he spoke at least as well as most of the crew and better than some of them.

"Give it back," Reuben said.

"Wait a bit," replied the monkey, opening and closing the marlin spike, and testing the point with his finger. "That may not be necessary. How much will you take for it? I offer fifteen round, ripe coconuts, delivered here to you immediately upon your agreement."

"Don't want coconuts." Reuben held out his hand.

The monkey raised his shoulders and let them fall. "I don't blame you. Neither do I." Regretfully, he returned the knife to Reuben. "You're from that big ship in the lagoon, aren't you? And you'll be going away in a day or two."

"I wish," Reuben told the monkey, "that I didn't have to go away."

The monkey scratched his head with his left hand, then with his right. His gray arms were long and thin, but very muscular. "Your mother would miss you."

"My mother's dead," Reuben confessed sadly. "My father too."

"Your sisters and brothers, then."

"I have only one brother," Reuben explained. "While my father was alive, my brother and I helped on the farm. But when my father died, my brother got it and I had to leave."

"Your troop, on the ship. Unless you had someone to take your place."

"No one would do that," Reuben said.

"Don't be too sure," the monkey told him. "I would trade this island for your clasp knife, those trousers, your striped shirt, your cap, and your place on the ship."

Reuben shook his head in wonder. "This beautiful island is worth a great deal more than our whole ship."

"Not to me," said the monkey. "You see, I have owned this island ever since I was born, and have never seen any other place."

Reuben nodded. "That was the way our farm was. When I could live there I didn't really care about it, so that when my brother told me I had to go, I felt that I'd just as soon do it, because I didn't want to work for him. But now it seems the dearest spot in all the world, next to this one."

Thus it was arranged. The monkey dressed himself in Reuben's clothes, putting his beautiful, curled tail down the left leg of Reuben's white duck trousers and the clasp knife into the pocket. And Reuben dressed himself in the monkey's (who had none). And when they heard some of the crew coming, he hid behind the banyan tree.

It was a watering party with buckets, for the ship had been mended, and refloated again, and they had come to refill its barrels and butts. Each sailor had two buckets, and when one set a full bucket down to fill another, the monkey picked it up and waited for him to object. He did not, and the monkey became quite friendly with him by the time that they had carried their buckets back to the ship.

The mates were not fooled. Let me say that at the outset, neither the bushy-black-bearded chief mate, nor the youthful third mate, nor the sleepy-eyed second mate, who never even appears in this story. All three knew perfectly well that the monkey was not Reuben; and if they did not imagine that he was a monkey, they must nonetheless have suspected that he was something not quite human and perhaps of the ape kind. This is shown clearly by the name they gave him, which was Jacko. But since Jacko was a better sailor than Reuben had ever been, and a prankish, lively fellow as well, they did not say a great deal about it.

As for the captain, his eyeglasses were so greasy that Jacko in Reuben's shirt looked the very image of Reuben to him. Once, it is true, the chief mate mentioned the matter to him, saying, "There's somethin' perqu'ler about one of our topmen, Capt'n."

"And what is that, Mr. Blackmire?" the captain had replied, looking at the chief mate over his eyeglasses in order to see him.

"Well, Capt'n, he's shorter than all the rest. And he's hairy, sir. Terribly hairy. Gray hair."

Scratching his own greasy gray beard with the point of his pen, the captain had inquired, "A disciplinary problem, Mr. Blackmire?"

"No, sir."

"Does his work?"

"Yes, sir." The chief mate had taken a step backward as he spoke, having divined whither their talk was bound.

"Keep an eye on him, Mr. Blackmire. Just keep an eye on him."

That was the end of it; and indeed, Jacko soon became such a valuable member of the crew that the chief mate was sorry he had brought the matter up.

But to explain to you how that was, I am going to have to explain first how whaling was carried on in those days, before the invention of the modern harpoon gun, and the equally modern explosive harpoon, and all the rest of the improvements and astonishing devices that have made whaling so easy and pleasant for everyone except the whales.

Those old harpoons, you see, hardly ever killed the whale—they did not penetrate deeply enough for that. The old harpoons were, in fact, really no more than big spears with barbed heads to which a long rope was attached as a sort of fishing line.

When the harpooner, standing in the bow of his whaleboat (you have seen pictures of Washington crossing the Delaware doing this), had thrown his harpoon, and it had gone a foot or two into the hump, as it usually was, of the poor whale, the whalers had only hooked their catch, not landed it. They had to play it, and when it was so tired that it could hardly swim and could not dive, though its life depended on it, they had to pull their boat alongside it and kill it with their whale lances, either by stabbing it from the boat, or actually springing out of the boat and onto the whale. And to say that all this was a difficult and a very dangerous business is like saying that learning to ride a tiger requires tenacity and a scratch-proof surface far above the common.

For a whale is as much bigger than the biggest tiger as the planet Jupiter is bigger than the big globe in a country school, and it is as much stronger than the strongest tiger as a full, round bumper of nitroglycerin is stronger than a cup of tea. And though it is not as savage as a tiger, the whale is fighting for its life.

Which Jacko, as I have implied, became very skilled in taking. No sailor on the ship was bolder than he with the whaling lance, none more ready to spring from the whaleboat onto the great, dark, slippery back, or to plunge the razor-sharp steel lancehead between his own feet, and raise the lance, and plunge it again and again till the whale's bright blood gushed forth not like a spring but like a full-grown river, and the whole of the sea for a mile around was dyed scarlet by it—just as certain rivers we have, that are bleeding their continents to death, dye the very oceans themselves for whole leagues beyond land with red or yellow mud that they have stolen away.

A day arrived (and in part it came as quickly as it did as a result of Jacko's efforts, let there be no doubt of that) when the great tuns in the ship's hold were nearly full. Then the captain, and the crew as well, calculated that one more whale would fill them to the brim. It was a pleasant prospect. Already the captain was thinking of his high white house in New Bedford and his grandchildren; and the sailors of weeks and even months ashore, of living well in an inn, and eating and drinking whenever they wished and never working, of farms and cottages and village girls, and stories around the fire.

Jacko was in the fo'c'sle that day, enlightening a few select friends as to the way the chief mate walked, and the way the captain lit his pipe, and the way in which a clever fellow may look between his own legs and see the world new, and other such things, when they heard the thrilling cry of "There . . . there . . . *thar* she blows!" from the maintop.

Three whales!

Jacko was the first on deck, the first at the davits, and the first into the first of the half-dozen whaleboats they launched. No oarsman pulled harder than he, his thin, gray back straining against Reuben's second-best striped shirt; and not a man on board cheered more heartily than he when Savannah Jefferson, the big brown harpooner with arms thicker than most men's thighs and a child's soft, sweet voice, cast his harpoon up and out, rising, bending, and falling like lightning to strike deep into the whale's back a boat's length behind the tail.

What a ride that whale gave them! There is nothing like it now, nothing at all. Mile after mile, as fast as the fastest speedboat, through mist and fog and floating ice. They could not slow or steer, and they would not cut free. At one moment they were sitting in water and bailing like so many madmen, nine-tenths swamped. At the next the whale was sounding, and like to pull them down with it. Long, long before it stopped and they were able to draw their boat up to it, they had lost sight of their ship.

But stop it did, eventually, and lay on the rough and heaving swell like the black keel of a capsized hulk, with its breath smoking in the air, and the long summer day (it was the twenty-first of December), like the whale, nearly spent.

"Lances!" bellowed the chief mate from his place in the stern.

Jacko was the first with his lance; nor did he content himself, as many another would have, with a mere jab at the whale from the boat. No, not he! As in times past he had leaped from the top of one tall palm to another, now he sprang from the gunnel of the whaleboat onto the whale's broad back.

And as he did, the whale, with one powerful blow of its tail, upset the whaleboat and tossed the crew, oars, lances, and spare harpoons into the freezing water.

A hand reached up—one lone hand, and that only for a moment—as though to grasp the top of a small wave. Jacko extended the shaft of his lance toward it, but the shaft was not long enough, nor Jacko quick enough, quick though he was. The hand vanished below the wave it had tried to grasp and never reappeared.

Then Jacko looked at the whale, or rather, as I should say, at the little round eye of it; and the whale at Jacko; and Jacko saw the whale for what it was, and himself for what he was, too. He took off Reuben's cap then and threw it into the sea, where it floated. Reuben's second-best shirt followed it, and floated too. Reuben's white duck trousers followed them both; but those trousers did not float like a duck or like anything else, for the weight of Reuben's clasp knife in the pocket sunk them.

"I am an animal like you," Jacko told the whale. "Not really like you, because you're very big, while I'm very small. And you're where you belong, while I'm thousands and thousands of miles from where I belong. But we're both animals— that's all I meant to say. If I don't molest you any more, ever again, will you let me right the boat, and bail it, and live on this terrible sea if I can?"

To which the whale said, "I will."

Then Jacko cut the harpoon line with the head of his lance, and let it slide into the sea. It is hard, very hard, to pull out a harpoon, because of the big, swiveling barbs on the head that open out and resist the pull. But Jacko worked the head back and forth with his long, gray, clever fingers, and cut when he had to with the head of the lance (those lance heads look very much like the blades of daggers), and eventually he got it out, and threw it into the sea, and the lance after it.

By that time it was nearly dark—so dark that he could hardly make out the upturned bottom of the whaleboat; but the whale knew where it was, and swam over to it until it bumped against its side. Jacko braced his long monkey-feet against the whale, grasped the gunnel through the freezing waves, and by heaving till it seemed his arms must break righted the whaleboat again, although it was still half full of seawater.

He leaped in with a loud splash, and the whale slid, silently and with hardly a ripple, beneath the dark sea.

Jacko bailed with his hands all that night, scooping out the cold seawater and throwing it over the side; and it is a good thing he did, for he would certainly have frozen to death otherwise. His thoughts were freed, as I have explained, and he thought about a great many things—about the beautiful island he had left behind, and how the sun had joined him there every morning in the top of his tall banyan tree; about finding bright shells and things to eat on the beach, and how he had scolded, sometimes, certain friendly little waves that came up to play with his toes.

All of which was pleasant enough. But again and again he thought of the ship, and wondered whether he would see it in the morning. He did not want to go back to it. In fact, he discovered that he hated the very thought of it, and its greasy smoke, and its cold, and the brutal treatment that he and others had received there, and the more brutal hunting of the peaceable whales. Yet he felt that if he did not see the ship in the morning he would certainly die.

Nor was that the worst of that terrible night, for he found himself haunted by the men who had been his companions in the whaleboat. When he went to the bow, it seemed to him that he could make out the shadowy form of Mr. Blackmire, the chief mate, seated in the stern with his hand upon the tiller. When he went to the stern, there was no one there; yet it seemed to him that he could make out the dark, dim shape of Savannah Jefferson in the bow, crouched and ready, grasping a harpoon.

Worst of all, he sometimes glimpsed the faces of the drowned sailors floating just beneath the waves, and he could not be certain that they were mere shenanigans of his imagination; their still lips seemed to ask him, silently and patiently, how it was that he deserved to live and they to die. At times he talked to them as he had when they were alive, and he found he had no answer to give them, save that it might be that he was only destined to die more slowly and more miserably. When he spoke to them in this way, he felt sure that the night would never end.

But that night, which seemed so very long to him, was actually quite short as measured by your clock. Our winter, in this northern hemisphere, is summer in the southern, so that at the same time that we have our longest winter night they have their shortest summer one. Morning came, and the water in the bottom of the whaleboat was no deeper than his ankles, but the ship was nowhere in sight.

Morning came, I said. But there was more to it than that, and it was far more beautiful than those plain words imply. Night faded—that was how it began. The stars winked out, one by one at first, and then by whole dozens and scores. A beautiful rosy flush touched the horizon, deepened, strengthened, and drove the night away before it as ten thousand angels with swords and bows and rods of power fanned out across the sky, more beautiful than birds and more terrible than the wildest storm. Jacko waved and called out to them, but if they heard him or saw him they gave no sign of it.

Soon the sun revealed its face, in the beginning no more than a sliver of golden light but rounded and lovely just the same, peeping above clouds in the northeast. Then the whole sun itself, warm and dazzling, and its friendly beams showed Jacko a little pole mast and a toylike boom, wrapped in a sail and lashed beneath the seats.

He set up the mast and climbed to the top (at which the whaleboat rolled alarmingly), but no ship could he see.

When he had climbed down again, he gave his head a good scratching, something that always seemed to help his thought processes. Since the ship was not here, it was clear to him that it was very likely somewhere else. And if that was the case, there seemed no point at all in his remaining where he was.

So he fitted the boom, which was not much thicker than a broomstick, to his little mast, and bent the small, three-cornered sail, and steered for the sun.

That was a very foolish thing to do, to be sure. The sun was in the northeast when it rose, but in the north at noon, and in the northwest as the long afternoon wore on, so that if you were to plot Jacko's course you would find that it looked rather like a banana, generally northward, but inclined to the east in the morning and rather favoring the west toward afternoon. But while Jacko did not know much about navigation (which he had always left to the captain), it was comforting to feel himself drawing ever nearer to the sun, and if the truth be told it was probably as good a course for looking for the ship as any of the other incorrect ones.

That day, which was in fact long, as I have tried to explain, seemed terribly short to poor Jacko. Soon evening came, the angels streamed back to the sun, night rose from the sea and spread her black wings, and Jacko was left alone, cold, hungry, and thirsty. He climbed his mast again so that he could keep the vanishing sun in sight as long as possible; and when it was gone, he dropped down into the bilges of the whaleboat and wept. In those days there were no laboratories, and so we may be fairly sure that he was the most miserable monkey in the world.

Still, it was not until the tenth hour of the night, when the new dawn was almost upon him, that his heart broke. When that happened, something that had always lived there, something that was very like Jacko himself, yet not at all like a monkey, went out from him. It left his broken heart, and left his skin as well, and left the whaleboat, and shot like an arrow over the dark sea, northeast after the sun. Jacko could not see it, but he knew that it was gone and that he was more alone now than he had ever been.

At which point a very strange thing happened. Among the many, many stars that had kindled in the northeast when the last light of the sun had gone, a new star rose (or so it seemed) and flew toward him—a star no different from countless others, but different indeed because it left its place in the heavens and approached him, nearer and nearer, until it hung just above his head.

"You mistake me," said the star.

"I don't even know you," replied Jacko, "but can you help me? Oh, please, help me if you can."

"You have seen me every day, throughout your entire life," replied the star. "I have always helped all of you, and I will help you again. But first you must tell me your story, so that I will know how to proceed."

And so Jacko told, more or less as you have heard it here, but in many more words, and with a wealth of gesture and expression which I should strive in vain to reproduce. It took quite a long time, as you have already seen. And during that long time the star said nothing, but floated above his head, a minute pinpoint of light; so that when he had finished at last Jacko said, "Are you really a star, and not a firefly?"

"I am a star," the star answered. If a small silver bell could form words when it spoke, it would no doubt sound very much like that star. "And this is my true appearance—or at least, it is as near my true appearance as you are able to comprehend. I am the star you call the sun, the star you pursued all day."

Jacko's mouth opened and shut. Then it opened and shut again—all this without saying one word.

"You think me large and very strong," the star said, "but there are many stars that are far larger and stronger than I. It is only because you stand so close to me that you think me a giant. Thus I show myself to you now as I really am, among my peers: a smallish, quite common and ordinary-looking star."

Jacko, who did not understand in the least, but who had been taught manners by the chief mate, said, "It's very kind of you to show yourself to me at all, sir."

"I do it every day," the star reminded him.

Jacko nodded humbly.

"Here is how I judge your case," the star continued. "Please interrupt if you feel that I am mistaken in anything that I say."

Jacko nodded, resolving not to object (as he too often had in the fo'c'sle) about trifles.

"You do not desire to be where you are."

Jacko nodded again, emphatically, both his hands across his mouth.

"You would prefer some me-warmed place, where fruiting trees were plentiful and men treated monkeys with great kindness. A place where there are wonderful things to see and climb on, of the sort you imagined when you left your island— monuments, and the like."

Jacko nodded a third time, more enthusiastically than ever, his hands still tight across his mouth.

"And yet you believe that you could be happy now, if only you might return to the island that was yours." The star sighed. "In that you are mistaken. Your island— it is no longer yours in any event—is visited from time to time by ships of men. The first man, as you know, has already made his home there, and more will be moving in soon. This age is not a good one for monkeys, and the age to come will be far worse."

At these words, Jacko felt his heart sink within him; it was only then that he realized it was whole once more—that the part of himself which had run away from him when his heart had broken had returned to him.

"Steer as I tell you," said the star, "and do not be afraid."

So poor Jacko took the tiller again, and trimmed their little sail; and it was a good thing he did, for the wind was rising and seemed almost to blow the star as though it were a firefly after all. For a few minutes he could still see it bright against the sail. By degrees it appeared to climb the mast, and for a long while it remained there, as if the whaleboat had hoisted a lantern with a little candle in it. But at last it blew forward and dropped lower, until it was hidden by the sail.

"Are you still there?" Jacko called.

"I am sitting in the bow," the star replied.

But while that was happening, far stranger things were taking place outside the boat. Night had backed away, and twilight come again. A fiery arch, like a burning rainbow, stretched clear across the sky. Ships came into view, only to vanish before

Jacko could hail them; and very strange ships they were—a towering junk, like a pagoda afloat; a stately galleon with a big cross upon its crimson foresail; and at last an odd, beaked craft, so long and narrow that it seemed almost a lance put to sea, that flew over the water on three pairs of wings.

"A point to starboard, helmsman," called the star. As it spoke, the twilight vanished. The shadow of their sail fell upon the water as sharp and black as that of the gnomon of a sundial, and around it every little wave sparkled and danced in the sunlight. Jacko steered a point to starboard, as he had been told, then turned his face toward the sun, grinned with happiness, and shut his eyes for a moment.

The sound of many voices made him open them again. A river's mouth was swallowing their whaleboat between sandy lips, and both those lips were black with people, thousands upon thousands of them, chanting and shouting.

"Where are we?" Jacko asked.

"This is Now." The star's clear voice came from the other side of the sail. "It is always Now, wherever I am." Beneath the lower edge of the sail, Jacko could see a man's bare, brown feet.

"Here and Now is your new home," the star continued.

"They will treat you well—better than you deserve—because you have come with me. But you must watch out for crocodiles."

"I will," Jacko promised.

"Then let down the sail so that they can see you. Our way will carry us as near the shore as we wish to go."

So Jacko freed the halyard, letting the little sail slip down the mast, and bounced up onto the tiller.

"Come here," said the star, "and sit upon my shoulder." Which now made perfect sense, because the star had become a tall, slender, brown man. Jacko leaped from the tiller to the mast, and from the mast onto the star's shoulder just as he had been told, though the great gold disc of the star's headdress was so bright it nearly blinded him. And at that a great cheer went up from all those thousands of people.

"Ra!" they shouted. "Ra, Ra, *Ra!*," so that Jacko might have thought they were watching a game, if he had known more about games. But some shouted, "Thoth!" as well.

"Ra is the name by which I am known Now," explained the star. "Do you see that old man with the necklace? He is my chief mistaker in this place. When I give the word, you must jump to him and take his hand. It will seem very far, but you must jump anyway. Do you understand?"

Jacko nodded. "I hope I don't fall in the water."

"You have my promise," the star said. "You will not fall in the water."

As he spoke, the whaleboat soared upward. It seemed to Jacko that some new kind of water, water so clear it could not be seen, must have been raining down on them, creating a new sea above the sea and leaving the river's mouth and all of its thousands of bowing people on the bottom.

Then the star said, "Go!" and he leaped over the side and seemed almost to fly.

If you that love books should ever come across *The Book of That Which Is in Tuat*, which is one of the very oldest books we have, I hope that you will look carefully at the picture called "The Tenth Hour of the Night." There you will see, marching to the right of Ra's glorious sun-boat, twelve men holding paddles. These are the twelve hours of the day. Beyond them march twelve women, all holding one long cord; these twelve women are the twelve hours of the night. Beyond even them— and thus almost at the head of this lengthy procession—are four gods, two with the heads of men and two with the heads of animals. Their names are Bant, Seshsha, Ka-Ament, and Renensebu.

And in front of *them*, standing upon the tiller of a boat, is one monkey.

It seems strange, to be sure, to find a monkey in such a procession as Ra's, but there is something about this particular monkey that is stranger still. Unlike the four gods, and the twelve women with the cord, and the twelve men with paddles, this monkey is actually looking back at Ra in his glorious sun-boat. And waving. Above this monkey's head, I should add, floats something that you will not find anywhere else in the whole of *The Book of That Which Is in Tuat*. It is a smallish, quite common and ordinary-looking, five-pointed star.

ON DEATH AND THE DEUCE

Rick Bowes

I have been a fan of Rick Bowes's work since the publication of his offbeat Urban Fantasy novel *Feral Cell* some years ago—and thus it is a pleasure to include him in this year's volume of *The Year's Best* with the following gritty contemporary fantasy tale about the fractured realities of alcoholism.

Bowes, who resides in New York City and has a background in theater, is also the author of the novels *Goblin Market* and *Warchild*, as well as works of short fiction. "On Death and the Deuce" is reprinted from the May issue of *The Magazine of Fantasy & Science Fiction*.

—T.W.

In the last days that the Irish ran Hell's Kitchen, I lived in that tenement neighborhood between the West Side docks and Times Square. An old lady of no charm whatsoever named McCready and called Mother rented furnished studios in an underheated fleabag on Tenth Avenue. Payment was cash only by the week or month, with anonymity guaranteed whether desired or not. Looking out the window one February morning, I spotted my Silent Partner heading south toward Forty-second Street.

He was already past me, so it was the clothes that caught my attention first. The camel-hair overcoat had been mine. The dark gray pants were from the last good suit I had owned. That morning I'd awakened from a drinking dream, and was still savoring the warm, safe feeling that comes with realizing it was all a nightmare and that I was sober. The sight of that figure three floors down filled my mouth with the remembered taste of booze. I tried to spit, but was too dry.

Hustlers called Forty-second the Deuce. My Silent Partner turned at that corner, and I willed him not to notice me. Just before heading east, he looked directly at my window. He wore shades, but his face was the one I feared seeing most. It was mine.

That made me too jumpy to stay in the twelve-by-fifteen-foot room. Reaching behind the bed, I found the place where the wall and floor didn't join. Inside was my worldly fortune: a slim .25 caliber Beretta, and beside it a wad of bills. Extracting six twenties, I put on a thick sweater and leather jacket and went out.

At that hour, nothing much was cooking in Hell's Kitchen. Two junkies went by, bent double by the wind off the Hudson. Up the block a super tossed away the belongings of a drag queen who the week before had gotten cut into bite-size chunks. My Silent Partner was not the kind to go for a casual walk in this weather.

Looking the way he had come, I saw the Club 596 sitting like a bunker at the corner of Forty-third. The iron grating on the front was ajar, but no lights were on inside. As I watched, a guy in a postman's uniform squeezed out the door and hurried away. The Westies, last of the Irish gangs—short, crazed, and violent—sat in the dark dispensing favors, collecting debts. And I knew what my Silent Partner had been up to.

Then I went to breakfast, put the incident to the back of my mind, and prepared for my daily session. The rest of my time was a wasteland, but my late afternoons were taken up with Leo Dunn.

He lived in a big apartment house over in the east sixties. Outside, the building gleamed white. The lobby was polished marble. Upstairs in his apartment, sunlight poured through windows curtained in gold and hit a glass table covered with pieces of silver and crystal. "Kevin, my friend." Mr. Dunn, tall and white-haired, came forward smiling and shook my hand. "How are you? Every time I see you come through this door, it gives me the greatest pleasure."

I sat down on the couch, and he sat across the coffee table from me. The first thing I thought to say was: "I had a drinking dream last night. This crowd watched like it was an Olympic event as I poured myself a shot and drank it. Then I realized what I'd done, and felt like dirt. I woke up, and it was as if a rock had been taken off my head."

Amused, Dunn nodded his understanding. But dreams were of no great interest to him. So, after pausing to be sure I was through, he drew a breath and was off. "Kevin, you have made the greatest commitment of your life. You stood up and said, 'Guilty as charged. I am a drunk.'"

Mr. Dunn's treatment for alcoholics was a talking cure: he talked, and I listened. He didn't just talk—he harangued; he argued like a lawyer; he gave sermons of fire. Gesturing to a closet door, he told me, "That is the record room where we store the evidence of our mistakes. Any boozehound has tales of people he trusted who screwed him over. But has there ever been anyone you knew that used you as badly and that you went back to as often as you have to booze?"

We had been over this material a hundred times in the past couple of weeks. "You're a bright boy, Kevin, and I wouldn't repeat myself if I hadn't learned that it was necessary. We go back to the record room." Again he pointed to the door. "We look for evidence of our stupidity."

For ten years, my habit and I had traveled from booze through the drug spectrum and back to booze. Then one morning on the apex of a bender, that fine moment when mortality is left behind and the shakes haven't started, I found myself standing at a bar reading a *New York Post* article. It was about some guy called Dunn who treated drunks.

The crash that followed was gruesome. Three days later I woke up empty, sweat-soaked, and terrified in a room I didn't remember renting. At first, it seemed that all I owned were the clothes I had been wearing. Gradually, in jacket and jean pockets, stuck in a boot, I discovered a vaguely familiar pistol, a thick roll of bills, and a page torn from the *Post*. The choice that I saw was clear; either to shoot myself or make a call.

My newly sober brain was blank and soft, and Mr. Dunn remolded it relentlessly. On the afternoon I am describing, he saw my attention wander, clicked a couple of ashtrays together on the table, picked up the gold lighter, and ignited a cigarette with a flourish. "How are you doing, Kevin?"

"O.K.," I told him. "Before I forget," I said, and placed five of the twenties from my stash on the table.

He put them in his pocket without counting and said, "Thank you, Kevin." But when he looked up at me, an old man with pale skin and very blue eyes, he wasn't smiling. "Any news on a job?" He had never questioned me closely, but I knew that my money bothered Mr. Dunn.

Behind him the light faded over Madison Avenue. "Not yet," I said. "The thing is, I don't need much to get by. Where I'm living is real cheap." At a hundred a week, Leo Dunn was my main expense. He was also what kept me alive. I recognized him as a real lucky kind of habit.

He went back to a familiar theme. "Kevin," he said, looking at the smoke from his cigarette. "For years, your addiction was your Silent Partner. When you decided to stop drinking, that was very bad news for him. Your Silent Partner wants to live as much as you do." At the mention of that name, I remembered what I had seen that morning.

Dunn said, "Your partner had the best racket in the world, skimming off an ever-increasing share of your life, your happiness. He is not just going to give up and go away. He will try treachery, intimidation, flattery, to get you back in harness."

He paused for a moment, and I said, "I saw him today, across the street. He saw me, too. He was wearing clothes that used to belong to me."

"What did he look like, Kevin?" I guess nothing a drunk could say would ever surprise Mr. Dunn.

"Just like me. But at the end of a three-week bender."

"What was he doing when you saw him?" This was asked very softly.

"Coming from a mob bar up the street, the 596 Club. He was trying to borrow money from guys who will whack you just because that's how they feel at the moment."

"Kevin," said Mr. Dunn. "Booze is a vicious, mind-altering substance. It gets us at its mercy by poisoning our minds, making us unable to distinguish between what is real and what isn't. Are you saying that you had to borrow money?" I shook my head. Very carefully, he asked, "Do you mean you remembered some aspect of your drinking self?"

"Something like that," I said. But what I felt was a double loss. Not only had my Silent Partner discovered where I lived, but Dunn didn't believe me. The partner had broken the perfect rapport between us.

At that point the lobby called to announce the next client. As Leo Dunn showed me to the door, his eyes searched mine. He wasn't smiling. "Kevin, you've done more than I would have thought possible when you first walked in here. But there's what they call a dry drunk, someone who's managed to stop drinking, but has not reached the state beyond that. I don't detect involvement in life from you, or real elation. I respect you too much to want to see you as just a dry drunk."

The next client was dressed like a stockbroker. He avoided looking at me in my street clothes. "Leo," he said, a little too loudly and too sincerely, "I'm glad to see you." And Dunn, having just directed a two-hour lecture at me, smiled and was ready to go again.

Outside, it was already dark. On my way across town, I went through Times Square down to the Deuce. It was rush hour. Spanish hustlers in maroon pants, hands jammed in jacket pockets, black hookers in leather miniskirts, stood on corners, all too stoned to know they were freezing to death. Around them, commuters poured down subway stairs and fled for Queens.

Passing the Victoria Hotel, I glanced in at the desk clerk sitting behind bulletproof glass. I had lived at the Victoria before my final bender. It was where those clothes the Silent Partner wore had been abandoned. Without remembering all the details, I sensed that it wasn't wise to go inside and inquire about my property.

Back on my block, I looked up at my bleak little window, dark and unwelcoming. Mother's was no place to spend an evening. Turning away, I started walking again; probably I ate dinner somewhere, maybe saw a movie. Without booze, I couldn't connect with anyone. Mostly I walked, watched crowds stream out of the theaters. A *Little Night Music* was playing, and A *Moon for the Misbegotten*. Then those rich tourists and nice couples from Westchester hurried into cabs and restaurants and left the streets quite empty.

In Arcade Parade on Broadway, goggle-eyed suit-and-tie johns watched the asses on kids bent over the pinball machines. Down the way a marquee advertised the double bill of *College Bound Babes* and *Bound to Please Girls*. Around a corner a tall guy with a smile like a knife slash chanted, "Got what you need," like a litany.

Glancing up, I realized we were in front of Sanctuary. Built to be a Methodist church, it had gotten famous in the late sixties as a disco. In those days a huge Day-Glo Satan loomed above the former altar; limos idled in front; a team of gorillas worked the door.

Now it was dim and dying, a trap for a particular kind of tourist. Inside, Satan flaked off the wall; figures stood in the shadows, willing to sell what you asked. I could remember in a hazy way spending my last money there to buy the Beretta. My trajectory on that final drunk—the arc that connected the pistol, the money, the absence of my Silent Partner—wasn't buried all that deeply inside me. I just didn't want to look.

At some point that night, the rhythm of the street, the cold logic of the Manhattan grid, took me way west, past the live sex shows and into the heart of the Kitchen. On long, dirty blocks of tenements, I went past small Mick bars with tiny front windows where lines of drinkers sat like marines, and guys in the back booths gossiped idly about last week's whack.

I walked until my hands and feet were numb, and I found myself over on Death Avenue. That's what the Irish of the Kitchen once called Eleventh because of the train tracks that ran there and killed so many of them. Now the trains were gone, the ships whose freight they hauled were gone, and those Irish themselves were fast disappearing. Though not born in the Kitchen, I identified with them a lot.

On Death, in a block of darkened warehouses, sat the Emerald Green Tavern. It was on a Saturday morning at the Emerald Green that I had found myself in a moment of utter clarity with a pistol and a pocketful of money, reading in a newspaper about Leo Dunn. I stood for a while remembering that. Then maybe the cold got to me, and I went home. My memory there is vague.

What I will never forget is the sight of a ship outlined in green and red lights. I was staring at it, and I was intensely cold. Gradually, I realized I was huddled against a pillar of the raised highway near the Hudson piers. One of the last of the cruise ships was docked there, and I thought how good it would be to have the money to sail down to the warm weather.

In fact, it would be so good to have any money at all. My worldly wealth was on me: suede boots and no socks, an overcoat and suit and no underwear. In one pocket were a penny, a dime, and a quarter—my wealth. In another were a set of standard keys and the gravity knife I'd had since college.

Then I knew why I had stolen the keys and where I was going to get money. And I recognized the state I was in: the brief, brilliant period of clarity at the end of a bender. My past was a wreck; my future held a terrifying crash. With nothing behind me and nothing to live for, I knew no fear and was a god.

With all mortal uncertainty and weakness gone, I was pure spirit as I headed down familiar streets. A block east of Death and north of the Deuce, I looked up at a lighted window on the third floor. I crossed the street, my overcoat open, oblivious to the cold.

Security at Mother's was based on there being nothing in the building worth taking. Drawing out the keys, I turned the street-door lock on my third try and went up the stairs, silently, swiftly. Ancient smells of boiled cabbages and fish, of damp carpet and cigarette smoke and piss, a hundred years of poverty, wafted around me. This was the kind of place a loser lived, a fool came to rest. Contempt filled me.

Light shone under his door. Finding a key the right shape, I transferred it to my left hand, drew out the knife with my right. The key went in without a sound. I held my breath and turned it. The lock clicked; the door swung into the miserable room with a bed, a TV on without the sound, a two-burner stove, a table. An all-too-familiar figure dozed in the only chair, shoes off, pants unbuttoned. Sobriety had made him stupid. Not even the opening of the door roused him. The click of the knife in my hand did that.

The eyes focused, then widened as the dumb face I had seen in ten thousand morning mirrors registered shock. "I got a little debt I want to collect," I said, and moved for him. Rage swept me, a feeling that I'd been robbed of everything: my body, my life. "You took the goddamn money. It's mine. My plan. My guts. You couldn't have pulled that scam in a thousand years."

For an instant the miserable straight head in front of me froze in horror. Then shoulder muscles tensed; stocking feet shot out as he tried to roll to the side and go for the .25. But he was too slow. My knife slashed, and the fool put out his hands. Oh, the terror in those eyes when he saw the blood on his palms and wrists. He fell back, tipping over the chair. The blade went for the stomach, cut through cloth and into flesh.

Eyes wide, his head hit the wall. The knife in my hand slashed his throat. The light in the eyes went out. The last thing I saw in them was a reflection of his humiliation at dying like that, pants fallen down, jockey shorts filling with dark red blood. His breath suddenly choked, became a drowning sound. An outstretched hand pointed to the loose board and the money.

* * *

"I was just cut down," I told Dunn the next morning. "It wasn't even a fight. I left that knife behind when I had to move, and the fucking Silent Partner had it and just cut me down." It was hard to get my throat to work.

"It was a dream, Kevin, a drinking dream like the one you told me yesterday. It has no power over your conscious mind. You came home and fell asleep sitting up. Then you had a nightmare. You say you fell off your chair and woke up on the floor. It was just a dream."

My eyes burned. "The expression my Silent Partner had on his face is the one I used to see sometimes in the mirror. Those moments when I was so far gone I could do anything."

"Nothing else has reached you like this, Kevin."

"Sorry. I couldn't sleep."

"Don't be sorry. This is part of the process. I don't know why, but this has to happen for the treatment to work. I've had detective sergeants bawl like babies, marines laugh until they cried. Until this, you haven't let anything faze you. Our stupid drinker's pride can take many forms."

"I won't be able to sleep as long as he's out there."

"Understand, Kevin, that I'm not a psychiatrist. I was educated by the Jesuits a long time ago. Dreams or how you feel about your mother don't mean much to me. But I hear myself say that, and spot my own stupid pride at work. If dreams are what you bring me, I'll use them." He paused, and I blew my nose. "What does your Silent Partner want, Kevin? You saw through his eyes in your dream."

"He wants to disembowel me!"

"The knife was the means, Kevin. Not the motive. What was he looking for?"

"My money. He knew where I had it."

"You keep money in your room? You don't have a job. But you pay me regularly in fairly crisp twenties and hundreds. It's stolen money, isn't it, Kevin?"

"I guess so. I don't remember."

"Earlier you mentioned that in the dream, you went for a gun. Is there blood on the money, Kevin? Did you hurt anyone? Do you know?"

"The gun hasn't been fired."

"I assume it's not registered, probably stolen. Get rid of it. Can you return the money?"

"I don't even know who it belonged to."

"You told me that he was in a calm eye when he came after you. That was his opportunity. You had that same kind of clarity when you found the article about me. You had the money with you then?"

"The gun, too."

"Kevin, let's say that some people's Silent Partners are more real than others. Then let's say that in a moment of clarity, you managed to give yours the slip and walked off with the money the two of you had stolen. Without him holding you back, you succeeded in reaching out for help. The money is the link. It's what still connects you to your drinking past. I don't want any of that money, and neither do you. Get rid of it."

"You mean throw it away?"

"The other day, you said your Silent Partner was borrowing from the West Side mob. If he's real enough to need money that badly, let him have it. No one, myself above all, ever loses his Silent Partner entirely. But this should give you both some peace."

"What'll I do for money? I won't be able to pay you."

"Do you think after all this time, I don't know which ones aren't going to pay me?" I watched his hands rearrange the crystal ashtrays, the gold lighter, as he said, "Let's look in the record room, where we will find that booze is a vicious, mind-altering substance, and that we have to be aware at every moment of its schemes." I raised my eyes. Framed in the light from the windows, Dunn smiled at me and said, "Keep just enough to live on for a couple of weeks until you find work. Which you will."

Afterward in my room, I took out the pistol and the money, put two hundred back in the wall, and placed the rest in a jacket pocket. The Beretta I carefully stuck under my belt at the small of my back. Then I went out.

At first, I walked aimlessly around the Kitchen. My Silent Partner had threatened me. It seemed my choices were to give up the money or to keep the money and give up Leo Dunn. The first I thought of as surrender; the second meant I'd be back on the booze. Then a third choice took shape. Payback. I would do to him just what he had tried to do to me.

Searching for him, I followed what I remembered of our route on the last night of our partnership. It had begun at Sanctuary. Passing by, I saw that the disco was no longer dying. It was dead. The doors were padlocked. On the former church steps, a black guy slept with his head on his knees. No sign of my Silent Partner.

But I finally recalled what had happened there. Sanctuary was a hunting ground. Tourists were the game. That last night I had run into four fraternity assholes in town with seven grand for a midwinter drug buy. Almost dead broke, I talked big about my connections. Before we left together, I bought the Beretta.

Following the trail, I walked by the Victoria. That's where I had taken them first. "Five guys showing up will not be cool," I said, and persuaded two of them to wait in my dismal room. "As collateral, you hold everything I own." That amounted to little more than some clothes and a few keepsakes like the knife. With the other two, I left the hotel that last time knowing I wouldn't be back. I recognized my Silent Partner's touch. He had been with me at that point.

Turning into an icy wind off the river, I took the same route that the frat boys and I had taken a few weeks before. At a doorway on a deserted side street near Ninth Avenue, we halted. I remembered telling them that this was the place. In the tenement hall, I put the pistol at the base of one kid's head and made him beg the other one to give me the money.

Standing in the doorway again, I recalled how the nervous sweat on my hand had made it hard to hold on to the .25. When those terrified kids had handed over the money, I discouraged pursuit by making them throw their shoes into the dark and lie face down with their hands behind their heads. The one I'd put the pistol on had pissed his pants. He wept and begged me not to shoot. Remembering that made my stomach turn. Right then my Partner had still been calling the shots.

The rest of that night was gone beyond recovery. But what had happened in those blank black hours wasn't important. I knew where the search for my partner was going to end. Death Avenue north of the Deuce had always been a favorite spot for both of us. The deserted warehouses, the empty railroad yards, made it feel like the end of the world.

Approaching the Emerald Green Tavern, I spotted a lone figure leaning on a lamppost, watching trailer trucks roll south. Only a lack of funds would have kept a man out on the street on a night like that. Touching the pistol for luck, stepping up behind my Silent Partner, I asked, "Whatcha doing?"

Not particularly surprised, not even turning all the way around, he replied, "Oh, living the life." I would never have his nonchalance. His face was hidden by shadows and dark glasses. That was just as well.

The air around him smelled of cheap booze. "We have to talk." I gestured toward the Emerald Green.

As we crossed the street, he told me, "I knew you'd show up. This is where we parted company. When I woke up days later, all I had were these clothes and a couple of keepsakes." I was reminded of the knife. My Silent Partner knew as soon as that crossed my mind. "Don't worry," he said. "I sold it." He went through the door first.

The Emerald Green was a typical Hell's Kitchen joint, with a bar that ran front to back, a few booths, and beer- and cigarette-soaked air unchanged since the Truman administration. The facilities were the one distinguishing feature of the place. The rest rooms lay down a flight of stairs and across a cellar/storage area. You could organize a firing squad down there, and the people above wouldn't know.

Or care. The customers that night were several guys with boozers' noses, an old woman with very red hair who said loudly at regular intervals, "Danny? Screw Danny," and a couple of Spanish guys off some night shift and now immobile at a table. The dead-eyed donkey of a bartender looked right through me and nodded at my Silent Partner. In here, he was the real one. We went to the far end of the bar near the cellar door, where we could talk. I ordered a ginger ale. My companion said, "Double Irish."

As we sat, he gave a dry chuckle. "Double Irish is about right for us." At no time did I turn and stare my Silent Partner in the face. But the filmed mirror behind the bar showed that he wore the rumpled jacket over a dirty T-shirt. The camel-hair coat was deeply stained. When the whiskey came, he put it away with a single gesture from counter to mouth. Up and in. I could taste it going down.

It was like living in a drinking dream. I touched the back of my belt and said, "You found out where I live."

"Yeah, Billy at the 596 told me you were staying at Mother's. Of course, what he said was that he had seen me going in and out. So I knew." Indoors, my partner smelled ripe. The back of his hand was dirty.

"You owe them money?" The last thing I needed was to get shot for debts he had run up.

"Not even five. My credit's no good," he said. "You left me with nothing. They locked me out of the hotel. Ripping off those kids was something you never could have done by yourself. You needed me." He signaled for a refill. The bartender's eyes shifted my way, since I was paying.

I shook my head, not sure I could have him drink again and not do it myself. "I've got the money on me. It's yours. So that we don't attract attention, what I want you to do is get up and go downstairs. After a couple of minutes, I'll join you."

"Pass the money to me under the bar." He didn't trust me.

"There's something else I want you to have." For a long moment he sat absolutely still. The TV was on with the sound off. It seemed to be all beer ads. "When you come back up here," I told him, "you will be able to afford enough doubles to kill yourself." That promise made him rise and push his way through the cellar door.

For a good two minutes, I sipped ginger ale and breathed deeply to calm myself. Then I followed him. Downstairs, there were puddles on the floor. The rest-room doors were open. Both were empty. One of the johns was broken and kept flushing. It sounded like an asthmatic trying to breathe.

The cellar was lighted by an overhead bulb above the stairs and one at the far end of the cellar near the rest rooms. Both lights swayed slightly, making it hard to focus. My Silent Partner had reached up and bumped them for just that reason. It was the kind of thing that I would not have thought of. He stood where the light didn't quite hit him.

When I reached the bottom of the stairs, I reached back and drew out the .25. He seemed to flicker before me. "Easy does it," he said. "You know how jumpy you are with guns." His tone was taunting, not intimidated.

I realized I could read him as easily as he could me. My Silent Partner wanted me to try to shoot him and find out that I couldn't. Then, after I failed, we could both go upstairs, have some drinks, and resume our partnership. Carefully, I ejected the clip and stuck it in my pocket. His eyes followed me as I put the empty pistol on the stairs. "You bought this; you get rid of it," I said. "My guess is, it's got a bad history."

"You'll never have another friend like me." His voice, my voice, had a whine to it, and I knew this was getting to him. I reached into my pocket and took out the money and a piece of torn newspaper. "You thought about what it's going to be like to be broke?" he asked. "It's not like you've got any skills."

I had thought of it, and it scared me. I hesitated. Then I noticed that the newspaper was the page with the Dunn article. Taking a deep breath, I riffled the money and told my Silent Partner: "Almost six grand. Just about everything I have." I put the cash on the stairs beside the Beretta and turned to go. "So long. It's been real."

"Oh, I'll keep in touch," he said in a whisper. Looking back, I saw nothing but a blur of light in the shadows.

On the stairs, I felt light-footed, like a burden had been laid down. This was relief, maybe even the happiness Mr. Dunn had mentioned. From his perch near the front, the bartender gave me a slightly wary look, like maybe I had come in at 2:00 A.M., drunk ginger ale, and had a conversation with myself. It occurred to me that if that's what happened, the first one to go take a leak was going to get a very nice surprise.

But as I went out into the cold, the bartender's gaze shifted, his hand reached for the pouring bottle, and I heard the cellar door swing open behind me.

This Is a Story Titled

THE MAN WHO ROWED CHRISTOPHER COLUMBUS ASHORE

Harlan Ellison

We are very pleased to include Harlan Ellison in this year's volume of *The Year's Best* with this superlative phantasia published in the year of the quinquecentennial of Columbus' voyage to the Americas. (Though the author assures us personally that it is mere coincidence that Columbus appears in this story at all and, despite the title, the story really has nothing at all to do with Christopher Columbus. He is also suitably mysterious when he says that "coincidence" *does* have a lot to do with this story.)

Ellison, who resides in Los Angeles, is one of the most lauded fantasists in America and a consummate artist in the short story form. He has published very nearly sixty books of fiction and essays (including the influential media critiques *The Glass Teat* and *The Other Glass Teat*), more than thirteen hundred stories, and is the editor of the landmark *Dangerous Visions* anthologies. *The Essential Ellison*, an 1,100-page retrospective of his 38-year career, is highly recommended.

Ellison has won more Hugo and Nebula Awards than any other writer, as well as the P.E.N. award for journalism, the British Fantasy Award, the Mystery Writers of America's Edgar Award, and numerous others (including nominations for the Emmy and the Grammy [in the Spoken Word category]). The following provocative tale (which has also been honored with inclusion in *The Best American Short Stories: 1993*) is reprinted from the July issue of *Omni* magazine.

—T.W.

LEVENDIS: On Tuesday the 1st of October, improbably dressed as an Explorer Scout, with his great hairy legs protruding from his knee-pants, and his heavily-festooned merit badge sash slantwise across his chest, he helped an old, arthritic black woman across the street at the jammed corner of Wilshire and Western. In fact, she didn't *want* to cross the street, but he half-pulled, half-dragged her, the old woman screaming at him, calling him a khaki-colored motherfucker every step of the way.

LEVENDIS: On Wednesday the 2nd of October, he crossed his legs carefully as he sat in the Boston psychiatrist's office, making certain the creases of his pants—he was wearing the traditional morning coat and ambassadorially-striped pants—remained sharp, and he said to George Aspen Davenport, MD, Ph.D., FAPA (who

had studied with Ernst Kris *and* Anna Freud), "Yes, that's it, now you've got it."
And Dr. Davenport made a note on his pad, lightly cleared his throat and phrased
it differently: "Your mouth is . . . vanishing? That is to say, your mouth, the facial
feature below your nose, it's uh disappearing?" The prospective patient nodded
quickly, with a bright smile. "Exactly." Dr. Davenport made another note, continued to ulcerate the inside of his cheek, then tried a third time: "We're speaking
now—heh heh, to maintain the idiom—we're speaking of your lips, or your tongue,
or your palate, or your gums, or your teeth, or—" The other man sat forward,
looking very serious, and replied, "We're talking *all* of it, Doctor. The whole,
entire, complete aperture and everything around, over, under, and within. My
mouth, the allness of my *mouth*. It's disappearing. What part of that is giving you
a problem?" Davenport hmmm'd for a moment, said, "Let me check something,"
and he rose, went to the teak and glass bookcase against the far wall, beside the
window that looked out on crowded, lively Boston Common, and he drew down a
capacious volume. He flipped through it for a few minutes, and finally paused at a
page on which he poked a finger. He turned to the elegant, gray-haired gentleman
in the consultation chair, and he said, "Lipostomy." His prospective patient tilted
his head to the side, like a dog listening for a clue, and arched his eyebrows
expectantly, as if to ask *yes, and lipostomy is what?* The psychiatrist brought the
book to him, leaned down and pointed to the definition. "Atrophy of the mouth."
The gray-haired gentleman, who looked to be in his early sixties, but remarkably
well-tended and handsomely turned-out, shook his head slowly as Dr. Davenport
walked back around to sit behind his desk. "No, I don't think so. It doesn't seem to
be withering, it's just, well, simply, I can't put it any other way, it's very simply
disappearing. Like the Cheshire cat's grin. Fading away." Davenport closed the
book and laid it on the desktop, folded his hands atop the volume, and smiled
condescendingly. "Don't you think this might be a delusion on your part? I'm
looking at your mouth right now, and it's right there, just as it was when you came
into the office." His prospective patient rose, retrieved his homburg from the sofa,
and started toward the door. "It's a good thing I can read lips," he said, placing the
hat on his head, "because I certainly don't need to pay your sort of exorbitant fee
to be ridiculed." And he moved to the office door, and opened it to leave, pausing
for only a moment to readjust his homburg, which had slipped down, due to the
absence of ears on his head.

LEVENDIS: On Thursday the 3rd of October, he overloaded his grocery cart with
okra and eggplant, giant bags of Kibbles 'n Bits 'n Bits 'n Bits, and jumbo boxes of
Huggies. And as he wildly careened through the aisles of the Sentry Market in La
Crosse, Wisconsin, he purposely engineered a collision between the carts of Kenneth Kulwin, a 47-year-old homosexual who had lived alone since the passing of
his father thirteen years earlier, and Anne Gillen, a 35-year-old legal secretary who
had been unable to find an escort to take her to her senior prom and whose social
life had not improved in the decades since that death of hope. He began screaming
at them, as if it had been *their* fault, thereby making allies of them. He was extremely
rude, breathing muscatel breath on them, and finally stormed away, leaving them
to sort out their groceries, leaving them to comment on his behavior, leaving them
to take notice of each other. He went outside, smelling the Mississippi River, and

he let the air out of Anne Gillen's tires. She would need a lift to the gas station, Kenneth Kulwin would tell her to call him "Kenny," and they would discover that their favorite movie was the 1945 romance, *The Enchanted Cottage*, starring Dorothy McGuire and Robert Young.

LEVENDIS: On Friday the 4th October, he came upon an interstate trucker dumping badly sealed cannisters of phenazine in an isolated picnic area outside Phillipsburg, Kansas; and he shot him three times in the head; and wedged the body into one of the large, nearly empty trash barrels near the picnic benches.

LEVENDIS: On Saturday the 5th of October, he addressed two hundred and forty-four representatives of the country & western music industry in the Chattanooga Room just off the Tennessee Ballroom of the Opryland Hotel in Nashville. He said to them, "What's astonishing is not that there is so much ineptitude, slovenliness, mediocrity and downright bad taste in the world . . . what *is* unbelievable is that there is so much *good* art in the world. Everywhere." One of the attendees raised her hand and asked, "Are you good, or evil?" He thought about it for less than twenty seconds, smiled, and replied, "Good, of course! There's only one real evil in the world: mediocrity." They applauded sparsely, but politely. Nonetheless, later at the reception, *no one* touched the Swedish meatballs, or the rumaki.

LEVENDIS: On Sunday the 6th of October, he placed the exhumed remains of Noah's ark near the eastern summit of a nameless mountain in Kurdistan, where the next infrared surveillance of a random satellite flyby would reveal them. He was careful to seed the area with a plethora of bones, here and there around the site, as well as within the identifiable hull of the vessel. He made sure to place them two-by-two: every beast after his kind, and all the cattle after their kind, and every creeping thing that creepeth upon the earth after his kind, and every fowl after his kind, and every bird of every sort. Two-by-two. Also the bones of pairs of gryphons, unicorns, stegosaurs, tengus, dragons, orthodontists, and the carbon-dateable 50,000-year-old bones of a relief pitcher for the Boston Red Sox.

LEVENDIS: On Monday the 7th of October, he kicked a cat. He kicked it a far distance. To the passersby who watched, there on Galena Street in Aurora, Colorado, he said: "I am an unlimited person, sadly living in a limited world." When the housewife who planned to call the police yelled at him from her kitchen window, "Who are you? What is your name!?!" he cupped his hands around his mouth so she would hear him, and he yelled back, "Levendis! It's a Greek word." They found the cat imbarked halfway through a tree. The tree was cut down, and the section with the cat was cut in two, the animal tended by a talented taxidermist who tried to quell the poor beast's terrified mewling and vomiting. The cat was later sold as bookends.

LEVENDIS: On Tuesday the 8th of October, he called the office of the District Attorney in Cadillac, Michigan, and reported that the blue 1988 Mercedes that had struck and killed two children playing in a residential street in Hamtramck just after sundown the night before, belonged to a pastry chef whose sole client was a Cosa Nostra *pezzonovante*. He gave detailed information as to the location of the chop shop where the Mercedes had been taken to be banged out, bondo'd, and repainted. He gave the license number. He indicated where, in the left front wheel-well, could be found a piece of the skull of the younger of the two little girls. Not only did the piece fit, like the missing section of a modular woodblock puzzle, but pathologists were able to conduct an accurate test that provided irrefutable evidence that would hold up under any attack in court: the medical examiner got past the basic ABO groups, narrowed the scope of identification with the five Rh tests, the M and N tests (also cap-S and small-s variations), the Duffy blood groups, and the Kidd types, both A and B; and finally he was able to validate the rare absence of Jr a, present in most blood-groups but missing in some Japanese-Hawaiians and Samoans. The little girl's name was Sherry Tualaulelei. When the homicide investigators learned that the pastry chef, his wife, and their three children had gone to New York City on vacation four days before the hit-and-run, and were able to produce ticket stubs that placed them seventh row center of the Martin Beck Theater, enjoying the revival of *Guys and Dolls*, at the precise moment the Mercedes struck the children, the Organized Crime Unit was called in, and the scope of the investigation was broadened. Sherry Tualaulelei was instrumental in the conviction and thirty-three year imprisonment of the pastry chef's boss, Sinio "Sally Comfort" Conforte, who had "borrowed" a car to sneak out for a visit to his mistress.

LEVENDIS: On Wednesday the 9th of October, he sent a fruit basket to Patricia and Faustino Evangelista, a middle-aged couple in Norwalk, Connecticut, who had given to their surviving son, the gun his beloved older brother had used to kill himself. The accompanying note read: *Way to go, sensitive Mom and Dad!*

LEVENDIS: On Thursday the 10th of October, he created a cure for bone-marrow cancer. Anyone could make it: the juice of fresh lemons, spiderwebs, the scrapings of raw carrots, the opaque and whitish portion of the toenail called the *lunula*, and carbonated water. The pharmaceutical cartel quickly hired a prestigious Philadelphia PR firm to throw its efficacy into question, but the AMA and FDA ran accelerated tests, found it to be potent, with no deleterious effects, and recommended its immediate use. It had no effect on AIDS, however. Nor did it work on the common cold. Remarkably, physicians praised the easing of their workload.

LEVENDIS: On Friday the 11th of October, he lay in his own filth on the sidewalk outside the British Embassy in Rangoon, holding a begging bowl. He was just to the left of the gate, half-hidden by the angle of the high wall from sight of the military guards on post. A woman in her fifties, who had been let out of a jitney just up the street, having paid her fare and having tipped as few rupees as necessary to escape a strident rebuke by the driver, smoothed the peplum of her shantung jacket over her hips, and marched imperially toward the Embassy gates. As she came abaft the derelict, he rose on one elbow and shouted at her ankles, "Hey, lady! I write these pomes, and I sell 'em for a buck inna street, an' it keeps juvenile delinquents offa the streets so's they don't spit on ya! So whaddaya think, y'wanna buy one?" The matron did not pause, striding toward the gates, but she said snappishly, "You're a businessman. Don't talk art."

This is a story titled
THE ROUTE OF ODYSSEUS

"You will find the scene of Odysseus's wanderings when you find the cobbler who sewed up the bag of winds."
Eratosthenes, late 3rd century, B.C

LEVENDIS: On Saturday the 12th of October, having taken the sidestep, he came to a place near Weimar in southwest Germany. He did not see the photographer snapping pictures of the scene. He stood among the cordwood bodies. It was cold for the spring; and even though he was heavily clothed, he shivered. He walked down the rows of bony corpses, looking into the black holes that had been eye sockets, seeing an endless chicken dinner, the bones gnawed clean, tossed like jackstraws in heaps. The stretched-taut groins of men and women, flesh tarpaulins where passion had once smoothed the transport from sleep to wakefulness. Entwined so cavalierly that here a woman with three arms, and there a child with the legs of a sprinter three times his age. A woman's face, looking up at him with soot for sight, remarkable cheekbones, high and lovely, she might have been an actress. Xylophones for chests and torsos, violin bows that had waved goodbye and hugged grandchildren and lifted in toasts to the passing of traditions, gourd whistles between eyes and mouths. He stood among the cordwood bodies and could not remain merely an instrument himself. He sank to his haunches, crouched and wept, burying his head in his hands, as the photographer took shot after shot, an opportunity like a gift from the editor. Then he tried to stop crying, and stood, and the cold cut him, and he removed his heavy topcoat and placed it gently over the bodies of two women and a man lying so close and intermixed that it easily served as a coverlet for them. He stood among the cordwood bodies, 24 April 1945, Buchenwald, and the photograph would appear in a book published forty-six years later, on Saturday the 12th of October. The photographer's roll ran out just an instant before the slim young man without a topcoat took the sidestep. Nor did he hear the tearful young man say, "Sertsa." In Russian, *sertsa* means soul.

LEVENDIS: On Sunday the 13th of October, he did nothing. He rested. When he thought about it, he grew annoyed. "Time does not become sacred until we have lived it," he said. But he thought: *to hell with it; even God knocked off for a day.*

LEVENDIS: On Monday the 14th of October, he climbed up through the stinking stairwell shaft of a Baltimore tenement, clutching his notebook, breathing through his mouth to block the smell of mildew, garbage, and urine, focusing his mind on the apartment number he was seeking, straining through the evening dimness in the wan light of one bulb hanging high above, barely illuminating the vertical tunnel, as he climbed and climbed, straining to see the numbers on the doors, going up, realizing the tenants had pulled the numbers *off* the doors to foil him and welfare investigators like him, stumbling over something oily and sobbing jammed into a corner of the last step, losing his grip on the rotting bannister and finding it just in time, trapped for a moment in the hopeless beam of washed-out light falling from above, poised in mid-tumble and then regaining his grip, hoping the welfare recipient under scrutiny would not be home, so he could knock off for the day, hurry back downtown and crosstown and take a shower, going up till he had reached the topmost landing, and finding the number scratched on the door-frame, and knocking, getting no answer, knocking again, hearing first the scream, then the sound of someone beating against a wall, or the floor, with a heavy stick, and then the scream again, and then another so closely following the first that it might have been one scream only, and he threw himself against the door, and it was old but never had been well-built, and it came away, off its hinges, in one rotten crack, and he was inside, and the most beautiful young black woman he had ever seen was tearing the rats off her baby. He left the check on the kitchen table, he did not have an affair with her, he did not see her fall from the apartment window, six storeys into a courtyard, and never knew if she came back from the grave to escape the rats that gnawed at her cheap wooden casket. He never loved her, and so was not there when what she became flowed back up through the walls of the tenement to absorb him and meld with him and become one with him as he lay sleeping penitently on the filthy floor of the topmost apartment. He left the check, and none of that happened.

LEVENDIS: On Tuesday the 15th of October, he stood in the Greek theatre at Aspendos, Turkey, a structure built two thousand years earlier, so acoustically perfect that every word spoken on its stage could be heard with clarity in any of its thirteen thousand seats, and he spoke to a little boy sitting high above him. He uttered Count Von Manfred's dying words, Schumann's overture, Byron's poem: "Old man, 'tis not so difficult to die." The child smiled and waved. He waved back, then shrugged. They became friends at a distance. It was the first time someone other than his mother, who was dead, had been kind to the boy. In years to come it would be a reminder that there was a smile out there on the wind. The little boy looked down the rows and concentric rows of seats: the man 'way down there was motioning for him to come to him. The child, whose name was Orhon, hopped and hopped, descending to the center of the ring as quickly as he could. As he came to the core, and walked out across the orchestra ring, he studied the man. This person was very tall, and he needed a shave, and his hat had an extremely wide brim, like the hat of Kül, the man who made weekly trips to Ankara, and he wore a long overcoat far too hot for this day. Orhon could not see the man's eyes because he wore dark glasses that reflected the sky. Orhon thought this man looked like a mountain bandit, only dressed more impressively. Not wisely for a day as torpid as this, but more impressively than Bilge and his men, who raided the farming villages. When he reached the tall man, and they smiled at each other, this person said to Orhon, "I am an unlimited person living in a limited world." The child did not know what to say to that. But he liked the man. "Why do you wear such heavy wool today? I am barefoot." He raised his dusty foot to show the man, and was embarrassed at the dirty cloth tied around his big toe. And the man said, "Because

I need a safe place to keep the limited world." And he unbuttoned his overcoat, and held open one side, and showed Orhon what he would inherit one day, if he tried very hard not to be a despot. Pinned to the fabric, each with the face of the planet, were a million and more timepieces, each one the Earth at a different moment, and all of them purring erratically like dozing sphinxes. And Orhon stood there, in the heat, for quite a long while, and listened to the ticking of the limited world.

LEVENDIS: On Wednesday the 16th of October, he chanced upon three skinheads in Doc Martens and cheap black leatherette, beating the crap out of an interracial couple who had emerged from the late show at the La Salle Theater in Chicago. He stood quietly and watched. For a long while.

LEVENDIS: On Thursday the 17th of October, he chanced upon three skinheads in Doc Martens and cheap black leatherette, beating the crap out of an interracial couple who had stopped for a bite to eat at a Howard Johnson's near King of Prussia on the Pennsylvania Turnpike. He removed the inch-and-a-half-thick ironwood dowel he always carried beside his driver's seat and, holding the 2½' long rod at its centerpoint, laid alongside his pants leg so it could not be seen in the semi-darkness of the parking lot, he came up behind the three as they kicked the black woman and the white man lying between parked cars. He tapped the tallest of the trio on his shoulder, and when the boy turned around—he couldn't have been more than seventeen—he dropped back a step, slid the dowel up with his right hand, gripped it tightly with his left, and drove the end of the rod into the eye of the skinhead, punching through behind the socket and pulping the brain. The boy flailed backward, already dead, and struck his partners. As they turned, he was spinning the dowel like a baton, faster and faster, and as the stouter of the two attackers charged him, he whipped it around his head and slashed straight across the boy's throat. The snapping sound ricocheted off the dark hillside beyond the restaurant. He kicked the third boy in the groin, and when he dropped, and fell on his back, he kicked him under the chin, opening the skinhead's mouth; and then he stood over him, and with both hands locked around the pole, as hard as he could, he piledrove the wooden rod into the kid's mouth, shattering his teeth, and turning the back of his skull to flinders. The dowel scraped concrete through the ruined face. Then he helped the man and his wife to their feet, and bullied the manager of the Howard Johnson's into actually letting them lie down in his office till the State Police arrived. He ordered a plate of fried clams and sat there eating pleasurably until the cops had taken his statement.

LEVENDIS: On Friday the 18th of October, he took a busload of Mormon school-children to the shallow waters of the Great Salt Lake in Utah, to pay homage to the great sculptor Smithson by introducing the art-ignorant children to the *Spiral Jetty*, an incongruously gorgeous line of earth and stone that curves out and away like a thought lost in the tide. "The man who made this, who dreamed it up and then *made* it, you know what he once said?" And they ventured that no, they didn't know what this Smithson sculptor had said, and the man who had driven the bus paused for a dramatic moment, and he repeated Smithson's words: "Establish enigmas, not explanations." They stared at him. "Perhaps you had to be there," he said, shrugging. "Who's for ice cream?" And they went to a Baskin-Robbins.

LEVENDIS: On Saturday the 19th of October, he filed a thirty-million-dollar lawsuit against the major leagues in the name of Alberda Jeannette Chambers, a 19-year-old lefthander with a fadeaway fast ball clocked at better than 96 mph; a dipsy-doodle slider that could do a barrel-roll and clean up after itself; an ERA of 2.10; who could hit from either side of the plate with a batting average of .360; who doubled as a peppery little shortstop working with a trapper's mitt of her own design; who had been refused tryouts with virtually every professional team in the United States (also Japan) from the bigs all the way down to the Pony League. He filed in Federal District Court for the Southern Division of New York State, and told Ted Koppel that Allie Chambers would be the first female player, mulatto or otherwise, in the Baseball Hall of Fame.

LEVENDIS: On Sunday the 20th of October, he drove out and around through the streets of Raleigh and Durham, North Carolina, in a rented van equipped with a public address system, and he endlessly reminded somnambulistic pedestrians and families entering eggs 'n grits restaurants (many of these adults had actually voted for Jesse Helms and thus were in danger of losing their *sertsa*) that perhaps they should ignore their bibles today, and go back and reread Shirley Jackson's short story, "One Ordinary Day, with Peanuts."

This is a story titled
THE DAFFODILS THAT ENTERTAIN

LEVENDIS: On Monday the 21st of October, having taken the sidestep, he wandered through that section of New York City known as the Tenderloin. It was 1892. Crosstown on 24th Street from Fifth Avenue to Seventh, then he turned uptown and walked slowly on Seventh to 40th. Midtown was rife with brothels, their red lights shining through the shadows, challenging the wan gaslit streetlamps. The Edison and Swan United Electric Light Co., Ltd., had improved business tremendously through the wise solicitations of a salesman with a Greek-sounding name who had canvassed the prostitution district west of Broadway only five years earlier, urging the installation of Mr. Joseph Wilson Swan and Mr. Thomas Alva Edison's filament lamps: painted crimson, fixed above the ominously yawning doorways of the area's many houses of easy virtue. He passed an alley on 36th Street, and heard a woman's voice in the darkness complaining, "You said you'd give me two dollars. You have to give it to me first! Stop! No, *first* you gotta give me the two dollars!" He stepped into the alley, let his eyes acclimate to the darkness so total, trying to hold his breath against the stench; and then he saw them. The man was in his late forties, wearing a bowler and a shin-length topcoat with an astrakhan collar. The sound of horse-drawn carriages clopped loudly on the bricks beyond the alley, and the man in the astrakhan looked up, toward the alley mouth. His face was strained, as if he expected an accomplice of the girl, a footpad or shoulder-hitter or bully-boy pimp to charge to her defense. He had his fly unbuttoned and his thin, pale penis extended; the girl was backed against the alley wall, the man's left hand at her throat; and he had hiked up her apron and skirt and petticoats, and was trying to get his right hand into her drawers. She pushed against him, but to no avail. He was large and strong. But when he saw the other man standing down there, near the mouth of the alley, he let her garments drop, and fished his organ back into his pants, but didn't waste time buttoning-up. "You there! Like to watch your betters at work, do you?" The man who had done the sidestep spoke softly: "Let the girl go. Give her the two dollars, and let her go." The man in the bowler took a step toward the mouth of the alley, his hands coming up in a standard pugilist's extension. He gave a tiny laugh that was a snort that was rude and derisive: "Oh so, fancy yourself something of the John L. Sullivan, do you, captain? Well, let's see how you and I and the Marquis Q get along . . ." and he danced forward, hindered considerably by the bulky overcoat. As he drew within double arm's-length of his opponent the younger man drew the taser from his coat pocket, fired at point-blank range, the barbs striking the pugilist in the cheek and neck, the charge lifting him off his feet and driving him back into the brick wall so hard that the filaments were wrenched loose, and the potential fornicator fell forward, his eyes rolled up in his head. Fell forward so hard he smashed three of his front teeth, broken at the gum-line. The girl tried to run, but the alley was a dead end. She watched as the man with the strange weapon came to her. She could barely see his face, and there had been all those killings with that Jack the Ripper in London a few years back, and there was talk that this Jack had been a Yankee and had come back to New York. She was terrified. Her name was Poppy Skurnik, she was an orphan, and she worked way downtown as a pieceworker in a shirtwaist factory. She made one dollar and sixty-five cents a week, for six days of labor, from seven in the morning until seven at night, and it was barely enough to pay for her lodgings at Baer's Rents. So she "supplemented" her income with a stroll in the Tenderloin, twice a week, never more, and prayed that she could continue to avoid the murderous attentions of gentlemen who liked to cripple girls after they'd topped them, continue to avoid the pressures of pimps and boy friends who wanted her to work for them, continue to avoid the knowledge that she was no longer "decent" but was also a long way from winding up in one of these red-light whorehouses. He took her gently by the hand, and started to lead her out of the alley, carefully stepping over the unconscious molester. When they reached the street, and she saw how handsome he was, and how young he was, and how premierely he was dressed, she also smiled. She was extraordinarily attractive, and the young man tipped his hat and spoke to her kindly, inquiring as to her name, and where she lived, and if she would like to accompany him for some dinner. And she accepted, and he hailed a carriage, and took her to Delmonico's for the finest meal she had ever had. And later, much later, when he brought her to his townhouse on upper Fifth Avenue, in the posh section, she was ready to do anything he required of her. But instead, all he asked was that she allow him to give her a hundred dollars in exchange for one second of small pain. And she felt fear, because she knew what these nabobs were like, *but a hundred dollars!* So she said yes, and he asked her to bare her left buttock, and she did it with embarrassment, and there was exactly one second of mosquito bite pain, and then he was wiping the spot where he had injected her with penicillin, with a cool and fragrant wad of cotton batting. "Would you like to sleep the night here, Poppy?" the young man asked. "My room is down the hall, but I think you'll be very comfortable in this one." And she was worried that he had done something awful to her, like inject her with a bad poison, but she didn't *feel* any different, and he seemed so nice, so she said yes, that would be a dear way to spend the evening, and he gave her ten ten-dollar bills, and wished her a pleasant sleep, and left the room, having saved her life, for she had contracted syphilis the week before, though she didn't know it; and within a year she would have been unable, by her appearance alone, to get men in the streets; and would have been let go at the shirtwaist factory; and would have been seduced and sold into one of the worst of the brothels; and would have been dead within another two years. But this night she slept well, between cool sheets with hand-embroidered lace edging, and when she rose the next day he was gone, and no one told her to leave the townhouse, and so she stayed on from day to day, for years, and eventually married and gave birth to three children, one of whom grew to maturity, married, had a child who became an adult and saved the lives of millions of innocent men, women, and children. But that night in 1892 she slept a deep, sweet, recuperative and dreamless sleep.

LEVENDIS: On Tuesday the 22nd of October, he visited a plague of asthmatic toads on Iisalmi, a small town in Finland; a rain of handbills left over from World War II urging the SS troops to surrender on Chejudo, an island off the southern coast of Korea; a shock wave of forsythia on Linares in Spain; and a fully-restored 1926 Ahrens-Fox model RK fire engine on a mini-mall in Clarksville, Arkansas.

LEVENDIS: On Wednesday the 23rd of October, he corrected every history book in America so that they no longer called it The Battle of Bunker Hill, but rather Breeds Hill where, in fact, the engagement of 17 June 1775 had taken place. He also invested every radio and television commentator with the ability to differentiate between "in a moment" and "momentarily," which were not at all the same thing, and the misuse of which annoyed him greatly. The former was in his job description; the latter was a matter of personal pique.

LEVENDIS: On Thursday the 24th of October, he revealed to the London *Times* and *Paris-Match* the name of the woman who had stood on the grassy knoll, behind the fence, in Dallas that day, and fired the rifle shots that killed John F. Kennedy. But no one believed Marilyn Monroe could have done the deed and gotten away unnoticed. Not even when he provided her suicide note that confessed the entire matter and tragically told in her own words how jealousy and having been jilted had driven her to hire that weasel Lee Harvey Oswald, and that pig Jack Ruby, and how she could no longer live with the guilt, goodbye. No one would run the story, not even the *Star*, not even *The Enquirer*, not even *TV Guide*. But he tried.

LEVENDIS: On Friday the 25th of October, he upped the intelligence of every human being on the planet by forty points.

LEVENDIS: On Saturday the 26th of October, he lowered the intelligence of every human being on the planet by forty-two points.

This is a story titled
AT LEAST ONE GOOD DEED A DAY, EVERY SINGLE DAY

LEVENDIS: On Sunday the 27th of October, he returned to a family in Kalgoorlie, SW Australia, a five-year-old child who had been kidnapped from their home in Bayonne, New Jersey, fifteen years earlier. The child was no older than before the family had immigrated, but he now spoke only in a dialect of Etruscan, a language that had not been heard on the planet for thousands of years. Having most of the day free, however, he then made it his business to kill the remaining seventeen American GIs being held MIA in an encampment in the heart of Laos. Waste not, want not.

LEVENDIS: On Monday the 28th of October, still exhilarated from the work and labors of the preceding day, he brought out of the highlands of North Viet Nam Capt. Eugene Y. Grasso, USAF, who had gone down under fire twenty-eight years earlier. He returned him to his family in Anchorage, Alaska, where his wife, remarried, refused to see him but his daughter whom he had never seen, would. They fell in love, and lived together in Anchorage, where their story provided endless confusion to the ministers of several faiths.

LEVENDIS: On Tuesday the 29th of October, he destroyed the last bits of evidence that would have led to the answers to the mysteries of the disappearances of Amelia Earhart, Ambrose Bierce, Benjamin Bathurst and Jimmy Hoffa. He washed the bones and placed them in a display of early American artifacts.

LEVENDIS: On Wednesday the 30th of October, he traveled to New Orleans, Louisiana, where he waited at a restaurant in Metairie for the former head of the Ku Klux Klan, now running for state office, to show up to meet friends. As the man stepped out of his limousine, wary guards on both sides of him, the traveler fired a Laws rocket from the roof of the eatery. It blew up the former KKK prexy, his guards, and a perfectly good Cadillac Eldorado. Leaving the electoral field open, for the enlightened voters of Louisiana, to a man who, as a child, had assisted Mengele's medical experiments, a second contender who had changed his name to avoid being arrested for child mutilation, and an illiterate swamp cabbage farmer from Baton Rouge whose political philosophy involved cutting the throats of peccary pigs, and thrusting one's face into the boiling blood of the corpse. Waste not, want not.

LEVENDIS: On Thursday the 31st of October, he restored to his throne the Dalai Lama, and closed off the mountain passes that provided land access to Tibet, and caused to blow constantly a cataclysmic snowstorm that did not affect the land below, but made any accessibility by air impossible. The Dalai Lama offered a referendum to the people: should we rename our land Shangri-La?

LEVENDIS: On Friday the 32nd of October, he addressed a convention of readers of cheap fantasy novels, saying, "We invent our lives (and other people's) as we live them; what we call 'life' is itself a fiction. Therefore, we must constantly strive to produce only good art, absolutely entertaining fiction." (He did *not* say to them: "I am an unlimited person, sadly living in a limited world.") They smiled politely, but since he spoke only in Etruscan, they did not understand a word he said.

LEVENDIS: On Saturday the 33rd of October, he did the sidestep and worked the oars of the longboat that brought Christopher Columbus to the shores of the New World, where he was approached by a representative of the native peoples, who laughed at the silly clothing the great navigator wore. They all ordered pizza and the man who had done the rowing made sure that venereal disease was quickly spread so that centuries later he could give a beautiful young woman an inoculation in her left buttock.

LEVENDIS: On Piltic the 34th of October, he gave all dogs the ability to speak in English, French, Mandarin, Urdu, and Esperanto; but all they could say was rhyming poetry of the worst sort, and he called it *doggerel*.

LEVENDIS: On Sqwaybe the 35th of October, he was advised by the Front Office that he had been having too rich a time at the expense of the Master Parameter, and he was removed from his position, and the unit was closed down, and darkness was pencilled in as a mid-season replacement. He was reprimanded for having called himself Levendis, which is a Greek word for someone who is full of the pleasure of living. He was reassigned, with censure, but no one higher up noticed that on his new assignment he had taken the name Sertsa.

This has been a story titled
SHAGGING FUNGOES

The author notes that the primary title of this story was courtesy of Mr. Frank P. Reynolds, via the late Mike Hodel; the author notes that this story was inspired by a short story written by the late Shirley Jackson (mentioned passim the preceding work); the author notes that assistance in the research for this work came from a great many people who were utterly confused by the nature of the questions asked them, not the least of whom were the late Dr. Isaac Asimov, Ms. Kristine Kathryn Rusch, and Mr. Len Wein; the author notes that he has been working on this story since 1978; and finally the author notes that he wrote this story for Robert Silverberg, because Robert Silverberg is a pain in the author's ass. No offense intended. And let's not forget the immortal Jorge Luis Borges.

GRAVES

Joe Haldeman

Joe Haldeman divides his time between homes in Gainesville, Florida, and in Cambridge, Massachusetts, where he is a visiting professor in the writing department of the Massachusetts Institute of Technology. He writes hard science fiction and is famous for his landmark novel of the 1970s, the award-winning *The Forever War*. He is the author of many other novels, including *Mindbridge, Worlds, Worlds Apart, Buying Time, The Hemingway Hoax*, and most recently, *Worlds Enough and Time*. His short stories have been gathered into two collections, *Infinite Dreams* and *Dealing in Futures*, and he is an award-winning poet as well.

Much of Haldeman's work, including *The Forever War* and "DX" (which appeared in *The Year's Best Fantasy: First Annual Collection*), was influenced by his experiences in the Vietnam War. "Graves" also takes place in Vietnam; the story is told by a member of "graves registration," the soldiers who catalog the bodies and body parts and property left on the battlefield. What makes this story so effective is the contrast between the cool professional manner of the narrator on the job and the terror he experiences when something unexpected occurs. It first appeared in *The Magazine of Fantasy & Science Fiction*.

—E.D.

I have this persistent sleep disorder that makes life difficult for me, but still I want to keep it. Boy, do I want to keep it. It goes back twenty years, to Vietnam. To Graves.

Dead bodies turn from bad to worse real fast in the jungle. You've got a few hours before rigor mortis makes them hard to handle, hard to stuff in a bag. By that time, they start to turn greenish, if they started out white or yellow, where you can see the skin. It's mostly bugs by then, usually ants. Then they go to black and start to smell.

They swell up and burst.

You'd think the ants and roaches and beetles and millipedes would make short work of them after that, but they don't. Just when they get to looking and smelling the worst, the bugs sort of lose interest, get fastidious, send out for pizza. Except for the flies. Laying eggs.

The funny thing is, unless some big animal got to it and tore it up, even after a week or so, you've still got something more than a skeleton, even a sort of a face. No eyes, though. Every now and then, we'd get one like that. Not too often, since soldiers usually don't die alone and sit there for that long, but sometimes. We called them "dry ones." Still damp underneath, of course, and inside, but kind of like a sunburned mummy otherwise.

You tell people what you do at Graves Registration, "Graves," and it sounds like about the worst job the army has to offer. It isn't. You just stand there all day and open body bags, figure out which parts maybe belong to which dog tag—not that it's usually that important—sew them up more or less with a big needle, account for all the wallets and jewelry, steal the dope out of their pockets, box them up, seal the casket, do the paperwork. When you have enough boxes, you truck them out to the airfield. The first week maybe is pretty bad. But after a hundred or so, after you get used to the smell and the god-awful feel of them, you get to thinking that opening a body bag is a lot better than ending up inside one. They put Graves in safe places.

Since I'd had a couple of years of college, premed, I got some of the more interesting jobs. Captain French, who was the pathologist actually in charge of the outfit, always took me with him out into the field when he had to examine a corpse in situ, which happened only maybe once a month. I got to wear a .45 in a shoulder holster, tough guy. Never fired it, never got shot at, except the one time.

That was a hell of a time. It's funny what gets to you, stays with you.

Usually when we had an in situ, it was a forensic matter, like an officer they suspected had been fragged or otherwise terminated by his own men. We'd take pictures and interview some people, and then Frenchy would bring the stiff back for autopsy, see whether the bullets were American or Vietnamese. (Not that that would be conclusive either way. The Vietcong stole our weapons, and our guys used the North Vietnamese AK-47s, when we could get our hands on them. More reliable than the M-16, and a better cartridge for killing. Both sides proved that over and over.) Usually Frenchy would send a report up to Division, and that would be it. Once he had to testify at a court-martial. The kid was guilty, but just got life. The officer was a real prick.

Anyhow, we got the call to come look at this in situ corpse about five in the afternoon. Frenchy tried to put it off until the next day, since if it got dark, we'd have to spend the night. The guy he was talking to was a major, though, and obviously proud of it, so it was no use arguing. I threw some C's and beer and a couple canteens into two rucksacks that already had blankets and air mattresses tied on the bottom. Box of .45 ammo and a couple hand grenades. Went and got a jeep while Frenchy got his stuff together and made sure Doc Carter was sober enough to count the stiffs as they came in. (Doc Carter was the one supposed to be in charge, but he didn't much care for the work.)

Drove us out to the pad, and lo and behold, there was a chopper waiting, blades idling. Should've started to smell a rat then. We don't get real high priority, and it's not easy to get a chopper to go anywhere so close to sundown. They even helped us stow our gear. Up, up and away.

I never flew enough in helicopters to make it routine. Kontum looked almost pretty in the low sun, golden red. I had to sit between two flamethrowers, though, which didn't make me feel too secure. The door gunner was smoking. The flame-thrower tanks were stenciled NO SMOKING.

We went fast and low out toward the mountains to the west. I was hoping we'd wind up at one of the big fire bases up there, figuring I'd sleep better with a few hundred men around. But no such luck. When the chopper started to slow down, the blades' whir deepening to a whuck-whuck-whuck, there was no clearing as far as the eye could see. Thick jungle canopy everywhere. Then a wisp of purple smoke showed us a helicopter-sized hole in the leaves. The pilot brought us down an inch at a time, nicking twigs. I was very much aware of the flamethrowers. If he clipped a large branch, we'd be so much pot roast.

When we touched down, four guys in a big hurry unloaded our gear and the flamethrowers and a couple cases of ammo. They put two wounded guys and one client on board and shooed the helicopter away. Yeah, it would sort of broadcast your position. One of them told us to wait; he'd go get the major.

"I don't like this at all," Frenchy said.

"Me neither," I said. "Let's go home."

"Any outfit that's got a major and two flamethrowers is planning to fight a real war." He pulled his .45 out and looked at it as if he'd never seen one before. "Which end of this do you think the bullets come out of?"

"Shit," I advised, and rummaged through the rucksack for a beer. I gave Frenchy one, and he put it in his side pocket.

A machine gun opened up off to our right. Frenchy and I grabbed the dirt. Three grenade blasts. Somebody yelled for them to cut that out. Guy yelled back he thought he saw something. Machine gun started up again. We tried to get a little lower.

Up walks this old guy, thirties, looking annoyed. The major.

"You men get up. What's wrong with you?" He was playin' games.

Frenchy got up, dusting himself off. We had the only clean fatigues in twenty miles. "Captain French, Graves Registration."

"Oh," he said, not visibly impressed. "Secure your gear and follow me." He drifted off like a mighty ship of the jungle. Frenchy rolled his eyes, and we hoisted our rucksacks and followed him. I wasn't sure whether "secure your gear" meant bring your stuff or leave it behind, but Budweiser could get to be a real collector's item in the boonies, and there were a lot of collectors out here.

We walked too far. I mean a couple hundred yards. That meant they were really spread out thin. I didn't look forward to spending the night. The goddamned machine gun started up again. The major looked annoyed and shouted, "Sergeant, will you please control your men?", and the sergeant told the machine gunner to shut the fuck up, and the machine gunner told the sergeant there was a fuckin' gook out there, and then somebody popped a big one, like a Claymore, and then everybody was shooting every which way. Frenchy and I got real horizontal. I heard a bullet whip by over my head. The major was leaning against a tree, looking bored, shouting, "Cease firing, cease firing!" The shooting dwindled down like popcorn getting done. The major looked over at us and said, "Come on. While there's still light." He led us into a small clearing, elephant grass pretty well trampled down. I guess everybody had had his turn to look at the corpse.

It wasn't a real gruesome body, as bodies go, but it was odd-looking, even for a dry one. Moldy, like someone had dusted flour over it. Naked and probably male, though incomplete: all the soft parts were gone. Tall; one of our Montagnard allies rather than an ethnic Vietnamese. Emaciated, dry skin taut over ribs. Probably old, though it doesn't take long for these people to get old. Lying on its back, mouth wide open, a familiar posture. Empty eye sockets staring skyward. Arms flung out in supplication, loosely, long past rigor mortis.

Teeth chipped and filed to points, probably some Montagnard tribal custom. I'd never seen it before, but we didn't "do" many natives.

Frenchy knelt down and reached for it, then stopped. "Checked for booby traps?"

"No," the major said. "Figure that's your job." Frenchy looked at me with an expression that said it was my job.

Both officers stood back a respectful distance while I felt under the corpse. Sometimes they pull the pin on a hand grenade and slip it under the body so that the body's weight keeps the arming lever in place. You turn it over, and *Tomato Surprise!*

I always worry less about a hand grenade than about the various weird serpents and bugs that might enjoy living underneath a decomposing corpse. Vietnam has its share of snakes and scorpions and megapedes.

I was lucky this time; nothing but maggots. I flicked them off my hand and watched the major turn a little green. People are funny. What does he think is going to happen to him when he dies? Everything has to eat. And he was sure as hell going to die if he didn't start keeping his head down. I remember that thought, but didn't think of it then as a prophecy.

They came over. "What do you make of it, Doctor?"

"I don't think we can cure him." Frenchy was getting annoyed at this cherry bomb. "What else do you want to know?"

"Isn't it a little . . . *odd* to find something like this in the middle of nowhere?"

"Naw. Country's full of corpses." He knelt down and studied the face, wiggling the head by its chin. "We keep it up, you'll be able to walk from the Mekong to the DMZ without stepping on anything but corpses."

"But he's been castrated!"

"Birds." He toed the body over, busy white crawlers running from the light. "Just some old geezer who walked out into the woods naked and fell over dead. Could happen back in the World. Old people do funny things."

"I thought maybe he'd been tortured by the VC or something."

"God knows. It could happen." The body eased back into its original position with a creepy creaking sound, like leather. Its mouth had closed halfway. "If you want to put 'evidence of VC torture' in your report, your body count, I'll initial it."

"What do you mean by that, Captain?"

"Exactly what I said." He kept staring at the major while he flipped a cigarette into his mouth and fired it up. Nonfilter Camels; you'd think a guy who worked with corpses all day long would be less anxious to turn into one. "I'm just trying to get along."

"You believe I want you to falsify—"

Now, "falsify" is a strange word for a last word. The enemy had set up a heavy machine gun on the other side of the clearing, and we were the closest targets. A round struck the major in the small of his back, we found on later examination. At the time, it was just an explosion of blood and guts, and he went down with his legs flopping every which way, barfing, then loud death rattle. Frenchy was on the ground in a ball, holding his left hand, going, "Shit shit shit." He'd lost the last joint of his little finger. Painful, but not serious enough, as it turned out, to get him back to the World.

I myself was horizontal and aspiring to be subterranean. I managed to get my pistol out and cocked, but realized I didn't want to do anything that might draw attention to us. The machine gun was spraying back and forth over us at about knee height. Maybe they couldn't see us; maybe they thought we were dead. I was scared shitless.

"Frenchy," I stage-whispered, "we've got to get outa here." He was trying to wrap his finger up in a standard first-aid-pack gauze bandage, much too large. "Get back to the trees."

"After you, asshole. We wouldn't get halfway." He worked his pistol out of the holster, but couldn't cock it, his left hand clamping the bandage and slippery with blood. I armed it for him and handed it back. "These are going to do a hell of a lot of good. How are you with grenades?"

"Shit. How you think I wound up in Graves?" In basic training, they'd put me on KP whenever they went out for live grenade practice. In school, I was always the last person when they chose up sides for baseball, for the same reason—though, to my knowledge, a baseball wouldn't kill you if you couldn't throw far enough. "I couldn't get one halfway there." The tree line was about sixty yards away.

"Neither could I, with this hand." He was a lefty.

Behind us came the "poink" sound of a sixty-millimeter mortar, and in a couple of seconds, there was a gray-smoke explosion between us and the tree line. The machine gun stopped, and somebody behind us yelled, "Add twenty!"

At the tree line, we could hear some shouting in Vietnamese, and a clanking of metal. "They're gonna bug out," Frenchy said. "Let's di-di."

We got up and ran, and somebody did fire a couple of bursts at us, probably an AK-47, but he missed, and then there were a series of poinks and a series of explosions pretty close to where the gun had been.

We rushed back to the LZ and found the command group, about the time the firing started up again. There was a first lieutenant in charge, and when things slowed down enough for us to tell him what had happened to the major, he expressed neither surprise nor grief. The man had been an observer from Battalion, and had assumed command when their captain was killed that morning. He'd take our word for it that the guy was dead—that was one thing we were trained observers in—and not send a squad out for him until the fighting had died down and it was light again.

We inherited the major's hole, which was nice and deep, and in his rucksack found a dozen cans and jars of real food and a flask of scotch. So, as the battle raged through the night, we munched pâté on Ritz crackers, pickled herring in sour-cream sauce, little Polish sausages on party rye with real French mustard. We drank all the scotch and saved the beer for breakfast.

For hours the lieutenant called in for artillery and air support, but to no avail. Later we found out that the enemy had launched coordinated attacks on all the local airfields and Special Forces camps, and every camp that held POWs. We were much lower priority.

Then, about three in the morning, Snoopy came over. Snoopy was a big C-130 cargo plane that carried nothing but ammunition and Gatling guns; they said it could fly over a football field and put a round into every square inch. Anyhow, it saturated the perimeter with fire, and the enemy stopped shooting. Frenchy and I went to sleep.

At first light, we went out to help round up the KIAs. There were only four dead, counting the major, but the major was an astounding sight, at least in context.

He looked sort of like a cadaver left over from a teaching autopsy. His shirt had been opened and his pants pulled down to his thighs, and the entire thoracic and abdominal cavities had been ripped open and emptied of everything soft, everything from esophagus to testicles, rib cage like blood-streaked fingers sticking rigid out of sagging skin, and there wasn't a sign of any of the guts anywhere, just a lot of dried blood.

Nobody had heard anything. There was a machine-gun position not twenty yards away, and they'd been straining their ears all night. All they'd heard was flies.

Maybe an animal feeding very quietly. The body hadn't been opened with a scalpel or a knife; the skin had been torn by teeth or claws—but seemingly systematically, throat to balls.

And the dry one was gone. Him with the pointed teeth.

There is one rational explanation. Modern warfare is partly mindfuck, and we aren't the only ones who do it, dropping unlucky cards, invoking magic and superstition. The Vietnamese knew how squeamish Americans were, and would mutilate bodies in clever ways. They could also move very quietly. The dry one? They might have spirited him away just to fuck with us. Show what they could do under our noses.

And as for the dry one's odd mummified appearance, the mold, there might be an explanation. I found out that the Montagnards in that area don't bury their dead; they put them in a coffin made from a hollowed-out log and leave them aboveground. So maybe he was just the victim of a grave robber. I thought the nearest village was miles away, like twenty miles, but I could have been wrong. Or the body could have been carried that distance for some obscure purpose—maybe the VC set it out on the trail to make the Americans stop in a good place to be ambushed.

That's probably it. But for twenty years now, several nights a week, I wake up sweating with a terrible image in my mind. I've gone out with a flashlight, and there it is, the dry one, scooping steaming entrails from the major's body, tearing them with its sharp teeth, staring into my light with black empty sockets, unconcerned. I reach for my pistol, and it's never there. The creature stands up, shiny with blood, and takes a step toward me—for a year or so, that was it; I would wake up. Then it was two steps, and then three. After twenty years it has covered half the distance and its dripping hands are raising from its sides.

The doctor gives me tranquilizers. I don't take them. They might help me stay asleep.

THE UGLY FILE
Ed Gorman

Ed Gorman lives in Cedar Rapids, Iowa, and writes a lot. He writes mystery, crime, horror (as Daniel Ransom), and western novels, including *Rough Cut, The Autumn Dead, A Cry of Shadows,* and *Night Kills*. He is also a prolific short story writer and his "Turn Away" won the Shamus Award. As an editor, he has been responsible for *The Black Lizard Anthologies of Crime Fiction, Stalkers, Mystery Scene* magazine, and many other publications.

Gorman writes in his recent collection, *Prisoners and Other Stories*, that "The Ugly File" is based on his experiences as a writer and producer of documentaries and commercials, when he interviewed women not unlike those in this story. Most stories I've read by Gorman are hard-boiled in tone, and often focus on psychos or tough guys. In contrast, the subject matter of "The Ugly File" is gut-wrenching, but its treatment by Gorman and his protagonist is deeply compassionate—which might be why I found the story so compelling. It was first published in *Borderlands 3*.

—E.D.

The cold rain didn't improve the looks of the housing development, one of those sprawling valleys of pastel-colored tract houses that had sprung from the loins of greedy contractors right at the end of WWII, fresh as flowers during that exultant time but now dead and faded.

I spent fifteen minutes trying to find the right address. Houses and streets formed a blinding maze of sameness.

I got lucky by taking what I feared was a wrong turn. A few minutes later I pulled my new station wagon up to the curb, got out, tugged my hat and raincoat on snugly, and then started unloading.

Usually Merle, my assistant, is on most shoots. He unloads and sets up all the lighting, unloads and sets up all the photographic umbrellas, and unloads and sets up all the electric sensors that trip the strobe lights. But Merle went on this kind of shoot once before and he said never again, "not even if you fire my ass." He was too good an assistant to give up, so now I did these particular jobs alone.

My name is Roy Hubbard. I picked up my profession of photography in Nam, where I was on the staff of a captain whose greatest thrill was taking photos of bloody

346

and dismembered bodies. He didn't care if the bodies belonged to us or them just as long as they had been somehow disfigured or dismembered.

In an odd way, I suppose, being the captain's assistant prepared me for the client I was working for today, and had been working for, on and off, for the past two months. The best-paying client I've ever had, I should mention here. I don't want you to think that I take any special pleasure, or get any special kick, out of gigs like this. I don't. But when you've got a family to feed, and you live in a city with as many competing photography firms as this one has, you pretty much take what's offered you.

The air smelled of wet dark earth turning from winter to spring. Another four or five weeks and you'd see cardinals and jays sitting on the blooming green branches of trees.

The house was shabby even by the standards of the neighborhood, the brown grass littered with bright cheap forgotten plastic toys and empty Diet Pepsi cans and wild rain-sodden scraps of newspaper inserts. The small picture window to the right of the front door was taped lengthwise from some long ago crack, and the white siding ran with rust from the drain spouts. The front door was missing its top glass panel.

I knocked, ducking beneath the slight overhang of the roof to escape the rain.

The woman who answered was probably no older than twenty-five but her eyes and the sag of her shoulders said that her age should not be measured by calendar years alone.

"Mrs. Cunningham?"

"Hi," she said, and her tiny white hands fluttered about like doves. "I didn't get to clean the place up very good."

"That's fine."

"And the two oldest kids have the flu so they're still in their pajamas and—"

"Everything'll be fine, Mrs. Cunningham." When you're a photographer who deals a lot with mothers and children, you have to learn a certain calm, doctorly manner.

She opened the door and I went inside.

The living room, and what I could see of the dining room, was basically a continuation of the front yard—a mine field of cheap toys everywhere and inexpensive furniture, of the sort you buy by the room instead of the piece, strewn with magazines and pieces of the newspaper and the odd piece of children's clothing.

Over all was a sour smell, one part the rainsodden wood of the exterior house, one part the lunch she had just fixed, one part the house cleaning this place hadn't had in a good long while.

The two kids with the flu, boy and girl respectively, were parked in a corner of the long, stained couch. Even from here I knew that one of them had diapers in need of changing. They showed no interest in me or my equipment. Out of dirty faces and dead blue eyes they watched one cartoon character beat another with a hammer on a TV whose sound dial was turned very near the top.

"Cindy's in her room," Mrs. Cunningham explained.

Her dark hair was in a pert little pony tail. The rest of her chunky self was packed into a faded blue sweat shirt and sweat pants. In high school she had probably been nice and trim. But high school was an eternity behind her now.

I carried my gear and followed her down a short hallway. We passed two messy bedrooms and a bathroom and finally we came to a door that was closed.

"Have you ever seen anybody like Cindy before?"

"I guess not, Mrs. Cunningham."

"Well, it's kind of shocking. Some people can't really look at her at all. They just sort of glance at her and look away real quick. You know?"

"I'll be fine."

"I mean, it doesn't offend me when people don't want to look at her. If she wasn't my daughter, I probably wouldn't want to look at her, either. Being perfectly honest, I mean."

"I'm ready, Mrs. Cunningham."

She watched me a moment and said, "You have kids?"

"Two little girls."

"And they're both fine?"

"We were lucky."

For a moment, I thought she might cry. "You don't know how lucky, Mr. Cunningham."

She opened the door and we went into the bedroom.

It was a small room, painted a fresh, lively pink. The furnishings in here—the bassinet, the bureau, the rocking horse in the corner—were more expensive than the stuff in the rest of the house. And the smell was better. Johnson's Baby Oil and Johnson's Baby Powder are always pleasant on the nose. There was a reverence in the appointments of this room, as if the Cunninghams had consciously decided to let the yard and the rest of the house go to hell. But this room—

Mrs. Cunningham led me over to the bassinet and then said, "Are you ready?"

"I'll be fine, Mrs. Cunningham. Really."

"Well," she said, "here you are then."

I went over and peered into the bassinet. The first look is always rough. But I didn't want to upset the lady so I smiled down at her baby as if Cindy looked just like every other baby girl I'd ever seen.

I even put my finger to the baby's belly and tickled her a little. "Hi, Cindy."

After I had finished my first three or four assignments for this particular client, I went to the library one day and spent an hour or so reading about birth defects. The ones most of us are familiar with are clubfoots and cleft palates and harelips and things like that. The treatable problems, that is. From there you work up to spina bifida and cretinism. And from there—

What I didn't know until that day in the library is that there are literally hundreds of ways in which infants can be deformed, right up to and including the genetic curse of The Elephant Man. As soon as I started running into words such as achondroplastic dwarfism and supernumerary chromosomes, I quit reading. I had no idea what those words meant.

Nor did I have any idea of what exactly you would call Cindy's malformation. She had only one tiny arm and that was so short that her three fingers did not quite reach her rib cage. It put me in mind of a flipper on an otter. She had two legs but only one foot and only three digits on that. But her face was the most terrible part of it all, a tiny little slit of a mouth and virtually no nose and only one good eye. The other was almond-shaped and in the right position but the eyeball itself was the deep, startling color of blood.

"We been tryin' to keep her at home here," Mrs. Cunningham said, "but she can be a lot of trouble. The other two kids make fun of her all the time and my husband can't sleep right because he keeps havin' these dreams of her smotherin' because she don't have much of a nose. And the neighbor kids are always tryin' to sneak in and get a look at her."

All the time she talked, I kept staring down at poor Cindy. My reaction was always the same when I saw these children. I wanted to find out who was in charge of a universe that would permit something like this and then tear his fucking throat out.

"You ready to start now?"

"Ready," I said.

She was nice enough to help me get my equipment set up. The pictures went quickly. I shot Cindy from several angles, including several straight-on. For some reason, that's the one the client seems to like best. Straight-on. So you can see everything.

I used VPS large format professional film and a Pentax camera because what I was doing here was essentially making many portraits of Cindy, just the way I do when I make a portrait of an important community leader.

Half an hour later, I was packed up and moving through Mrs. Cunningham's front door.

"You tell that man—that Mr. Byerly who called—that we sure do appreciate that $2000 check he sent."

"I'll be sure to tell him," I said, walking out into the rain.

"You're gonna get wet."

"I'll be fine. Goodbye, Mrs. Cunningham."

Back at the shop, I asked Merle if there had been any calls and he said nothing important. Then, "How'd it go?"

"No problems," I said.

"Another addition to the ugly file, huh?" Then he nodded to the three filing cabinets I'd bought years back at a government auction. The top drawer of the center cabinet contained the photos and negatives of all the deformed children I'd been shooting for Byerly.

"I still don't think that's funny, Merle."

"The ugly file?" He'd been calling it that for a couple weeks now and I'd warned him that I wasn't amused. I have one of those tempers that it's not smart to push on too hard or too long.

"Uh-huh," I said.

"If you can't laugh about it then you have to cry about it."

"That's a cop-out. People always say that when they want to say something nasty and get away with it. I don't want you to call it that any more, you fucking understand me, Merle?"

I could feel the anger coming. I guess I've got more of it than I know what to do with, especially after I've been around some poor goddamned kid like Cindy.

"Hey, boss, lighten up. Shit, man, I won't say it any more, OK?"

"I'm going to hold you to that."

I took the film of Cindy into the dark room. It took six hours to process it all through the chemicals and get the good, clear proofs I wanted.

At some point during the process, Merle knocked on the door and said, "I'm goin' home now, all right?"

"See you tomorrow," I said through the closed door

"Hey, I'm sorry I pissed you off. You know, about those pictures."

"Forget about it, Merle. It's over. Everything's fine."

"Thanks. See you tomorrow."

"Right."

When I came out of the dark room, the windows were filled with night. I put the proofs in a manilla envelope with my logo and return address on it and then went out the door and down the stairs to the parking lot and my station wagon.

The night was like October now, raw and windy. I drove over to the freeway and took it straight out to Mannion Springs, the wealthiest of all the wealthy local suburbs.

On sunny afternoons, Mary and I pack up the girls sometimes and drive through Mannion Springs and look at all the houses and daydream aloud of what it would be like to live in a place where you had honest-to-God maids and honest-to-God butlers the way some of these places do.

I thought of Mary now, and how much I loved her, more the longer we were married, and suddenly I felt this terrible, almost oppressive loneliness, and then I thought of little Cindy in that bassinet this afternoon and I just wanted to start crying and I couldn't even tell you why for sure.

The Byerly place is what they call a shingle Victorian. It had dormers of every kind and description—hipped, eyebrow and gabled. The place is huge but has far fewer windows than you'd expect to find in a house this size. You wonder if sunlight can ever get into it.

I'd called Byerly before leaving the office. He was expecting me.

I parked in the wide asphalt drive that swept around the grounds. By the time I reached the front porch, Byerly was in the arched doorway, dressed in a good dark suit.

I walked right up to him and handed him the envelope with the photos in it.

"Thank you," he said. "You'll send me a bill?"

"Sure," I said. I was going to add, "That's my favorite part of the job, sending out the bill," but he wasn't the kind of guy you joke with. And if you ever saw him, you'd know why.

Everything about him tells you he's one of those men who used to be called aristocratic. He's handsome, he's slim, he's athletic, and he seems to be very, very confident in everything he does—until you look at his eyes, at the sorrow and weariness of them, at the trapped gaze of a small and broken boy hiding in those eyes.

Of course, on my last trip out here I learned why he looks this way. Byerly was out and the maid answered the door and we started talking and then she told me all about it, in whispers of course, because Byerly's wife was upstairs and would not have appreciated being discussed this way.

Four years ago, Mrs. Byerly gave birth to their only child, a son. The family physician said that he had never seen a deformity of this magnitude. The child had a head only slighter larger than an apple and had no eyes and no arms whatsoever. And it made noises that sickened even the most doctorly of doctors . . .

The physician even hinted that the baby might be destroyed, for the sake of the entire family.

Mrs. Byerly had a nervous breakdown and went into a mental hospital for nearly a year. She refused to let her baby be taken to a state institution. Mr. Byerly and three shifts of nurses took care of the boy.

When Mrs. Byerly got out of the hospital everybody pretended that she was doing just fine and wasn't really crazy at all. But then Mrs. Byerly got her husband to hire me to take pictures of deformed babies for her. She seemed to draw courage from knowing that she and her son were not alone in their terrible grief.

All I could think of was those signals we send deep into outer space to see if some other species will hear them and let us know that we're not alone, that this isn't just some frigging joke, this nowhere planet spinning in the darkness . . .

When the maid told me all this, it broke my heart for Mrs. Byerly and then I didn't feel so awkward about taking the pictures anymore. Her husband had his personal physician check out the area for the kind of babies we were looking for and Byerly would call the mother and offer to pay her a lot of money . . . and then I'd go over there and take the pictures of the kid . . .

Now, just as I was just about to turn around and walk off the porch, Byerly said, "I understand that you spent some time here two weeks ago talking to one of the maids."

"Yes."

"I'd prefer that you never do that again. My wife is very uncomfortable about our personal affairs being made public."

He sounded as I had sounded with Merle earlier today. Right on the verge of being very angry. The thing was, I didn't blame him. I wouldn't want people whispering about me and my wife, either

"I apologize, Mr. Byerly. I shouldn't have done that."

"My wife has suffered enough." The anger had left him. He sounded drained. "She's suffered way too much, in fact."

And with that, I heard a child cry out from upstairs.

A child—yet not a child—a strangled, mournful cry that shook me to hear.

"Good night," he said.

He shut the door very quickly, leaving me to the wind and rain and night.

After awhile, I walked down the wide steps to my car and got inside and drove straight home.

As soon as I was inside, I kissed my wife and then took her by the hand and led her upstairs to the room our two little girls share.

We stood in the doorway, looking at Jenny and Sara. They were asleep.

Each was possessed of two eyes, two arms, two legs; and each was possessed of song and delight and wonderment and tenderness and glee.

And I held my wife tighter than I ever had, and felt an almost giddy gratitude for the health of our little family.

Not until much later, near midnight it was, my wife asleep next to me in the warmth of our bed—not until much later did I think again of Mrs. Byerly and her photos in the upstairs bedroom of that dark and shunned Victorian house, up there with her child trying to make frantic sense of the silent and eternal universe that makes no sense at all.

ELFHOUSES
Midori Snyder

The daughter of a French poet and an American scholar of Asian languages, Midori Snyder grew up in the United States and Africa and studied African myth and languages at the University of Wisconsin. Snyder's multicultural background fuels her rich story-telling skills, as evidenced in her novels *Soul-String, New Moon, Sadar's Keep,* and *Belden's Fire.* Her latest is *Hannah's Garden,* a book created in collaboration with British artist Brian Froud.

Snyder currently lives with her husband and two children in Milwaukee, Wisconsin. The following gentle coming-of-age tale comes from an unusual source, Volume #64 of *Mothering* magazine.

—T.W.

(For Deirdre)

When I was 12, everything made me angry. I woke in the morning with irritation the flavor of tart green apples on my tongue. Every word I spoke was sharp, and my mood was sour.

I quarreled with everyone. It usually began at breakfast, as my younger sister Bridget would absently kick the table leg while eating her cereal.

"Watch it!" I growled one day, annoyed at her dreamy face as the milk splashed from her spoon.

"Leave me alone," she snapped.

"You're such a slob," I sneered.

"Mom!"

My mother turned from the counter, holding up the knife still thick with peanut butter. Her other hand cradled the sandwich bread. Above the frown, her dark eyes settled on me accusingly. "Stop nagging your sister, Jeanie. You'll be late for school."

Blood flushed my indignant face. Grabbing my books, I stormed out of the kitchen, letting the back door slam.

Walking to school, I reviewed the origins of my dissatisfaction. To be 12 years old was horrible. I was too old for most of the things that had once given me pleasure. Stuffed animals and dolls gathered dust on the upper shelves of my bookcase. Sometimes when I missed them, I consented to play with Bridget, who still found them interesting. Such occasions were rare, however. Doll play was babyish, I had decided just after Susan, my best friend, had gotten her first bra.

And that was the second problem. Though I had small, flat breasts, they were clearly destined to be something one day. I wanted a bra. I had fine, gold hair on my shins and beneath my arms, and I wanted to shave. My eyes seemed small, and I wanted to wear makeup. Some of my mother's friends would nudge me and wink. "Have you started your periods yet?" they would inquire, and my cheeks would pink with embarrassment. I was in between everything, and I wanted to be grown up. At 12 years old, I was close, very close—but as far as my parents were concerned, not close enough.

It wasn't until the Saturday after Easter, when the sun grew bright and the air finally warm after the long winter, that things began to change. I was sitting in the kitchen arguing with my parents.

"Why can't I wear makeup? Susan's mom lets her. She even wore it to church last week. And what's wrong with shaving my legs? They look awful. All the girls—" I stopped as my father's face clouded.

He rolled his eyes and looked over at my mother. She was at the sink, calmly washing two apples. On the counter were two cheese sandwiches, one on top of the other. I saw the shadow of a smile on her face.

"Get a sweater, Jeanie," she said evenly. "I want you to come with me to Fairy's Bluff."

"Daddy," I pleaded, angry that they were ignoring my outburst. My father got up from the kitchen table, his hands in his pockets. He stood by my mother, looking at her expectantly. For a moment, my heart lifted. Surely, he meant to nudge her into talking, I thought.

She looked back, her eyes half-lidded in a sleepy smile. My father shrugged, and briefly cupped her cheek with one hand. My happiness fell as I saw the wordless agreement pass between them. On his way out of the kitchen, he stroked my head, smoothing down my hair. Then, whistling softly between his teeth, he left me alone with my mother.

"I don't want to go," I said sullenly.

"You don't have a choice."

"Take Bridget," I tried, offering my little sister.

My mother shook her head and went on packing lunch. "She's too young. Now, get the thermos. Do you want tea or juice?" she asked, turning her face to me.

I glared back, hiding the mild surprise I felt at being given a choice of beverage. "Tea," I snapped, grasping at anything that sounded grown up.

"Water's boiled," she answered briskly. "Make the tea, then add some milk to the thermos before you pour it in." She put a sandwich, an apple, and a piece of cake into each bag. Carrot sticks came next, and a small bag of trail mix.

"I'll get the car and meet you out front," she said, scooping up the lunch and two buckets that waited by the door.

Alone in the kitchen, pouring the milk and amber-colored tea into the thermos,

I sighed miserably. I'm never going to get what I want, I thought. I screwed the cap on the thermos angrily, thinking of Susan at church. She had turned around in the pew to wave at me, and her lips had been a rosy pink. In the middle of the homily, she had casually raised the fallen bra strap off her upper arm. I, meantime, had gritted my teeth and looked away at the stained glass windows.

My mother was waiting for me in the car, the motor idling quietly. She had one elbow resting out the open window. On her head, she was wearing a scarf with the pattern of green ivy all over it. I had always liked that scarf on my mother. When I was little, I thought it looked like a fairy crown of leaves covering her dark hair.

I slipped into the front seat beside her, and we drove off toward the country. As the neighborhoods and shopping malls gradually gave way to the spreading fields of nearby farms, some of my anger abated. I stared curiously at my mother, searching her face for signs of myself as an adult.

She had a strong, clean profile. Her smooth, prominent forehead curved out over intelligent eyes. Her nose was a little crooked—the result of a childhood break— though it lent an interesting angle to her face. Her mouth was generous, and she smiled often. Dark hair had escaped the edges of her scarf and curled around her temples. She had a good figure, sturdy and wide hipped. I followed the lines of her muscled forearms down to her squared hands. She gripped the wheel with confidence, her knuckles large and white where they rose above the shiny metal.

Had I not been so absorbed in my anger, I might have been happier at that moment. It was a ritual of my mother's to go every spring to Fairy's Bluff—to pick wild asparagus along the roadsides and then gather mushrooms, especially the hooded morels, in the dark woods of the bluff. She would go for the day, with lunch in tow, and always return with a quiet gleam in her eyes as she settled, tired but satisfied, into a chair. Kicking off her shoes, she scattered little clods of black dirt from the heels of her socks. On her clothes, she carried the soft fragrance of the woods.

I had joined her the previous year for the first time. Looking back on it as we rode along, I realized I must have been a big pain. I tired quickly, complained about the long walk, stepped on the mushrooms I was supposed to pick, and fussed at the dirt that got into my sandwich. My mother tried being patient, but by the end of the day, she became frustrated and very sharp with me. She tossed the buckets in the back seat, and the mushrooms spilled out into the footwells. Her lips were pressed tightly together as she drove home, faster than usual. My father met us at the door, with quizzical eyes. Bridget, holding his hand, sucked on a Popsicle.

"Too early," she had said to him, and I knew it was me she was talking about, not the lack of mushrooms or asparagus.

Well, it'll be different this year, I thought as I saw the cliffs of Fairy's Bluff rising in the distance. I'm older, I told myself, squaring my shoulders. Catching my mother's sidelong glance, I wondered at her smile.

We spent the early part of the day searching for newly risen stalks of asparagus along the back roads that wound around the bluff. My mother knew just where the asparagus hid amid the dried grasses of the old year. The sun was hot on my back as I waded through the tangled grass looking for the arrowed heads. Finding a small patch of green, I leaned down close to the earth, the dusty perfume of sun-heated straw filling my nostrils. A black stag beetle clambered over the stalks, raising an indignant claw at me as I cut away at the base of the green asparagus.

"Be sure you leave some behind," my mother called from her patch farther down the road. "We want there to be some for next year."

So close to the earth and sheltered from the road by the brambles and grasses, I stared at the green stalks of asparagus. They were sturdy sentries, rising up out of the hard soil. Dark green whorls of leaves were packed tightly against the tip of each shaft, which faded to a pale cream at the woody base. I cut the stalks, the sun warming my back and the hum of insects filling my ears.

It was nearly midday when my mother came up to me, her bucket full of green spears. Her expression had softened, and a streak of dirt ran across her forehead. Sweat circled her throat like a necklace of dew.

As tired and thirsty as I was, I refused to show any signs of it.

"Come on. We'll head into the woods," she said, taking my half-filled bucket and emptying the asparagus into a cooler in the car. Setting our empty buckets aside, she grabbed the lunch bags, handed me the thermos, and set off.

I followed her, my eyes squinting against the bright noonday sun. At the edge of the woods, she stopped, poised half in the shadows of the trees. I saw my mother inhale slowly. She closed her eyes. Her lips parted with the breath of her exhalation. Then slipping the scarf from her head, she entered the woods, the new leaves casting a pale green light over her shoulders.

I hesitated at the edge of the shadowed forest and sniffed. The scent was rich and dark. The odor of rotted trees, wet soil, and sharp, resinous pine was distinct and commanding, filling my mouth with the dense flavor of earth. I exhaled, awed as the pale green shadows speckled the skin of my arms and dappled the front of my white shirt.

In the muted silence of the forest, I saw my mother bending down by an old pine, its ancient branches brushing a welcome across her shoulders. Her hair hung loosely around her face, clinging in damp curls at her neck. She glanced at me, and a stray shaft of sunlight glinted in her eyes, making them sparkle in the green shadows.

"Come, Jeanie. Look here," she called, and her voice sounded musical.

I drew near, almost cautiously, as the forest light caressed my mother and transformed her into the image of a green fairy, newly wakened from a winter sleep beneath the carpet of pine needles. She was on her knees before the base of an old, gnarled pine tree. Pine needles were tangled in her curly hair, and the white remains of a sticky cobweb clung to her arm. Her hand was cupped around the bright pink blossom of a lady's slipper blooming in the shadow of the old tree. Shaped like an orchid, the rosy bowl of the flower hung suspended over the dull brown of the forest floor. Two pale pink wings graced the throat of the blossom.

"Oh," I exclaimed, and knelt to examine the flower. "It's beautiful." Gently, I touched the green leaves, and the pink bowl of the flower trembled on its delicate stalk.

"And very rare," my mother added softly, sitting back on her heels, her hands resting on top of her thighs. She touched my shoulder softly, and I turned to face her. She smiled at me. "When you're angry, your cheeks blush just that color."

My eyes widened, and I frowned. "That red, huh?"

"That beautiful," she replied, and stood up. "Come on," she urged. "I want to collect the morels before we stop for lunch."

My mother moved quietly through the woods, her hand affectionately patting the rough, patchy bark of familiar trees. As she brushed back the carpet of dried needles, the mottled brown caps of the morels appeared.

In the silence of the forest, I thought about my yearnings for adulthood, which at home in the kitchen had seemed so clear and in the woods had become confusing. I felt both frightened and excited by the life that lay ahead. Emotions bubbled like thawed sap, and the sour taste of my anger was suddenly sliced by the pungent aroma of the pines mingled with the leaven of humus. It was a smell that promised new growth out of the old; it was a taste that came as a harbinger of the future I craved.

My head swirled with half-understood thoughts, and as I bent to pick a morel, I hesitated, struck by shyness. The morel was a lovely brown, its wide, elongated cap tucked neatly around a slender shaft. My hand hovered above the mushroom, and I stared at it, recognizing its sensual shape for the first time. I glanced awkwardly at my mother. With gentle fingers, so as not to bruise the shaft, she plucked a mushroom from the forest floor. She held it up to the light, admiring the color. Then smiling at me, she placed it with the others in her basket. I reached down and plucked mine.

The shaft was smooth, the flesh springy to the touch. It had a moist fragrance that tickled my nose. Clinging to the crevasses in its cap were tiny clods of dirt. A pale milk-white spider huddled in one fold, and very carefully, I coaxed it onto my finger before releasing it to the forest floor.

"There's a nice clearing over by those rocks, where we can eat lunch," my mother said, pointing to a spot just beyond the pine trees. The sun filtered through a break in the trees and settled on a gathering of boulders. Brilliant green moss covered the curves on their humped backs like a velvet cloth.

My legs were tired, and I was aware now that my stomach growled for a cheese sandwich. Placing the morel carefully in my bucket, I joined my mother by the rocks.

Though there was sunlight, she sat in the shade, the green light of the forest veiling her face. I sat beside her and watched as she unwrapped the sandwiches and handed me one. Her fingers were dusted with dirt, and a few black particles speckled the bread. I shrugged and, not even caring to brush them away, took the sandwich and started to eat.

We chewed quietly for a while. Then, I grew impatient. "Mom," I said, trying not to sound pleading, "why can't I be like Susan? What's wrong with wearing makeup?"

My mother's eyes were lidded, her mouth softened with disappointment. She put her sandwich down and shook her head. "Jeanie," she said, "why do you ask for so little?"

I scowled, confused by her reply.

She raised her eyes to me. "Do you remember when you were younger, and we used to build elfhouses?"

In spite of my anger, I smiled at the memory. "Yeah, you told Bridget and me that elves lived in the tangled roots of big old trees. We used to sweep out passages to make little houses."

"And then you put in rocks and acorns as tables and chairs," my mother said, laughing.

"We also made rugs out of moss." I paused, and then added, "It was fun."

"You believed in the magic of elfhouses then, didn't you?" my mother asked.

I shrugged as a pang of sadness pierced my heart. What did any of that have to do with *now*? I was growing up, wasn't I? I wasn't supposed to believe in those things anymore. "I guess so," I replied sourly.

"And no more?" my mother whispered.

Looking up at her, I was overcome with fear. In the shimmering green light, her hair entangled with the twigs and leaves of the forest, my mother appeared as a stranger to me. The sunlight cast a hard gleam in her eyes, and they glowed like those of an animal caught at night in the headlights. Her shirt was opened at the throat, and lines of sweat trickled between the cleft of her breasts, streaking the fine coating of dirt on her skin. Along the ridge of her collarbone, the green light of the forest clung like moss.

She plunged her hand into the loose soil around the rocks, withdrew something, and held it between us in her closed fist. As she opened her hand, I saw a tiny brown bulb with a fine webbing of roots extending from its base.

"Magic doesn't leave us as we grow older, Jeanie," she said softly, "we abandon magic. It remains always within us, and we need only choose to see it."

As I watched, a slender green stalk emerged from the tip of the brown bulb. It grew before my eyes, splitting through the papery thinness of its covering in an eager search for sunlight.

My mother fanned the roots of the bulb with careful fingers and replaced it in the soil. Tamped down in its bed of dirt, the green stalk continued to rise, its leaves unfurling like flags.

I stared at it, fascinated. Then I looked at my mother, who was gazing at me in private amusement. "How did you do that?" I asked, breathless.

"Ask for more, Jeanie—of yourself and of the world about you," my mother urged. "You will find there is an endless store of mystery. It will grow as you grow. And if you let it, it will deepen into something loving and powerful." She sighed and pushed back her hair. "You may get a bra, and in time you will wear makeup and probably shave your legs, though I suspect you may come to hate those things as much as you now want them. *Don't forget what makes you truly special.*" She brushed my cheek with her hand, and the skin of my face tingled. "Come on, finish your lunch. We still have a lot of collecting to do."

The rest of the afternoon passed me by as if I were floating on the surface of a quiet pond. I drifted, aware of the whispering wind in the leaves, the gentle rasp of insects, and the dry rustle of creatures in the underbrush. A wood dove cooed, and as her mate answered from another tree, I smiled knowingly. Although I was still impatient to be grown up, my mother had gifted me with vision, and I could calmly hear my yearnings echoed in the waking forest.

Like that small bulb my mother had unearthed, I, too, had roots resting firmly against the earth, roots that dug deep for sustenance. Along with the bright flag of youth that was forcing its way through the soil, with a longing to bloom lush and beautiful like the lady's slipper, came a downward pull, and a new kind of knowing. As my mother had shown me, the strength and beauty of the flower was not in its brilliance, but in the solid core that lay beneath the surface. Listening to the roots that coursed within me, I could hear the murmured songs of nature and feel the ancient history that joined me to the world of nature. I would not have to sacrifice the wonderment of childhood for the shiny trappings of adulthood. As a child, I had built houses of magic for elves; as an adult, I would *become* a house of magic, every door opening to reveal yet another mystery.

We returned at twilight, just as the sun began slanting over the tops of the trees. My father met us at the door, and next to him was my sister Bridget, with one sock on and the other dangling from her hand. My father's gaze shifted from my mother's face to mine. I saw him nod in recognition, and then he sighed. All my clamoring for the things of adulthood had not impressed him. In the day spent with my mother, however, a change had occurred in me. He saw that change and, giving me his shy smile, patted my shoulder encouragingly.

CANDLES ON THE POND

Sue Ellen Sloca

Sue Ellen Sloca, who hails from Iowa, is a new writer in the fantasy field. I was unfamiliar with her work until the following tale, written at the Clarion workshop in Michigan, was sent to me by Pulphouse Press (published as part of their Paperback Short Story series).

"Candles on the Pond" is a deceptively quiet and carefully crafted tale that creates the myths and rituals of an imaginary world to address issues of growth and coming-of-age. These rituals may take different forms from culture to culture in our own world as well as in imaginary worlds, yet still they resonate in the hearts of all of us who have made the long journey from childhood to adulthood.

—T.W.

1

When I was five, I learned the answer to the riddle of the Pond.

I, Dahni, daughter of the Middagland, was born without a soul.

My mother expected only my sister Neel.

For Neel she braved the chambered caves below the Pond to gather honeycomb. For Neel she tempered the wax, mixed it with blood, dipped the braided wick and poured the candle. When my sister's soul awoke and stirred within my mother's womb, it was Neel for whom Grandfather Mose breathed on the wick to light her candle.

My mother wove a single birthing blanket.

Grandfather Mose told me that it stormed the night my mother summoned him.

His wattle-and-daub roundhouse lay on an island in the pond, across the pale green water from my village, which, like others of the Middag, rose like a circle of old stumps, brown and blended, between the water and the deep wood.

When the pains began, my mother went alone to the bank. Standing ankle-deep in the ooze at the spot where fallen trees formed two crossed fingers, she shouted over the wind.

The old man came. Some said that he walked on the water's crest. Others, that he waded, barefoot, his leggings drawn above his knees, defying the wrath of the storm.

When the pains peaked, my mother grew afraid and confessed her secret: that she had lain with one of the Nameless from beyond the Pond. That she feared for her child. Grandfather Mose moistened her cracked lips, kneaded the pit of her back, and promised her that her child would wear a name.

Red and kicking, fists curled, arms beating, my sister greeted air. With her first indignant howl, her candle shrieked into flame before he could hold it to her mouth. It burned without wavering. He damped it with a handful of muddy moss and named her Neel, "life-strong."

My mother cried out in joyous relief, and the pains began again. After a day and yet another night, filled with wave upon wave of life-contorting pain, he unbanked her candle. It flickered. It smoked. She tossed and twisted, moaning and begging for death.

Ashen-faced, Grandfather Mose bowed his head, and allowed her family, her friends—those of the village who would—to file by her bed of fur-cushioned rushes and drip wax from their own lit candles into the clay pot that held her flame. Her candle steadied, burning with a thin, clear fire. Her eyes closed.

At dawn her candle sputtered and died.

And I was taken from her womb: blue, limp and cold. Reluctantly I breathed on my own. Grandfather Mose wrapped me in his head scarf, placed me against my sister's warmth, and named me Dahni, "candleless."

On mornings when it did not rain, before the sun would burn the mist off the Pond—while the garden was too wet to work—Neel and I would race each other to the sunning rock on our side of the Pond. There we would kick off our moccasins and shimmy out of our leggings.

Should the wind lift Neel's kirtle above her knees, she would giggle, flap her hands, hop on one foot and be a bird. I knew why she would pull the green, mossy cloth into deep folds to blouse above her sash, but I did not reveal to our aunts how much of her legs she allowed to show. We shared secrets, Neel and I.

Neel's skin and hair were the color of sorrel honey. Early on she learned that a well-placed kick worked to deter those of our cousins who would tease.

I was a pale ghost of Neel; I left my hair braided in its thin, single plait. Early on I learned that words could hurt.

Once, when I grew bold enough to ask why we were so unlike, Grandfather Mose drew on his barrelreed pipe, exhaled, billowing smoke, and sat gray-wreathed and silent for so long that I thought that his ears were failing along with his eyes. Finally he said that I alone wore my father's coloring.

I buried his words under the flat rock where we left our clothes, and lived for mornings heavy with haze, when I would lock hands with Neel and wade across the shallows, squishing my toes in the muck, to fill my head with his stories.

I can remember all of Grandfather Mose's tales, but the one that I would ask for again and again was Why We Neither Fish Nor Net Birds. He would tell it like this.

On the morning of the first day the Maker awoke. It was dark. It was cold. And he was hungry.

He stood up, parting the clouds with his shoulders, and the sun rose. He smiled at the light, and the air around him warmed. After the long night, it felt good— he laughed for the joy of morning—and his breath shimmered into birds.

When it grew so warm that he no longer needed his clothes, he let them slide to his feet. His furs became trees, and the soft cloth of his kirtle, the grass.

All morning long he danced with the birds. He clapped his hands, squeezing clouds into rain. He whirled, whipping air into wind. His heels dug valleys; his toes kicked earth into hills. He loved the Children of the Wind and found life sweet.

At midday, he remembered that he was hungry. He planted bluecorn; gathered tubers and nuts; hunted rabbits and ground squirrels. He ate and ate until he grew too fat to dance. Still unsatisfied, he shaped and breathed beeswax to life, and to his likenesses gave both words and birdsong. He loved the Children of the Wax and found life sweet.

Tired from his labor, he rested.

While he slept, his likenesses listened to the songs-that-remembered-flight within their heads. And banding together, they wove a net from his hair, trapped the birds and pulled off their wings.

In the evening when he awoke, he wept. His tears pooled on the birds-without-wings, becoming a green and shallow Pond. Wingstubs sprouted into fins.

Then, angry, he gave his likenesses death. One by one they grew old . . . died, and left him alone.

He loved the Children of the Mud and found life bittersweet.

He closed his eyes and darkness fell. And in his dreams he remembered the birds—remembered whose songs he had given man—grieved, and promised that morning would come again. That on the second day his children would take turns, becoming bird, man, fish . . . bird, man, fish.

And that is why we neither fish nor net birds.

As a child I grew to dread yeardays. I remember well Neel's fifth.

Preparations for the celebration of her candling began several days before the village-wide feast. The youngest of my mother's sisters set off into the deep woods with her bow and snares and hunting dog. My uncle, who always saved a smile for me, laid aside his weaving to twine rushes and ferns into the stiff mats that were to serve as ground covers.

While the rest of my aunts and older girl cousins shelled pine nuts, mashed bilberries into a paste, and otherwise began to prepare the meal, they argued among themselves as to whether red or yellow ochre would best express the color of Neel's name when it grew time to paint her face. On one thing they agreed: that she was old enough to crack the corn for the communal flatbread.

I remember bending my head to the smell of sweet fern, heavy and fragrant; I remember sorting rushes by size and soaking them in a hollowed-log trough. I hear the popping crack of the corn. I see Neel's face, flushed with concentration and pride.

After a short while, Neel complained that cracking corn was hard work. I splashed an armful of rushes into the trough, and as I turned to pick up the next bundle, my uncle slid a sprig of fern into my hair.

Both of them spoke at once.

"It's not fair," she said. "Dahni doesn't have to help."

"If you'd rather crack corn, go ahead," he told me. "It's your day, too, little fin."

All my pent-up feelings erupted. "I hate you!" I said to Neel. "I wish you were dead."

I ran from the roundhouse.

My eyes stinging, I fled down the path that wound to the Pond. Through the thin leather of my soles I felt the uneven edges of stone, the crush of too-dry leaves, crunching as I ran.

At the edge of the Pond I left the path, snagging my kirtle as I plunged through a greenbriar thicket to reach our sunwarmed rock—Neel's and mine. There I lay on my stomach, my head on my arms, and cried. Eventually I fell asleep.

When a shivering breeze woke me, my rock bed lay in shadow. I sat up and rubbed my eyes. A wedge of flatbread loosely wrapped in a fern lay beside me on the moss. I looked around and saw no one. I brushed the bread free of ants, and ate it hungrily.

As I chewed, I watched the Pond.

Two trees grew level with the surface of the Pond, their trunks crossing, their branches rising leafed and vined, their roots anchored in the soil. The under one wore leggings of mud-green turtles at the junction of water and wood. I lay turtle-still, feeling the cool of the wind as it whispered among the trees and ruffled the heads of the long-stalked maiden's caps—broad, lacy clusters of white that grew with the green of the weeds on the earth-and-tree-root mounds near my rock.

A splash.

I jerked my head to the sound, but saw only water-rings rippling, widening, their waves damping as they enlarged. Disappointed, I watched until the water quieted.

Carp were bottom-dwellers, shiny and silver-finned; I had never seen one jump.

Neel. I sat up abruptly, remembering. A spray of sweet fern fell from my hair. I pitched it into the water. It drifted, floating on the slow-moving sludge an arm's length away from my rock. I gathered a handful of stones and tossed them at the frond, until it sank.

My splash—*my* water-rings.

Why did I still feel like weeping?

While I watched my spot, a bubble broke—burst—from below, sending rings rippling outwards. I blinked. Intent, I studied the water. Wherever the wind died, wave-rings bubbled, met, and merged. Mouthfuls of air rose to the surface, like words, I thought. Like the language of fish.

I hugged my knees, at peace with the Pond.

2

When I was ten, I learned that my answer to the riddle was wrong.

Neel was born able to master the tasks expected of us.

At ten, I had barely learned to string a bow when she was chosen to accompany my aunt and adults from other neighboring families on the hunt. That her place was to care for the dogs and check the traplines, that she rarely returned with a woodchuck herself, dampened neither her pride nor my worry that I would ever fit the role.

After I tended my share of the garden, I would set out alone for the Pond, intending to practice my archery. There I would pause, barefoot, to leave tracks in the mud, to flush frogs from the thicket of heart-leaved weeds that choked the shore, to watch ducks. When the sun was level with the tops of the trees, I would return home, eager to describe what I had seen to Neel, to remember much later—at dusk—that I had left my practice bow on the rock, unstrung.

If only I had a candle, I thought.

The night that I asked her, Neel agreed to share her candle.

It was dark, and we lay, shoulder-to-shoulder, whispering. Night sounds spoke too loudly for her, and she burrowed beneath our furs. Within the cocoon our voices touched, warm and mothering.

"How can we split a candle?" I asked.

"Grandfather Mose will know."

The quiet rhythm of breathing, hers and mine, filled me. I curled into the sound; perhaps I slept.

Some time later I became aware that she was awake. Lying hands-behind-her-head, she stared into the dark. She asked me whether I thought she was pretty, adding, quickly, that I could share the man to whom she would be candlefast at fifteen.

I closed my eyes, but could not sleep.

It was several days before I found an opportunity to talk with Grandfather Mose. The Nameless arrived to disrupt his routine.

They had visited my village nearly every summer that I could remember, appearing between the end of the spring rains and the start of the autumn winds—when the creek that drained the Pond was deep enough to float a canoe.

They had skin the color of dried cornhusks. Neel was convinced that they came from beyond where the sun fell. I wasn't sure, though their hair, which grew no longer than rabbit-cropped grass, was darker than hers and ranged in color from brown to almost black.

Grandfather Mose had told us that they came to learn from our ways, which I thought strange. Had they no teller of tales among the elders of their village? When I ventured this to Neel, she said that I wasted too much time in thought.

That day as I lay drowsing on my rock, listening to the Pond, I saw their canoe emerge from behind the scrub pines on the lee side of Grandfather Mose's island. It slid through the water, long and sleek and silver-skinned. There were three of the Nameless in the boat: two adult males and a boy.

I sat up, intrigued.

A boy. I wondered if it bothered him that he lacked a name.

They set up camp on the level strip between the roundhouse and the shore on Grandfather Mose's island. I watched from my rock as they pitched sloping tents, dug a fire pit and circled it with flat sitting-rocks. There, in the next few days, the men gathered to smoke with Grandfather Mose. I rarely saw the boy. I pondered that. Did the old man's stories not interest him?

Neel called me silly, but I kept my vigil. Whenever I could, I slipped away to the Pond to lie belly-flat on my moss-furred rock, to watch and wait.

Late on the third day, I arrived as the afternoon sun set fire to the water. A raccoon pawed through the ashes of their cooking pit.

Smoke drifted in wind-spun curls above the roof of the roundhouse. I watched for a while, and when I saw no signs that either the men or the boy were in camp, I waded across the Pond, skirting their tents, and paused outside the doorflap to clear my throat—to announce myself—before entering.

The interior was dim and smoky and smelled of molding reeds. I oriented myself by the orange glow of Grandfather Mose's pipe. At first I didn't see the boy, but he must have seen me, for he was standing when I reached the old man's side.

He was shorter than I by half a head, and chunky square of waist, of shoulders and chin. He fingered a shiny disk that he wore on a thong around his neck and eyed me as if he couldn't decide whether or not I would bite, like Neel face to face with a squirrel.

Grandfather Mose motioned for both of us to sit.

"Dahni," he said, pointing at me.

I nodded.

"Peter Jeff Tarr."

The boy smiled hesitantly. I remember feeling confused.

At dusk when Grandfather Mose ended his stories, I tiptoed home barefoot.

Late that night, as I lay in the dark beside Neel, I wondered how much of our language Peter Jeff Tarr had understood. Somehow it did not seem right to mention our meeting to her.

Peter Jeff Tarr.

I rolled it slowly like Grandfather Mose, then tried it fast, blurring the notes like the call of a bird.

He had a word. What did it mean to lack a name?

And how could Neel and I share a candle?

For two days after our meeting it rained, and I pulled at the corners of the questions as I cracked corn, as I scraped pelts, as I cleaned porcupine quills to be dyed and stitched on baskets—until my head ached.

At dawn on the first clear morning after the storm, I escaped. Trees dripped with after-rain. Birds awakened the wind with chirrupy crees. The odor of earth, of decay and new growth, was thick enough to bite.

At my rock I found Grandfather Mose—waiting for me—he said. I sat crosslegged beside him, facing the water, the seat of my pants becoming a wick for the wet, spongy moss.

He questioned me about little things, nodding gravely at my answers as if it mattered to him what I thought. When he fell silent I drew a deep breath and asked, "How can I cut Neel's candle in half?"

"Can a soul be split? If I knew that, I would be the Maker himself."

He was lying. Angry at him, at the Maker, at Neel, I jumped up and would have run away had the tone of his voice not held me fast.

"Sit down!"

He gestured at the Pond. "Look closely. What do you see?"

I lay on my stomach and stared, squinted, closed one eye and then the other, leaned so low over the water that I nearly fell in headfirst. Opaque, muddy-green, floating with branches and wet-browning leaves, the water was . . . water. When I said as much, he told me the tale of the Rabbit Who Wanted to Be a Deer.

A long time ago, when the woods were young, the animals envied one another.

Rabbit was always hungry. He chewed tender weeds and dandelion fluffs, which tickled his nose. So while he ate, he would stop to scratch with his hind feet. But when he noticed that Deer could stretch to nibble tree buds and bend to graze on grass, he complained to the Maker.

"I dress like Deer; wear a tail like Deer. It's not fair that Deer is so tall and I am so short."

The Maker sighed, and blinked, and Rabbit became a Deer.

Rabbit chewed shoots from overhead trees, and he rejoiced. But when he fed on flowers, and needed to scratch, he found that his hind hoofs would not reach his nose. He itched and itched and itched, until in tears, he begged the Maker for relief.

The Maker frowned, and blinked, and Rabbit became himself, and he rejoiced. But ever afterwards, when not asleep, his nose twitched.

But I didn't want *stories*.

When the tale ended, I opened myself and words emerged, all hot and jumbled and begging with hurt. He lifted my chin and tilted my head to his, and the words trickled to a stop. His eyes were the marbled brown of the Pond after a summer rain, cloudy and swimming with thoughts.

I wanted answers cut as crisply as leaves.

I cried, and he held me on his lap—as old as I was—and sang a song without words as he rocked me to silence.

Afterwards I wanted only to sleep, but he pointed to the water—bubbling, produced a sound, and asked me to repeat it. Bewildered, I did so. Again. A leaf-floating. The rock-unmoving. Again . . . again.

The sounds reused the same distortions of mouth and tongue that formed the word for the boy. Gradually it dawned; he was teaching me to speak with the Nameless ones.

In the days that followed, the language lessons continued. I taught Neel and for us they became a private game. In the garden as we worked, weeding adjacent rows of squash and beans on hands and knees, Neel would ask What is the Nameless word for this or that? and I would answer in fat patties of sound bitten off from the ends and middles of actual words and mushed together when I didn't know the proper name. And then we would burst into just-to-be-silly laughter, and I would look at her, and for a moment so intensely filling that I ached . . . would sense that this could be enough.

And yet.

On afternoons when I lay on my rock, bathed by the wind, I scraped away moss and scratched a picture of a candle onto the granite with a stone, wrist-to-elbow long, life-thick, with a flame as tall and wide as my hand, which would last until the next hard rain.

One afternoon as I sat staring at the water, pondering the strange ways of the Nameless who had spent the morning "measuring" things in the village, I heard someone approach. Twigs snapped, leaves crunched too loudly for stealth. I held my breath and sat gray and motionless, trying to blend into the rock, hoping not to be seen if I were wanted for some disagreeable chore.

"Hullo."

I turned. The boy, Peter Jeff Tarr, stood where the path dwindled into grass-embedded mud, studying me. His smile faded as I stared at the sunball red of his shirt. I remembered my manners and fumbled to reply in his language. Perhaps I spoke too loudly. Perhaps I chose inaptly. The corners of his mouth twitched, recalling Rabbit. I laughed. He laughed. And we shed words.

I parted low-sweeping branches to show him where to look for brown-furred water rats at play. I lifted handfuls of musty leaves to show him where to find toadcups, fruity and orange-gold. Despite my urging—I ate one first—he would not put one in his mouth. "Grandfather Mose" I named the old man's pipes that grew in deep shade, hand-high and curved like flowers carved from wax. He grinned and dared me to walk the trees whose trunks, still rooted, extended over the Pond. *He* fell in.

I lent him my leggings, and while his pants dried, we talked in broken words, part his, part mine. Thinking of Neel, I asked him where he came from.

"Iowa," he said.

"You have sun there?"

"Oh, yes. And corn."

He stood up to show me how tall it grew in his village: above his head. I was impressed. But when he pantomimed the stripping of its tassels—his chore, he said—I thought of flowers for the Maker's bees destroyed, and ears of corn misshapen and unkerneled—and understood more of why his people had come to learn from us.

Feeling brave, I asked him whether it saddened him that he lacked a name.

"I have a name," he said. "Peter Jeff Tarr."

"A word. What does it *mean?*"

He looked confused. "Nothing. It's just my name. What I answer to."

I told him how my name embodied me, showed him my drawing and confided that I, also, lacked.

Had he a candle of his own at home? I asked, ashamed of my directness—grateful that I could not see his face as he traced the lines on the rock with his finger. No, he said, but if he wanted one he could always "buy" one, or make one, he added, with a sideways glance at me.

"Make one for myself?"

He started to explain how, but I waved him to silence. What I had not heard was of a candle made for other than a child between the time of her mother's last blood and the stirring of her soul, by any but her mother.

He would have talked further, but I was too full of what he planted in me to continue. He dressed, and started up the path, then turned—retraced his steps, and laid the shiny disk he wore around his neck on the rock in front of me. Scratched onto one side of it was his name, he said, and on the other, a picture of an old man. "Saint Christopher" he called his Grandfather Mose.

I glanced at it briefly, then tossed it back to him.

He put it on the rock again. "For you," he said. "In return for the Pond."

That year, when the Nameless left, I watched their canoe until it slid out of sight behind a screen of scrub pines on Grandfather Mose's island. I closed my eyes, and saw it flying through the clear green water, paddles dipping, sunlight burning silver on its hull. And I saw him, Peter Jeff Tarr, standing shadowed in a field of tree-tall corn.

In front of me I heard a splash. I squeezed my eyes more tightly shut, pressed his disk into the hollow of my throat, and pictured Iowa.

3

When I was fifteen, I learned that the riddle was misformed.

That next spring when the rains subsided and the Pond rose, I waited for the Nameless to return. It pains me to remember how many times a day I paused, mid-task, to listen for the shouts of greeting, to stare at the water, watching for the silver canoe.

When it arrived, and Peter Jeff Tarr was not among them, I found compelling reasons to be elsewhere when Grandfather Mose told stories. When Neel asked why, I spoke of pressing work. My uncle began to treat me as an adult; no longer was I "little fin." Neel did not understand. They're only stories, she said.

Grandfather Mose did not insist that I attend, but kept me at his side, a silent sponge, when he exchanged words with them. To see to an old man's needs, he said.

Over that summer my skill in speaking their tongue improved; I grew able to transform thoughts into words without provoking smiles.

Before they left that year, I had healed enough inside to ask them from what land they had come. California. Maine. The world beyond the Pond expanded by two.

Peter Jeff Tarr. Summers came and went, and with them others of his kind. I learned to call them "anthropologists." I discovered that they knew how to capture words, strip off their wings, and save them on cornhusk-thin sheets and in strange "metal" baskets against the coming snows. I asked Grandfather Mose if I might learn how to make the marks that remembered, but he said no.

Minnesota. Indiana. France, a village much like ours, whose speaker struggled with the words. When I asked her for a story, Grandfather Mose said no. Ohio. Georgia. Michigan. The Pond shrank as my list enlarged.

The years dripped through my fingers, as I grew. A smile above a square chin paled to the touch of a silver disk. Peter Jeff Tarr. Dreams of a magic place called Iowa where candles grew like corn, rank and lush, faded with the memory of his face.

*   *   *

In the spring of the year that Neel and I were to turn fifteen, I decided that I would make my own candle. It rained that day, as on the morning of the day when I resolved that I would gather myself to confide in Neel after tempers settled.

That morning within the crowded babies-crying, wet-dogs-shaking, looms-clicking, corn-cracking, pine-bark-smoking womb of the roundhouse, water dripped through gaps in the thatch. Neel and I spent the afternoon arguing over whose task it ought to have been to move our sleeping furs away from the leak. That night we huddled near the central fire in borrowed blankets without speaking, without sleeping.

Neel broke first, as always. Grandfather Mose had agreed to terms; by fall she would be candlefast.

Neel and a man.

She did not repeat her offer to share him, made on impulse years before.

I turned my face from the fire and pulled darkness over my head. I may have asked her the customary questions; she may have answered them. What I remember of the day we parted lives was the sound of my own silence.

For days after, Neel and I barely spoke.

I surrendered my claim on our furs, and moved my blanket to the opposite wall of the roundhouse, professing a sudden interest in sleeping with the dogs. She laid aside her bow and traplines and absorbed herself in quilling her candlefast clothes.

When the spring rains stopped, and still she acted like a mud-brained guppy, I remarked to the dogs that her behavior proved that it was a man who had pulled the wings off the first bird. My uncle laughed as if he enjoyed this immensely, saying that when I was joined to a man, I would understand.

His teasing struck a nerve. I fled to my rock, the only spot where I could breathe, unbraided my hair, and stared at my mirror image, rippled in the wind-stirred water. How could *I* be candlefast?

I hid my face in my knees. Overhead the willows bent their shadowy branches, cradled me as I wept. Would I ever be whole?

Hands touched my shoulders. I whirled to push them away.

Neel.

She reached for a strand of my hair, waist-long, like her own, but lighter by several shades, and curled it around her fingers, shivered in the brisk wind, then asked me for the Nameless word for hair.

We had not played our game since we were ten. I looked at Neel and saw my *sister*, not another part of me. I dredged my voice from the bottom of the Pond, scraped the silt of years from its tone, and asked her to tell me about the man to whom she was to be candlefast.

That night I moved my blanket alongside her furs.

After that day Neel took it upon herself to share what she was taught by our aunts on how to become a proper woman to her man. She joined me at sunfall at the Pond. I lay on the shore, plucked grass, and lashed curls of bark into leaky canoes until it grew too dark to watch them chart the water's drift while she explained the latest in mysteries.

Mostly I listened with only one ear. But the night she talked about candles I sat up straight and chewed on my sourgrass.

After a woman was with child, Neel said, she would lower herself into the caves that underlay the Pond to harvest honeycomb. The wax she would render, tint with her blood and mix with drippings from the candles of villagers who wished to share with her child. The wick she would braid from cornsilk, angora, and hanks of her hair—the longer the strands, the taller her child—and dip, suspend by a stick in a tall clay pot, and cover with cooling wax.

Aside from the danger—the caves were known for their treacherous footing— the process sounded within my reach.

"But why would a woman wait until she was sick with child?" I asked, affecting what I hoped was a casual tone.

"The bees," Neel said. "It's said they can sense the change in a woman's smell and will not attack."

I almost choked on my mouthful of grass.

I needed a man.

Who could I trust?

Without a candle I was like the Nameless woman from France who slept in Grandfather Mose's roundhouse to avoid unwanted hands. I knew what it meant when men looked at me; I would not have them whispering lies.

I pondered the problem as summer arrived. Alone on my rock I would stare at the cornhusk paleness of my wrists, and curse my mother for lying with a Nameless man. In this sour temper the answer appeared.

I shivered as I touched the disk at my throat, and began to watch for the silver canoe.

During the waiting days, I steeled myself for the worst and practiced my invitation. One night? One hour? How long did it take to make a child? I regretted that I had paid so little attention to Neel when she tried to teach me the bitter details.

The morning the Nameless beached their canoe on his island, Grandfather Mose summoned me. The previous year I had lived with him while they were in camp; he would need me again.

The day was already sticky-hot, without a whisper of breeze. My kirtle was wet in patches and clung to my skin. I fastened my braid to the top of my head, rolled my moccasins into my blanket, and set off barefoot for the Pond.

Intending to strip, submerge, and cool off before spending the afternoon bored with formalities, stewing in sun, I stopped at my rock.

There, on the moss. One of them, seated facing the water, his back to me, his hair rabbit-short, his shirt the color of glowing coals.

I opened my mouth and swallowed . . . air. The speech I had practiced dissolved into words that coiled in my throat and refused to crawl out. Under his clothes he was only a man—I knew what *they* looked like. And yet.

"Hello," I said.

He turned.

He squinted, his forehead wrinkling.

I wanted to beat my wings and fly from the spot, but I could not lift my feet from the mud-caked grass.

"Dahni?"

He stood up and crossed the few paces that separated us. Now a head taller than I, his body proportions fitted his blocky stature. His eyes crinkled as he smiled. He extended his hand.

I stepped backward and shook my head. It wasn't supposed to be like this.

"Don't you remember me, Dahni?"

Nodding, I clutched at the silver disk and whispered his name. "Peter Jeff Tarr."

Nothing went right for me that summer.

By night I slept by Grandfather Mose's side; I sponged him cool when he woke in the prickly heat, and fetched him water when he coughed. Often I threatened to refuse him his pipe, but I never did.

By day I grew to know Peter Jeff Tarr.

We talked about him. He told me of "school" and of how he planned to attend the "university" when he had passed his test of manhood. He told me of his father who, as in his previous visit, belonged to the team of "anthropologists." Winters he spent with his mother, he said, and summers with his father. I thought it sad that his people did not allow a man to live in his woman's roundhouse.

We talked about me. I introduced him to Neel.

Mostly we explored the Pond. We traced the curvature of the shore; he drew a "map." I taught him to name and recognize plants, to know which trefoil cluster of leaves, when crushed, raises water blisters on the skin, and which signals that a knuckle-sized bulb, edible and crunchy-sweet, lies buried in clay below the mud.

We climbed on the rocks and swam in the Pond. We lay like turtles on the logs that grew over the water, sunning ourselves, trailing our toes, and laughing like silly children. We shared meals and stories, and long silent moments attuned to the quiet of the Pond.

With Peter Jeff Tarr, I played and forgot.

As the summer slumbered to a close, and the day of his leaving approached, I awoke and remembered my plan.

That night, at dusk, as we sat on my rock, I scraped away the matted moss and scratched the outline of a candle in the granite with his pocket knife. He watched without question as I drew, and when I had finished, I unlaced the front of my kirtle, and guided his hands to my breasts.

"Teach me," I said.

Peter Jeff Tarr. I touched his smile in my sleep. The night before he left, he promised that he would return for me, to take me home to Iowa.

At dawn the next day the silver canoe spilled out of my sight.

Did I carry his child?

The question rattled my dreams. I would wake up sweating. I took to walking the shore of the Pond by dark, until the calm of the water settled inside, and I could sleep.

As I waited for signs, I stole the supplies I would need and hid them in the hollow of a rotten log in the forest behind the roundhouse. A pine burl torch. A knife of sharpened bone. Head scarves to cover my ankles, neck and face; strips of leather to wrap around my wrists and palms: protective covering. A net-string pouch for holding honeycomb.

Six, seven, eight days passed. I must have grown cross and ill-tempered. Neel took me aside and asked me how long I was planning to mourn the departure of Peter Jeff Tarr. I lied. I told her I feared that I carried his child.

Instantly she was all concern, hugging me and assuring me that I need not worry until two moons had passed without blood—that she had been told that babies frequently changed their minds in the first full moon. I could scarcely sit through her remedies for inducing them early.

The following night I waited until even the dogs had curled their tails and tucked their heads in sleep. I dressed, scooped up a pot of still-glowing coals, and slipped outside. The moon was high and wan.

I recovered my gear, lit my torch, and made my way through the woods to the opening of the caves, a sinkhole hidden by brush and blackberry bramble on the high ground above the village. As I wrapped myself securely, leaving only my eyes and fingers exposed, I watched the Maker's bees stream in and out of the hole.

They were bigger than honeybees, as large as hummingbirds. I had hoped to find them sluggish in the late-night chill. Three times I had to remind myself why I had chosen to steal the wax.

Gingerly I tested the crumbly soil at the mouth of the cave. Gripping the torch, I lowered myself with my free hand, using my toes to feel for buried roots and rock ledges that would support my weight. After what seemed like too few steps if Neel's account were accurate, my feet hit level ground. As I turned to face the passage I heard a high, shrill squeak. I pulled back suddenly. The ground beneath me gave way. I slipped—slid—hit the solid rock floor of the cave with a jolt that knocked the torch from my hand.

I saw it arc—caught a glimmer of water—to fall with a clunk and a hiss. Its glow vanished, leaving me alone with the dark. And the bats.

Another squeal. I dropped to my knees and crawled toward the sound of rushing water. Keeping it at my right, I scrambled, coughing and sneezing, through ankle-deep piles of dusty dung until I found the squeeze-hole in the rock that led to the next chamber. There I paused to catch my breath, grateful that I was not attempting this while swollen with child.

The air was cool, weeping with moisture, one with the rock that closed on all sides. The sound of the water steadied me. The water. The bats, as underground birds. Words whispered in me: Bird, man, fish. Bird, man, fish. I had not guessed that the Maker layered the world. To come back as a carp I might enjoy. But as a bat? Shuddering, I reminded myself it was time to move on.

I picked my way on my hands and knees, using my fingertips as feelers. Gradually I grew aware that a distant humming drew me. I crawled more quickly. I wanted—I needed—to drink at the source.

As the noise grew louder, the darkness thinned. Soon I was able to see my path clearly. I stood up and walked. The humming swelled as the passage turned. I followed, and gasped as I entered the chamber. Luminous cones, long and white, hung from the ceiling, like icicles dripped from wax. The mid-section of each was black with bees. Cautiously I stepped closer. The cones were made of six-sided chambers, each large enough to hatch a bee. Their lower portions were uneven, as if they had been cut and reconstructed many times.

The hive. Honeycomb.

I opened my bag, drew my knife, and cut deeply into the nearest cone: wax enough for me and my child.

The humming stopped.

I knew that I ought to run, but the silence would not let me move.

The Maker saw.

He knew.

He knew that I was not with child.

I screamed as the bees attacked. My hands and eyes were on fire. I beat them off with my bag. I dropped my bag and blinded, ran. Stumbled. Fell against rock. Curled on the floor and hid my hands and eyes. Bees stung my back and my legs through my clothes.

I rolled, screaming, and fell into water. Cool cool. Burning with fire, I dove. I kicked myself lower . . . lower . . . lower.

Gasping, I surfaced and gulped air. I struggled against the current. I swam I breathed I swam I breathed I swam I breathed. I lost track of time.

I must have been climbing higher within the netting of caves beneath the Pond. I must have passed out.

Grandfather Mose found me washed up on the sandy soil at the edge of the Pond. He dragged me into his roundhouse, removed the damper of muddy moss from his candle—used it to pack my swollen eyes—and asked the Maker to accept the exchange.

By the time he thought me out of danger, his candle had burned to a thin glaze of wax at the bottom of the clay pot.

In his care, I replenished my strength and regained the use of my eyes, although I knew they would need protection from strong light for a time—perhaps for the rest of my life.

I was still living with Grandfather Mose when the fall winds began to whip the surface of the Pond to a froth. As the day of Neel's candlefasting approached, I knew that I could not return to share the same roof with her and her man, with my family, as if nothing important had happened.

I did not belong.

I could not belong.

The Maker had seen to that.

I stood on the shore, threw stones at the water until my arms ached, and cursed him for saving my life.

And then, exhausted, I drew myself into a ball, and would have shut out the world, but the silver disk dangled between my knees. Peter Jeff Tarr. If he could come to me, I thought, surely I could go to him. On foot I could follow the creek to its outlet; I, myself, could find Iowa.

When I told Grandfather Mose that I could no longer stay in the Middag, he reached for his pipe, and busied himself in packing the spoon-cut lip of the reed with the dried weeds that he claimed were beneficial. And he told me that he had extracted an oath from the Nameless when I was born: that when he was dead, they would care for me as one of their own.

My head swam; drowning in questions, I could not word them fast enough.

Curtly he brushed them all aside and unbanked his candle; blew on it until its flame grew round and huge. When I voiced my alarm, he ordered me out of his sight.

Dizzy, I fled to my rock and asked the Pond: Should I try to find Peter Jeff Tarr myself? Or wait for the Nameless Ones to find me?

Awaiting an answer, I watched the water. During a lull in the wind, bubbles rose and broke into shimmering rings, into halos ever expanding, their auras growing like widening flames, like candles glowing on the Pond.

And I knew, then, that I could never leave the Pond.

I sat.

Soul-quiet.

At home with myself.

When suddenly, in front of me, I heard a splash, and saw it—this time, a carp—rising like a shaft of silver sunlight, fins and tail-flaps beating, flying for the space of a gasp.

I hugged myself and returned to Grandfather Mose. I knelt at his side and cupped my hands over his candle, preserving its flame.

"Teach me how to tell stories," I said. "Teach me how to speak for the pond."

Today Grandfather Mose is dead, and it is I, Dahni, daughter of the Middagland, who stands hands-cupped against the glare and scans the far horizon for the Nameless Ones. The evening sun bleeds red upon the green peace of the water.

I write this in my own hand. When you read this—that I send back with them this year—know, Peter Jeff Tarr, that I give you my story, in return for the Pond.

TREE OF LIFE, BOOK OF DEATH

Grania Davis

"Tree of Life, Book of Death" is a fascinating blend of history, magic, and Jewish folklore. The tale is oddly reminiscent of Hans Christian Andersen's "The Snow Queen"—if the former had been written not in Northern lands of ice and snow, but in the war-torn Carpathian hills between Poland and the Ukraine.

Grania Davis resides in California and is the author of *Moonbird*, *The Rainbow Annals*, *Marco Polo and the Sleeping Beauty* (with Avram Davidson), and a number of children's books. The following tale is reprinted from the March issue of *F & SF*.

—T.W.

The village teemed with death. Located as it was in an armpit of rocky land in the Carpathian foothills, between Poland and the Ukraine, the village shtetl caught endless tidal waves of warring armies. It became a rest stop for angry, golden-haired Slavic soldiers, who tried to unwind by killing Jews and raping dark-haired Jewish women. After many generations the surviving Jews of the village became famous for their golden hair.

Then the Hapsburg empress decreed that Jews were allowed to leave the shtetlach, to settle in safe and prosperous walled towns. The tolerant Hapsburg empress knew of the legendary founding princess of Prague, who brought good fortune to her people by allowing the Jews to settle beneath her ancient castle walls. The golden-haired Jews of the village welcomed the imperial decree, and praised its wisdom. They packed their meager belongings, pickled the scanty vegetables in their stony gardens, and prepared to depart for better lives in the bustling Slovakian market town of Gidlov.

Only one golden-haired Jewish woman did not pickle and did not pack, for she was in the throes of giving birth. The woman named Schulka lay in the back of the wagon, clutching her belly, which was big as a nobleman's house. The midwife bustled back and forth between her own packing, and supervising this improvised birthing couch, while Schulka's sisters hastily gathered her belongings with their own.

The entire village departed as a caravan, traveling the rutted dirt roads together for safety. Just before the horse-drawn wagons lurched to a start, Schulka gave birth in a burst of sweat and blood. The midwife held up two healthy, squalling twin girls, with little rings of golden fuzz crowning their heads, and little birthmarks shaped like tears of blood at the napes of their necks.

Schulka lay back in the wagon with a contented sigh, and said her twin daughters should be named Chava and Eva, and they should live like princesses in the rich walled town. Then Schulka sighed deeply again—and died in a pool of blood.

Schulka's weeping sisters took charge of the infants, and embroidered their names on their little nightshirts, so they wouldn't be confused. For it was their loving duty to honor their late sister's wishes. They fed the twins on goat's milk and honey, until the wagons stopped at a rustic town for the night. There they found a robust peasant woman whose baby girl had just died of fever, whom they hired as a wet nurse. As night fell, Chava's and Eva's tiny lips were contentedly fastened to the ample bosom of a strange, red-haired peasant woman in a strange town.

"Such a twisted dagger of fate," wept the eldest sister, Tamarka, wiping her plump cheeks on the corner of her babushka scarf. "But thank God, Schulka's sweet princesses will live."

But the peasant woman was crazed by the death of her only child, and during the night she heard the voice of the Holy Mother whisper in her grief-maddened mind. The voice said that the soul of her dead baby girl had entered the little body of Eva, who must be saved and baptized in the sacred church. So the red-haired peasant woman, named Maria, hid Eva in a hunter's hut in the forest during the night.

In the morning the weeping peasant woman told Tamarka that a one-eyed Gypsy had climbed through the open shutters of her house, and stolen tiny Eva. Maria told how she gave chase, but the wily one-eyed gypsy moved like a cat in the dark and escaped. Tanta Tamarka and the peasant wept in their aprons over the fate of poor Eva. Maria promised to continue searching for the golden-haired infant, with the blood-drop birthmark at the nape of her neck.

Little Chava was placed in the care of a young nursing cousin, Leah, who could handle one more baby, but not two. Then the wagon caravan pulled away from the rustic town, where wildflowers grew from the thatched roofs, and storks nested in the chimneys.

"Fate twists like a dagger in my heart," kvetched Tamara to Leah, as the wagon jounced onto the rutted dirt road with Chava, the one remaining twin. The grieving women didn't notice a robust, red-haired peasant slip into the forest to claim Eva as her own.

The village Jews thrived in the town of Gidlov, which was a lively East Slovakian trading post on the road between Poland and the Ukraine. They established their homes and shops on a square at the eastern edge of town, where they built a great synagogue, grand as any church, to thank God for their good fortune. The Great Synagogue of Gidlov had walls and ceiling colorfully painted in delicate filigree, windows of dazzling stained glass, and altarpieces of heavy silver and gold. A jumble of mossy tombstones crowded the rear wall. The temple's beauty and fame attracted scholars from afar, and even a wandering wunder-rebbe from Muscovy.

Chava also grew and thrived in Gidlov. Her golden hair gleamed as she walked among the crumbling gray buildings, beneath the drizzly gray sky. As a young girl, she showed talent with words and skill with a drawing brush, and she became known as a poet and painter. She said she did not wish to marry, and her family didn't press the matter—because she had the same delicate build as her poor mother who died in childbirth.

Chava and her father boarded with Tanta Tamarka's family, and her papa and uncle drove drayage wagons, carrying trading goods to the merchants' shops. Chava spent her time at her drawing board, and helped her aunt with chores around their bustling courtyard.

Yet always there was the sense of something missing—of *someone* missing. Chava knew the story of how her twin sister was stolen as an infant by a one-eyed Gypsy. She often frequented Gypsy fairs, hoping to see a delicate, golden-haired girl among the swarthy Rom faces.

One drizzly spring day, just as the apple trees were forming fruit against the gray sky, a Gypsy circus came to Gidlov from the steppelands of the Huns. The Rom set up their tents and their booths in a meadow outside the town walls. Everyone in Gidlov was excited by the Gypsy circus. Gentiles and Jews flocked to hear the wild music and to watch the lithe sword jugglers. The townfolk wandered among Gypsy booths selling fur hats and leather boots, embroidered felt capes and amber beads, icons and housewares and spicy hot goulash.

Chava took her sketchbook to the Gypsy fair, for she loved to draw the Oriental Rom faces, so exotic, like tales from Egypt and India. She stopped to sketch an old fortune-teller, with a clip-tailed white monkey perched on one shoulder. The fortune-teller peered at his amber divination beads. He became aware of her presence, and turned to gaze at her. Then Chava saw that he had only one dark eye, and she gave a little cry.

The one-eyed Gypsy beckoned her to come closer. "Don't be afraid," he said with a gap-toothed smile. "I am only an old gray fool without an eye, and my wise companion is only an old white monkey without a tail. We can't harm you . . . but we can tell what will ease the empty place in your heart."

"You and your people have already harmed me—you created the empty place in my heart," said Chava.

"Me harm . . . what harm . . . never harm . . . ?" burbled the old Gypsy. "Such foolish talk. Come closer now; come closer. My fleas promise not to jump on you . . . though you never can trust Gypsy fleas. Come gaze at the amber beads . . . it costs only a smile . . . and see what can be seen." The old man scratched at the fleas on his burly chest.

"Where is my twin?" Chava demanded. "A one-eyed Gypsy stole her when we were just newborn babes."

"And you think it was *me?*" laughed the Gypsy, his one black eye flashing. "Me looking after a squalling, soggy baby? No, thanks; I have enough trouble looking after my mischievous monkey . . . and my famished fleas." He scratched beneath his chin, and his monkey did the same. "I apologize for the unworthy Rom who did such a terrible deed. Between you and me, did he demand a big ransom?"

"There was never any demand for ransom," said Chava.

"You think we steal babies for love or charity?" scoffed the old Gypsy, scratching inside an ear while his monkey did likewise. "Why would he steal her, if not for ransom? It's hard to sell such a tiny babe, still needing to suck and too young to work. My wily Rom mind smells rotten goulash. Come, look with me at the amber beads." The white monkey reached out its little hand and beckoned Chava to come closer.

She knelt down on the felt blanket, facing the old Gypsy and his divination beads. The fortune-teller gazed intently into the clear amber, and stroked the beads with his grimy fingers, as if coaxing them to reveal their secrets. Then he closed his single eye.

"Ah," he said. "Aha!"

"What?" cried Chava.

"The fleas," he said. "They're chewing my groin! Also, I see a red-haired peasant woman carrying a baby into the forest. Who was she? How was she involved?" The clip-tailed white monkey anxiously scratched its groin.

"She was the wet nurse my aunt hired . . . the night my mother died . . . the night my sister was taken."

"Ah, aha! They're nibbling in my ears!" The monkey scratched frantically in its ears. The old Gypsy opened his jet-black eye and gazed again at the beads. "That's it! Your sister is still alive. The thieving wet nurse knows where to find her. And you must move quickly, my princess—because your sister is in great danger!" The white monkey chittered and bounced up and down with alarm.

Tanta Tamarka grew hysterical, and Papa raged when Chava told them the Gypsy's words. "A dagger twists in my heart! A beautiful young woman like you mustn't wander alone to such places—or you'll disappear, too," kvetched Tamarka, as she mixed the herring with sour cream and boiled potatoes in the steamy kitchen, and set the bowl on the wooden table.

Chava helped her aunt slice the rye bread and poppy-seed strudel, and herded her younger cousins to the table. She didn't reply, for there was nothing to say. Papa poured himself a glass of hot tea. "You should stay at home and help your aunt in the kitchen," he grumbled. "This isn't the Grand Hotel."

Chava nodded silently, and the family talk shifted to other problems, especially the infected foot of their strongest drayage horse. The horses were their livelihood— and far more important than any wandering daughter.

But Chava's mind continued to wander all that night and the next day, to the Carpata Mountains where her baby sister was stolen. Was her twin really in great danger—and how could puny Chava find and help her?

Then she recalled the mushroom pickers, the groups of young folks who went up in the Carpatas after the spring snowmelt to gather mushrooms in the forest. They always had a good time, singing loud and jolly songs, and they returned looking tan and fit, with baskets of mushrooms to sell in the market. Surely her family would let her pick mushrooms this summer. It would be good for her health, and she could earn a few coins, and she could slip away to mountain villages to search for her missing sister.

Tanta Tamarka and Papa agreed that the mountain air would do her good, so Chava went to speak to the mushroom merchant. As she walked along the gray cobbled streets, beneath the gray sky, she nearly collided with someone dressed all in black. It was the Muscovy wunder-rebbe, lost in his mystical dreams. Chava apologized demurely.

"Your secret surrounds you like a cloud, and prevents you from seeing clearly," kvetched the wunder-rebbe.

"What secret?"

"How should I know? It's a secret, isn't it? If you want to tell me, then I'll know what secret."

Chava laughed at his illogic. "If I tell you, then it won't be a secret."

"No, but maybe you'll be able to see more clearly." His eyes gleamed with a mad and holy warmth.

Chava impulsively decided to tell him—about the one-eyed Gypsy's words, and her plan to seek mushrooms in the Carpata Mountains—and to search for her lost twin, Eva.

"You are like two halves of a broken heart. If you don't find her, who will?" mused the scholar, twisting a chestnut-colored earlock beneath his stiff black hat. "But if she is truly in great danger, then you will be in great danger, too. Oy, little one, such a difficult secret . . . what to do?" He gazed at her with his wild and holy eyes, the color of a deep lake in a storm. Then he gestured to Chava to follow him to the Great Synagogue.

The interior of the synagogue always thrilled Chava. Whenever she sat in the women's section during holidays, her mind strayed from the prayers to the rich hues of the filigree on the arched ceilings, the glittering chandeliers of Bohemian crystal, the marble columns, glowing stained-glass windows, and red-velvet hangings worked with gold. If only she'd been born sooner . . . and a man . . . she could have been an artist painting her soul into the walls of the holy temple.

Chava thought the wunder-rebbe would guide her to the gilded altar to say a prayer for her safety. Instead, he led her up a flight of narrow wooden stairs that led to the dusty attic, lit only by two narrow grimy windows. In the dim light, Chava saw that the wunder-rebbe's skin had a golden glow. Though he was shrouded in a long black woolen coat and a black felt hat, his powerful hands and gentle, bearded face were illuminated with warm golden light.

In one corner of the dingy attic was a mound of powdery gray earth beside an urn of scummy water. The wunder-rebbe poured the water onto the earth and kneaded it into a mound of clay. As he worked, sweat poured profusely from his brow and scented the air with honey. He chanted an eerie and discordant melody. Chava watched and listened silently as the simple clay figure of a sturdy boy took form.

When the figurine was complete, the wunder-rebbe set it upright on the floor and traced the Hebrew letters for Chava and Eva on its brow. "This is the younger brother that your mother would have borne if she had lived. His name is Asher. He is known for great strength and for loyalty to his beloved sisters. He will go with you to seek mushrooms and your missing twin."

"But he is made only of fragile clay," said Chava, feeling a sudden flash of fear as the attic filled with vibrant warmth.

"We are all made of fragile clay," thundered the wunder-rebbe. His holy madman's eyes glinted with wild light.

Then the wunder-rebbe filled his lungs so his chest expanded like the trunk of a massive tree. He blasted air in the face of the clay boy, who turned ruddy like an overheated horseshoe. The wunder-rebbe's skin blazed with a golden glow, and the scent of boiling honey filled the attic. He clasped the shoulders of the clay boy with his gentle hands, alive with golden fire, and he blew into the boy's face three times. Each time the clay flesh gained—and retained—more color.

At last the clay had the tone of human flesh, yet the boy was still a simple figurine. Chava held her breath with terror and awe. How could she believe—or not believe—what she saw and felt? The wunder-rebbe chanted strange words in a strange melody while kneading the boy's flesh with his long, pulsing hands. His mad and holy eyes flashed golden lightning.

Suddenly the wunder-rebbe shouted in a voice like thunder, "Awake, Asher. Awake!"

And a sturdy lad stood in the attic, yawning and smiling winsomely. Hebrew letters formed pale scars on his forehead.

"Awake, Asher," whispered the wunder-rebbe gently.

"Oh Rabbi, was I asleep?" smiled the boy, rubbing the soft down on his cheeks. "I must have dozed off at my studies."

"It's time to wake up, Asher," repeated the rabbi, pulling playfully at the boy's golden forelock that curled beneath his cap. "Go with your sister Chava into the mountains to pick mushrooms. And you must stay with her and protect her from all harm."

"No harm will come to my sister," said Asher slowly, as if reciting a memorized prayer.

"Good boy," said the wunder-rebbe. He sighed deeply, and his skin returned to its normal pallor. "Oy, it's getting late. Let's climb down from this stuffy attic. Asher can stay with me tonight. Go speak to the mushroom merchant, Chava, and leave for the mountains at once—and next time be careful whom you bump into on the street."

The mountains were shrouded with mists, and wildflowers formed bright mosaics in rocky clearings in the forests. Chava wished she had time for her drawing board, as she and Asher joined the frolicking band of mushroom pickers along narrow and obscure pathways. They followed the muddy routes of mountain streams, to hidden glens where fairy rings of mushrooms grew. Then they fanned out to fill their baskets.

Asher was a warm and lively lad. He made friends with everyone before the first day was done. All were drawn to the sturdy and playful boy with the winsome smile. Soon he was leading mischievous games with the other boys, while his quiet and delicate sister trailed behind, wishing for her pen.

They camped like Gypsies each night, in the forest, or on the outskirts of rustic wooden villages; where smoke rose like sighs from the chimneys, and soft lamplight gleamed from windows not yet shuttered for the night. Here their leader could buy fresh milk and rye bread, cheese, and other provisions. At each village, Chava wandered like a shadow at dusk along rutted alleys, stopping at carved wooden gates to ask wistfully if anyone knew of her lost twin. No one had seen or heard of Eva.

Then one evening, in a shabby village where pigs and chickens poked for garbage in the muddy lanes, Chava approached a group of women who gossiped around a well with a long wooden handle. As she drew near, a buxom peasant woman whose red hair was streaked with gray crossed herself and began to scream shrilly.

"My God! Holy Mother! Why did you come here, child. Did you fly back like a ghost to torment your poor auntie for her sins? Holy God! Don't you know they'll hunt you if you escape—and me, too. *He* will destroy you if he finds you're gone. They'll be waking soon. Hurry back quickly, my child!"

Chava realized she'd found the lying peasant woman, Maria—who now mistook her for Eva. "I came to see you, Auntie," she said, moving toward the woman, who crossed herself again and drew back against the stone rim of the well.

"You mustn't! You know you can't escape! It was wrong to sell you to him, my child. I know it was wrong, and I suffer the fires of Hell every day," she wept. "But what was I to do, child? You were too weak to work in the fields, like my own darling daughter who flies with the angels. And no one wanted such a weakling as a servant. Then they saw you. *He* saw you, and said you looked like a fragile porcelain figurine. I had no other choice. He offered me a good price and promised to treat you like a lady. But that's not why I sold you. You were never really mine, and I know that now. I love you, child, but I wasn't never meant to keep you. He is cold and cruel. Hurry back before your master wakes!"

"I can't do that, Auntie, because I'm not Eva. I'm her twin sister, Chava."

"Holy Mother of God!" shrieked the woman, crossing herself vehemently. "How did you find me?"

"You found me," said Chava. "I was picking mushrooms in the forest with my brother when I came upon you."

"Your brother?" asked Maria in a calmer voice. "Then your poor father remarried? He was so upset the day your sainted mother died."

"Then was the story of the thieving one-eyed Gypsy a lie?" asked Chava.

"A lie? No, no, not a lie. Thank God, he returned her to a hut in the forest the next day," said the peasant woman, twisting her apron nervously with her big red hands.

"Then why didn't you send for my father?" demanded Chava.

"I . . . I forgot the name of the town where you were going. Your aunt wrote it on a paper . . . but I can't read." She made a feeble attempt at a gap-toothed smile.

"Your priests can read," said Chava.

"Yes, but I got fond of her. I cared for her like my own, I did, though she was a sickly child. And I never asked for a penny from anyone until she was grown."

"You tore us apart!" cried Chava. "Does she know about me? Does she know who she is?"

"She thinks she's a foundling, the runt of my litter," said Maria, wiping her eyes and nose with her apron. "I even had her baptized in the holy church to save her soul."

Now it was Chava's turn to weep. Eva was eternally lost to her as a sister. Yet surely the wunder-rebbe could undo what had been done—if they could find her.

"You must tell me where my sister is," demanded Chava. "For I heard that she's in great danger. Tell me at once, and tell me truly—no lies or tales. Where is Eva?"

"You'll cause her more harm by bothering them," wept the woman. "She's in no great danger if you leave her be. But if *he* catches you snooping around, he'll snare you both like butterflies in a glass."

"Who are *they*? Why are they so beastly cruel? . . . Who is *he*?"

"I can't rightly say for sure. They are strange, child. Not like regular folks. They pay for everything with gold, and keep to themselves. You never see them at holy days or fairs. Sometimes they appear at dusk, like you, looking to buy honey or fruit. They never eat meat, far as I know. Their skin is cold and pale as moonlight, their hair is colorless as flax, and their eyes are icy blue. They use lots of fancy words, and their accent is strange. They never smile, like their faces would crack. Their master, Lord Gringore, is very strict. At first we thought they were some kind of Protestants, but now I don't know."

"And you sold poor Eva to these fanatics? Where do they live?"

"Better than working her to death in the potato fields. They have a dreary village at the far end of the road . . . atop the highest ridge, always covered with clouds. The sun never shines up there, and the wind howls like a wolf pack. You can't grow nothing there, only twisted trees. Why would anyone live in such a lonely place?"

"Maybe they want to be left alone."

"We leave them well alone, and you'd better do likewise, child. If you value Eva's life—and your own."

Asher was curled up with the other boys, like a litter of drowsy pups, when Chava returned to the mushroom pickers' camp. She gazed warmly at his sleeping face, nestled in golden curls. She'd grown fond of the rascal in the short time they'd been together, as if he really were her brother. How would he react to their quest?

After their breakfast of porridge and milk, she drew him aside. "Asher," she said, "we must leave the camp today and go up into the mountains."

"But why?" he asked with a merry smile.

"My little sister was stolen—long before you were born—and now she's in great danger. We must find Eva quickly."

"But I want to stay with my friends," said Asher. "We play such crazy games. And the new mushrooms must be packed for shipping to the towns. . . . They spoil so fast. I'm the strongest boy in the camp, and I promised to help."

"Wake up Asher!" said Chava sharply. "You must protect your sisters from harm."

"My sisters must not be harmed," said Asher slowly, as if reciting a memorized prayer. He rubbed the twin pale scars on his forehead.

It was a slow and laborious climb up the rutted roadway to the high ridge of the Carpatas, and the meager provisions they'd taken from the mushroom camp were quickly exhausted. They reached the end of the narrow road at dusk. Swirling mists obscured their sight, and winds howled like wolves.

"Sister, that is a very strange village that lies ahead," said Asher quietly.

"Strange, indeed," agreed Chava, shivering in the cold wind.

Along the roadway leading up to the village were gnarled dead trees whose branches were cut at odd angles. And these branches were sharpened into pointed stakes. Sharpened tree stakes were set around the rim of the village like a weird wall. Chava shivered again, and this time it wasn't only the cold.

The houses were built of wooden shingles, with thatched roofs and delicately carved wooden porches, much like any other mountain village. But unlike other villages at dusk, there was no bustle of peasants gossiping at their gates, drawing water from the well, and settling in for the night. No children or dogs played in the alleys, and no smoke rose from the chimneys despite the cold wind.

"I think it's deserted," said Asher. "No one lives here anymore."

"I think you're wrong," said Chava as they wandered the narrow lanes. "Look at the cracks at the edges of the shutters. You can see candlelight flicker in some of the rooms."

The alley opened onto a narrow square, with a rustic, wood-shingled church topped with graceful onion domes. Chava and Asher held hands and stared. In the churchyard, where the cemetery should have been, was a tangle of sharpened tree stakes.

"This place scares me," said Asher, slowly rubbing the scars on his forehead.

"What do you want?" asked a woman's voice behind them.

Asher and Chava turned and gasped. The young woman was like a mirror image of Chava, with the same delicate features and golden hair.

"Oh Eva! Sister, we've found you! Thank God. You must come away with us at once."

"What do you want here?" repeated the woman coldly.

"We want you!" cried Chava. "Are you blind? Can't you see that we're two peas in a pod? You are my twin, stolen at birth, and this is our brother. We came to take you home."

"This is my home," said the woman.

"No, no. You were sold here as a servant, by the peasant woman who kept you from your true family. You are confused, Eva."

"How do you know my name?" asked the woman.

"Because I'm your twin!" cried Chava. "Look, if you don't believe me. Look at the birthmark on my neck, just like yours." Chava drew aside her wind-tangled hair and revealed the blood-drop birthmark at the nape of her neck.

Eva scowled and felt behind her own neck. "It means nothing," she said. "Many women have yellow hair and marks on their skin. I don't know you, and I don't want to know you. Please go away. We don't want strangers here."

"Are you mad, Eva?" said Asher. "Look closely at your twin's face. It's like looking in a mirror."

"We allow no such vanities as mirrors here," she said.

"Come with us, Eva," pleaded Asher. "We play lots of fun games and eat lots of good food. We pick mushrooms in the forest and . . . well, I can't remember much before then."

"Eva! Send them away and come inside now," called a deep male voice from a big house near the churchyard of sharpened tree stakes.

"You must leave at once," said Eva. And she turned and swiftly slipped inside the house.

They followed her onto the carved wooden porch and rapped on the door. It opened a crack, and dim candlelight revealed a tall and gaunt man, with hair and skin so pale that he seemed to shimmer.

"What do you want? We don't welcome strangers here," said the man in a hollow, rumbling voice.

"Eva is my twin. I came to see her."

"You have seen her," he rumbled. "She does not recall any twin."

"We were separated at birth, and. . . ."

"Oh, come in, then; come in," said the man. He gazed at them with ice-blue eyes and opened the door a bit wider. "You are persistent in your childish delusion. You think my kitchen wench is your lost sister because she vaguely resembles you. Meanwhile, it's getting late, and you have no place to spend the night. If you two innocents are eaten by wolves, every peasant in the mountains will be after my head. So come in, then. Get warm, and have some supper and some sleep, and you'll soon see that Eva hardly resembles you at all."

"But she *does* . . . ," began Asher. Chava hushed him.

They wiped their boots and entered the parlor, which was elegantly furnished in white-and-gold antiques, quite unexpected in such an isolated place. A prismatic crystal chandelier cast glinting light on the lavish gilded furnishings, and on the tall man's hair and skin, which were almost transparently pale.

"I am Lord Gringore," he rumbled. "I have retired from the complex life of the royal court to live simply in this mountain retreat. You may share my rustic home tonight, children, and be on your way at dawn."

"I want to talk to Eva," insisted Chava.

"Very well," said Lord Gringore with a resigned sigh. "Eva, dear, please give our young guests some supper, and keep them amused while I read in my study. We eat simply here, but healthfully."

Eva brought bowls of curds, honey and wild berries, and brown bread and sweet butter to the table. Asher dug in like a boy who hasn't eaten in weeks, while Chava and Eva gazed at each other.

"You truly don't recognize me?" asked Chava.

"I never saw you before. Why should I recognize you?" asked Eva stiffly.

"But surely you see the resemblance between us . . . and the birthmark. . . ."

"I am very common. Many frail women look like me. I feel nothing special toward you. . . . I feel nothing."

"Are you happy here? Does he treat you well?" asked Chava.

"Lord Gringore is . . . unusual," said Eva slowly. "I am content to be in his presence."

"Awake, Eva!" said Asher. He glanced up from his bowl with eyes blazing soft fire. "Gringore has you bewitched, doesn't he?"

Eva seemed startled. Chava looked at Asher and nodded. The lad was right. Eva spoke and moved like someone in a trance.

The room was comfortable, with feather beds and down pillows, and Chava realized she was exhausted. She hadn't slept well since leaving home, and she sank into slumber like a pebble in a pond. She rose to consciousness again with a strange sound . . . of weeping. Chava sat up and saw that Asher was also awake.

"It sounds like Eva," he whispered.

They slipped quietly from the room and saw that a crystal lamp was still burning in Lord Gringore's study. "You mindless doll!" they heard him snarl.

"Please, Lord. I meant nothing by it!" wept Eva.

Chava and Asher crept to either side of the doorway and peered inside. Lord Gringore stood tall and arrogant in a white satin dressing robe that reflected the sheen of his skin. Eva stood before him in a white velvet nightgown, with her head meekly bowed.

Gringore grasped Eva's narrow wrist tightly in his long white fingers. "You encouraged them, you fool; I heard you." His pale eyes flashed cold blue fire.

"I tried not to, Lord. Truly I tried."

Eva's long sleeve slipped back, and Chava saw that her sister's arm was stained with livid bruises.

"Try harder, or know my rage," Gringore rumbled. His free hand grabbed a thick coil of golden hair and twisted Eva's head sideways. Her breath fluttered like a trapped bird.

Asher put his fingertips to the scars on his forehead, as if deep in thought. Then his face hardened with resolve. "No one will harm my sister!" he shouted, striding forcefully into the room.

"Be gone, little boy," scowled Lord Gringore.

"Only if Eva comes with us."

"Do you want to go with these ragged mushroom pickers, Eva?" he sneered.

"Oh no, my lord, I want to be with you."

"But he hurts you, Eva," said Asher, looking puzzled.

"He never means to. . . . He is very kind."

"You heard the wench," said Gringore. "Now be gone and leave us alone." He grabbed Asher's sturdy shoulder and pushed him toward the door.

"Eva is bewitched!" said Asher, and he shoved Lord Gringore's narrow shoulder with his powerful arm.

Gringore laughed in a resonant tone. "You are made of flimsy stuff, lad; you shouldn't play too rough." His long white hand formed a fist and cracked Asher's jaw—which crumbled slowly at the blow like a broken earthenware jar.

Chava screamed with rage . . . and sorrow . . . and fear.

Asher didn't cry out or bleed, and seemed to feel no pain. He stood in a shocked daze, holding the jagged wound where his jaw had been, and staring at the scattered clay shards on the oriental rug.

"No harm will come to my sisters," he stammered, and pummeled wildly at Lord Gringore with his own fists.

"Still haven't learned, lad," said Gringore, dodging the blows skillfully. He aimed his hand like a shimmering hammer at Asher's left shoulder—which shattered at the impact and crashed to the floor.

"Stop, Asher; please stop. He'll kill you!" wept Chava.

Asher stood very still with his arms hanging limply at his sides. The edge of his right jaw and a big chunk of his left shoulder lay scattered on the carpet in jagged shards of clay. His good right hand stroked the scars on his forehead. Tears welled in his eyes and streamed down his ruddy cheeks. "Awake, Asher. No harm must come to your sisters," he whispered in a voice now slurred by his shattered jaw.

"Asher!" sobbed Chava. "Go back to Gidlov. Find the wunder-rebbe. Only he can heal you."

Asher nodded slowly, then turned abruptly and fled.

Chava darted after him, then stopped. Should she follow her injured brother, or stay with Eva? Lord Gringore made the decision for her by locking the door with a firm click.

The book-lined room was silent except for the hissing crystal lamp and Chava's sobs.

Lord Gringore's chuckle was a hollow tone in his throat, like an old bell. The lamplight blazed on his gleaming hair and skin. His pale blue eyes flashed frozen light as they fixed on Chava. "At last," he said, "the lovely twins are reunited."

Chava decided to watch and wait. She would appear to join Eva in Lord Gringore's service, while she observed him and his dreadful power over her sister. Gringore grew cool and indifferent toward her, as though it didn't matter if she departed or stayed.

The day of the full moon, Eva was in a frenzied bustle in the kitchen. "They are gathering here tonight," she fretted to Chava as she nervously sliced newly ripe apples and strained soured milk curds, which she mixed with honey. Chava calmly helped her slice and strain, much as she helped Tanta Tamarka in the kitchen. Eva tensely tucked a wisp of hair behind her ear, and Chava wondered why this simple meal caused her twin such dread.

At moonrise the twelve guests arrived from the few occupied houses in the village of sharpened tree stakes. Chava quickly saw that they were unlike any guests ever seen in her aunt's parlor. They seemed to be cut from the same brittle mold as Lord Gringore: tall and arrogant and pale, with translucent skin and hair, and glassy blue eyes. The six ladies sparkled like windblown snowflakes in robes of glinting white silk, with beads of cut crystal flashing at their necks and wrists. The six men moved stiffly, in flowing white felt capes.

The long table was set simply for thirteen, with a white lace cloth, glowing silver spoons, and cut crystal goblets and bowls that glistened beneath the crystal chandelier. Lord Gringore stood at the head, and the men and women rigidly faced each other from opposite sides. As they took their seats with silent grace, Chava thought they seemed like a brightly lit pageant of lifeless puppets.

Lord Gringore silently gestured to Chava to pour mead in the goblets; and silently, she obeyed. Eva meekly served the apples, curds, and honey from a heavy crystal tureen. Lord Gringore raised his glass in a curt salute, and the weird banquet began. Chava waited for conversation, prayer, laughter . . . any sign of life, but she waited in vain. There was no sound except the chiming of silver against crystal.

They ate and drank very little, as if they rarely felt hunger. Then they stopped with frozen smiles, and listened expectantly. Lord Gringore tapped his goblet with his spoon, which sang out a deep, clear tone. The others tapped their goblets in turn, so an eerie melody rang out from the silver-and crystal carillon. Chava listened and wondered at this unearthly gathering. Who were these strange beings, and where did they come from? Were they humankind, or shadowy creatures of moonlight and mist? The uncanny chiming faded away. Then, with silent grace, they rose in unison from the long table, bowed somberly, and floated away in the pale moonlight.

The twins swiftly cleared the table, then Lord Gringore ordered Eva into the kitchen. She fled with a look of great relief, like a creature freed from slaughter. Gringore beckoned Chava to the seat beside him. "Sit with me for a moment, child. The moon is setting, and I am weary and filled with angst," he rumbled.

"Your friends were very odd," said Chava. "They ate almost nothing and spoke not one word."

"Many kinds of ancient beings dwell in the shadows of these mountains," said Gringore with a timeless sigh. "And not all thrive in warmth and sunlight like you and your timid twin."

"Are you not humankind?" asked Chava.

"No more or less humankind than your sweet brother."

Chava fell silent, for there were many strange things that she would never understand.

Lord Gringore's long fingers, cool and pale as moonlight, reached out to take her hand. "Your blood has the warmth of sunlight . . . warmth that can renew me," he murmured. Chava drew back in revulsion and fear. Then she felt his luminous gaze pull her closer . . . closer to his brittle touch. His icy fingertips hungrily stroked her cheek.

"So soft, child. Yes, I need your warmth to revive me as the moon wanes," he whispered. He stared irresistibly into her eyes with cold and consuming fire, and his caressing fingers strayed to the blood-drop birthmark at the nape of her neck. His breath quickened.

"Please, my lord," she began, trembling. But even Chava no longer knew whether she begged him to stop—or begged for his unearthly touch.

There was a loud, banging crash—and Asher burst into the room. Beside him was the one-eyed Gypsy and his clip-tailed white monkey, who gazed at them with wise and benevolent eyes. Gringore's spell was broken, and Chava leaped up to embrace her brother. Eva scurried in from the kitchen to observe the commotion.

"Who *are* you?" demanded Lord Gringore. His angry face was taut as a drum.

"I am a simple man of the steppeland Rom people," said the Gypsy with a flourishing bow. "I met this lad in the forest, and we made a good match. You see, he is strong and loyal, but lacks a shoulder and a jaw. I am wily, but lack an eye, and my clever monkey lacks a tail—so among us we are complete and whole. Asher said we'd find his sisters here, and I see two lovely ladies waiting to greet us, like two identical dill pickles in a barrel."

"Get out!" roared Gringore. His eyes raged liked beasts.

"Oh, but my feet are tired, and my fleas need a rest," said the Gypsy with a sly smile, twirling his mustaches. He stood with his burly back blocking the door, caught Chava's eye, and glanced at Eva. Chava positioned herself so she could block any sudden move by her sister. Asher and Lord Gringore faced each other in the center of the room.

"You're not too bright, lad," said Gringore. "You've returned for another lesson."

"I'll remain until my sisters are free," said Asher. His speech was slurred by his broken jaw and his left arm was limp beneath his shattered shoulder.

Gringore snarled like an animal torn from its prey, then abruptly lashed out with his lightning fist. Asher's eyes clouded with pain as his left ear smashed to the floor.

Chava and Eva moved closer and fearfully clasped hands. How long could Asher withstand such cruel blows?

This time, Asher didn't stop to weep in confused grief. Instead, he drew in his breath until his broad chest was round as a barrel. Then he blasted air at Lord Gringore's face. At the same time, he deftly aimed a mighty kick at Gringore's vicious right arm—which burst into bloodless fragments of glittering crystal that shattered to the floor.

They all stared in shock, and the monkey hooted. Asher glanced at Chava with the remnant of a proud, boyish grin.

Eva screamed in terror and fell to the ground to gather the bits of broken crystal that had been Lord Gringore's arm. Chava pulled Eva to her feet and held her tightly.

Gringore gazed at his splintered arm with a mild ennui. "You see, child, many kinds of beings live in these mountains. Some are made of flesh and some of dust," he said wearily to Chava. "My people are as old as the crystal rocks themselves."

Gringore and Asher began to circle each other warily, like two torn stags whose final strength was summoned for this deadly battle. Then, in a whirl of motion too swift for Chava to see, they collided in an explosive blur. There were horrible sounds of cracking crystal and bursting pottery. Sharp fragments of glistening glass and gritty clay flew around the room. The white monkey stared with wise old eyes and chittered with excitement.

At last there was silence. Pieces of pulverized crystal and clay, and scraps of torn cloth, were thrown around the room. Some of the larger bits still retained the form of an eye or a nose or a hand, but they were lifeless. Asher and Lord Gringore were gone.

Chava and Eva both knelt weeping on the floor to gather the shards. Chava carefully piled on the oriental rug the clay fragments that had been the laughing and mischievous lad named Asher.

Eva began to collect the cold crystal remnants of Lord Gringore, then she paused and glanced shyly at Chava, like someone just waking from sleep. She pulled up her sleeve to reveal the bruises on her arm. "He hurt me," she said slowly. "And he would have hurt you, too. He wasn't humankind, you know. He and his people are cruel creatures that were born of mountain crystal and sired by moonlight. When the moon wanes, they lose their strength and must drain the vitality of someone warm. He enchanted me and drank my essence like wine, and he would have done the same to you."

"Yes, I know, sister," said Chava.

". . . Sister," said Eva softly, as though she'd just heard the word for the first time. "Yes, I see that now, like an image in the mirror. And the mark on your neck . . . is just like mine. Oh . . . Sister!" She fell weeping and laughing into Chava's arms.

The one-eyed Gypsy snuffled and wiped a tear from his grimy cheek as he and his monkey scratched wistfully at their fleas.

"We have a brother, too," said Chava. "We must gather every clay bit and take him home with us—to be healed."

"I will help you . . . Sister," said Eva. Her face glowed with wonder at her newfound free will. "I will travel with you to our home, for I have never had a home. And perhaps Lord Gringore's secret hoard of gold would also be helpful."

"Gold?" said the Gypsy. "Did you say *gold?*" He strutted and cavorted with his hooting monkey. "Gold is heavy stuff. Such delicate ladies mustn't burden themselves. Allow your humble Rom servant to carry the gold through the treacherous mountain pathways." He winked and leered broadly, and the monkey chittered.

"You shall carry a third of the gold where you will, and I'll carry the rest," said Eva with newly discovered strength. "Chava will carry Asher's remains in a silken shroud."

"Will the other crystal-folk try to follow us?" asked Chava fearfully as they left the house.

"I think not," said Eva. "For the moon is setting, and now they are at rest."

"May they rest in their unholy peace," said the one-eyed Gypsy fortune-teller, fingering his amber beads. The white monkey gazed at the dark village with wise compassionate eyes.

Thus they slipped quietly from the village of sharpened tree stakes, on the high Carpathian ridge, in the waning moonlight.

Though it was shabby and gray, the town of Gidlov had never looked more beautiful to Chava. The one-eyed Gypsy had accompanied them safely to the meadow at the edge of town, where he and Chava first met. Then, with a flourishing bow and a jaunty scratch at his fleas, the Gypsy vanished, with his white monkey and portion of gold, into the river valley mists.

Chava and Eva stood alone on a rise overlooking the town, with Asher's remains in a silken pouch. "I never saw so many houses," said Eva. Her pallid face showed some healthy color after their trek through the wooded slopes. "Perhaps we can use some of the gold to get a little cottage. For your . . . our family doesn't know me yet, and I'm not familiar with their ways. We could all live in a sunny cottage surrounded by flower gardens, where Asher could play his games. And you could teach me to use a drawing brush, for I always wanted to learn. What do you think . . . Sister?"

"I think that's a splendid idea," said Chava. "But first we must take our brother to the wunder-rebbe to be healed."

"Such a grand building!" cried Eva when they reached the Great Synagogue. "Is it a church? But where is the cross?"

"You have much to learn about your people," said Chava.

They found the wunder-rebbe absorbed in his prayers, swaying back and forth with earlocks aflutter, as if rocked by divine winds. Chava didn't want to disturb him, but her mission couldn't wait.

"Rabbi! I freed my sister—but Asher was destroyed."

The wunder-rebbe paused in his chanting, chestnut earlocks still quivering, and opened his eyes peacefully. He looked from one twin to the other, and a smile lit his gentle eyes like sunlight on a holy lake. "Such a joy to see two halves united and whole again," he said.

"I found a sister and lost a brother. Asher must also become whole again," cried Chava opening the silken pouch to reveal the shattered clay shards.

"Oy. Such a sweet boy . . . such a beating. Such a twisted dagger of fate. Come with me upstairs," said the rabbi.

They followed him from the dazzling temple of gilt and filigree, up the narrow stairs to the dark and dusty attic. There the rabbi poured Asher's remains onto the pile of dusty clay on the floor.

"You should understand, Chavale, little one, that the Tree of Life creates the pages of the Book of Death. They are one and the same," said the wunder-rebbe.

"Yes, but Asher must live and laugh again," wept Chava, longing for her brother's frolicking games and winsome smile.

"Did he ever really live in this world?" asked the rabbi. He placed his gentle hands on Asher's remains, and his skin glowed golden again. The scent of warm honey filled the room. He chanted in a voice so sweet that Chava sensed angels pausing in flight to listen.

She felt sorrowful yet soothed.

"Sleep now, Asher. Return to peaceful dust," murmured the wunder-rebbe. "You have done well, lad, and now you may rest."

Golden light filled the room, and the universe opened. Then Asher crumbled into the lifeless clay dust from which he had been born.

PUJA

D. R. McBride

D. R. McBride lives in Las Vegas. Under his full name, Dennis McBride, he writes nonfiction books and articles. D. R. McBride has sold more than a dozen short stories to small presses and anthologies, including *Noctulpa*'s *Souls in Pawn* issue and *Grue* magazine, from which this chilling story comes.

"Puja" is a story of culture shock. Although the protagonist, a native of Calcutta, has lived in the United States for many years, he is not prepared to meet someone from the realm of the mad.

—E.D.

"You'll like her," said Mrs. Compton. "She's a little eccentric, but she'll be a good neighbor."

"I didn't think twenty miles would seem so far," Mr. Bannerjee said.

"Any closer to town and you couldn't afford it."

Bannerjee and Mrs. Compton passed green hills and forest as they drove north out of Schenectady. It was like a Union Pacific Railroad calendar: blue sky, a river, picturesque white houses and old barns.

There was space, air and freedom here Mr. Bannerjee hadn't known in the hot crush of Brooklyn, or in the mad streets of Calcutta where he grew up.

Bannerjee had come to the United States when he was forty; he'd managed a theater on Flatbush Avenue, never married. He'd saved a little money so he could get out of New York when he retired and enjoy the last years of his modest life. There wasn't much money—but enough to retire upstate if he was thrifty and found a place he could afford.

With this in mind, he'd come to Mrs. Compton's real estate office in Schenectady.

"I want a small house," Bannerjee said. "Somewhere I can live quietly."

Mrs. Compton was condescending; Mr. Bannerjee was not well dressed and his skin was darker than the carpet on her office floor.

"Mr. Bennyjoe . . ." she began.

"Bannerjee, please."

"Bannerjee, yes. How much money do you have?"

"Why don't you just show me what you have and I'll tell you if I'm interested."

Compton pulled out a thick binder from a shelf behind her desk and thumped it down impatiently. She spoke as she turned the plastic sleeves into which had been inserted Polaroid snapshots of property around Schenectady. "Here's a charming Cape Cod," she said. "$125,000."

The house was tiny and there was a tract development nearby. The pond which backed the property looked shallow and brackish. "Excessive," Bannerjee said.

"Then here's a colonial with an acre, and the interstate runs along one side. $110,000."

"No," Bannerjee said.

"No?"

"No, Mrs. Compton. I don't want to buy. What do you have for rent?"

Mrs. Compton looked as though Mr. Bannerjee had just thrust his brown hand up her dress.

"Rent?"

"Rent."

Compton slammed the binder shut and pulled another, considerably thinner, from the shelf.

They looked at two or three places before Bannerjee saw the house next door to Mrs. Hammond: small, unpretentious, twenty miles north of Schenectady near a wooded hill with a small stream.

"Mrs. Hammond grows roses," Mrs. Compton said. "She has a big gray cat and no neighbors. Nice lady, nice house. She only wants three hundred a month."

It seemed too reasonable to be true.

But it turned out to be just what Bannerjee wanted. The house was ordinary: a single large bedroom, a sunny kitchen whose window faced Mrs. Hammond's house, and a white picket fence bisecting the property. Reclined on this picket fence lazily switching his tail and purring loudly enough to be heard across the yard, was Mrs. Hammond's cat.

"Muffin," Compton said.

And Mrs. Hammond *was* nice. A nice American lady with a nice American face: open, and ingenuous. Her eyes were pale and glistened; her hair was white and a little wild, her figure intact. She'd been tending her roses and wore gloves when she shook Mr. Bannerjee's hand.

Mrs. Compton introduced them.

"You're from India, then?" Mrs. Hammond asked Mr. Bannerjee. "I've never been there. But I saw *Ghandi*. Let me show you my roses."

They crossed the lawn. "I've raised roses for twenty years," Mrs. Hammond began, "since my son was killed. I dote on them. They're my children now." She cupped one enormous red rose in her hand and smelled it. "Like Heaven."

"I couldn't grow them in New York," Bannerjee said. "The air was bad and the winos kept stepping on them. I like it here . . ."

But Mrs. Hammond had drifted away to her roses and her careful, delicate pruning.

Mrs. Compton whispered in his ear. "Her son died in Viet Nam. Maybe she's a little more eccentric than I remember."

Mrs. Hammond turned to them.

"When would you like to move in, Mr. Bannerjee?"

It took Bannerjee two weeks to move up from his shabby apartment in New York, and he felt as though he'd been let free from prison. He settled into his little house, arranged his furniture, and fixed a small altar for Kali in one corner of his bedroom.

Bannerjee had worshiped the goddess since he was a child acolyte in the temple at Kalighat. Even though he'd been in America twenty-five years and had lost most of his Asian habits, he'd never felt comfortable giving up the cruel black goddess. She was the deity of disaster and plague, of death and destruction and placating her was assurance of a good, safe life.

Maybe true, maybe not, but better, Bannerjee thought, to worship her with skepticism than abandon her and risk trouble. So he offered every morning a little rice, a flower, a dash of cologne, occasionally a piece of fruit. Nothing too terrible had ever happened to him, so perhaps there was something to it.

Mrs. Hammond called over the fence one day to invite Bannerjee for lemonade on her front porch. It was July and the day was sultry.

Bannerjee found Mrs. Hammond swinging in her comfortable old porch swing with Muffin beside her. A small wicker table was set with a pitcher and two tall glasses of ice. Sweat drooled down the sides of the glass pitcher.

"Mr. Bannerjee," Mrs. Hammond began when he sat down, "you must have had an interesting life growing up in India."

"I suppose I did."

"What part of India are you from?"

"I was born in Calcutta."

"I see," Mrs. Hammond said. "You know, my son Frank was killed in Viet Nam."

"I know. I'm sorry."

"And now my Henry's dead, too." Mrs. Hammond shook her head and looked across the yard to her roses. "All the men in my life are dead."

Bannerjee was a little embarrassed. He wanted to excuse himself.

"But I have my roses and Muffin," she said dreamily. "Cats and roses, roses and cats."

"Well," Bannerjee said. "I'm next door. You're not entirely alone. If there's anything I can do . . ."

Before he could finish, Mrs. Hammond drained her lemonade with a loud gulp. Then she chewed her ice. Her teeth ground and grated.

Bannerjee sipped his lemonade and looked at the roses again. They were vivid in the afternoon sun, like little bloody eruptions.

"Cats and roses," Mrs. Hammond said again as though it were a chant.

And then she took a large bite from her lemonade glass.

Bannerjee stared.

He watched her bite through the glass again.

She cut her tongue; she ground blood and glass between her teeth. Her gaze was distant and pink drool crept down her chin and along her jaw.

Muffin hissed.

When Mrs. Hammond had eaten the last of her glass, she dabbed at her red mouth with a white handkerchief until the blood stopped.

394 D. R. McBride

She turned to Bannerjee. "You know, I hate old ladies who sit around talking about their troubles. Don't you, Mr. Bannerjee?"

Bannerjee was fascinated by a crusty bit of dried blood at the corner of Mrs. Hammond's mouth, and he watched it dance as she spoke.

"What?" he asked.

"I asked if you hate old ladies who sit around and talk about everything that's wrong."

"I suppose I do." He paused. "Mrs. Hammond, are you all right?"

Her smile was sincere and affectionate. "Why, yes. Why do you ask?"

Bannerjee shook his head.

"Now don't you worry about me, Mr. Bannerjee," Mrs. Hammond said. Muffin had moved to the furthest corner of the porch swing. "I've got my roses and Muffin and my lovely house. Everything I need. And a devoted new neighbor."

Mr. Bannerjee wondered if he'd just hallucinated. But there was a deep cut on Mrs. Hammond's lip, a bloody handkerchief in her hand, and only one lemonade glass.

Bannerjee set his glass down and rose to go.

"So soon?" Mrs. Hammond asked. "We were just getting to know one another."

"I'm afraid I still have unpacking to do," Bannerjee lied. "Please excuse me, Mrs. Hammond. Perhaps you'll come for tea one day." He prayed she wouldn't accept.

"If you need help, Mr. Bannerjee, just call me." Then she added, "And if I want anything, I'll come to you."

For the next couple of days Bannerjee tried sorting out what had happened.

Was eating glass something Mrs. Hammond did customarily? Did she do it compulsively or did she plan it to put him off? Eating glass was an unreasonable thing to do, but not unheard of in circuses and certain religions. Besides, Bannerjee was from India and was no stranger to strange things.

At the market one day Mr. Bannerjee paused to read an article in the *National Enquirer:* "Dad Downs Razor Blades and Light Bulbs." A color photograph pictured a middle-aged gentleman with a mouthful of razor blades and a plate of light bulbs set before him like a feast.

Maybe Mrs. Hammond wasn't so strange after all.

The middle of August passed and rain swept in the afternoons eastward over the wooded hills. Mrs. Hammond's roses blossomed profusely and she brought Bannerjee an armful twice a week.

She stroked their soft petals.

"Roses have always been my favorite," she said.

"Sad that Schenectady is too cold to grow jasmine," Bannerjee said, recalling the fragrant nights of his childhood in Calcutta.

"But roses," Mrs. Hammond said. "There's no comparison."

Bannerjee laid a rose out for Kali each morning in gratitude for the good fortune of his quiet, comfortable life.

Bannerjee noticed, too, a subtle change in Mrs. Hammond when the rain came. He couldn't make out what that change was—it wasn't physical and she was still

pleasant when she spoke to him. But there was a distance in her manner now as
though she regarded him from the top of a high hill. And there was an uncomfortable
linger in her stare which made Bannerjee anxious.

He added a few minutes to his morning devotions and kept his glassware locked
up.

One afternoon when clouds rolled over the sun, Mr. Bannerjee went out to get
his mail from the box in front of his house. On his way back, he glanced at Mrs.
Hammond's yard. The sun came out at that moment, blinding him, and he shaded
his eyes.

He thought he saw something large scuttling through Mrs. Hammond's rose
garden. Something white and red.

Perhaps a dog had gotten in.

Then the sun slipped once again behind the clouds, and in the shade Bannerjee
saw Mrs. Hammond squatted like an ape among her rose bushes. She purred like
a delighted child, snapped off a long, thick, thorny branch and chewed it like celery.

Bannerjee's heart skipped.

Mrs. Hammond had already stripped her bushes of their blooms and was gnawing
the shrubs themselves now.

Muffin sat in his customary spot on the fence watching Bannerjee watch Mrs.
Hammond.

Suddenly Mrs. Hammond paused, sniffed the wind, and turned around.

Bannerjee dropped his mail and stooped to retrieve it. He hoped Mrs. Hammond
hadn't seen him.

But when he stood up she was staring at him with half a thorny branch hanging
from her bloody mouth. Blood smeared her chin and throat; thorns had torn her
hands and scored her face. Blood seeped from the ragged gashes.

But it wasn't that which made Bannerjee's skin crawl.

It was her grin, her smile, the strange curl of Mrs. Hammond's lips that was part
sneer, part surprise, part . . .

Desire.

Bannerjee called silently on Kali Ma to protect him.

As calmly as he could, Bannerjee waved, then retreated into his house. He paused
inside the door and peered through the window.

Mrs. Hammond had turned back to her botanical feast and Bannerjee heard her
munching. His own mouth watered.

In the days which followed, Bannerjee regained much of the religious devotion he
thought he'd lost. He moved Kali's altar from his bedroom to a prominent spot in
his living room near the television. He lit jasmine candles. He performed puja twice
a day now as he had when he was a child in Calcutta, and he meditated after lunch
on the gruesome picture of Kali tacked to the wall. The goddess wore a girdle of
human skulls; in one of her four black hands she carried a sword to destroy evil,
and in another she carried a dripping severed head.

Her tongue was long and red and fearsome.

Bannerjee was beginning to be a little afraid.

By the first of September when nothing else seemed to have gone wrong next door, Bannerjee decided Kali had responded to his prayers and put things right with Mrs. Hammond. He began feeling cautiously paternal toward the old woman: but for himself and Muffin there was no one around for miles, and surely Mrs. Hammond was lonely.

Bannerjee knew loneliness, too.

Besides, this was America: live and let live. If Mrs. Hammond confined her appetites to glass and rose bushes, it was really none of Bannerjee's business. He should strive to be friendly, even if she was a little peculiar.

Bannerjee was a good cook. Maybe he could cook something to share with Mrs. Hammond, something Indian, something exotic and spicy.

He spent one whole afternoon cooking a mutton curry; he stood in his little kitchen stirring the green, steamy sauce.

In another pot the mutton simmered.

He swallowed his fear and called Mrs. Hammond.

"Well, Mr. Bannerjee," she said. "Where on earth have you been? Are you ill?" Her voice was bright.

"Oh no, Mrs. Hammond. I like to be alone. But I thought perhaps you'd like to take dinner with me this evening. I've made curry."

"Curry, Mr. Bannerjee, how delightful! I've never had it. Shall I come over?"

"No. I'll bring it to you in about an hour."

"I'll be on my front porch," Mrs. Hammond said. "I'll be waiting for you."

Bannerjee prodded the mutton with a fork and sampled the curry. He decided he must learn to be a better neighbor. Too many years in New York had made him suspicious and uncharitable.

As he poured the sauce and mutton into dishes to carry over to Mrs. Hammond's house, Bannerjee heard an abrupt shriek. It raised his hackles, but when he looked outside, he saw nothing unusual.

He carried the dinner he'd cooked on a teak tray. When he reached Mrs. Hammond's front steps, he saw her sitting on the porch swing with her knitting bag in her lap. The porch rail hid her face, but Bannerjee heard her mumbling and growling.

When he gained the porch and saw Mrs. Hammond, she was perfectly still. But an enormous lump swelled in her throat.

And the lump moved.

Between her teeth Bannerjee saw Muffin's tail switch violently before it disappeared into Mrs. Hammond's mouth.

Mr. Bannerjee went back to Mrs. Compton's real estate office the next day.

"Mr. Banjo," Compton said. She made it clear his visit was an unwelcome distraction. She had also changed her hair; it was an explosion of henna.

"Bannerjee," said Mr. Bannerjee. "I'm no longer happy at Mrs. Hammond's. I wish to move."

"Why?"

"Her cat keeps me awake."

"I doubt you'll find anything cheaper," Compton said. "We can look but it'll be a waste of time."

And it was: there was nothing else in Compton's binders that Bannerjee could afford, and none of the other agents Bannerjee visited that day could help.

He was stuck.

Bannerjee felt Kali had deceived him. Perhaps she laughed at him; he felt abandoned and adrift.

But worse was the change Bannerjee noticed in himself. He'd always been proud of his tolerance, of his generosity toward the plague of human nature, but he no longer felt tolerant or sympathetic where Mrs. Hammond was concerned. And despite Bannerjee's eastern inclination to find the obtuse and bizarre credible, he found he could not accept the obtuse and bizarre out of context. In India Mrs. Hammond by now would have gained a following, and devotees would have raised a temple in her honor.

But in Schenectady she was just plain frightening.

He sat in the dark safety of his curtained living room watching and listening.

He noted that Mrs. Hammond had stopped going out and there were terrible noises from her house. He heard loud groans, the crack of shattering stone, the sharp splinter of wood. He could see Mrs. Hammond's silhouette at night cast on the drawn shades of her windows, passing restlessly from room to room.

One night Mrs. Hammond's lights went out and they never came back on.

September melted into October, and autumn blazed along the hills. Evenings grew longer and crisper; the stars were brighter and the wind whistled along the marshy banks of the stream behind Bannerjee's house.

But Bannerjee saw no smoke from Mrs. Hammond's chimney though temperatures outside dropped below freezing.

At seven o'clock one morning the phone woke Bannerjee.

"Hello?"

"Mr. Banjo?" The voice of an old woman, but not Mrs. Hammond.

"Bannerjee."

"Yes. I'm Gladys, Florence Hammond's sister."

"I didn't know she had a sister."

"She has three of them, Mr. Banshee."

"Can I help you?"

"Well, none of us has heard from Florence in a long time and we can't get her on the phone. It rings, but she doesn't answer."

"She's over there," Bannerjee said. "I can hear her."

"She gave me your phone number in case of emergency and we're worried. She hasn't been the same since her husband died. Would you do us a favor?"

Bannerjee was afraid he knew what she was going to ask.

"Would you go over and see if she's all right? Ask her to call us or answer her phone."

Bannerjee was silent.

"Mr. Bannerjee? We'd be very grateful."

"Is it necessary?"

"I'm afraid it is. I live in Dubuque. I can't do it myself."

"Very well."

"And then you'll call me back?" Gladys asked. "Here's my number."

Bannerjee sat on the edge of his bed watching the picture of Kali on the living room wall through the opened door of his bedroom. *Give me courage, Mother,* he prayed. *I'm your poor servant.*

He dressed and went next door. There were loud crashes from inside, but when he rapped they stopped. He hunched his shoulders and shivered.

"Mrs. Hammond?" he called. "Your sister telephoned. She's worried. Are you all right?"

Silence.

"Mrs. Hammond? Are you sick? Should I call a doctor? I heard you in there."

Nothing.

He knocked but Mrs. Hammond ignored him.

He put his hand on the cold brass knob.

He turned it.

The door swung on empty air.

Mrs. Hammond's house was a shell, and if Bannerjee had stepped over the threshold he'd have plummeted to the basement.

He held on to the doorframe with both hands and saw Mrs. Hammond standing on the concrete floor ten feet below.

Her mouth was so stuffed with wood and nails that she couldn't close it. Her face was bruised and distorted, her lips black and swollen. She resumed chewing, and her teeth made a horrible, rocky sound as she bit through nails and ground wood into paste.

She swallowed.

She smiled.

"Come in, Mr. Bannerjee," she croaked. "Long time no see."

From behind the locked door of his bedroom, Bannerjee dialed Gladys.

"Mr. Benchmark?" she said. "How's Florence?"

"Your sister's fine. She said she'll call you."

"You sound out of breath, Mr. Banksheet."

"Bannerjee, goddamn it."

Gladys drew her breath sharply. "I see. Thank you."

Bannerjee went into his bathroom and threw up.

Winter settled among the naked trees and dying fields. Bannerjee listened to the patter of cold rain on his roof and watched drab English sparrows peck in the ruins of Mrs. Hammond's rose garden.

Bannerjee prayed for a miracle and wondered why Kali, the spiritual mother of his childhood, the namesake of his birthplace, had abandoned him.

He trapped a sparrow in the front yard with a string and a box, and sacrificed it to Kali in his living room: he twisted its head off with his bare hands. It pecked and screamed till the end and Bannerjee left its bloody pieces on his altar.

Bannerjee stripped and bathed in the stream behind his house as he had done in the Ganges at Varanasi. Only now there was a snow flurry and he caught a bad cold.

In his fever Bannerjee imagined India, the velvety green slopes of tea plantations in the Himalayas around Darjeeling; the slow, muddy Hooghly as it wound across the scorched plains of Calcutta and through the great mildewy pile of the city itself. He recalled a garden in Calcutta, walled off from the noise and dirt of the Chowringhee, a garden with a clear fountain, a macaw in a bamboo cage, a small green snake lurking in the shade of a banyan tree.

But here in upstate New York there was no color, no light, no warmth. Mrs. Hammond was silent and her house was dark.

Bannerjee imagined her walking round and round in her cold basement.

He had a morbid curiosity about what her bowel movements must look like. And he wondered when her appetite might bring her up from the hole which had been her cellar. Maybe she'd crawl up the inside walls of her house like a white-haired termite. Perhaps one cold afternoon he'd see Mrs. Hammond's face poke through a widening hole in the wall as she gnawed her way through it.

Would she smile then?

Would she recognize Mr. Bannerjee and speak to him, working her mandibles in a parody of speech?

And when she finished off her own house, there was her dead lawn, the trees, and her garage still to go.

And why not the earth itself?

Bannerjee imagined her snuffling along the ground on her tattered stomach, her mouth opened like a shovel, scooping up the frozen black earth like chocolate ice cream, round and round, deeper and deeper.

One still, starry night Bannerjee fell asleep in his chair and dreamed of Kali.

The goddess reared up from a bleeding plain and reached for him with a thin, bloody hand. Her eyes were shot with red and yellow, and swimming in her black, bottomless pupils were a headless gray cat and sparrows with human faces. She shuddered; she closed her eyes. Her thin red tongue darted from between her fangs. She massaged herself.

She trembled and the earth quaked.

Bannerjee awoke immediately and slowly began to understand. How could he have been so stupid not to have realized before?

Bannerjee had seen goats sacrificed in the sunny courtyard of Kalighat south of Calcutta; even tied together and awaiting the priest's knife against their throats, the goats had mounted one another.

He'd seen a devotee of Kali immolate himself on the banks of Lal Diggee, the smoky red flames dancing across the rank water.

And in secret places on the Maidan after midnight on certain nights of the year, Kali received the flesh of abandoned babies.

How could Bannerjee have trifled with the goddess and thought it was she who trifled with him?

Bannerjee bathed and shaved and dressed. He put on his coat and overshoes because it was cold and the snow was deep.

He walked to Mrs. Hammond's house.

He mounted the steps to her front porch.

He opened her front door and balanced himself on the threshold. The stench inside was incredible.

It was gloomy down there but the sun was rising and cast a little light. Something moved from a dark corner of the basement.

Mrs. Hammond stared up at Bannerjee from her pit.

She was hideous: drawn, yellow, bruised, and crusted with blood. Her clothes were shreds and Bannerjee saw the dried, flat bags of her breasts. Her hair was matted and filthy, her legs thin and oozing with sores. Black toenails showed through holes in her tennis shoes, and scattered at her feet were the half-eaten bodies of brown rats.

Mrs. Hammond grinned and moved her lips as though trying to speak, but no words came. Just a soughing breath through her broken teeth.

Her mouth watered.

Bannerjee breathed deeply the rank air which rose from the creature below.

He closed his eyes, pictured the warm, walled garden of his childhood, offered a single, simple prayer to Kali.

Then he jumped.

HERMIONE AND THE MOON
Clive Barker

British writer Clive Barker was born in Liverpool in 1952 and began his career as an illustrator and playwright. In the mid-1980s he took the horror field by storm with the publication of the six graphic and intense volumes of *Books of Blood*, as well as his motion picture *Hellraiser*. He now ranks with Stephen King, Dean Koontz, and Peter Straub as one of today's best-known names in horror fiction.

The following story, however, is not for the hardcore "gore" horror fans but for lovers of shivery ghostly tales—a gentle and moving Halloween tale that comes, surprisingly, from the pages of *The New York Times* daily paper.

—T.W.

It was not only painters who were connoisseurs of light, Hermione had come to learn in the three days since her death; so too were those obliged to shun it. She was a member of that fretful clan now—a phantom in the world of flesh—and if she hoped to linger here for long she would have to avoid the sun's gift as scrupulously as a celibate avoided sin, and for much the same reason. It tainted, corrupted and finally drove the soul into the embrace of extinction.

She wasn't so unhappy to be dead. She had failed at love, failed at marriage, failed at friendship, failed at motherhood. That last stung the sharpest. If she could have plunged back into life to change one thing, she would have left the broken romances in pieces and gone to her 6-year-old son Finn to say: Trust your dreams and take the world lightly, for it means nothing, even in the losing.

She had shared these ruminations with one person only. His name was Rice—an ethereal nomad like herself who had died wasted and crazed from the plague but was now in death returned to corpulence and wit. Together they had spent that third day behind the blinds of his shunned apartment, listening to the babble of the street and exchanging tidbits. Toward evening, conversation turned to the subject of light.

"I don't see why the sun hurts us and the moon doesn't," Hermione reasoned. "The moon's reflected sunlight, isn't it?"

"Don't be so logical," Rice replied, "or so damned *serious*."

"And the stars are little suns. Why doesn't starlight hurt us?"

"I never liked looking at the stars," Rice replied. "They always made me feel lonely. Especially toward the end. I'd look up and see all that empty immensity and . . ." He caught himself in midsentence. "Damn you, woman, listen to me! We're going to have to get out of here and *party*."

She drifted to the window.

"Down there?" she said.

"Down there."

"Will they see us?"

"Not if we go naked."

She glanced at him. He was starting to unbutton his shirt.

"I can see you perfectly well," she told him.

"But you're dead, darling. The living have a lot more trouble." He tugged off his shirt and joined her at the window. "Shall we dare the dusk?" he asked her, and without waiting for a reply, raised the blind. There was just enough power in the light to give them both a pleasant buzz.

"I could get addicted to this," Hermione said, taking off her dress and letting the remnants of the day graze her breasts and belly.

"Now you're talking," said Rice. "Shall we take the air?"

All Hallows' Eve was a day away, a night away, and every store along Main Street carried some sign of the season. A flight of paper witches here, a cardboard skeleton there.

"Contemptible," Rice remarked as they passed a nest of rubber bats. "We should protest."

"It's just a little fun," Hermione said.

"It's our holiday, darling. The Feast of the Dead. I feel like . . . like Jesus at a Sunday sermon. How dare they *simplify* me this way?" He slammed his phantom fists against the glass. It shook, and the remote din of his blow reached the ears of a passing family, all of whom looked toward the rattling window, saw nothing and, trusting their eyes, moved on down the street.

Hermione gazed after them.

"I want to go and see Finn," she said.

"Not wise," Rice replied.

"Forget wise," she said. "I want to see him."

Rice already knew better than to attempt persuasion, so up the hill they went, toward her sister Elaine's house, where she assumed the boy had lodged since her passing.

"There's something you should know . . ." Rice said as they climbed. "About being dead."

"Go on."

"It's difficult to explain. But it's no accident we feel safe under the moon. We're *like* the moon, reflecting the light of something living, something that loves us. Does that make any sense?"

"Not much."

"Then it's probably the truth."

She stopped her ascent and turned to him. "Is this meant as a warning of some kind?" she asked.

"Would it matter if it were?"

"Not much."

He grinned. "I was the same. A warning was always an invitation."

"End of discussion?"

"End of discussion."

There were lamps burning in every room of Elaine's house, as if to keep the night and all it concealed at bay.

How sad, Hermione thought, to live in fear of shadows. But then didn't the day now hold as many terrors for her as the night did for Elaine? Finally, it seemed, after 31 years of troubled sisterhood, the mirrors they had always held up to each other—fogged until this moment—were clear. Regret touched her, that she had not better known this lonely woman whom she had so resented for her lack of empathy.

"Stay here," she told Rice. "I want to see them on my own."

Rice shook his head. "I'm not missing this," he replied, and followed her up the path, then across the lawn toward the dining room window.

From inside came not two voices but three: a woman, a boy and a man whose timbre was so recognizable it stopped Elaine in her invisible tracks.

"Thomas," she said.

"Your ex?" Rice murmured.

She nodded. "I hadn't expected . . ."

"You'd have preferred him not to come and mourn you?"

"That doesn't sound like mourning to me," she replied.

Nor did it. The closer to the window they trod, the more merriment they heard. Thomas was cracking jokes and Finn and Elaine were lapping up his performance.

"He's such a *clown!*" Hermione said. "Just listen to him."

They had reached the windowsill now, and peered in. It was worse than she'd expected. Thom had Finn on his knee, his arms wrapped around the child. He was whispering something in the boy's ear, and as he did so a grin appeared on Finn's face.

Hermione could not remember ever being seized by such contrary feelings. She was glad not to find her sweet Finn weeping—tears did not belong on that guileless face. But did he have to be quite so content, quite so forgetful of her passing? And as to Thom the clown, how could he so quickly have found his way back into his son's affections, having been an absentee father for five years? What bribes had he used to win back Finn's favor, master of empty promises that he was?

"Can we go trick-or-treating tomorrow night?" the boy was asking.

"Sure we can, partner," Thomas replied. "We'll get you a mask and a cape and . . ."

"You too," Finn replied. "You have to come too."

"Anything you want."

"Creep," Hermione said.

"From now on . . ."

"He never even *wrote* to the boy while I was alive."

". . . anything you want."

"Maybe he's feeling guilty," Rice suggested.

"Guilty?" she hissed, clawing at the glass, longing to have her fingers at Thomas's lying throat. "He doesn't know the meaning of the word."

Her voice had risen in pitch and volume and Elaine—who had always been so insensitive to nuance—seemed to hear its echo. She rose from the table and turned her troubled gaze toward the window.

"Come away," Rice said, taking hold of Hermione's arm. "Or this is going to end badly."

"I don't care," she said.

Her sister was crossing to the window now and Thomas was sliding Finn off his knee, rising as he did so, a question on his lips.

"There's somebody . . . watching us," Elaine murmured. There was fear in her voice.

Thomas came to her side and slipped his arm around her waist.

Hermione expelled what she thought was a shuddering sigh, but at the sound of it the window shattered, a hail of glass driving man, woman and child back from the sill.

"Away!" Rice demanded, and this time she conceded; went with him, across the lawn, out into the street, through the benighted town and finally home to the cold apartment where she could weep out the rage and frustration she felt.

Her tears had not dried by dawn; nor even by noon. She wept for too many reasons. At last, however, her unhappiness found a salve.

"I want to touch him one last time," she told Rice.

"Finn?"

"Of course Finn."

"You'll scare the bejeezus out of him."

"He'll never know it's me."

She had a plan. If she was invisible when naked, then she would clothe every part of herself and put on a mask and find him in the streets, playing trick-or-treat. She would smooth his fine hair with her palm or lay her fingers on his lips, then be gone, forever, out of the twin states of living death and Idaho.

"I'm warning you," she told Rice, "you shouldn't come."

"Thanks for the invitation," he replied a little ruefully, "I accept."

His clothes had been boxed and awaited removal. They untaped the boxes and dressed in motley. The cardboard they tore up and shaped into crude masks—horns for her, elfin ears for him. By the time they were ready for the streets, All Hallows' Eve had settled on the town.

It was Hermione who led the way back toward Elaine's house, but she set a leisurely pace. Inevitable meetings did not have to be hurried to, and she was certain she would encounter Finn if she let instinct lead her.

There were children at every corner, dressed for the business of the night. Ghouls, zombies and fiends, freed to be cruel by mask and darkness, as she was freed to be loving. One last time, and then away.

"Here he comes," she heard Rice say, but she'd already recognized Finn's jaunty step.

"You distract Thom," she told Rice.

"My pleasure," came the reply, and the revenant was away from her side in an instant.

Thom saw him coming and sensed something awry. He reached to snatch hold of Finn, but Rice pitched himself against the solid body, his ether forceful enough to throw Thom to the ground. Thom let out a ripe curse, and, rising the next instant, snatched hold of Rice. He might have landed a blow, but he caught sight of Hermione as she closed on Finn, and instead turned and snatched at her mask.

It came away in his hands, and the sight of her face drew from him a shout of horror. He retreated a step, then another.

"Jesus . . . Jesus . . ." he said.

She advanced on him, Rice's warning ringing in her head.

"What do you see?" she demanded.

By the way of reply he heaved up his dinner in the gutter.

"He sees decay," Rice said. "He sees rot."

"Mom?"

She heard Finn's voice behind her; felt his hand tug at her sleeve. "Mom, is that you?"

Now it was she who let out a cry of distress, she who trembled.

"Mom?" he said again.

She wanted so much to turn, to touch his hair, his cheek, to kiss him goodbye. But Thom had seen rot in her. Perhaps the child would see the same, or worse.

"Turn around," he begged.

"I . . . can't . . . Finn."

"Please."

And before she could stop herself, she was turning, her hands dropping from her face.

The boy squinted. Then he smiled.

"You're so *bright*," he said.

"I am?"

She seemed to see her radiance in his eyes as she touched his cheeks, his lips, his brow. So this was what it felt like to be a moon, she thought, to reflect a living light. It was a fine condition.

"Finn . . . ?"

Thom was summoning the boy to his side.

"He's frightened of you," Finn explained.

"I know. I'd better go."

The boy nodded gravely.

"Will you explain to him?" she asked Finn. "Tell him what you saw?"

Again, the boy nodded. "I won't forget," he said.

That was all she needed. She left him with his father and let Rice lead her away, through darkened alleys and empty parking lots to the edge of town. They discarded their costumes as they went. By the time they reached the freeway, they were once more naked and invisible.

"Maybe we'll wander a while," Rice suggested. "Go down South."

"Sure," she replied. "Why not?"

"Key West for Christmas. New Orleans for Mardi Gras. And maybe next year we'll come back here. See how things are going."

She shook her head. "Finn belongs to Thom now," she said. "He belongs to life."

"And to whom do we belong?" Rice asked, a little sadly.

She looked up. "You know damn well," she said, and pointed to the moon.

ABSENCE OF BEAST

Graham Masterton

Graham Masterton is the author of many novels of terror and suspense, including *The Burning*, *Walkers*, and *The Manitou*, which was adapted for film. He has also written historical fiction and several books of nonfiction. He is the editor of the anthology *Scare Care*.

"Absence of Beast" continues the theme of familial relationships, with a story about the special relationship between a young boy and his grandfather. It is reprinted from *Dark Voices 4*.

—E.D.

Robert knelt on the window-seat with his hands pressed against the window-pane, watching the leaves scurrying across the lawn below him. The clouds hurried across the sky at a delirious, unnatural speed, and the trees thrashed as if they were trying to uproot themselves in sheer panic.

The gale had been blowing up all afternoon, and now it was shrieking softly under the doors, buffeting the chimneystacks, and roaring hollow-mouthed in the fireplaces.

It was the trees that alarmed Robert the most. Not because of their helpless bowing and waving, but because of the strange shapes that kept appearing between their leafless branches. Every tree seemed to be crowded with witches and trolls and indescribable demons, their gaping mouths formed by the way in which two twigs crossed over each other, their eyes by a few shivering leaves which had managed to cling on, despite October's storms.

And at the far end of the long curving driveway stood the giant oak, in whose uppermost branches raged the monster that Robert feared above all. A complicated arrangement of twigs and offshoots formed a spiny-backed beast like a huge wild boar, with four curving tusks, and a tiny bright malevolent eye that—in actual fact—was a rain-filled puddle almost two hundred yards further away. But when the wind blew stronger, the eye winked and the beast churned its hunched-up back, and Robert wanted nothing more in the world than to take his eyes away from it, and not to see it.

But it was there; and he couldn't take his eyes away—any more than he could fail to see the blind Venetian mask in the tapestry curtains, or the small grinning dog in the pattern of the cushions, or the scores of purple-cloaked strangers who appeared in the wallpaper, their backs mysteriously and obdurately turned to the world of reality. Robert lived among secret faces, and living patterns, and inexplicable maps.

He was still kneeling on the window-seat when his grandfather came into the room, with a plate of toast and a glass of cold milk. His grandfather sat beside him and watched him for a long time without saying anything, and eventually reached out with a papery-skinned hand and touched his shoulder, as if he were trying to comfort him.

"Your mother rang," said his grandfather. "She said she'd try to come down tomorrow afternoon."

Robert looked at his grandfather sideways. Robert was a thin, pale boy, with an unfashionably short haircut, and protruding ears, and a small, finely-featured face. His eyes shone pale as agates. He wore a gray school jumper and gray shorts and black lace-up shoes.

"I brought you some toast," said his grandfather. White-haired, stooped; but still retaining a certain elegance. Anybody walking into the library at that moment would have realized at once that they were looking at grandfather and grandson. Perhaps it was the ears. Perhaps it was more than that. Sometimes empathy can skip a generation: so that young and old can form a very special closeness, a closeness that even mothers are unable to share.

Robert took a piece of toast and began to nibble at one corner.

"You didn't eat very much lunch, I thought you might be hungry," his grandfather added. "Oh, for goodness' sake don't feel guilty about it. I don't like steak-and-kidney pie either, especially when it's all kidney and no steak, and the pastry's burned. But cook will insist on making it."

Robert frowned. He had never heard an adult talking about food like this before. He had always imagined that adults liked everything, no matter how disgusting it was. After all, they kept telling *him* to eat fish and cauliflower and kidney-beans and fatty lamb, even though his gorge rose at the very sight of them. His mother always made him clear the plate, even if he had to sit in front of it for hours and hours after everybody else had finished, with the dining-room gradually growing darker and the clock ticking on the wall.

But here was his grandfather not only telling him that steak-and-kidney pie was horrible, but he didn't have to eat it. It was extraordinary. It gave him the first feeling for a long time that everything might turn out for the better.

Because, of course, Robert hadn't had much to be happy about—not since Christmas, and the Christmas Eve dinner party. His father had raged, his mother had wept, and all their guests had swayed and murmured in hideous embarrassment. Next morning, when Robert woke up, his mother had packed her suitcase and gone, and his grandfather had come to collect him from home. He had sat in his grandfather's leather-smelling Daimler watching the clear raindrops trickle indecisively down the windscreen, while his father and his grandfather had talked in the porch with an earnestness that needed no subtitles.

"You probably haven't realized it, but for quite a long time your mother and father haven't been very happy together," his grandfather had told him, as they drove through Pinner and Northwood in the rain. "It just happens sometimes, that people simply stop loving each other. It's very sad, but there's nothing that anybody can do about it."

Robert had said nothing, but stared out at the rows of suburban houses with their wet orange-tiled roofs and their mean and scrubby gardens. He had felt an ache that he couldn't describe, but it was almost more than he could bear. When they stopped at The Bell on Pinner Green so that grandfather could have a small whisky and a sandwich, and Robert could have a Coca-Cola and a packet of crisps, there were tears running down his cheeks and he didn't even know.

He had now spent almost three weeks at Falworth Park. His great-grandfather had once owned all of it, the house and farm and thirty-six acres; but death duties had taken most of it, and now his grandfather was reduced to living in eight rooms on the eastern side of the house, while another two families occupied the west and south wings.

"You're not bored, are you?" his grandfather asked him, as they sat side by side on the window-seat. "I think I could find you some jigsaws."

Robert shook his head.

"You've been here for hours."

Robert looked at him quickly. "I like looking at the trees."

"Yes," said his grandfather. "Sometimes you can see faces in them, can't you?"

Robert stared at his grandfather with his mouth open. He didn't know whether to be frightened or exhilarated. How could his grandfather have possibly known that he saw faces in the trees? He had never mentioned it to anybody, in case he was laughed at. Either his grandfather could read his mind, or else—

"See there?" his grandfather said, almost casually, pointing to the young oaks that lined the last curve in the driveway. "The snarl-cats live in those trees; up in the high branches. And the hobgobblings live underneath them; always hunched up, always sour and sly."

"But there's nothing there," said Robert. "Only branches."

His grandfather smiled, and patted his shoulder. "You can't fool me, young Robert. It's what you see *between* the branches that matters."

"But there's nothing there, not really. Only sky."

His grandfather turned back and stared at the trees. "The world has an outside as well as an inside, you know. How do I know you're sitting here next to me? Because I can see you, because you have a positive shape. But you also have a *negative* shape, which is the shape which is formed by where you're *not*, rather than where you are."

"I don't understand," Robert frowned.

"It's not difficult," his grandfather told him. "All you have to do is look for the things that aren't there, instead of the things that are. Look at that oak tree, the big one, right at the end of the driveway. I can see a beast in that oak tree, can't you? Or rather, the negative shape of a beast. An *absence* of beast. But in its own way, that beast is just as real as you are. It has a recognizable shape, it has teeth and claws. You can see it. And, if you can see it . . . how can it be any less real than you are?"

Robert didn't know what to say. His grandfather sounded so matter-of-fact. Was he teasing him, or did he really mean it? The wind blew and the rain pattered against the window, and in the young oaks close to the house the snarl-cats swayed in their precarious branches and the hunched hobgobblings shuffled and dodged.

"Let me tell you something," said his grandfather. "Back in the 1950s, when I was looking for minerals in Australia, I came across a very deep ravine in the Olgas in which I could see what looked like copper deposits. I wanted to explore the ravine, but my Aborigine guide refused to go with me. When I asked him why, he said a creature lived there—a terrible creature called Woolrabunning, which means 'you were here but now you have gone away again.'

"Well, of course I didn't believe him. Who would? So late one afternoon I went down into that ravine alone. It was very quiet, except for the wind. I lost my way, and it was almost dark when I found the markers that I had left for myself. I was right down at the bottom of the ravine, deep in shadow. I heard a noise like an animal growling. I looked up, and I *saw* that creature, as clearly as I can see you. It was like a huge wolf, except that its head was larger than a wolf, and its shoulders were heavier. It was formed not from flesh or fur but entirely from the sky in between the trees and the overhanging rocks."

Robert stared at his grandfather, pale-faced. "What did you do?" he whispered.

"I did the only thing I could do. I ran. But do you know something? It chased me. I don't know how, to this day. But as I was scaling the ravine, I could hear its claws on the rocks close behind me, and I could hear it panting, and I swear that I could feel its hot breath on the back of my neck.

"I fell, and I gashed my leg. Well . . . I don't know whether the Woolrabunning gashed my leg, or whether I cut it on a rock or a thorn-bush. But look . . . you can judge for yourself."

He lifted his left trouser-leg and bared his white, skinny calf. Robert leaned forward, and saw a deep blueish scar that ran down from his knee, and disappeared into the top of his Argyle sock.

"Thirty stitches, I had to have in that," said his grandfather. "I was lucky I didn't bleed to death. You can touch it if you want to. It doesn't hurt."

Robert didn't want to touch it, but he stared at it for a long time in awe and fascination. *Not a beast*, he thought to himself, *but an absence of beast. Look for the things that aren't there, rather than the things that are.*

"Do you know what my guide said?" asked his grandfather. "He said I should have given the Woolrabunning something to eat. Then the blighter would have left me alone."

The next day, after lunch, Robert went for a walk on his own. The gale had suddenly died down, and although the lawns and the rose-gardens were strewn with leaves and twigs, the trees were silent and frigidly still. Robert could hear nothing but his own footsteps, crunching on the shingle driveway, and the distant echoing rattle of a train.

He passed the two stone pillars that marked the beginning of the avenue. There was a rampant stone lion on each of them, with a shield that bore a coat of arms. One of the lions had lost its right ear and part of its cheek, and both were heavily cloaked in moss. Robert had always loved them when he was smaller. He had christened them Pride and Wounded. They had been walking between them—his mother, his father and him—when his mother had said to his father, "All you worry about is your wounded pride." Then he had learned at nursery school that a group of lions is called a pride, and somehow his mother's words and the lions had become inextricably intermingled in his mind.

He laid his hand on Wounded's broken ear, as if to comfort him. Then he turned to Pride, and stroked his cold stone nose. If only they could come alive, and walk through the park beside him, these two, their breath punctuating the air in little foggy clouds. Perhaps he could train them to run and fetch sticks.

He walked up the avenue alone. The snarl-cats perched in the upper branches of the trees, watching him spitefully with leaf-shaped eyes. The hobgobblings hid themselves in the crooks and crotches of the lower branches. Sometimes he glimpsed one of them, behind a tree-trunk, but as soon as he moved around to take a closer look, of course the hobgobbling had vanished; and the shape that had formed its face had become something else altogether, or just a pattern, or nothing at all.

He stopped for a while, alone in the park, a small boy in a traditional tweed coat with a velvet collar, surrounded by the beasts of his own imagination. He felt frightened: and as he walked on, he kept glancing quickly over his shoulder to make sure that the snarl-cats and the hobgobblings hadn't climbed down from the trees and started to sneak up behind him, tip-toeing on their claws so that they wouldn't make too much of a scratching noise on the shingle.

But he had to go to the big oak, to see the hump-backed creature that dominated all the rest—the Woolrabunning of Falworth Park. You were here, and now you have gone again. But all the time you're still here, because I can see the shape of you.

At last the big oak stood directly in front of him. The hog-like beast looked different from this angle, leaner, with a more attenuated skull. *Meaner*, if anything. Its hunched-up shoulders were still recognizable, and if anything its jaws were crammed even more alarmingly with teeth. Robert stood staring at it for a long time, until the gentle whisper of freshly-falling drizzle began to cross the park.

"Please don't chase after me," said Robert, to the beast that was nothing but sky-shapes in the branches of a tree. "Here . . . I've brought you something to eat."

Carefully, he took a white paper napkin out of his coat pocket, and laid it in the grass at the foot of the oak. He unfolded it, to show the beast his offering. A pork chipolata, smuggled from lunch. Pork chipolatas were his favourite, especially the way that grandfather insisted they had to be cooked, all burst and crunchy and overdone, and so Robert was making a considerable sacrifice.

"All hail," he said to the beast. He bowed his head. Then he turned around and began to walk back to the house, at a slow and measured pace.

This time, he didn't dare to turn around. Would the beast ignore his offering, and chase after him, the way that the Woolrabunning had chased after grandfather, and ripped his leg? Should he start running, so that he would at least have a chance of reaching the house and shutting the door before the beast could catch up with him? Or would that only arouse the beast's hunting instincts, and start him running, too?

He walked faster and faster between the trees where the snarl-cats lived, listening as hard as he could for the first heavy loping of claws. Soon he was walking so fast that to all intents and purposes he was running with his arms swinging and his legs straight. He hurried between Pride and Wounded, and it was then that he heard the shingle crunching behind him and the soft deep roaring of—

A gold-colored Jaguar XJS, making its way slowly toward the house.

Because of the afternoon gloom, the Jaguar had its headlights on, so that at first it was impossible for Robert to see past the dazzle, and make out who was driving. Then the car swept past him, and he saw a hand waving, and a familiar smile, and he ran behind it until it had pulled up beside the front door.

"Mummy!" he cried, as she stepped out of the passenger-seat. He flung his arms around her waist and held her tight. She felt so warm and familiar and lovely that he could scarcely believe that she had ever left him.

She ruffled his hair and kissed him. She was wearing a coat with a fur collar that he hadn't ever seen her wearing before, and she smelled of a different perfume. A rich lady's perfume. She had a new brooch, too, that sparkled and scratched his cheek when she bent forward to kiss him.

"That was a funny way to run," she told him. "Gerry said you looked like a clockwork soldier."

Gerry?

"This is Gerry," said his mother. "I brought him along so that you could meet him."

Robert looked up, frowning. He sensed his mother's tension. He sensed that something wasn't quite right. A tall man with dark combed-back hair came around the front of the car with his hand held out. He had a sooty-black three o'clock shadow and eyes that were bright blue like two pieces of Mediterranean sky cut out of a travel-brochure.

"Hallo, Robert," he said, still holding his hand out. "My name's Gerry. I've heard a lot about you."

"Have you?" swallowed Robert. He glanced at his mother for some sort of guidance, some sort of explanation; but all his mother seemed to be capable of doing was smiling and nodding.

"I hear you're keen on making model aeroplanes," said Gerry.

Robert blushed. His aeroplane models were very private to him: partly because he didn't think that he was very good at making them (although his mother always thought he was, even when he stuck too much polystyrene cement on the wings, or broke the decals, or stuck down the cockpit canopy without bothering to paint the pilot). And partly because—well—they were *private*, that's all. He couldn't understand how Gerry could have known about them. Not unless his mother had told Gerry almost everything about him.

Why would she have done that? Who was this "Gerry"? Robert had never even seen him before, but "Gerry" seemed to think that he had a divine right to know all about Robert's model aeroplanes, and drive Robert's mother around in his rotten XJS, and behave as if he practically owned the place.

Robert's grandfather came out of the house. He was wearing his mustard Fair Isle jumper. He had an odd look on his face that Robert had never seen before. Agitated, ill-at-ease, but defiant, too.

"Oh, *daddy*, so marvelous to see you," said Robert's mother, and kissed him. "This is Gerry. Gerry—this is daddy."

"Sorry we're early," smiled Gerry, shaking hands. "We made *much* better time on the M40 than I thought we would. Lots of traffic, you know, but fairly fast-moving."

Robert's grandfather stared at the XJS with suspicion and animosity. "Well, I expect you can travel quite quickly in a thing like that."

"Well, it's funny, you know," said Gerry. "I never think of her as a 'thing.' I always think of her as a 'she.' "

Robert's grandfather looked away from the XJS and (with considerable ostenta-tiousness) didn't turn his eyes toward it again. In a thin voice, almost as if he were speaking to himself, he said, "A thing is an 'it' and only a woman is a 'she.' I've always thought that men who lump women in with ships and cars and other assorted junk deserve nothing more than ships and cars and other assorted junk."

"Well," flustered Gerry. "*Chacun à son gôut.*" At the same time, he gave Robert's mother one of those looks which meant, *You said he was going to be difficult. You weren't joking, were you?* Robert's mother, in return, shrugged and tried bravely to look as if this wasn't going to be the worst weekend in living memory. She had warned Gerry, after all. But Gerry had insisted on "meeting the sprog and granddad, too . . . it all comes with the territory."

Robert stood close to the Jaguar's boot as Gerry tugged out the suitcases.

"What do you think of these, then?" Gerry asked him. "Hand-distressed pigskin, with solid brass locks. Special offer from Diner's Club."

Robert sniffed. "They smell like sick."

Gerry put down the cases and closed the boot. He looked at Robert long and hard. Perhaps he thought he was being impressive, but Robert found his silence and his staring to be nothing but boring, and looked away, at Wounded and Pride, and thought about running beside them through the trees.

"I *had* hoped that we could be friends," said Gerry.

Friends? How could we be friends? I'm nine and you're about a hundred. Besides, I don't want any friends, not at the moment. I've got Wounded and Pride and grandfather, and mummy, too. Why should I want to be friends with you?

"What about it?" Gerry persisted. "Friends? Yes? Fanites?"

"You're too old," said Robert, plainly.

"What the hell do you mean, too old? I'm thirty-eight. I'm not even forty. Your mother's thirty-six, for God's sake."

Robert gave a loud, impatient sigh. "You're too *old* to be friends with me, that's what I meant."

Gerry hunkered down, so that his large sooty-shaven face was on the same level as Robert's. He leaned one elbow against the XJS with the arrogance of ownership, but also to stop himself from toppling over. "I don't mean that sort of friends. I mean friends like father and son."

Robert was fascinated by the wart that nestled in the crease in Gerry's nose. He wondered why Gerry hadn't thought of having it cut off. Couldn't he see it? He must have seen it, every morning when he looked in the mirror. It was so warty. If *I* had a wart like that, I'd cut it off myself. But supposing it bled forever, and never stopped? Supposing I cut it off, and nothing would stop the blood pumping out? What was better, dying at the age of nine, or having a wart as big as Gerry's wart for ever and ever?

"Do you think that's possible?" Gerry coaxed him.

"What?" asked Robert, in confusion.

"Do you think that could be possible? Do you think that you could try to do that for me? Or at least for your mother, if not for me?"

"But mummy hasn't got a wart."

It seemed for a moment as if the whole universe had gone silent. Then Robert saw Gerry's hand coming towards him, and the next thing he knew he was lying on his side on the shingle, stunned, seeing stars, and Gerry was saying in an echoing voice, "I picked up the suitcase . . . I didn't realize he was there . . . he just came running towards me. He must have caught his face on the solid-brass corner."

He refused to come down for supper and stayed in bed and read *The Jumblies* by Edward Lear. "*They went to sea in a sieve they did . . . in a sieve they went to sea.*" He liked the lines about "*. . . the Lakes, and the Terrible Zone, and the hills of the Chankly Bore.*" It all sounded so strange and sad and forbidding, and yet he longed to go there. He longed to go anywhere, rather than here, with his mother's laughter coming up the stairs, flat and high, not like his mother's laughter at all. What had Gerry done to her, to make her so perfumed and deaf and unfamiliar? She had even believed him about hitting his face on the suitcase. And what could Robert say, while his mother was cuddling him and stroking his hair? *Gerry hit me?*

Children could say lots of things but they couldn't say things like that. Saying *Gerry hit me* would have taken more composure and strength than Robert could ever have summoned up.

His grandfather came up with a tray of shepherd's pie and a glass of Coca-Cola with a straw.

"Are you all right?" he asked, sitting on the end of Robert's bed and watching him eat. Outside it was dark, but the bedroom curtains were drawn tight, and even though the wallpaper was filled with mysterious cloaked men who refused to turn around, no matter what, Robert felt reassured that they never would; or at least, not tonight. The night was still silent. The Coca-Cola made a prickling noise.

Robert said, "I hate Gerry."

His grandfather's tissue-wrinkled hand rested on his knee. "Yes," he said. "Of course you do."

"He's got a wart."

"So have I."

"Not a big one, right on the side of your nose."

"No—not a big one, right on the side of my nose."

Robert forked up shepherd's pie while his grandfather watched him with unaccustomed sadness. "I've got to tell you something, Robert."

"What is it?"

"Your mother . . . well, your mother's very friendly with Gerry. She likes him a lot. He makes her happy."

Robert slowly stopped chewing. He swallowed once, and then silently put down his fork. His grandfather said, uncomfortably, "Your mother wants to marry him, Robert. She wants to divorce your father and marry Gerry."

"How can she marry him?" asked Robert, aghast.

There was a suspicious sparkle in the corner of his grandfather's eye. He squeezed

Robert's knee, and said, "I'm sorry. She loves him. She really loves him, and he makes her happy. You can't run other people's lives for them, you know. You can't tell people who to love and who not to love."

"*But he's got a wart!*"

Robert's grandfather lifted the tray of supper away, and laid it on the floor. Then he took hold of Robert in his arms and the two of them embraced, saying nothing, but sharing a common anguish.

After a long time, Robert's grandfather said, quite unexpectedly, "What did you want that sausage for?"

Robert felt himself blush. "What sausage?"

"The sausage you sneaked off your plate at lunchtime and wrapped in a napkin and put in your pocket."

At first Robert couldn't speak. His grandfather knew so much that it seemed to make him breathless. But eventually he managed to say, "I gave it to the beast. The beast in the big oak tree. I asked him not to chase me."

His grandfather stroked his forehead two or three times, so gently that Robert could scarcely feel it. Then he said, "You're a good boy, Robert. You deserve a good life. You should do whatever you think fit."

"I don't know what you mean."

His grandfather stroked his forehead again, almost dreamily. "What I mean is, you shouldn't let a good sausage go to waste."

Not long after midnight, the gales suddenly rose up again. The trees shook out their skirts, and began to dance Dervish-like and furious in the dark. Robert woke up, and lay stiffly listening—trying to hear the rushing of feet along the shingle driveway, or the scratching of claws against the window. He had a terrible feeling that tonight was the night—that all the snarl-cats and hobgobblings would leap from the trees and come tearing through the house—whirled by the gale, whipped by the wind— all teeth and reddened eyes and bark-brown breath.

Tonight was the night!

He heard a window bang, and bang again. Then he heard his mother screaming. Oh, God! Gerry was murdering her! Tonight was the night, and Gerry was murdering her! He scrambled out of bed, and found his slippers, and pulled open the door, and then he was running slap-slap-slap along the corridor screaming *Mummy— mummy—mummy—*

And collided into his mother's bedroom door. And saw by the lamplight. Gerry's big white bottom, with black hair in the crack; and his red shining cock plunging in and out. And his mother's face. Transfigured. Staring at him. Sweaty and flushed and distressed. A sweaty saint. But despairing too.

Robert. Her voice sounded as if he were drowning in the bath.

He ran out again. *Robert*, his mother called, but he wouldn't stop running. Downstairs, across the hallway, and the front door bursting open, and the gale blowing wildly in. Then he was rushing across the shingle, past Wounded and Pride, and all the dancing snarl-cats and hobgobblings.

The night was so noisy that he couldn't think. Not that he wanted to think. All he could hear was blustering wind and whining trees and doors that banged like cannon-fire. He ran and he ran and his pajama-trousers flapped, and his blood bellowed in his ears. At last—out of the darkness at the end of the avenue—the big oak appeared, bowing and dipping a little in deference to the wind, but not much more than a full-scale wooden warship would have bowed and dipped, in the days when these woods were used for ocean-going timber.

He stood in front of it, gasping. He could see the beast, leaping and dipping in the branches. "*Woolrabunning!*" he screamed at it. "*Woolrabunning!*"

Beneath his feet, the shingle seemed to surge. The wind shouted back at him with a hundred different voices. "*Woolrabunning!*" he screamed, yet again. Tears streaked his cheeks. "*Help me, Woolrabunning!*"

The big oak tossed and swayed as if something very heavy had suddenly dropped down from its branches. Robert strained his eyes in the wind and the darkness, but he couldn't see anything at all. He was about to scream out to the Woolrabunning one more time, when something *huge* came crashing toward him, something huge and invisible that spattered the shingle and claw-tore the turf.

He didn't have time to get out of the way. He didn't have time even to cry out. Something bristly and solid knocked him sideways, spun him onto his back, and then rushed past him with a swirl of freezing, fetid air. Something invisible. Something he couldn't see. A beast. Or an absence of beast.

He climbed to his feet, shocked and bruised. The wind lifted up his hair. He could hear the creature running toward the house. Hear it, but not see it. Only the shingle, tossed up by heavy, hurrying claws. Only the faintest warping of the night.

He couldn't move. He didn't dare to think what would happen now. He heard the front door of the house racketing open. He heard glass breaking, furniture falling. He heard banging and shouting and then a scream like no scream that he had ever heard before, or ever wanted to hear again.

Then there was silence. Then he started to run.

The bedroom was decorated with blood. It slid slowly down the walls in viscous curtains. And worse than the blood were the torn ribbons of flesh that hung everywhere like a saint's day carnival. And the ripest of smells, like slaughtered pigs. Robert stood in the doorway and he could scarcely understand what he was looking at.

Eventually his grandfather laid his hand on his shoulder. Neither of them spoke. They had no idea what would happen now.

They walked hand in hand along the windy driveway, between Wounded and Pride, between the trees where the snarl-cats and the hobgobblings roosted.

As they passed Wounded and Pride, the two stone lions stiffly turned their heads, and shook off their mantles of moss, and dropped down from their plinths with soft intent, and followed them.

Then snarl-cats jumped down from the trees, and followed them, too; and humpbacked hobgobblings, and dwarves, and elves, and men in purple cloaks. They walked together, a huge and strangely-assorted company, until they reached the big oak, where they stopped, and bowed their heads.

Up above them, in the branches, the Woolrabunning roared and roared; a huge cry of triumph and blood-lust that echoed all the way across Falworth Park, and beyond.

Robert held his grandfather's hand as tight as tight. "Absence of beast!" he whispered, thrilled. "Absence of beast!"

And his grandfather touched his face in the way that a man touches the face of somebody he truly loves. He kept the bloody carving-knife concealed behind his back; quite unsure if he could use it, either on Robert or on himself. But he had always planned to cut his throat beneath the big oak in Falworth Park, one day; so perhaps this was as good a night as any.

Even when their positive shapes were gone, their negative shapes would still remain, him and Robert and the snarl-cats and the sly hobgobblings; and perhaps that was all that anybody could ever ask.

RAT CATCHER

Steve Rasnic Tem

Like Steve Rasnic Tem's other story in this volume, "Hungry," "Rat Catcher" is about a fiercely protective parent. Like "Hungry," the supernatural element is subdued, yet its effect is no less horrifying. "Rat Catcher" first appeared in the dark suspense anthology *Dark at Heart*.

—E.D.

Jimmy hadn't caught four hours sleep all week. Normally he was a dead man about five seconds after he hit the sheets. In fact he liked telling people "I work like a bastard for my sleepeye." Not that he didn't lie there staring at the ceiling a few hours now and then, but not like this, not for days, not for a week. Sometimes he might lie awake counting the tiles because he was trying to remember something, even though he might not know he was trying to remember something. Some special butt-saving part of his brain would nag at him until he'd think of that anniversary, birthday, or special favor for his boss that he'd completely forgotten. "Ah, Jimmy, thank you," he'd say when he remembered these things, flat on his back in bed. Sometimes Tess would nudge him with her elbow a little when this happened, pretending to be asleep but still letting him know he'd saved his butt by just a hair this time (she figured he'd forgotten something having to do with her and most of the time she was right).

But not this time. He didn't think his lack of sleep had anything to do with her. Not this time. What he forgot this time, he knew, came from somewhere deeper than that, from somewhere further back, off where the dog bled in the dark and the rats gathered round to lick the blood.

"Ah, Jimmy, thank you . . ." he said, but quietly, not wanting Tess to hear. *Off where the dog bled in the dark . . .*

Maybe he felt the scratching before he actually heard it. Later he'd wonder about that. He felt it up in his scalp, long and hard like fingernails scratching through a wooden door, the fingers bleeding from the effort and the mind spinning dizzy from the pain. Jimmy raised his head and looked toward the bedroom door—they always kept it open half-way and the hall light on because Miranda was just down the hall and at five years old she still *hated* the dark, almost as bad as Jimmy used to hate the dark. Almost as bad as he hated it now. They kept the door open because Jimmy wanted to be sure and hear her when she screamed, which she still did about once every two weeks. He didn't want to lose any time getting into his little girl's room.

Tess was always telling him that he coddled the kids. That was a funny word— he didn't think he'd ever heard anyone else use it besides his grandma, back when he was a kid. And maybe Tess was right. He'd never been able to talk much about what it is you do with kids—being a dad to them, disciplining them, that kind of thing—not the way Tess could. Sometimes she gave him these books to read, books on parenting by experts. He never got much out of them.

All Jimmy knew was to pay attention to them, love and protect them. And tell them when they did wrong, though after a while you couldn't stop them from doing wrong, just slow them down a little. Just doing that much wasn't easy, not like it sounded. The kids would find out soon enough that the world was worse than they'd ever imagined, and maybe they'd hate him a little at first because of that. But all he could do was try to keep them alive and teach them a few things that would help them keep themselves alive. And maybe someday they'd figure out he'd loved them and that he'd meant the best for them, even with all the mistakes he'd made. He figured love was mostly mistakes that turned out okay. And maybe he'd get lucky. Maybe he wouldn't be dead when that someday came around.

A small black dog, maybe a cat, came racing by the open door, in and out of the little bit of light like a shadow pulled by a rubber band. On its way to Miranda's room, looked like. But they didn't own a dog, not since they put old Wooly to sleep. And their cat was white as a clean pillowcase.

Kids scream for all kinds of reasons. But even for the silly ones Jimmy had never been able to stand it. When Miranda's scream tore so ragged out of the dark he was up and heading out of the door without even pulling down the covers. Tess made a little gasp of surprise behind him as the headboard rocked back and banged the wall. The whole house was shaking with his legs pounding down the hallway and Miranda screaming.

As soon as he reached his little girl's door he caught the sharp smell of pee, and when he slammed the light switch on he fully expected to find the rat up on the bed with her, marking her with his teeth and claws and marking the bed with his pee just to let Jimmy know whose was whose. But there was just Miranda huddled by herself, her face red as a beet (how do little kids make their faces go that color?), and the damp gray flower opening up all around her tiny behind.

"Daddy! A big mousy! Big mousy!" she screamed, words he would have expected from her two years ago but not now (Dad! I'm a *big* girl now!), pointing a whole pudgy and shaking fist toward her open closet door. Jimmy ran back into the hallway and Miranda started screaming again; he could hear the baby squalling in the back room and Tess and Robert were out in the hall, Tess shouting *What's wrong!*, but Jimmy could hardly hear her over Miranda's *Daddy!* He waved a hand at Tess trying to get her to stay back, jerked open the hall closet door and grabbed the heavy broom, and ran back into his daughter's room.

Where he slammed her closet door as far back as it would go and held the broom up, waiting.

Miranda's screams had choked off into hard, snotty breathing. He could feel Tess and Robert behind him at the door, Tess no doubt holding Robert's jaw in that way she had when she wanted him to know he shouldn't talk just now. Daddy's real busy.

Suddenly there was movement at the bottom of the closet: Miss Raggedy Ella fell over and Jimmy could see that half her face had been torn away into clouds of cotton and he just started waling away with the broom on Miss Ella and Barbie and Tiny Tears and Homer Hippo and the whole happy-go-lucky bunch until they were all dancing up and down and laughing with those big wide permanent grins painted on their faces (except for Miss Ella, who now had no mouth to speak of) and screaming just like Miranda did. "Daddy, stop! You're hurting them!"

"It's a rat! A rat, goddamit!" He didn't know who he was yelling at; he just didn't know how they could be bothering him when there were rats in the house.

Eventually he stopped and when there wasn't any more movement he used the straw end of the broom to pull out Miranda's toys from the bottom of the closet one by one until it was empty.

He found a flap of loose wallpaper along the back wall above the yellowed baseboard. He lifted the flap up with the broom handle and discovered a four-inch hole in the plaster and lathe.

It took Miranda a long time to go back to sleep that night. She was trying to forget something but that part of her brain expert at saving your butt wasn't letting her forget so easily. Instead Jimmy knew that memory was getting filed back there where the rats lick the blood off the wounded dog.

Tess kept telling him, "It's all over now. Go to sleep, honey." And finally he pretended he had.

And thought about the rats he didn't want to think about living in his house, sniffing around his kids. He wasn't about to forget that one. He wasn't about to forget any of it.

He'd never thought that his momma had a dirty house, and he didn't think the other ladies in the neighborhood thought so either else they wouldn't have kept coming over to the house, drinking coffee, eating little cakes his momma made and getting icing all over the Bicycle cards they played with. But this was Kentucky and it was pretty wet country up their valley down the ridge from the mines and half the rooms in that big old house they didn't use except for storage, and fully two-thirds of all those dressers his momma kept around were full of stuff—clothing, old letters, picture albums, bedding—and were never opened. His momma never threw away anything, especially if it came down from "the family," and she had taken charge of all of grandma's old stuff, who had never thrown away anything in her life either.

So it was that he found the nest of hairless little baby rats in that dresser drawer one day. He wasn't supposed to be messing with that dresser anyway. His momma would have switched him skinny if she'd have caught him in one of her dressers.

Back then they'd looked like nasty little miniature piglets to him, squirming and squealing for their momma's hairy rat-tit, but not quite real-looking, more like puppets, a dirty old man hiding inside the dresser making them squirm with transparent fishing line. He'd slammed the drawer shut right away and good thing, too, because if he hadn't then maybe that dirty old man would have reached his burnt arm out of the drawer and pulled him in. Jimmy's momma had never told him to be scared of rats but she sure as hell had told him about the ragged, dirty old men who stayed down by the tracks and prowled the streets at night looking for young boys to steal.

He never told his momma about the rats either and they just seemed to grow right along with him, hiding in their secret places inside his momma's house. Like the rats he'd heard about up in the mines that grew big as beavers because they could hide there where nobody bothered them. He'd heard that sometimes the miners would even share their lunches with them. Then the summer he was twelve the rats seemed to be everywhere, in all the closets in the house and you could hear them in the ceilings and inside the floors running back and forth between the support beams under your feet and his momma got pretty much beside herself. He'd hear her crying in her bed at night sounding like his dear sweet little Miranda now.

He remembered feeling so bad because he was the man of the house, had been since he was a baby in fact and he knew he was supposed to do something about the rats but at twelve years old he didn't know what.

Then one day this big rat that should have been a raccoon or a beaver it was so big—a *mine* rat, he just knew it—came out from behind the refrigerator (that always felt so warm on the outside, smelling like hot insulation, perfect for a rat house) and ran around the kitchen while they were eating, its gray snake tail making all these S's and question marks on the marbled linoleum behind it. Jimmy's momma had screamed, "Do something!" and he had—he picked up the thick old broom and chased it, and that big hairy thing ran right up her leg and she screamed and peed all over herself and it dropped like she'd hit it and Jimmy broke the broom over it, but it started running again and he chased it down the cellar steps whacking it and whacking it with that broken piece of broom until the broom broke again over the rat's back and still it just kept going, now making its S's and question marks all over the dusty cellar floor so that it looked like a thousand snakes had been wrestling down there.

Jimmy kept thinking this had to be the momma rat. In fact over the next year or so he'd *prayed* that what he had seen down there had been the momma, and not one of her children.

The rat suddenly went straight up the cellar wall and into a foot-high crawlspace that spread out under the living room floor.

"You get it, son?" his mother had called down from the kitchen door, her voice shaking like his grandma's used to.

He started to call back that he'd lost it, when he looked up at the crawlspace, then dragged an old chair over to the wall, and climbed up on the splintered seat for a better look.

Back in the darkness of the crawlspace there seemed to be a solider black, and a strong wet smell, and a hard scratch against the packed earth that shook all the way back out to the opening where his two hands gripped the wall.

The scratching deepened and ran and suddenly his face was full of the sound of it as he fell back away from the wall with the damp and heavy black screeching and clawing at his face.

His momma called some people in and they got rid of the nests in the dressers and closets but they never did find the big dark momma he had chased into the cellar. At night he'd think about where that rat must have got to and he tried to forget what wasn't good to forget.

There was one more thing (isn't there always, he thought). They'd had a dog. Not back when he'd first seen the big momma rat, but later, because his momma had felt bad about what happened and he'd always wanted a dog, so she gave it to him. Jimmy named it Spot, which was pretty dumb but "Spot" had been a name that had represented all dogs for him since he was five or six, so he named his first dog Spot even though she was a solid-color, golden spaniel.

Just having Spot around made him feel better, although as far as he knew a dog couldn't help you much with a rat. Maybe she should have gotten him a cat instead, but he couldn't imagine a cat of any size dealing with that big momma rat.

Jimmy didn't think much about that dog anymore. Ah, Jimmy, thank you.

They had Spot four years. Jimmy was sixteen when the rats came back, a few at a time, and quite a bit smaller than the way he remembered them, but still there seemed to be a lot more of them each week and he'd dreamed enough about what was going to happen to him and his momma when there were enough of those rats.

Then he was down in the cellar one day when he saw this big shadow crawling around the side of the furnace, and heard the scratching that was as nervous and deep as an abscess. He ran upstairs and got his dead daddy's shotgun that his momma had kept cleaned and oiled since the day his daddy died, and took it down to the dark, damp cellar, and waited awhile until the scratching came again, and then that crawling shadow came again, and then he just took aim, and fired.

When he went over to look at the body, already wondering how he was going to dispose of that awful thing without upsetting his momma when she got home, he found his beautiful dog instead.

He'd started crying then, and shaking her, and ran back up the steps to get some towels (but why had she been crawling, and why hadn't she just trotted on over to him like she'd always done?), and when he got back down to the cellar with his arms full of every sheet and towel he could get his hands on, there had been all these rats gathered around the body of his dog, licking off the blood.

And now there were rats in his house, around his children.

The rat catcher, Homer Smith, was broad and rounded as an old Ford. Tess called Jimmy at work to tell him that the "rat man" had finally gotten there and Jimmy took the time off to go and meet him. When Jimmy first saw him the rat catcher was butt-wedged under the front porch, his big black boots soles out like balding tires, his baggy gray pants sliding off his slug-white ass as he pushed his way further into the opening until all of a sudden Jimmy was thinking of this huge, half-naked fellow crawling around under their house chasing rats. And he was trying not to giggle about that picture in his head when suddenly the rat catcher backed out and lifted himself and pulled his pants up all in one motion too quick to believe. Homer Smith was big and meaty and red-faced like he'd been shouting all morning and looking into his face Jimmy knew there was nothing comical about this man at all.

"You got rats," Homer Smith said, like it wasn't true until he'd said it. Jimmy nodded, watching the rat catcher's lips pull back into a grin that split open the lower half of his bumpy brown face. But the high fatty cheeks were as smooth and unmoved as before, the eyes circled in white as if the man had spent so much time squinting that very little sun ever got to those areas. The eyes inside the circles were fixed black marbles with burning highlights. "Some call me out to look at their rats and it comes up nothing but little mousies they coulda chased away their own selves with a lighter and a can of hairspray. If they had a little hair on their chests that is." Miranda's "mousies" sounded lewd and obscene coming from Smith's greasy red lips. "But rats now, they don't burn out so good. That hair of theirs stinks to high heaven while it's burning, but your good size mean-ass rat, he don't mind burning so much. And you, son . . ." He raised his fist. "You got rats."

Jimmy stared at the things wriggling in the rat catcher's fist: blind, pale and constantly moving, six, maybe eight little hairless globs of flesh, all alike, all as blank and featureless as the rat catcher's fingers and thumb, which now wriggled with the rat babies like their own long-lost brothers and sisters. "How many?" Jimmy asked, glancing down at his feet.

"How many what?" Smith asked, gazing at his fistfull of slick wriggle. He reached over with a finger from the other hand and flicked one of the soft bellies. It had a wet, fruity sound. Jimmy could see a crease in the rat skin from the hard edge of the nail. A high-pitched squeak escaped the tiny mouth.

Jimmy turned away, not wanting to puke on his new shoes. "How many rats? How many days to do the job? Any of that," he said weakly.

The rat catcher grinned again and tossed the babies to the ground where they made a sound like dishrags slapping linoleum. "Oh, you got *lots*, mister. Lots of rats and lots and lots of days for doing this job. You'll be seeing lots of me the next few weeks."

And of course the rat catcher hadn't lied. He arrived each morning about the time Jimmy was leaving for work, heavy gauge cages and huge wood and steel traps slung across his back and dangling from his fingers. "Poison don't do much good with these kind o' rats," Smith told him. "They eat it like candy and shit it right out again. 'Bout all it does is turn their assholes blue." Jimmy wasn't about to ask the rat catcher how he'd come by the information.

If he planned it right Jimmy would get home each afternoon just as Smith was loading the last sack or barrel marked "waste" up on his pickup. The idea that there were barrels of rats in his house was something Jimmy tried not to think about.

If he planned it wrong, however, which happened a lot more often than he liked, he'd get there just as the rat catcher was filling the sacks and barrels with all the pale dead babies and greasy-haired adults he'd been piling up at one corner of the house all day. Babies were separated from the shredded rags and papers they'd been nested in, then tossed into the sacks by the handsfull, so many of them that after a while Jimmy couldn't see them as dead animals anymore, or even as meat, more like vegetables, like bags full of radishes or spring potatoes. The adults Smith dropped into the barrels one at a time, swinging them a little by their slick pink tails and slinging them in. When the barrels were mostly empty, the sound the rats made when they hit was like mushy softballs. But as the barrels filled the rats made hardly a sound at all on that final dive: no more than a soft pat on a baby's behind, or a sloppy kiss on the cheek.

Jimmy had figured Smith was bound to be done after a few days. But the man became like a piece of household equipment, always there, always moving, losing his name as they started calling him by Tess's name for him, "the rat man," as if he looked like what he was after, when they were able to mention him at all. Because sometimes he made them too jumpy even to talk about, and the both of them would stay up nights thinking about him, even though they'd each pretend to the other that they were asleep. A week later he was still hauling the rats out of there. It seemed impossible. Jimmy started having dreams about a mine tunnel opening up under their basement, and huge, crazy-eyed mine rats pouring out.

"I don't like having that man around my kids," Tess said one day.

Jimmy looked up from his workbench, grabbing onto the edge of it to keep his hands from shaking. "What's he done?"

"He hasn't *done* anything, exactly. It's just the way he looks, the way he moves."

Jimmy thought about the rats down in their basement, the rats in their walls. "He's doing a job, honey. When he's done with the job he'll get out of here and we won't be seeing him anymore."

"He gives me the creeps. There's something, I don't know, a little strange about him."

Jimmy thought the rat man was a lot strange, actually, but he'd been trying not to think too much about that. "Tell you what, I've got some things I can do at home tomorrow. I'll just stick around all day, see if he's up to anything."

Jimmy spent the next day doing paperwork at the dining room table. Every once in a great while he'd see the rat man going out to his truck with a load of vermin, then coming back all slick smiles and head nodding at the window. Then Jimmy would hear him in the basement, so loud sometimes it was like the rat man was squeezing himself up inside the wall cavities and beating on them with a hammer.

But once or twice he saw the rat man lingering by one of the kid's windows, and once he was scratching at the baby's screen making meow sounds like some great big cat, a scary, satisfied-looking expression on his face. Then the rat man looked like the derelicts his momma had always warned him about, the ones that had a "thing" for children. But still Jimmy wasn't sure they should do anything about the rat man. Not with the kind of rat problem they had.

When he talked to her about it that night Tess didn't agree. "He's weird, Jimmy. But it's more than that. It's the way the kids act when he's around."

"And how's that?"

"They're scared to death of him. Miranda sticks herself off in a corner somewhere with her dolls. Robert gets whiny and unhappy with everything, and you *know* that's not like him. He just moves from one room to the next all day and he doesn't seem to like any of his toys or anything he's doing. But the baby, she's the worst."

Jimmy started to laugh but caught himself in time, hoping Tess hadn't seen the beginnings of a smile on his lips. Not that this was funny. Far from it. But this idea of how the baby was reacting to the rat man? They called their youngest child "the baby" instead of by her name, because she didn't feel like a Susan yet. She didn't feel like anything yet, really—she seemed to have no more personality than the baby rats the rat man had thrown down outside the house. Tess would have called him disgusting, saying that about his own daughter, but he knew she felt pretty much the same way. Some babies were born personalities; Susan just wasn't one of those. This was one of those things that made mommies and daddies old before their time: waiting to see if the baby was going to grow into a person, waiting to see if the baby was going to turn out having much of a brain at all.

So the idea of "the baby" feeling anything at all about the rat man made no sense to Jimmy. He felt a little relieved, in fact, that maybe they'd made too much out of this thing. Maybe they'd let their imaginations get away from them. Then he realized that Tess was staring at him suspiciously. "The *baby*?" he finally said. "What's wrong with the baby?"

"Susan," Tess replied, as if she'd been reading his mind. "Susan is too quiet. Like she's being careful. You know the way a dog or a cat stops sometimes and gets real still because it senses something dangerous nearby? That's Susan. She's hardly even crying anymore. And you try to make her laugh—dance that teddy bear with the bright blue bib in front of her, or shake her rattle by her face—and she doesn't make a sound. Like she knows the rat man's nearby and she doesn't want to make a noise 'cause then he'll figure out where she is."

In his head Jimmy saw the rat man prowling through the dark house, his baby holding her breath, her eyes moving restlessly over the bedroom shadows. "Maybe he'll be done soon."

"Christ, Jimmy, I want him out of here! And I know you do, too!"

"What reason could I give him? We're just talking about 'feelings' here. We don't really know anything."

"What *reasons* do we need? We hired the man—we can fire him just as easy."

"Easy?"

"You're scared of him, Jimmy! I've never seen you so scared. But these are our *kids* we're talking about!"

"He makes me a little nervous, I admit," he said. "What you said about Susan makes me nervous as hell. And I am thinking about the kids right now, and how I can keep things safe for them around here."

"So we just let him stay? We just let him sneak around our kids doing god-know's-what?"

"We don't know he's doing anything except acting a little eccentric. We could fire him and the police could force him off our property, but that doesn't help us any with what might happen later."

"Later," she repeated. Jimmy couldn't bear how scared she looked. "What are we going to do?"

"I'm staying home again tomorrow. I'll park the car down the street and hide in the house. If he's doing anything he shouldn't he probably figures he can avoid your one pair of eyes. But tomorrow you'll be following your normal schedule and I'll be your extra pair of eyes. Between the two of us we shouldn't miss much." Jimmy looked down at the floor, thinking of the beams and pipes and electrical conduit hidden there. He listened for the rats, but the only scratches he heard were the ones inside his head.

The rat man came out exactly at nine in the A.M. like always. You could set your clock by him. He started unloading all his equipment, including the sacks and the metal barrel he threw the adult rats in. Jimmy crouched low by the master bedroom window, watching for anything and everything the rat man did. The first sign of weirdness, he thought, and he'd be hauling his kids' asses out of there. Tess went to work in the kitchen; they agreed it'd be best to pretend she was having a normal day.

The rat man disappeared around the corner of the house with the big metal barrel. Jimmy was thinking about shifting to another room when he came back, holding four stiff rats by the tails, their black coats grayed with dust. *No way he could've caught and killed them that quick*, he thought. The rats appeared to have been dead a good day at least. Jimmy watched as the rat man waddled up to the corner where the house turned into an "L," the corner with the window to the baby's room. He watched as the rat man dangled the stiff rats against the rusting screen, clucking and cooing, rubbing his fingers up and down the smooth, hairless tails, talking to Jimmy's baby through the screen and smiling like he didn't realize where he was, like he was off in another place entirely.

Off where dogs bleed in the dark and the rats gather round to lick the blood.

All day long Jimmy watched as the rat man sneaked dead adult rats and hairless baby rats out of his rusted green pickup and planted them in the crawl spaces under the house only to haul them out again and replace them in the barrel and the sacks. The same ones, over and over. Jimmy wondered how many rats they'd actually had in the first place. A dozen? Six? Four? Just the one, trapped back under Miranda's bedroom, and coming into the rat man's hand easier than a hungry kitten?

Now and then the rat man would come out with something wrapped in a towel or a rag, cradling it carefully in his arms like it was his own baby. Jimmy couldn't quite credit the gentleness he was seeing in the rat man; he looked silly, really. Jimmy wondered why the rat man would want some of the rats bundled up.

Right after the rat man left for the day Jimmy told the whole story to Tess. "I wasn't about to confront him on it here," he said.

"Well, if he's just a con artist then we can call the police."

"He's a helluva lot more than that—I think we've both figured that one. That little office he has in town is closed and there's no home phone number listed. So I'm going to have to go out to his place tonight. I'm going to tell him not to come around here anymore."

"What if he says no?"

"He's not allowed to say no, honey. I'm not going to let him."

"What if I say no, Jimmy?" Her voice shook.

"I don't think you're going to say no. I think you're going to be thinking about the kids, and that crazy man dangling rats in front of their faces like they were baby toys." He stroked her shoulder. After a few seconds she looked away. And Jimmy grabbed his coat and went out to the car.

The rat man lived out past the empty industrial parks on the north end of the city. Here the municipal services weren't so good, the streets full of ragged holes like they'd just run short of asphalt, the signs faded, with a permanent, pasted-on look to the trash layering the ditchlines.

It wasn't hard finding the right house. "The rat catcher man? He lives down the end of that street don't-cha-know." The old man was eager to tell him even more information about the rat man, but these were stories Jimmy didn't want to hear.

The rat man's house didn't look much different from any other house in that neighborhood. It was a smallish box, covered with that aluminum siding you're supposed to be able to wash off with a hose. A small porch contained a broken porch swing. There were green curtains in the window. A brown Christmas wreath hung on the front door even though it was April. Two trash cans at the curb overflowed with paper and rotten food. And the foot-high brown grass moved back and forth like a nervous shag carpet.

What was different about the rat man's yard was all the tires that had been piled there, stacked into wobbly-looking towers eight or nine feet tall, bunches of them sitting upright like a giant black snake run through a slicer, tangled together in some parts of the yard like a slinky run through the washer. Some of the tires were full of dirt and had weeds growing out of them. Some of the tires looked warped and burnt like they'd had to be scraped off somebody's car after some fiery journey.

But it was the nervous grass that kept pulling at Jimmy's gaze. It wiggled and shook like the ground underneath it was getting ready to turn somersaults.

When Jimmy moved through it on the way to the rat man's door it scratched at the sides of his boots. When Jimmy climbed the porch steps it slicked long, trembling fingers up around his ankles, making slow S-curves and question marks that set him shivering almost—it was crazy—with delight.

When Jimmy actually got to the door he could hear the layers of scratch and whisper building behind him, but he didn't turn around. The scratching got louder and Jimmy found himself angry. He started to knock on the rat man's door but once he got his hand curled into a fist he just held it there, looked at it and made the fist so tight the fingers went white. The scratching was in his ears and in his scalp now, and suddenly he was in a rage at the rat man, and couldn't get that picture out of his head: the rat man dangling those dead monster babies in front of Jimmy's baby's window.

He held back his fist before he punched through the rotting door and instead moved to the dingy yellow window at the back of the rat man's porch. He let go of the fist and used the open hand to shield his eyes from the late afternoon glare when he pressed his face against the glass.

He saw the rat man's back bobbing up and down like a greasy old sack moving restlessly with its full complement of dying rat babies. The walls of the room were lined with a hodge-podge of shelving: gray planks and old wooden doors cut into strips and other salvage rigged in rows and the shelves full of glass jars like his grandmother's root cellar packed with a season's worth of canning.

Jimmy couldn't tell what was in those jars. It looked like yellow onions, potatoes maybe.

The rat man was taking something out of a sack. He moved, and Jimmy could see a small table, and little bundles of rags on it. The rat man picked up the bundles gently and filled his arms with them. Then he headed toward a dark brown, greasy-looking door at the back of the room.

Jimmy stepped off the porch and moved toward the side of the house. The rat man's grass seemed to move with him, pushing against his shoes and rippling as he passed. He looked down and now and then saw a gray or black hump rise briefly over the grass tops before sinking down inside again.

The first window on that side was dark and even with his face pushed up into the dirty screen he could see nothing. A tall dresser or something had been pushed up against the window on the other side.

The second window glowed with a dim yellow light. Jimmy moved toward it, through grass alive with clumps and masses that rubbed against his boots, crawled over his ankles, and scratched at his pants legs.

A heavy curtain had been pulled across the window, but it gapped enough in the middle to give Jimmy a peep-hole. Inside, the rat man was unwrapping the bundles. Around the room were more shelves, but here they had been filled with children's toys: dolls, teddy bears, stuffed monkeys and rabbits, tops and cars and jack-in-the-boxes and every kind of wind-up or pull-toy Jimmy had ever seen. Some of them looked shiny brand-new as if they'd just come out of the box. Others looked as old as Jimmy and older, the painted wood or metal dark brown or gray with layers of oily-looking dust.

The rat man put his new toys up on the shelf: a Miss Raggedy Ella doll, Tiny Tears, Homer Hippo, GI Joe, a plastic Sherman tank, a baby rattle, and a teddy bear with a bright blue bib. Toys that belonged to Jimmy's kids. And then the rat man picked up the last, slightly larger bundle, and placed it in a pink bassinet in the middle of the room, where he unwrapped it and rearranged the faded blankets.

Suddenly Jimmy felt the rats clawing at his ankles, crawling up his legs.

He turned so quickly—thinking he'd run to the porch and break through the door—that he stumbled and fell on his knees. Instantly he had rats crawling up on his back, raking at his legs, several hanging by their claws and teeth from the loose front of his shirt. He stood and brushed them off him, finally grabbing one that just wouldn't let go with his hands around its belly and squeezing until it screamed and dropped.

All around him the towered and twisting mass of tires was alive with dark rats, scrambling over each other as they climbed and tumbled through the insides and over the outsides of the black casings. He didn't make it to the porch without losing a few hunks of skin here and there. *The rats gathered round to lick the blood . . .*

The rat man's door disintegrated the second time Jimmy plowed into it with his shoulder, but not without a couple of hard splinters lodging painfully into the top of his arm. He stumbled into the front room and crashed into the far wall where the shelves of old wood began pulling away from the wall, dumping row after row of Mason jars onto the floor.

His feet slid on the spilled gunk. He could feel soft lumps smashing under the soles of his shoes. He staggered and grabbed the edge of a shelf, bringing down more of the jars. He started moving toward the greasy brown door at the back of the room as if in slow-motion, looking down at his shoes and moving carefully so that he wouldn't slash himself on the broken glass, but all the time screaming, yelling at himself to get his ass in gear and get to that bedroom at the back of the rat man's house.

He saw, but didn't think about, the bodies of the hundreds of hairless little rat babies bursting open under his shoes and smearing across every inch of the wooden floor.

He felt himself sliding, beginning to fall, as he jerked the door open and headed down a pitch black hallway toward a dim yellow rectangle of light at the other end. He pushed at the invisible walls of the hallway to keep himself upright and raced toward that rectangle, the walls going away around him as in a dream.

He wasn't aware of pushing open the door to the back room. It just seemed to dissolve at the touch of his hands.

Homer Smith, the rat man, was bent over the pink bassinet, cooing and making little wet laughing sounds. Later Jimmy would wonder why it was the rat man hadn't paid any attention to the ruckus in the front part of his house.

Homer looked up, his hands still inside the bassinet, as Jimmy hit him across the face as hard as he could. He fell to his knees with a noise like thunder, then looked up at Jimmy, then looked around at all his toys, smiled a little, like he wanted Jimmy to play with him. *Off where the dog bled in the dark . . .* Jimmy kicked him in the ribs this time, with boots still smeared and sticky.

Homer doubled over without a sound, then he looked up at Jimmy again, and his face was as soft and unfocused as a baby's.

Jimmy thought about his baby in the bassinet, but couldn't quite bring himself to look yet. He glanced around the room instead and saw the broom propped in one corner. He stepped over to it, still aware that Homer wasn't moving, picked it up and brought it down across Homer's left cheekbone. The straw-end snapped off like a dry, dusty flowerhead and Jimmy used the broken handle to whip Homer's face until it was a bloody, frothy pudding, Homer's head snapping back and forth with each blow but still Homer stayed upright, leaning forward on his knees. Jimmy couldn't believe it, and it scared him something terrible.

He kept thinking about the baby, but couldn't keep his eyes off the baby catcher, the baby snatcher. Finally he took the ragged, broken end of the broom handle and held it a couple of feet from Homer's throat. Jimmy could feel the weight of the pink bassinet behind him, and the thing wrapped up inside it, not moving, not crying, keeping still as if watching to see what would happen, but Jimmy knew it wasn't just keeping still. It was dead. Susan was dead. He hadn't checked on her before he came out here after the rat man and he should have known, watching the rat man carrying all those swaddled objects out of his house like that. He should have *known*.

At last Homer Smith raised his bloody head and stared at the sharp stick Jimmy had poised at his throat and seeing what Jimmy was ready to do Homer began to cry a wet, blood-filled cry, like a baby, just like a baby Jimmy thought, and it reminded him of lots of things, not all of it bad, as he drove the sharp end of that stick as hard as he could into the soft skin of Homer's throat.

The dying took a few minutes, Homer trying to pull the stick out but not being able to. Jimmy threw up over the bassinet until he had nothing left to heave. Finally he got to his feet again and stood over his baby, hesitated, then slowly unwrapped the blanket from around her.

And found two dead black rats there, curled around each other like Siamese twins. Homer had dressed each in baby doll clothes.

Jimmy felt the scratching up in his scalp, long and hard like fingernails clawing through a wooden door, long before he actually heard it. And then the sounds of hundreds of pale tongues, lapping.

He turned and looked *off where the dog bled in the dark* at Homer Smith's body, and the hundreds of rats gathered round to lick the blood.

WILL
THE QUESTION OF THE GRAIL

Jane Yolen

While best known for her multi–award winning children's books and magical novels for adults, Jane Yolen is also a distinguished poet, folklore scholar, and editor of the Jane Yolen Books imprint at Harcourt, Brace & Co. She lives in rural western Massachusetts and in St. Andrews, Scotland. Her most recent novel is *Briar Rose*, a tour-de-force retelling of the Sleeping Beauty legend set against the backdrop of World War II.

Yolen's poetry has been published in a wide variety of venues; the two poems on the following pages both come from small press editions. "The Question of the Grail" comes from the *Grails* anthology published by Unnameable Press in Atlanta, Georgia. "Will" is one of three Yolen poems published as beautiful limited-edition broadsides by Lawrence Schimel's A Midsummer Night's Press in New Haven, Connecticut, and also appeared in the *Magazine of Speculative Poetry*.

—T.W. & E.D.

WILL

The past will not lie buried.
Little bones and teeth
harrowed from grave's soil,
tell different tales.
My father's bank box told me,
in a paper signed by his own hand,
the name quite clearly: William.
All the years he denied it,
that name, that place of birth,
that compound near Kiev,
and I so eager for the variants
with which he lived his life.
In the middle of my listening,
death,
that old interrupter,
with the unkindness of all coroners,
revealed his third name to me.
Not William, not Will, but Wolf.
Wolf.
And so at last I know the story,
my old wolf, white against the Russian Snows,
the cracking of his bones,
the stretching sinews,
the coarse hair growing boldly
on the belly, below the eye.
Why grandfather, my children cry,
what great teeth you have,
before he devours them
as he devoured me,
all of me, bones and blood,
all of my life.

THE QUESTION OF THE GRAIL

Answer: Christ's vessel.
What is the question?

We could argue ships, the weight
of boats upon the Galilee,
the width and breadth of arks,
the wooden scow scurrying between
Avalon and eternity.

We could argue cups, the weight
of jewels in the ham-fist of kings,
the belching cauldron of Annwyn,
a simple Semitic glass
holding incarnate blood.

But I rather argue a woman's weight,
the bowls of my breasts, my cup-like womb,
the mound fitted for blood,
for salt in equal measure,
for the treasuring of life,
for divine revelation,
for the granting of it—
bowls, cups, mounds—
and the pattern of the maze.

IN THE SEASON OF THE DRESSING OF THE WELLS

John Brunner

John Brunner is a British science fiction writer best known for his prescient novels *Stand on Zanzibar*, *The Sheep Look Up*, *The Shockwave Rider*, and numerous others. This prolific author has also published thrillers, fantasy, mainstream novels, and volumes of poetry. He has won the Hugo Award, the British Science Fiction Award, and the French Prix Apolo.

"In the Season of the Dressing of the Wells" is a gorgeous piece of fantasy exploring the potent folk traditions of rural England. It is reprinted from *After the King: Stories in Honor of J. R. R. Tolkien* and it is easily one of the very best novellas of the year.

—T.W.

Ears numb with the thunder of exploding shells, eyes stinging and throat raw from poison gas, Ernest Peake forced himself to grope for the bell-pull alongside his bed. He had woken with his fists clenched and his heart pounding, and he felt so exhausted he might as well not have slept at all.

Better if I hadn't, perhaps . . .

The door opened. Tinkler, who had been his batman in France and Flanders, entered and drew the curtains. As daylight flooded in he said, "Another bad night, sir."

It wasn't a question. The tangled state of the bedclothes was evidence.

Among pillboxes on the bedside table stood a bottle of tincture of valerian, a glass, and a jug of water. Measuring out the prescribed dose, he diluted, stirred and offered it. Resignedly Ernest gulped it down. It did seem to be helping, and Dr. Castle had shown him an article describing its success in other cases of shell-shock . . .

Every one of them alone like me, inside the prison of his skull.

"Would you like your tea now, sir?" Tinkler inquired.

"Yes, and run my bath. And I'll take breakfast up here."

"Very good, sir. What shall I lay out?"

Rising with difficulty, silently cursing the bullet-shattered kneecap that made his left leg permanently stiff, Ernest gazed at the clear sky and shrugged.

"Looks like a day for blazer and flannels."

"With respect, sir, it is Sunday, and—"

"To hell with what day it is!" Ernest roared, and was instantly contrite. "I'm sorry. My nerves are on edge again. Bad dreams. You can go to church if you want."

"Yes, sir," Tinkler murmured. "Thank you, sir."

Waiting for his tea, Ernest stared glumly at the sunlit view from his window. The grounds of Welstock Hall had—like so many others—been turned over to vegetables during the War, and those parts which even his patriotic uncle Sir Roderick had been unwilling to see dug and trenched had been left to the weeds. But there were signs of a return to normal. Of course, staff was almost impossible to get, but one elderly man and two fifteen-year-old boys were doing their best. The tennis-court was not yet restored, but the lawn was neatly mown and set with croquet hoops, and a good half of the surrounding beds were bright with flowers. The tower of the church was visible from here, though its nave was hidden by dense-leaved trees and shrubs, as was all but a corner of the adjacent vicarage.

Normally it was an idyllic prospect, and one that had often made him wonder what it would have been like to spend his childhood here instead of in India, educated by tutors. Uncle Roderick and Aunt Aglaia, who were childless, had repeatedly suggested he be sent home to school and spend the holidays at Welstock. But his parents had always declined the offer, and at heart he wasn't sorry. So much more had changed in England than was ever likely to in that far-off, ancient, and slow-moving country a quarter of the world away, so he had far less to regret the passing of.

Today, though, sunk as he was in the recollected misery of nightmare, the very pleasure-dome of Kubla Khan could not have dispersed the clouds that shrouded his mind, wounded as surely by the War as his stiff leg.

Tinkler delivered the tea-tray. Before heading for the bathroom, he inquired, "Have you made any plans for today, sir?"

Ernest turned from the window with a sigh. His eye fell on the folding easel propped against a table that bore a large stiff-covered portfolio of paper, a box of water-colors, and other accoutrements proper to an artist.

Shall I ever become one? Even a bad one? They say I have a certain talent . . . But I can't seem to see any longer. I can't see what's there, only what's lying in ambush behind it. All the hidden horrors of the world . . .

"I'll probably go out sketching," he said at random.

"Should I ask Cook to prepare a lunch-basket?"

"I don't know!" Ernest barely prevented himself from snapping a second time. "I'll decide after breakfast."

"Very good, sir," Tinkler responded, and was gone.

Bathed, shaved, dressed, but having hardly touched his breakfast, Ernest made his slow way across the entrance hall. Every least action nowadays cost him vast mental effort, and as for making major decisions . . . Preoccupied with his bad manners towards Tinkler, who had stuck by him as loyally as any friend well could, he was within arm's reach of the door that led to the terrace and garden beyond when a harsh unwelcome voice bade him good morning.

Turning, across the parquet floor he confronted his Aunt Aglaia, clad in the unrelieved black she had adopted on her husband's death from influenza. That had been three years ago, so the customary time for mourning was long past, but she seemed determined to do as Queen Victoria had done for Albert. There was no resemblance in any other respect; the little monarch would barely have come up to her ample and efficiently-corseted bosom.

Worse still, her attitudes appeared to have become as rigid as her undergarments. On the few occasions he had met her when on leave from the Front, while Uncle Roderick was still alive, Ernest had thought of her as tolerably pleasant, if somewhat over-conscious of her status as wife of the Lord of the Manor. Now, however, she had taken to describing herself as the *châtelaine* of Welstock, hence the official guardian of not merely her estate but also the lives and behavior of her tenants and dependants. Among whom, very much against his will, was Ernest.

Before he had time to return her greeting, she went on, "That is scarcely suitable attire for Divine Service!"

Morbid religiosity was among her new attributes. She had reinstituted "family" prayers, which Ernest resignedly attended on the grounds that it was "not done" to reveal to servants any disagreement between those who employed them. But he thought it was so much cant.

Now, through the open door of the breakfast-room, he could see a maid clearing the table. Keeping his voice down in case the girl was in earshot, he said as civilly as possible, "I'm not coming to church, Aunt Aglaia."

She advanced on him. "Young man, I've put up with a great deal from you on account of your alleged ill-health! But you are beginning to try my patience. You've been here a month now, and Dr. Castle assures me you are making good progress. Perhaps one of these days you will choose to consider the hospitality I am extending you and even, as I sincerely hope, your duty towards your Creator!"

The blood drained from Ernest's face; he could feel the whiteness of his cheeks. Locking his fingers together for fear that otherwise he might strike this hypocritical old bitch, he grated between his teeth, "I owe nothing to the god that authorized such foulness as the War!"

And, before she could brand him a blasphemer, he tugged the door open and limped into blinding sunshine hatless and without his stick.

A single bell was chiming from the church. To his distorted perception it sounded like the tolling of a knell.

"Mr. Peake? Mr. Peake!"

A soft, inquiring voice. Ernest came to himself with a start. He was leaning on the wall dividing the grounds of the Hall from those of the vicarage. The bell had stopped. Facing him was a slender girl, face shaded by a broad-brimmed hat, wearing a plain dress of the same dark gray as her large, concerned eyes.

Even as he wondered frantically whether he had been crying out aloud—he knew he sometimes did—his hand rose automatically to lift a nonexistent hat.

"Good morning, Miss Pollock," he forced out. "I'm sorry if I disturbed you."

"Not at all. I was just taking a turn around the garden while Grandfather puts some final touches to his sermon."

Feverishly eager to counter any bad impression he might have made: "Well, as you've no doubt deduced I shan't be there to hear it, I'm afraid. You see, as I've been trying to explain to my aunt, I lost my faith when I saw what was allowed to happen over there. I couldn't believe any more in a loving, beneficent, all-wise—" Suddenly aware that he was virtually babbling, he broke off in mid-word.

To his surprise and relief, there was no sign that Miss Pollock had taken offense. Indeed, she was saying, "Yes, I can understand. Gerald—my fiancé—he said very similar things the last time he came home on leave."

Oh, yes. I heard about Gerald, didn't I? Bought his at—Cambrai, I think it was. Tanks.

While he was still fumbling around for something else to say, from the direction of the house came a grinding of carriage-wheels on gravel, the sign that Lady Peake was about to depart for church. She could have walked this way in half the time it took to go around by the drive, but of course that would never have done.

She could also have well afforded a motor-car, and indeed Uncle Roderick had owned one before the War, but she had never approved, and more than once had mentioned how glad she'd been when their chauffeur joined up and her husband told him to drive to London in it and turn it over to the Army.

Miss Pollock glanced past Ernest's shoulder. "Ah, there's your aunt coming out. I'd better go back and rouse Grandfather. He does tend to lose track of time nowadays. Oh, by the way, in fine weather we like to take afternoon tea in the garden. Perhaps you'd care to join us?"

"Why—why, that's very kind of you," Ernest stammered.

"There's no need to fix a date in advance. Any time you're free, just ask one of the maids to pop over and say you're coming. Now I really must rush. Good morning!"

And she was gone, leaving Ernest to wonder all over again whether he had been talking aloud to himself when she noticed him, and if so, what he had been saying.

As ever, his charming surroundings, aglow with the onset of summer, seemed permeated with menace, like the germs in fertile soil that could bloat and burst the human frame.

Gas gangrene. But what is gangrened in me is my mind . . .

The Hall, the vicarage and the church stood on the crest of a low hill, with the rest of the village scattered on level ground below and on the flank of another hill opposite. In olden days it had been a weary and toilsome climb to attend Divine Service, especially for children and the old, and many were content to proceed no further than a spring that formerly had gushed out near the bottom of the slope, for its waters were held to possess the power of cleansing and absolution.

Early in the last century, though, the incumbent Lord of the Manor had had the spring covered, and athwart its site had caused to be constructed a slanting paved track, rising from what was still called Old Well Road, that offered greater ease of access. He also had planted, either side of the lych-gate, a pair of magnificent chestnut trees. Beneath their shade, uncomfortable in their dark Sunday clothes on such a warm morning, were foregathered most of the inhabitants of Welstock, among whom, despite the fine weather, there were few smiles to be seen. Tragedy had struck the little community again, during the past week. Young George Gibson, who had been gassed in France and taken prisoner, and come home to cough his life away, had died at last, leaving his wife with three children.

As ever, the villagers had separated into two groups. To the left were the women-folk and young children, ebbing and flowing around the schoolmistress, Miss Hicks. Apart from regrets at George Gibson's death, their talk was mainly of high prices, illness—every hint of fever might signal another outbreak of the dreaded influenza—cottages out of repair and, with little optimism for the bride and groom, a forthcoming marriage. It was not a good time, they all agreed, to think of bringing more children into the world.

To the right were the fathers and grandfathers, surrounded by single young men—few of those, for more and more of their age-group were drifting away from the countryside in search of the glamour, and the better wages, to be found in cities. Beyond them again hung about a bored fringe of boys old enough to work but not yet concerned with the matters that so preoccupied their elders.

At the focus of this group were to be found Hiram Stoddard, smith and farrier—and incidentally wicket-keeper for the village cricket-team—and his brother Jabez who kept the Plough Inn, exchanging news and views with the local farmers. Within this cluster, but not of it, was the most prosperous of the latter, Henry Ames. He had moved here from the next county. Having lived in the area a bare ten years, he was still regarded as a foreigner, and though people were civil to him and his family they kept their distance. He was the only one among them still invariably addressed as Mister.

The men too wore grave countenances as they chatted. At first their talk, like the women's, was of George Gibson and his bereaved family; soon, though, they moved on to more pressing subjects. They spoke of the shortage of labor—George had been a farmhand, living in a cottage on the Peake estate; they dismissed the theorists who argued that farming would soon become entirely mechanized, for none among them (always excepting Mr. Ames) could afford the expensive new machinery, and so many horses had been killed during the War that it was proving hard to breed up to former levels, while much the same applied to other kinds of livestock, vastly diminished because there had not been enough hands to tend them . . . No doubt of it: times were hard, if anything harder than in wartime. Someone mentioned the politicians' promise of "homes fit for heroes" and the sally was greeted with derisive chuckles, lacking mirth.

Attempting to divert the conversation into a more cheerful path, Hiram broached the early arrival of summer and the promise of a good hay-crop. Mention of grass led by natural stages to mowing, mowing to the need to prepare the cricket-pitch, and that in turn to further depressed bouts of silence, as they remembered the many former players who would not again turn out for the team.

At length Hiram said with feigned heartiness, "Well, 'tes time to wait on her ladyship and ask to borrow the three-gang mower. I'll go after service. Who'll come with me?"

There were four or five reluctant offers. In the days of Sir Roderick it would have been a pleasant prospect—he'd have consented at once, and more than likely seen them off with a mug of beer apiece. Dealing with her ladyship, on the other hand . . .

As though sensing their thoughts, Gaffer Tatton said in his creaky voice, "Bad times, bain't they? *Bad* times!"

The group parted to let him through to its heart. He was leaning on an oaken stick he had cut before the rheumatism sapped his limbs and bowed his back, and panting from his climb up the slope. In his day he had been a carpenter and wheelwright, and an accomplished carver. But that day was long past, and not again would skills like his be called for. As he was fond of saying, if it could all be done in factories in wartime, they'd stick to the same now there was peace, leaving no space for the craftsman on his own. His dismal predictions had certainly been borne out so far, and though some of the younger sort made mock of him behind his back, others were coming to heed his old man's wisdom.

Halting, he gazed about him with bleared eyes.

"These times be sent to try us, bain't they? And small wonder. *It's the year.* And last time we neglected un. So it's for two."

Understanding, the older men shifted uneasily from foot to foot, looking as though they would rather change the subject. When one of the boys from the outer ring, puzzled, asked for enlightenment, and Mr. Ames looked relieved at someone putting the question in his own mind, there was shifting of eyes as well as feet. Gaffer, however, was not to be diverted from his theme.

"Shoulda been in '15," he emphasized. "'Course, with the War and all . . . She'll 'uv forgiven it. But not this time. Bain't there warnings? Sir Roderick gone! 'Im as should be the rightful heir lying under a curse!"

Some of his listeners winced. Even to them, that was straining the description of Mr. Ernest's condition which they had teased out of his man Mr. Tinkler. He had taken to dropping in at the Plough on evenings off, and despite being "one o' they Lunnon folks" by birth had shown himself to be a square fellow with a fund of anecdotes and a remarkable capacity for the local cider.

Nonetheless, so long after the War, and still in such a pitiable state—!

"Fragile," Mr. Tinkler had once said, and repeated the word with approval. "Yes, fragile! To do with what they call 'the artistic temperament,' you know. For those who have it, it's often as much a curse as a blessing."

He had at least uttered the word, if not in the sense that Gaffer Tatton meant it . . .

But the old man was still in full spate. Now, charging ahead on the assumption that the person they had been arranging to wait on when he arrived must be the vicar, he was saying, "And rightly too! Bain't none too long until Ascensiontide! If we don't make him bless the wells—"

With a cough Hiram interrupted. "We were talking about borrowing the gang-mower from the Hall for the cricket-field. After service we're going to call on her ladyship and—"

Gaffer's cheeks purpled. "And I thought you were talking about the dressing! Bain't *she* one of our ills, and a warning?"

It was in the minds of not a few of his listeners to admit how completely they agreed with him, but they had no chance, for just at that moment up rolled her carriage. To a chorus of "Good morning, m'lady!" she descended, nodding acknowledgement of raised hats and touched caps, and paraded up the path between the gravestones.

Dutifully, they fell in behind.

And paid scant attention to the service.

*   *   *

Bit late mowing the cricket-field, aren't they?

The thought emerged unexpectedly into Ernest's mind as he wandered around the grounds of the Hall dogged by phantoms. Giving up all intention of painting, he had let his feet carry him where they would. Fragments of memory from a wartime summer leave fell into place as he gazed at what might have been taken for an ordinary meadow; indeed, a crop of hay had lately been reaped from it, and its grass was barely longer than wheat-stubble. But still too long for a good square-cut to drive the ball to its boundary.

All of a sudden the view was overlain with images from the past. Surely the pavilion must be on his left . . . Yes, there it was, its green planks in need of fresh paint, its tallywag board hanging awry after the winter winds.

A terrible ache arose within him. Short of a batsman because someone had just been called up, they had asked him to play for the village, and he'd agreed, and he'd made forty—off pretty poor bowling, admittedly, but enough to tip the balance so that Welstock won by two wickets.

And it was my last game.

He turned his back and hobbled towards the house, trying not to weep.

On his way he passed the summerhouse where croquet gear was stored in a weatherproof chest. He had a vague recollection of saying, "Croquet's about the most strenuous game I'll ever be fit for again!" Alert as ever to an unspoken command, Tinkler had set out the hoops and pegs.

For want of any better way to pass the time until lunch, he opened the chest, picked up a mallet and a ball at random, and set to listlessly driving around the lawn. All the time, though, he was preoccupied by recollected sights and sounds. For once, blessedly, they did not all concern the hell of the trenches. But awareness of the service at the church brought to mind Hindu processions following idols smeared with *ghee* and hung with garlands, and from there it was a short mental leap to his father's bearer Gul Khan, who was such a demon bowler and such a patient coach. During the hot season, in Simla . . .

"What the hell, though, is the bloody *point?*" he whispered, and slammed his mallet down as though it were a golf club. Squarely hit, the ball struck one of the hoops and knocked it clear out of the turf. He threw the mallet after it and turned back towards the house.

And was, on the instant, very calm.

Here, walking up the gravel drive, were six men in black suits and hats. He recognized them, though he could not certify their names save one. At their head, brawny and stolid, that was surely Mr. Stoddard, captain and wicket-keeper of the last side he would ever play for . . .

Once again he must have spoken aloud without intention, for a quiet voice at his back said, "Yes, sir. Mr. Hiram Stoddard, that is. There's also Mr. Jabez Stoddard, but he keeps the Plough Inn and had to go and open up."

And, apologetically: "Catching sight of you as we left the church, I excused myself to her ladyship and took the short cut."

"Thank you, Tinkler." For the moment Ernest felt quite in control of himself. "Any idea what brings them here?"

"None at all, sir."

"Is my aunt coming straight back?"

"No, sir. She intends to call on Mr. Gibson's family."

"You mean the poor devil who just died? Hmm! One point to my aunt, then. I didn't think she was so charitably inclined, except insofar as she considers it an obligation . . . Tinkler, is something wrong?"

"It's not my place, sir, to—"

"Out with it!" Ernest realized he was panting. Why?

"Since you insist, sir," Tinkler said after a pause, "I'm not entirely convinced about the charitable motive for her visit. I"—a discreet cough—"I detected a certain what you might call *gleam* in her ladyship's eye."

Ernest came to a dead stop and rounded on his manservant. "You've noticed it too?" he burst out.

Meeting his gaze dead level, Tinkler said, "Where did you last see it?" There wasn't even the echo of a "sir" this time.

"In—in the mad eyes of that general who sent us over the top at . . ."

"Say it!" He was in command. "I don't want to remember any more than you do. He killed ten thousand of us with that order, didn't he? And you and me survived by a miracle . . . But *say it!*"

"Mal . . ." Ernest's tongue was like a monstrous sponge blocking the name. He gulped and swayed and ultimately forced it out:

"*Malenchines!*"

"Yes. It was there. And I hoped never to see it again, neither. But I have . . . Now, sir, I'll go and find out what they want."

"No, Tinkler, *We'll* go."

As though uttering the terrible name had lifted a burden from his soul, Ernest was able to greet Mr. Stoddard and his companions and refer to their last encounter with scarcely a qualm. When they explained their errand he said at once he was sure it would be all right, though he was by no means so convinced as he sounded, and went on to inquire about prospects for the coming season.

The villagers exchanged glances. At length Mr. Stoddard shrugged.

"We've done poorly since the War. But there are a few good players coming along. Could do with more practice, though, and more coaching."

Is that a hint?

Assuming it was, Ernest forced a smile. "Well, I might offer a bit of help there," he said. Against his will a trace of bitterness crept back into his voice as he added, "My playing days are over, though, I'm afraid. Croquet is about my limit now, and I can't even find partners for that . . ."

Struck by a sudden thought, he glanced around. "Don't suppose any of you play, do you?"

A worried expression came and went on Tinkler's face, but Ernest paid no attention.

"It can be quite a good game, you know. Not much exercise, but a lot of skill. If you can spare a few minutes I'll show you. Tinkler, would you replace that hoop and bring me a mallet and a couple of balls?"

Strangely excited for the first time in years, he proceeded to initiate them into the mysteries of running a hoop, making one's peg, croquet and roquet and becoming a rover, with such enthusiasm that the visitors' stiffness melted and the youngest said at length, "Tell 'ee what, Mr. Ernest, I wouldn't mind 'aving a go some time!"

"Good man!" Ernest exclaimed. "And I tell you what, as well. I just remembered something. I was wandering around while I was on leave here once, and I came across some nets in one of the outbuildings. They may still be there. Have you got enough nets for practice?"

"No, sir!" said Hiram Stoddard promptly.

"Then let's go and—"

A gentle cough interrupted him. It was Tinkler. Her ladyship's carriage was rolling towards the house.

"Ah, fine! We can arrange about the mower. Aunt! Aunt Aglaia!"

Descending with the assistance of her groom and coachman Roger, who had been too young for the Army, Lady Peake fixed her nephew with a stony gaze.

"You are profaning the Sabbath!" she barked.

"What? Oh, you mean this?" Ernest waved the croquet mallet. "Not at all. I was just showing these people the rudiments in the hope they might give me a game some day."

He might as well have been addressing the air. She went on as though he had not spoken.

"And what are these—persons—doing here?"

"Oh, they came to borrow the three-gang mower. For the cricket-field. Uncle Roderick always used to—"

"Your uncle is no longer among us! And when, pray, was this *implement* to be put to use?"

Hiram had removed his hat and not replaced it. Turning it around between his large callused hands, he muttered, "We thought we might make a start this afternoon, m'lady."

An expression of triumph crossed Lady Peake's face.

"So, like my nephew, you are a breaker of commandments. 'The seventh day is the Sabbath of the Lord Thy God. In it thou shalt do no manner of work!' You may not borrow my mower, today or any other day. Return to the bosom of your families and pray to be forgiven."

She waddled away towards the house.

"Sorry, Mr. Stoddard," said young Roger. "But you know what she's like. 'Course, it don't apply to people working for 'er, do it? Like to see the look on 'er face if I answered back the same way: 'No, m'lady, can't drive you to church, can I? It'd be working on the Lord's Day!' "

For a second it looked as though Hiram was about to tell him off for being over-forward, but he changed his mind.

"I'm awfully sorry," Ernest muttered. "Never expected her to react like that . . . What will you do now?"

"Go back to the old way, I suppose, sir. Turn out men with scythes. Aren't that many left, though, that can mow a good tidy outfield, let alone a proper pitch. One of them dying skills Gaffer Tatton always talks about. If you'll excuse us, sir, we'd best make for the Plough before the rest of 'em head home for dinner, see who we can round up for the job."

"Hang on! I'll come with you! Just let me get my hat and stick! Roger, warn Cook I'll be late for lunch!"

As he hobbled towards the house, they looked questions at Tinkler. He hesitated. At length he said, "It's not exactly *comeelfoh*, is it? But his heart's in the right place. Only his wits are astray. And a chance to stand up to her ladyship may be just what he needs. I'll be there to keep an eye on him."

At which they relaxed. But only a little.

Startled silence fell beneath the low timbered ceiling of the Plough's single bar as they recognized who had come to join the company, and conversation was slow to resume. Only Gaffer Tatton, in his usual seat in the chimney-corner, went on talking as though nothing out of the ordinary were happening.

Or, at least, nothing so trivial as the presence of gentry.

He had finally stopped grousing about the lack of a fire to warm his aching bones, and had drifted on to the other subject preoccupying his mind—and, if truth be told, not his alone: the neglect of an ancient ceremony, to which he attributed their continuing misfortune. Making a valiant attempt to distract the visitor's attention, Hiram led the way to the bar, re-introduced his brother Jabez the landlord and presented several of the others, even going so far as to include Mr. Ames.

Aware of the problem, Jabez said heartily, "Well, sir, since it's the first time you've honored my premises, let me offer you a glass! What'll it be?"

Ernest looked about him uncertainly. For the past few minutes he had been out of touch with himself, anger at his aunt having taken control. Now, in this unfamiliar setting, among people who clearly were uneasy at his presence, he was at a loss. He glanced at Tinkler, who said suavely, "I can recommend Mr. Stoddard's cider, sir. He makes it himself."

"By all means," Ernest agreed.

"Well, thank you, Mr. Tinkler," the landlord said, reaching for mugs. "Allow me to offer you the same."

And, as he turned the tap on the barrel, everyone tried to pick up the talk where it had left off. Instead the bad news about the mower circulated, trailing gloom around the room, and renewed silence.

Hiram invited his companions to take seats at the one partly-vacant table. Belatedly noticing them, and plainly still under the impression that it was the vicar they had been to see, Gaffer demanded their news.

"She won't let us 'ave the mower," Hiram said loudly and clearly. "Got to use scythes!"

Confused, Gaffer countered, "Don't use scythes in well-dressing! Bain't nothing used bar what's natural!"

"I don't quite get the drift of this," Ernest ventured.

"Oh, don't concern yourself with it, sir," Hiram said. "Got a bit of a bee in 'is bonnet, Gaffer do."

"He seems very upset," Ernest persisted.

And indeed he was, even though someone had made haste to refill his mug. His voice rose to the pitch of a revival preacher, despite attempts to hush him, and at last there was nothing for it but to explain.

"The way of it, sir, you see," Hiram sighed, "is this. Back before the War, come Ascensiontide, we had a local—ah—"

"Custom?" supplied a voice from the background.

"Custom, yes, a very good term. Thank you—" He glanced around and finished in a tone of surprise, "Mr. Ames! Used to make up sort of decorations, pictures out of flowers and leaves and alder-cones and such, and put them to the wells."

"And the wall below the church," someone inserted.

"Yes, in Old Well Road too. Three places." Hiram ran a finger around his collar as though it were suddenly too tight. "Then we'd get vicar to come and speak a blessing on 'em."

Gaffer's attention was completely engaged now. Leaning forward, mug in both hands, he nodded vigorously. "Ah, an' every seventh year—"

"Every seventh year, yes," Hiram interrupted loudly, "we had a sort of feast, as well. We'd roast a sheep, or a pig, and share it out among everybody, making sure bits got taken to the old folk or those sick abed."

"It sounds like a fascinating tradition," Ernest said, staring. "Has it fallen into disuse?"

"Ha'n't been kept up since the War."

"But why?"

There was an awkward pause. Eventually Hiram found no one else was willing to answer, so it was up to him again.

"Vicar used to say it were truly a heathen custom made over. I wouldn't know about that. But I daresay he's not un'appy."

"An' what would 'er ladyship say?" called Jabez from behind the bar, forgetting himself for a moment.

His brother glowered at him, but by now the cider was having an effect on Ernest. Since falling ill he had seldom touched alcohol; besides, he had had almost no breakfast.

Draining his mug, he said, "You're right, Tinkler. It is good, this stuff. Here, bring me another. And for Mr. Stoddard too, and Mr.—Oh, drinks all round, why not? Here!" He pulled banknotes from his wallet.

Somewhat reluctantly Tinkler complied. Meantime Ernest turned to Hiram and continued.

"Well, I don't see what my aunt has to do with it, you know. How did Sir Roderick feel?"

" 'E were in favor," Hiram grunted.

"That's the truth!" chimed in someone from the background. "Remember 'ow, if there were visitors, 'e'd bring 'em round along of us? Or come by later in the day with 'em, with their Kodaks and all?"

The older men uttered a chorus of confirmation.

Returning with the full mugs, Tinkler murmured, "Here you are, sir."

Ernest gulped a mouthful and set his aside. By now his attention was fully engaged.

"Well, if your major problem is with the vicar, I can put in a word, at least. Miss Pollock has invited me to tea at the vicarage, and I can bring up the matter then. Would you mind?"

It was clear from their faces that they wouldn't, and Hiram said, "That's very generous, sir. Here!"—loudly—"I think we should drink Mr. Ernest's health!"

"Hear hear!"

Absent-mindedly drinking along with them, Ernest wiped his lip and took up another point that particularly interested him.

"What kind of—of decorations, or pictures?"

"Always Bible stories," Hiram said.

"To do with water? Walking on the waves, Jonah and the whale, that kind of thing?"

Headshakes. By now everyone in the bar was crowding around the table, so that Gaffer complained about not being able to see. They ignored him.

"No, just any that came to mind. 'Course . . ."

"Yes?"

"They was mostly the work of one that's gone."

"You mean one particular person used to work out the designs for you?"

"That's right, sir. Mr. Faber it were. Taken off in the same way as your poor uncle, but the year before."

"Bain't no one left got 'is skill an' touch," came a doleful voice.

Ernest hesitated. He glanced at Tinkler for advice, as had become his habit. Surprisingly, this time he wore a completely blank expression—indeed, was elaborately pretending not to notice. Abruptly annoyed, Ernest drank half of what was left in his mug and reached a decision.

"If you don't think it's out of place," he said, "you may know . . . Tinkler!"

"Yes, sir?"

"Talked about me in here at all, have you?"

"Well, sir"—looking pained—"no more than is called for by ordinary politeness, I assure you."

"Don't worry, man! I only wanted to find out if they know that I do a bit of drawing and painting."

"That, sir, of course."

"Well, then . . ." Ernest took a deep breath. "Would you mind if I proposed a few ideas?"

Mingled doubt and excitement showed on all faces. Gaffer complained again about not knowing what was going on, and someone bent to explain. Before the murmured debate reached a conclusion he cut it short, rising effortfully to his feet.

"Don't turn it down! Remember it's the seventh year, and if we don't do it right then *she*—"

A dozen voices drowned out the rest.

"That's very handsome of you, sir," Hiram declared, and it was settled.

Feeling a renewal of that particular excitement which had possessed him earlier, Ernest said, "Well, now! You mentioned people sometimes took photographs of the—do you say well-dressings?"

"That's right, sir."

"So if I could look at a few of those, get the general idea . . . Tinkler, is something wrong?"

"Sir, I've noticed people are starting to look at the clock. Perhaps we should ask if they're expected home for dinner."

There was a rustle of relief, and Ernest rose in embarrassment. "I'm sorry, I wasn't thinking about the time!"

"Not at all, sir, not at all," Hiram countered. "But—well, there are some whose wives do be expecting 'em. As to the photographs, though . . . Jabez!"

The landlord looked round.

"Weren't there an album some place, with pictures in?"

"Why, indeed there were. I'll hunt around for un!"

"Excellent!" Ernest cried. "And I'll talk to the vicar as I promised. Tinkler, where did I put my hat . . .? Ah, thanks. Well, good afternoon, gentlemen!"

There was a long pause after the door swung shut. At last Jabez voiced the feelings of them all.

"*Proper* gentleman, 'e be. Calling *us* gentlemen! That'd've been Sir Roderick's way."

"But not," said his brother, " 'er ladyship's!"

At which, amid cynical laughter, the company made to disperse, only to be checked by an exclamation from Mr. Ames: "Just a moment!"

All heads turned.

Lapels aside, thumbs in the armholes of his waistcoat, wearing an expression that bordered on defiance, he said, "If you'll accept the support of Mr. Ernest, I dare to hope you'll accept the like from me. I have a porker I've been fattening for Mankley show. After living in the district for so long, and knowing"—a glance at Gaffer—"what store you set by the well-dressing feast, I hope you'll let me donate it for Ascensiontide instead."

For a long moment there was a sense of uncertainty. Hiram resolved the matter. Advancing on Ames, he offered his hand.

"Spoken as handsomely as Mr. Ernest!" he exclaimed. "Jabez! Before we go, draw one more mug—*for Henry!*"

"What be they going on about?" Gaffer demanded crossly.

The offer was explained to him, and also that in accepting it Hiram had addressed Mr. Ames by his Christian name.

Gaffer beamed.

" 'Tes like I always say," he declared. "Do right by 'er and she'll do right by us. Bain't it already begun?"

On returning to the Hall Tinkler insisted that his master eat something, and brought him cold meat, bread and pickles in the summerhouse. Lady Peake was taking her customary afternoon nap, so they were spared recriminations about her nephew's absence from the lunch-table.

Talking feverishly with his mouth full, Ernest at first exclaimed over and over about the excitement of finding a pre-Christian ceremony in a modern English village, and gave Tinkler positive orders to call at the vicarage and tell Miss Pollock he proposed to take up her invitation this very afternoon. Little by little the food and cider combined to make him drowsy, and in the end he muttered something about taking forty winks. Satisfied he was indeed asleep, Tinkler returned the tray to the kitchen and undertook his errand.

When he came back less than half an hour later, however, he found his master awake again and plagued by his old uncertainties. On being told that he was engaged for tea at four o'clock, he lapsed into his usual despondency.

"It's no use, Tinkler," he muttered. "I'm not up to it. You'll have to go back and apologize. How can I face the vicar? I don't believe in his religion! I'm likely to insult him in an unguarded moment, aren't I?"

"No, sir."

"What?" Ernest glanced up, blinking. "But you know damn' well I don't give a farthing for his mumbo-jumbo!"

"Yes, sir. But as a result of what has transpired today I am also aware that you take great interest in the survival of old customs. So does Mr. Pollock."

"But Mr. Stoddard said—"

"He seems to be mistaken. While I was at the vicarage I took the liberty of mentioning the subject to Mrs. Kail the housekeeper. She's local. And a very affable person, I may say. It is her opinion that were it up entirely to the vicar there would be no objection to resuming the ceremony."

Slowly—sluggishly—Ernest worked it out. He said at last, "You mean my aunt is once again the fly in the ointment?"

"It would appear so, sir."

"Hmm . . ." He glanced towards the house, towards the drawn curtains of his aunt's room. "In that case . . . All right, Tinkler. I'll put a bold face on it. But you come too. Go and pump Mrs.—did you say Kail? Yes?—and if I make a mess of it maybe you can think of a better approach next time."

He turned his gaze in the direction of the few cottages visible from here.

"They seem like decent people," he muttered, half inaudibly. "I don't want to let them down . . ."

"Good afternoon, Mr. Peake," said the vicar. His bespectacled face was deeply lined and his movements were stiff from arthritis, but his voice remained firm and resonant. "So glad you could join us. Do sit down."

Awkwardly, Ernest took his place at the table that had been set out in a shady arbor. Miss Pollock smiled at him and inquired whether he preferred Indian or China tea, then proffered plates of cakes and dainty fish-paste sandwiches.

But her smile struck Ernest as forced, and once again he wondered whether he was doing the right thing. His nerve had almost failed him again at the last moment, and he had been half minded to turn back, but Tinkler had kept on going and at last he had stumbled to catch up.

"I'm especially pleased you've come," the vicar continued, wiping a trace of tea from his upper lip with a wide white napkin. "I—ah—I have been hoping for a little chat with you."

About what? Instantly Ernest was on edge. Was there, after all, to be an argument about his non-attendance at church? In that case, the best form of defense was certainly attack. He countered, "As a matter of fact, padre"—the colloquial military term for a chaplain sprang automatically to his lips—"there's something I'd like to discuss with you as well. Apparently the people in the village . . ."

But the words trailed away. Miss Pollock had leaned forward, her expression troubled.

"If you don't mind, Mr. Peake, Grandfather did broach his subject first. And it concerns your aunt."

"It would," Ernest muttered.

"Excuse me?" the vicar said, cupping a hand to his ear. "I'm becoming a little hard of hearing, I'm afraid."

Disregarding him, his granddaughter said fiercely, "Have you heard what she's decided to do now?"

This sounded alarming. Ernest shook his head. "I'm afraid not. To be candid, I'm rather avoiding her at the moment."

"It's a scandal and a shame!" Under the table she stamped her small foot on the grass. Her grandfather laid a restraining touch on her arm, but she shook it off.

"I'm sorry, Grandfather, but I will not be silenced! What she intends to do is— is downright un-Christian!"

The old man sighed.

"Uncharitable at least, I must concede . . . But Mr. Peake doesn't yet know what we are talking about, does he?"

The girl swung to face the visitor.

"You heard about poor George Gibson's death?"

"Yes, of course."

"You know he was a laborer on your aunt's estate—not that he could do much work after being gassed?"

This time, a nod.

"And that he left a wife and three children?"

Another nod.

"Well, Sir Roderick said in his will he could stay in his cottage for life because he'd been wounded in the War. Now he's gone, your aunt intends to throw the family out. She told Mrs. Gibson today. They have one week."

"But that's disgraceful!" Ernest exclaimed. "Why?"

The vicar gave a gentle cough. She ignored it.

"Mrs. Gibson's youngest was born in March 1919."

For a moment Ernest failed to make the connection. Then he realized what the date implied. Slowly he said, "I take it you mean the youngest child is not her husband's?"

"How could it be? He'd been a prisoner of war since '17!" She leaned forward, her eyes beseeching. "But he'd forgiven her! He treated the child as he did his own—I saw. Why can't your aunt do the same? What gives her the right to pass this kind of 'moral' judgment? One week for the poor wretch to find a new home, or else it'll be the bailiffs and eviction!"

She was almost panting with the force of her tirade. In passing Ernest marvelled at how lovely it made her look. Previously he had thought of her as a rather pallid girl, meekly content to exist in her grandfather's shadow, but now there was color flaming in her cheeks and righteous anger in her voice.

At length he said, "Whoso shall offend one of these little ones . . ."

In a tone of unexpected cordiality the vicar said, "I gather from Alice that you are one of the unfortunates who lost his faith owing to the War, but I must say that is precisely the text that has been running through my own mind. An attitude such as your aunt's belongs to the old covenant which Our Lord came to replace with the gospel of love. We no longer think it proper that the sins of the ancestors should be visited on the children, and it is they who will suffer the worst."

Wasn't the War the visiting of our forebears' sins upon us, the young cannon-fodder?

But Ernest bit back the bitter comment. He said after a pause, "I have scant influence with my aunt, I'm afraid. What I can do, though, I certainly will."

"Thank you," Alice said, leaning forward and laying her slim hand on his. "Thank you very much. More tea? And now: what was it that you wanted to discuss with us?"

"Well, you see . . ." And clumsily he brought it out. By the time he was done the vicar had finished his tea and was sitting back with a reflective expression, polishing his glasses on his napkin.

"Ah yes. They do take the well-dressing very seriously, don't they? And indeed I myself see little harm in it. Of course one is aware that it began as a pagan custom, but then so did Christmas, being timed to coincide with the Roman Saturnalia."

"The tradition really is that ancient?"

"Oh, yes. And formerly very widespread, though Welstock is the only place in the West Country where it is, or was, kept up. The most notable survivals are in Derbyshire, where several villages adhere to the custom. Its nature is much altered, naturally. The 'feast' you referred to was originally a sacrifice, indeed a human sacrifice, to the patron spirit of water. The Romans knew her as Sabellia, but that was a corruption of an even earlier name. She was also an embodiment of springtime, associated, as one might expect, with the fertility of plants and animals. Including—ah—human animals."

"Yet you saw no objection to continuing the rite?" Ernest couldn't keep the puzzlement out of his voice.

"It's been efficiently disinfected, as it were," answered the vicar with a thin smile. "Indeed the villagers no longer know that there was a heathen spirit, or goddess, connected with the ceremony. At least I never heard any of them mention her name. They do still refer to 'she,' but pronouns in the local dialect tend to be somewhat interchangeable, and at worst they tend to identify her with the Virgin. That smacks of Mariolatry, of course, which I am professionally unable to countenance, but at least it lacks specifically pagan associations."

"And I think it's rather fun," Alice said. "I remember when I was a little girl, following the procession around from well to well. The pictures Mr. Faber used to make were so clever, too! And using such ordinary bits and pieces! Grandfather!" She turned to the vicar. "I think Mr. Peake has had a wonderful idea! Let's put our feet down, and insist on reviving the well-dressing this year!"

"I'm absolutely on your side," Ernest said fervently. "If you'll forgive me saying so, despite her apparent devoutness I cannot regard my aunt as—"

"As a good advertisement for religion?" the vicar interpolated gently. "No more, alas, can I. To my mind, these simple souls who want to celebrate the miracle of water, even more than bread the staff of life, have a deeper faith than she will ever attain—save, of course," he added, as to reproach himself for lack of charity, "by the grace of God, which I trust will reveal to her the beam in her own eye . . . Mr. Peake, I believe you have convinced me!"

He gave the table an open-palmed slap that made the teacups rattle, and winced as though regretting the impulse.

"We'll strike a bargain, shall we? We shall both defy Lady Peake! I shall announce that the well-dressing is to be resumed; you, for your part, will do your best to save the Gibson family from eviction."

It's not going to be easy . . .

But the thought only flashed across Ernest's mind for a fraction of a second. At once he was extending his hand to the vicar.

"Agreed, padre! It's a deal!"

When tea was over, Alice offered to accompany him to the gate. He was about to protest that it wasn't necessary when he realized that she wanted to say something more, out of hearing of her grandfather.

And when she uttered it, he was astounded.

At the very last moment before they separated she caught him by the arm.

"Mr. Peake—or may I call you Ernest? My name is Alice, as you know."

"Please do," he stammered.

"Ernest, do your utmost for Mrs. Gibson, won't you? What happened to her is so—so understandable! It could have happened to anybody during the War. It could . . ." She withdrew a pace, standing bolt upright, and looked him straight in the eyes.

"It could have happened to me."

"You mean—"

"Yes. I was Gerald's mistress. And before you ask, I do not feel in the least like a Fallen Woman! I'm only glad that he had the chance to become a complete man before his life was cut short . . . Have I shocked you? I apologize if so."

Ernest looked at her as though for the first time. He read defiance in her face, noted that her small hands were clenched, remembered that her voice had trembled as she made her admission. To his amazement, he heard himself say, "No, Alice. You haven't shocked me, not at all. My only feeling is that your Gerald was a very lucky man."

"Thank you," she whispered, and darted forward and gave him a brief kiss on the cheek before hastening away.

"Wait!" Ernest cried.

"I can't!"

"But I forgot to send a message to Tinkler—my man! Tell him I'm returning to the Hall!"

"Yes! Yes, of course! Goodbye!"

All the way home Ernest's head was spinning in a maelström of confused impressions. But the strongest was this: that for the first time (and in how unexpected a setting!) he had met a girl with more courage than a man.

By sheer force of will he compelled himself to be polite to his aunt at the dinner-table, chatting—for so long as the maid was in the room—about his visit to the vicarage (which mellowed her a trifle), the beauty of the area, and his vague plans to paint several views of it. He was unable to resist a few indirect comments about the plight of rural communities nowadays, but managed to avoid any overt references to either the Gibson children or her refusal to lend her mower to the cricket-team. Not until coffee was served in the drawing-room, and they were alone, did he steer the talk around to the former of those two subjects.

Then, adopting his most reasonable tone, he observed that the vicar, and particularly Miss Pollock, seemed very worried about the fate hanging over Mrs. Gibson and especially her children.

But at the mere mention of the name Lady Peake's face froze as hard as marble.

"You will oblige me by making no further mention of the matter. The woman is a sinner, and she must be punished for her sin."

"But, aunt, it's not the fault of the children that—"

"Be silent, sir! It is the duty of those in a position of authority to ensure that Christian values are upheld. That is what I am doing."

Oh, what's the use? But at least I tried . . .

"I see," he said after a pause. "Well, I must ask you to excuse me. I have some work to do."

"Work?"

"Yes"—setting aside his empty cup. "Amongst other things, I found out today about the well-dressing ceremony. It's to be revived this year, and I've offered to prepare some designs for it." He rose with a slight bow.

"You will do nothing of the kind!" his aunt thundered. "It's naked paganism!"

"You think so?" Ernest was very conscious of the way his heart was pounding, but he kept his voice steady. "The vicar doesn't. Indeed he said it has been completely Christianized with the passing of the years. And the designs I have in mind have an immaculately biblical basis. Good evening, aunt, and if I don't see you again before bedtime, good night."

He closed the door before she could erupt again.

Once in his room, however, staring at the first sheet from his portfolio, he suddenly found his mind as blank as the paper. He kept imagining what Mrs. Gibson's state of mind must be, alone in her isolated cottage, perhaps with the children crying, not knowing whether they would have a roof over their heads a week from now. He was still sitting, pencil in lax fingers, when Tinkler came in to turn down the bed, lay out his pajamas, and mix his final draught of tincture of valerian. On his way to draw the curtains, he inquired sympathetically, "Shortage of inspiration, sir?"

Tossing the pencil angrily aside, Ernest rose and began to pace the room. "Yes," he muttered. "I thought I had a lot of ideas. I thought for instance I might base something on the story of the three wise men, and show scenes from various parts of the Empire where one might imagine them to have hailed from. My people once took me to a church in Goa, in India, where they claim to have originally been converted by the Apostle Thomas. And I've seen services in Singapore, too, and Hong Kong. I was very young at the time, but I still remember a lot of details. But it seems—well—somehow wrong!" Slumping back into his chair, he concluded, "You've talked to the local folk much more than I have. Any suggestions?"

Tinkler hesitated for a moment. At length he said, "If I'm not presuming, sir—"

"Out with it!"

"Well, sir, are there not stories from the New Testament that would be more relevant to the present situation? For example, how about the woman taken in adultery?"

For an instant Ernest sat as though thunderstruck. Then he snapped his fingers.

"Of course! And Mary Magdalene—and the woman who met Jesus at the well! *That's* apt, if you like! There's a Bible under the night-table, isn't there? Pass it to me, there's a good chap."

Complying, Tinkler said, "Will there be anything else?"

"Hm? Oh—no, not tonight. You can turn in."

"Thank you, sir. Good night."

And he was gone, having uncharacteristically forgotten to draw the curtains.

By the time the church clock struck eleven-thirty Ernest was surrounded by a dozen rough sketches. Without seeing the promised photographs of Mr. Faber's creations he had no idea whether they would prove acceptable, but he had a subconscious conviction that they would, for into the background of each he had contrived to incorporate a haughty, self-righteous figure modelled on his aunt. At first he had considered portraying her full-face, but then bethought himself of the difficulty of showing fine detail using a mosaic of natural objects bedded in clay, and concluded it would be best to depict her turning her back on those in need of help. Was that not most appropriate?

Yawning, stretching, he set aside the drawings and rose. Turning to the window, meaning to close the curtains, he checked in mid-movement.

Beyond the trees that fringed the left side of the garden, there was a fitful red glow.

For a moment he thought his eyes were playing tricks. Then he whistled under his breath.

"That's a house on fire, or I'm a Dutchman . . . Tinkler! *Tinkler!*" And, seizing the blazer he had hung on the back of his chair with one hand, with the other he tugged frantically on the bell-pull.

He met his valet in a nightshirt on the landing, looking sleepily puzzled, and explained in a rush.

"Get some clothes on! Rouse the coachman and tell him to wake everyone he can! There isn't a fire-engine in Welstock, is there?"

"I believe it has to come from the next village, sir."

"Then tell them to bring buckets and ladders. Dr. Castle had better be woken up, too; someone might be hurt."

"Where is the fire, sir? " Tinkler demanded.

"Over *that* way, but you can't miss it. I'll go via the vicarage and have the bells rung . . . What's wrong?"

"There's only one cottage near the house on that side of the estate, sir. And that's Mrs. Gibson's."

"What is this *infernal* row?" a stern voice demanded. Through her partly-opened bedroom door his aunt was peering.

"There's a house on fire, and Tinkler says it must be the Gibsons'!"

He couldn't see his aunt's expression, but he could picture it. Because he heard her say, "It's a visitation, then."

"*What?*" Beside himself with rage, Ernest took a pace toward her. But Tinkler caught his arm.

"The alarm, sir—the church bells! That's the important thing."

"Yes. Yes, you're right. The rest can wait. But not for long . . ."

And he was hobbling down the stairs, outside into the clear spring night, across the garden towards the vicarage. From here the smoke was already pungent, and he could hear faint cries.

By shouting and hammering on the oaken door, he managed to rouse a middle-aged woman armed with a poker whom he took for Mrs. Kail. He uttered instructions as though he were again briefing his men against an enemy attack: *do this now, then do that, then come and help.* And was off again, struggling through thorns and underbrush on the straightest line to the burning cottage. Before he reached it a ragged clang was sounding from the tower.

The fire had obviously begun in an ill-repaired chimney, for it was still uttering most of the smoke. But by now the adjacent thatch was well alight. Outside, weeping and terrified, were three scantily-clad children. Where was their mother—? He glimpsed her through the open door, striving to rescue her pitiful possessions. At that moment she turned back with her arms full of oddments, coughing and choking and with tears streaming from her reddened eyes. She had on nothing but a soiled linen shift.

Limping forward, he shouted that she mustn't go inside again, but she seemed not to hear, and he had to hurry after and drag her away by force. She fought to break his grip, whimpering.

"I've raised the alarm! Help will be here soon! Look to your children!"

There was a sudden crackling of trodden sticks behind him, and he turned gratefully to the first of the promised helpers, whom he took for a young man in the dimness.

"See if you can find a ladder! We'll need a bucket-chain until the engine comes! Where can we get water—? *Alice!*"

To his amazement, it was indeed. She had donned, practically enough, boots and trousers and an old jersey. Women in trousers or breeches had been a common enough sight during the War, but he hadn't seen one since and certainly had not expected to in Welstock. He was still at a loss when more half-glimpsed figures arrived at the double, laden with buckets and an invaluable ladder.

"I'll take care of her and the children," Alice said. "Take them to the vicarage and calm them down. You get things organized. There's a pump round the back."

Her coolness steadied his own racing thoughts. He issued brisk orders. By the time the fire-engine negotiated the rutted lane that was the only access to the cottage the unburnt portion of the thatch had been saturated and despite the mingled smoke and steam coachman Roger, who had been first to the top of the ladder, had begun to douse the glowing rafters.

Realizing that hoses were playing on the roof, Ernest discovered his eyes were full of tears. Some were due to smoke, no doubt, but he felt that more stemmed from the sight of this small tragedy, one more burden inflicted on an innocent victim.

"You can come away now," a soft voice said at his side. "You've done wonders. Without you, the whole place would have been in ruins."

Blearily he looked at Alice. He wasn't the only one. Now they had been relieved, the volunteers were staring at her too, and one or two of their expressions were disapproving, as to say, "Her, in trousers? Shocking!"

He heard the imagined words in the voice of his aunt, and remembered what Tinkler had said about the glint in her eyes . . . Where was he, anyhow? Oh, over there, talking to the Stoddards.

"I don't want to go back under that woman's roof," he said without intention. "Know what she said when I told her Mrs. Gibson's house was burning down? She said it was a visitation on her!"

"You don't have to," Alice answered. "Not tonight. I can make up a bed at the vicarage. And I'll run you a bath, too. You need one."

For the first time Ernest realized he was grimy from head to toe with smoke.

And utterly exhausted.

"All right," he muttered. "Thanks. Let Tinkler know."

Oddly, during what was left of the night, for the first time in years his sleep was free from fearful dreams.

It was broad daylight. Opening his eyes, he discovered himself in a narrow bed, in a small room under the eaves, wearing—good heavens—his skin. Memory surged back. Alice had apologized for the fact that her grandfather had retired again and she didn't want to disturb him by creeping into his room in search of nightwear he could borrow, but produced a large towel that she said would do to cover him returning from his bath.

Someone, though, had stolen into this room while he was asleep. Neatly arranged on a chair were clean clothes, his own, and underneath a pair of shoes awaited him.

Bless you, Tinkler!

Abruptly he discovered he was ravenous. Rising, dressing hastily, he went downstairs, finding his way by guesswork. This was an old and rambling house, with many misleading passages and stairways, but eventually he located the entrance hall—and Mr. Pollock.

"Good morning, young fellow! I understand from Alice that you did sterling work last night!"

Embarrassed, Ernest shrugged. "I just happened to be the only person awake, I suppose. I spotted the fire by sheer chance."

"Professionally," the vicar murmured, "I tend not to think in terms of 'sheer chance' . . . The Gibsons, you'll be glad to know, are in reasonable spirits this morning; Mrs. Kail is looking after them. But we'll talk about that later. In the meantime, how about breakfast?"

"I'll get it for him," Alice said, appearing in one of the hall's many doorways. She looked amazingly fresh, considering the experiences of the night. Looking at her—she had put on a brown dress this morning, as plain as her usual gray—Ernest wondered how, even for a moment and in trousers, he could have mistaken her for a boy.

"There's no need," he protested. "Tinkler can—"

"Tinkler has gone to fetch the rest of your belongings."

He stared blankly. The vicar explained.

"I hope you won't be upset, Mr. Peake, but—well, you did say, I believe, that you couldn't face another night under your aunt's roof?"

"I . . . Well, yes, actually I did."

"It would appear that the feeling is mutual. First thing this morning, I received a note from her ladyship to the effect that if I proceed with plans to revive the well-dressing she will report me to my bishop and invoke ecclesiastical discipline. Apparently I am embroiling you, who are already a soul in danger of damnation, in pagan rites that will doom you past redemption. Fortunately"—his usual thin smile—"I happen to know that my bishop is, like myself, something of an antiquary, and had taken the precaution of notifying him of my intentions. I confidently predict that he will cast his vote in my favor."

"You must forgive us, Ernest," Alice said. "But we have taken the liberty of temporarily re-planning your life. We consulted Mr. Tinkler, and it was his view as well as ours that you might be better able to concentrate on your designs for the well-dressings here rather than at the Hall. Do you mind very much?"

"Do I mind?" Ernest blurted. "I'd give anything to be out of that—that Gorgon's lair! I can't say how grateful I am!"

"There are," the vicar said sententiously, "many in Welstock this morning who are equally grateful to yourself . . . Alice, my dear: you promised Mr. Peake some breakfast?"

"Of course. Right away. Come along!"

Ernest could scarcely believe the transformation in his life. About noon a delegation from the village waited on him—he had to use the archaic term, for they were so determined to make it a formal occasion—led by Hiram Stoddard, who presented his publican brother's apologies, as well as Henry Ames, who practically overnight seemed to have been accepted as a full member of the community, and into the bargain Gaffer Tatton, who declared more than once that it would have taken far worse than rheumatism to keep him at home today. Apparently he was some sort of distant cousin of the Gibsons; probably, Ernest thought wryly, they all were.

They moved a vote of thanks to him in the drawing-room and uttered three solemn cheers, which struck him as rather silly since there were only eight of them, but kindly intended. Trying not to seem unappreciative, he contrived at last to drag the conversation around to something that interested him far more, and sent Tinkler for his sketches.

"Of course, I still haven't seen your brother's photographs, Mr. Stoddard," he said as he diffidently removed them from the portfolio. "But would something on these lines serve? You'll notice"—he recalled and consciously echoed Tinkler's remark—"they are in a sense relevant to certain recent events around here."

For a moment they seemed not to catch the reference. Then, unexpectedly, Gaffer Tatton banged the floor with his stick. "'Tes the very thing!" he exclaimed. "Bain't it to do *her* honor as we dress the wells? She'm bound to be pleased. Don't all on 'em show ladies?"

Ernest was about to comment light-heartedly—light-headedly?—that "lady" was perhaps a misnomer for somebody like Mary Magdalene, when he realized it would have struck a false note. Grave, they were all nodding their agreement.

"Well, sir, we'll get the boards cut by the weekend," Hiram said. "And puddle the clay ready. Can you tell us what colors you have in mind, so we can set the young 'uns to gathering the right bits and pieces?"

"I haven't finished working that out," Ernest admitted. "But I can give you a rough idea. For instance . . ."

And spent a happy quarter of an hour explaining.

It was not until they had left that an odd, disturbing point occurred to him.

The central female figure in each of his three designs bore a remarkable likeness—in his imagination, at least—to Alice Pollock.

What had Gaffer Tatton said? That "she" would certainly be pleased! But he, equally certainly, must have been thinking of a different "she" . . .

Customary doubt assailed him yet again. This time, though, he drove it back, secure in the conviction he had found a worthwhile task at last.

"You may be pleased to hear," the vicar said at lunch a few days later, "that the eviction of the Gibsons from their cottage may not prove as simple as Lady Peake might hope."

Ernest, who had been thinking as little as possible about his aunt and as much as possible about the wells, came to himself with a start.

"How is that?" he inquired.

"The chief fire-officer who attended the conflagration has submitted a report, a copy of which I saw this morning. He says the chimney of the cottage had been long neglected, and its upkeep is not the responsibility of the tenant, but of the landlord. A high proportion of the Gibsons' belongings were inevitably damaged, many beyond recall. One of my nephews is a solicitor, and he informs me that the possibility arises of a claim for financial recompense."

"You mean the Gibsons might get some money out of my aunt?" The family were lodging as best they could in one of the vicarage stables, but while this was tolerable in warm weather their stay could not be indefinitely prolonged.

"Blood from a stone," Alice sighed. "But it's worth a try."

"I meant to ask!" Ernest exclaimed. "Sorry to change the subject, but what did the bishop say?"

A twinkle came and went in Mr. Pollock's eyes. "At the risk of sounding vain, I think I may claim that my knowledge of my superiors is as much—ah—*superior* to her ladyship's as is my acquaintance with the principles of doctrine. He went so far as to ask why I had let such an interesting old custom lapse for so long."

"*She* will be pleased," Ernest murmured.

"I beg your pardon?"

"Nothing—nothing. Just quoting someone from the village, one of the people who've been advising me about the well-dressings. By the way, I'm not quite as sure as you about their having completely forgotten the patron spirit of water. But we can discuss that some other time. For now, just remind me of the date of Ascension Day. Since moving here I've lost track of time."

"It's next Thursday," Alice supplied.

"Really! Then I'd better tell them to get a move on!"

"Don't."

"Excuse me . . . ?"

"I said don't!"—with a smile. "They set too much store by this to brook delay. Everything you need will be ready, that I promise."

That evening, strolling in the garden after dinner, he dared to kiss her for the first time. And on Sunday he attended church and sat beside her, ;and took much pleasure in ignoring his aunt's glares.

The glint was in her eye again, though, and thinking of it made shivers tremble down his spine.

The wells that had drawn the first settlers to the site of this village would, Ernest felt, more properly have been called springs. The first he visited was the closest to his own vision of a well, being surrounded by a stone coping and covered with a makeshift roof, but that was of corrugated iron, and there was neither windlass nor bucket and chain. The second was even more disappointing, for its water had been diverted to first a pump in the main square, then public taps at various points nearby, and eventually individual homes. Now only isolated cottages—like the Gibsons'—lacked at least cold water in the scullery. As to the third, which supplied the part of the village nearest the Hall, there was no sign of it at all below the stone facing that supported the track up to the church. (There were two others, in the grounds of the Hall and the vicarage, but they had of course never been available for general use . . . or dressing at Ascensiontide.)

Leaning on his stick in unconscious imitation of his guide Gaffer Tatton, whom he sometimes found hard to understand, he ventured, "One would scarcely imagine there was a well below here, would one?"

"Ah, but there be!" was the prompt response. "Don't go too close, will 'ee, sir? I recall last time the cover on it were made good—see, 'tes under mould now, and that there grass." He pointed at the base of the wall with his stick. "Deepest on 'em all, it were. Time and past time we dug un out and mended tiles."

"Tiles?"

"Can't see en, but they're there. I recall helping to mend un. I were a boy then. Saw the way on un. Jes' a few tiles. Ah, but good mortar! Best kind! Mr. Howard the builder, 'twere as done it. Still, 'tes in the nature o' things. Don't last for ever, do un? And 'tes time and past time we mended un again. She don't care for being overlooked, she don't."

Greatly daring, Ernest countered, "She . . . ?"

"Ah, 'tes all old stories, sir. We tell un round the chimney-corner come winter, that we do. Fine day like this bain't no time for such chitter-chatter . . . Well, sir, what do you think o' the way they changed your drawings for to fit the boards?"

"I think there's more talent in the village than people admit," Ernest answered honestly. "They could have worked something out by themselves. I don't think you needed me."

"Ah, sir!" Gaffer Tatton leaned firmly on his stick again, staring his companion directly in the eyes. "That's where you be wrong. If you'll excuse me. It's you exactly that we do be needing."

And, before Ernest could inquire what he meant, he was consulting an old pocket-watch.

"Time be a-wasting, sir. Waits for no man, as they say."

"Just a moment!" Ernest exclaimed. "When you said 'she,' were you referring to—?"

"I bain't saying more, sir," the old man grunted. "There be some as believes and some as don't. Though when you've lived in Welstock long as me—"

"I haven't had to," Ernest said.

It was the other's turn to be puzzled. He said, "Do I understand 'ee right, sir?"

"I hope so." Ernest drew back a pace or two and gazed up at the Hall, silhouetted against the bright sky. "*She* can be kind, but she can also be cruel. Isn't that so?"

Gaffer Tatton was totally at a loss. Eventually, however, he found words.

"I knew it!" he burst out. "Couldn't a-drawn them pictures 'less . . ."

"Well? Go on!"—impatiently.

"The rest bain't for me to say, sir, but for you to find out. Same as we all do. Same as we all must. But I'll tell 'ee this: you'm on the right track. Good day!"

"What do you think he meant?" Ernest fretted to Alice after dinner that night.

"Could he have been talking about nature?" she suggested.

"I suppose so, but—"

"Nature personified? You hinted that you don't believe grandfather when he claims they've all forgotten the origin of well-dressing."

"It fits," he admitted. "People always say 'Mother' Nature, don't they? Even though—"

"What?"

He drew a deep breath. "Living here instead of at the Hall, even though I recall what my aunt has said and done, I find it incredibly hard to believe the cruel side of her."

"You aren't talking about your aunt," Alice said perceptively.

"No, I'm not."

"But she's an aspect of the female principle, too."

"I can't think of her that way!"

"Then what about Kali—Kali Durga?"

Taken aback, he demanded, "How do you know about her?"

"From Grandfather's library, of course. You were brought up in India, a place I've never been and very likely never shall, and it's no secret that I want to know more about you, is it? So I've made a start. Grandfather has a lot of old books about missionary work abroad . . . Did you ever witness one of her ceremonies?"

"No, and I'm rather glad!"

"I think I'd be interested—provided, of course, I could just watch from a distance . . . But do you accept my point? There are all those millions of people, much closer to the primitive state than we are, or at any rate believe we are, and they know nature can be cruel as well as kind."

"Yes, of course. But if you're thinking of the well-dressing—"

"Every seventh year there used to be a human sacrifice. Grandfather said so. This year Mr. Ames is offering a pig. Did you ever hear a pig squeal when they slaughter it—? Oh, that was a rotten thing to say. I keep forgetting, because you're such a nice person. You've heard men scream while they were dying, haven't you?"

"Did"—his mouth was suddenly dry as though he had found himself confronting an unexpected rival—"did Gerald tell you about that?"

"He had to tell someone."

"Yes. Yes, of course." Ernest licked his lips.

"Have you ever told anyone? Tinkler?"

"I don't have to tell him. We went through it together."

The glint in my aunt's eyes, the same as that general's—and he recognized it too . . .

"Then a doctor?"

"The doctors I've talked to weren't there. Maybe they can imagine it, but they never saw it."

"Surely, though, doctors too see people die. Horribly, sometimes. In railway accidents, for instance—or burning houses. Worse yet, after operations that went wrong."

"An accident can't be helped. War is deliberate."

"Yes, of course . . . So you haven't ever found anyone to tell?"

He shook his head.

"Then what about me?" She reached for his hand and drew him unresisting to a seat. "I know you think of India as an old unchanging land, but there are more things in England that haven't changed than most people are prepared to admit. Under the veneer of 'tradition' and 'ancient custom' there remain the superstitions that were once a religious faith. Isn't the central mystery of Christianity a human sacrifice? And, come to that, communion involves symbolic cannibalism!"

"What would your grandfather say if—?"

"If he heard me talking like this? He'd accuse me of plagiarism."

"You mean it was he who—?"

"He's a very broad-minded person. Hadn't you noticed? Why do you think I can spend so much time unchaperoned?"

Ernest looked a desperate question that he did not dare to formulate in words.

"I can read your thoughts from your face," Alice murmured. "Did he know about me and Gerald? I don't know. I never asked. I never shall. He very likely guessed, but he never behaved any differently towards me, and when the bad news came"— a quiver in her voice—"he was wonderful . . . Are you jealous of Gerald?"

"No. Sometimes I wonder why not. But I can't be. I find myself wishing that I'd met him. I think we'd have been friends."

"I think so, too." She squeezed his hand. "Now tell me what you couldn't say to anyone before."

"I'll try," he whispered. "I will try . . ."

And out it came, like pus from a boil: the remembered and the imaginary horrors, the images from a borderland between nightmare come alive and reality become nightmare; what it was like to realize you were obeying the orders of a crazy man, and had no escape from them; how it felt to choke one's guts up in a gale of poison gas, to watch one's comrades' very bodies rotting in the putrefaction of the sodden trenches, to shake a man's hand knowing it must be for the last time, for impersonal odds decreed that one or the other of you would be dead by sundown; taking aim at an enemy sniper spotted in a treetop or a belfry, as coolly as at a sitting rabbit, and not remembering until the flailing arms had vanished that the target was a human being like oneself . . .

And endlessly the howling-crashing of the shells, the chatter of machine guns, the racket, the hell-spawned racket that had silenced the very songbirds in the man-made desolation all around.

She sat very still, face pale in the dim light, without expression, never letting go his hand no matter how he cramped her fingers. When he finished he was crying, tears creeping down his cheeks like insects.

But he felt purged. And what she said, as she drew him close and kissed his tears away, was this:

"I met a woman from London who visited the Hall during the war. She called on us and boasted about her 'war work.' It consisted in handing out white feathers to men who weren't in uniform. I remember how I wished I could have kidnapped her and sent her to the Front with the VAD's."

He said, completely unexpectedly, "I love you."

"Yes. I know," was her reply. "I'm glad."

"You—knew?"

"Oh, my dear!" She let go his hand at last and leaned back, laughing aloud. "That's something that you've never learned to hide! The talk in the servants' hall has been of nothing else all week, and all around the village, I imagine. Your aunt, I hear, is absolutely scandalized, but since her setback vis-à-vis the bishop—"

"Stop, for pity's sake! You're making my head spin!"

At once she was contrite.

"Yes, of course. It was a dreadful thing to pour your heart out as you did, and I should have left you in peace immediately. But"—she was rising and withdrawing—"if anyone has bad dreams tonight, let it be me who wasn't there and wished she could have been, to help."

And she was gone, as instantly as the embodiment of . . .

Suddenly I know who She is, that Gaffer Tatton spoke of. The thought came unbidden. It seemed to echo from the waters that underlay the hill, and phrases from childhood crowded his mind: the waters beneath the earth. . .

Also he remembered Kali, garlanded with human skulls, and could not stop himself from shuddering.

"Well, Mr. Ernest!" Hiram Stoddard said. "What do you think of what we've made out of your sketches? Have we done them justice?"

Ernest stared at the three great boards on which his designs had been interpreted by pressing odds and ends, all natural, into white soft clay. Half his mind wanted to say that this wasn't what he had envisaged, this transformation into bones and leaves and cones and feathers—yet the other, perhaps the older and the wiser half, approved at once. How ingeniously, for example, in every case, they had caught the implication of another, older woman's half-turned back as she spurned the central figure, calling her a sinner justifiably due for punishment! Indeed, they had added something by taking something away. His detestation of his aunt had led him, as he abruptly recognized, to give too much emphasis to her effigy. Now, as he studied the pictures ranked before him, he noticed that the villagers had left her prominent in the first that would be blessed tomorrow, reduced her in the second, left her isolated in a corner of the third which would be set in Old Well Road . . .

Primitive it may be, he thought. *But many of the major French artists, and not a few of our own, have turned to the art not just of primitives but of savages in recent years. Maybe it's because of the savagery we so-called civilized nations have proved capable of . . . Yes, they're right. Their changes are correct.*

He said as much aloud, and those who had been anxiously standing by relaxed and set off to install the boards at their appointed places, ready for tomorrow morning's ceremony. Only at the last moment did it occur to him that he must take one final glance.

Checking in dismay as he called them back, they waited for his ultimate verdict.

But it was all right after all. He already knew that the resemblance between the main female figures and Alice had been efficiently disguised by its interpretation into whatever could be pressed into the clay, with pebbles for eyes and twigs and leaves for hair. For a moment, though, he had been afraid that he might have put too much of himself into the other major figure, who was Jesus . . .

"Don't you fret, sir," muttered Gaffer Tatton at his side, arriving heralded by the stump-stump of his stick. "You do understand. Didn't need me to tell 'ee."

And he was gone again before Ernest could reply, and the board-carriers, escorted by a gang of cheering children and Miss Hicks the teacher, seizing the chance for an open-air history lecture, were on their way to the wells.

He lay long awake that night, as though on the eve of his first one-man show, the kind of thing he had dreamed of when as a boy in India he had marvelled at the images contrived from *ghee* and leaves and petals to celebrate a Hindu festival. Why had he not noticed the connection sooner? Perhaps the iron curtain of the War had shut it out. But tonight he could sense a pulsing in the very landscape, as though an aboriginal power were heaving underground.

The waters beneath the earth. . .

Waking afraid in darkness, feeling as though the old and solid house were rocking back and forth like Noah's Ark, he groped for matches on the bedside table. There was an electric generator at the Hall, but the vicarage was still lit by lamps and candles. When he could see, he forced out faintly, "Alice!"

She was closing the door behind her. In a flimsy nightgown and barefoot, she stole across the floor as if she knew which boards might creak and could avoid them.

"I didn't mean to come," she said in a musing voice, as though puzzled at herself. "Not yet, at any rate. Not until tomorrow when it's over. But I couldn't stop myself. Do you feel something changing, Ernest?"

The match burned his fingers. By touch she prevented him from lighting another, and guided the box back to the table. He heard it rattle as it fell. Something else fell too, with a faint swishing sound, and she was beside him, arms and legs entwined with his.

"Do you feel something changing?" she insisted.

"I feel as though the whole world is changing!"

"Perhaps it is. But not for the worse. Not now, at any rate . . . Oh, my beloved! *Welcome back from hell!*"

Her hands were tugging at his pajamas, and in a moment there was nothing but the taste and scent of love, and its pressure, and delight.

"If . . ." he said later, into darkness.

Understanding him at once, she interrupted. "So what? You're going to marry me, I hope."

"Of course. Even so—"

She closed his lips with a finger. "Remember this is a part of the world where the old ways endure. Did anyone you met here condemn Mrs. Gibson, for example?"

"Just my aunt."

"Did anybody tell you how soon after the wedding Mrs. Gibson bore her first?"

"Ah—no!"

"It must have been conceived last time the seventh year came round. They didn't marry until he got his call-up papers, though they were long engaged. The second followed one of his leaves, and you know about the third. They take it as natural. Some may think ill of us. I won't. Nor they."

"I won't think ill of you! Ever!" He sealed the promise with a frantic kiss.

"Even if I steal away now?"

"Alice darling—"

"I cannot be found here in the morning, can I? No matter how tolerant Grandfather is! No, you must let me go." She was suiting action to word, sliding out of bed, donning her nightgown again. "We have a lifetime before us. Let's not squander it in advance."

"You're right," he sighed. "I wish I had half your sense."

"And I wish I had half the presence of mind you showed when Mrs. Gibson's fire broke out. Between us"—she bent to bestow a final kiss on his forehead—"we should make quite a team . . . *What was that?*"

The air had been rent by a scream: faint, distant, but unbelievably shrill, like the cry of a damned soul.

Sitting up, Ernest snatched at a possibility.

"It sounded like a stuck pig! Mr. Ames has offered a pig for tomorrow—does the tradition include sacrificing it at midnight?"

"Not that I know of! But it'll have woken half the neighborhood, whatever it is! I must fly!"

And she was gone.

For a moment Ernest was determined to ignore the noise. He wanted to lie back and recall the delicious proof of love that she had given him. It was no use, though. Within moments he heard noises from below. The rest of the household was awake. After what he had done on the night of the fire, it behooved him to rouse himself. He was already struggling back into his clothes when Tinkler tapped on the door.

"Coming!" he said resignedly.

And, when he descended to the hallway, found Alice there—attired again in jersey and trousers, and looking indescribably beautiful.

Not just looking. Being. Something has entered into that girl . . . Wrong. She was a girl. Now she's a woman.

And an extraordinary corollary followed.

I wonder whether anybody else will notice.

They did.

This time it wasn't he who wore the mantle of authority. She did. She quieted Mrs. Kail, sent her to tell her grandfather he could go back to sleep, and found a lantern and set forth with him down towards Old Well Road and the site of the third of the well-dressings.

Where others had already begun to gather, also bearing lanterns. Among them was Gaffer Tatton, fully dressed. Sensing Ernest's surprise, Alice murmured, "He lives in that cottage opposite. And alone. I don't suppose he takes his clothes off very often."

Ernest couldn't help smiling. That explained a lot!

But why was he so happy? Why was he blatantly holding his companion's hand as they joined the others? He couldn't work it out. He felt as though he were in the grip of a power beyond himself, and kept looking to Alice for guidance.

But she offered none, and none came from anyone else, until they had reached the bottom of the slope and were able to see what the rest of the people were staring at.

The well-dressing was unharmed. But, immediately before it, at the spot where Gaffer Tatton had told him grass was growing on leaf-mould that had accumulated over nothing stronger than tiles and mortar, there was a gaping hole.

And, lying on the ground nearby, there was a mallet.

Realization slowly dawned. Ernest said faintly, "Is it . . . ?"

"We think so, sir." Hiram Stoddard emerged into the circle of light cast by the lanterns. "It were young Roger as tipped us off. Here, young feller, you're old enough to speak for yourself."

And Roger the coachman was thrust forward from the crowd.

"Well, sir," he began awkwardly, "since you left the Hall her ladyship has been acting stranger and stranger. In the middle of the night we heard her getting up. I was roused by May—that's her maid, sir, as sleeps in the room next to hers. She said the mistress had gone out, muttering to herself like." An enormous gulp. "She said she thought—excuse me, sir—she must have taken leave of her senses!"

"So?"

Ernest would have liked to be the one to say that. In fact it was Alice. Very calm, totally heedless of what the men around might think of her masculine attire.

"Well, sir . . ." Roger shifted uneasily from foot to foot. "As you know, sir, there's a mallet kept next to the dinner gong at the Hall. I saw it were gone. I couldn't think on anyone else as mighta taken it."

Ernest bent to pick up the mallet. He said, turning it over, "Yes, I recognize it. You think she set out to smash the well-dressings?"

Everyone relaxed, most noticeably Gaffer Tatton, who nudged those nearest to him in the ribs.

"It would fit," Alice said in a strained voice. "Only she didn't know how weak the cover was. Being so fat . . ."

"Ah!"—from Gaffer Tatton. "She'll do for two, she will."

The others pretended not to understand, but even Ernest got the point. At length:

"Weren't nothing anybody could do," Hiram declared, and there was a murmur of agreement.

Ernest glanced from face to face. He knew, in that moment, that this was what they'd hoped might happen. It would be no use arguing that if they had turned out sooner in response to the scream they might have saved his aunt's life. Anyway, why should they? He would not have wanted to . . .

Again he sensed the presence of a power beneath the ground. Here, in the lonely small hours of the night, he could clearly hear for the first time the rushing of the water far below.

No longer pure, of course.

"Bring hooks and ropes," he ordered gruffly. "We'll pull her up. And people who use the water from this well had best avoid it for the time being."

"We thought of that, sir," Hiram said. "Those who draw on it will let their taps run the rest of the night."

"Wash her away," said Gaffer Tatton with a gap-toothed smile, and plodded back across the road to home.

"Will you carry on with the well-dressing?" Ernest said, red-eyed at an early breakfast-table.

"Yes, of course."

"You don't think it's inappropriate in the circumstances?"

"My dear Mr. Peake—or may I now address you as Ernest, given the degree of affection that you display towards my granddaughter?"

He is a wise old owl, isn't he? And doesn't he look pleased?

"Of course," he said mechanically.

"Well, then, my dear Ernest: you don't think it inappropriate, do you?"

"Absolutely not!"

"Then we shall go ahead. In fact"—he produced a watch that reminded Ernest of Gaffer Tatton's—"it's time to leave."

Virtually the entire village had turned out for the procession, despite this being officially a working day. The vicar went at its head, attended by Roger the coachman bearing a stoup of holy water and a bundle of herbs bound to make a kind of brush, with which he asperged the decorations at each well before pronouncing a benediction. The church choir came next, singing a traditional hymn, and after there followed the villagers roughly in order of age, while the rear was brought up by the children from the school under Miss Hicks's stern direction, except for one boy and one girl who had been allotted the coveted duty of leading the way with branches of greenery.

Listening to the singing—quiet at first, then lusty—it occurred to Ernest that since his arrival he had never seen so many smiles at once.

During the blessing of the second well, he felt a shy tug at the hand with which he wasn't clasping Alice's. He glanced down to see a woman's face, drawn and lined under prematurely gray hair. It was Mrs. Gibson.

"Me and my littluns got a lot to thank 'ee for already," she whispered. "Now all on us folk got 'ee to thank for bringing back the well-dressing . . . God bless 'ee, Mr. Ernest!"

And she had withdrawn into the throng.

But across the group he caught the eye of Gaffer Tatton, and he was beaming as to say, "What did I tell 'ee?"

Then at last it was time to make for their final destination, the one in Old Well Road. The air was tense with expectation. The ceremony here proceeded exactly as before, with the same prayers and the same quotations about the Water of Life. But more was clearly expected, and of a sudden it came.

Abandoning any prepared text, the vicar surveyed his congregation and said abruptly, "Friends! For I trust after so many years of tribulation I may call you so!"

The smiles came back, in even greater number.

"There are some who have called it wrong, indeed evil, to keep up the tradition we have today renewed. I am not one of them."

Nor are we, was the silent response.

"We all know that our very lives are a miracle—that we are born, that we can think and reason, and that we can learn to praise our Creator: yes, that's a miracle!"

Almost, there was an outburst of applause. The Stoddard brothers frowned it down.

"For the food we eat, and the water we drink: should we not give thanks? And that the land yields bountifully, and our cattle and our other livestock? And, indeed, that we can leave children to follow in our footsteps when we, as must inevitably ensue, are called to join the company of the righteous . . . Met here today, we have acknowledged our indebtedness to the Maker of all things. Today in particular we have celebrated the gift of water. It behooves us all, and always, to remember it is one of many gifts, and the greatest of these is love. God bless you all!"

And he turned back to the well-dressing on which Ernest and all its makers had lavished so much care, and recited the Doxology at the top of his voice. Many of the listeners joined in.

Gaffer Tatton, though, was not among them. He had made for home, bent perhaps on the kind of errand that an old man's weak bladder might make urgent. Just as the vicar finished, however, he burst out once more from his cottage door.

"It's sweet!"

Every head turned.

"The water's sweet! Bain't no more taint to un! I drunk this water all me life, and 'spite o' her as went *she's* made it clean again!"

"He means," Alice began, whispering close to Ernest's ear, and he cut her short.

"I know. What he means is that no matter how awful she was, and how long she lay in the well, she didn't foul the water . . . When we get married, my love, would you mind if we did it twice?"

"How can that be?" She drew back to arm's length, studying him with her wide gray eyes.

"We'll do it once for me, the man, in the name of the Father and the Son. And we'll do it once for you, in the name of—*her*. How about it?"

"But no one knows her name!"

"Does it matter? We know she's there, don't we?"

She thought awhile, and eventually nodded.

"Yes, I've known for years, like Gaffer Tatton. I'm surprised you found out so quickly, but I'm terribly glad . . . Shall we live at the Hall?"

"Most of the time, I suppose. After all, I'm the heir. But I want to take you on honeymoon to India. Even if I can't promise a private view of Kali-worship."

Smiling, she pressed his hand. "I think I've seen enough of the wicked side of the female principle for the time being—" She broke off, aghast. "Ernest, this is terrible! She's scarcely cold, and here we are talking about a honeymoon! We ought to be planning her funeral!"

"Excuse me, Mr. Ernest."

They turned to find the Stoddard brothers at their side.

"Before we go, we'd just like to offer our congratulations and say we hope you'll both be very happy."

How in the world—?

Then he recalled what Alice had said about the talk in the servants' hall, and all around the village. He let his face relax into a grin.

"Thanks awfully! What time's the feast tonight? We'll see you there!"

Afterwards, when Mr. Ames's pig had been distributed in slices, special care being taken to deliver enough to Mrs. Gibson and her children, he said to Alice in the darkness of her room, "I don't think we need the second wedding after all."

"Hmm?"—nuzzling his neck with soft warm lips.

"As far as *she's* concerned we're married, aren't we?"

"Mm-hm. That's what surprised me when you mentioned it . . . Can we again?"

"I think so—Yes! Oh, *yes!*"

Later, though, just before, for the first time, they went to sleep in one another's arms, having agreed to stop worrying about scandal or offending old Mr. Pollock—or even Tinkler—he said musingly, "It's funny, though."

"What is?"

"How close a connection there is between what you see in India and what you find at home."

"But why?" She raised herself on one elbow, her breasts enchantingly visible in the faint light from the window. "Isn't it the same with science?"

"What?"

"You wouldn't expect science to stop working because it's a different country, would you?"

"No, of course not!"

"Well, then!" She lay down again. "Why not the same with religion? After all, we're all human."

"You mean—"

"What I mean," she said firmly, "is that whoever *she* is who guards the wells of Welstock, and brought you and me so splendidly together, she can't be anything else except another aspect of what you are, and I am, and everybody else. That goes for India too, and every countless world we find our way to in our dreams. Which is where, with my lord's permission, I propose to adjourn to. Good night."

He lay awake a while longer, pondering what she had said, and at last inquired, "How do you think the villagers will take to having people here with views like ours?"

"So long as we honor the mistress of the water," came the sleepy answer, "why in the world should they worry?"

Yes indeed. Why should they?

His doubts resolved, the new lord of the manor of Welstock dozed off contentedly beside his lady.

THE BLUE STONE EMPEROR'S THIRTY-THREE WIVES

Sara Gallardo

Sara Gallardo was born in Buenos Aires in 1931 and died in 1988. She worked as a journalist, traveling extensively throughout Latin America, Europe, and the Orient. She is the author of several novels and short stories set in Southern Argentina and Patagonia and imbued with mythic elements. Among her works are *Enero, El País del humo* and *Páginas de Sara Gallardo*.

The first English translation of Gallardo's poetic tale "The Blue Stone Emperor's Thirty-three Wives" appeared in 1992. Translated from the Spanish by Elizabeth Rhodes, it comes from the anthology *Secret Weavers: Stories of the Fantastic by Women of Argentina and Chile*, published by White Pine Press in Fredonia, New York.

—T.W.

1

Behind the great king hangs a painted leather hide. It can waver; it is the wind. Or not waver; the queen is listening. I count within myself those dead at his command. Those dead at his hands are within me. Foolish women, those who bewail their lost youth; they do not know the secrets of fermentation. May they see drunkenness beneath the stars; if water is for daytime then alcohol is for power.

Alcohol is old age. I lost my teeth; my nourishment is to influence. I braid my gray hair; what gets braided without me?

I have a whim, nonetheless. I'd like to have that girl killed. And her child in her arms.

2

For me, stretching leather. Eating. Going for water. Sewing the skins, preparing the threads, weaving. Looking at the smoke, whether it will rain tomorrow. Relieving myself calmly among the rushes. Seasoning the venison through the wound in the flesh. Preparing maté and drinking it. Dying ostrich feathers.

To each day its own. A good life. Sleeping.

3

I make people travel. Careful, horseman. Not a word of what we said can be repeated. The most terrible of the kings moans like a calf. I never needed beauty.

I am the one who travels. Door of journeys.

It is true that I take risks; I see death at every step. How can you fasten my body of a thousand lives to only one man?

No one is as young nor as old as I.

4

I tortured them, the women. I still thirst. I saw them die, naming unknown people in other languages. I did not satiate myself. If each grazing were the subject of humiliation and each star an eye to blind, my anxieties would go on.

5

Wool, wool, morning has come. Shake off the dew, scare off the cold. If you take in what is red, you warm your eye. Tie the strands of life together.* Grid what is black, cross what is white. The form of the woof; the woof is my shape. Here the line of silence, the border, madness, the little tracks of the skunk, the tips of the night, footsteps, footprints, tracks. Life is between these steps: the yes, the no, the now, the never.

This is the poncho I wove for the king.

6

Friend, give your mouth to me. Spread your legs for me. I used to pick fleas from your hair. Fat ones to you, medium ones to me, skinny to die between my finger-nails. Something happened. To be the king's wife matters little to me. To be the king's wife matters little to you. Is it possible to hide it? There are so many eyes.

7

I won't speak of another time, of another language, of another man, other children.

Here the wind, the horror.

To rock to sleep, I am the oven and the bread. Nine bakings. Nine loaves of bread.

I see six with the riding master. One, the bola balls. One, the lance. One, the dagger. One, the hobbled gallop. One, the race on foot. One, the stretching out.

They will talk among themselves. I will be a single ear: horses, horses. Only horses. Can any other words matter to me? Can they?

There are two more; then run close to my steps. What steps do I hear if not those?

One remains, asleep. Happy lap. I had a garden. There are no petals besides those eyes.

Nine loaves of bread. I ran in this same wind to kill other children.

---

*Translator's note: The first four sentences of this paragraph are rhyming proverbs from the oral tradition. Since their elements figure in later sections of the story, they are translated literally. The first one might otherwise be rendered, "Out of bed, sleepyhead."

8

To go along, without footprints. Ant. Air. Nothing.

9

I glory in his glory.
   I repeat that the wind might carry:
   Two thousand five hundred leagues of confederation.
   Two thousand lancers.
   Four horses per lancer.
   Thus is counted the greatness of my king.
   I walk weighed down with splendors.
   Why did he mount me but once?

10

The Marquis whispered: the carriage is tied. Madame, all we have to do is flee.
She lifted her mask. Her heavenly pupils were farewell. A ring with a seal on it
slipped through her hands.
   I can't remember what came next . . .

11

I will always see him as ridiculous. Every night guarding his females. He found me
with my friend. He buried my face in a blow. He went off to bed. In the morning,
he called my companion. He asked him for twenty sheep.
   I was blind after that.
   Twenty sheep.
   In the land of shadow, I still see him. Ridiculous.

12

My grandmother—it was so long ago on the other side of the great mountain—
had an ear for the dead. Strolling through the countryside she used to say:
   "Here, some buried people. Dig, you'll see."
   We dug. The bones appeared.
   With the years, that same ear opened itself to me.
   Others know where the enemy is by the smell of the wind. I deal with the dead.
   Looking for an herb to dye the wool, I walk a lot. At some point, someone dead
calls.
   They call, like a warrior in the alcohol of dreams, like the creatures in the night.
Their yellow bones are not dust any more. I tell them to sleep.
   "We walk by day. Soon the night will come."

13

Everything was glorious there. With my cousin, I used to run horse races. We
broke them in. Mine used to halt without reins, didn't drink, knew how to wait.
We had a specimen, the most beautiful: Nahuel, horse of my father. We were
almost children.

One night I heard the witch sing like the water in the cauldron. She was talking with the devil. The smoke of her fire responded:

"What scared you, lord?"

"I shall tell you, I shall tell you."

"What drove you away?"

"I shall tell you."

"Return to me, I am an orphan, I can no longer fly."

"The small one that eats from the hand of the leader scares me. Its neigh startles me, its odor scares me, its mane drowns me. Its feet break my powers. Each time it swallows fodder, I am asphyxiated."

"Fear not, my lord, you shall return. He shall die."

I dragged myself over and awoke my cousin. I told him what I'd heard. Nahuel, horse of my father, heard. He turned around in his stall. My cousin spoke into my ear: "Go to sleep." I didn't sleep. Almost a child, he cut the witch's throat. She woke up facing the fire burnt down to the bone.

There was a scream in the morning. We were playing with our horses.

What a meeting, what talk, what arms raised, the boys hid, the women filed their nails. My father put on his blanket, the woolen crown.

"She is dead," he said. "Dead she will remain."

There was a lot of low talking, not in front of him. Who killed her, why weren't people punished? He didn't know why himself. But a great prosperity followed.

What for?

The king of kings—but a king among kings—asked for my hand.

I said to my cousin:

"We show our horses, don't we?"

And we escaped. My father mounted Nahuel. Nahuel caught up with us.

My father carried his lance. He raised it and shouted.

"It is true that I love you like a son. It is true that you were going to be leader."

He killed my cousin. He shut himself up in his tent. He drank for three days. On the third I said to him:

"Your prosperity is due to the one you killed. Nahuel as witness. Your prosperity attracted the king of kings. Now you will see what he leaves you."

They carried me covered with silver to the old man of the blue stone.

Nahuel has died, my father is a beggar, his dispersed tribe gnaws at remains.

14

He was born. I always feared it: blue eyes. The king, my cousin and uncle, came to see him. The wives hid their delight. I awaited death. He smiled:

"Good blood," he said. "He will be a king."

15

I wish he would die, defeated. I wish, foot on the ground, he would find himself chained up by soldiers without leaders. I wish that his children would betray him and that he would find out, that he would lose his manhood.

I wish he would die. And his race would be erased from the earth. I with it.

Cursing him.

16

My father found me trying to fly. I never understood men's taste. Women's less. Lives of shadows.

Now I know. I search for buried snake's eggs. Toads. Sleeping bats. May the enchantress receive my adulation.

I shall learn.

17

A traveller saw me: hopeless, dying, very beautiful.

It was a mistake. I never existed.

Outside I hear the birds' song.

18

I am two. I have two names, and I am two. One morning I lost my first tooth. My mother—who used to cry all the time—said:

"Maria of the Angels, bury it, and a miracle will sprout."

I buried it next to the tent. The next day I went to get the miracle. I didn't see anything. I sat down and waited. When I returned, my mother—she was counting her bones—had died. Beaten to death. It seemed she was smiling.

No one else called me Maria of the Angels. Only I used to say it. No one used to say miracle.

When I buried my eighth tooth, I screamed in the middle of the field.

"Miracles! I won't wait any more! I will forget how to say Mary of the Angels! I will only be White Cloud."

That night, asleep, I heard a song. It spoke that which I never heard:

"Seaworthy boat, light oar.

Castle by the river, keep me from cold.

Mountain snow, goes where I go.

Angels, saints, sing their songs."

I asked a man, an interpreter, with a red beard: "What does boat mean, and seaworthy, and oar, and castle, and snow, and mountain." He said it. He repeated it to me gathering wood, carrying water.

One day an old man came:

"The king of kings who lives on the other side of the desert makes known what he has found out from the red-bearded man. A white, fat, blonde, girl child lives here. He demands that she be brought. He will send this much livestock, this many vessels, this much silver."

"What girl child is that?" I asked.

I was warmly received. We were poor. That king didn't know our people, or our leader.

Now I am a wife far from there. I have two names, and I am two.

When I find my mother, she will tell me why.

19

The pleasure I have left is to contemplate the new.

The dew in the brush. The coming out of the new queen, the favorite, with her child in her arms. She laughs. The king wants her close.

In the spider's web, dew drops.

In the afternoon, I lock myself in, light the fire.

In the afternoon, there is no dew in the brush. The web is loaded with insects. The dust clouds fly on the horizon.

20

Sometimes we run into the king. If he feels like it, he greets me and continues on his way. I don't know where youth went.

We have been accomplices.

It's not that he needs them. In the triumph, the punishment, the killing, the glory, the lust.

But only I saw his tears.

21

I gave myself to the mystery.

What was it?

A path of darkness

toward a land which perhaps does not exist.

I am faithful. I persevere.

22

This happened when we crossed the great mountain. Playing, my brother and I went up to where the ice is very quiet.

In a cave, a small girl was sleeping.

Gold in her crowns, on her chest. Her sandals were made of green beads. Little face mask of pearls. She was sleeping.

When we went down, he died from the cold. I lived.

We never told anything.

They call me wife of the king. I use a silver necklace.

Whoever did not see the princess who sleeps in the mountain will never know about kings.

23

I waited ten years. And he saw me.

He was coming back from the war. Black blood flowed from his chest. I saw his children, his grandchildren. The feathers of his lances, also black, crazy with victory. Women, the aged, dogs, children were one single howl. And the captive females the color of death.

I held his glance. His horse brushed by close to my feet. I did not move. My grandmother hit me.

They celebrated for many days. The warriors slept, vomited. I waited. The king walked among the tents. I saw the leather skin at my house open.

I never said his name. He never said mine. I was the king, he the girl. I learned to rule, he to laugh.

They usually talk. They know little of love.

24
The moon has a halo; kings are travelling.
 My brother arrived.
 The rain erases all the signals. I cry.
 My brothers left.

25
The story, which still gives people something to talk about, really went like this.
 My cousin had a favorite dog, used to biting people's heels. I saw that that young man had his heel wounded.
 I got some poison seeds and held them in my hand.
 While dying wool with the old queen, I cried. She promised me a pearl necklace if I would tell her why. A bead necklace.
 I said: "My cousin and her sisters are preparing a poison. That young man brought them the seed. They want to kill the king."
 I opened my hand and showed them to her.
 My cousin, her sisters, that young man, were burned alive.
 They have been dust and ash for seven years. I use the bead necklace.
 That fire keeps me awake.
 I asked him for his love; he laughed at me. And he visited my cousin at night?

26 and 27
We are sisters and we are different. The day of that double banquet—that hecatomb—we were working together. Unannounced the little leader and his two hundred men arrived for a visit. They were given lunch. They were eating and his brother arrived, four hundred lances in the dust. Another banquet.
 And they satiated themselves both times.
 The king inspected the rows of eaters and drinkers in person. He talked and laughed.
 I guarantee it was a proud day. To be the wife of a king, to feed six hundred men, and laugh.
 But my sister said: "I know what the salt of a king's kitchen is like. Tears and sweat. Grief and fatigue."

28
While filling the king's pipe, I've heard how he dictates his letters. The men who serve him make lines and dots, like the white men do.
 In the afternoons, I sit down. I am old. Words do not interest me.
 I see the birds. Lines, dots. Every afternoon in the sky, the same letter.
 Always the same, that I cannot say.
 Defeat, end.

29
My brother, lord of the apple tree country, wanted an alliance with the great one. His wife promised me. When I arrived, he was out hunting ostriches. He returned at night, left for the war. Later he wanted to see me.
 He didn't like me.

He performed the ceremony for an alliance with the lord of the apple trees.
He never touched me.
I didn't have any women friends.
The witch asked a favor of me. I listen to all the conversations for her; I spy on
every tent.
They call me names. The young boys set traps at my feet. I get hit.
Still, my mother told me stories; she promised me happiness.

30

I dreamed: I lost a tooth.
What will I do without it, what will it do without me?
Wind has come come up over the river.
What will he do without me, what will I do without him?

31

It was raining. And it rained my lament. It is sad to be a wife of the old king. It
was night, under the blanket. In autumn, things are like that.
My husband's son entered the darkness. He had been drinking. Perhaps he made
a mistake.
What happened was a coming out into brilliance on a battle horse. It was running.
It was conquering.

32

On the day of the first battle, his father told him:
"Let no woman matter more to you than war."
On the day of the first banquet, his father told him:
"No woman takes you further than alcohol."
On the day of the first sacrifice, his father told him:
"He who ties himself to a woman separates himself from the mystery."
He knew battle, alcohol, mystery. He tells me: "There are three shadows next to
your red skirt."

33

I have seen a vision that is not a lie in the water of the well. I saw the king's funeral.
It will not be long now. His horse dressed in silver will go with him. His wives in
a line, their skulls broken. His favorite one, dressed in red, will carry her child in
her arms. They will wrench it away from her at the same time they kill her. Thus
I saw the funeral, with thirty-two wives. I am escaping tonight.

ALICE IN PRAGUE, OR THE CURIOUS ROOM

Angela Carter

Many of us in the fantasy field have been greatly inspired by the work of Angela Carter—one of the finest writers in the English language for her richly surrealistic novels and dark, sensual adult fairy tales. It was with great sadness that I learned of her early death in 1992.

Born in South Yorkshire, England, in 1940, Carter published her first novel, *Shadow Dance*, in 1965; won the John Llewellyn Rhys Prize for her second novel, *The Magic Toyshop* (highly recommended); and won the Somerset Maugham Award for her third novel, *Several Perceptions*. Novels published since include *Heroes and Villains*, *Nights at the Circus*, and (the last of her career) *Wise Children*. She is also the author of several collections of short stories and two works of nonfiction. Of particular interest to fantasy readers are her various translations and retellings of fairy tales, particularly the *Old Wives' Fairy Tale Book* in the Pantheon Fairy Tale Library; and her brilliant collection of adult stories based on fairy tales: *The Bloody Chamber* (from which her screenplay for the Neil Jordan–directed movie "The Company of Wolves" was drawn).

The following story, which first appeared in *The Village Voice Literary Supplement*, was written in praise of Jan Svankmajer, the animator of Prague, and his film of *Alice*. It was one of the very last stories ever penned by Angela Carter, and it is an honor to reprint it here.

—T.W.

In the city of Prague, once, it was winter.

Outside the curious room, there is a sign on the door which says: "Forbidden." Inside, inside, oh, come and see! The celebrated DR. DEE.

The celebrated Dr. Dee, looking for all the world like Santa Claus on account of his long, white beard and apple cheeks, is contemplating his crystal, the fearful sphere that contains everything that is, or was, or ever shall be.

It is a round ball of solid glass and gives a deceptive impression of weightlessness, because you can see right through it and we falsely assume an equation between lightness and transparency, that what the light shines through cannot be there and so must weigh nothing. In fact, the Doctor's crystal ball is heavy enough to inflict a substantial injury and the Doctor's assistant, Ned Kelly, the Man in the Iron Mask, often weighs the ball in one hand or tosses it back and forth from one to the other hand as he ponders the fragility of the hollow bone, his master's skull, as it pores heedless over some tome.

Ned Kelly would blame the murder on the angels. He would say the angels came out of the sphere. Everybody knows the angels live there.

The crystal resembles:

an aqueous humour, frozen;

a glass eye, although without any iris or pupil—just the sort of transparent eye, in fact, which the adept might construe as apt to see the invisible;

a tear, round, as it forms within the eye, for a tear acquires its characteristic shape of a pear, what we think of as a "tear" shape, only in the act of falling;

the shining drop that trembles, sometimes, on the tip of the doctor's well-nigh senescent, tending towards the flaccid, yet nevertheless sustainable and discernible morning erection, and always reminds him of

a drop of dew,

a drop of dew endlessly about to fall from the unfolded petals of a rose and, therefore, like the tear, retaining the perfection of its circumference only by refusing to sustain free fall, remaining what it is, because it refuses to become what it might be, the antithesis of metamorphosis;

and yet, in old England, far away, the sign of the Do Drop Inn will always, that jovial pun, show an ablate spheroid, heavily tinseled, because the sign-painter, in order to demonstrate the idea of "drop," needs must represent the dew in the act of falling and therefore, for the purposes of this comparison, *not* resembling the numinous ball weighing down the angelic doctor's outstretched palm.

For Dr. Dee, the invisible is only another unexplored country, a brave new world.

The hinge of the sixteenth century, where it joins with the seventeenth century, is as creaky and judders open as reluctantly as the door in a haunted house. Through that door, in the distance, we may glimpse the distant light of the Age of Reason, but precious little of that is about to fall on Prague, the capital of paranoia, where the fortune-tellers live on Golden Alley in cottages so small a good-sized doll would find itself cramped, and there is one certain house on Alchemist's Street that only becomes visible during a thick fog. (On sunny days, you see a stone.) But, even in the fog, only those born on the Sabbath can see the house, anyway.

Like a lamp guttering out in a recently vacated room, the Renaissance flared, faded and extinguished itself. The world had suddenly revealed itself as bewilderingly infinite, but since the imagination remained, for, after all, it is only human, finite, our imaginations took some time to catch up. If Francis Bacon will die in 1626 a martyr to experimental science, having contracted a chill whilst stuffing a dead hen with snow on Highgate Hill to see if that would keep it fresh, in Prague, where Dr. Faustus once lodged in Charles Square, Dr. Dee, the English expatriate alchemist, awaits the manifestation of the angel in the Archduke Rudolph's curious room, and we are still fumbling our way towards the end of the previous century.

The Archduke Rudolph keeps his priceless collection of treasures in this curious room; he numbers the doctor amongst these treasures and is therefore forced to number the doctor's assistant, the unspeakable and iron-visaged Kelly too.

The Archduke Rudolph has crazy eyes. These eyes are the mirrors of his soul.

It is very cold this afternoon, the kind of weather that makes a person piss. The moon is up already, a moon the color of candlewax and, as the sky discolors when the night comes on, the moon grows more white, more cold, white as the source of all the cold in the world, until, when the winter moon reaches its chill meridian, everything will freeze—not only the water in the jug and the ink in the well, but the blood in the vein, the aqueous humour.

Metamorphosis.

In their higgly-piggly disorder, the twigs on the bare trees outside the thick window resemble those random scratchings made by common use that you only see when you lift your wine glass up to the light. A hard frost has crisped the surface of the deep snow on the Archduke's tumbled roofs and turrets. In the snow, a raven: caw!

Dr. Dee knows the language of birds and sometimes speaks it, but what the birds say is frequently banal; all the raven said, over and over, was: "Poor Tom's a-cold!"

Above the Doctor's head, slung from the low-beamed ceiling, dangles a flying turtle, stuffed. In the dim room we can make out, amongst much else, the random juxtaposition of an umbrella, a sewing machine, and a dissecting table; a raven and a writing desk; an aged mermaid, poor wizened creature, cramped in a foetal position in a jar, her ream of gray hair suspended adrift in the viscous liquid that preserves her, her features rendered greenish and somewhat distorted by the flaws in the glass.

Dr. Dee would like, for a mate to this mermaid, to keep in a cage, if alive, or, if dead, in a stoppered bottle, an angel.

It was an age in love with wonders.

Dr. Dee's assistant, Ned Kelly, the Man in the Iron Mask, is also looking for angels. He is gazing at the sheeny, reflective screen of his scrying disc, which is made of polished coal. The angels visit him more frequently than they do the Doctor, but, for some reason, Dr. Dee cannot see Kelly's guests, although they crowd the surface of the scrying disc, crying out in their high, piercing voices in the species of bird-creole with which they communicate. It is a great sadness to him.

Kelly, however, is phenomenally gifted in this direction and notes down on a pad the intonations of their speech which, though he doesn't understand it himself, the Dr. excitedly makes sense of.

But, today, no go.

Kelly yawns. He stretches. He feels the pressure of the weather on his bladder.

*　*　*

The privy at the top of the tower is a hole in the floor behind a cupboard door. It is situated above another privy, with another hole, above another privy, another hole, and so on, down seven further privies, seven more holes, until your excreta at last hurtles into the cesspit far below. The cold keeps the smell down, thank God.

Dr. Dee, ever the seeker after knowledge, has calculated the velocity of a flying turd.

Although a man could hang himself in the privy with ease and comfort, securing the rope about the beam above and launching himself into the void to let gravity break his neck for him, Kelly, whether at stool or making water, never allows the privy to remind him of the "long drop" nor even, however briefly, to admire his own instrument for fear the phrase "well-hung" recalls the noose which he narrowly escaped in his native England for fraud, once, in Lancaster; for forgery, once, in Rutlandshire; and for performing a confidence trick in Ashby-de-la-Zouche.

But his ears were cropped for him in the pillory at Walton-le-Dale, after he dug up a corpse from a churchyard for purposes of necromancy, or possibly of grave-robbing, and this is why, in order to conceal this amputation, he always wears the iron mask modeled after that which will be worn by a namesake three hundred years hence in a country that does not yet exist, an iron mask like an upturned bucket with a slit cut for his eyes.

Kelly, unbuttoning, wonders if his piss will freeze in the act of falling; if, today, it is cold enough in Prague to let him piss an arc of ice.

No.

He buttons up again.

Women loathe this privy. Happily, few venture here, into the magician's tower, where the Archduke Rudolph keeps his collection of wonders, his proto-museum, his "Wunderkammer," his "cabinet des curiosités," that curious room of which we speak.

There's a theory, one I find persuasive, that the quest for knowledge is, at bottom, the search for the answer to the question: "Where was I before I was born?"

In the beginning, was . . . what?

Perhaps, in the beginning, there was a curious room, a room like this one, crammed with wonders; and now the room and all it contains are forbidden you, although it was made just for you, had been prepared for you since time began, and you will spend all your life trying to remember it.

Kelly once took the Archduke aside and offered him, at a price, a little piece of the beginning, a slice of the fruit of the Tree of the Knowledge of Good and Evil itself, which Kelly claimed he had obtained from an Armenian who had found it on Mount Ararat, growing in the shadows of the wreck of the Ark. The slice had dried out with time and looked very much like a dehydrated ear.

The Archduke soon decided it was a fake, that Kelly had been fooled. The Archduke is not gullible. Rather, he has a boundless desire to know everything and an exceptional generosity of belief. At night, he stands on top of the tower and watches the stars in the company of Tycho Brahe and Johannes Kepler, yet by day, he makes no move nor judgment before he consults the astrologers in their zodiacal hats and yet, in those days, either an astrologer or an astronomer would be hard put to describe the difference between their disciplines.

He is not gullible. But he has his peculiarities.

The Archduke keeps a lion chained up in his bedroom as a species of watchdog or, since the lion is a member of the *felis* family and not a member of the *cave canem* family, a giant guard-cat. For fear of the lion's yellow teeth, the Archduke had them pulled. Now that the poor beast cannot chew, he must subsist on slop. The lion lies with his head on his paws, dreaming. If you could open up his brain this moment, you would find nothing there but the image of a beefsteak.

Meanwhile, the Archduke, in the curtained privacy of his bed, embraces something, God knows what.

Whatever it is, he does it with such energy that the bell hanging over the bed becomes agitated due to the jolting and rhythmic lurching of the bed, and the clapper jangles against the sides.

Ting-a-ling!

The bell is cast out of *electrum magicum*. Paracelsus said that a bell cast out of *electrum magicum* would summon up the spirits. If a rat gnaws the Archduke's toe during the night, his involuntary start will agitate the bell immediately so the spirits can come and chase the rat away, for the lion, although *sui generis* a cat, is not sufficiently a cat in spirit to perform the domestic functions of a common mouser, not like the little calico beastie who keeps the good Doctor company and often, out of pure affection, brings him furry tributes of those she has slain.

Though the bell rings, softly at first, and then with increasing fury as the Archduke nears the end of his journey, no spirits come. But there have been no rats either.

A split fig falls out of the bed onto the marble floor with a soft, exhausted plop, followed by a hand of bananas, that spread out and go limp, as if in submission.

"Why can't he make do with meat, like other people," whined the hungry lion.

Can the Archduke be effecting intercourse with a fruit salad?

Or, with Carmen Miranda's hat?

Worse.

The hand of bananas indicates the Archduke's enthusiasm for the newly discovered Americas. Oh, brave new world! There is a street in Prague called "New World" (*Nový Svet*). The hand of bananas is freshly arrived from Bermuda via his Spanish kin, who know what he likes. He has a particular enthusiasm for weird plants, and every week comes to converse with his mandrakes, those warty, shaggy roots that originate (the Archduke shudders pleasurably to think about it) in the sperm and water spilled by a hanged man.

The mandrakes live at ease in a special cabinet. It falls to Ned Kelly's reluctant duty to bathe each of these roots once a week in milk and dress them up in fresh linen nightgowns. Kelly, reluctantly, since the roots, warts and all, resemble so many virile members, and he does not like to handle them, imagining they raucously mock his manhood as he tends them, believing they unman him.

The Archduke's collection also boasts some magnificent specimens of the *coco-de-mer*, or double coconut, which grows in the shape, but exactly the shape, of the pelvic area of a woman, a foot long, heft and clefted, I kid you not. The Archduke and his gardeners plan to effect a vegetable marriage and will raise the progeny— *man-de-mer* or *coco-drake*—in his own greenhouses. (The Archduke himself is a confirmed bachelor.)

The bell ceases. The lion sighs with relief and lays his head once more upon his heavy paws: "Now I can sleep!"

Then, from under the bed curtains, on either side of the bed, begins to pour a veritable torrent that quickly forms into dark, viscous, livid puddles on the floor.

But, before you accuse the Archduke of the unspeakable, dip your finger in the puddle and lick it.

Delicious!

For these are sticky puddles of freshly squeezed grape juice, and apple juice, and peach juice, juice of peach, plum, pear, or raspberry, strawberry, cherry ripe, blackberry, black currant, white currant, red . . . The room brims with the delicious ripe scent of summer pudding, even though, outside, on the frozen tower, the crow still creaks out his melancholy call: "Poor Tom's a-cold!"

And it is midwinter.

Night was. Widow Night, an old woman in mourning, with big, black wings, came beating against the window; they kept her out with lamps and candles.

When he went back into the laboratory, Ned Kelly found that Dr. Dee had nodded off to sleep as the old man often did, nowadays, toward the end of the day, the crystal ball having rolled from palm to lap as he lay back in the black oak chair, and now, as he shifted at the impulse of a dream, it rolled again off his lap, down onto the floor, where it landed with a soft thump on the rushes—no harm done— and the little calico cat disabled it at once with a swift blow of her right paw, then began to play with it, batting it that way and this before she administered the *coup de grace.*

With a gusty sigh, Kelly once more addressed his scrying disc, although today he felt barren of invention. He ironically reflected that, if just so much as one wee feathery angel ever, even the one time, should escape the scrying disc and flutter into the laboratory, the cat would surely get it.

Not, Kelly knew, that such a thing was possible.

If you could see inside Kelly's brain, you would discover a calculating machine.

Widow Night painted the windows black.

Then, all at once, the cat made a noise like sharply crumpled paper, a noise of enquiry and concern. A rat? Kelly turned to look. The cat, head on one side, was considering with such scrupulous intensity that its pricked ears met at the tips something lying on the floor beside the crystal ball, so that at first it looked as if the glass eye had shed a tear.

But look again.

Kelly looked again and began to sob and gibber.

The cat rose up and backed away all in one liquid motion, hissing, its bristling tail stuck straight up, stiff as a broom handle, too scared to permit even the impulse of attack upon the creature, about the size of a little finger that popped out of the crystal ball as if the ball had been a bubble.

But its passage has not cracked or fissured the ball; it is still whole, has sealed itself up again directly after the departure of the infinitesimal child who, so suddenly released from her sudden confinement, now experimentally stretches out her tiny limbs to test the limits of the new invisible circumference around her.

Kelly stammered: "There must be some rational explanation!"

Although they were too small for him to see them, her teeth still had the transparency and notched edges of the first stage of the second set; her straight, fair hair was cut in a stern fringe; she scowled and sat upright, looking about her with evident disapproval.

The cat, cowering ecstatically, now knocked over an alembic and a quantity of *elixir vitae* ran away through the rushes. At the bang, the Doctor woke and was not astonished to see her.

He bade her a graceful welcome in the language of the tawny pipit.

How did she get there? She was kneeling on the mantelpiece of the sitting-room of the place she lived, looking at herself in the mirror. Bored, she breathed on the glass until it clouded over and then, with her finger, she drew a door. The door opened. She sprang through and, after a brief moment's confusing fish-eye view of a vast, gloomy chamber, scarcely illuminated by five candles in one branched stick and filled with all the clutter in the world, her view was obliterated by the clawed paw of a vast cat extended ready to strike, hideously increasing in size as it approached her, and then, splat! she burst out of "time will be" into "time was," for the transparent substance which surrounded her burst like a bubble and there she was, in her pink frock, lying on some rushes under the gaze of a tender ancient with a long, white beard and a man with a coal scuttle on his head.

Her lips moved but no sound came out; she had left her voice behind in the mirror. She flew into a tantrum and beat her heels upon the floor, weeping furiously. The Doctor, who, in some remote time past, raised children of his own, let her alone until, her passion spent, she heaved and grunted on the rushes, knuckling her eyes; then he peered into the depths of a big china bowl on a dim shelf and produced from out of it a strawberry.

The child accepted the strawberry suspiciously, for it was, although not large, the size of her head. She sniffed it, turned it round and round, and then essayed just one little bite out of it, leaving behind a tiny ring of white within the crimson flesh. Her teeth were perfect.

At the first bite, she grew a little.

Kelly continued to mumble: "There must be some rational explanation."

The child took a second, less tentative bite, and grew a little more. The mandrakes in their white nightgowns woke up and began to mutter among themselves.

Reassured at last, she gobbled the strawberry all up, but she had been falsely reassured; now her flaxen crown bumped abruptly against the rafters, out of the range of the candlestick so they could not see her face but a gigantic tear splashed with a metallic clang upon Ned Kelly's helmet, then another, and the Doctor, with some presence of mind, before they needed to hurriedly construct an Ark, pressed a phial of *elixir vitae* into her hand. When she drank it, she shrank down again until soon she was small enough to sit on his knee, her blue eyes staring with wonder at his beard, as white as ice cream and as long as Sunday.

But she had no wings.

Kelly, the faker, knew there *must* be a rational explanation but he could not think of one.

She found her voice at last. "Tell me," she said, "the answer to this problem: the Governor of Kgoujni wants to give a very small dinner party, and invites his father's brother-in-law, his brother's father-in-law, his father-in-law's brother, and his brother-in-law's father. Find the number of guests."[1]

At the sound of her voice, which was as clear as a looking-glass, everything in the curious room gave a shake and a shudder and, for a moment, looked as if it were painted on gauze, like a theatrical effect, and might disappear if a bright light were shone on it. Dr. Dee stroked his beard, reflectively. He could provide answers to many questions, or knew where to look for answers. He had gone and caught a falling starre—didn't a piece of it lie beside the stuffed dodo? To impregnate the aggressively phallic mandrake, with its masculinity to the power of two, as implied by its name, was a task which, he pondered, the omnivorous Archduke, with his enthusiasm for erotic esoterica, might prove capable of. And the answer to the other two imponderables posed by the poet were obtainable, surely, through the intermediary of the angels, if only one scried long enough.

He truly believed that nothing was unknowable. That is what makes him modern.

But, to the child's question, he can imagine no answer.

Kelly, forced against his nature to suspect the presence of another world that would destroy his confidence in tricks, is sunk in introspection, and has not even heard her.

However, such magic as there is in *this* world, as opposed to the worlds that can be made out of dictionaries, can only be real when it is artificial and Dr. Dee himself, whilst a member of the Cambridge Footlights, at university, before his beard was white or long, directed a famous production of Aristophanes's *Peace* at Trinity College, in which he sent a grocer's boy right up to heaven, laden with his basket, as if to make deliveries, on the back of a giant beetle.

Architas made a flying dove of wood. At Nuremburg, according to Boterus, an adept constructed both an eagle and a fly and set them to flutter and flap across his laboratory, to the astonishment of all. In olden times, the statues that Daedalus built raised their arms and moved their legs due to the action of weights, and of shifting deposits of mercury. Albertus Magnus, the Great Sage, cast a head in brass that spoke.

Are they animate or not, these beings that jerk and shudder into such a semblance of life? Do these creatures believe themselves to be human? And if they do, at what point might they, by virtue of the sheer intensity of their belief, become so?

(In Prague, the city of the Golem, an image can come to life.)

The Doctor thinks about these things a great deal and thinks the child upon his knee, babbling about the inhabitants of another world, must be a little automaton popped up from God knows where.

Meanwhile, the door marked "Forbidden" opened up again.
It came in.

It rolled on little wheels, a wobbling, halting, toppling progress, a clockwork land galleon, tall as a mast, advancing at a stately if erratic pace, nodding and becking and shedding inessential fragments of its surface as it came, its foliage rustling, now stuck and perilously rocking at a crack in the stone floor with which its wheels cannot cope, now flying helter-skelter, almost out of control, wobbling, clicking, whirring, an eclectic juggernaut evidently almost on the point of collapse; it has been a heavy afternoon.

But, although it looked as if eccentrically self-propelled, Arcimboldo the Milanese pushed it, picking up bits of the thing as they fell off, tutt-tutting at its ruination, pushing it, shoving it, occasionally picking it up bodily and carrying it. He was smeared all over with its secretions and looked forward to a good wash once it had been returned to the curious room from whence it came. There, the Doctor and his assistant will take it apart until the next time.

This thing before us, although it is not, was not and never will be alive, *has* been animate and will be animate again, but, at the moment, not, for now, after one final shove, it stuck stock still, wheels halted, wound down, uttering one last, gross, mechanical sigh.

A nipple dropped off. The Doctor picked it up and offered it to the child. Another strawberry! She shook her head.

The size and prominence of the secondary sexual characteristics indicate this creature is, like the child, of the feminine gender. She lives in the fruit bowl where the Doctor found the first strawberry. When the Archduke wants her, Arcimboldo, who designed her, puts her together again, arranging the fruit of which she is composed on a wicker frame, always a little different from the last time according to what the greenhouse can provide. Today, her hair is largely composed of green muscat grapes, her nose a pear, eyes filbert nuts, cheeks russet apples somewhat wrinkled—never mind! The Archduke has a penchant for older women. When the painter got her ready, she looked like Carmen Miranda's hat on wheels, but her name was "Summer."

But now, what devastation! Hair mashed, nose squashed, bosom pureed, belly juiced. The child observed this apparition with the greatest interest. She spoke again. She queried earnestly:

"If 70 per cent have lost an eye, 75 per cent an ear, 80 per cent an arm, 85 per cent a leg: what percentage, *at least*, must have lost all four?"[2]

Once again, she stumped them. They pondered, all three men, and at last slowly shook their heads. As if the child's question were the last straw, "Summer" now disintegrated—subsided, slithered, slopped off her frame into her fruit bowl, whilst shed fruit, some almost whole, bounced to the rushes around her. The Milanese, with a pang, watched his design disintegrate.

It is not so much that the Archduke likes to pretend this monstrous being is alive, for nothing inhuman is alien to him; rather, he does not care whether she is alive or no, that what he wants to do is to plunge his member into her artificial strangeness, perhaps as he does so imagining himself an orchard and this embrace, this plunge into the succulent flesh, which is not flesh as we know it, which is, if you like, the living metaphor—"fica," explains Arcimboldo, displaying the orifice—this intercourse with the very flesh of summer will fructify his cold kingdom, the snowy country outside the window, where the creaking raven endlessly laments the inclement weather.

"Reason becomes the enemy which withholds from us so many possibilities of pleasure," said Freud.

One day, when the fish within the river freeze, the day of the frigid lunar noon, the Archduke will come to Dr. Dee, his crazy eyes resembling, the one, a blackberry, the other, a cherry, and say: transform me into a harvest festival!

So he did; but the weather got no better.

Peckish, Kelly absently demolished a fallen peach, so lost in thought he never noticed the purple bruise, and the little cat played croquet with the peach stone while Dr. Dee, stirred by memories of his English children long ago and far away, stroked the girl's flaxen hair.

"Whither comest thou?" he asked her.

The question stirred her again into speech.

"A and B began the year with only £1000 apiece," she announced, urgently.

The three men turned to look at her as if she were about to pronounce some piece of oracular wisdom. She tossed her blonde head. She went on. "They borrowed nought; they stole nought. On the next New Year's Day they had £60,000 between them. How did they do it?"[3]

They could not think of a reply. They continued to stare at her, words turning to dust in their mouths.

"How did they do it?" she repeated, now almost with desperation, as if, if they only could stumble on the correct reply, she would be precipitated back, diminutive, stern, rational, within the crystal ball and thence be tossed back through the mirror to "time will be," or, even better, to the book from which she had sprung.

"Poor Tom's a-cold," offered the raven. After that, came silence.

The answers to Alice's conundrums: [1]One. [2]Ten. [3]They went that day to the Bank of England. A stood in front of it, while B went round and stood behind it.

(Problems and answers from *A Tangled Tale*, Lewis Carroll, London, 1885.)

Alice was invented by a logician and therefore comes from the world of nonsense, that is, from the world of non-sense—the opposite of common sense; this world is constructed by logical deduction and is created by language, although language shivers into abstractions within it.

REPLACEMENTS
Lisa Tuttle

Lisa Tuttle, a Texan successfully transplanted to Scotland, has published three novels, *Familiar Spirit, Gabriel,* and *Lost Futures,* and three collections, *A Nest of Nightmare, A Spaceship Built of Stone and Other Stories,* and *Memories of the Body.* She has also written several works of nonfiction and edited the anthology *Skin of the Soul.*

Tuttle's short stories often take on the volatile subject of male-female relations and illuminate the inadvertent wounds the genders sometimes inflict on one another. In "Replacements" she gives physical form to the very realistic male fear of displacement when a newborn is added to the dynamic of a relationship. The story is reprinted from the anthology *MetaHorror.*

—E.D.

Walking through gray north London to the tube station, feeling guilty that he hadn't let Jenny drive him to work and yet relieved to have escaped another pointless argument, Stuart Holder glanced down at a pavement covered in a leaf-fall of fast-food cartons and white paper bags and saw, amid the dog turds, beer cans and dead cigarettes, something horrible.

It was about the size of a cat, naked looking, with leathery, hairless skin and thin, spiky limbs that seemed too frail to support the bulbous, ill-proportioned body. The face, with tiny bright eyes and a wet slit of a mouth, was like an evil monkey's. It saw him and moved in a crippled, spasmodic way. Reaching up, it made a clotted, strangled noise. The sound touched a nerve, like metal between the teeth, and the sight of it, mewling and choking and scrabbling, scaly claws flexing and wriggling, made him feel sick and terrified. He had no phobias, he found insects fascinating, not frightening, and regularly removed, unharmed, the spiders, wasps and mayflies which made Jenny squeal or shudder helplessly.

But this was different. This wasn't some rare species of wingless bat escaped from a zoo, it wasn't something he would find pictured in any reference book. It was something that should not exist, a mistake, something alien. It did not belong in his world.

A little snarl escaped him and he took a step forward and brought his foot down hard.

486

The small, shrill scream lanced through him as he crushed it beneath his shoe and ground it into the road.

Afterwards, as he scraped the sole of his shoe against the curb to clean it, nausea overwhelmed him. He leaned over and vomited helplessly into a red-and-white-striped box of chicken bones and crumpled paper.

He straightened up, shaking, and wiped his mouth again and again with his pocket handkerchief. He wondered if anyone had seen, and had a furtive look around. Cars passed at a steady crawl. Across the road a cluster of schoolgirls dawdled near a man smoking in front of a newsagent's, but on this side of the road the fried chicken franchise and bathroom suppliers had yet to open for the day and the nearest pedestrians were more than a hundred yards away.

Until that moment, Stuart had never killed anything in his life. Mosquitoes and flies of course, other insects probably, a nest of hornets once, that was all. He had never liked the idea of hunting, never lived in the country. He remembered his father putting out poisoned bait for rats, and he remembered shying bricks at those same vermin on a bit of waste ground where he had played as a boy. But rats weren't like other animals; they elicited no sympathy. Some things had to be killed if they would not be driven away.

He made himself look to make sure the thing was not still alive. Nothing should be left to suffer. But his heel had crushed the thing's face out of recognition, and it was unmistakably dead. He felt a cool tide of relief and satisfaction, followed at once, as he walked away, by a nagging uncertainty, the imminence of guilt. Was he right to have killed it, to have acted on violent, irrational impulse? He didn't even know what it was. It might have been somebody's pet.

He went hot and cold with shame and self-disgust. At the corner he stopped with five or six others waiting to cross the road and because he didn't want to look at them he looked down.

And there it was, alive again.

He stifled a scream. No, of course it was not the same one, but another. His leg twitched; he felt frantic with the desire to kill it, and the terror of his desire. The thin wet mouth was moving as if it wanted to speak.

As the crossing-signal began its nagging blare he tore his eyes away from the creature squirming at his feet. Everyone else had started to cross the street, their eyes, like their thoughts, directed ahead. All except one. A woman in a smart business suit was standing still on the pavement, looking down, a sick fascination on her face.

As he looked at her looking at it, the idea crossed his mind that he should kill it for her, as a chivalric, protective act. But she wouldn't see it that way. She would be repulsed by his violence. He didn't want her to think he was a monster. He didn't want to be the monster who had exulted in the crunch of fragile bones, the flesh and viscera merging pulpily beneath his shoe.

He forced himself to look away, to cross the road, to spare the alien life. But he wondered, as he did so, if he had been right to spare it.

Stuart Holder worked as an editor for a publishing company with offices an easy walk from St. Paul's. Jenny had worked there, too, as a secretary, when they met five years ago. Now, though, she had quite a senior position with another publishing house, south of the river, and recently they had given her a car. He had been supportive of her ambitions, supportive of her learning to drive, and proud of her on all fronts when she succeeded, yet he was aware, although he never spoke of it, that something about her success made him uneasy. One small, niggling, insecure part of himself was afraid that one day she would realize she didn't need him anymore. That was why he picked at her, and second-guessed her decisions when she was behind the wheel and he was in the passenger seat. He recognized this as he walked briskly through more crowded streets towards his office, and he told himself he would do better. He would have to. If anything drove them apart it was more likely to be his behavior than her career. He wished he had accepted her offer of a ride today. Better any amount of petty irritation between husband and wife than to be haunted by the memory of that tiny face, distorted in the death he had inflicted. Entering the building, he surreptitiously scraped the sole of his shoe against the carpet.

Upstairs two editors and one of the publicity girls were in a huddle around his secretary's desk; they turned on him the guilty-defensive faces of women who have been discussing secrets men aren't supposed to know.

He felt his own defensiveness rising to meet theirs as he smiled. "Can I get any of you chaps a cup of coffee?"

"I'm sorry, Stuart, did you want . . . ?" As the others faded away, his secretary removed a stiff white paper bag with the NEXT logo printed on it from her desktop.

"Joke, Frankie, joke." He always got his own coffee because he liked the excuse to wander, and he was always having to reassure her that she was not failing in her secretarial duties. He wondered if Next sold sexy underwear, decided it would be unkind to tease her further.

He felt a strong urge to call Jenny and tell her what had happened, although he knew he wouldn't be able to explain, especially not over the phone. Just hearing her voice, the sound of sanity, would be a comfort, but he restrained himself until just after noon, when he made the call he made every day.

Her secretary told him she was in a meeting. "Tell her Stuart rang," he said, knowing she would call him back as always.

But that day she didn't. Finally, at five minutes to five, Stuart rang his wife's office and was told she had left for the day.

It was unthinkable for Jenny to leave work early, as unthinkable as for her not to return his call. He wondered if she was ill. Although he usually stayed in the office until well after six, now he shoved a manuscript in his briefcase and went out to brave the rush hour.

He wondered if she was mad at him. But Jenny didn't sulk. If she was angry she said so. They didn't lie or play those sorts of games with each other, pretending not to be in, "forgetting" to return calls.

As he emerged from his local underground station Stuart felt apprehensive. His eyes scanned the pavement and the gutters, and once or twice the flutter of paper made him jump, but of the creatures he had seen that morning there were no signs. The body of the one he had killed was gone, perhaps eaten by a passing dog, perhaps returned to whatever strange dimension had spawned it. He noticed, before he turned off the high street, that other pedestrians were also taking a keener than usual interest in the pavement and the edge of the road, and that made him feel vindicated somehow.

London traffic being what it was, he was home before Jenny. While he waited for the sound of her key in the lock he made himself a cup of tea, cursed, poured it down the sink, and had a stiff whisky instead. He had just finished it and was feeling much better when he heard the street door open.

"Oh!" The look on her face reminded him unpleasantly of those women in the office this morning, making him feel like an intruder in his own place. Now Jenny smiled, but it was too late. "I didn't expect you to be here so early."

"Nor me. I tried to call you, but they said you'd left already. I wondered if you were feeling all right."

"I'm fine!"

"You look fine." The familiar sight of her melted away his irritation. He loved the way she looked: her slender, boyish figure, her close-cropped, curly hair, her pale complexion and bright blue eyes.

Her cheeks now had a slight hectic flush. She caught her bottom lip between her teeth and gave him an assessing look before coming straight out with it. "How would you feel about keeping a pet?"

Stuart felt a horrible conviction that she was not talking about a dog or a cat. He wondered if it was the whisky on an empty stomach which made him feel dizzy.

"It was under my car. If I hadn't happened to notice something moving down there I could have run over it." She lifted her shoulders in a delicate shudder.

"Oh, God, Jenny, you haven't brought it home!"

She looked indignant. "Well, of course I did! I couldn't just leave it in the street—somebody else might have run it over."

Or stepped on it, he thought, realizing now that he could never tell Jenny what he had done. That made him feel even worse, but maybe he was wrong. Maybe it was just a cat she'd rescued. "What is it?"

She gave a strange, excited laugh. "I don't know. Something very rare, I think. Here, look." She slipped the large, woven bag off her shoulder, opening it, holding it out to him. "Look. Isn't it the sweetest thing?"

How could two people who were so close, so alike in so many ways, see something so differently? He only wanted to kill it, even now, while she had obviously fallen in love. He kept his face carefully neutral although he couldn't help flinching from her description. "*Sweet?*"

It gave him a pang to see how she pulled back, holding the bag protectively close as she said, "Well, I know it's not pretty, but so what? I thought it was horrible, too, at first sight. . . ." Her face clouded, as if she found her first impression difficult to remember, or to credit, and her voice faltered a little. "But then, then I realized how *helpless* it was. It needed me. It can't help how it looks. Anyway, doesn't it kind of remind you of the Psammead?"

"The what?"

"Psammead. You know, *The Five Children and It?*"

He recognized the title but her passion for old-fashioned children's books was something he didn't share. He shook his head impatiently. "That thing didn't come out of a book, Jen. You found it in the street and you don't know what it is or where it came from. It could be dangerous, it could be diseased."

"Dangerous," she said in a withering tone.

"You don't know."

"I've been with him all day and he hasn't hurt me, or anybody else at the office, he's perfectly happy being held, and he likes being scratched behind the ears."

He did not miss the pronoun shift. "It might have rabies."

"Don't be silly."

"Don't *you* be silly; it's not exactly native, is it? It might be carrying all sorts of foul parasites from South America or Africa or wherever."

"Now you're being racist. I'm not going to listen to you. *And* you've been drinking." She flounced out of the room.

If he'd been holding his glass still he might have thrown it. He closed his eyes and concentrated on breathing in and out slowly. This was worse than any argument they'd ever had, the only crucial disagreement of their marriage. Jenny had stronger views about many things than he did, so her wishes usually prevailed. He didn't mind that. But this was different. He wasn't having that creature in his home. He had to make her agree.

Necessity cooled his blood. He had his temper under control when his wife returned. "I'm sorry," he said, although she was the one who should have apologized. Still looking prickly, she shrugged and would not meet his eyes. "Want to go out to dinner tonight?"

She shook her head. "I'd rather not. I've got some work to do."

"Can I get you something to drink? I'm only one whisky ahead of you, honest."

Her shoulders relaxed. "I'm sorry. Low blow. Yeah, pour me one. And one for yourself." She sat down on the couch, her bag by her feet. Leaning over, reaching inside, she cooed, "Who's my little sweetheart, then?"

Normally he would have taken a seat beside her. Now, though, he eyed the pale, misshapen bundle on her lap and, after handing her a glass, retreated across the room. "Don't get mad, but isn't having a pet one of those things we discuss and agree on beforehand?"

He saw the tension come back into her shoulders, but she went on stroking the thing, keeping herself calm. "Normally, yes. But this is special. I didn't plan it. It happened, and now I've got a responsibility to him. Or her." She giggled. "We don't even know what sex you are, do we, my precious?"

He said carefully, "I can see that you had to do something when you found it, but keeping it might not be the best thing."

"I'm not going to put it out in the street."

"No, no, but . . . don't you think it would make sense to let a professional have a look at it? Take it to a vet, get it checked out . . . maybe it needs shots or something."

She gave him a withering look and for a moment he faltered, but then he rallied. "Come on, Jenny, be reasonable! You can't just drag some strange animal in off the street and keep it, just like that. You don't even know what it eats."

"I gave it some fruit at lunch. It ate that. Well, it sucked out the juice. I don't think it can chew."

"But you don't know, do you? Maybe the fruit juice was just an aperitif, maybe it needs half its weight in live insects every day, or a couple of small, live mammals. Do you really think you could cope with feeding it mice or rabbits fresh from the pet shop every week?"

"Oh, Stuart."

"Well? Will you just take it to a vet? Make sure it's healthy? Will you do that much?"

"And then I can keep it? If the vet says there's nothing wrong with it, and it doesn't need to eat anything too impossible?"

"Then we can talk about it. Hey, don't pout at me; I'm not your father, I'm not telling you what to do. We're partners, and partners don't make unilateral decisions about things that affect them both; partners discuss things and reach compromises . . ."

"There can't be any compromise about this."

He felt as if she'd doused him with ice water. "What?"

"Either I win and I keep him or you win and I give him up. Where's the compromise?"

This was why wars were fought, thought Stuart, but he didn't say it. He was the picture of sweet reason, explaining as if he meant it, "The compromise is that we each try to see the other person's point. You get the animal checked out, make sure it's healthy and I, I'll keep an open mind about having a pet, and see if I might start liking . . . him. Does he have a name yet?"

Her eyes flickered. "No . . . we can choose one later, together. If we keep him."

He still felt cold and, although he could think of no reason for it, he was certain she was lying to him.

In bed that night as he groped for sleep Stuart kept seeing the tiny, hideous face of the thing screaming as his foot came down on it. That moment of blind, killing rage was not like him. He couldn't deny he had done it, or how he had felt, but now, as Jenny slept innocently beside him, as the creature she had rescued, a twin to his victim, crouched alive in the bathroom, he tried to remember it differently.

In fantasy, he stopped his foot, he controlled his rage and, staring at the memory of the alien animal, he struggled to see past his anger and his fear, to see through those fiercer masculine emotions and find his way to Jenny's feminine pity. Maybe his intuition had been wrong and hers was right. Maybe, if he had waited a little longer, instead of lashing out, he would have seen how unnecessary his fear was.

Poor little thing, poor little thing. It's helpless, it needs me, it's harmless so I won't harm it.

Slowly, in imagination, he worked towards that feeling, *her* feeling, and then, suddenly, he was there, through the anger, through the fear, through the hate to . . . not love, he couldn't say that, but compassion. Glowing and warm, compassion filled his heart and flooded his veins, melting the ice there and washing him out into the sea of sleep, and dreams where Jenny smiled and loved him and there was no space between them for misunderstanding.

He woke in the middle of the night with a desperate urge to pee. He was out of bed in the dark hallway when he remembered what was waiting in the bathroom. He couldn't go back to bed with the need unsatisfied, but he stood outside the bathroom door, hand hovering over the light switch on this side, afraid to turn it on, open the door, go in.

It wasn't, he realized, that he was afraid of a creature no bigger than a football and less likely to hurt him; rather, he was afraid that he might hurt it. It was a stronger variant of that reckless vertigo he had felt sometimes in high places, the fear, not of falling, but of throwing oneself off, of losing control and giving in to self-destructive urges. He didn't *want* to kill the thing—had his own feelings not undergone a sea change, Jenny's love for it would have been enough to stop him—but something, some dark urge stronger than himself, might make him.

Finally he went down to the end of the hall and outside to the weedy, muddy little area which passed for the communal front garden and in which the rubbish bins, of necessity, were kept, and, shivering in his thin cotton pajamas in the damp, chilly air, he watered the sickly forsythia, or whatever it was, that Jenny had planted so optimistically last winter.

When he went back inside, more uncomfortable than when he had gone out, he saw the light was on in the bathroom, and as he approached the half-open door, he heard Jenny's voice, low and soothing. "There, there. Nobody's going to hurt you, I promise. You're safe here. Go to sleep now. Go to sleep."

He went past without pausing, knowing he would be viewed as an intruder, and got back into bed. He fell asleep, lulled by the meaningless murmur of her voice, still waiting for her to join him.

Stuart was not used to doubting Jenny, but when she told him she had visited a veterinarian who had given her new pet a clean bill of health, he did not believe her.

In a neutral tone he asked, "Did he say what kind of animal it was?"

"He didn't know."

"He didn't know what it was, but he was sure it was perfectly healthy."

"God, Stuart, what do you want? It's obvious to everybody but you that my little friend is healthy and happy. What do you want, a birth certificate?"

He looked at her "friend," held close against her side, looking squashed and miserable. "What do you mean, 'everybody'?"

She shrugged. "Everybody at work. They're all jealous as anything." She planted a kiss on the thing's pointy head. Then she looked at him, and he realized that she had not kissed him, as she usually did, when he came in. She'd been clutching that thing the whole time. "I'm going to keep him," she said quietly. "If you don't like it, then . . ." Her pause seemed to pile up in solid, transparent blocks between them. "Then, I'm sorry, but that's how it is."

So much for an equal relationship, he thought. So much for sharing. Mortally wounded, he decided to pretend it hadn't happened.

"Want to go out for Indian tonight?"

She shook her head, turning away. "I want to stay in. There's something on telly. You go on. You could bring me something back, if you wouldn't mind. A spinach bahjee and a couple of nans would do me."

"And what about . . . something for your little friend?"

She smiled a private smile. "He's all right. I've fed him already." Then she raised her eyes to his and acknowledged his effort. "Thanks."

He went out and got take-away for them both, and stopped at the off-license for the Mexican beer Jenny favored. A radio in the off-license was playing a sentimental song about love that Stuart remembered from his earliest childhood: his mother used to sing it. He was shocked to realize he had tears in his eyes.

That night Jenny made up the sofa bed in the spare room, explaining, "He can't stay in the bathroom; it's just not satisfactory, you know it's not."

"He needs the bed?"

"I do. He's confused, everything is new and different, I'm the one thing he can count on. I have to stay with him. He needs me."

"He needs you? What about me?"

"Oh, Stuart," she said impatiently. "You're a grown man. You can sleep by yourself for a night or two."

"And that thing can't?"

"Don't call him a thing."

"What am I supposed to call it? Look, you're not its mother—it doesn't need you as much as you'd like to think. It was perfectly all right in the bathroom last night—it'll be fine in here on its own."

"Oh? And what do you know about it? You'd like to kill him, wouldn't you? Admit it."

"No," he said, terrified that she had guessed the truth. If she knew how he had killed one of those things she would never forgive him. "It's not true, I don't—I couldn't hurt it any more than I could hurt you."

Her face softened. She believed him. It didn't matter how he felt about the creature. Hurting it, knowing how she felt, would be like committing an act of violence against her, and they both knew he wouldn't do that. "Just for a few nights, Stuart. Just until he settles in."

He had to accept that. All he could do was hang on, hope that she still loved him and that this wouldn't be forever.

The days passed. Jenny no longer offered to drive him to work. When he asked her, she said it was out of her way and with traffic so bad a detour would make her late. She said it was silly to take him the short distance to the station, especially as there was nowhere she could safely stop to let him out, and anyway the walk would do him good. They were all good reasons, which he had used in the old days himself, but her excuses struck him painfully when he remembered how eager she had once been for his company, how ready to make any detour for his sake. Her new pet accompanied her everywhere, even to work, snug in the little nest she had made for it in a woven carrier bag.

"Of course things are different now. But I haven't stopped loving you," she said when he tried to talk to her about the breakdown of their marriage. "It's not like I've found another man. This is something completely different. It doesn't threaten you; you're still my husband."

But it was obvious to him that a husband was no longer something she particularly valued. He began to have fantasies about killing it. Not, this time, in a blind rage, but as part of a carefully thought-out plan. He might poison it, or spirit it away somehow and pretend it had run away. Once it was gone he hoped Jenny would forget it and be his again.

But he never had a chance. Jenny was quite obsessive about the thing, as if it were too valuable to be left unguarded for a single minute. Even when she took a bath, or went to the toilet, the creature was with her, behind the locked door of the bathroom. When he offered to look after it for her for a few minutes she just smiled, as if the idea was manifestly ridiculous, and he didn't dare insist.

So he went to work, and went out for drinks with colleagues, and spent what time he could with Jenny, although they were never alone. He didn't argue with her, although he wasn't above trying to move her to pity if he could. He made seemingly casual comments designed to convince her of his change of heart so that eventually, weeks or months from now, she would trust him and leave the creature with him—and then, later, perhaps, they could put their marriage back together.

One afternoon, after an extended lunch break, Stuart returned to the office to find one of the senior editors crouched on the floor beside his secretary's empty desk, whispering and chuckling to herself.

He cleared his throat nervously. "Linda?"

She lurched back on her heels and got up awkwardly. She blushed and ducked her head as she turned, looking very unlike her usual high-powered self. "Oh, uh, Stuart, I was just—"

Frankie came in with a pile of photocopying. "Uh-huh," she said loudly.

Linda's face got even redder. "Just going," she mumbled, and fled.

Before he could ask, Stuart saw the creature, another crippled bat–without–wings, on the floor beside the open bottom drawer of Frankie's desk. It looked up at him, opened its slit of a mouth and gave a sad little hiss. Around one matchstick-thin leg it wore a fine golden chain which was fastened at the other end to the drawer.

"Some people would steal anything that's not chained down," said Frankie darkly. "People you wouldn't suspect."

He stared at her, letting her see his disapproval, his annoyance, disgust, even. "Animals in the office aren't part of the contract, Frankie."

"It's not an animal."

"What is it, then?"

"I don't know. You tell me."

"It doesn't matter what it is, you can't have it here."

"I can't leave it at home."

"Why not?"

She turned away from him, busying herself with her stacks of paper. "I can't leave it alone. It might get hurt. It might escape."

"Chance would be a fine thing."

She shot him a look, and he was certain she knew he wasn't talking about *her* pet. He said, "What does your boyfriend think about it?"

"I don't have a boyfriend." She sounded angry but then, abruptly, the anger dissipated, and she smirked. "I don't have to have one, do I?"

"You can't have that animal here. Whatever it is. You'll have to take it home."

She raised her fuzzy eyebrows. "Right now?"

He was tempted to say yes, but thought of the manuscripts that wouldn't be sent out, the letters that wouldn't be typed, the delays and confusions, and he sighed. "Just don't bring it back again. All right?"

"Yowza."

He felt very tired. He could tell her what to do but she would no more obey than would his wife. She would bring it back the next day and keep bringing it back, maybe keeping it hidden, maybe not, until he either gave in or was forced into firing her. He went into his office, closed the door, and put his head down on his desk.

That evening he walked in on his wife feeding the creature with her blood.

It was immediately obvious that it was that way round. The creature might be a vampire—it obviously was—but his wife was no helpless victim. She was wide awake and in control, holding the creature firmly, letting it feed from a vein in her arm.

She flinched as if anticipating a shout, but he couldn't speak. He watched what was happening without attempting to interfere and gradually she relaxed again, as if he wasn't there.

When the creature, sated, fell off, she kept it cradled on her lap and reached with her other hand for the surgical spirit and cotton wool on the table, moistened a piece of cotton wool and tamped it to the tiny wound. Then, finally, she met her husband's eyes.

"He has to eat," she said reasonably. "He can't chew. He needs blood. Not very much, but . . ."

"And he needs it from you? You can't . . . ?"

"I can't hold down some poor scared rabbit or dog for him, no." She made a shuddering face. "Well, really, think about it. You know how squeamish I am. This is so much easier. It doesn't hurt."

It hurts me, he thought, but couldn't say it. "Jenny . . ."

"Oh, don't start," she said crossly. "I'm not going to get any disease from it, and he doesn't take enough to make any difference. Actually, I like it. We both do."

"Jenny, please don't. Please. For me. Give it up."

"No." She held the scraggy, ugly thing close and gazed at Stuart like a dispassionate executioner. "I'm sorry, Stuart, I really am, but this is nonnegotiable. If you can't accept that you'd better leave."

This was the showdown he had been avoiding, the end of it all. He tried to rally his arguments and then he realized he had none. She had said it. She had made her choice, and it was nonnegotiable. And he realized, looking at her now, that although she reminded him of the woman he loved, he didn't want to live with what she had become.

He could have refused to leave. After all, he had done nothing wrong. Why should he give up his home, this flat which was half his? But he could not force Jenny out onto the streets with nowhere to go; he still felt responsible for her.

"I'll pack a bag, and make a few phone calls," he said quietly. He knew someone from work who was looking for a lodger, and if all else failed, his brother had a spare room. Already, in his thoughts, he had left.

He ended up, once they'd sorted out their finances and formally separated, in a flat just off the Holloway Road, near Archway. It was not too far to walk if Jenny cared to visit, which she never did. Sometimes he called on her, but it was painful to feel himself an unwelcome visitor in the home they once had shared.

He never had to fire Frankie; she handed in her notice a week later, telling him she'd been offered an editorial job at The Women's Press. He wondered if pets in the office were part of the contract over there.

He never learned if the creatures had names. He never knew where they had come from, or how many there were. Had they fallen only in Islington? (Frankie had a flat somewhere off Upper Street.) He never saw anything on the news about them, or read any official confirmation of their existence, but he was aware of occasional oblique references to them in other contexts, occasional glimpses.

One evening, coming home on the tube, he found himself looking at the woman sitting opposite. She was about his own age, probably in her early thirties, with strawberry blond hair, greenish eyes, and an almost translucent complexion. She was strikingly dressed in high, soft-leather boots, a long black woolen skirt, and an enveloping cashmere cloak of cranberry red. High on the cloak, below and to the right of the fastening at the neck, was a simple, gold circle brooch. Attached to it he noticed a very fine golden chain which vanished inside the cloak, like the end of a watch fob.

He looked at it idly, certain he had seen something like it before, on other women, knowing it reminded him of something. The train arrived at Archway, and as he rose to leave the train, so did the attractive woman. Her stride matched his. They might well leave the station together. He tried to think of something to say to her, some pretext for striking up a conversation. He was after all a single man again now, and she might be a single woman. He had forgotten how single people in London contrived to meet.

He looked at her again, sidelong, hoping she would turn her head and look at him. With one slender hand she toyed with her gold chain. Her cloak fell open slightly as she walked, and he caught a glimpse of the creature she carried beneath it, close to her body, attached by a slender golden chain.

He stopped walking and let her get away from him. He had to rest for a little while before he felt able to climb the stairs to the street.

By then he was wondering if he had really seen what he thought he had seen. The glimpse had been so brief. But he had been deeply shaken by what he saw or imagined, and he turned the wrong way outside the station. When he finally realized, he was at the corner of Jenny's road, which had once also been his. Rather than retrace his steps, he decided to take the turning and walk past her house.

Lights were on in the front room, the curtains drawn against the early winter dark. His footsteps slowed as he drew nearer. He felt such a longing to be inside, back home, belonging. He wondered if she would be pleased at all to see him. He wondered if she ever felt lonely, as he did.

Then he saw the tiny, dark figure between the curtains and the window. It was spread-eagled against the glass, scrabbling uselessly; inside, longing to be out.

As he stared, feeling its pain as his own, the curtains swayed and opened slightly as a human figure moved between them. He saw the woman reach out and pull the creature away from the glass, back into the warm, lighted room with her, and the curtains fell again, shutting him out.

THE GHOST VILLAGE
Peter Straub

Peter Straub is the author of the novels *Marriages, Under Venus, Julia, If You Could See Me Now, Ghost Story, Shadowland, Floating Dragon, The Talisman* (with Stephen King), *Koko, Mystery,* and most recently, *The Throat,* as well as the collection *Houses Without Doors,* the omnibus *Wild Animals,* and two volumes of poetry, *Open Air* and *Leeson Park and Belsize Square.*

Some of Straub's most effective fiction has used the Vietnam War as a backdrop for his explorations of the behavior of men under extreme conditions. "The Ghost Village" is only partly about the American "invaders" and serves to remind us of the universal nature of horror. This powerful novella is from *MetaHorror.*

—E.D.

This story skillfully explores the horror of human minds forced to acknowledge things that are usually kept secret, terribly secret, among those who have witnessed, and are incapable of preventing, evil deeds.

—T.W.

1

In Vietnam I knew a man who went quietly and purposefully crazy because his wife wrote him that his son had been sexually abused—"messed with"—by the leader of their church choir. This man was a black six-foot-six grunt named Leonard Hamnet, from a small town in Tennessee named Archibald. Before writing, his wife had waited until she had endured the entire business of going to the police, talking to other parents, returning to the police with another accusation, and finally succeeding in having the man charged. He was up for trial in two months. Leonard Hamnet was no happier about that than he was about the original injury.

"I got to murder him, you know, but I'm seriously thinking on murdering her too," he said. He still held the letter in his hands, and he was speaking to Spanky Burrage, Michael Poole, Conor Linklater, SP4 Cotton, Calvin Hill, Tina Pumo, the magnificent M. O. Dengler, and myself. "All this is going on, my boy needs help, this here Mr. Brewster needs to be dismantled, needs to be *racked* and *stacked,*

497

and she don't tell me! Makes me want to put her *down*, man. Take her damn head off and put it up on a stake in the yard, man. With a sign saying: *Here is one stupid woman.*"

We were in the unofficial part of Camp Crandall known as No Man's Land, located between the wire perimeter and a shack, also unofficial, where a cunning little weasel named Wilson Manly sold contraband beer and liquor. No Man's Land, so called because the C.O. pretended it did not exist, contained a mound of old tires, a pisstube, and a lot of dusty red ground. Leonard Hamnet gave the letter in his hand a dispirited look, folded it into the pocket of his fatigues, and began to roam around the heap of tires, aiming kicks at the ones that stuck out furthest. "One stupid woman," he repeated. Dust exploded up from a burst, worn-down wheel of rubber.

I wanted to make sure Hamnet knew he was angry with Mr. Brewster, not his wife, and said, "She was trying—"

Hamnet's great glistening bull's head turned toward me.

"Look at what the woman did. She nailed that bastard. She got other people to admit that he messed with their kids too. That must be almost impossible. And she had the guy arrested. He's going to be put away for a long time."

"I'll put that bitch away, too," Hamnet said, and kicked an old gray tire hard enough to push it nearly a foot back into the heap. All the other tires shuddered and moved. For a second it seemed that the entire mound might collapse.

"This is my *boy* I'm talking about here," Hamnet said. "This shit has gone far enough."

"The important thing," Dengler said, "is to take care of your boy. You have to see he gets help."

"How'm I gonna do that from here?" Hamnet shouted.

"Write him a letter," Dengler said. "Tell him you love him. Tell him he did right to go to his mother. Tell him you think about him all the time."

Hamnet took the letter from his pocket and stared at it. It was already stained and wrinkled. I did not think it could survive many more of Hamnet's readings. His face seemed to get heavier, no easy trick with a face like Hamnet's. "I got to get home," he said. "I got to get back home and take *care* of these people."

Hamnet began putting in requests for compassionate leave relentlessly—one request a day. When we were out on patrol, sometimes I saw him unfold the tattered sheet of notepaper from his shirt pocket and read it two or three times, concentrating intensely. When the letter began to shred along the folds, Hamnet taped it together.

We were going out on four-and five-day patrols during that period, taking a lot of casualties. Hamnet performed well in the field, but he had retreated so far within himself that he spoke in monosyllables. He wore a dull, glazed look, and moved like a man who had just eaten a heavy dinner. I thought he looked like he had given up, and when people gave up they did not last long—they were already very close to death, and other people avoided them.

We were camped in a stand of trees at the edge of a paddy. That day we had lost two men so new that I had already forgotten their names. We had to eat cold C rations because heating them with C-4 it would have been like putting up billboards and arc lights. We couldn't smoke, and we were not supposed to talk. Hamnet's C rations consisted of an old can of Spam that dated from an earlier war and a can of peaches. He saw Spanky staring at the peaches and tossed him the can. Then he dropped the Spam between his legs. Death was almost visible around him. He fingered the note out of his pocket and tried to read it in the damp gray twilight.

At that moment someone started shooting at us, and the Lieutenant yelled "*Shit!*", and we dropped our food and returned fire at the invisible people trying to kill us. When they kept shooting back, we had to go through the paddy.

The warm water came up to our chests. At the dikes, we scrambled over and splashed down into the muck on the other side. A boy from Santa Cruz, California, named Thomas Blevins got a round in the back of his neck and dropped dead into the water just short of the first dike, and another boy named Tyrell Budd coughed and dropped down right beside him. The F.O. called in an artillery strike. We leaned against the backs of the last two dikes when the big shells came thudding in. The ground shook and the water rippled, and the edge of the forest went up in a series of fireballs. We could hear the monkeys screaming.

One by one we crawled over the last dike onto the damp but solid ground on the other side of the paddy. Here the trees were much sparser, and a little group of thatched huts was visible through them.

Then two things I did not understand happened, one after the other. Someone off in the forest fired a mortar round at us—just one. One mortar, one round. That was the first thing. I fell down and shoved my face in the muck, and everybody around me did the same. I considered that this might be my last second on earth, and greedily inhaled whatever life might be left to me. Whoever fired the mortar should have had an excellent idea of our location, and I experienced that endless moment of pure, terrifying helplessness—a moment in which the soul simultaneously clings to the body and readies itself to let go of it—until the shell landed on top of the last dike and blew it to bits. Dirt, mud, and water slopped down around us, and shell fragments whizzed through the air. One of the fragments sailed over us, sliced a hamburger-sized wad of bark and wood from a tree, and clanged into Spanky Burrage's helmet with a sound like a brick hitting a garbage can. The fragment fell to the ground, and a little smoke drifted up from it.

We picked ourselves up. Spanky looked dead, except that he was breathing. Hamnet shouldered his pack and picked up Spanky and slung him over his shoulder. He saw me looking at him.

"I gotta take *care* of these people," he said.

The other thing I did not understand—apart from why there had been only one mortar round—came when we entered the village.

Lieutenant Harry Beevers had yet to join us, and we were nearly a year away from the events at Ia Thuc, when everything, the world and ourselves within the world, went crazy. I have to explain what happened. Lieutenant Harry Beevers killed thirty children in a cave at Ia Thuc and their bodies disappeared, but Michael Poole and I went into that cave and knew that something obscene had happened in there. We smelled evil, we touched its wings with our hands. A pitiful character named Victor Spitalny ran into the cave when he heard gunfire, and came pinwheeling out right away, screaming, covered with welts or hives that vanished almost as soon as he came out into the air. Poor Spitalny had touched it too. Because I was twenty and already writing books in my head, I thought that the cave was the place where the other *Tom Sawyer* ended, where Injun Joe raped Becky Thatcher and slit Tom's throat.

When we walked into the little village in the woods on the other side of the rice paddy, I experienced a kind of foretaste of Ia Thuc. If I can say this without setting off all the Gothic bells, the place seemed intrinsically, inherently wrong—it was too quiet, too still, completely without noise or movement. There were no chickens, dogs, or pigs; no old women came out to look us over, no old men offered conciliatory smiles. The little huts, still inhabitable, were empty—something I had never seen before in Vietnam, and never saw again. It was a ghost village, in a country where people thought the earth was sanctified by their ancestors' bodies.

Poole's map said that the place was named Bong To.

Hamnet lowered Spanky into the long grass as soon as we reached the center of the empty village. I bawled out a few words in my poor Vietnamese.

Spanky groaned. He gently touched the sides of his helmet. "I caught a head wound," he said.

"You wouldn't have a head at all, you was only wearing your liner," Hamnet said.

Spanky bit his lips and pushed the helmet up off his head. He groaned. A finger of blood ran down beside his ear. Finally the helmet passed over a lump the size of an apple that rose up from under his hair. Wincing, Spanky fingered this enormous knot. "I see double," he said. "I'll never get that helmet back on."

The medic said, "Take it easy, we'll get you out of here."

"Out of *here?*" Spanky brightened up.

"Back to Crandall," the medic said.

Spitalny sidled up, and Spanky frowned at him. "There ain't nobody here," Spitalny said. "What the fuck is going on?" He took the emptiness of the village as a personal affront.

Leonard Hamnet turned his back and spat.

"Spitalny, Tiano," the Lieutenant said. "Go into the paddy and get Tyrell and Blevins. Now."

Tattoo Tiano, who was due to die six and a half months later and was Spitalny's only friend, said, "You do it this time, Lieutenant."

Hamnet turned around and began moving toward Tiano and Spitalny. He looked as if he had grown two sizes larger, as if his hands could pick up boulders. I had forgotten how big he was. His head was lowered, and a rim of clear white showed above the irises. I wouldn't have been surprised if he had blown smoke from his nostrils.

"Hey, I'm gone, I'm already there," Tiano said. He and Spitalny began moving quickly through the sparse trees. Whoever had fired the mortar had packed up and gone. By now it was nearly dark, and the mosquitos had found us.

"So?" Poole said.

Hamnet sat down heavily enough for me to feel the shock in my boots. He said, "I have to go home, Lieutenant. I don't mean no disrespect, but I cannot take this shit much longer."

The Lieutenant said he was working on it.

Poole, Hamnet, and I looked around at the village.

Spanky Burrage said, "Good quiet place for Ham to catch up on his reading."

"Maybe I better take a look," the Lieutenant said. He flicked the lighter a couple of times and walked off toward the nearest hut. The rest of us stood around like fools, listening to the mosquitos and the sounds of Tiano and Spitalny pulling the dead men up over the dikes. Every now and then Spanky groaned and shook his head. Too much time passed.

The Lieutenant said something almost inaudible from inside the hut. He came back outside in a hurry, looking disturbed and puzzled even in the darkness.

"Underhill, Poole," he said, "I want you to see this."

Poole and I glanced at each other. I wondered if I looked as bad as he did. Poole seemed to be couple of psychic inches from either taking a poke at the Lieutenant or exploding altogether. In his muddy face his eyes were the size of hen's eggs. He was wound up like a cheap watch. I thought that I probably looked pretty much the same.

"What is it, Lieutenant?" he asked.

The Lieutenant gestured for us to come to the hut, then turned around and went back inside. There was no reason for us not to follow him. The Lieutenant was a jerk, but Harry Beevers, our next Lieutenant, was a baron, an earl among jerks, and we nearly always did whatever dumb thing he told us to do. Poole was so ragged and edgy that he looked as if he felt like shooting the Lieutenant in the back. I felt like shooting the Lieutenant in the back, I realized a second later. I didn't have an idea in the world what was going on in Poole's mind. I grumbled something and moved toward the hut. Poole followed.

The Lieutenant was standing in the doorway, looking over his shoulder and fingering his sidearm. He frowned at us to let us know we had been slow to obey him, then flicked on the lighter. The sudden hollows and shadows in his face made him resemble one of the corpses I had opened up when I was in graves registration at Camp White Star.

"You want to know what it is, Poole? Okay, you tell me what it is."

He held the lighter before him like a torch and marched into the hut. I imagined the entire dry, flimsy structure bursting into heat and flame. This Lieutenant was not destined to get home walking and breathing, and I pitied and hated him about equally, but I did not want to turn into toast because he had found an American body inside a hut and didn't know what to do about it. I'd heard of platoons finding the mutilated corpses of American prisoners, and hoped that this was not our turn.

And then, in the instant before I smelled blood and saw the Lieutenant stoop to lift a panel on the floor, I thought that what had spooked him was not the body of an American POW but of a child who had been murdered and left behind in this empty place. The Lieutenant had probably not seen any dead children yet. Some part of the Lieutenant was still worrying about what a girl named Becky Rodden-burger was getting up to back at Idaho State, and a dead child would be too much reality for him.

He pulled up the wooden panel in the floor, and I caught the smell of blood. The Zippo died, and darkness closed down on us. The Lieutenant yanked the panel back on its hinges. The smell of blood floated up from whatever was beneath the floor. The Lieutenant flicked the Zippo, and his face jumped out of the darkness. "Now. Tell me what this is."

"It's where they hide the kids when people like us show up," I said. "Smells like something went wrong. Did you take a look?"

I saw in his tight cheeks and almost lipless mouth that he had not. He wasn't about to go down there and get killed by the Minotaur while his platoon stood around outside.

"Taking a look is your job, Underhill," he said.

For a second we both looked at the ladder, made of peeled branches lashed together with rags, that led down into the pit.

"Give me the lighter," Poole said, and grabbed it away from the Lieutenant. He sat on the edge of the hole and leaned over, bringing the flame beneath the level of the floor. He grunted at whatever he saw, and surprised both the Lieutenant and myself by pushing himself off the ledge into the opening. The light went out. The Lieutenant and I looked down into the dark open rectangle in the floor.

The lighter flared again. I could see Poole's extended arm, the jittering little fire, a packed-earth floor. The top of the concealed room was less than an inch above the top of Poole's head. He moved away from the opening.

"What is it? Are there any—" The Lieutenant's voice made a creaky sound. "Any bodies?"

"Come down here, Tim," Poole called up.

I sat on the floor and swung my legs into the pit. Then I jumped down.

Beneath the floor, the smell of blood was almost sickeningly strong.

"What do you see?" the Lieutenant shouted. He was trying to sound like a leader, and his voice squeaked on the last word.

I saw an empty room shaped like a giant grave. The walls were covered by some kind of thick paper held in place by wooden struts sunk into the earth. Both the thick brown paper and two of the struts showed old bloodstains.

"Hot," Poole said, and closed the lighter.

"Come *on*, damn it," came the Lieutenant's voice. "Get out of there."

"Yes, sir," Poole said. He flicked the lighter back on. Many layers of thick paper formed an absorbent pad between the earth and the room, and the topmost, thinnest layer had been covered with vertical lines of Vietnamese writing. The writing looked like poetry, like the left-hand pages of Kenneth Rexroth's translations of Tu Fu and Li Po.

"Well, well," Poole said, and I turned to see him pointing at what first looked like intricately woven strands of rope fixed to the bloodstained wooden uprights. Poole stepped forward and the weave jumped into sharp relief. About four feet off the ground, iron chains had been screwed to the uprights. The thick pad between the two lengths of chain had been soaked with blood. The three feet of ground between the posts looked rusty. Poole moved the lighter closer to the chains, and we saw dried blood on the metal links.

"I want you guys out of there, and I mean *now*," whined the Lieutenant.

Poole snapped the lighter shut.

"I just changed my mind," I said softly. "I'm putting twenty bucks into the Elijah fund. For two weeks from today. That's what, June twentieth?"

"Tell it to Spanky," he said. Spanky Burrage had invented the pool we called the Elijah fund, and he held the money. Michael had not put any money into the pool. He thought that a new Lieutenant might be even worse than the one we had. Of course he was right. Harry Beevers was our next Lieutenant. Elijah Joys, Lieutenant Elijah Joys of New Utrecht, Idaho, a graduate of the University of Idaho and basic training at Fort Benning, Georgia, was an inept, weak Lieutenant, not a disastrous one. If Spanky could have seen what was coming, he would have given back the money and prayed for the safety of Lieutenant Joys.

Poole and I moved back toward the opening. I felt as if I had seen a shrine to an obscene deity. The Lieutenant leaned over and stuck out his hand—uselessly, because he did not bend down far enough for us to reach him. We levered ourselves up out of the hole stiff-armed, as if we were leaving a swimming pool. The Lieutenant stepped back. He had a thin face and thick, fleshy nose, and his Adam's apple danced around in his neck like a jumping bean. He might not have been Harry Beevers, but he was no prize. "Well, how many?"

"How many what?" I asked.

"How many are there?" He wanted to go back to Camp Crandall with a good body count.

"There weren't exactly any bodies, Lieutenant," said Poole, trying to let him down easily. He described what we had seen.

"Well, what's that good for?" He meant, *How is that going to help me?*

"Interrogations, probably," Poole said. "If you questioned someone down there, no one outside the hut would hear anything. At night, you could just drag the body into the woods."

Lieutenant Joys nodded. "Field Interrogation Post," he said, trying out the phrase. "Torture, Use of, Highly Indicated." He nodded again. "Right?"

"Highly," Poole said.

"Shows you what kind of enemy we're dealing with in this conflict."

I could no longer stand being in the same three square feet of space with Elijah Joys, and I took a step toward the door of the hut. I did not know what Poole and I had seen, but I knew it was not a Field Interrogation Post, Torture, Use of, Highly Indicated, unless the Vietnamese had begun to interrogate monkeys. It occurred to me that the writing on the wall might have been names instead of poetry—I thought that we had stumbled into a mystery that had nothing to do with the war, a Vietnamese mystery.

For a second music from my old life, music too beautiful to be endurable, started playing in my head. Finally I recognized it: "The Walk to the Paradise Gardens," from *A Village Romeo and Juliet* by Frederick Delius. Back in Berkeley, I had listened to it hundreds of times.

If nothing else had happened, I think I could have replayed the whole piece in my head. Tears filled my eyes, and I stepped toward the door of the hut. Then I froze. A ragged Vietnamese boy of seven or eight was regarding me with great seriousness from the far corner of the hut. I knew he was not there—I knew he was a spirit. I had no belief in spirits, but that's what he was. Some part of my mind as detached as a crime reporter reminded me that "The Walk to the Paradise Gardens" was about two children who were about to die, and that in a sense the music *was* their death. I wiped my eyes with my hand, and when I lowered my arm, the boy was still there. He was beautiful, beautiful in the ordinary way, as Vietnamese children nearly always seemed beautiful to me. Then he vanished all at once, like the flickering light of the Zippo. I nearly groaned aloud. That child had been murdered in the hut: he had not just died, he had been murdered.

I said something to the other two men and went through the door into the growing darkness. I was very dimly aware of the Lieutenant asking Poole to repeat his description of the uprights and the bloody chain. Hamnet and Burrage and Calvin Hill were sitting down and leaning against a tree. Victor Spitalny was wiping his hands on his filthy shirt. White smoke curled up from Hill's cigarette, and Tina Pumo exhaled a long white stream of vapor. The unhinged thought came to me with an absolute conviction that *this* was the Paradise Gardens. The men lounging in the darkness; the pattern of the cigarette smoke, and the patterns they made, sitting or standing; the in-drawing darkness, as physical as a blanket; the frame of the trees and the flat gray-green background of the paddy.

My soul had come back to life.

Then I became aware that there was something wrong about the men arranged before me, and again it took a moment for my intelligence to catch up to my intuition. Every member of a combat unit makes unconscious adjustments as members of the unit go down in the field; survival sometimes depends on the number of people you know are with you, and you keep count without being quite aware of doing it. I had registered that two men too many were in front of me. Instead of seven, there were nine, and the two men that made up the nine of us left were still behind me in the hut. M. O. Dengler was looking at me with growing curiosity, and I thought he knew exactly what I was thinking. A sick chill went through me. I saw Tom Blevins and Tyrell Budd standing together at the far right of the platoon, a little muddier than the others but otherwise different from the rest only in that, like Dengler, they were looking directly at me.

Hill tossed his cigarette away in an arc of light. Poole and Lieutenant Joys came out of the hut behind me. Leonard Hamnet patted his pocket to reassure himself that he still had his letter. I looked back at the right of the group, and the two dead men were gone.

"Let's saddle up," the Lieutenant said. "We aren't doing any good around here."

"Tim?" Dengler asked. He had not taken his eyes off me since I had come out of the hut. I shook my head.

"Well, what was it?" asked Tina Pumo. "Was it juicy?"

Spanky and Calvin Hill laughed and slapped hands.

"Aren't we gonna torch this place?" asked Spitalny.

The Lieutenant ignored him. "Juicy enough, Pumo. Interrogation Post. Field Interrogation Post."

"No shit," said Pumo.

"These people are into torture, Pumo. It's just another indication."

"Gotcha." Pumo glanced at me and his eyes grew curious. Dengler moved closer.

"I was just remembering something," I said. "Something from the world."

"You better forget about the world while you're over here, Underhill," the Lieutenant told me. "I'm trying to keep you alive, in case you hadn't noticed, but you have to cooperate with me." His Adam's apple jumped like a begging puppy.

As soon as he went ahead to lead us out of the village, I gave twenty dollars to Spanky and said, "Two weeks from today."

"My man," Spanky said.

The rest of the patrol was uneventful.

The next night we had showers, real food, alcohol, cots to sleep in. Sheets and pillows. Two new guys replaced Tyrell Budd and Thomas Blevins, whose names were never mentioned again, at least by me, until long after the war was over and Poole, Linklater, Pumo, and I looked them up, along with the rest of our dead, on the Wall in Washington. I wanted to forget the patrol, especially what I had seen and experienced inside the hut. I wanted the oblivion which came in powdered form.

I remember that it was raining. I remember the steam lifting off the ground, and the condensation dripping down the metal poles in the tents. Moisture shone on the faces around me. I was sitting in the brothers' tent, listening to the music Spanky Burrage played on the big reel-to-reel recorder he had bought on R & R in Taipei. Spanky Burrage never played Delius, but what he played was paradisal: great jazz from Armstrong to Coltrane, on reels recorded for him by his friends back in Little Rock and which he knew so well he could find individual tracks and performances without bothering to look at the counter. Spanky liked to play disc jockey during these long sessions, changing reels and speeding past thousands of feet of tape to play the same songs by different musicians, even the same song hiding under different names—"Cherokee" and "KoKo," "Indiana" and "Donna Lee"—or long series of songs connected by titles that used the same words—"I Thought About You" (Art Tatum), "You and the Night and the Music" (Sonny Rollins), "I Love You" (Bill Evans), "If I Could Be with You" (Ike Quebec), "You Leave Me Breathless," (Milt Jackson), even, for the sake of the joke, "Thou Swell," by Glenroy Breakstone. In his single-artist mode on this day, Spanky was ranging through the work of a great trumpet player named Clifford Brown.

On this sweltering, rainy day, Clifford Brown's music sounded regal and un-earthly. Clifford Brown was walking to the Paradise Gardens. Listening to him was like watching a smiling man shouldering open an enormous door to let in great dazzling rays of light. We were out of the war. The world we were in transcended pain and loss, and imagination had banished fear. Even SP4 Cotton and Calvin Hill, who preferred James Brown to Clifford Brown, lay on their bunks listening as Spanky followed his instincts from one track to another.

After he had played disc jockey for something like two hours, Spanky rewound the long tape and said, "Enough." The end of the tape slapped against the reel. I looked at Dengler, who seemed dazed, as if awakening from a long sleep. The memory of the music was still all around us: light still poured in through the crack in the great door. I felt as though I had returned from a long journey.

Spanky finished putting the Clifford Brown reel back into its cardboard box. Someone in the rear of the tent switched on Armed Forces Radio. Spanky looked at me and shrugged. Leonard Hamnet took his letter out of his pocket, unfolded it, and read it through very slowly.

"Leonard," I said, and he swung his big buffalo's head toward me. "You still putting in for compassionate leave?"

He nodded. "You know what I gotta do."

"Yes," Dengler said, in a slow quiet voice.

"They gonna let me take care of my people. They gonna send me back."

He spoke with a complete absence of nuance, like a man who had learned to get what he wanted by parroting words without knowing what they meant.

Dengler looked at me and smiled. For a second he seemed as alien as Hamnet. "What do you think is going to happen? To us, I mean. Do you think it'll just go on like this day after day until some of us get killed and the rest of us go home, or do you think it's going to get stranger and stranger?" He did not wait for me to answer. "I think it'll always sort of look the same, but it won't be—I think the edges are starting to melt. I think that's what happens when you're out here long enough. The edges melt."

"Your edges melted a long time ago, Dengler," Spanky said, and applauded his own joke.

Dengler was still staring at me. He always resembled a serious, dark-haired child, and never looked as though he belonged in uniform. "Here's what I mean, kind of," he said. "When we were listening to that trumpet player—"

"*Brownie*, Clifford *Brown*," Spanky whispered.

"—I could see the notes in the air. Like they were written out on a long scroll. And after he played them, they stayed in the air for a long time."

"Sweetie-*pie*," Spanky said softly. "You pretty hip, for a little ofay square."

"When we were back in that village, last week," Dengler said. "Tell me about that."

I said that he had been there too.

"But something happened to you. Something special."

"I put twenty bucks in the Elijah fund," I said.

"Only twenty?" Cotton asked.

"What was in that hut?" Dengler asked.

I shook my head.

"All right," Dengler said. "But it's happening, isn't it? Things are changing."

I could not speak. I could not tell Dengler in front of Cotton and Spanky Burrage that I had imagined seeing the ghosts of Blevins, Budd, and a murdered child. I smiled and shook my head.

"Fine," Dengler said.

"What the fuck you sayin' is *fine*?" Cotton said. "I don't mind listening to that music, but I do draw the line at this bullshit." He flipped himself off his bunk and pointed a finger at me. "What date you give Spanky?"

"Fifteenth."

"He last longer than that." Cotton tilted his head as the song on the radio ended. Armed Forces Radio began playing a song by Moby Grape. Disgusted, he turned back to me. "Check it out. End of August. He be so tired, he be *sleepwalkin'*. Be halfway through his tour. The fool will go to pieces, and that's when he'll get it."

Cotton had put thirty dollars on August thirty-first, exactly the midpoint of Lieutenant Joys' tour of duty. He had a long time to adjust to the loss of the money, because he himself stayed alive until a sniper killed him at the beginning of February. Then he became a member of the ghost platoon that followed us wherever we went. I think this ghost platoon, filled with men I had loved and detested, whose names I could or could not remember, disbanded only when I went to the Wall in Washington, D.C., and by then I felt that I was a member of it myself.

2

I left the tent with a vague notion of getting outside and enjoying the slight coolness that followed the rain. The packet of Si Van Vo's white powder rested at the bottom of my right front pocket, which was so deep that my fingers just brushed its top. I decided that what I needed was a beer.

Wilson Manly's shack was all the way on the other side of camp. I never liked going to the enlisted men's club, where they were rumored to serve cheap Vietnamese beer in American bottles. Certainly the bottles had often been stripped of their labels, and to a suspicious eye the caps looked dented; also, the beer there never quite tasted like the stuff Manly sold.

One other place remained, farther away than the enlisted men's club but closer than Manly's shack and somewhere between them in official status. About twenty minutes' walk from where I stood, just at the curve in the steeply descending road to the airfield and the motor pool, stood an isolated wooden structure called Billy's. Billy himself, supposedly a Green Beret Captain who had installed a handful of bar girls in an old French command post, had gone home long ago, but his club had endured. There were no more girls, if ever had been, and the brand-name liquor was about as reliable as the enlisted men's club's beer. When it was open, a succession of slender Montagnard boys who slept in the nearly empty upstairs rooms served drinks. I visited these rooms two or three times, but I never learned where the boys went when Billy's was closed. They spoke almost no English. Billy's did not look anything like a French command post, even one that had been transformed into a bordello: it looked like a roadhouse.

A long time ago, the building had been painted brown. The wood was soft with rot. Someone had once boarded up the two front windows on the lower floor, and someone else had torn off a narrow band of boards across each of the windows, so that light entered in two flat white bands that traveled across the floor during the day. Around six thirty the light bounced off the long foxed mirror that stood behind the row of bottles. After five minutes of blinding light, the sun disappeared beneath the pine boards, and for ten or fifteen minutes a shadowy pink glow filled the barroom. There was no electricity and no ice. Fingerprints covered the glasses. When you needed a toilet, you went to a cubicle with inverted metal boot-prints on either side of a hole in the floor.

The building stood in a little grove of trees in the curve of the descending road, and as I walked toward it in the diffuse reddish light of the sunset, a mud-spattered jeep painted in the colors of camouflage gradually came into view to the right of the bar, emerging from invisibility like an optical illusion. The jeep seemed to have floated out of the trees behind it, to be a part of them.

I heard low male voices, which stopped when I stepped onto the soft boards of the front porch. I glanced at the jeep, looking for insignia or identification, but the mud covered the door panels. Something white gleamed dully from the back seat. When I looked more closely, I saw in a coil of rope an oval of bone that it took me a moment to recognize as the top of a painstakingly cleaned and bleached human skull.

Before I could reach the handle, the door opened. A boy named Mike stood before me, in loose khaki shorts and a dirty white shirt much too large for him. Then he saw who I was. "Oh," he said. "Yes. Tim. Okay. You can come in." His real name was not Mike, but Mike was what it sounded like. He carried himself with an odd defensive alertness, and he shot me a tight, uncomfortable smile. "Far table, right side."

"It's okay?" I asked, because everything about him told me that it wasn't.

"Yesss." He stepped back to let me in.

I smelled cordite before I saw the other men. The bar looked empty, and the band of light coming in through the opening over the windows had already reached the long mirror, creating a bright dazzle, a white fire. I took a couple of steps inside, and Mike moved around me to return to his post.

"Oh, hell," someone said from off to my left. "We have to put up with *this?*"

I turned my head to look into the murk of that side of the bar, and saw three men sitting against the wall at a round table. None of the kerosene lamps had been lighted yet, and the dazzle from the mirror made the far reaches of the bar even less distinct.

"Is okay, is okay," said Mike. "Old customer. Old friend."

"I bet he is," the voice said. "Just don't let any women in here."

"No women," Mike said. "No problem."

I went through the tables to the furthest one on the right.

"You want whiskey, Tim?" Mike asked.

"Tim?" the man said. "*Tim?*"

"Beer," I said, and sat down.

A nearly empty bottle of Johnnie Walker Black, three glasses, and about a dozen cans of beer covered the table before them. The soldier with his back against the wall shoved aside some of the beer cans so that I could see the .45 next to the Johnnie Walker bottle. He leaned forward with a drunk's guarded coordination. The sleeves had been ripped off his shirt, and dirt darkened his skin as if he had not bathed in years. His hair had been cut with a knife, and had once been blond.

"I just want to make sure about this," he said. "You're not a woman, right? You swear to that?"

"Anything you say," I said.

"No woman walks into this place." He put his hand on the gun. "No nurse. No wife. No *anything*. You got that?"

"Got it," I said. Mike hurried around the bar with my beer.

"Tim. Funny name. Tom, now—that's a name. Tim sounds like a little guy— like him." He pointed at Mike with his left hand, the whole hand and not merely the index finger, while his right still rested on the .45. "Little fucker ought to be wearing a dress. Hell, he practically *is* wearing a dress."

"Don't you like women?" I asked. Mike put a can of Budweiser on my table and shook his head rapidly, twice. He had wanted me in the club because he was afraid the drunken soldier was going to shoot him, and now I was just making things worse.

I looked at the two men with the drunken officer. They were dirty and exhausted—whatever had happened to the drunk had also happened to them. The difference was that they were not drunk yet.

"That is a complicated question," the drunk said. "There are questions of responsibility. You can be responsible for yourself. You can be responsible for your children and your tribe. You are responsible for anyone you want to protect. But can you be responsible for women? If so, how responsible?"

Mike quietly moved behind the bar and sat on a stool with his arms out of sight. I knew he had a shotgun under there.

"You don't have any idea what I'm talking about, do you, Tim, you rear-echelon dipshit?"

"You're afraid you'll shoot any women who come in here, so you told the bartender to keep them out."

"This wise-ass sergeant is personally interfering with my state of mind," the drunk said to the burly man on his right. "Tell him to get out of here, or a certain degree of unpleasantness will ensue."

"Leave him alone," the other man said. Stripes of dried mud lay across his lean, haggard face.

The drunken officer Beret startled me by leaning toward the other man and speaking in a clear, carrying Vietnamese. It was an old-fashioned, almost literary Vietnamese, and he must have thought and dreamed in it to speak it so well. He assumed that neither I nor the Montagnard boy would understand him.

This is serious, he said, *and I am serious. If you wish to see how serious, just sit in your chair and do nothing. Do you not know of what I am capable by now? Have you learned nothing? You know what I know. I know what you know. A great heaviness is between us. Of all the people in the world at this moment, the only ones I do not despise are already dead, or should be. At this moment, murder is weightless.*

There was more, and I cannot swear that this was exactly what he said, but it's pretty close. He may have said that murder was *empty*.

Then he said, in that same flowing Vietnamese that even to my ears sounded as stilted as the language of a third-rate Victorian novel: *Recall what is in our vehicle (carriage); you should remember what we have brought with us, because I shall never forget it. Is it so easy for you to forget?*

It takes a long time and a lot of patience to clean and bleach bone. A skull would be more difficult than most of a skeleton.

Your leader requires more of this nectar, he said, and rolled back in his chair, looking at me with his hand on his gun.

"Whiskey," said the burly soldier. Mike was already pulling the bottle off the shelf. He understood that the officer was trying to knock himself out before he would find it necessary to shoot someone.

For a moment I thought that the burly soldier to his right looked familiar. His head had been shaved so close he looked bald, and his eyes were enormous above the streaks of dirt. A stainless-steel watch hung from a slot in his collar. He extended a muscular arm for the bottle Mike passed him while keeping as far from the table as he could. The soldier twisted off the cap and poured into all three glasses. The man in the center immediately drank all the whiskey in his glass and banged the glass down on the table for a refill.

The haggard soldier who had been silent until now said, "Something is gonna happen here." He looked straight at me. "Pal?"

"That man is nobody's pal," the drunk said. Before anyone could stop him, he snatched up the gun, pointed it across the room, and fired. There was a flash of fire, a huge explosion, and the reek of cordite. The bullet went straight through the soft wooden wall, about eight feet to my left. A stray bit of light slanted through the hole it made.

For a moment I was deaf. I swallowed the last of my beer and stood up. My head was ringing.

"Is it clear that I hate the necessity for this kind of shit?" said the drunk. "Is that much understood?"

The soldier who had called me pal laughed, and the burly soldier poured more whiskey into the drunk's glass. Then he stood up and started coming toward me. Beneath the exhaustion and the stripes of dirt, his face was taut with anxiety. He put himself between me and the man with the gun.

"I am not a rear-echelon dipshit," I said. "I don't want any trouble, but people like him do not own this war."

"Will you maybe let me save your ass, Sergeant?" he whispered. "Major Bachelor hasn't been anywhere near white men in three years, and he's having a little trouble readjusting. Compared to him, we're all rear-echelon dipshits."

I looked at his tattered shirt. "Are you his babysitter, Captain?"

He gave me an exasperated look, and glanced over his shoulder at the Major. "Major, put down your damn weapon. The sergeant is a combat soldier. He is on his way back to camp."

I don't care what he is, the Major said in Vietnamese.

The Captain began pulling me toward the door, keeping his body between me and the other table. I motioned for Mike to come out with me.

"Don't worry, the Major won't shoot him, Major Bachelor loves the Yards," the Captain said. He gave me an impatient glance because I had refused to move at his pace. Then I saw him notice my pupils. "God damn," he said, and then he stopped moving altogether and said "God damn" again, but in a different tone of voice.

I started laughing.

"Oh, this is—" He shook his head. "This is really—"

"Where have you *been*?" I asked him.

John Ransom turned to the table. "Hey, I know this guy. He's an old football friend of mine."

Major Bachelor shrugged and put the .45 back on the table. His eyelids had nearly closed. "I don't care about football," he said, but he kept his hand off the weapon.

"Buy the sergeant a drink," said the haggard officer.

"Buy the fucking sergeant a drink," the Major chimed in.

John Ransom quickly moved to the bar and reached for a glass, which the confused Mike put into his hand. Ransom went through the tables, filled his glass and mine, and carried both back to join me.

We watched the Major's head slip down by notches toward his chest. When his chin finally reached the unbuttoned top of his ruined shirt, Ransom said, "All right, Bob," and the other man slid the .45 out from under the Major's hand. He pushed it beneath his belt.

"The man is out," Bob said.

Ransom turned back to me. "He was up three days straight with us, God knows how long before that." Ransom did not have to specify who *he* was. "Bob and I got some sleep, trading off, but he just kept on talking." He fell into one of the chairs at my table and tilted his glass to his mouth. I sat down beside him.

For a moment no one in the bar spoke. The line of light from the open space across the windows had already left the mirror, and was now approaching the place on the wall that meant it would soon disappear. Mike lifted the cover from one of the lamps and began trimming the wick.

"How come you're always fucked up when I see you?"

"You have to ask?"

He smiled. He looked very different from when I had seen him preparing to give a sales pitch to Senator Burrman at Camp White Star. His body had thickened and hardened, and his eyes had retreated far back into his head. He seemed to me to have moved a long step nearer the goal I had always seen in him than when he had given me the zealot's word about stopping the spread of Communism. This man had taken in more of the war, and that much more of the war was inside him now.

"I got you off graves registration at White Star, didn't I?"

I agreed that he had.

"What did you call it, the body squad? It wasn't even a real graves registration unit, was it?" He smiled and shook his head. "I took care of your Captain McCue, too—he was using it as a kind of dumping ground. I don't know how he got away with it as long as he did. The only one with any training was that sergeant, what's his name. Italian."

"DeMaestro."

Ransom nodded. "The whole operation was going off the rails." Mike lit a big kitchen match and touched it to the wick of the kerosene lamp. "I heard some things—" He slumped against the wall and swallowed whiskey. I wondered if he had heard about Captain Havens. He closed his eyes. "Some crazy stuff went on back there."

I asked if he was still stationed in the highlands up around the Laotian border. He almost sighed when he shook his head.

"You're not with the tribesmen anymore? What were they, Khatu?"

He opened his eyes. "You have a good memory. No, I'm not there anymore." He considered saying more, but decided not to. He had failed himself. "I'm kind of on hold until they send me up around Khe Sahn. It'll be better up there—the Bru are tremendous. But right now, all I want to do is take a bath and get into bed. Any bed. Actually, I'd settle for a dry level place on the ground."

"Where did you come from now?"

"Incountry." His face creased and he showed his teeth. The effect was so unsettling that I did not immediately realize that he was smiling. "Way incountry. We had to get the Major out."

"Looks more like you had to pull him out, like a tooth."

My ignorance made him sit up straight. "You mean you never heard of him? Franklin Bachelor?"

And then I thought I had, that someone had mentioned him to me a long time ago.

"In the bush for years. Bachelor did stuff that ordinary people don't even *dream* of—he's a legend."

A legend, I thought. Like the Green Berets Ransom had mentioned a lifetime ago at White Star.

"Ran what amounted to a private army, did a lot of good work in Darlac Province. He was out there on his own. The man was a hero. That's straight. Bachelor got to places we couldn't even get close to—he got *inside* an NVA encampment, you hear me, *inside* the encampment and *silently* killed about an entire division."

Of all the people in the world at this minute, I remembered, the only ones he did not detest were already dead. I thought I must have heard it wrong.

"He was absorbed right into Rhade life," Ransom said. I could hear the awe in his voice. "The man even got married. Rhade ceremony. His wife went with him on missions. I hear she was beautiful."

Then I knew where I had heard of Franklin Bachelor before. He had been a captain when Ratman and his platoon had run into him after a private named Bobby Swett had been blown to pieces on a trail in Darlac Province. Ratman had thought his wife was a black-haired angel.

And then I knew whose skull lay wound in rope in the back seat of the jeep.

"I did hear of him," I said. "I knew someone who met him. The Rhade woman, too."

"His *wife*," Ransom said.

I asked him where they were taking Bachelor.

"We're stopping overnight at Crandall for some rest. Then we hop to Tan Son Nhut and bring him back to the States—Langley. I thought we might have to strap him down, but I guess we'll just keep pouring whiskey into him."

"He's going to want his gun back."

"Maybe I'll give it to him." His look told me what he thought Major Bachelor would do with his .45, if he was left alone with it long enough. "He's in for a rough time at Langley. There'll be some heat."

"Why Langley?"

"Don't ask. But don't be naïve, either. Don't you think they're . . ." He would not finish that sentence. "Why do you think we had to bring him out in the first place?"

"Because something went wrong."

"Oh, everything went wrong. Bachelor went totally out of control. He had his own war. Ran a lot of sidelines, some of which were supposed to be under shall we say tighter controls?"

He had lost me.

"Ventures into Laos. Business trips to Cambodia. Sometimes he wound up in control of airfields Air America was using, and that meant he was in control of the cargo."

When I shook my head, he said, "Don't you have a little something in your pocket? A little package?"

A secret world—inside this world, another, secret world.

"You understand, I don't care what he did any more than I care about what *you* do. I think Langley can go fuck itself. Bachelor wrote the book. In spite of his sidelines. In spite of whatever *trouble* he got into. The man was effective. He stepped over a boundary, maybe a lot of boundaries—but tell me that you can do what we're supposed to do without stepping over boundaries."

I wondered why he seemed to be defending himself, and asked if he would have to testify at Langley.

"It's not a trial."

"A debriefing."

"Sure, a debriefing. They can ask me anything they want. All I can tell them is what I saw. That's *my* evidence, right? What I saw? They don't have any evidence, except maybe this, uh, these human remains the Major insisted on bringing out."

For a second, I wished that I could see the sober shadowy gentlemen of Langley, Virginia, the gentlemen with slicked-back hair and pinstriped suits, question Major Bachelor. They thought *they* were serious men.

"It was like Bong To, in a funny way." Ransom waited for me to ask. When I did not, he said, "A ghost town, I mean. I don't suppose you've ever heard of Bong To."

"My unit was just there." His head jerked up. "A mortar round scared us into the village."

"You saw the place?"

I nodded.

"Funny story." Now he was sorry he had ever mentioned it. "Well, think about Bachelor, now. I think he must have been in Cambodia or someplace, doing what he does, when his village was overrun. He comes back and finds everybody dead, his wife included. I mean, I don't think *Bachelor* killed those people—they weren't just dead, they'd been made to beg for it. So Bachelor wasn't there, and his assistant, a Captain Bennington, must have just run off—we never did find him. Officially, Bennington's MIA. It's simple. You can't find the main guy, so you make sure he can see how mad you are when he gets back. You do a little grievous bodily harm on his people. They were not nice to his wife, Tim, to her they were especially not nice. What does he do? He buries all the bodies in the village graveyard, because that's a sacred responsibility. Don't ask me what else he does, because you don't have to know this, okay? But the bodies are buried. Generally speaking. Captain Bennington never does show up. We arrive and take Bachelor away. But sooner or later, some of the people who escaped are going to come back to that village. They're going to go on living there. The worst thing in the world happened to them in that place, but they won't leave. Eventually, other people in their family will join them, if they're still alive, and the terrible thing will be a part of their lives. Because it is not thinkable to leave your dead."

"But they did in Bong To," I said.

"In Bong To, they did."

I saw the look of regret on his face again, and said that I wasn't asking him to tell me any secrets.

"It's not a secret. It's not even military."

"It's just a ghost town."

Ransom was still uncomfortable. He turned his glass around and around in his hands before he drank. "I have to get the Major into camp."

"It's a real ghost town," I said. "Complete with ghosts."

"I honestly wouldn't be surprised." He drank what was left in his glass and stood up. He had decided not to say any more about it. "Let's take care of Major Bachelor, Bob," he said.

"Right."

Ransom carried our bottle to the bar and paid Mike. I stepped toward him to do the same, and Ransom said, "Taken care of."

There was that phrase again—it seemed I had been hearing it all day, and that its meaning would not stay still.

Ransom and Bob picked up the Major between them. They were strong enough to lift him easily. Bachelor's greasy head rolled forward. Bob put the .45 into his pocket, and Ransom put the bottle into his own pocket. Together they carried the Major to the door.

I followed them outside. Artillery pounded hills a long way off. It was dark now, and light from the lanterns spilled out through the gaps in the windows.

All of us went down the rotting steps, the Major bobbing between the other two.

Ransom opened the jeep, and they took a while to maneuver the Major into the back seat. Bob squeezed in beside him and pulled him upright.

John Ransom got in behind the wheel and sighed. He had no taste for the next part of his job.

"I'll give you a ride back to camp," he said. "We don't want an MP to get a close look at you."

I took the seat beside him. Ransom started the engine and turned on the lights. He jerked the gearshift into reverse and rolled backwards. "You know why that mortar round came in, don't you?" he asked me. He grinned at me, and we bounced onto the road back to the main part of camp. "He was trying to chase you away from Bong To, and your fool of a Lieutenant went straight for the place instead." He was still grinning. "It must have steamed him, seeing a bunch of round-eyes going in there."

"He didn't send in any more fire."

"No. He didn't want to damage the place. It's supposed to stay the way it is. I don't think they'd use the word, but that village is supposed to be like a kind of monument." He glanced at me again. "To shame.'

For some reason, all I could think of was the drunken Major in the seat behind me, who had said that you were responsible for the people you wanted to protect. Ransom said, "Did you go into any of the huts? Did you see anything unusual there?"

"I went into a hut. I saw something unusual."

"A list of names?"

"I thought that's what they were."

"Okay," Ransom said. "You know a little Vietnamese?"

"A little."

"You notice anything about those names?"

I could not remember. My Vietnamese had been picked up in bars and markets, and was almost completely oral.

"Four of them were from a family named Trang. Trang was the village chief, like his father before him, and his grandfather before him. Trang had four daughters. As each one got to the age of six or seven, he took them down into that underground room and chained them to the posts and raped them. A lot of those huts have hidden storage areas, but Trang must have modified his after his first daughter was born. The funny thing is, I think everybody in the village knew what he was doing. I'm not saying they thought it was okay, but they let it happen. They could pretend they didn't know: the girls never complained, and nobody every heard any screams. I guess Trang was a good-enough chief. When the daughters got to sixteen, they left for the cities. Sent back money, too. So maybe they thought it was okay, but I don't think they did, myself, do you?"

"How would I know? But there's a man in my platoon, a guy from—"

"I think there's a difference between private and public shame. Between what's acknowledged and what is not acknowledged. That's what Bachelor has to cope with, when he gets to Langley. Some things are acceptable, as long as you don't talk about them." He looked sideways at me as we began to approach the northern end of the camp proper. He wiped his face, and flakes of dried mud fell off his cheek. The exposed skin looked red, and so did his eyes. "Because the way I see it, this is a whole general issue. The issue is: what is *expressible*? This goes way beyond the tendency of people to tolerate thoughts, actions, or behavior they would otherwise find unacceptable."

I had never heard a soldier speak this way before. It was a little bit like being back in Berkeley.

"I'm talking about the difference between what is expressed and what is described," Ransom said. "A lot of experience is unacknowledged. Religion lets us handle some of the unacknowledged stuff in an acceptable way. But suppose—just suppose—that you were forced to confront extreme experience directly, without any mediation?"

"I have," I said. "You have, too."

"More extreme than combat, more extreme than terror. Something like that happened to the Major: he *encountered* God. Demands were made upon him. He had to move out of the ordinary, even as *he* defined it."

Ransom was telling me how Major Bachelor had wound up being brought to Camp Crandall with his wife's skull, but none of it was clear to me.

"I've been learning things," Ransom told me. He was almost whispering. "Think about what would make all the people of a village pick up and leave, when sacred obligation ties them to that village."

"I don't know the answer," I said.

"An even more sacred obligation, created by a really spectacular sense of shame. When a crime is too great to live with, the memory of it becomes sacred. Becomes the crime itself—"

I remembered thinking that the arrangement in the hut's basement had been a shrine to an obscene deity.

"Here we have this village and its chief. The village knows but does not know what the chief has been doing. They are used to consulting and obeying him. Then—one day, a little boy disappears."

My heart gave a thud.

"A little boy. Say: three. Old enough to talk and get into trouble, but too young to take care of himself. He's just gone—*poof*. Well, this is Vietnam, right? You turn your back, your kid wanders away, some animal gets him. He could get lost in the jungle and wander into a claymore. Someone like you might even shoot him. He could fall into a boobytrap and never be seen again. It could happen.

"A couple of months later, it happens again. Mom turns her back, where the hell did Junior go? This time they really look, not just Mom and Grandma, all their friends. They scour the village. The *villagers* scour the village, every square foot of that place, and then they do the same to the rice paddy, and then they look through the forest.

"And guess what happens next. This is the interesting part. An old woman goes out one morning to fetch water from the well, and she sees a ghost. This old lady is part of the extended family of the first lost kid, but the ghost she sees isn't the kid's—it's the ghost of a disreputable old man from another village, a drunkard, in fact. A local no-good, in fact. He's just standing near the well with his hands together, he's hungry—that's what these people know about ghosts. The skinny old bastard wants *more*. He wants to be *fed*. The old lady gives a squawk and passes out. When she comes to again, the ghost is gone.

"Well, the old lady tells everybody what she saw, and the whole village gets in a panic. Evil forces have been set loose. Next thing you know, two thirteen-year-old girls are working in the paddy, they look up and see an old woman who died when they were ten—she's about six feet away from them. Her hair is stringy and gray and her fingernails are about a foot long. She used to be a friendly old lady, but she doesn't look too friendly now. She's hungry too, like all ghosts. They start screaming and crying, but no one else can see her, and she comes closer and closer, and they try to get away but one of them falls down, and the old woman is on her like a cat. And do you know what she does? She rubs her filthy hands over the screaming girl's face, and licks the tears and slobber off her fingers.

"The next night, another little boy disappears. Two men go looking around the village latrine behind the houses, and they see two ghosts down in the pit, shoving excrement into their mouths. They rush back into the village, and then they both see half a dozen ghosts around the chief's hut. Among them are a sister who died during the war with the French and a twenty-year-old first wife who died of dengue fever. They want to eat. One of the men screeches, because not only did he see his dead wife, who looks something like what we could call a vampire, he saw her pass into the chief's hut without the benefit of the door.

"These people believe in ghosts, Underhill, they know ghosts exist, but it is extremely rare for them to see these ghosts. And these people are like psychoanalysts, because they do not believe in accidents. Every event contains meaning.

"The dead twenty-year-old wife comes back out through the wall of the chief's hut. Her hands are empty but dripping with red, and she is licking them like a starving cat.

"The former husband stands there pointing and jabbering, and the mothers and grandmothers of the missing boys come out of their huts. They are as afraid of what they're thinking as they are of all the ghosts moving around them. The ghosts are part of what they know they know, even though most of them have never seen one until now. What is going through their minds is something new: new because it was hidden.

"The mothers and grandmothers go to the chief's door and begin howling like dogs. When the chief comes out, they push past him and they take the hut apart. And you know what they find. They found the end of Bong To."

Ransom had parked the jeep near my battalion headquarters five minutes before, and now he smiled as if he had explained everything.

"But what *happened?*" I asked. "How did you hear about it?"

He shrugged. "We learned all this in interrogation. When the women found the underground room, they knew the chief had forced the boys into sex, and then killed them. They didn't know what he had done with the bodies, but they knew he had killed the boys. The next time the VC paid one of their courtesy calls, they told the cadre leader what they knew. The VC did the rest. They were disgusted— Trang had betrayed *them*, too—betrayed everything he was supposed to represent. One of the VC we captured took the chief downstairs into his underground room and chained the man to the posts, wrote the names of the dead boys and Trang's daughters on the padding that covered the walls, and then . . . then they did what they did to him. They probably carried out the pieces and threw them into the excrement-pit. And over months, bit by bit, not all at once but slowly, everybody in the village moved out. By that time, they were seeing ghosts all the time. They had crossed a kind of border."

"Do you think they really saw ghosts?" I asked him. "I mean, do you think they were real ghosts?"

"If you want an expert opinion, you'd have to ask Major Bachelor. He has a lot to say about ghosts." He hesitated for a moment, and then leaned over to open my door. "But if you ask me, sure they did."

I got out of the jeep and closed the door.

Ransom peered at me through the jeep's window. "Take better care of yourself."

"Good luck with your Bru."

"The Bru are fantastic." He slammed the jeep into gear and shot away, cranking the wheel to turn the jeep around in a giant circle in front of the battalion headquarters before he jammed it into second and took off to wherever he was going.

Two weeks later Leonard Hamnet managed to get the Lutheran chaplain at Crandall to write a letter to the Tin Man for him, and two days after that he was in a clean uniform, packing up his kit for an overnight flight to an Air Force base in California. From there he was connecting to a Memphis flight, and from there the Army had booked him onto a six-passenger puddlejumper to Lookout Mountain.

When I came into Hamnet's tent he was zipping his bag shut in a zone of quiet afforded him by the other men. He did not want to talk about where he was going or the reason he was going there, and instead of answering my questions about his flights, he unzipped a pocket on the side of his bag and handed me a thick folder of airline tickets.

I looked through them and gave them back. "Hard travel," I said.

"From now on, everything is easy," Hamnet said. He seemed rigid and constrained as he zipped the precious tickets back into the bag. By this time his wife's letter was a rag held together with scotch tape. I could picture him reading and rereading it, for the thousandth or two thousandth time, on the long flight over the Pacific.

"They need your help," I said. "I'm glad they're going to get it."

"That's right." Hamnet waited for me to leave him alone.

Because his bag seemed heavy, I asked about the length of his leave. He wanted to get the tickets back out of the bag rather than answer me directly, but he forced himself to speak. "They gave me seven days. Plus travel time."

"Good," I said, meaninglessly, and then there was nothing left to say, and we both knew it. Hamnet hoisted his bag off his bunk and turned to the door without any of the usual farewells and embraces. Some of the other men called to him, but he seemed to hear nothing but his own thoughts. I followed him outside and stood beside him in the heat. Hamnet was wearing a tie and his boots had a high polish. He was already sweating through his stiff khaki shirt. He would not meet my eyes. In a minute a jeep pulled up before us. The Lutheran chaplain had surpassed himself.

"Goodbye, Leonard," I said, and Hamnet tossed his bag in back and got into the jeep. He sat up straight as a statue. The private driving the jeep said something to him as they drove off, but Hamnet did not reply. I bet he did not say a word to the stewardesses, either, or to the cab drivers or baggage handlers or anyone else who witnessed his long journey home.

3

On the day after Leonard Hamnet was scheduled to return, Lieutenant Joys called Michael Poole and myself into his quarters to tell us what had happened back in Tennessee. He held a sheaf of papers in his hand, and he seemed both angry and embarrassed. Hamnet would not be returning to the platoon. It was a little funny. Well, of course it wasn't funny at all. The whole thing was terrible—that was what it was. Someone was to blame, too. Irresponsible decisions had been made, and we'd all be lucky if there wasn't an investigation. We were closest to the man, hadn't we seen what was likely to happen? If not, what the hell was our excuse?

Didn't we have any inkling of what the man was planning to do?

Well, yes, at the beginning, Poole and I said. But he seemed to have adjusted.

We have stupidity and incompetence all the way down the line here, said Lieutenant Elijah Joys. Here is a man who manages to carry a semi-automatic weapon through security at three different airports, bring it into a courthouse, and carry out threats he made months before, without anybody stopping him.

I remembered the bag Hamnet had tossed into the back of the jeep; I remembered the reluctance with which he had zipped it open to show me his tickets. Hamnet had not carried his weapon through airport security. He had just shipped it home in his bag and walked straight through customs in his clean uniform and shiny boots.

As soon as the foreman had announced the guilty verdict, Leonard Hamnet had gotten to his feet, pulled the semi-automatic pistol from inside his jacket, and executed Mr. Brewster where he was sitting at the defense table. While people shouted and screamed and dove for cover, while the courthouse officer tried to unsnap his gun, Hamnet killed his wife and his son. By the time he raised the pistol to his own head, the security officer had shot him twice in the chest. He died on the operating table at Lookout Mountain Lutheran Hospital, and his mother had requested that his remains receive burial at Arlington National Cemetery.

His mother. Arlington. I ask you.

That was what the Lieutenant said. *His mother. Arlington. I ask you.*

A private from Indianapolis named E. W. Burroughs won the six hundred and twenty dollars in the Elijah Fund when Lieutenant Joys was killed by a fragmentation bomb thirty-two days before the end of his tour. After that we were delivered unsuspecting into the hands of Harry Beevers, the Lost Boss, the worst lieutenant in the world. Private Burroughs died a week later, down in Dragon Valley along with Tiano and Calvin Hill and lots of others, when Lieutenant Beevers walked us into a mined field where we spent forty-eight hours under fire between two companies of NVA. I suppose Burroughs' mother back in Indianapolis got the six hundred and twenty dollars.

Honorable Mentions
1992

Aiken, Joan, "A Nasty, Muddy Ghost Dog," *Short Circuits.*

Akagawa, Jiro, "Beat Your Neighbor Out of Doors," *Ellery Queen's Mystery Magazine*, March.

Alcalá, Kathleen, "Gypsy Lover," *Mrs. Vargas & the Dead Naturalist.*

———, "Reading the Road," *Ibid.*

Alcock, Vivien, "Save the Elephant, the Ant, and Billikins," *Short Circuits.*

Aldiss, Brian W., "Common Clay," *Fantasy & Science Fiction*, Dec.

———, "Horse Meat," *Interzone* 65.

Aldridge, Ray, "Winedark," *F&SF*, Aug.

Ames, John Edward, "Cisisbeo," *Bizarre Sex & Other Crimes of Passion.*

Amies, Christopher, "Rain," *The Weerde.*

Andelman, Joan, "A Sunday in December," *Lovers & Other Monsters.*

Ansary, Mir Tamin, "The Cooper Junction Loop," *Jabberwocky*, spring/summer.

Anton, Karl, "The Dying God," *Weirdbook Encores* 12.

Aquino, John T., "The Sad Wizard," *The Camelot Chronicles.*

Arnzen, Michael A., "Spring Ahead, Fall Back," *Palace Corbie* 2.

Arthurs, Bruce, "Shadows Do Not Bleed," *Sword & Sorceresses IX.*

Atwood, Margaret, "Let Us Now Praise Stupid Women," *This Magazine*, Sept.

———, "There Was Once," *Ibid.*

Baker, Scott, "The Lurking Duck," (novella) *Foundations of Fear.*

Ballentine, Lee and Boston, Bruce, "Gulling South," *New Pathways*, winter.

Bannister, Jo, "A Poisoned Chalice," *EQMM*, May.

———, "Howler," *EQMM*, Oct.

———, "The Witness," *EQMM*, March.

Barnham, Chris, "Barrowpath," *Darklands* 2.

Barrett, Neal, Jr., "Uteropolis II," *Slightly Off Center.*

Baudino, Gael, "Tidings of Comfort and Joy," *The Magic of Christmas.*

Baxter, Stephen, "In the Manner of Trees," *Interzone* 62.

Beagle, Peter S., "The Naga," *After the King.*

Beechcroft, William, "Turkey Durkin and the Catfish," *EQMM*, Oct.

Begamudre, Ven, "Vishnu's Navel," *A Planet of Eccentrics.*

Behunin, Judith R., "Sometimes (Mood of June Morning)" (poem), *Eldritch Tales* 27.

Berman, Ruth, "Alder-Woman," *Fantasy Macabre* 15.

Blanchard, Stephen, "The Fat People," *Interzone* 61.

Blumenthal, Jay, "Parallel Universe" (poem), *The South Carolina Review*, spring.

Bograd, Larry, "The Reincarnation of Sweetlips," *Short Circuit.*

Bond, Jonathan, "SYSTEMatic Shocks," *Pulphouse* 9.

Boren, Terry, "Three Views of a Staked Plain," *Interzone* 57.

Borton, Douglas, "Venice, California," *Freak Show.*

Boston, Bruce and Frazier, Robert, "Aerial Reconnaissance of a Conflagration at the Heart," *Chronicles of the Mutant Rain Forest.*

Boston, Bruce, "Clothed and Naked in the Mutant Rain Forest," *Dreams & Nightmares* 38.
————, "What Trees Dream About in Their Prodigious Sleep," *Isaac Asimov's Science Fiction Magazine*, August.
Braly, David, "The Ominous Stroll," *Alfred Hitchcock's Mystery Magazine*, Feb.
————, "The Cattleman's Club," *AHMM*, July.
Braunbeck, Gary A., "By Civilized Means," *Cemetery Dance*, spring.
————, "Drowning with Others," *Dark Crimes* 2.
————, "Natural Enemies," *The Tome*, summer.
Brèque, Jean-Daniel, "Coffee," *Darklands* 2.
Briggs, Pamela, "Party of One," *The Urbanite #2: The Party Issue*.
Brite, Poppy Z., "The Sixth Sentinel," *Borderlands* 3.
————, "How to Get Ahead in New York," *Gauntlet* 4.
Brown, Molly, "The Vengeance of Grandmother Wu," *Interzone* 61.
Brown, Simon, "Shadows," *Aurealis* 7.
Bryant, Edward, "Country Mouse," *F&SF*, March.
Budrys, Algis, "Grabow and Collicker and I," *F&SF*, May.
Burke, John, "One Day You'll Learn," *Darklands* 2.
Burns, Cliff, "Strays," *Premonitions* 1.
Burrello, Dan, "The Songs of My Young," *Lovers & Other Monsters*.
Cadigan, Pat, "A Deal with God," *Grails: Quests, Visitations, and Other Occurrences*.
————, "Mother's Milt," *Omni Best Science Fiction Two*.
————, "Naming Names," *Narrow Houses*.
————, "No Prisoners," *Alternate Kennedys.*,
————, "New Life for Old," *Aladdin: Master of the Lamp*.
Cahoon, Brad, "The Arachnarium," *Deathrealm* #16.
Calvert, David, "Dispatches," *Midnight Graffiti*, fall.
Campbell, Ramsey, "End of the Line," *MetaHorror*.
————, "The Dead Must Die," *Narrow Houses*.
————, "The Limits of Fantasy," *Gauntlet* #3.
————, "Welcomeland," *Weird Tales*, spring.
Cantrell, Lisa, "A Good Day's Work," *New Mystery* 3.
Card, Orson Scott, "Atlantis," *Grails*.
Carroll, Jonathan, "Learning to Leave," *Narrow Houses*.
————, "Uh-Oh City," *F&SF*, June.
————, "The Life of My Crime," *Omni*, Feb.
Cassutt, Michael, "Night Life," *Borderlands* 3.
————, "Perpetual Light," *Grails*.
Castro, Adam-Troy, "Synchronicity," *Pulphouse* 9.
Chehak, Susan Taylor, "Coulda Been You," *Sisters in Crime* 5.
Clarke, A. G., "Sirensong," *Intimate Armageddons*.
Clawson, Calvin, "The Torcher," *Forbidden Lines* 11.
Clayton, Ash, "Stand Not Alone Against Eternity," *Prisoners of the Night* 6.
Collins, Barbara & Collins, Max Allan, "Cat Got Your Tongue," *Cat Crimes III*.
Collins, Nancy A., "Cold Turkey" (novella), Crossroads Press.

Constantine, Storm, "A Change of the Season," *The Weerde.*
———, "The Law of Being," *Eurotemps.*
Cooper, Dennis, "Container," *Wrong.*
Cornell, Paul, "Sunflower Pump," *The Weerde.*
Coward, Mat, "Cold Calling," *Mind's Eye.*
Craig, Brian, "The Woman in the Mirror," *The Dedalus Book of Femmes Fatales.*
Crawford, Dan, "Extra Cheese, and I Have Your Coupon," *AHMM,* July.
———, "Local History," *Deathrealm* 17.
Curtis, Ashley, "Anomalies of the Heart," *AHMM,* July.
Daniel, Tony, "The Natural Hack," *Amazing,* March.
Dean, David, "Angela's Baby," *EQMM,* Sept.
Dedman, Stephen, "A Death in Casablanca," *Strange Plasma* 5.
de Lint, Charles, "Conjure Man," *After the King.*
———, "Mr. Truepenny," Cheap Street (chapbook).
Delaplace, Barbara, "Black Ice," *Aladdin.*
Derose, Criss, "The Mystery of the Dark Comedian" (poem), *Tekeli-li!* 4.
Devereaux, Robert, "Spell Check," *Bizarre Bazaar '92.*
DiChario, Nicholas A., "The Winterberry," *Alternate Kennedys.*
Doolittle, Sean, "A Safer Place," *Palace Corbie,* Aug.
Dorr, James S. L., "Crumbs," *Palace Corbie,* Autumnal.
———, "Fetuscam," *Abortion Stories.*
———, *"The Birdcatchers" (poem), The Tome,* summer.
Dorrell, Paul, "Jason," Constable *New Crimes 1.*
Dowling, Terry, "They Found the Angry Moon," *Intimate Armageddons.*
Drago, Ty, "The Attendant," *After Hours* 15.
Dumars, Denise, "Incident in a New York Office" (poem), *Eldritch Tales* 27.
Dunmore, Helen, "Annina," *Caught in a Story.*
Edelman, Scott, "The Kindest Cut," *Suicide Art,* Necronomicon Press (chapbook).
———, "Suicide Art," *Ibid.*
Elflandsson, Galad, "Waiting," *Northern Frights.*
Elko, Bronwynn, "Blueblood," *Writers of the Future* Volume VIII.
Ellis, Mary, "Wings," *Glimmer Train* 4.
Engstrom, Elizabeth, "Project Stone" (novella), *Nightmare Flower.*
———, "The Old Woman Upstairs," *Ibid.*
Epperson, S. K., "The Cause," *Gauntlet* 4.
Fainlight, Ruth, "The Fishscale Shirt," *Caught in a Story.*
Fearn, Michael, "Railway Mania," *The Weerde.*
Fenn, Lionel, "The Awful Truth in Arthur's Barrow," *Grails.*
Ferguson, Andrew C., "The Devil's Advocate," *Dementia* 13.
Ferret, "God-Worm Coming," *New Pathways* 20.
Ford, Steven M., "Set a Place for Arthur," *Aboriginal SF,* fall.
Foster, Alan Dean, "Lay Your Head on My Pilose," *Future Crime.*
Fowler, Christopher, "Black Day at Bad Rock," *In Dreams.*
———, "Evil Eye," *Narrow Houses.*
Fox, Daniel, "High-Flying, Adored," *Dark Voices* 4.
Frey, Mary, "Behind the Waterfall," *Sword & Sorceresses* IX.
Friesner, Esther M., "All Vows," *Asimov's Science Fiction,* Nov.

Frost, R. J., "State of the Art," *Dementia 13*.
Fuqua, C. S., "Mama's Boy," *Cemetery Dance*, spring.
Fusco, Adam Corbin, "Shell," *Cemetery Dance*, fall.
Gaiman, Neil, "Chivalry," *Grails*.
Gallagher, Stephen, "Homebodies," *Dark at Heart*.
Gannon, S. R., "Jessie," *After Hours 14*.
Garcia y Robertson, R., "Breakfast Cereal Killers," *IASFM*, June.
Garnett, David, "Off the Track," *Interzone 63*.
Gates, David Edgerley, "How to Electrocute an Elephant," *Story*, summer.
Gleisser, Benjamin, "Restaurant of the Damned," *After Hours 15*.
Goddin, Jeffrey, "The Soul of the King's Daughter," *Weirdbook 27*.
———, "The Straw Man," *Space & Time*, summer.
Goldstein, Lisa, "Alfred," *ASFM*, Dec.
Gordon, John, "Death Wish," *The Burning Baby and Other Ghosts*.
———, "The Key," *Ibid*.
———, "Under the Ice," *Ibid*.
Gorman, Ed, "Mother Darkness," *Constable New Crimes 1*.
———, "The Long Silence After," *Dark at Heart*.
Gorodischer, Angela, "Letters from an English Lady," translated by Monica Bruno, *Secret Weavers*.
Gramlich, Charles A., "The Lady Wore Black," *Prisoners of the Night 6*.
Haldeman II, Jack C., "Ashes to Ashes," *Grails*.
Haldeman, Philip, "The Composer in Residence," *Weirdbook 27*.
Hall, David C., "He Waits for You," *EQMM*, Sept.
Hand, Elizabeth, "Engels Unaware," *Interzone 66*.
———, "The Have-nots," *IASFM*, June.
———, "In the Month of Athyr," *Best Omni Science Fiction Two*.
Harrison, M. John, "GIFCO," *MetaHorror*.
Hellweg, Paul, "The Coke Boy," *IASFM*, May.
Hensley, Chad, "Pilgrimage" (poem), *Deathrealm 17*.
Henighan, Tom, "Dark Christmas," *Strange Attractors*.
Higgins, Graham, "Jabberwockish," *Villains!*.
Hines, Judy, "Nearly Tomorrow," *Darklands 2*.
Hodge, Brian, "Jocko," *Cemetery Dance*, winter.
———, "Love Is Where You Buy It," *Gauntlet #3*.
———, "Like a Pilgrim to the Shrine," *Dracula: Prince of Darkness*.
Holder, Nancy, "The Ghost of Tivoli," Pulphouse Short Story Paperback.
Holdstock, Robert, "The Silvering," *Narrow Houses*.
Holliday, Liz, "Blind Fate," *The Weerde*.
———, "Third Person Singular," *Temps*.
Holt, Esther J., "The Orange Sofa," *AHMM*, Sept.
Hopkins, Brian, "The Night Was Kind to Loretta," *The Tome*, summer.
Howe, Robert J., "Little Boy Black and Blue," *Weird Tales*, spring.
Huff, Tanya, "Underground," *Northern Frights*.
Hughes, Philip, "Cut and Print," *Carnage Hall 3*.
Hyde, Gregory R., "Do You Hear What I Hear?" *The Blood Review Christmas Card*.

Ings, Simon, "Bruised Time," *New Worlds* 2.
Isle, Sue, "A Sprig of Aconite," *Intimate Armageddons*.
Jenhoff, Marvyne, "Cinderella and All the Slippers: The Story of a Story," *The Fiddlehead*, summer.
Jessen, Pamela J., "Cuttings," Roadkill Press (chapbook).
Johnson, George Clayton, "The Ring of Truth," *MetaHorror*.
Johnson, Kij, "Questing," *Tales of the Unanticipated* 10.
Jones, Jenny, "Hide and Seek," *Eurotemps*.
Jordan, Deane, "Making Change," *EQMM*, Oct.
Joyce, Graham, "Last Rising Sun," *In Dreams*.
———, "Under the Pylon," *Darklands* 2.
Julian, Astrid, "Bringing Sissy Home," *Writers of the Future Volume VIII*.
Kane, Kristopher P., "Side Show," *Deathrealm* 16.
Katzir, Yehudit, "Fellini's Shoes," *Closing the Sea*.
Kaveney, Roz, "Totally Trashed," *Eurotemps*.
———, "A Wolf to Man," *The Weerde*.
Keefauver, Brad, "A New Dimension in Jogging," *Weirdbook Encores* 12.
Kelly, Andrew, "The Cowgirl Who Rode the Lonesome Trail," *Doppelganger* 14.
Kelly, Ronald, "Beneath Black Bayou," *Dark at Heart*.
———, "Thinning of the Herd," *2AM*, spring.
Kenan, Randall, "Things of This World; Or, Angels Unawares," *Let the Dead Bury Their Dead*.
Kennett, Rick, "Out of the Storm," *Chills* 14.
———, "The Outsider," *Ghosts & Scholars* 14.
———, "The Seas of Castle Hill Road," *Eidolon* 9.
Kernaghan, Eileen, "The Weighmaster of Flood," *Ark of Ice*.
Kessel, John, "Man," *IASFM*, May.
Kidd, A. F., "Saint Sebastian and the Mona Lisa," *Aurealis* 9.
Kilworth, Garry, "1948," *Strange Plasma* 5.
———, "The Cave Painting," *Omni Best Science Fiction Two*.
———, "My Lady Lydia," *SF&F U.K.* 2.
King, Stephen, "Chattery Teeth," *Cemetery Dance*, fall.
———, "You Know They Got a Hell of a Band," *Shock Rock*.
Klause, Annette Curtis, "The Hoppins," *Short Circuits*.
Knight, Ellen, "Trompe-L'Oeil," *Weirdbook* 27.
Koja, Kathe, "By the Mirrors of My Youth," *Universe* 2.
———, "The Company of Storms," *F&SF*, June.
———, "Leavings," *Borderlands* 3.
———, "The Prince of Nox," *Still Dead*.
Koman, Victor, "Bootstrap Enterprise," *F&SF*, Feb.
Konrad, George, "On the Adolescence of Middle-Aged Men," translated by Imre Goldstein, *The Paris Review*, spring.
Kress, Nancy, "Eoghan," *Alternate Kennedys*.
Laidlaw, Marc, "The Vulture Maiden," *F&SF*, Aug.
Lannes, Roberta, "I Walk Alone," *Still Dead*.
Laymon, Richard, "Kitty Litter," *Cat Crimes II*.
Le Guin, Ursula, "Climbing to the Moon," *American Short Fiction*.

Lee, Tanith, "Beautiful Lady," *The Book of the Dead*.
———, "Exalted Hearts," *Grails*.
———, "The Glass Dagger," *The Book of the Dead*.
———, "The Lily Garden," *Weird Tales*, spring.
———, "The Moon Is a Mask," *The Book of the Dead*.
Lewis, D. F., "Weggs Padgett," *Fantasy Macabre* 15.
Lipinski, Miroslaw, "The Travelling Coffin," *Ibid*.
Little, Bentley, "Big Al's," *Eldritch Tales* 26.
Livings, Martin J., "Ghost Card," *Eidolon* 10.
Lovegrove, James, "The Landlady's Dog," *Narrow Houses*.
Lovesey, Peter, "The Man Who Ate People," *EQMM*, Oct.
Luft, Lya, "The Left Wing of the Angel," *One Hundred Years After Tomorrow*.
Lyons, Rebecca, "Nana's Magic," *After Hours* 14.
MacGregor, T. J., "Wild Card," *Sisters in Crime* 5.
Maclay, John, "Just a Closer Walk with Thee," *Borderlands* 3.
———, "Meat Men," *Mindwarps*.
———, "The Flats," *Ibid*.
Malzberg, Barry N., "Grand Tour," *Aladdin*.
———, "On the Heath," *Ibid*.
———, "Ship Full of Jews," *Omni*, April.
———, & Dann, Jack, "Life in the Air," *Amazing*, April.
Mandrake, Jill, "The Alligator People," *Event*, spring.
Mapes, Diane, "Nesting," *Interzone* 59.
———, "She-Devil," *Interzone* 63.
———, "The Man in the Red Suit," *ASFM*, Dec.
Marshall, Don, "As Ye Sow So Shall Ye . . ." *AHMM*, mid-Dec.
Massie, Elizabeth, "Abed," *Still Dead*.
———, "Brazo de Dios," *Borderland* 3.
———, "Meat," *The Tome*, summer.
Masterton, Graham, "Laird of Dunain," *The Mammoth Book of Vampire Stories*.
Matheson, Richard Christian, "Groupies," *Shock Rock*.
———, "Mutilator," *MetaHorror*.
Mayfair, Linda Lee, "Dance with the Devil," *2AM*, spring.
McCarthy, Wil, "Looking for Pablo," *Grails*.
McConnell, Chan, "DONt/WALK," *Still Dead*.
McCrumb, Sharyn, "Nine Lives to Live," *Cat Crimes II*.
McDonald, Ian, "Brody Loved the Masaii Woman," *The Dedalus Book of Femmes Fatales*.
McDowell, Ian, "My Father's Face," *Amazing*, July.
McHugh, Maureen F. "The Beast," *IASFM*, March.
McKillip, Patricia A., "The Fellowship of the Dragon," *After the King*.
Metzger, Thom, "Body Body," *Final Warning*.
Meyer, Adam, "Mind Games," *Doppelganger* 14.
———, "Swimmer," *Souls in Pawn*.
Michaels, Frank, "Mrs. Edgecliff," *AHMM*, Aug.
Miller, Frances A., "Something Different," *Short Circuits*.
Moler, Lee, "Drood Hollow, West Virginia," *Freak Show*.

Monath, Jay, "A Clown's Story," *Fiction International*.
Monteleone, Thomas F., "Oyster Bay, New York," *Freak Show*.
Morrell, David, "Nothing Will Hurt You," *MetaHorror*.
———, "The Shrine," *Dark at Heart*.
Morris, Mary McGarry, "The Perfect Tenant," *Glimmer Train* 1.
Morrow, James, "Isabella of Castile Answers Her Mail," *Amazing*, April.
Mullins, Kevin, "Love," *Darklands* 2.
Naparsteck, Martin, "The 9:13," *EQMM*, Feb.
Nasir, Jamil, "Sunlight," *Aboriginal SF*, fall.
———, "The Heaven Tree," *IASFM*, Feb.
Nelson, Amy, "Narcissus," *Fantasy Macabre* 15.
Newman, Kim, "Organ Donors," *Darklands* 2.
———, "Red Reign" (novella), *The Mammoth Book of Vampire Stories*.
———, "Week Woman," *Dark Voices* 4.
Nickels, Tim, "Born in the Forest," *Back Brain Recluse* 21.
Noble, Carol T., "Beach Weather," *Ibid*.
Norris, Gregory L., "Dorian's Party," *The Urbanite 2: The Party Issue*.
Novakovich, Josip, "Bricks," *Prairie Schooner*, spring.
Oates, Joyce Carol, "Extenuating Circumstances," *Sisters in Crime 5*.
———, "Schroeder's Stepfather," *EQMM*, April.
———, "The Artist," *Omni*, June.
———, "The Ice Pack," *Raritan*, winter.
———, "The Model," *EQMM*, October.
———, "The Premonition," *Playboy*, Dec.
Ocampo, Silvina, "The House of Sugar," translated by Nina M. Scott, *Secret Weavers*.
Olson, Donald, "Deadly Wednesday," *EQMM*, mid-Dec.
Olson, Lance, "Losing Things" (poem), *Weirdbook Encores* 12.
Olujic, Grozdana, "The Man Who Went Looking for His Face," *Conjunctions* 18.
Osier, Jeffrey, "Sanctuary," *The Silver Web*, summer.
———, "What I Had to Do . . . ." *Not One of Us* 9.
O'Brien, Jr., Edward, "The Unpleasantness at Marlowe's," *Crypt of Cthulhu* 80.
O'Driscoll, Mike, "Foreign Land," *Darklands* 2.
Palmer, Stuart, "The Discontinuum Kitchen," *Interzone* 55.
Parker, Mike, "The Stuntman," *Critical Quarterly* Vol. 34 #1.
Partridge, Norman, "Apotropaics," *Cemetery Dance*, winter.
———, "Candy Bars for Elvis," *Cemetery Dance*, spring.
———, "Johnny Halloween," *Cemetery Dance*, fall.
———, "Last Kiss," *New Crimes 3*.
———, "Mr. Fox," *Mr. Fox & Other Feral Tales*.
———, "Tombstone Moon," *Souls in Pawn*.
Penney, Bridget, "Sister Anne," *Honeymoon with Death & Other Stories*.
———, "Spike and Scissors," *Ibid*.
———, "Honeymoon with Death," *Ibid*.
Philbrick, W. R., "The Cure," *Dracula: Prince of Darkness*.
Pilkington, Ace G., "Half Sisters" (poem), *IASFM*, March.

Platt, Charles, "Dark Desires," *Pulphouse*, July.
Plieger, C. Maria, "A Cold Fragrant Air," *Writers of the Future VIII*.
Pronzini, Bill, "Liar's Dice," *EQMM*, Nov.
Ptacek, Kathryn, "Healing Touch," *Eldritch Tales* 27.
———, "Palmomita, New Mexico," *Freak Show*.
Purdy, James, "Kitty Blue," *Conjunctions* 18.
Ragan, Jacie, "What Kind of Cook" (poem), *Dreams & Nightmares* 39.
Rainey, Mark, "The Grey House," *Crypt of Cthulhu St. John's Eve*.
Rainey, Stephen M., "The Herald at Midnight," *Not One of Us* 9.
———, "The Last Show at Verdi's Supper Club," *After Hours* 16.
Randal, John W., "Dead Sky Eyes," *Aboriginal SF*, winter.
Ransom, Daniel, "Night Cries," *Dracula: Prince of Darkness*.
Raymond, Derek, "Changeless Susan," *Constable New Crimes 1*.
Reed, Kit, "The Hall of New Faces," *F&SF*, Oct./Nov.
Reeves-Stevens, Garfield, "Tear Down," *Northern Frights*.
Reiter, Thomas, "Rootstocks and Cuttings" (poem), *The Caribbean Writer*, Vol.
    6.
Resnick, Mike, "The Revolt of the Sugar Plum Fairies," *After the King*.
Reynolds, Alastair, "Digital to Analogue," *In Dreams*.
Richerson, Carrie, "A Dying Breed," *F&SF*, Oct/Nov.
———, "Apotheosis," *Souls in Pawn*.
Rios, Alberto Alvaro, "Susto," *Mid-American Review*, Vol XXI, #1.
Rogal, Stan, "Skin Deep," *Glimmer Train* 3.
Rowlands, Betty, "Here Comes a Chopper," *EQMM*, May.
Royle, Nicholas, "Night Shift Sister," *In Dreams*.
———, "Tracks," *Interzone* 55.
Russell, Douglas, "The Sorcerer's Remains," *Weirdbook* 27.
Russell, J. S., "Undiscovered Countries," *Still Dead*.
Russo, Patricia, "Mirror Images," *Tales of the Unanticipated* 10.
Ryan, James, "The Laughing Man," *The Urbanite 2: The Party Issue*.
Sallee, Wayne Allen, "Blood from a Turnip," *Dracula: Prince of Darkness*.
———, "Every Mother's Son," *Constable New Crimes 1*.
———, "What Would Mamaw Say," *Bizarre Sex and Other Crimes of Passion*.
Salmonson, Jessica Amanda, "The Oak," *The Goddess Under Siege*.
Sampson, Robert, "The Yellow Clay Bowl," *Grails*.
Saxton, Josephine, "A Strange Sort of Friend," *The Weerde*.
Schossau, P. K., "Where Angels Fear," *AHMM*, March.
Schow, David J., "Action," *Dark at Heart*.
Schweitzer, Darrell & van Hollander, Jason, "The Caravan of the Dead,"
    Weirdbook 27.
Sequeira, George W., "Catch Me When You Can—From Hell," *Terror Australis*
    3.
Shepard, Lucius, "Beast of the Heartland," *Playboy*, Sept.
Sherman, C. H., "Teacher," *Lovers & Other Monsters*.
Shirley, John, " 'I Want to Get Married!' Says the World's Smallest Man," *Mid-
    night Graffiti*.
Shockley, W. M., "A Father's Gift," *IASFM*, April.

Simmons, Dan, "Elm Haven, Illinois," *Freak Show*.
————, "This Year's Class Picture," *Still Dead*.
Simpson, Helen, "Four Bare Legs in a Bed," *Four Bare Legs in a Bed*.
Skipp, John & Spector, Craig, "The Ones You Love," *Still Dead*.
Slatton, Diane T., "Seventh Son of a Seventh Son," *Abortion Stories*.
Smeds, David, "The Flower That Does Not Wither," *Swords & Sorceresses IX*.
Smith, Dean Wesley, "The Blind Poet," *2AM*, spring.
Smith, William, "Pawned Teeth," *Dementia 13 #7*.
Smyth, George W., "The Man from Madagascar," *Thin Ice XII*.
Somtow, S. P., "Hunting the Lion," *Weird Tales*, spring.
————, "The Steel American," *Grails*.
Springer, Nancy, "Damnbanna" (novella), Axolotl Press (chapbook)/*F&SF*, Dec.
————, "Don't Look Back," *F&SF*, Oct/Nov.
Stableford, Brian, "Salome," *The Dedalus Book of Femmes Fatales*.
————, "The Innsmouth Heritage." Necronomicon Press (chapbook).
————, "Upon the Gallows-Tree," *Narrow Houses*.
Starkey, David, "Flesh," *Aberations 6*.
————, "Savior Complex," *Mean Lizards 1992*.
————, "A Disturbance in the Universe," *Tales of the Unanticipated* 10.
Stevens, B. J., "This Little Piggy Gets . . ." *Terror Australis* 3.
Stevens-Arce, James, "The Devil's Sentrybox," *Amazing*, March.
Strickland, Brad, "Okenfenokee Swamp, Georgia," *Freak Show*.
Stross, Charles, "Execution Night," *Villains!*
Sullivan, Thomas, "Deep Down Under," *Dark at Heart*.
Taff, John F. D., "The Two of Guns," *Eldritch Tales* 26.
Tarr, Judith, "Death and the Lady," *Grails*.
Taylor, Lucy, "Deer Season," *Northern Frights*.
————, "Games," *Bizarre Sex and Other Crimes of Passion*.
————, "Heels," *Unnatural Acts*.
————, "Rush," *Unnatural Acts*.
————, "Slips," *Ibid*.
Tem, Melanie, "Repentance," *Grue* 14.
————, "Trails of Crumbs," *ASFM*, Nov.
Tem, Steve Rasnic, "Breaking the Rules," *Narrow Houses*.
————, "Decodings," *Decoded Mirrors: 3 Tales After Lovecraft*.
————, "Going North," *Northern Frights*.
————, "Guardian Angels," *Decoded Mirrors: 3 Tales After Lovecraft*.
————, "Mirror Man," *Ibid*.
————, "Squeezer," *New Crimes* 3.
————, "The Dying," *Jabberwocky*, spring/summer.
————, "Vintage Domestic," *The Mammoth Book of Vampire Stories*.
————, "Blue Alice," *The Dedalus Book of Femmes Fatales*.
Temple, William F., "The Healer," *Interzone*, Nov.
Tessier, Thomas, "Addicted to Love," *Shock Rock*.
————, "In Praise of Folly," *MetaHorror*.
————, "The Banshee," *Borderlands 3*.
Thomas, Scott, "Little Mercy," *Elegia*, fall.

Thompson, Joyce, "Synecdoche," *F&SF*, August.
Thomson, June, "Secrets," *EQMM*, March.
Timlin, Mark, "Ai No Corrida," *Constable New Crimes 1*.
————, "Riders on the Storm," *In Dreams*.
Tremblay, Mildred, "Ruby's Child," *Dark Forms Gliding*.
VanderMeer, Jeff, "Flesh," *Midnight Zoo*, vol. 1 issue 2.
————, "Mahout," *ASFM*, mid-Dec.
Vasey, Glen, "One Step at a Time," *Still Dead*.
Velde, Vivian Vande, "Thanksgiving Troll," *Disney Adventure*.
Wade, Susan, "Living in Memory," *Amazing*, Oct.
Wagner-Hankins, Maggie, "Witch and Cousin," *AHMM*, Dec.
Wainer, Jack, "Miss Ain't Behaving," *Far Point 4*.
Waldrop, Howard, "The Effects of Alienation," *Omni*, June.
Wallace, Daniel, "In Heaven These Days," *Story Magazine*, summer.
Wallace, Marilyn, "Reunion," *Deadly Allies*.
Watson, Ian, "Looking Down on You," *F&SF*, Oct/Nov.
————, "The Tale of the Peg and the Brain," *Narrow Houses*.
Webb, Don, "Rest Cure," bOING-bOING 8.
————, "The Photographer" (poem), *Psychos*.
Wehrstein, Karen, "Cold," *Northern Frights*.
Weiner, Andrew, "The Map," *Ibid*.
Wells, J. A., "Like Cats," *Prisoners of the Night 6*.
West, Suzi, "Hog-Fat and Useless," *After Hours 15*.
Westall, Robert, "Aunt Florrie," *Short Circuits*.
Wheeler, Wendy, "Franklin's Salamander," *Crafters*.
Wilber, Rick, "Ice Covers the Hole," *F&SF*, Dec.
Williams, Conrad, "Ancient Flavours," *Back Brain Recluse 21*.
Williams, Sean, "Going Nowhere," *Intimate Armageddons*.
Williamson, Chet, "Bird-in-Hand, Pennsylvania," *Freak Show*.
————, "Mushrooms," *Dark at Heart*.
Williamson, J. N., "The Girl of My Dreams," *Narrow Houses*.
Wiloch, Thomas, "Never Disappear" (poem), *Psychos*.
Wilson, F. Paul, "Bob Dylan, Troy Jonson, and the Speed Queen," *Shock Rock*.
————, "The Lord's Work," *Dracula: Prince of Darkness*.
Wilson, Gahan, "Come One, Come All," *Still Dead*.
Wilson, Sam, "Winter Night, with Kittens," *Writers of the Future Volume VIII*.
Wimberger, Lisa, "The Girl with the Curious Eyes," *Deathrealm 17*.
Windsor, Patricia, "Teeth," *Short Circuits*.
Winter, Douglas E., "Bright Lights, Big Zombie," *Still Dead*.
Woodworth, Stephen, "Scary Monsters," *Writers of the Future Volume VIII*.
Wright, David, "Everyday Things," *Northwest Review*, Vol 28 #3.
Wu, William F., "Missing Person," *Amazing*, April.
Yarbro, Chelsea Quinn, "Investigating Jericho," *F&SF*, April.
Yolen, Jane, "The Winter's King," *After the King*.
————, "The Gift of the Magicians," *Christmas Bestiary*.
Young, Elizabeth, "Lethality," *Darklands 2*.
Yourgrau, Barry, "Honky Tonk," *A Man Jumps Out of an Airplane*.

About the Editors

ELLEN DATLOW has been Fiction Editor at *Omni* for more than a decade, and in that time has published award-winning stories by many of the finest writers in science fiction, fantasy, and horror. She has also edited a number of anthologies, including *Blood Is Not Enough*, *Alien Sex*, *The Omni Books of Science Fiction*, and A *Whisper of Blood*, and has co-edited the previous five volumes in the *Year's Best Fantasy and Horror* series with Terri Windling. She lives in New York.

TERRI WINDLING, five-time winner of the World Fantasy Award, developed the Ace Books Fantasy imprint in the 1980s, where she published the first novels of Steven Brust, Emma Bull, Charles de Lint, Sheri S. Tepper, and many others. She now runs the Endicott Studio, a transatlantic company specializing in myth-related work for print, visual art, and film medias. She is also a consulting editor for Tor Books' fantasy line. Windling created the ongoing *Adult Fairy Tales* series of novels, the *Borderland* "punk urban fantasy" series, and co-created the *Brian Froud's Faerielands* series. She has published numerous anthologies, including *Snow White, Rose Red* with Ellen Datlow, has two novels forthcoming in 1994 from Tor and Bantam Books, an animated children's film forthcoming from Lightyear Entertainment, and a TV movie in development at Columbia Pictures for NBC. She lives in Devon, England, and Tucson, Arizona.

About the Artist

THOMAS CANTY is one of the most distinguished artists working in the fantasy field. He has won the World Fantasy Award for his distinctive book jacket and cover illustrations, and is a noted book designer working in a number of diverse fields, as well as with various small presses. He has also created children's picture-book series for St. Martin's Press and Ariel Books. He lives in Massachusetts.

About the Media Critic

EDWARD BRYANT is a major author of horror and science fiction. He has won Hugo and Nebula Awards for short fiction. He also works in radio, writes book reviews for major journals and newspapers, and is a charming and able speaker. He lives in Colorado.

About the Packager

JAMES FRENKEL has been a publisher, packager, and editor for over twenty years. Editor of Dell's science fiction imprint in the late 1970s, he published Bluejay Books, a major trade publisher in the field in the mid-1980s. He is currently a consulting editor for Tor Books. He lives in Madison, Wisconsin, with his wife, Joan D. Vinge, with whom he is collaborating on several fiction anthologies.

publisher in the field in the mid-1980s. He is currently a consulting editor for Tor Books. He also edits the Collier Nucleus series of classic SF and fantasy reprints. He lives in Madison, Wisconsin, with his wife, Joan D. Vinge, with whom he is collaborating on several fiction anthologies.